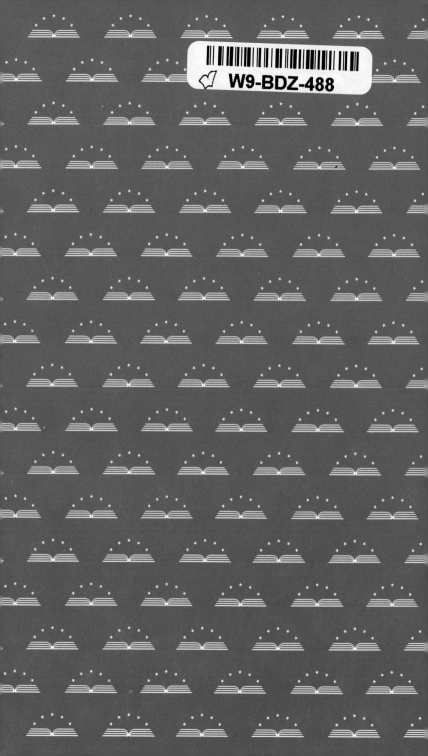

JAMES BALDWIN

JAMES BALDWIN

EARLY NOVELS AND STORIES

Go Tell It on the Mountain
Giovanni's Room
Another Country
Going To Meet the Man

THE LIBRARY OF AMERICA

Go Tell It on the Mountain copyright 1952, 1953 by James
Baldwin; copyright renewed; reprinted by permission of
Doubleday, a division of Bantam Doubleday Dell Publishing
Group Inc. *Giovanni's Room* copyright 1956 by James
Baldwin; copyright renewed; reprinted by permission of
Doubleday, a division of Bantam Doubleday Dell Publishing
Group Inc. *Another Country* copyright 1962, 1960 by James
Baldwin; copyright renewed. Published by Vintage Books,
reprinted by permission of the James Baldwin Estate. *Going
To Meet the Man* copyright 1948, 1951, 1957, 1958, 1960, 1965
by James Baldwin; copyright renewed. Published by Vintage
Books; reprinted by permission of the James Baldwin Estate.

The paper used in this publication meets the
minimum requirements of the American National Standard for
Information Sciences—Permanence of Paper for Printed
Library Materials, ANSI Z39.48—1984.

Distributed to the trade
in the United States by Penguin Putnam, Inc.
and in Canada by Penguin Books Canada Ltd.

Library of Congress Catalog Number: 97–23028
For cataloging information, see end of Notes.
ISBN 1–883011–51–5

First Printing
The Library of America—97

Manufactured in the United States of America

TONI MORRISON
SELECTED THE CONTENTS FOR THIS VOLUME

Contents

GO TELL IT
ON THE MOUNTAIN

For
My Father and Mother

They that wait upon the Lord shall renew their strength; they shall mount up with wings like eagles; they shall run and not be weary, they shall walk and not faint.

Contents

THE SEVENTH DAY

*And the Spirit and the bride say,
Come. And let him that heareth
say, Come. And let him that is
athirst come. And whosoever will,
let him take the water of life freely.*

I looked down the line,
And I wondered.

EVERYONE had always said that John would be a preacher when he grew up, just like his father. It had been said so often that John, without ever thinking about it, had come to believe it himself. Not until the morning of his fourteenth birthday did he really begin to think about it, and by then it was already too late.

His earliest memories—which were in a way, his only memories—were of the hurry and brightness of Sunday mornings. They all rose together on that day; his father, who did not have to go to work, and led them in prayer before breakfast; his mother, who dressed up on that day, and looked almost young, with her hair straightened, and on her head the close-fitting white cap that was the uniform of holy women; his younger brother, Roy, who was silent that day because his father was home. Sarah, who wore a red ribbon in her hair that day, and was fondled by her father. And the baby, Ruth, who was dressed in pink and white, and rode in her mother's arms to church.

The church was not very far away, four blocks up Lenox Avenue, on a corner not far from the hospital. It was to this hospital that his mother had gone when Roy, and Sarah, and Ruth were born. John did not remember very clearly the first time she had gone, to have Roy; folks said that he had cried and carried on the whole time his mother was away; he remembered only enough to be afraid every time her belly began to swell, knowing that each time the swelling began it would not end until she was taken from him, to come back with a stranger. Each time this happened she became a little more of a stranger herself. She would soon be going away again, Roy said—he knew much more about such things than John. John had observed his mother closely, seeing no swelling yet, but his father had prayed one morning for the "little voyager soon to be among them," and so John knew that Roy spoke the truth.

Every Sunday morning, then, since John could remember,

they had taken to the streets, the Grimes family on their way
to church. Sinners along the avenue watched them—men still
wearing their Saturday-night clothes, wrinkled and dusty now,
muddy-eyed and muddy-faced; and women with harsh voices
and tight, bright dresses, cigarettes between their fingers or
held tightly in the corners of their mouths. They talked, and
laughed, and fought together, and the women fought like the
men. John and Roy, passing these men and women, looked
at one another briefly, John embarrassed and Roy amused.
Roy would be like them when he grew up, if the Lord did
not change his heart. These men and women they passed on
Sunday mornings had spent the night in bars, or in cat houses,
or on the streets, or on rooftops, or under the stairs. They
had been drinking. They had gone from cursing to laughter,
to anger, to lust. Once he and Roy had watched a man and
woman in the basement of a condemned house. They did it
standing up. The woman had wanted fifty cents, and the man
had flashed a razor.

John had never watched again; he had been afraid. But Roy
had watched them many times, and he told John he had done
it with some girls down the block.

And his mother and father, who went to church on Sundays, they did it too, and sometimes John heard them in the
bedroom behind him, over the sound of rat's feet, and rat
screams, and the music and cursing from the harlot's house
downstairs.

Their church was called the *Temple of the Fire Baptized*. It
was not the biggest church in Harlem, nor yet the smallest,
but John had been brought up to believe it was the holiest
and best. His father was head deacon in this church—there
were only two, the other a round, black man named Deacon
Braithwaite—and he took up the collection, and sometimes
he preached. The pastor, Father James, was a genial, well-fed
man with a face like a darker moon. It was he who preached
on Pentecost Sundays, and led revivals in the summertime,
and anointed and healed the sick.

On Sunday mornings and Sunday nights the church was
always full; on special Sundays it was full all day. The Grimes
family arrived in a body, always a little late, usually in the
middle of Sunday school, which began at nine o'clock. This

lateness was always their mother's fault—at least in the eyes of their father; she could not seem to get herself and the children ready on time, ever, and sometimes she actually remained behind, not to appear until the morning service. When they all arrived together, they separated upon entering the doors, father and mother going to sit in the Adult Class, which was taught by Sister McCandless, Sarah going to the Infant's Class, John and Roy sitting in the Intermediate, which was taught by Brother Elisha.

When he was young, John had paid no attention in Sunday school, and always forgot the golden text, which earned him the wrath of his father. Around the time of his fourteenth birthday, with all the pressures of church and home uniting to drive him to the altar he strove to appear more serious and therefore less conspicuous. But he was distracted by his new teacher, Elisha, who was the pastor's nephew and who had but lately arrived from Georgia. He was not much older than John, only seventeen, and he was already saved and was a preacher. John stared at Elisha all during the lesson, admiring the timbre of Elisha's voice, much deeper and manlier than his own, admiring the leanness, and grace, and strength, and darkness of Elisha in his Sunday suit, wondering if he would ever be holy as Elisha was holy. But he did not follow the lesson, and when, sometimes, Elisha paused to ask John a question, John was ashamed and confused, feeling the palms of his hands become wet and his heart pound like a hammer. Elisha would smile and reprimand him gently, and the lesson would go on.

Roy never knew his Sunday school lesson either, but it was different with Roy—no one really expected of Roy what was expected of John. Everyone was always praying that the Lord would change Roy's heart, but it was John who was expected to be good, to be a good example.

When Sunday school service ended there was a short pause before morning service began. In this pause, if it was good weather, the old folks might step outside a moment to talk among themselves. The sisters would almost always be dressed in white from crown to toe. The small children, on this day, in this place, and oppressed by their elders, tried hard to play without seeming to be disrespectful of God's house. But sometimes, nervous or perverse, they shouted, or threw hymn-books, or began to cry, putting their parents, men or women of God, under the necessity of proving—by harsh means or tender—who, in a sanctified household, ruled. The older children, like John or Roy, might wander down the avenue, but not too far. Their father never let John and Roy out of his sight, for Roy had often disappeared between Sunday school and morning service and had not come back all day.

The Sunday morning service began when Brother Elisha sat down at the piano and raised a song. This moment and this music had been with John, so it seemed, since he had first drawn breath. It seemed that there had never been a time when he had not known this moment of waiting while the packed church paused—the sisters in white, heads raised, the brothers in blue, heads back; the white caps of the women seeming to glow in the charged air like crowns, the kinky, gleaming heads of the men seeming to be lifted up—and the rustling and the whispering ceased and the children were quiet; perhaps someone coughed, or the sound of a car horn, or a curse from the streets came in; then Elisha hit the keys, beginning at once to sing, and everybody joined him, clapping their hands, and rising, and beating the tambourines.

The song might be: *Down at the cross where my Saviour died!*

Or: *Jesus, I'll never forget how you set me free!*

Or: *Lord, hold my hand while I run this race!*

They sang with all the strength that was in them, and clapped their hands for joy. There had never been a time when John had not sat watching the saints rejoice with terror in his heart, and wonder. Their singing caused him to believe in the presence of the Lord; indeed, it was no longer a question of belief, because they made that presence real. He did not feel it himself, the joy they felt, yet he could not doubt that it was, for them, the very bread of life—could not doubt it, that is, until it was too late to doubt. Something happened to their faces and their voices, the rhythm of their bodies, and to the air they breathed; it was as though wherever they might be became the upper room, and the Holy Ghost were riding on the air. His father's face, always awful, became more awful now; his father's daily anger was transformed into prophetic wrath. His mother, her eyes raised to heaven, hands arced before her, moving, made real for John that patience, that endurance, that long suffering, which he had read of in the Bible and found so hard to imagine.

On Sunday mornings the women all seemed patient, all the men seemed mighty. While John watched, the Power struck someone, a man or woman; they cried out, a long, wordless crying, and, arms outstretched like wings, they began the Shout. Someone moved a chair a little to give them room, the rhythm paused, the singing stopped, only the pounding feet and the clapping hands were heard; then another cry, another dancer; then the tambourines began again, and the voices rose again, and the music swept on again, like fire, or flood, or judgment. Then the church seemed to swell with the Power it held, and, like a planet rocking in space, the temple rocked with the Power of God. John watched, watched the faces, and the weightless bodies, and listened to the timeless cries. One day, so everyone said, this Power would possess him; he would sing and cry as they did now, and dance before his King. He watched young Ella Mae Washington, the seventeen-year-old granddaughter of Praying Mother Washington, as she began to dance. And then Elisha danced.

At one moment, head thrown back, eyes closed, sweat standing on his brow, he sat at the piano, singing and playing; and then, like a great, black cat in trouble in the jungle, he stiffened and trembled, and cried out. *Jesus, Jesus, oh Lord Jesus!* He struck on the piano one last, wild note, and threw up his hands, palms upward, stretched wide apart. The tambourines raced to fill the vacuum left by his silent piano, and his cry drew answering cries. Then he was on his feet, turning, blind, his face congested, contorted with this rage, and the muscles leaping and swelling in his long, dark neck. It seemed that he could not breathe, that his body could not contain this passion, that he would be, before their eyes, dispersed into the waiting air. His hands, rigid to the very fingertips, moved outward and back against his hips, his sightless eyes looked upward, and he began to dance. Then his hands closed into fists, and his head snapped downward, his sweat loosening the grease that slicked down his hair; and the rhythm of all the others quickened to match Elisha's rhythm; his thighs moved terribly against the cloth of his suit, his heels beat on the floor, and his fists moved beside his body as though he were beating his own drum. And so, for a while, in the center of the dancers, head down, fists beating, on, on, unbearably, until it seemed the walls of the church would fall for very sound; and then, in a moment, with a cry, head up, arms high in the air, sweat pouring from his forehead, and all his body dancing as though it would never stop. Sometimes he did not stop until he fell—until he dropped like some animal felled by a hammer—moaning, on his face. And then a great moaning filled the church.

There was sin among them. One Sunday, when regular service was over, Father James had uncovered sin in the congregation of the righteous. He had uncovered Elisha and Ella Mae. They had been "walking disorderly"; they were in danger of straying from the truth. And as Father James spoke of the sin that he knew they had not committed yet, of the unripe fig plucked too early from the tree—to set the children's teeth on edge—John felt himself grow dizzy in his seat and could not look at Elisha where he stood, beside Ella Mae, before the altar. Elisha hung his head as Father James spoke, and the congregation murmured. And Ella Mae was not so beautiful now as she was when she was singing and testifying, but looked like a sullen, ordinary girl. Her full lips were loose and her eyes were black—with shame, or rage, or both. Her grandmother, who had raised her, sat watching quietly, with folded hands. She was one of the pillars of the church, a powerful evangelist and very widely known. She said nothing in Ella Mae's defense, for she must have felt, as the congregation felt, that Father James was only exercising his clear and painful duty; he was responsible, after all, for Elisha, as Praying Mother Washington was responsible for Ella Mae. It was not an easy thing, said Father James, to be the pastor of a flock. It might look easy to just sit up there in the pulpit night after night, year in, year out, but let them remember the awful responsibility placed on his shoulders by almighty God—let them remember that God would ask an accounting of him one day for every soul in his flock. Let them remember this when they thought he was hard, let them remember that the Word was hard, that the way of holiness was a hard way. There was no room in God's army for the coward heart, no crown awaiting him who put mother, or father, sister, or brother, sweetheart, or friend above God's will. Let the church cry amen to this! And they cried: "Amen! Amen!"

The Lord had led him, said Father James, looking down on the boy and girl before him, to give them a public warning before it was too late. For he knew them to be sincere young people, dedicated to the service of the Lord—it was only that, since they were young, they did not know the pitfalls Satan laid for the unwary. He knew that sin was not in their minds—not yet; yet sin was in the flesh; and should they continue with their walking out alone together, their secrets and laughter, and touching of hands, they would surely sin a sin beyond all forgiveness. And John wondered what Elisha was thinking—Elisha, who was tall and handsome, who played basketball, and who had been saved at the age of eleven in the improbable fields down south. *Had* he sinned? Had he been tempted? And the girl beside him, whose white robes now seemed the merest, thinnest covering for the nakedness of breasts and insistent thighs—what was her face like when she was alone with Elisha, with no singing, when they were not surrounded by the saints? He was afraid to think of it, yet he could think of nothing else; and the fever of which they stood accused began also to rage in him.

After this Sunday Elisha and Ella Mae no longer met each other each day after school, no longer spent Saturday afternoons wandering through Central Park, or lying on the beach. All that was over for them. If they came together again it would be in wedlock. They would have children and raise them in the church.

This was what was meant by a holy life, this was what the way of the cross demanded. It was somehow on that Sunday, a Sunday shortly before his birthday, that John first realized that this was the life awaiting him—realized it consciously, as something no longer far off, but imminent, coming closer day by day.

John's birthday fell on a Saturday in March, in 1935. He awoke on this birthday morning with the feeling that there was menace in the air around him—that something irrevoca-

ble had occurred in him. He stared at a yellow stain on the
ceiling just above his head. Roy was still smothered in the
bedclothes, and his breath came and went with a small, whistling sound. There was no other sound anywhere; no one in
the house was up. The neighbors' radios were all silent, and
his mother hadn't yet risen to fix his father's breakfast. John
wondered at his panic, then wondered about the time; and
then (while the yellow stain on the ceiling slowly transformed
itself into a woman's nakedness) he remembered that it was
his fourteenth birthday and that he had sinned.

His first thought, nevertheless, was: "Will anyone remember?" For it had happened, once or twice, that his birthday
had passed entirely unnoticed, and no one had said "Happy
Birthday, Johnny," or given him anything—not even his
mother.

Roy stirred again and John pushed him away, listening to
the silence. On other mornings he awoke hearing his mother
singing in the kitchen, hearing his father in the bedroom behind him grunting and muttering prayers to himself as he put
on his clothes; hearing, perhaps, the chatter of Sarah and the
squalling of Ruth, and the radios, the clatter of pots and pans,
and the voices of all the folk near by. This morning not even
the cry of a bedspring disturbed the silence, and John seemed,
therefore, to be listening to his own unspeaking doom. He
could believe, almost, that he had awakened late on that great
getting-up morning; that all the saved had been transformed
in the twinkling of an eye, and had risen to meet Jesus in the
clouds, and that he was left, with his sinful body, to be bound
in hell a thousand years.

He had sinned. In spite of the saints, his mother and his
father, the warnings he had heard from his earliest beginnings,
he had sinned with his hands a sin that was hard to forgive.
In the school lavatory, alone, thinking of the boys, older, bigger, braver, who made bets with each other as to whose urine
could arch higher, he had watched in himself a transformation
of which he would never dare to speak.

And the darkness of John's sin was like the darkness of the
church on Saturday evenings; like the silence of the church
while he was there alone, sweeping, and running water into
the great bucket, and overturning chairs, long before the

saints arrived. It was like his thoughts as he moved about the tabernacle in which his life had been spent; the tabernacle that he hated, yet loved and feared. It was like Roy's curses, like the echoes these curses raised in John: he remembered Roy, on some rare Saturday when he had come to help John clean the church, cursing in the house of God, and making obscene gestures before the eyes of Jesus. It was like all this, and it was like the walls that witnessed and the placards on the walls which testified that the wages of sin was death. The darkness of his sin was in the hardheartedness with which he resisted God's power; in the scorn that was often his while he listened to the crying, breaking voices, and watched the black skin glisten while they lifted up their arms and fell on their faces before the Lord. For he had made his decision. He would not be like his father, or his father's fathers. He would have another life.

For John excelled in school, though not, like Elisha, in mathematics or basketball, and it was said that he had a Great Future. He might become a Great Leader of His People. John was not much interested in his people and still less in leading them anywhere, but the phrase so often repeated rose in his mind like a great brass gate, opening outward for him on a world where people did not live in the darkness of his father's house, did not pray to Jesus in the darkness of his father's church, where he would eat good food, and wear fine clothes, and go to the movies as often as he wished. In this world John, who was, his father said, ugly, who was always the smallest boy in his class, and who had no friends, became immediately beautiful, tall, and popular. People fell all over themselves to meet John Grimes. He was a poet, or a college president, or a movie star; he drank expensive whisky, and he smoked Lucky Strike cigarettes in the green package.

It was not only colored people who praised John, since they could not, John felt, in any case really know; but white people also said it, in fact had said it first and said it still. It was when John was five years old and in the first grade that he was first noticed; and since he was noticed by an eye altogether alien and impersonal, he began to perceive, in wild uneasiness, his individual existence.

They were learning the alphabet that day, and six children

at a time were sent to the blackboard to write the letters they had memorized. Six had finished and were waiting for the teacher's judgment when the back door opened and the school principal, of whom everyone was terrified, entered the room. No one spoke or moved. In the silence the principal's voice said:

"Which child is that?"

She was pointing at the blackboard, at John's letters. The possibility of being distinguished by her notice did not enter John's mind, and so he simply stared at her. Then he realized, by the immobility of the other children and by the way they avoided looking at him, that it was he who was selected for punishment.

"Speak up, John," said the teacher, gently.

On the edge of tears, he mumbled his name and waited. The principal, a woman with white hair and an iron face, looked down at him.

"You're a very bright boy, John Grimes," she said. "Keep up the good work."

Then she walked out of the room.

That moment gave him, from that time on, if not a weapon at least a shield; he apprehended totally, without belief or understanding, that he had in himself a power that other people lacked; that he could use this to save himself, to raise himself; and that, perhaps, with this power he might one day win that love which he so longed for. This was not, in John, a faith subject to death or alteration, nor yet a hope subject to destruction; it was his identity, and part, therefore, of that wickedness for which his father beat him and to which he clung in order to withstand his father. His father's arm, rising and falling, might make him cry, and that voice might cause him to tremble; yet his father could never be entirely the victor, for John cherished something that his father could not reach. It was his hatred and his intelligence that he cherished, the one feeding the other. He lived for the day when his father would be dying and he, John, would curse him on his deathbed. And this was why, though he had been born in the faith and had been surrounded all his life by the saints and by their prayers and their rejoicing, and though the tabernacle in which they worshipped was more completely real to him than the several precarious homes in which he and his family had lived, John's heart was hardened against the Lord. His father was God's minister, the ambassador of the King of Heaven, and John could not bow before the throne of grace without first kneeling to his father. On his refusal to do this had his life depended, and John's secret heart had flourished in its wickedness until the day his sin first overtook him.

In the midst of all his wonderings he fell asleep again, and when he woke up this time and got out of bed his father had gone to the factory, where he would work for half a day. Roy was sitting in the kitchen, quarreling with their mother. The baby, Ruth, sat in her high chair banging on the tray with an oatmeal-covered spoon. This meant that she was in a good mood; she would not spend the day howling, for reasons known only to herself, allowing no one but her mother to touch her. Sarah was quiet, not chattering today, or at any rate not yet, and stood near the stove, arms folded, staring at Roy with the flat black eyes, her father's eyes, that made her look so old.

Their mother, her head tied up in an old rag, sipped black coffee and watched Roy. The pale end-of-winter sunlight filled the room and yellowed all their faces; and John, drugged and morbid and wondering how it was that he had slept again and had been allowed to sleep so long, saw them for a moment like figures on a screen, an effect that the yellow light intensified. The room was narrow and dirty; nothing could alter its dimensions, no labor could ever make it clean. Dirt was in the walls and the floorboards, and triumphed beneath the sink where roaches spawned; was in the fine ridges of the pots and pans, scoured daily, burnt black on the bottom, hanging above the stove; was in the wall against which they hung, and revealed itself where the paint had cracked and leaned outward in stiff squares and fragments, the paper-thin underside webbed with black. Dirt was in every corner, angle, crevice of the monstrous stove, and lived behind it in delirious communion with the corrupted wall. Dirt was in the baseboard that John scrubbed every Saturday, and roughened the cupboard shelves that held the cracked and gleaming dishes. Under this dark weight the walls leaned, under it the ceiling, with a great crack like lightning in its center, sagged. The windows gleamed like beaten gold or silver, but now John saw, in the yellow light, how fine dust veiled their doubtful glory. Dirt crawled in the gray mop hung out of the windows to dry. John thought with shame and horror, yet in angry hardness of heart: *He who is filthy, let him be filthy still.* Then he looked at his mother, seeing, as though she were someone else, the dark, hard lines running downward from her eyes, and the deep, perpetual scowl in her forehead, and the downturned, tightened mouth, and the strong, thin, brown, and bony hands; and the phrase turned against him like a two-edged sword, for was it not he, in his false pride and his evil imagination, who was filthy? Through a storm of tears that did not reach his eyes, he stared at the yellow room; and the room shifted, the light of the sun darkened, and his mother's face changed. Her face became the face that he gave her in his dreams, the face that had been hers in a photograph he had seen once, long ago, a photograph taken before he was born. This face was young and proud, uplifted, with a smile that made the wide mouth beautiful and glowed in the enormous eyes. It was the face of a girl who knew that no evil could undo her, and who could laugh, surely, as his mother did not laugh now. Between the two faces there stretched a darkness and a mystery that John feared, and that sometimes caused him to hate her.

Now she saw him and she asked, breaking off her conversation with Roy: "You hungry, little sleepyhead?"

"Well! About time you was getting up," said Sarah.

He moved to the table and sat down, feeling the most bewildering panic of his life, a need to touch things, the table and chairs and the walls of the room, to make certain that the room existed and that he was in the room. He did not look at his mother, who stood up and went to the stove to heat his breakfast. But he asked, in order to say something to her, and to hear his own voice:

"What we got for breakfast?"

He realized, with some shame, that he was hoping she had prepared a special breakfast for him on his birthday.

"What you *think* we got for breakfast?" Roy asked scornfully. "You got a special craving for something?"

John looked at him. Roy was not in a good mood.

"I ain't said nothing to you," he said.

"Oh, I *beg* your pardon," said Roy, in the shrill, little-girl tone he knew John hated.

"What's the *matter* with you today?" John asked, angry, and trying at the same time to lend his voice as husky a pitch as possible.

"Don't you let Roy bother you," said their mother. "He cross as two sticks this morning."

"Yeah," said John, "I reckon." He and Roy watched each other. Then his plate was put before him: hominy grits and a scrap of bacon. He wanted to cry, like a child: "But, Mama, it's my birthday!" He kept his eyes on his plate and began to eat.

"You can *talk* about your Daddy all you want to," said his mother, picking up her battle with Roy, "but *one* thing you can't say—you can't say he ain't always done his best to be a father to you and to see to it that you ain't never gone hungry."

"I been hungry plenty of times," Roy said, proud to be able to score this point against his mother.

"Wasn't *his* fault, then. Wasn't because he wasn't *trying* to feed you. That man shoveled snow in zero weather when he ought've been in bed just to put food in your belly."

"Wasn't just *my* belly," said Roy indignantly. "He got a belly, too, I *know*—it's a *shame* the way that man eats. I sure ain't asked him to shovel no snow for me." But he dropped his eyes, suspecting a flaw in his argument. "I just don't want him beating on me all the time," he said at last. "I ain't no dog."

She sighed, and turned slightly away, looking out of the window. "Your Daddy beats you," she said, "because he loves you."

Roy laughed. "That ain't the kind of love I understand, old lady. What you reckon he'd do if he didn't love me?"

"He'd let you go right on," she flashed, "right on down to hell where it looks like you is just determined to go any-how! Right on, Mister Man, till somebody puts a knife in you, or takes you off to jail!"

"Mama," John asked suddenly, "is Daddy a good man?"

He had not known that he was going to ask the question, and he watched in astonishment as her mouth tightened and her eyes grew dark.

"That ain't no kind of question," she said mildly. "You don't know no better men, do you?"

"Looks to me like he's a mighty good man," said Sarah. "He sure is praying all the time."

"You children is young," their mother said, ignoring Sarah and sitting down again at the table, "and you don't know how lucky you is to have a father what worries about you and tries to see to it that you come up right."

"Yeah," said Roy, "we don't know how lucky we *is* to have a father what don't want you to go to movies, and don't want you to play in the streets, and don't want you to have no friends, and he don't want this and he don't want that, and he don't want you to do *nothing*. We so *lucky* to have a father who just wants us to go to church and read the Bible and beller like a fool in front of the altar and stay home all nice and quiet, like a little mouse. Boy, we sure is lucky, all right. Don't know what I done to be so lucky."

She laughed. "You going to find out one day," she said, "you mark my words."

"Yeah," said Roy.

"But it'll be too late, then," she said. "It'll be too late when you come to be . . . sorry." Her voice had changed. For a moment her eyes met John's eyes, and John was frightened. He felt that her words, after the strange fashion God sometimes chose to speak to men, were dictated by Heaven and were meant for him. He was fourteen—was it too late? And this uneasiness was reinforced by the impression, which at that moment he realized had been his all along, that his mother was not saying everything she meant. What, he wondered, did she say to Aunt Florence when they talked together? Or to his father? What were her thoughts? Her face would never tell. And yet, looking down at him in a moment that was like a secret, passing sign, her face did tell him. Her thoughts were bitter.

"I don't care," Roy said, rising. "When *I* have children I ain't going to treat them like this." John watched his mother; she watched Roy. "I'm *sure* this ain't no way to be. Ain't got no right to have a houseful of children if you don't know how to treat them."

"You mighty grown up this morning," his mother said. "You be careful."

"And tell me something else," Roy said, suddenly leaning over his mother, "tell me how come he don't never let me talk to him like I talk to you? He's my father, ain't he? But he don't never listen to me—no, I all the time got to listen to him."

"Your father," she said, watching him, "knows best. You listen to your father, I guarantee you you won't end up in no jail."

Roy sucked his teeth in fury. "I ain't looking to go to no *jail*. You think that's all that's in the world is jails and churches? You ought to know better than that, Ma."

"I know," she said, "there ain't no safety except you walk humble before the Lord. You going to find it out, too, one day. You go on, hardhead. You going to come to grief."

And suddenly Roy grinned. "But you be there, won't you, Ma—when I'm in trouble?"

"You don't know," she said, trying not to smile, "how long the Lord's going to let me stay with you."

Roy turned and did a dance step. "That's all right," he said. "I know the Lord ain't as hard as Daddy. Is he, boy?" he demanded of John, and struck him lightly on the forehead.

"Boy, let me eat my breakfast," John muttered—though his plate had long been empty, and he was pleased that Roy had turned to him.

"That sure is a crazy boy," ventured Sarah, soberly.

"Just listen," cried Roy, "to the little saint! Daddy ain't never going to have no trouble with her—*that* one, she was born holy. I bet the first words she ever said was: 'Thank you, Jesus.' Ain't that so, Ma?"

"You stop this foolishness," she said, laughing, "and go on about your work. Can't nobody play the fool with you all morning."

"Oh, is you got work for me to do this morning? Well, I declare," said Roy, "what you got for me to do?"

"I got the woodwork in the dining-room for you to do.

And you going to do it, too, before you set foot out of *this* house."

"Now, why you want to talk like that, Ma? Is I said I wouldn't do it? You know I'm a right good worker when I got a mind. After I do it, can I go?"

"You go ahead and do it, and we'll see. You better do it right."

"I *always* do it right," said Roy. "You won't know your old woodwork when *I* get through."

"John," said his mother, "you sweep the front room for me like a good boy, and dust the furniture. I'm going to clean up in here."

"Yes'm," he said, and rose. She *had* forgotten about his birthday. He swore he would not mention it. He would not think about it any more.

To sweep the front room meant, principally, to sweep the heavy red and green and purple Oriental-style carpet that had once been that room's glory, but was now so faded that it was all one swimming color, and so frayed in places that it tangled with the broom. John hated sweeping this carpet, for dust rose, clogging his nose and sticking to his sweaty skin, and he felt that should he sweep it forever, the clouds of dust would not diminish, the rug would not be clean. It became in his imagination his impossible, lifelong task, his hard trial, like that of a man he had read about somewhere, whose curse it was to push a boulder up a steep hill, only to have the giant who guarded the hill roll the boulder down again—and so on, forever, throughout eternity; he was still out there, that hapless man, somewhere at the other end of the earth, pushing his boulder up the hill. He had John's entire sympathy, for the longest and hardest part of his Saturday mornings was his voyage with the broom across this endless rug; and, coming to the French doors that ended the living-room and stopped the rug, he felt like an indescribably weary traveler who sees his home at last. Yet for each dustpan he so laboriously filled at the doorsill demons added to the rug twenty more; he saw in the expanse behind him the dust that he had raised settling again into the carpet; and he gritted his teeth, already on edge because of the dust that filled his mouth, and nearly wept to think that so much labor brought so little reward.

Nor was this the end of John's labor; for, having put away the broom and the dustpan, he took from the small bucket under the sink the dustrag and the furniture oil and a damp cloth, and returned to the living-room to excavate, as it were, from the dust that threatened to bury them, his family's goods and gear. Thinking bitterly of his birthday, he attacked the mirror with the cloth, watching his face appear as out of a cloud. With a shock he saw that his face had not changed, that the hand of Satan was as yet invisible. His father had always said that his face was the face of Satan—and was there not something—in the lift of the eyebrow, in the way his rough hair formed a V on his brow—that bore witness to his father's words? In the eye there was a light that was not the light of Heaven, and the mouth trembled, lustful and lewd, to drink deep of the wines of Hell. He stared at his face as though it were, as indeed it soon appeared to be, the face of a stranger, a stranger who held secrets that John could never know. And, having thought of it as the face of a stranger, he tried to look at it as a stranger might, and tried to discover what other people saw. But he saw only details: two great eyes, and a broad, low forehead, and the triangle of his nose, and his enormous mouth, and the barely perceptible cleft in his chin, which was, his father said, the mark of the devil's little finger. These details did not help him, for the principle of their unity was undiscoverable, and he could not tell what he most passionately desired to know: whether his face was ugly or not.

And he dropped his eyes to the mantelpiece, lifting one by one the objects that adorned it. The mantelpiece held, in brave confusion, photographs, greeting cards, flowered mottoes, two silver candlesticks that held no candles, and a green metal serpent, poised to strike. Today in his apathy John stared at them, not seeing; he began to dust them with the exaggerated care of the profoundly preoccupied. One of the mottoes was pink and blue, and proclaimed in raised letters, which made the work of dusting harder:

Come in the evening, or come in the morning,
Come when you're looked for, or come without warning,
A thousand welcomes you'll find here before you,
And the oftener you come here, the more we'll adore you.

And the other, in letters of fire against a background of gold, stated:

For God so loved the world, that He gave His only begotten Son, that whosoever should believe in Him should not perish, but have everlasting life.

John iii, 16

These somewhat unrelated sentiments decorated either side of the mantelpiece, obscured a little by the silver candlesticks. Between these two extremes, the greeting cards, received year after year, on Christmas, or Easter, or birthdays, trumpeted their glad tidings; while the green metal serpent, perpetually malevolent, raised its head proudly in the midst of these trophies, biding the time to strike. Against the mirror, like a procession, the photographs were arranged.

These photographs were the true antiques of the family, which seemed to feel that a photograph should commemorate only the most distant past. The photographs of John and Roy, and of the two girls, which seemed to violate this unspoken law, served only in fact to prove it most iron-hard: they had all been taken in infancy, a time and a condition that the children could not remember. John in his photograph lay naked on a white counterpane, and people laughed and said that it was cunning. But John could never look at it without feeling shame and anger that his nakedness should be here so unkindly revealed. None of the other children was naked; no, Roy lay in his crib in a white gown and grinned toothlessly into the camera, and Sarah, somber at the age of six months, wore a white bonnet, and Ruth was held in her mother's arms. When people looked at these photographs and laughed, their laughter differed from the laughter with which they greeted the naked John. For this reason, when visitors tried to make advances to John he was sullen, and they, feeling that for some reason he disliked them, retaliated by deciding that he was a "funny" child.

Among the other photographs there was one of Aunt Florence, his father's sister, in which her hair, in the old-fashioned way, was worn high and tied with a ribbon; she had been very young when this photograph was taken, and had just come North. Sometimes, when she came to visit, she called the photograph to witness that she had indeed been beautiful in her youth. There was a photograph of his mother, not the one John liked and had seen only once, but one taken immediately after her marriage. And there was a photograph of his father, dressed in black, sitting on a country porch with his hands folded heavily in his lap. The photograph had been taken on a sunny day, and the sunlight brutally exaggerated the planes of his father's face. He stared into the sun, head raised, unbearable, and though it had been taken when he was young, it was not the face of a young man; only something archaic in the dress indicated that this photograph had been taken long ago. At the time this picture was taken, Aunt Florence said, he was already a preacher, and had a wife who was now in Heaven. That he had been a preacher at that time was not astonishing, for it was impossible to imagine that he had ever been anything else; but that he had had a wife in the so distant past who was now dead filled John with a wonder by no means pleasant. If she had lived, John thought, then he would never have been born; his father would never have come North and met his mother. And this shadowy woman, dead so many years, whose name he knew had been Deborah, held in the fastness of her tomb, it seemed to John, the key to all those mysteries he so longed to unlock. It was she who had known his father in a life where John was not, and in a country John had never seen. When he was nothing, nowhere, dust, cloud, air, and sun, and falling rain, *not even thought of,* said his mother, *in Heaven with the angels,* said his aunt, she had known his father, and shared his father's house. She had loved his father. She had known his father when lightning flashed and thunder rolled through Heaven, and his father said: "Listen. God is talking." She had known him in the mornings of that far-off country when his father turned on his bed and opened his eyes, and she had looked into those eyes, seeing what they held, and she had not been afraid. She had seen him baptized, *kicking like a mule and howling,* and she had seen him weep when his mother died; *he was a right young man then,* Florence said. Because she had looked into those eyes before they had looked on John, she knew what John would never know—the purity of his father's eyes when John was not reflected in their depths. She could have told him—

had he but been able from his hiding-place to ask!—how to make his father love him. But now it was too late. She would not speak before the judgment day. And among those many voices, and stammering with his own, John would care no longer for her testimony.

When he had finished and the room was ready for Sunday, John felt dusty and weary and sat down beside the window in his father's easy chair. A glacial sun filled the streets, and a high wind filled the air with scraps of paper and frosty dust, and banged the hanging signs of stores and storefront churches. It was the end of winter, and the garbage-filled snow that had been banked along the edges of sidewalks was melting now and filling the gutters. Boys were playing stickball in the damp, cold streets; dressed in heavy woolen sweaters and heavy pants, they danced and shouted, and the ball went *crack!* as the stick struck it and sent it speeding through the air. One of them wore a bright-red stocking cap with a great ball of wool hanging down behind that bounced as he jumped, like a bright omen above his head. The cold sun made their faces like copper and brass, and through the closed window John heard their coarse, irreverent voices. And he wanted to be one of them, playing in the streets, unfrightened, moving with such grace and power, but he knew this could not be. Yet, if he could not play their games, he could do something they could not do; he was able, as one of his teachers said, to think. But this brought him little in the way of consolation, for today he was terrified of his thoughts. He wanted to be with these boys in the street, heedless and thoughtless, wearing out his treacherous and bewildering body.

But now it was eleven o'clock, and in two hours his father would be home. And then they might eat, and then his father would lead them in prayer, and then he would give them a Bible lesson. By and by it would be evening and he would go to clean the church, and remain for tarry service. Suddenly, sitting at the window, and with a violence unprecedented, there arose in John a flood of fury and tears, and he bowed his head, fists clenched against the windowpane, crying, with teeth on edge: "What shall I do? What shall I do?"

Then his mother called him; and he remembered that she

was in the kitchen washing clothes and probably had something for him to do. He rose sullenly and walked into the
kitchen. She stood over the washtub, her arms wet and soapy
to the elbows and sweat standing on her brow. Her apron,
improvised from an old sheet, was wet where she had been
leaning over the scrubbing-board. As he came in, she straightened, drying her hands on the edge of the apron.

"You finish your work, John?" she asked.

He said: "Yes'm," and thought how oddly she looked at
him; as though she were looking at someone else's child.

"That's a good boy," she said. She smiled a shy, strained
smile. "You know you your mother's right-hand man?"

He said nothing, and he did not smile, but watched her,
wondering to what task this preamble led.

She turned away, passing one damp hand across her forehead, and went to the cupboard. Her back was to him, and
he watched her while she took down a bright, figured vase,
filled with flowers only on the most special occasions, and
emptied the contents into her palm. He heard the chink of
money, which meant that she was going to send him to the
store. She put the vase back and turned to face him, her palm
loosely folded before her.

"I didn't never ask you," she said, "what you wanted for
your birthday. But you take this, son, and go out and get
yourself something you think you want."

And she opened his palm and put the money into it, warm
and wet from her hand. In the moment that he felt the warm,
smooth coins and her hand on his, John stared blindly at her
face, so far above him. His heart broke and he wanted to put
his head on her belly where the wet spot was, and cry. But he
dropped his eyes and looked at his palm, at the small pile of
coins.

"It ain't much there," she said.

"That's all right." Then he looked up, and she bent down
and kissed him on the forehead.

"You getting to be," she said, putting her hand beneath
his chin and holding his face away from her, "a right big boy.
You going to be a mighty fine man, you know that? Your
mama's counting on you."

And he knew again that she was not saying everything she

meant; in a kind of secret language she was telling him today
something that he must remember and understand tomorrow.
He watched her face, his heart swollen with love for her and
with an anguish, not yet his own, that he did not understand
and that frightened him.

"Yes, Ma," he said, hoping that she would realize, despite
his stammering tongue, the depth of his passion to please her.

"I know," she said, with a smile, releasing him and rising,
"there's a whole lot of things you don't understand. But
don't you fret. The Lord'll reveal to you in His own good
time everything He wants you to know. You put your faith in
the Lord, Johnny, and He'll surely bring you out. Everything
works together for good for them that love the Lord."

He had heard her say this before—it was her text, as *Set
thine house in order* was his father's—but he knew that today
she was saying it to him especially; she was trying to help him
because she knew he was in trouble. And this trouble was also
her own, which she would never tell to John. And even
though he was certain that they could not be speaking of the
same things—for then, surely, she would be angry and no
longer proud of him—this perception on her part and this
avowal of her love for him lent to John's bewilderment a reality that terrified and a dignity that consoled him. Dimly, he
felt that he ought to console her, and he listened, astounded,
at the words that now fell from his lips:

"Yes, Mama. I'm going to try to love the Lord."

At this there sprang into his mother's face something startling, beautiful, unspeakably sad—as though she were looking
far beyond him at a long, dark road, and seeing on that road
a traveler in perpetual danger. Was it he, the traveler? or herself? or was she thinking of the cross of Jesus? She turned back
to the washtub, still with this strange sadness on her face.

"You better go on now," she said, "before your daddy gets
home."

In Central Park the snow had not yet melted on his favorite
hill. This hill was in the center of the park, after he had left
the circle of the reservoir, where he always found, outside the
high wall of crossed wire, ladies, white, in fur coats, walking
their great dogs, or old, white gentlemen with canes. At a

point that he knew by instinct and by the shape of the buildings surrounding the park, he struck out on a steep path over-
grown with trees, and climbed a short distance until he
reached the clearing that led to the hill. Before him, then, the
slope stretched upward, and above it the brilliant sky, and
beyond it, cloudy, and far away, he saw the skyline of New
York. He did not know why, but there arose in him an exultation and a sense of power, and he ran up the hill like an
engine, or a madman, willing to throw himself headlong into
the city that glowed before him.

But when he reached the summit he paused; he stood on
the crest of the hill, hands clasped beneath his chin, looking
down. Then he, John, felt like a giant who might crumble
this city with his anger; he felt like a tyrant who might crush
this city beneath his heel; he felt like a long-awaited conqueror
at whose feet flowers would be strewn, and before whom multitudes cried, Hosanna! He would be, of all, the mightiest,
the most beloved, the Lord's anointed; and he would live in
this shining city which his ancestors had seen with longing
from far away. For it was his; the inhabitants of the city had
told him it was his; he had but to run down, crying, and they
would take him to their hearts and show him wonders his eyes
had never seen.

And still, on the summit of that hill he paused. He remembered the people he had seen in that city, whose eyes held no
love for him. And he thought of their feet so swift and brutal,
and the dark gray clothes they wore, and how when they
passed they did not see him, or, if they saw him, they smirked.
And how their lights, unceasing, crashed on and off above
him, and how he was a stranger there. Then he remembered
his father and his mother, and all the arms stretched out to
hold him back, to save him from this city where, they said,
his soul would find perdition.

And certainly perdition sucked at the feet of the people who
walked there; and cried in the lights, in the gigantic towers;
the marks of Satan could be found in the faces of the people
who waited at the doors of movie houses; his words were
printed on the great movie posters that invited people to sin.
It was the roar of the damned that filled Broadway, where
motor cars and buses and the hurrying people disputed every

inch with death. *Broadway:* the way that led to death *was* broad, and many could be found thereon; but narrow was the way that led to life eternal, and few there were who found it. But he did not long for the narrow way, where all his people walked; where the houses did not rise, piercing, as it seemed, the unchanging clouds, but huddled, flat, ignoble, close to the filthy ground, where the streets and the hallways and the rooms were dark, and where the unconquerable odor was of dust, and sweat, and urine, and homemade gin. In the narrow way, the way of the cross, there awaited him, only humiliation forever; there awaited him, one day, a house like his father's house, and a church like his father's, and a job like his father's, where he would grow old and black with hunger and toil. The way of the cross had given him a belly filled with wind and had bent his mother's back; they had never worn fine clothes, but here, where the buildings contested God's power and where the men and women did not fear God, here he might eat and drink to his heart's content and clothe his body with wondrous fabrics, rich to the eye and pleasing to the touch. And then what of his soul, which would one day come to die and stand naked before the judgment bar? What would his conquest of the city profit him on that day? To hurl away, for a moment of ease, the glories of eternity!

These glories were unimaginable—but the city was real. He stood for a moment on the melting snow, distracted, and then began to run down the hill, feeling himself fly as the descent became more rapid, and thinking: "I can climb back up. If it's wrong, I can always climb back up." At the bottom of the hill, where the ground abruptly leveled off onto a gravel path, he nearly knocked down an old white man with a white beard, who was walking very slowly and leaning on his cane. They both stopped, astonished, and looked at one another. John struggled to catch his breath and apologize, but the old man smiled. John smiled back. It was as though he and the old man had between them a great secret; and the old man moved on. The snow glittered in patches all over the park. Ice, under the pale, strong sun, melted slowly on the branches and the trunks of trees.

He came out of the park at Fifth Avenue where, as always, the old-fashioned horse-carriages were lined along the curb, their drivers sitting on the high seats with rugs around their knees, or standing in twos and threes near the horses, stamping their feet and smoking pipes and talking. In summer he had seen people riding in these carriages, looking like people out of books, or out of movies in which everyone wore old-fashioned clothes and rushed at nightfall over frozen roads, hotly pursued by their enemies who wanted to carry them back to death. *"Look back, look back,"* had cried a beautiful woman with long blonde curls, *"and see if we are pursued!"*— and she had come, as John remembered, to a terrible end. Now he stared at the horses, enormous and brown and patient, stamping every now and again a polished hoof, and he thought of what it would be like to have one day a horse of his own. He would call it Rider, and mount it at morning when the grass was wet, and from the horse's back look out over great, sun-filled fields, his own. Behind him stood his house, great and rambling and very new, and in the kitchen his wife, a beautiful woman, made breakfast, and the smoke rose out of the chimney, melting into the morning air. They had children, who called him Papa and for whom at Christmas he bought electric trains. And he had turkeys and cows and chickens and geese, and other horses besides Rider. They had a closet full of whisky and wine; they had cars—but what church did they go to and what would he teach his children when they gathered around him in the evening? He looked straight ahead, down Fifth Avenue, where graceful women in fur coats walked, looking into the windows that held silk dresses, and watches, and rings. What church did they go to? And what were their houses like when in the evening they took off these coats, and these silk dresses, and put their jewelry in a box, and leaned back in soft beds to think for a moment before they slept of the day gone by? Did they read a verse from the Bible every night and fall on their knees to pray? But no, for their thoughts were not of God, and their way was not God's way. They were in the world, and of the world, and their feet laid hold on Hell.

Yet in school some of them had been nice to him, and it was hard to think of them burning in Hell forever, they who were so gracious and beautiful now. Once, one winter when he had been very sick with a heavy cold that would not leave him, one of his teachers had bought him a bottle of cod liver oil, especially prepared with heavy syrup so that it did not taste so bad: this was surely a Christian act. His mother had said that God would bless that woman; and he had got better. They were kind—he was sure that they were kind—and on the day that he would bring himself to their attention they would surely love and honor him. This was not his father's opinion. His father said that all white people were wicked, and that God was going to bring them low. He said that white people were never to be trusted, and that they told nothing but lies, and that not one of them had ever loved a nigger. He, John, was a nigger, and he would find out, as soon as he got a little older, how evil white people could be. John had read about the things white people did to colored people; how, in the South, where his parents came from, white people cheated them of their wages, and burned them, and shot them—and did worse things, said his father, which the tongue could not endure to utter. He had read about colored men being burned in the electric chair for things they had not done; how in riots they were beaten with clubs; how they were tortured in prisons; how they were the last to be hired and the first to be fired. Niggers did not live on these streets where John now walked; it was forbidden; and yet he walked here, and no one raised a hand against him. But did he dare to enter this shop out of which a woman now casually walked, carrying a great round box? Or this apartment before which a white man stood, dressed in a brilliant uniform? John knew he did not dare, not today, and he heard his father's laugh: *"No, nor tomorrow neither!"* For him there was the back door, and the dark stairs, and the kitchen or the basement. This world was not for him. If he refused to believe, and wanted to break his neck trying, then he could try until the sun re-fused to shine; they would never let him enter. In John's mind then, the people and the avenue underwent a change, and he feared them and knew that one day he could hate them if God did not change his heart.

He left Fifth Avenue and walked west towards the movie houses. Here on 42nd Street it was less elegant but no less strange. He loved this street, not for the people or the shops but for the stone lions that guarded the great main building

of the Public Library, a building filled with books and unimaginably vast, and which he had never yet dared to enter.
He might, he knew, for he was a member of the branch in
Harlem and was entitled to take books from any library in the
city. But he had never gone in because the building was so
big that it must be full of corridors and marble steps, in the
maze of which he would be lost and never find the book he
wanted. And then everyone, all the white people inside, would
know that he was not used to great buildings, or to many
books, and they would look at him with pity. He would enter
on another day, when he had read all the books uptown, an
achievement that would, he felt, lend him the poise to enter
any building in the world. People, mostly men, leaned over
the stone parapets of the raised park that surrounded the library, or walked up and down and bent to drink water from
the public drinking-fountains. Silver pigeons lighted briefly on
the heads of the lions or the rims of fountains, and strutted
along the walks. John loitered in front of Woolworth's, staring
at the candy display, trying to decide what candy to buy—and
buying none, for the store was crowded and he was certain
that the salesgirl would never notice him—and before a vender
of artificial flowers, and crossed Sixth Avenue where the Au-
tomat was, and the parked taxis, and the shops, which he
would not look at today, that displayed in their windows dirty
postcards and practical jokes. Beyond Sixth Avenue the movie
houses began, and now he studied the stills carefully, trying
to decide which of all these theaters he should enter. He
stopped at last before a gigantic, colored poster that represented a wicked woman, half undressed, leaning in a doorway,
apparently quarreling with a blond man who stared wretchedly into the street. The legend above their heads was:
"There's a fool like him in every family—and a woman next
door to take him over!" He decided to see this, for he felt identified with the blond young man, the fool of his family, and he
wished to know more about his so blatantly unkind fate.

And so he stared at the price above the ticket-seller's window and, showing her his coins, received the piece of paper
that was charged with the power to open doors. Having once
decided to enter, he did not look back at the street again for
fear that one of the saints might be passing and, seeing him,

might cry out his name and lay hands on him to drag him back. He walked very quickly across the carpeted lobby, looking at nothing, and pausing only to see his ticket torn, half of it thrown into a silver box and half returned to him. And then the usherette opened the doors of this dark palace and with a flashlight held behind her took him to his seat. Not even then, having pushed past a wilderness of knees and feet to reach his designated seat, did he dare to breathe; nor, out of a last, sick hope for forgiveness, did he look at the screen. He stared at the darkness around him, and at the profiles that gradually emerged from this gloom, which was so like the gloom of Hell. He waited for this darkness to be shattered by the light of the second coming, for the ceiling to crack upward, revealing, for every eye to see, the chariots of fire on which descended a wrathful God and all the host of Heaven. He sank far down in his seat, as though his crouching might make him invisible and deny his presence there. But then he thought: *"Not yet. The day of judgment is not yet,"* and voices reached him, the voices no doubt of the hapless man and the evil woman, and he raised his eyes helplessly and watched the screen.

The woman was most evil. She was blonde and pasty white, and she had lived in London, which was in England, quite some time ago, judging from her clothes, and she coughed. She had a terrible disease, tuberculosis, which he had heard about. Someone in his mother's family had died of it. She had a great many boy friends, and she smoked cigarettes and drank. When she met the young man, who was a student and who loved her very much, she was very cruel to him. She laughed at him because he was a cripple. She took his money and she went out with other men, and she lied to the student—who was certainly a fool. He limped about, looking soft and sad, and soon all John's sympathy was given to this violent and unhappy woman. He understood her when she raged and shook her hips and threw back her head in laughter so furious that it seemed the veins of her neck would burst. She walked the cold, foggy streets, a little woman and not pretty, with a lewd, brutal swagger, saying to the whole world: "You can kiss my ass." Nothing tamed or broke her, nothing touched her, neither kindness, or scorn, nor hatred, nor love. She had never thought of prayer. It was unimaginable that she would ever bend her knees and come crawling along a dusty floor to anybody's altar, weeping for forgiveness. Perhaps her sin was so extreme that it could not be forgiven; perhaps her pride was so great that she did not need forgiveness. She had fallen from that high estate which God had intended for men and women, and she made her fall glorious because it was so complete. John could not have found in his heart, had he dared to search it, any wish for her redemption. He wanted to be like her, only more powerful, more thorough, and more cruel; to make those around him, all who hurt him, suffer as she made the student suffer, and laugh in their faces when they asked pity for their pain. *He* would have asked no pity, and his pain was greater than theirs. Go on, girl, he whispered, as the student, facing her implacable ill will, sighed and wept. Go on, girl. One day he would talk like that, he would face them and tell them how much he hated them, how they had made him suffer, how he would pay them back!

Nevertheless, when she came to die, which she did eventually, looking more grotesque than ever, as she deserved, his thoughts were abruptly arrested, and he was chilled by the expression on her face. She seemed to stare endlessly outward and down, in the face of a wind more piercing than any she had felt on earth, feeling herself propelled with speed into a kingdom where nothing could help her, neither her pride, nor her courage, nor her glorious wickedness. In the place where she was going, it was not these things that mattered but something else, for which she had no name, only a cold intimation, something that she could not alter in any degree, and that she had never thought of. She began to cry, her depraved face breaking into an infant's grimace; and they moved away from her, leaving her dirty in a dirty room, alone to face her Maker. The scene faded out and she was gone; and though the movie went on, allowing the student to marry another girl, darker, and very sweet, but by no means so arresting, John thought of this woman and her dreadful end. Again, had the thought not been blasphemous, he would have thought that it was the Lord who had led him into this theater to show him an example of the wages of sin. The movie ended and people stirred around him; the newsreel came on, and while girls in bathing suits paraded before him and boxers growled and fought, and baseball players ran home safe and presidents and kings of countries that were only names to him moved briefly across the flickering square of light John thought of Hell, of his soul's redemption, and struggled to find a compromise between the way that led to life everlasting and the way that ended in the pit. But there was none, for he had been raised in the truth. He could not claim, as African savages might be able to claim, that no one had brought him the gospel. His father and mother and all the saints had taught him from his earliest childhood what was the will of God. Either he arose from this theater, never to return, putting behind him the world and its pleasures, its honors, and its glories, or he remained here with the wicked and partook of their certain punishment. Yes, it was a narrow way—and John stirred in his seat, not daring to feel it God's injustice that he must make so cruel a choice.

As John approached his home again in the late afternoon, he saw little Sarah, her coat unbuttoned, come flying out of the house and run the length of the street away from him into the far drugstore. Instantly, he was frightened; he stopped a moment, staring blankly down the street, wondering what could justify such hysterical haste. It was true that Sarah was full of self-importance, and made any errand she ran seem a matter of life or death; nevertheless, she had been sent on an errand, and with such speed that her mother had not had time to make her button up her coat.

Then he felt weary; if something had really happened it would be very unpleasant upstairs now, and he did not want to face it. But perhaps it was simply that his mother had a headache and had sent Sarah to the store for some aspirin. But if this were true, it meant that he would have to prepare supper, and take care of the children, and be naked under his father's eyes all the evening long. And he began to walk more slowly.

There were some boys standing on the stoop. They watched him as he approached, and he tried not to look at them and to approximate the swagger with which they walked. One of them said, as he mounted the short, stone steps and started into the hall: "Boy, your brother was hurt real bad today."

He looked at them in a kind of dread, not daring to ask for details; and he observed that they, too, looked as though they had been in a battle; something hangdog in their looks suggested that they had been put to flight. Then he looked down, and saw that there was blood at the threshold, and blood spattered on the tile floor of the vestibule. He looked again at the boys, who had not ceased to watch him, and hurried up the stairs.

The door was half open—for Sarah's return, no doubt—and he walked in, making no sound, feeling a confused impulse to flee. There was no one in the kitchen, though the light was burning—the lights were on all through the house. On the kitchen table stood a shopping-bag filled with groceries, and he knew that his Aunt Florence had arrived. The washtub, where his mother had been washing earlier, was open still, and filled the kitchen with a sour smell.

There were drops of blood on the floor here too, and there had been small, smudged coins of blood on the stairs as he walked up.

All this frightened him terribly. He stood in the middle of the kitchen, trying to imagine what had happened, and preparing himself to walk into the living-room, where all the family seemed to be. Roy had been in trouble before, but this new trouble seemed to be the beginning of the fulfillment of a prophecy. He took off his coat, dropping it on a chair, and was about to start into the living-room when he heard Sarah running up the steps.

He waited, and she burst through the door, carrying a clumsy parcel.

"What happened?" he whispered.

She stared at him in astonishment, and a certain wild joy. He thought again that he really did not like his sister. Catching her breath, she blurted out, triumphantly: "Roy got stabbed with a knife!" and rushed into the living-room.

Roy got stabbed with a knife. Whatever this meant, it was sure that his father would be at his worst tonight. John walked slowly into the living-room.

His father and mother, a small basin of water between them, knelt by the sofa where Roy lay, and his father was washing the blood from Roy's forehead. It seemed that his mother, whose touch was so much more gentle, had been thrust aside by his father, who could not bear to have anyone else touch his wounded son. And now she watched, one hand in the water, the other, in a kind of anguish, at her waist, which was circled still by the improvised apron of the morning. Her face, as she watched, was full of pain and fear, of tension barely supported, and of pity that could scarcely have been expressed had she filled all the world with her weeping. His father muttered sweet, delirious things to Roy, and his hands, when he dipped them again in the basin and wrung out the cloth, were trembling. Aunt Florence, still wearing her hat and carrying her handbag, stood a little removed, looking down at them with a troubled, terrible face.

Then Sarah bounded into the room before him, and his mother looked up, reached out for the package, and saw him. She said nothing, but she looked at him with a strange, quick intentness, almost as though there were a warning on her tongue which at the moment she did not dare to utter. His Aunt Florence looked up, and said: "We been wondering where you was, boy. This bad brother of yours done gone out and got hisself hurt."

But John understood from her tone that the fuss was, possibly, a little greater than the danger—Roy was not, after all, going to die. And his heart lifted a little. Then his father turned and looked at him.

"Where you been, boy," he shouted, "all this time? Don't you know you's needed here at home?"

More than his words, his face caused John to stiffen instantly with malice and fear. His father's face was terrible in anger, but now there was more than anger in it. John saw now what he had never seen there before, except in his own vindictive fantasies: a kind of wild, weeping terror that made the face seem younger, and yet at the same time unutterably older and more cruel. And John knew, in the moment his father's eyes swept over him, that he hated John because John was not lying on the sofa where Roy lay. John could scarcely meet his father's eyes, and yet, briefly, he did, saying nothing, feeling in his heart an odd sensation of triumph, and hoping in his heart that Roy, to bring his father low, would die.

His mother had unwrapped the package and was opening a bottle of peroxide. "Here," she said, "you better wash it with this now." Her voice was calm and dry; she looked at his father briefly, her face unreadable, as she handed him the bottle and the cotton.

"This going to hurt," his father said—in such a different voice, so sad and tender!—turning again to the sofa. "But you just be a little man and hold still; it ain't going to take long."

John watched and listened, hating him. Roy began to moan. Aunt Florence moved to the mantelpiece and put her handbag down near the metal serpent. From the room behind him, John heard the baby begin to whimper.

"John," said his mother, "go and pick her up like a good boy." Her hands, which were not trembling, were still busy: she had opened the bottle of iodine and was cutting up strips of bandage.

John walked into his parents' bedroom and picked up the squalling baby, who was wet. The moment Ruth felt him lift her up she stopped crying and stared at him with a wide-eyed, pathetic stare, as though she knew that there was trouble in the house. John laughed at her so ancient-seeming distress—he was very fond of his baby sister—and whispered in her ear as he started back to the living-room: "Now, you let your big brother tell you something, baby. Just as soon as you's able to stand on your feet, you run away from *this* house, run far away." He did not quite know why he said this, or where he wanted her to run, but it made him feel instantly better.

His father was saying, as John came back into the room: "I'm sure going to be having some questions to ask you in a minute, old lady. I'm going to be wanting to know just how come you let this boy go out and get half killed."

"Oh, no, you ain't," said Aunt Florence. "You ain't going to be starting none of that mess this evening. You know right doggone well that Roy don't never ask *nobody* if he can do *nothing*—he just go right ahead and do like he pleases. Elizabeth sure can't put no ball and chain on him. She got her hands full right here in this house, and it ain't her fault if Roy got a head just as hard as his father's."

"You got a awful lot to say, look like for once you could keep from putting your mouth in my business." He said this without looking at her.

"It ain't my fault," she said, "that you was born a fool, and always done been a fool, and ain't never going to change. I swear to my Father you'd try the patience of Job."

"I done told you before," he said—he had not ceased working over the moaning Roy, and was preparing now to dab the wound with iodine—"that I didn't want you coming in here and using that gutter language in front of my children."

"Don't you worry about my language, brother," she said with spirit, "you better start worrying about your *life*. What these children hear ain't going to do them near as much harm as what they *see*."

"What they *see*," his father muttered, "is a poor man trying to serve the Lord. *That's* my life."

"Then I guarantee *you*," she said, "that they going to do their best to keep it from being *their* life. *You* mark my words."

He turned and looked at her, and intercepted the look that passed between the two women. John's mother, for reasons that were not at all his father's reasons, wanted Aunt Florence to keep still. He looked away, ironically. John watched his mother's mouth tighten bitterly as she dropped her eyes. His father, in silence, began bandaging Roy's forehead.

"It's just the mercy of God," he said at last, "that this boy didn't lose his eye. Look here."

His mother leaned over and looked into Roy's face with a sad, sympathetic murmur. Yet, John felt, she had seen instantly the extent of the danger to Roy's eye and to his life, and was beyond that worry now. Now she was merely marking time, as it were, and preparing herself against the moment when her husband's anger would turn, full force, against her.

His father now turned to John, who was standing near the French doors with Ruth in his arms.

"You come here, boy," he said, "and see what them white folks done done to your brother."

John walked over to the sofa, holding himself as proudly

beneath his father's furious eyes as a prince approaching the scaffold.

"Look here," said his father, grasping him roughly by one arm, "look at your brother."

John looked down at Roy, who gazed at him with almost no expression in his dark eyes. But John knew by the weary, impatient set of Roy's young mouth that his brother was asking that none of this be held against him. It wasn't his fault, or John's, Roy's eyes said, that they had such a crazy father.

His father, with the air of one forcing the sinner to look down into the pit that is to be his portion, moved away slightly so that John could see Roy's wound.

Roy had been gashed by a knife, luckily not very sharp, from the center of his forehead where his hair began, downward to the bone just above his left eye: the wound described a kind of crazy half-moon and ended in a violent, fuzzy tail that was the ruin of Roy's eyebrow. Time would darken the half-moon wound into Roy's dark skin, but nothing would bring together again the so violently divided eyebrow. This crazy lift, this question, would remain with him forever, and emphasize forever something mocking and sinister in Roy's face. John felt a sudden impulse to smile, but his father's eyes were on him and he fought the impulse back. Certainly the wound was now very ugly, and very red, and must, John felt, with a quickened sympathy towards Roy, who had not cried out, have been very painful. He could imagine the sensation caused when Roy staggered into the house, blinded by his blood; but just the same, he wasn't dead, he wasn't changed, he would be in the streets again the moment he was better.

"You see?" came now from his father. "It was white folks, some of them white folks *you* like so much that tried to cut your brother's throat."

John thought, with immediate anger and with a curious contempt for his father's inexactness, that only a blind man, however white, could possibly have been aiming at Roy's throat; and his mother said with a calm insistence:

"And he was trying to cut theirs. Him and them bad boys."

"Yes," said Aunt Florence, "I ain't heard you ask that boy nary a question about how all this happened. Look like you just determined to raise cain any*how* and make everybody in this house suffer because something done happened to the apple of your eye."

"I done asked you," cried his father in a fearful exasperation, "to stop running your *mouth*. Don't none of this concern you. This is *my* family and this is my house. You want me to slap you side of the head?"

"You slap me," she said, with a placidity equally fearful, "and I *do* guarantee you you won't do no more slapping in a hurry."

"Hush now," said his mother, rising, "ain't no need for all this. What's done is done. We ought to be on our knees, thanking the Lord it weren't no worse."

"Amen to that," said Aunt Florence, "*tell* that foolish nigger something."

"You can tell that foolish *son* of yours something," he said to his wife with venom, having decided, it seemed, to ignore his sister, "him standing there with them big buckeyes. You can tell him to take this like a warning from the Lord. *This* is what white folks does to niggers. I been telling you, now you see."

"*He* better take it like a warning?" shrieked Aunt Florence. "*He* better take it? Why, Gabriel, it ain't *him* went halfway across this city to get in a fight with white boys. This boy on the sofa went *deliberately*, with a whole lot of other boys, all the way to the west side, just *looking* for a fight. I declare, I do wonder what goes on in your head."

"You know right well," his mother said, looking directly at his father, "that Johnny don't travel with the same class of boys as Roy goes with. You done beat Roy too many times, here, in this very room for going out with them bad boys. Roy got hisself hurt this afternoon because he was out doing something he didn't have no business doing, and that's the end of it. You ought to be thanking your Redeemer he ain't dead."

"And for all the care you take of him," he said, "he might as well be dead. Don't look like you much care whether he lives, or dies."

"*Lord*, have mercy," said Aunt Florence.

"He's my son, too," his mother said, with heat. "I carried

him in my belly for nine months and I know him just like I know his daddy, and they's just *exactly* alike. Now. You ain't got no *right* in the world to talk to me like that."

"I reckon you *know*," he said, choked, and breathing hard, "all about a mother's love. I sure reckon on you telling me how a woman can sit in the house all day and let her own flesh and blood go out and get half butchered. Don't you tell me you don't know no way to stop him, because I remember *my* mother, God rest her soul, and *she'd* have found a way."

"She was my mother, too," said Aunt Florence, "and I recollect, if you don't, you being brought home many a time more dead than alive. She didn't find no way to stop *you*. She wore herself out beating on you, just like you been wearing yourself out beating on this boy here."

"My, my, *my*," he said, "you got a lot to say."

"I ain't doing a thing," she said, "but trying to talk some sense into your big, black, hardhead. You better stop trying to blame everything on Elizabeth and look to your own wrongdoings."

"Never mind, Florence," his mother said, "it's all over and done with now."

"I'm out of this house," he shouted, "every day the Lord sends, working to put the food in these children's mouths. Don't you think I got a right to ask the mother of these children to look after them and see that they don't break their necks before I get back home?"

"You ain't got but one child," she said, "that's liable to go out and break his neck, and that's Roy, and you know it. And I don't know how in the world you expect me to run this house, and look after these children, and keep running around the block after Roy. *No,* I can't stop him, I done told you that, and you can't stop him neither. You don't know *what* to do with this boy, and that's why you all the time trying to fix the blame on somebody. Ain't nobody to *blame,* Gabriel. You just better pray God to stop him before somebody puts another knife in him and puts him in his grave."

They stared at each other a moment in an awful pause, she with a startled, pleading question in her eyes. Then, with all his might, he reached out and slapped her across the face. She crumpled at once, hiding her face with one thin hand, and

Aunt Florence moved to hold her up. Sarah watched all this with greedy eyes. Then Roy sat up, and said in a shaking voice:

"Don't you slap my mother. That's my *mother*. You slap her again, you black bastard, and I swear to God I'll kill you."

In the moment that these words filled the room, and hung in the room like the infinitesimal moment of hanging, jagged light that precedes an explosion, John and his father were staring into each other's eyes. John thought for that moment that his father believed the words had come from him, his eyes were so wild and depthlessly malevolent, and his mouth was twisted into such a snarl of pain. Then, in the absolute silence that followed Roy's words, John saw that his father was not seeing him, was not seeing anything unless it were a vision. John wanted to turn and flee, as though he had encountered in the jungle some evil beast, crouching and ravenous, with eyes like Hell unclosed; and exactly as though, on a road's turning, he found himself staring at certain destruction, he found that he could not move. Then his father turned and looked down at Roy.

"What did you say?" his father asked.

"I told you," said Roy, "not to touch my mother."

"You cursed me," said his father.

Roy said nothing; neither did he drop his eyes.

"Gabriel," said his mother, "Gabriel. Let us pray. . . ."

His father's hands were at his waist, and he took off his belt. Tears were in his eyes.

"Gabriel," cried Aunt Florence, "ain't you done playing the fool for tonight?"

Then his father raised his belt, and it fell with a whistling sound on Roy, who shivered, and fell back, his face to the wall. But he did not cry out. And the belt was raised again, and again. The air rang with the whistling, and the *crack!* against Roy's flesh. And the baby, Ruth, began to scream.

"My Lord, my Lord," his father whispered, *"my Lord, my Lord."*

He raised the belt again, but Aunt Florence caught it from behind, and held it. His mother rushed over to the sofa and caught Roy in her arms, crying as John had never seen a woman, or anybody, cry before. Roy caught his mother around the neck and held on to her as though he were drowning.

His Aunt Florence and his father faced each other.

"Yes, Lord," Aunt Florence said, "you was born wild, and you's going to die wild. But ain't no use to try to take the whole world with you. You can't change nothing, Gabriel. You ought to know that by now."

John opened the church door with his father's key at six o'clock. Tarry service officially began at eight, but it could begin at any time, whenever the Lord moved one of the saints to enter the church and pray. It was seldom, however, that anyone arrived before eight thirty, the Spirit of the Lord being sufficiently tolerant to allow the saints time to do their Saturday-night shopping, clean their houses, and put their children to bed.

John closed the door behind him and stood in the narrow church aisle, hearing behind him the voices of children playing, and ruder voices, the voices of their elders, cursing and crying in the streets. It was dark in the church; street lights had been snapping on all around him on the populous avenue; the light of the day was gone. His feet seemed planted on this wooden floor; they did not wish to carry him one step further. The darkness and silence of the church pressed on him, cold as judgment, and the voices crying from the window might have been crying from another world. John moved forward, hearing his feet crack against the sagging wood, to where the golden cross on the red field of the altar cloth glowed like smothered fire, and switched on one weak light.

In the air of the church hung, perpetually, the odor of dust and sweat; for, like the carpet in his mother's living-room, the dust of this church was invincible; and when the saints were praying or rejoicing, their bodies gave off an acrid, steamy smell, a marriage of the odors of dripping bodies and soaking, starched white linen. It was a storefront church and had stood, for John's lifetime, on the corner of this sinful avenue, facing the hospital to which criminal wounded and dying were carried almost every night. The saints, arriving, had rented this abandoned store and taken out the fixtures; had painted the walls and built a pulpit, moved in a piano and camp chairs, and bought the biggest Bible they could find. They put white curtains in the show window, and painted across this window TEMPLE OF THE FIRE BAPTIZED. Then they were ready to do the Lord's work.

And the Lord, as He had promised to the two or three first gathered together, sent others; and these brought others and created a church. From this parent branch, if the Lord blessed, other branches might grow and a mighty work be begun throughout the city and throughout the land. In the history of the Temple the Lord had raised up evangelists and teachers and prophets, and called them out into the field to do His work; to go up and down the land carrying the gospel, or to raise other temples—in Philadelphia, Georgia, Boston, or Brooklyn. Wherever the Lord led, they followed. Every now and again one of them came home to testify of the wonders the Lord had worked through him, or her. And sometimes on a special Sunday they all visited one of the nearer churches of the Brotherhood.

There had been a time, before John was born, when his father had also been in the field; but now, having to earn for his family their daily bread, it was seldom that he was able to travel further away than Philadelphia, and then only for a very short time. His father no longer, as he had once done, led great revival meetings, his name printed large on placards that advertised the coming of a man of God. His father had once had a mighty reputation; but all this, it seemed, had changed since he had left the South. Perhaps he ought now to have a church of his own—John wondered if his father wanted that; he ought, perhaps, to be leading, as Father James now led, a great flock to the Kingdom. But his father was only a caretaker in the house of God. He was responsible for the replacement of burnt-out light bulbs, and for the cleanliness of the church, and the care of the Bibles, and the hymn-books, and the placards on the walls. On Friday night he conducted the Young Ministers' Service and preached with them. Rarely did he bring the message on a Sunday morning; only if there was no one else to speak was his father called upon. He was a kind of fill-in speaker, a holy handyman.

Yet he was treated, so far as John could see, with great respect. No one, none of the saints in any case, had ever reproached or rebuked his father, or suggested that his life was anything but spotless. Nevertheless, this man, God's minister, had struck John's mother, and John had wanted to kill him—and wanted to kill him still.

John had swept one side of the church and the chairs were still piled in the space before the altar when there was a knocking at the door. When he opened the door he saw that it was Elisha, come to help him.

"Praise the Lord," said Elisha, standing on the doorstep, grinning.

"Praise the Lord," said John. This was the greeting always used among the saints.

Brother Elisha came in, slamming the door behind him and stamping his feet. He had probably just come from a basketball court; his forehead was polished with recent sweat and his hair stood up. He was wearing his green woolen sweater, on which was stamped the letter of his high school, and his shirt was open at the throat.

"You ain't cold like that?" John asked, staring at him.

"No, little brother, I ain't cold. You reckon everybody's frail like you?"

"It ain't only the little ones gets carried to the graveyard," John said. He felt unaccustomedly bold and lighthearted; the arrival of Elisha had caused his mood to change.

Elisha, who had started down the aisle toward the back room, turned to stare at John with astonishment and menace. "Ah," he said, "I see you fixing to be sassy with Brother Elisha tonight—I'm going to have to give you a little correction. You just wait till I wash my hands."

"Ain't no need to wash your hands if you come here to work. Just take hold of that mop and put some soap and water in the bucket."

"Lord," said Elisha, running water into the sink, and talking, it seemed, to the water, "that sure is a sassy nigger out there. I sure hope he don't get hisself hurt one of these days, running his mouth thataway. Look like he just *won't* stop till somebody busts him in the eye." He sighed deeply, and began to lather his hands. "Here I come running all the way so he wouldn't bust a gut lifting one of them chairs, and all he got to say is 'put some water in the bucket.' Can't do nothing with a nigger nohow." He stopped and turned to face John. "Ain't you got no manners, boy? You better learn how to talk to old folks."

"You better get out here with that mop and pail. We ain't got all night."

"Keep on," said Elisha. "I see I'm going to have to give you your lumps tonight."

He disappeared. John heard him in the toilet, and then over the thunderous water he heard him knocking things over in the back room.

"*Now* what you doing?"

"Boy, leave me alone. I'm fixing to work."

"It sure sounds like it." John dropped his broom and walked into the back. Elisha had knocked over a pile of camp chairs, folded in the corner, and stood over them angrily, holding the mop in his hand.

"I keep telling you not to hide that mop back there. Can't nobody get at it."

"I always get at it. Ain't everybody as clumsy as you."

Elisha let fall the stiff gray mop and rushed at John, catching him off balance and lifting him from the floor. With both arms tightening around John's waist he tried to cut John's breath, watching him meanwhile with a smile that, as John struggled and squirmed, became a set, ferocious grimace. With both hands John pushed and pounded against the shoulders and biceps of Elisha, and tried to thrust with his knees against Elisha's belly. Usually such a battle was soon over, since Elisha was so much bigger and stronger and as a wrestler so much more skilled; but tonight John was filled with a determination not to be conquered, or at least to make the conquest dear. With all the strength that was in him he fought against Elisha, and he was filled with a strength that was almost hatred. He kicked, pounded, twisted, pushed, using his lack of size to confound and exasperate Elisha, whose damp fists, joined at the small of John's back, soon slipped. It was a deadlock; he could not tighten his hold, John could not break it. And so they turned, battling in the narrow room, and the odor of Elisha's sweat was heavy in John's nostrils. He saw the veins rise on Elisha's forehead and in his neck; his breath became jagged and harsh, and the grimace on his face

became more cruel; and John, watching these manifestations
of his power, was filled with a wild delight. They stumbled
against the folding-chairs, and Elisha's foot slipped and his
hold broke. They stared at each other, half grinning. John
slumped to the floor, holding his head between his hands.

"I didn't hurt you none, did I?" Elisha asked.

John looked up. "Me? No, I just want to catch my breath."

Elisha went to the sink, and splashed cold water on his face
and neck. "I reckon you going to let me work now," he said.

"It wasn't *me* that stopped you in the first place." He stood
up. He found that his legs were trembling. He looked at
Elisha, who was drying himself on the towel. "You teach me
wrestling one time, okay?"

"No, boy," Elisha said, laughing, "I don't want to wrestle
with *you*. You too strong for me." And he began to run hot
water into the great pail.

John walked past him to the front and picked up his broom.
In a moment Elisha followed and began mopping near the
door. John had finished sweeping, and he now mounted to
the pulpit to dust the three thronelike chairs, purple, with
white linen squares for the head-pieces and for the massive
arms. It dominated all, the pulpit: a wooden platform raised
above the congregation, with a high stand in the center for
the Bible, before which the preacher stood. There faced the
congregation, flowing downward from this height, the scarlet
altar cloth that bore the golden cross and the legend: JESUS
SAVES. The pulpit was holy. None could stand so high unless
God's seal was on him.

He dusted the piano and sat down on the piano stool to
wait until Elisha had finished mopping one side of the church
and he could replace the chairs. Suddenly Elisha said, without
looking at him:

"Boy, ain't it time you was thinking about your soul?"

"I guess so," John said with a quietness that terrified him.

"I know it looks hard," said Elisha, "from the outside, especially when you young. But you believe me, boy, you can't
find no greater joy than you find in the service of the Lord."

John said nothing. He touched a black key on the piano
and it made a dull sound, like a distant drum.

"You got to remember," Elisha said, turning now to look

at him, "that you think about it with a carnal mind. You still got Adam's mind, boy, and you keep thinking about your friends, you want to do what they do, and you want to go to the movies, and I bet you think about girls, don't you, Johnny? Sure you do," he said, half smiling, finding his answer in John's face, "and you don't want to give up all that. But when the Lord saves you He burns out all that old Adam, He gives you a new mind and a new heart, and then you don't find no pleasure in the world, you get all your joy in walking and talking with Jesus every day."

He stared in a dull paralysis of terror at the body of Elisha. He saw him standing—had Elisha forgotten?—beside Ella Mae before the altar while Father James rebuked him for the evil that lived in the flesh. He looked into Elisha's face, full of questions he would never ask. And Elisha's face told him nothing.

"People say it's hard," said Elisha, bending again to his mop, "but, let me tell you, it ain't as hard as living in this wicked world and all the sadness of the world where there ain't no pleasure nohow, and then dying and going to Hell. Ain't nothing as hard as that." And he looked back at John. "You see how the Devil tricks people into losing their souls?"

"Yes," said John at last, sounding almost angry, unable to bear his thoughts, unable to bear the silence in which Elisha looked at him.

Elisha grinned. "They got girls in the school I go to"—he was finished with one side of the church and he motioned to John to replace the chairs—"and they nice girls, but their minds ain't on the Lord, and I try to tell them the time to repent ain't tomorrow, it's today. They think ain't no sense to worrying now, they can sneak into Heaven on their deathbed. But I tell them, honey, ain't everybody lies down to die—people going all the time, just like that, today you see them and tomorrow you don't. Boy, they don't know what to make of old Elisha because he don't go to movies, and he don't dance, and he don't play cards, and he don't go with them behind the stairs." He paused and stared at John, who watched him helplessly, not knowing what to say. "And boy, some of them is real nice girls, I mean *beautiful* girls, and when you got so much power that *they* don't tempt you then you know you saved sure enough. I just look at them and I tell them Jesus saved me one day, and I'm going to go all the way with *Him*. Ain't no woman, no, nor no man neither going to make me change my mind." He paused again, and smiled and dropped his eyes. "That Sunday," he said, "that Sunday, you remember?—when Father got up in the pulpit and called me and Ella Mae down because he thought we was about to commit sin—well, boy, I don't want to tell no lie, I was mighty hot against the old man that Sunday. But I thought about it, and the Lord made me to see that he was right. Me and Ella Mae, we didn't have nothing on our minds at all, but look like the devil is just everywhere—sometime the devil he put his hand on you and look like you just can't breathe. Look like you just a-burning up, and you got to do something, and you can't do nothing; I been on my knees many a time, weeping and wrestling before the Lord—*crying*, Johnny—and calling on Jesus' name. That's the only name that's got power over Satan. That's the way it's been with *me* sometime, and I'm *saved*. What you think it's going to be like for you, boy?" He looked at John, who, head down, was putting the chairs in order. "Do you want to be saved, Johnny?"

"I don't know," John said.

"Will you try him? Just fall on your knees one day and ask him to help you to pray?"

John turned away, and looked out over the church, which now seemed like a vast, high field, ready for the harvest. He thought of a First Sunday, a Communion Sunday not long ago when the saints, dressed all in white, ate flat, unsalted Jewish bread, which was the body of the Lord, and drank red grape juice, which was His blood. And when they rose from the table, prepared especially for this day, they separated, the men on the one side, and the women on the other, and two basins were filled with water so that they could wash each other's feet, as Christ had commanded His disciples to do. They knelt before each other, woman before woman, and man before man, and washed and dried each other's feet. Brother Elisha had knelt before John's father. When the service was over they had kissed each other with a holy kiss. John turned again and looked at Elisha.

Elisha looked at him and smiled. "You think about what I said, boy."

When they were finished Elisha sat down at the piano and played to himself. John sat on a chair in the front row and watched him.

"Don't look like nobody's coming tonight," he said after a long while. Elisha did not arrest his playing of a mournful song: "Oh, Lord, have mercy on me."

"They'll be here," said Elisha.

And as he spoke there was a knocking on the door. Elisha stopped playing. John went to the door, where two sisters stood, Sister McCandless and Sister Price.

"Praise the Lord, son," they said.

"Praise the Lord," said John.

They entered, heads bowed and hands folded before them around their Bibles. They wore the black cloth coats that they wore all week and they had old felt hats on their heads. John felt a chill as they passed him, and he closed the door.

Elisha stood up, and they cried again: "Praise the Lord!" Then the two women knelt for a moment before their seats to pray. This was also passionate ritual. Each entering saint, before he could take part in the service, must commune for a moment alone with the Lord. John watched the praying women. Elisha sat again at the piano and picked up his mournful song. The women rose, Sister Price first, and then Sister McCandless, and looked around the church.

"Is we the first?" asked Sister Price. Her voice was mild, her skin was copper. She was younger than Sister McCandless by several years, a single woman who had never, as she testified, known a man.

"No, Sister Price," smiled Brother Elisha, "Brother Johnny here was the first. Him and me cleaned up this evening."

"Brother Johnny is mighty faithful," said Sister McCandless. "The Lord's going to work with him in a mighty way, you mark my words."

There were times—whenever, in fact, the Lord had shown His favor by working through her—when whatever Sister McCandless said sounded like a threat. Tonight she was still very much under the influence of the sermon she had preached the night before. She was an enormous woman, one of the biggest and blackest God had ever made, and He had blessed her with a mighty voice with which to sing and preach, and she was going out soon into the field. For many years the Lord had pressed Sister McCandless to get up, as she said, and move; but she had been of timid disposition and feared to set herself above others. Not until He laid her low, before this very altar, had she dared to rise and preach the gospel. But now she had buckled on her traveling shoes. She would cry aloud and spare not, and lift up her voice like a trumpet in Zion.

"Yes," said Sister Price, with her gentle smile, "He says that he that is faithful in little things shall be made chief over many."

John smiled back at her, a smile that, despite the shy gratitude it was meant to convey, did not escape being ironic, or even malicious. But Sister Price did not see this, which deepened John's hidden scorn.

"Ain't but you two who cleaned the church?" asked Sister McCandless with an unnerving smile—the smile of the prophet who sees the secrets hidden in the hearts of men.

"Lord, Sister McCandless," said Elisha, "look like it ain't never but us two. I don't know what the other young folks does on Saturday nights, but they don't come nowhere near here."

Neither did Elisha usually come anywhere near the church on Saturday evenings; but as the pastor's nephew he was entitled to certain freedoms; in him it was a virtue that he came at all.

"It sure is time we had a revival among our young folks," said Sister McCandless. "They cooling off something terrible. The Lord ain't going to bless no church what lets its young people get so lax, no sir. He said, because you ain't neither hot or cold I'm going to spit you outen my mouth. That's the Word." And she looked around sternly, and Sister Price nodded.

"And Brother Johnny here ain't even saved yet," said Elisha. "Look like the saved young people would be ashamed to let him be more faithful in the house of God than they are."

56

GO TELL IT ON THE MOUNTAIN

"He said that the first shall be last and the last shall be first," said Sister Price with a triumphant smile.

"Indeed, He did," agreed Sister McCandless. "This boy going to make it to the Kingdom before any of them, you wait and see."

"Amen," said Brother Elisha, and he smiled at John.

"Is Father going to come and be with us tonight?" asked Sister McCandless after a moment.

Elisha frowned and thrust out his lower lip. "I don't reckon so, Sister," he said. "I believe he going to try to stay home tonight and preserve his strength for the morning service. The Lord's been speaking to him in visions and dreams and he ain't got much sleep lately."

"Yes," said Sister McCandless, "that sure is a praying man. I tell you, it ain't every shepherd tarries before the Lord for his flock like Father James does."

"Indeed, that is the truth," said Sister Price, with animation. "The Lord sure done blessed us with a good shepherd."

"He mighty hard sometimes," said Sister McCandless, "but the Word is hard. The way of holiness ain't no joke."

"He done made me to know that," said Brother Elisha with a smile.

Sister McCandless stared at him. Then she laughed. "Lord," she cried, "I *bet* you can say so!"

"And I loved him for that," said Sister Price. "It ain't every pastor going to set down his own nephew—in front of the whole church, too. And Elisha hadn't committed no big fault."

"Ain't no such thing," said Sister McCandless, "as a little fault or a big fault. Satan get his foot in the door, he ain't going to rest till he's in the room. You is in the Word or you *ain't*—ain't no halfway with God."

"You reckon we ought to start?" asked Sister Price doubtfully, after a pause. "Don't look to me like nobody else is coming."

"Now, don't you sit there," laughed Sister McCandless, "and be of little faith like that. I just believe the Lord's going to give us a great service tonight." She turned to John. "Ain't your daddy coming out tonight?"

"Yes'm," John replied, "he said he was coming."

"There!" said Sister McCandless. "And your mama—is she coming out, too?"

"I don't know," John said. "She mighty tired."

"She ain't so tired she can't come out and pray a *little* while," said Sister McCandless.

For a moment John hated her, and he stared at her fat, black profile in anger. Sister Price said:

"But I declare, it's a wonder how that woman works like she does, and keeps those children looking so neat and clean and all, and gets out to the house of God almost every night. Can't be nothing but the Lord that bears her up."

"I reckon we might have a little song," said Sister McCandless, "just to warm things up. I sure hate to walk in a church where folks is just sitting and talking. Look like it takes all my spirit away."

"Amen," said Sister Price.

Elisha began a song: "This may be my last time," and they began to sing:

> *"This may be the last time I pray with you,*
> *This may be my last time, I don't know."*

As they sang, they clapped their hands, and John saw that Sister McCandless looked about her for a tambourine. He rose and mounted the pulpit steps, and took from the small opening at the bottom of the pulpit three tambourines. He gave one to Sister McCandless, who nodded and smiled, not breaking her rhythm, and he put the rest on a chair near Sister Price.

> *"This may be the last time I sing with you,*
> *This may be my last time, I don't know."*

He watched them, singing with them—because otherwise they would force him to sing—and trying not to hear the words that he forced outward from his throat. And he thought to clap his hands, but he could not; they remained tightly folded in his lap. If he did not sing they would be upon him, but his heart told him that he had no right to sing or to rejoice.

> *"Oh, this*
> *May be my last time*
> *This*
> *May be my last time*
> *Oh, this*
> *May be my last time . . ."*

And he watched Elisha, who was a young man in the Lord; who, a priest after the order of Melchizedek, had been given power over death and Hell. The Lord had lifted him up, and turned him around, and set his feet on the shining way. What were the thoughts of Elisha when night came, and he was alone where no eye could see, and no tongue bear witness, save only the trumpet-like tongue of God? Were his thoughts, his bed, his body foul? What were his dreams?

> *"This may be my last time,*
> *I don't know."*

Behind him the door opened and the wintry air rushed in. He turned to see, entering the door, his father, his mother, and his aunt. It was only the presence of his aunt that shocked him, for she had never entered this church before: she seemed to have been summoned to witness a bloody act. It was in all her aspect, quiet with a dreadful quietness, as she moved down the aisle behind his mother and knelt for a moment beside his mother and father to pray. John knew that it was the hand of the Lord that had led her to this place, and his heart grew cold. The Lord was riding on the wind tonight. What might that wind have spoken before the morning came?

PART TWO

THE PRAYERS OF THE SAINTS

And they cried with a loud voice,
saying, How long, O Lord, holy
and true, dost thou not judge and
avenge our blood on them that dwell
on the earth?

ONE

Florence's Prayer

Light and life to all He brings,
Risen with healing in His wings!

F LORENCE raised her voice in the only song she could remember that her mother used to sing:

> *"It's me, it's me, it's me, oh, Lord,*
> *Standing in the need of prayer."*

Gabriel turned to stare at her, in astonished triumph that
his sister should at last be humbled. She did not look at him.
Her thoughts were all on God. After a moment, the congregation and the piano joined her:

> *"Not my father, not my mother,*
> *But it's me, oh, Lord."*

She knew that Gabriel rejoiced, not that her humility might
lead her to grace, but only that some private anguish had
brought her low: her song revealed that she was suffering, and
this her brother was glad to see. This had always been his
spirit. Nothing had ever changed it; nothing ever would. For
a moment her pride stood up; the resolution that had brought
her to this place tonight faltered, and she felt that if Gabriel
was the Lord's anointed, she would rather die and endure
Hell for all eternity than bow before His altar. But she strangled her pride, rising to stand with them in the holy space
before the altar, and still singing:

> *"Standing in the need of prayer."*

Kneeling as she had not knelt for many years, and in this
company before the altar, she gained again from the song the
meaning it had held for her mother, and gained a new meaning for herself. As a child, the song had made her see a
woman, dressed in black, standing in infinite mists alone, waiting for the form of the Son of God to lead her through that

white fire. This woman now returned to her, more desolate; it was herself, not knowing where to put her foot; she waited, trembling, for the mists to be parted that she might walk in peace. That long road, her life, which she had followed for sixty groaning years, had led her at last to her mother's starting-place, the altar of the Lord. For her feet stood on the edge of that river which her mother, rejoicing, had crossed over. And would the Lord now reach out His hand to Florence and heal and save? But, going down before the scarlet cloth at the foot of the golden cross, it came to her that she had forgotten how to pray.

Her mother had taught her that the way to pray was to forget everything and everyone but Jesus; to pour out of the heart, like water from a bucket, all evil thoughts, all thoughts of self, all malice for one's enemies; to come boldly, and yet more humbly than a little child, before the Giver of all good things. Yet, in Florence's heart tonight hatred and bitterness weighed like granite, pride refused to abdicate from the throne it had held so long. Neither love nor humility had led her to the altar, but only fear. And God did not hear the prayers of the fearful, for the hearts of the fearful held no belief. Such prayers could rise no higher than the lips that uttered them.

Around her she heard the saints' voices, a steady, charged murmur, with now and again the name of *Jesus* rising above, sometimes like the swift rising of a bird into the air of a sunny day, sometimes like the slow rising of the mist from swamp ground. Was this the way to pray? In the church that she had joined when she first came North one knelt before the altar once only, in the beginning, to ask forgiveness of sins; and this accomplished, one was baptized and became a Christian, to kneel no more thereafter. Even if the Lord should lay some great burden on one's back—as He had done, but never so heavy a burden as this she carried now—one prayed in silence. It was indecent, the practice of common niggers to cry aloud at the foot of the altar, tears streaming for all the world to see. She had never done it, not even as a girl down home in the church they had gone to in those days. Now perhaps it was too late, and the Lord would suffer her to die in the darkness in which she had lived so long.

In the olden days God had healed His children. He had caused the blind to see, the lame to walk, and He had raised dead men from the grave. But Florence remembered one phrase, which now she muttered against the knuckles that bruised her lips: "Lord, help my unbelief."

For the message had come to Florence that had come to Hezekiah: *Set thine house in order, for thou shalt die and not live.* Many nights ago, as she turned on her bed, this message came to her. For many days and nights the message was repeated; there had been time, then, to turn to God. But she had thought to evade him, seeking among the women she knew for remedies; and then, because the pain increased, she had sought doctors; and when the doctors did no good she had climbed stairs all over town to rooms where incense burned and where men or women in traffic with the devil gave her white powders, or herbs to make tea, and cast spells upon her to take the sickness away. The burning in her bowels did not cease—that burning which, eating inward, took the flesh visibly from her bones and caused her to vomit up her food. Then one night she found death standing in the room. Blacker than night, and gigantic, he filled one corner of her narrow room, watching her with eyes like the eyes of a serpent when his head is lifted to strike. Then she screamed and called on God, turning on the light. And death departed, but she knew he would be back. Every night would bring him a little closer to her bed.

And after death's first silent vigil her life came to her bedside to curse her with many voices. Her mother, in rotting rags and filling the room with the stink of the grave, stood over her to curse the daughter who had denied her on her deathbed. Gabriel came, from all his times and ages, to curse the sister who had held him to scorn and mocked his ministry. Deborah, black, her body as shapeless and hard as iron, looked on with veiled, triumphant eyes, cursing the Florence who had mocked her in her pain and barrenness. Frank came, even he, with that same smile, the same tilt of his head. Of them all she would have begged forgiveness, had they come with ears to hear. But they came like many trumpets; even if they had come to hear and not to testify it was not they who could forgive her, but only God.

The piano had stopped. All around her now were only the voices of the saints.

"Dear Father"—it was her mother praying—"we come before You on our knees this evening to ask You to watch over us and hold back the hand of the destroying angel. Lord, sprinkle the doorpost of this house with the blood of the Lamb to keep all the wicked men away. Lord, we praying for every mother's son and daughter everywhere in the world but we want You to take special care of this girl here tonight, Lord, and don't let no evil come nigh her. We know you's able to do it, Lord, in Jesus' name, Amen."

This was the first prayer Florence heard, the only prayer she was ever to hear in which her mother demanded the protection of God more passionately for her daughter than she demanded it for her son. It was night, the windows were shut tightly with the shades drawn, and the great table was pushed against the door. The kerosene lamps burned low and made great shadows on the newspaper-covered wall. Her mother, dressed in the long, shapeless, colorless dress that she wore every day but Sunday, when she wore white, and with her head tied up in a scarlet cloth, knelt in the center of the room, her hands hanging loosely folded before her, her black face lifted, her eyes shut. The weak, unsteady light placed shadows under her mouth and in the sockets of her eyes, making the face impersonal with majesty, like the face of a prophetess, or like a mask. Silence filled the room after her "Amen," and in the silence they heard, far up the road, the sound of a horse's hoofs. No one moved. Gabriel, from his corner near the stove, looked up and watched his mother.

"I ain't afraid," said Gabriel.

His mother turned, one hand raised. "You hush, now!"

Trouble had taken place in town today. Their neighbor Deborah, who was sixteen, three years older than Florence, had been taken away into the fields the night before by many white men, where they did things to her to make her cry and bleed. Today, Deborah's father had gone to one of the white men's houses, and said that he would kill him and all the other white men he could find. They had beaten him and left him for dead. Now, everyone had shut their doors, praying and waiting, for it was said that the white folks would come to-night and set fire to all the houses, as they had done before.

In the night that pressed outside they heard only the horse's hoofs, which did not stop; there was not the laughter they would have heard had there been many coming on this road, and no calling out of curses, and no one crying for mercy to white men, or to God. The hoofbeats came to the door and passed, and rang, while they listened, ever more faintly away. Then Florence realized how frightened she had been. She watched her mother rise and walk to the window. She peered out through a corner of the blanket that covered it.

"They's gone," she said, "whoever they was." Then: "Blessed be the name of the Lord," she said.

Thus had her mother lived and died; and she had often been brought low, but she had never been forsaken. She had always seemed to Florence the oldest woman in the world, for she often spoke of Florence and Gabriel as the children of her old age, and she had been born, innumerable years ago, during slavery, on a plantation in another state. On this plantation she had grown up as one of the field workers, for she was very tall and strong; and by and by she had married and raised children, all of whom had been taken from her, one by sickness and two by auction; and one, whom she had not been allowed to call her own, had been raised in the master's house. When she was a woman grown, well past thirty as she reckoned it, with one husband buried—but the master had given her another—armies, plundering and burning, had come from the North to set them free. This was in answer to the prayers of the faithful, who had never ceased, both day and night, to cry out for deliverance.

For it had been the will of God that they should hear, and pass thereafter, one to another, the story of the Hebrew children who had been held in bondage in the land of Egypt; and how the Lord had heard their groaning, and how His heart was moved; and how He bid them wait but a little season till He should send deliverance. Florence's mother had known this story, so it seemed, from the day that she was born. And while she lived—rising in the morning before the sun came up, standing and bending in the fields when the sun was high, crossing the fields homeward while the sun went down at the gates of Heaven far away, hearing the whistle of the foreman and his eerie cry across the fields; in the whiteness of winter when hogs and turkeys and geese were slaughtered, and lights burned bright in the big house, and Bathsheba, the cook, sent over in a napkin bits of ham and chicken and cakes left over by the white folks—in all that befell: in her joys, her pipe in the evening, her man at night, the children she suckled, and guided on their first short steps; and in her tribulations, death, and parting, and the lash, she did not forget that deliverance was promised and would surely come. She had only to endure and trust in God. She knew that the big house, the house of pride where the white folks lived, would come down: it was written in the Word of God. They, who walked so proudly now, had not fashioned for themselves or their children so sure a foundation as was hers. They walked on the edge of a steep place and their eyes were sightless—God would cause them to rush down, as the herd of swine had once rushed down, into the sea. For all that they were so beautiful, and took their ease, she knew them, and she pitied them, who would have no covering in the great day of His wrath.

Yet, she told her children, God was just, and He struck no people without first giving many warnings. God gave men time, but all the times were in His hand, and one day the time to forsake evil and do good would all be finished: then only the whirlwind, death riding on the whirlwind, awaited those people who had forgotten God. In all the days that she was growing up, signs failed not, but none heeded. "Slaves done ris," was whispered in the cabin and at the master's gate: slaves in another county had fired the masters' houses and fields and dashed their children to death against the stones. "Another slave in hell," Bathsheba might say one morning, shooing the pickaninnies away from the great porch: a slave had killed his master, or his overseer, and had gone down to Hell to pay for it. "I ain't got long to stay here," someone crooned beside her in the fields, someone who would be gone by morning on his journey north. All these signs, like the plagues with which the Lord had afflicted Egypt, only hardened the hearts of these people against the Lord. They thought the lash would save them, and they used the lash; or the knife, or the gallows, or the auction block; they thought that kindness would save them, and the master and mistress came down, smiling, to the cabins, making much of the pickaninnies and bearing gifts. These were great days, and they all, black and white, seemed happy together. But when the Word has gone forth from the mouth of God nothing can turn it back.

The word was fulfilled one morning, before she was awake. Many of the stories her mother told meant nothing to Florence; she knew them for what they were, tales told by an old black woman in a cabin in the evening to distract her children from their cold and hunger. But the story of this day she was never to forget; it was a day for which she lived. There was a great running and shouting, said her mother, everywhere outside, and, as she opened her eyes to the light of that day, so bright, she said, and cold, she was certain that the judgment trumpet had sounded. While she still sat, amazed, and wondering what, on the judgment day, would be the best behavior, in rushed Bathsheba, and behind her many tumbling children and field hands and house niggers, all together, and Bathsheba shouted: "Rise up, rise up, Sister Rachel, and see the Lord's deliverance! He done brought us out of Egypt, just like He promised, and we's free at last!" Bathsheba grabbed her, tears running down her face; she, dressed in the clothes in which she had slept, walked to the door to look out on the new day God had given them.

On that day she saw the proud house humbled; green silk and velvet blowing out of windows, and the garden trampled by many horsemen, and the big gate open. The master and mistress, and their kin, and one child she had borne were in that house—which she did not enter. Soon it occurred to her that there was no longer any reason to tarry here. She tied her things in a cloth that she put on her head, and walked out through the big gate, never to see that country any more.

And this became Florence's deep ambition: to walk out one morning through the cabin door, never to return. Her father, whom she scarcely remembered, had departed that way one morning not many months after the birth of Gabriel. And not only her father; every day she heard that another man or woman had said farewell to this iron earth and sky, and started on the journey north. But her mother had no wish to go

North where, she said, wickedness dwelt and Death rode mighty through the streets. She was content to stay in this cabin and do washing for the white folks, though she was old and her back was sore. And she wanted Florence, also, to be content—helping with the washing, and fixing meals and keeping Gabriel quiet.

Gabriel was the apple of his mother's eye. If he had never been born, Florence might have looked forward to a day when she would be released from her unrewarding round of labor, when she might think of her own future and go out to make it. With the birth of Gabriel, which occurred when she was five, her future was swallowed up. There was only one future in that house, and it was Gabriel's—to which, since Gabriel was a man-child, all else must be sacrificed. Her mother did not, indeed, think of it as sacrifice, but as logic: Florence was a girl, and would by and by be married, and have children of her own, and all the duties of a woman; and this being so, her life in the cabin was the best possible preparation for her future life. But Gabriel was a man; he would go out one day into the world to do a man's work, and he needed, therefore, meat, when there was any in the house, and clothes, whenever clothes could be bought, and the strong indulgence of his womenfolk, so that he would know how to be with women when he had a wife. And he needed the education that Florence desired far more than he, and that she might have got if he had not been born. It was Gabriel who was slapped and scrubbed each morning and sent off to the one-room schoolhouse—which he hated, and where he managed to learn, so far as Florence could discover, almost nothing at all. And often he was not at school, but getting into mischief with other boys. Almost all of their neighbors, and even some of the white folks, came at one time or another to complain of Gabriel's wrongdoing. Their mother would walk out into the yard and cut a switch from a tree and beat him—beat him, it seemed to Florence, until any other boy would have fallen down dead; and so often that any other boy would have ceased his wickedness. Nothing stopped Gabriel, though he made Heaven roar with his howling, though he screamed aloud, as his mother approached, that he would never be such a bad boy again. And, after the beating, his pants still down around his knees and his face wet with tears and mucus, Gabriel was made to kneel down while his mother prayed. She asked Florence to pray, too, but in her heart Florence never prayed. She hoped that Gabriel would break his neck. She wanted the evil against which their mother prayed to overtake him one day.

In those days Florence and Deborah, who had become close friends after Deborah's "accident," hated all men. When men looked at Deborah they saw no further than her unlovely and violated body. In their eyes lived perpetually a lewd, uneasy wonder concerning the night she had been taken in the fields. That night had robbed her of the right to be considered a woman. No man would approach her in honor because she was a living reproach, to herself and to all black women and to all black men. If she had been beautiful, and if God had not given her a spirit so demure, she might, with ironic gusto, have acted out that rape in the fields forever. Since she could not be considered a woman, she could only be looked on as a harlot, a source of delights more bestial and mysteries more shaking than any a proper woman could provide. Lust stirred in the eyes of men when they looked at Deborah, lust that could not be endured because it was so impersonal, limiting communion to the area of her shame. And Florence, who was beautiful but did not look with favor on any of the black men who lusted after her, not wishing to exchange her mother's cabin for one of theirs and to raise their children and so go down, toil-blasted, into as it were a common grave, reinforced in Deborah the terrible belief against which no evidence had ever presented itself: that all men were like this, their thoughts rose no higher, and they lived only to gratify on the bodies of women their brutal and humiliating needs.

One Sunday at a camp-meeting, when Gabriel was twelve years old and was to be baptized, Deborah and Florence stood on the banks of a river along with all the other folks and watched him. Gabriel had not wished to be baptized. The thought had frightened and angered him, but his mother insisted that Gabriel was now of an age to be responsible before God for his sins—she would not shirk the duty, laid on her by the Lord, of doing everything within her power to bring him to the throne of grace. On the banks of a river, under the violent light of noon, confessed believers and children of Gabriel's age waited to be led into the water. Standing out, waist-deep and robed in white, was the preacher, who would hold their heads briefly under water, crying out to Heaven as the baptized held his breath: "I indeed have baptized you with water: but He shall baptize you with the Holy Ghost." Then, as they rose sputtering and blinded and were led to the shore, he cried out again: "Go thou and sin no more." They came up from the water, visibly under the power of the Lord, and on the shore the saints awaited them, beating their tambourines. Standing near the shore were the elders of the church, holding towels with which to cover the newly baptized, who were then led into the tents, one for either sex, where they could change their clothes.

At last, Gabriel, dressed in an old white shirt and short linen pants, stood on the edge of the water. Then he was slowly led into the river, where he had so often splashed naked, until he reached the preacher. And the moment that the preacher threw him down, crying out the words of John the Baptist, Gabriel began to kick and sputter, nearly throwing the preacher off balance; and though at first they thought that it was the power of the Lord that worked in him, they realized as he rose, still kicking and with his eyes tightly shut, that it was only fury, and too much water in his nose. Some folks smiled, but Florence and Deborah did not smile. Though Florence had also been indignant, years before when the slimy water entered her incautiously open mouth, she had done her best not to sputter, and she had not cried out. But now, here came Gabriel, floundering and furious up the bank, and what she looked at, with an anger more violent than any she had felt before, was his nakedness. He was drenched, and his thin, white clothes clung like another skin to his black body. Florence and Deborah looked at one another, while the singing rose to cover Gabriel's howling, and Deborah looked away.

Years later, Deborah and Florence had stood on Deborah's porch at night and watched a vomit-covered Gabriel stagger up the moonlit road, and Florence had cried out: "I hate him! I hate him! Big, black, prancing tomcat of a nigger!" And Deborah had said, in that heavy voice of hers: "You know, honey, the Word tell us to hate the sin but not the sinner."

In nineteen hundred, when she was twenty-six, Florence walked out through the cabin door. She had thought to wait until her mother, who was so ill now that she no longer stirred out of bed, should be buried—but suddenly she knew that she would wait no longer, the time had come. She had been working as cook and serving-girl for a large white family in town, and it was on the day her master proposed that she become his concubine that she knew her life among these wretched had come to its destined end. She left her employment that same day (leaving behind her a most vehement conjugal bitterness), and with part of the money that with cunning, cruelty, and sacrifice she had saved over a period of years, bought a railroad ticket to New York. When she bought it, in a kind of scarlet rage, she held like a talisman at the back of her mind the thought: "I can give it back, I can sell it. This don't mean I got to go." But she knew that nothing could stop her.

And it was this leave-taking that came to stand, in Florence's latter days, and with many another witness, at her bedside. Gray clouds obscured the sun that day, and outside the cabin window she saw that mist still covered the ground. Her mother lay in bed, awake; she was pleading with Gabriel, who had been out drinking the night before, and who was not really sober now, to mend his ways and come to the Lord. And Gabriel, full of the confusion, and pain, and guilt that were his whenever he thought of how he made his mother suffer, but that became nearly insupportable when she taxed him with it, stood before the mirror, head bowed, buttoning his shirt. Florence knew that he could not unlock his lips to speak; he could not say yes to his mother, and to the Lord; and he could not say no.

"Honey," their mother was saying, "don't you *let* your old mother die without you look her in the eye and tell her she going to see you in glory. You hear me, boy?"

In a moment, Florence thought with scorn, tears would fill his eyes, and he would promise to "do better." He had been promising to "do better" since the day he had been baptized.

She put down her bag in the center of the hateful room.

"Ma," she said, "I'm going. I'm a-going this morning."

Now that she had said it, she was angry with herself for not

having said it the night before, so that they would have had
time to be finished with their weeping and their arguments.
She had not trusted herself to withstand the night before; but
now there was almost no time left. The center of her mind
was filled with the image of the great, white clock at the rail-
way station, on which the hands did not cease to move.

"You going where?" her mother asked sharply. But she
knew that her mother had understood, had indeed long before this moment known that this time would come. The
astonishment with which she stared at Florence's bag was not
altogether astonishment, but a startled, wary attention. A danger imagined had become present and real, and her mother
was already searching for a way to break Florence's will. All
this Florence knew in a moment, and it made her stronger.
She watched her mother, waiting.

But at the tone of his mother's voice Gabriel, who had
scarcely heard Florence's announcement, so grateful had he
been that something had occurred to distract from him his
mother's attention, dropped his eyes and saw Florence's trav-
eling-bag. And he repeated his mother's question in a
stunned, angry voice, understanding it only as the words hit
the air:

"Yes, girl. Where you think you going?"

"I'm going," she said, "to New York. I got my ticket."

And her mother watched her. For a moment no one said a
word. Then, Gabriel, in a changed and frightened voice,
asked:

"And when you done decide that?"

She did not look at him, nor answer his question. She continued to watch her mother. "I got my ticket," she repeated.
"I'm going on the morning train."

"Girl," asked her mother, quietly, "is you sure you know
what you's doing?"

She stiffened, seeing in her mother's eyes a mocking pity.
"I'm a woman grown," she said. "I know what I'm doing."

"And you going," cried Gabriel, "this morning—just like
that? And you going to walk off and leave your mother—just
like that?"

"You hush," she said, turning to him for the first time, "she
got you, ain't she?"

This was indeed, she realized as he dropped his eyes, the bitter, troubling point. He could not endure the thought of being left alone with his mother, with nothing whatever to put between himself and his guilty love. With Florence gone, time would have swallowed up all his mother's children, except himself; and *he*, then, must make amends for all the pain that she had borne, and sweeten her last moments with all his proofs of love. And his mother required of him one proof only, that he tarry no longer in sin. With Florence gone, his stammering time, his playing time, contracted with a bound to the sparest interrogative second, when he must stiffen himself, and answer to his mother, and all the host of Heaven, yes or no.

Florence smiled inwardly a small, malicious smile, watching his slow bafflement, and panic, and rage; and she looked at her mother again. "She got you," she repeated. "She don't need me."

"You going north," her mother said, then. "And when you reckon on coming back?"

"I don't reckon on coming back," she said.

"You come crying back soon enough," said Gabriel, with malevolence, "soon as they whip your butt up there four or five times."

She looked at him again. "Just don't you try to hold your breath till then, you hear?"

"Girl," said her mother, "you mean to tell me the Devil's done made your heart so hard you can just leave your mother on her dying bed, and you don't care if you don't never see her in this world no more? Honey, you can't tell me you done got so evil as all that?"

She felt Gabriel watching her to see how she would take this question—the question that, for all her determination, she had dreaded most to hear. She looked away from her mother, and straightened, catching her breath, looking outward through the small, cracked window. There, outside, beyond the slowly rising mist, and farther off than her eyes could see, her life awaited her. The woman on the bed was old, her life was fading as the mist rose. She thought of her mother as already in the grave; and she would not let herself be strangled by the hands of the dead.

"I'm going, Ma," she said. "I got to go."

Her mother leaned back, face upward to the light, and began to cry. Gabriel moved to Florence's side and grabbed her arm. She looked up into his face and saw that his eyes were full of tears.

"You can't go," he said. "You can't go. You can't go and leave your mother thisaway. She need a woman, Florence, to help look after her. What she going to do here, all alone with me?"

She pushed him from her and moved to stand over her mother's bed.

"Ma," she said, "don't be like that. Ain't a blessed thing for you to cry about so. Ain't a thing can happen to me up North can't happen to me here. God's everywhere, Ma. Ain't no need to worry."

She knew that she was mouthing words; and she realized suddenly that her mother scorned to dignify these words with her attention. She had granted Florence the victory—with a promptness that had the effect of making Florence, however dimly and unwillingly, wonder if her victory was real. She was not weeping for her daughter's future, she was weeping for the past, and weeping in an anguish in which Florence had no part. And all of this filled Florence with a terrible fear, which was immediately transformed into anger. "Gabriel can take care of you," she said, her voice shaking with malice. "Gabriel ain't never going to leave you. Is you, boy?" and she looked at him. He stood, stupid with bewilderment and grief, a few inches from the bed. "But me," she said, "I got to go." She walked to the center of the room again, and picked up her bag.

"Girl," Gabriel whispered, "ain't you got no feelings at all?"

"Lord!" her mother cried; and at the sound her heart turned over; she and Gabriel, arrested, stared at the bed. "Lord, Lord, Lord! Lord, have mercy on my sinful daughter! Stretch out your hand and hold her back from the lake that burns forever! Oh, my Lord, my Lord!" and her voice dropped, and broke, and tears ran down her face. "Lord, I done my best with all the children what you give me. Lord, have mercy on my children, and my children's children."

"Florence," said Gabriel, "please don't go. Please don't go. You ain't really fixing to go and leave her like this?"

Tears stood suddenly in her own eyes, though she could not have said what she was crying for. "Leave me be," she said to Gabriel, and picked up her bag again. She opened the door; the cold, morning air came in. "Good-by," she said. And then to Gabriel: "Tell her I said good-by." She walked through the cabin door and down the short steps into the frosty yard. Gabriel watched her, standing frozen between the door and the weeping bed. Then, as her hand was on the gate, he ran before her, and slammed the gate shut.

"Girl, where you going? What you doing? You reckon on finding some men up North to dress you in pearls and diamonds?"

Violently, she opened the gate and moved out into the road. He watched her with his jaw hanging, and his lips loose and wet. "If you ever see me again," she said, "I won't be wearing rags like yours."

All over the church there was only the sound, more awful than the deepest silence, of the prayers of the saints of God. Only the yellow, moaning light shone above them, making their faces gleam like muddy gold. Their faces, and their attitudes, and their many voices rising as one voice made John think of the deepest valley, the longest night, of Peter and Paul in the dungeon cell, one praying while the other sang; or of endless, depthless, swelling water, and no dry land in sight, the true believer clinging to a spar. And, thinking of tomorrow, when the church would rise up, singing, under the booming Sunday light, he thought of the light for which they tarried, which, in an instant, filled the soul, causing (throughout those iron-dark, unimaginable ages before John had come into the world) the new-born in Christ to testify: Once I was blind and now I see.

And then they sang: "Walk in the light, the beautiful light. Shine all around me by day and by night, Jesus, the light of the world." And they sang: "Oh, Lord, Lord, I want to be ready, I want to be ready. I want to be ready to walk in Jerusalem just like John."

To walk in Jerusalem just like John. Tonight, his mind was awash with visions: nothing remained. He was ill with doubt and searching. He longed for a light that would teach him, forever and forever, and beyond all question, the way to go; for a power that would bind him, forever and forever, and beyond all crying, to the love of God. Or else he wished to stand up now, and leave this tabernacle and never see these people any more. Fury and anguish filled him, unbearable, unanswerable; his mind was stretched to breaking. For it was time that filled his mind, time that was violent with the mysterious love of God. And his mind could not contain the terrible stretch of time that united twelve men fishing by the shores of Galilee, and black men weeping on their knees tonight, and he, a witness.

My soul is a witness for my Lord. There was an awful silence at the bottom of John's mind, a dreadful weight, a dreadful speculation. And not even a speculation, but a deep, deep turning, as of something huge, black, shapeless, for ages dead on the ocean floor, that now felt its rest disturbed by a faint, far wind, which bid it: "Arise." And this weight began to move at the bottom of John's mind, in a silence like the silence of the void before creation, and he began to feel a terror he had never felt before.

And he looked around the church, at the people praying there. Praying Mother Washington had not come in until all of the saints were on their knees, and now she stood, the terrible, old, black woman, above his Aunt Florence, helping her to pray. Her granddaughter, Ella Mae, had come in with her, wearing a mangy fur jacket over her everyday clothes. She knelt heavily in a corner near the piano, under the sign that spoke of the wages of sin, and now and again she moaned. Elisha had not looked up when she came in, and he prayed in silence: sweat stood on his brow. Sister McCandless and Sister Price cried out every now and again: "Yes, Lord!" or: "Bless your name, Jesus!" And his father prayed, his head lifted up and his voice going on like a distant mountain stream.

But his Aunt Florence was silent; he wondered if she slept. He had never seen her praying in a church before. He knew that different people prayed in different ways: had his aunt always prayed in such a silence? His mother, too, was silent, but he had seen her pray before, and her silence made him feel that she was weeping. And why did she weep? And why did they come here, night after night after night, calling out to a God who cared nothing for them—if, above this flaking ceiling, there was any God at all? Then he remembered that the fool has said in his heart, There is no God—and he dropped his eyes, seeing that over his Aunt Florence's head Praying Mother Washington was looking at him.

Frank sang the blues, and he drank too much. His skin was the color of caramel candy. Perhaps for this reason she always thought of him as having candy in his mouth, candy staining the edges of his straight, cruel teeth. For a while he wore a tiny mustache, but she made him shave it off, for it made him look, she thought, like a half-breed gigolo. In details such as this he was always very easy—he would always put on a clean shirt, or get his hair cut, or come with her to Uplift meetings where they heard speeches by prominent Negroes about the future and duties of the Negro race. And this had given her, in the beginning of their marriage, the impression that she controlled him. This impression had been entirely and disastrously false.

When he had left her, more than twenty years before, and after more than ten years of marriage, she had felt for that moment only an exhausted exasperation and a vast relief. He had not been home for two days and three nights, and when he did return they quarreled with more than their usual bitterness. All of the rage she had accumulated during their marriage was told him in that evening as they stood in their small kitchen. He was still wearing overalls, and he had not shaved, and his face was muddy with sweat and dirt. He had said nothing for a long while, and then he had said: "All right, baby. I guess you don't never want to see me no more, not a miserable, black sinner like me." The door closed behind him, and she heard his feet echoing down the long hall, away. She stood alone in the kitchen, holding the empty coffeepot that she had been about to wash. She thought: "He'll come back, and he'll come back drunk." And then she had thought, looking about the kitchen: "Lord, wouldn't it be a blessing if he didn't never come back no more." The Lord had given her what she said she wanted, as was often, she had found, His bewildering method of answering prayer. Frank never did come back. He lived for a long while with another woman, and when the war came he died in France.

Now, somewhere at the other end of the earth, her husband lay buried. He slept in a land his fathers had never seen. She wondered often if his grave was marked—if there stood over it, as in pictures she had seen, a small white cross. If the Lord had ever allowed her to cross that swelling ocean she would have gone, among all the millions buried there, to seek out his grave. Wearing deep mourning, she would have laid on it, perhaps, a wreath of flowers, as other women did; and stood for a moment, head bowed, considering the unspeaking ground. How terrible it would be for Frank to rise on the day of judgment so far from home! And he surely would not scruple, even on that day, to be angry at the Lord. "Me and the Lord," he had often said, "don't always get along so well. He running the world like He thinks I ain't got good sense." How had he died? Slow or sudden? Had he cried out? Had death come creeping on him from behind, or faced him like a man? She knew nothing about it, for she had not known that he was dead until long afterward, when boys were coming home and she had begun searching for Frank's face in the streets. It was the woman with whom he had lived who had told her, for Frank had given this woman's name as his next of kin. The woman, having told her, had not known what else to say, and she stared at Florence in simple-minded pity. This made Florence furious, and she barely murmured: "Thank you," before she turned away. She hated Frank for making this woman official witness to her humiliation. And she wondered again what Frank had seen in this woman, who, though she was younger than Florence, had never been so pretty, and who drank all the time, and who was seen with many men.

But it had been from the first her great mistake—to meet him, to marry him, to love him as she so bitterly had. Looking at his face, it sometimes came to her that all women had been cursed from the cradle; all, in one fashion or another, being given the same cruel destiny, born to suffer the weight of men. Frank claimed that she got it all wrong side up: it was men who suffered because they had to put up with the ways of women—and this from the time that they were born until the day they died. But it was she who was right, she knew; with Frank she had always been right; and it had not been her fault that Frank was the way he was, determined to live and die a common nigger.

But he was always swearing that he would do better; it was, perhaps, the brutality of his penitence that had kept them together for so long. There was something in her which loved to see him bow—when he came home, stinking with whisky, and crept with tears into her arms. Then he, so ultimately master, was mastered. And holding him in her arms while, finally, he slept, she thought with the sensations of luxury and power: "But there's lots of good in Frank. I just got to be patient and he'll come along all right." To "come along" meant that he would change his ways and consent to be the husband she had traveled so far to find. It was he who, unforgivably, taught her that there are people in the world for whom "coming along" is a perpetual process, people who are destined never to arrive. For ten years he came along, but when he left her he was the same man she had married. He had not changed at all.

He had never made enough money to buy the home she wanted, or anything else she really wanted, and this had been part of the trouble between them. It was not that he could not make money, but that he would not save it. He would take half a week's wages and go out and buy something he wanted, or something he thought she wanted. He would come home on Saturday afternoons, already half drunk, with some useless object, such as a vase, which, it had occurred to him, she would like to fill with flowers—she who never noticed flowers and who would certainly never have bought any. Or a hat, always too expensive or too vulgar, or a ring that looked as though it had been designed for a whore. Sometimes it occurred to him to do the Saturday shopping on his way home, so that she would not have to do it; in which case he would buy a turkey, the biggest and most expensive he could find, and several pounds of coffee, it being his belief that there was never enough in the house, and enough breakfast cereal to feed an army for a month. Such foresight always filled him with such a sense of his own virtue that, as a kind

of reward, he would also buy himself a bottle of whisky; and—
lest she should think that he was drinking too much—invite
some ruffian home to share it with him. Then they would sit
all afternoon in her parlor, playing cards and telling indecent
jokes, and making the air foul with whisky and smoke. She
would sit in the kitchen, cold with rage and staring at the
turkey, which, since Frank always bought them unplucked and
with the head on, would cost her hours of exasperating,
bloody labor. Then she would wonder what on earth had possessed her to undergo such hard trials and travel so far from
home, if all she had found was a two-room apartment in a
city she did not like, and a man yet more childish than any
she had known when she was young.

Sometimes from the parlor where he and his visitor sat he
would call her:

"Hey, Flo!"

And she would not answer. She hated to be called "Flo,"
but he never remembered. He might call her again, and when
she did not answer he would come into the kitchen.

"What's the matter with you, girl? Don't you hear me a-
calling you?"

And once when she still made no answer, but sat perfectly
still, watching him with bitter eyes, he was forced to make
verbal recognition that there was something wrong.

"What's the matter, old lady? You mad at me?"

And when in genuine bewilderment he stared at her, head
to one side, the faintest of smiles on his face, something began
to yield in her, something she fought, standing up and snarling at him in a lowered voice so that the visitor might not
hear:

"I wish you'd tell me just how you think we's going to live
all week on a turkey and five pounds of coffee?"

"Honey, I ain't bought nothing we didn't *need*!"

She sighed in helpless fury, and felt tears springing to her
eyes.

"I done told you time and again to give *me* the money
when you get paid, and let *me* do the shopping—'cause you
ain't got the sense that you was born with."

"Baby, I wasn't doing a thing in the world but trying to
help you out. I thought maybe you wanted to go somewhere

tonight and you didn't want to be bothered with no shopping."

"Next time you want to do me a favor, you tell me first, you hear? And how you expect me to go to a show when you done brought this bird home for me to clean?"

"Honey, I'll clean it. It don't take no time at all."

He moved to the table where the turkey lay and looked at it critically, as though he were seeing it for the first time. Then he looked at her and grinned. "That ain't nothing to get mad about."

She began to cry. "I declare I don't know what gets into you. Every week the Lord sends you go out and do some more foolishness. How do you expect us to get enough money to get away from here if you all the time going to be spending your money on foolishness?"

When she cried, he tried to comfort her, putting his great hand on her shoulder and kissing her where the tears fell.

"Baby, I'm sorry. I thought it'd be a nice surprise."

"The only surprise I want from you is to learn some sense! *That'd* be a surprise! You think I want to stay around here the rest of my life with these dirty niggers you all the time bring home?"

"Where you expect us to live, honey, where we ain't going to be with niggers?"

Then she turned away, looking out of the kitchen window. It faced an elevated train that passed so close she always felt that she might spit in the faces of the flying, staring people.

"I just don't like all that ragtag . . . looks like you think so much of."

Then there was silence. Although she had turned her back to him, she felt that he was no longer smiling and that his eyes, watching her, had darkened.

"And what kind of man you think you married?"

"I thought I married a man with some get up and go to him, who didn't just want to stay on the bottom all his life!"

"And what you want me to do, Florence? You want me to turn white?"

This question always filled her with an ecstasy of hatred. She turned and faced him, and, forgetting that there was someone sitting in the parlor, shouted:

"You ain't got to be white to have some self-respect! You reckon I slave in this house like I do so you and them common niggers can sit here every afternoon throwing ashes all over the floor?"

"And who's common now, Florence?" he asked, quietly, in the immediate and awful silence in which she recognized her error. "Who's acting like a common nigger now? What you reckon my friend is sitting there a-thinking? I declare, I wouldn't be surprised none if he wasn't a-thinking: 'Poor Frank, he sure found him a common wife.' Anyway, he ain't putting his ashes on the floor—he putting them in the ashtray, just like he knew what a ashtray was." She knew that she had hurt him, and that he was angry, by the habit he had at such a moment of running his tongue quickly and incessantly over his lower lip. "But we's a-going now, so you can sweep up the parlor and sit there, if you want to, till the judgment day."

And he left the kitchen. She heard murmurs in the parlor, and then the slamming of the door. She remembered, too late, that he had all his money with him. When he came back, long after nightfall, and she put him to bed and went through his pockets, she found nothing, or almost nothing, and she sank helplessly to the parlor floor and cried.

When he came back at times like this he would be petulant and penitent. She would not creep into bed until she thought that he was sleeping. But he would not be sleeping. He would turn as she stretched her legs beneath the blankets, and his arm would reach out, and his breath would be hot and sour-sweet in her face.

"Sugar-plum, what you want to be so evil with your baby for? Don't you know you done made me go out and get drunk, and I wasn't a-fixing to do that? I wanted to take you out somewhere tonight." And, while he spoke, his hand was on her breast, and his moving lips brushed her neck. And this caused such a war in her as could scarcely be endured. She felt that everything in existence between them was part of a mighty plan for her humiliation. She did not want his touch, and yet she did: she burned with longing and froze with rage. And she felt that he knew this and inwardly smiled to see how easily, on this part of the battlefield, his victory could be assured. But at the same time she felt that his tenderness, his passion, and his love were real.

"Let me alone, Frank. I want to go to sleep."

"No you don't. You don't want to go to sleep so soon. You want me to talk to you a little. You know how your baby loves to talk. Listen." And he brushed her neck lightly with his tongue. "You hear that?"

He waited. She was silent.

"Ain't you got nothing more to say than that? I better tell you something else." And then he covered her face with kisses; her face, neck, arms, and breasts.

"You stink of whisky. Let me alone."

"Ah. I ain't the only one got a tongue. What you got to say to this?" And his hand stroked the inside of her thigh.

"Stop."

"I ain't going to stop. This is sweet talk, baby."

Ten years. Their battle never ended; they never bought a home. He died in France. Tonight she remembered details of those years which she thought she had forgotten, and at last she felt the stony ground of her heart break up; and tears, as difficult and slow as blood, began to trickle through her fingers. This the old woman above her somehow divined, and she cried: "Yes, honey. You just let go, honey. Let Him bring you low so He can raise you up." And was this the way she should have gone? Had she been wrong to fight so hard? Now she was an old woman, and all alone, and she was going to die. And she had nothing for all her battles. It had all come to this: she was on her face before the altar, crying to God for mercy. Behind her she heard Gabriel cry: "Bless your name, Jesus!" and, thinking of him and the high road of holiness he had traveled, her mind swung like a needle, and she thought of Deborah.

Deborah had written her, not many times, but in a rhythm that seemed to remark each crisis in her life with Gabriel, and once, during the time she and Frank were still together, she had received from Deborah a letter that she had still: it was locked tonight in her handbag, which lay on the altar. She had always meant to show this letter to Gabriel one day, but she never had. She had talked with Frank about it late one night while he lay in bed whistling some ragtag tune and she sat before the mirror and rubbed bleaching cream into her skin. The letter lay open before her and she sighed loudly, to attract Frank's attention.

He stopped whistling in the middle of a phrase; mentally, she finished it. "What you got there, sugar?" he asked, lazily.

"It's a letter from my brother's wife." She stared at her face in the mirror, thinking angrily that all these skin creams were a waste of money, they never did any good.

"What's them niggers doing down home? It ain't no bad news, is it?" Still he hummed, irrepressibly, deep in his throat.

"No . . . well, it ain't no good news neither, but it ain't nothing to surprise *me* none. She say she think my brother's got a bastard living right there in the same town what he's scared to call his own."

"No? And I thought you said your brother was a preacher."

"Being a preacher ain't never stopped a nigger from doing his dirt."

Then he laughed. "You sure don't love your brother like you should. How come his wife found out about this kid?"

She picked up the letter and turned to face him. "Sound to *me* like she *been* knowing about it but she ain't never had the nerve to say nothing." She paused, then added, reluctantly: "Of course, she ain't really what you might call *sure*. But she ain't a woman to go around thinking things. She mighty worried."

"Hell, what she worried about it now for? Can't nothing be done about it *now*."

"She wonder if she ought to ask him about it."

"And do she reckon if she ask him, he going to be fool enough to say yes?"

She sighed again, more genuinely this time, and turned back to the mirror. "Well . . . he's a preacher. And if Deborah's right, he ain't got no right to be a preacher. He ain't no better'n nobody else. In *fact*, he ain't no better than a murderer."

He had begun to whistle again; he stopped. "Murderer? How so?"

"Because he done let this child's mother go off and die

when the child was born. That's how so." She paused. "And it sound just like Gabriel. He ain't never thought a minute about nobody in this world but himself."

He said nothing, watching her implacable back. Then: "You going to answer this letter?"

"I reckon."

"And what you going to say?"

"I'm going to tell her she ought to let him know she know about his wickedness. Get up in front of the congregation and tell them too, if she has to."

He stirred restlessly, and frowned. "Well, you know more about it than me. But I don't see where that's going to do no good."

"It'll do *her* some good. It'll make him treat her better. You don't know my brother like I do. There ain't but one way to get along with him, you got to scare him half to death. That's all. He ain't *got* no right to go around running his mouth about how holy he is if he done turned a trick like that."

There was silence; he whistled again a few bars of his song; and then he yawned, and said: "Is you coming to bed, old lady? Don't know why you keep wasting all your time and *my* money on all them old skin whiteners. You as black now as you was the day you was born."

"You wasn't there the day I was born. And I know you don't want a coal-black woman." But she rose from the mirror, and moved toward the bed.

"I ain't never said nothing like that. You just kindly turn out that light and I'll make you to know that black's a mighty pretty color."

She wondered if Deborah had ever spoken; and she wondered if she would give to Gabriel the letter that she carried in her handbag tonight. She had held it all these years, awaiting some savage opportunity. What this opportunity would have been she did not know; at this moment she did not want to know. For she had always thought of this letter as an instrument in her hands which could be used to complete her brother's destruction. When he was completely cast down she would prevent him from ever rising again by holding before him the evidence of his blood-guilt. But now she thought she would not live to see this patiently awaited day. She was going to be cut down.

And the thought filled her with terror and rage; the tears dried on her face and the heart within her shook, divided between a terrible longing to surrender and a desire to call God into account. Why had he preferred her mother and her brother, the old, black woman, and the low, black man, while she, who had sought only to walk upright, was come to die, alone and in poverty, in a dirty, furnished room? She beat her fists heavily against the altar. He, *he* would live, and, smiling, watch her go down into the grave! And her mother would be there, leaning over the gates of Heaven, to see her daughter burning in the pit.

As she beat her fists on the altar, the old woman above her laid hands on her shoulders, crying: "Call on Him, daughter! Call on the Lord!" And it was as though she had been hurled outward into time, where no boundaries were, for the voice was the voice of her mother but the hands were the hands of death. And she cried aloud, as she had never in all her life cried before, falling on her face on the altar, at the feet of the old, black woman. Her tears came down like burning rain. And the hands of death caressed her shoulders, the voice whispered and whispered in her ear: "God's got your number, knows where you live, death's got a warrant out for you."

TWO

Gabriel's Prayer

Now I been introduced
To the Father and the Son,
And I ain't
No stranger now.

W HEN Florence cried, Gabriel was moving outward in
fiery darkness, talking to the Lord. Her cry came to him
from afar, as from unimaginable depths; and it was not his
sister's cry he heard, but the cry of the sinner when he is taken
in his sin. This was the cry he had heard so many days and
nights, before so many altars, and he cried tonight, as he had
cried before: "Have your way, Lord! Have your way!"

Then there was only silence in the church. Even Praying
Mother Washington had ceased to moan. Soon someone
would cry again, and the voices would begin again; there
would be music by and by, and shouting, and the sound of
the tambourines. But now in this waiting, burdened silence it
seemed that all flesh waited—paused, transfixed by something
in the middle of the air—for the quickening power.

This silence, continuing like a corridor, carried Gabriel back
to the silence that had preceded his birth in Christ. Like a
birth indeed, all that had come before this moment was
wrapped in darkness, lay at the bottom of the sea of forgetfulness, and was not now counted against him, but was related
only to that blind, and doomed, and stinking corruption he
had been before he was redeemed.

The silence was the silence of the early morning, and he
was returning from the harlot's house. Yet all around him
were the sounds of the morning: of birds, invisible, praising
God; of crickets in the vines, frogs in the swamp, of dogs miles
away and close at hand, roosters on the porch. The sun was
not yet half awake; only the utmost tops of trees had begun
to tremble at his turning; and the mist moved sullenly, before
Gabriel and all around him, falling back before the light that

87

rules by day. Later, he said of that morning that his sin was
on him; then he knew only that he carried a burden and that
he longed to lay it down. This burden was heavier than the
heaviest mountain and he carried it in his heart. With each
step that he took his burden grew heavier, and his breath
became slow and harsh, and, of a sudden, cold sweat stood
out on his brow and drenched his back.

All alone in the cabin his mother lay waiting; not only for
his return this morning, but for his surrender to the Lord. She
lingered only for this, and he knew it, even though she no
longer exhorted him as she had in days but shortly gone by.
She had placed him in the hands of the Lord, and she waited
with patience to see how He would work the matter.

For she would live to see the promise of the Lord fulfilled.
She would not go to her rest until her son, the last of her
children, he who would place her in the winding-sheet, should
have entered the communion of the saints. Now she, who had
been impatient once, and violent, who had cursed and
shouted and contended like a man, moved into silence, con-
tending only, and with the last measure of her strength, with
God. And this, too, she did like a man: knowing that she had
kept the faith, she waited for Him to keep His promise.
Gabriel knew that when he entered she would not ask him
where he had been; she would not reproach him; and her eyes,
even when she closed her lids to sleep, would follow him
everywhere.

Later, since it was Sunday, some of the brothers and sisters
would come to her, to sing and pray around her bed. And she
would pray for him, sitting up in bed unaided, her head lifted,
her voice steady; while he, kneeling in a corner of the room,
trembled and almost wished that she would die; and trembled
again at this testimony to the desperate wickedness of his
heart; and prayed without words to be forgiven. For he had
no words when he knelt before the throne. And he feared to
make a vow before Heaven until he had the strength to keep
it. And yet he knew that until he made the vow he would
never find the strength.

For he desired in his soul, with fear and trembling, all the
glories that his mother prayed he should find. Yes, he wanted
power—he wanted to know himself to be the Lord's anointed,

His well-beloved, and worthy, nearly, of that snow-white dove which had been sent down from Heaven to testify that Jesus was the son of God. He wanted to be master, to speak with that authority which could only come from God. It was later to become his proud testimony that he hated his sins—even as he ran towards sin, even as he sinned. He hated the evil that lived in his body, and he feared it, as he feared and hated the lions of lust and longing that prowled the defenseless city of his mind. He was later to say that this was a gift bequeathed him by his mother, that it was God's hand on him from his earliest beginnings; but then he knew only that when each night came, chaos and fever raged in him; the silence in the cabin between his mother and himself became something that could not be borne; not looking at her, facing the mirror as he put on his jacket, and trying to avoid his face there, he told her that he was going to take a little walk—he would be back soon.

Sometimes Deborah sat with his mother, watching him with eyes that were no less patient and reproachful. He would escape into the starry night and walk until he came to a tavern, or to a house that he had marked already in the long daytime of his lust. And then he drank until hammers rang in his distant skull; he cursed his friends and his enemies, and fought until blood ran down; in the morning he found himself in mud, in clay, in strange beds, and once or twice in jail; his mouth sour, his clothes in rags, from all of him arising the stink of his corruption. Then he could not even weep. He could not even pray. He longed, nearly, for death, which was all that could release him from the cruelty of his chains.

And through all this his mother's eyes were on him; her hand, like fiery tongs, gripped the lukewarm ember of his heart; and caused him to feel, at the thought of death, another, colder terror. To go down into the grave, unwashed, unforgiven, was to go down into the pit forever, where terrors awaited him greater than any the earth, for all her age and groaning, had ever borne. He would be cut off from the living, forever; he would have no name forever. Where he had been would be silence only, rock, stubble, and no seed; for him, forever, and for his, no hope of glory. Thus, when he came to the harlot, he came to her in rage, and he left her in

vain sorrow—feeling himself to have been, once more, most
foully robbed, having spent his holy seed in a forbidden darkness where it could only die. He cursed the betraying lust that
lived in him, and he cursed it again in others. But: "I remember," he was later to say, "the day my dungeon shook and
my chains fell off."

And he walked homeward, thinking of the night behind
him. He had seen the woman at the very beginning of the
evening, but she had been with many others, men and
women, and so he had ignored her. But later, when he was
on fire with whisky, he looked again directly at her, and saw
immediately that she had also been thinking of him. There
were not so many people with her—it was as though she had
been making room for him. He had already been told that
she was a widow from the North, in town for only a few days
to visit her people. When he looked at her she looked at him
and, as though it were part of the joking conversation she was
having with her friends, she laughed aloud. She had the lie-
gap between her teeth, and a big mouth; when she laughed,
she belatedly caught her lower lip in her teeth, as though she
were ashamed of so large a mouth, and her breasts shook. It
was not like the riot that occurred when big, fat women
laughed—her breasts rose and fell against the tight cloth of
her dress. She was much older than he—around Deborah's
age, perhaps thirty-odd—and she was not really pretty. Yet
the distance between them was abruptly charged with her, and
her smell was in his nostrils. Almost, he felt those moving
breasts beneath his hand. And he drank again, allowing, unconsciously, or nearly, his face to fall into the lines of innocence and power which his experience with women had told
him made their love come down.

Well (walking homeward, cold and tingling) yes, they did
the thing. Lord, how they rocked in their bed of sin, and how
she cried and shivered; Lord how her love came down! Yes
(walking homeward through the fleeing mist, with the cold
sweat standing on his brow), yet, in vanity and the pride of
conquest, he thought of her, of her smell, the heat of her body
beneath his hands, of her voice, and her tongue, like the
tongue of a cat, and her teeth, and her swelling breasts, and

how she moved for him, and held him, and labored with him, and how they fell, trembling and groaning, and locked together, into the world again. And, thinking of this, his body freezing with his sweat, and yet altogether violent with the memory of lust, he came to a tree on a gentle rise, beyond which, and out of sight, lay home, where his mother lay. And there leaped into his mind, with the violence of water that has burst the dams and covered the banks, rushing uncontrolled toward the doomed, immobile houses—on which, on rooftops and windows, the sun yet palely shivers—the memory of all the mornings he had mounted here and passed this tree, caught for a moment between sins committed and sins to be committed. The mist on this rise had fled away, and he felt that he stood, as he faced the lone tree, beneath the naked eye of Heaven. Then, in a moment, there was silence, only silence, everywhere—the very birds had ceased to sing, and no dogs barked, and no rooster crowed for day. And he felt that this silence was God's judgment; that all creation had been stilled before the just and awful wrath of God, and waited now to see the sinner—*he* was the sinner—cut down and banished from the presence of the Lord. And he touched the tree, hardly knowing that he touched it, out of an impulse to be hidden; and then he cried: "Oh, Lord, have mercy! Oh, Lord, have mercy on me!"

And he fell against the tree, sinking to the ground and clutching the roots of the tree. He had shouted into silence and only silence answered—and yet, when he cried, his cry had caused a ringing to the outermost limits of the earth. This ringing, his lone cry rolling through creation, frightening the sleeping fish and fowl, awakening echoes everywhere, river, and valley, and mountain wall, caused in him a fear so great that he lay for a moment silent and trembling at the base of the tree, as though he wished to be buried there. But that burdened heart of his would not be still, would not let him keep silence—would not let him breathe until he cried again. And so he cried again; and his cry returned again; and still the silence waited for God to speak.

And his tears began—such tears as he had not known were in him. "I wept," he said later, "like a little child." But no child had ever wept such tears as he wept that morning on his face before Heaven, under the mighty tree. They came from deeps no child discovers, and shook him with an ague no child endures. And presently, in his agony, he was screaming, each cry seeming to tear his throat apart, and stop his breath, and force the hot tears down his face, so that they splashed his hands and wet the root of the tree: "Save me! Save me!" And all creation rang, but did not answer. "I couldn't hear nobody pray."

Yes, he was in that valley where his mother had told him he would find himself, where there was no human help, no hand outstretched to protect or save. Here nothing prevailed save the mercy of God—here the battle was fought between God and the Devil, between death and everlasting life. And he had tarried too long, he had turned aside in sin too long, and God would not hear him. The appointed time had passed and God had turned His face away.

"Then," he testified, "I heard my mother singing. She was a-singing for me. She was a-singing low and sweet, right there beside me, like she knew if she just called Him, the Lord would come." When he heard this singing, which filled all the silent air, which swelled until it filled all the waiting earth, the heart within him broke, and yet began to rise, lifted of its burden; and his throat unlocked; and his tears came down as though the listening skies had opened. "Then I praised God, Who had brought me out of Egypt and set my feet on the solid rock." When at last he lifted up his eyes he saw a new Heaven and a new earth; and he heard a new sound of singing, for a sinner had come home. "I looked at my hands and my hands were new. I looked at my feet and my feet were new. And I opened my mouth to the Lord that day and Hell won't make me change my mind." And, yes, there was singing everywhere; the birds and the crickets and the frogs rejoiced, the distant dogs leaping and sobbing, circled in their narrow yards, and roosters cried from every high fence that here was a new beginning, a blood-washed day!

And this was the beginning of his life as a man. He was just past twenty-one; the century was not yet one year old. He moved into town, into the room that awaited him at the top of the house in which he worked, and he began to preach.

He married Deborah in that same year. After the death of his mother, he began to see her all the time. They went to the house of God together, and because there was no one, any more, to look after him, she invited him often to her home for meals, and kept his clothes neat, and after he had preached they discussed his sermons; that is, he listened while she praised.

He had certainly never intended to marry her; such an idea was no more in his mind, he would have said, than the possibility of flying to the moon. He had known her all his life; she had been his older sister's older friend, and then his mother's faithful visitor; she had never, for Gabriel, been young. So far as he was concerned, she might have been born in her severe, her sexless, long and shapeless habit, always black or gray. She seemed to have been put on earth to visit the sick, and to comfort those who wept, and to arrange the last garments of the dying.

Again, there was her legend, her history, which would have been enough, even had she not been so wholly unattractive, to put her forever beyond the gates of any honorable man's desire. This, indeed, in her silent, stolid fashion, she seemed to know: where, it might be, other women held as their very charm and secret the joy that they could give and share, she contained only the shame that she had borne—shame, unless a miracle of human love delivered her, was all she had to give. And she moved, therefore, through their small community like a woman mysteriously visited by God, like a terrible example of humility, or like a holy fool. No ornaments ever graced her body; there was about her no tinkling, no shining, and no softness. No ribbon falsified her blameless and implacable headgear; on her woolen head there was only the barest minimum of oil. She did not gossip with the other women—she had nothing, indeed, to gossip about—but kept her communication to yea and nay, and read her Bible, and prayed. There were people in the church, and even men carrying the gospel, who mocked Deborah behind her back; but their mockery was uneasy; they could never be certain but that they might be holding up to scorn the greatest saint among them, the Lord's peculiar treasure and most holy vessel.

"You sure is a godsend to me, Sister Deborah," Gabriel

would sometimes say. "I don't know what I'd do without you."

For she sustained him most beautifully in his new condition; with her unquestioning faith in God, and her faith in him, she, even more than the sinners who came crying to the altar after he had preached, bore earthly witness to his calling; and speaking, as it were, in the speech of men she lent reality to the mighty work that the Lord had appointed to Gabriel's hands.

And she would look up at him with her timid smile. "You hush, Reverend. It's me that don't never kneel down without I thank the Lord for *you*."

Again: she never called him Gabriel or "Gabe," but from the time that he began to preach she called him Reverend, knowing that the Gabriel whom she had known as a child was no more, was a new man in Christ Jesus.

"You ever hear from Florence?" she sometimes asked.

"Lord, Sister Deborah, it's me that ought to be asking *you*. That girl don't hardly never write to me."

"I ain't heard from her real lately." She paused. Then: "I don't believe she so happy up there."

"And serve her right, too—she ain't had no business going away from here like she did, just like a crazy woman." And then he asked, maliciously: "She tell you if she married yet?"

She looked at him quickly, and looked away. "Florence ain't thinking about no husband," she said.

He laughed. "God bless you for your pure heart, Sister Deborah. But if that girl ain't gone away from here a-looking for a husband, my name ain't Gabriel Grimes."

"If she'd a wanted a husband look to me like she could a just picked one out right here. You don't mean to tell me she done traveled all the way North just for that?" And she smiled strangely, a smile less gravely impersonal. He, seeing this, thought that it certainly did a strange thing to her face: it made her look like a frightened girl.

"You know," he said, watching her with more attention, "Florence ain't never thought none of these niggers around here was good enough for her."

"I wonder," she ventured, "if she *ever* going to find a man good enough for her. She so proud—look like she just won't let nobody come near her."

"Yes," he said, frowning, "she so proud the Lord going to bring her low one day. You mark my words."

"Yes," she sighed, "the Word sure do tell us that pride goes before destruction."

"And a haughty spirit before a fall. That's the Word."

"Yes," and she smiled again, "ain't no shelter against the Word of God, is there, Reverend? You is just got to be in it, that's all—'cause every word is true, and the gates of Hell ain't going to be able to stand against it."

He smiled, watching her, and felt a great tenderness fill his heart. "You just *stay* in the Word, little sister. The windows of Heaven going to open up and pour down blessings on you till you won't know where to put them."

When she smiled now it was with a heightened joy. "He done blessed me already, Reverend. He blessed me when He saved your soul and sent you out to preach His gospel."

"Sister Deborah," he said, slowly, "all that sinful time— was you a-praying for me?"

Her tone dropped ever so slightly. "We sure was, Reverend. Me and your mother, we was a-praying all the time."

And he looked at her, full of gratitude and a sudden, wild conjecture: he had been real for her, she had watched him, and prayed for him during all those years when she, for him, had been nothing but a shadow. And she was praying for him still; he would have her prayers to aid him all his life long— he saw this, now, in her face. She said nothing, and she did not smile, only looked at him with her grave kindness, now a little questioning, a little shy.

"God bless you, sister," he said at last.

It was during this dialogue, or hard on the heels of it, that the town was subjected to a monster revival meeting. Evangelists from all the surrounding counties, from as far south as Florida and as far north as Chicago, came together in one place to break the bread of life. It was called the Twenty-Four Elders Revival Meeting, and it was the great occasion of that summer. For there were twenty-four of them, each one given his night to preach—to shine, as it were, before men, and to glorify his Heavenly Father. Of these twenty-four, all of them men of great experience and power, and some of them men of great fame, Gabriel, to his astonished pride, was asked to be one. This was a great, a heavy honor for one so young in the faith, and in years—who had but only yesterday been lying, vomit-covered, in the gutters of sin—and Gabriel felt his heart shake with fear as this invitation came to him. Yet he felt that it was the hand of God that had called him out so early to prove himself before such mighty men.

He was to preach on the twelfth night. It was decided, in view of his possible failure to attract, to support him on either side with a nearly equal number of war horses. He would have, thus, the benefit of the storm they would certainly have stirred up before him; and should he fail to add substantially to the effect they had created, there would be others coming after him to obliterate his performance.

But Gabriel did not want his performance—the most important of his career so far, and on which so much depended—to be obliterated; he did not want to be dismissed as a mere boy who was scarcely ready to be counted in the race, much less to be considered a candidate for the prize. He fasted on his knees before God and did not cease, daily and nightly, to pray that God might work through him a mighty work and cause all men to see that, indeed, God's hand was on him, that he was the Lord's anointed.

Deborah, unasked, fasted with him, and prayed, and took his best black suit away, so that it would be clean and mended and freshly pressed for the great day. And she took it away again, immediately afterward, so that it would be no less splendid on the Sunday of the great dinner that was officially to punctuate the revival. This Sunday was to be a feast day for everyone, but more especially for the twenty-four elders, who were, that day, to be gloriously banqueted at the saints' expense and labor.

On the evening when he was to preach, he and Deborah walked together to the great, lighted, lodge hall that had but lately held a dance band, and that the saints had rented for the duration of the revival. The service had already begun; lights spilled outward into the streets, music filled the air, and passers-by paused to listen and to peek in through the half-open doors. He wanted all of them to enter; he wanted to run through the streets and drag all sinners in to hear the Word of God. Yet, as they approached the doors, the fear held in check so many days and nights rose in him again, and he thought how he would stand tonight, so high, and all alone, to vindicate the testimony that had fallen from his lips, that God had called him to preach.

"Sister Deborah," he said, suddenly, as they stood before the doors, "you sit where I can see you?"

"I sure will do that, Reverend," she said. "You go on up there. Trust God."

Without another word he turned, leaving her in the door, and walked up the long aisle to the pulpit. They were all there already, big, comfortable, ordained men; they smiled and nodded as he mounted the pulpit steps; and one of them said, nodding toward the congregation, which was as spirited as any evangelist could wish: "Just getting these folks warmed up for you, boy. Want to see you make them *holler* tonight."

He smiled in the instant before he knelt down at his throne-like chair to pray; and thought again, as he had been thinking for eleven nights, that there was about his elders an ease in the holy place, and a levity, that made *his* soul uneasy. While he sat, waiting, he saw that Deborah had found a seat in the very front of the congregation, just below the pulpit, and sat with her Bible folded on her lap.

When, at last, the Scripture lesson read, the testimonies in, the songs sung, the collection taken up, he was introduced— by the elder who had preached the night before—and found himself on his feet, moving toward the pulpit where the great Bible awaited him, and over that sheer drop the murmuring congregation; he felt a giddy terror that he stood so high, and with this, immediately, a pride and joy unspeakable that God had placed him there.

He did not begin with a "shout" song, or with a fiery testimony; but in a dry, matter-of-fact voice, which trembled only a little, asked them to look with him at the sixth chapter of Isaiah, and the fifth verse; and he asked Deborah to read it aloud for him.

And she read, in a voice unaccustomedly strong: " 'Then said I, Woe is me! for I am undone; because I am a man of unclean lips, and I dwell in the midst of a people of unclean lips: for mine eyes have seen the King, the Lord of hosts.' "

Silence filled the lodge hall after she had read this sentence. For a moment Gabriel was terrified by the eyes on him, and by the elders at his back, and could not think how to go on. Then he looked at Deborah, and began.

These words had been uttered by the prophet, Isaiah, who had been called the Eagle-eyed because he had looked down the dark centuries and foreseen the birth of Christ. It was Isaiah also who had prophesied that a man should be as a hiding-place from the wind and tempest, Isaiah who had described the way of holiness, saying that the parched ground should become a pool, and the thirsty land springs of water: the very desert should rejoice, and blossom as the rose. It was Isaiah who had prophesied, saying: "Unto us a child is born, unto us a son is given; and the government shall be upon His shoulder." This was a man whom God had raised in righteousness, whom God had chosen to do many mighty works, yet this man, beholding the vision of God's glory, had cried out: "Woe is me!"

"Yes!" cried a woman. *"Tell it!"*

"There is a lesson for us all in this cry of Isaiah's, a meaning for us all, a hard saying. If we have never cried this cry then we have never known salvation; if we fail to live with this cry, hourly, daily, in the midnight hour, and in the light of the noonday sun, then salvation has left us and our feet have laid hold on Hell. Yes, bless our God forever! When we cease to tremble before Him we have turned out of the way."

"Amen!" cried a voice from far away. "Amen! You preach it, boy!"

He paused for only a moment and mopped his brow, the heart within him great with fear and trembling, and with power.

"For let us remember that the wages of sin is death; that it is written, and cannot fail, the soul that sinneth, it shall die. Let us remember that we are born in sin, in sin did our mothers conceive us—sin reigns in all our members, sin is the foul heart's natural liquid, sin looks out of the eye, amen, and leads to lust, sin is in the hearing of the ear, and leads to folly, sin sits on the tongue, and leads to murder. Yes! Sin is the only heritage of the natural man, sin bequeathed us by our natural father, that fallen Adam, whose apple sickens and will sicken all generations living, and generations yet unborn! It was sin that drove the son of the morning out of Heaven, sin that drove Adam out of Eden, sin that caused Cain to slay his brother, sin that built the tower of Babel, sin that caused the fire to fall on Sodom—sin, from the very foundations of the world, living and breathing in the heart of man, that causes women to bring forth their children in agony and darkness, bows down the backs of men with terrible labor, keeps the empty belly empty, keeps the table bare, sends our children, dressed in rags, out into the whorehouses and dance halls of the world!"

"Amen! Amen!"

"Ah. Woe is me. Woe is *me*. Yes, beloved—there is no righteousness in man. All men's hearts are evil, all men are liars—only God is true. Hear David's cry: 'The Lord is my rock, and my fortress, and my deliverer; my God, my strength, in whom I will trust; my buckler, and the horn of my salvation, and my high tower.' Hear Job, sitting in dust and ashes, his children dead, his substance gone, surrounded by false comforters: 'Yea, though He slay me, yet will I trust Him.' And hear Paul, who had been Saul, a persecuter of the redeemed, struck down on the road to Damascus, and going forth to preach the gospel: 'And if ye be Christ's, then ye are Abraham's seed, and heirs according to the promise!' "

"Oh, yes," cried one of the elders, "bless our God forever!"

"For God had a plan. He would not suffer the soul of man to die, but had prepared a plan for his salvation. In the beginning, way back there at the laying of the foundations of the world, God had a plan, *amen!* to bring all flesh to a knowledge of the truth. In the beginning was the Word and the Word was with God and the Word was God—yes, and in Him was life, *hallelujah!* and this life was the light of men. Dearly beloved, when God saw how men's hearts waxed evil, how they turned aside, each to his own way, how they married and gave in marriage, how they feasted on ungodly meat and drink, and lusted, and blasphemed, and lifted up their hearts in sinful pride against the Lord—oh, then, the Son of God, the blessed lamb that taketh away the sins of the world, this Son of God who was the Word made flesh, the fulfillment of the promise—oh, then, He turned to His Father, crying: 'Father, prepare me a body and I'll go down and redeem sinful man.' "

"So *glad* this evening, praise the Lord!"

"Fathers, here tonight, have you ever had a son who went astray? Mothers, have you seen your daughters cut down in the pride and fullness of youth? Has any man here heard the command which came to Abraham, that he must make his son a living sacrifice on God's altar? Fathers, think of your sons, how you tremble for them, and try to lead them right, try to feed them so they'll grow up strong; think of your love for *your* son, and how any evil that befalls him cracks up the heart, and think of the pain that *God* has borne, sending down His only begotten Son, to dwell among men on the sinful earth, to be persecuted, to suffer, to bear the cross and *die*—not for His *own* sins, like our natural sons, but for the sins of *all* the world, to take away the sins of *all* the world—that we might have the joy bells ringing deep in our hearts tonight!"

"Praise Him!" cried Deborah, and he had never heard her voice so loud.

"Woe is me, for when God struck the sinner, the sinner's eyes were opened, and he saw himself in all his foulness naked before God's glory. Woe is me! For the moment of salvation is a blinding light, cracking down into the heart from Heaven—Heaven so high, and the sinner so low. *Woe is me!* For unless God raised the sinner, he would never rise again!"

"Yes, Lord! I was there!"

How many here tonight had fallen where Isaiah fell? How many had cried—as Isaiah cried? How many could testify, as Isaiah testified, "Mine eyes have seen the King, the Lord of hosts"? Ah, whosoever failed to have this testimony should never see His face, but should be told, on that great day: "Depart from me, ye that work iniquity," and he hurled forever into the lake of fire prepared for Satan and all his angels. Oh, would the sinner rise tonight, and walk the little mile to his salvation, here to the mercy seat?

And he waited. Deborah watched him with a calm, strong smile. He looked out over their faces, their faces all upturned to him. He saw joy in those faces, and holy excitement, and belief—and they all looked up to him. Then, far in the back, a boy rose, a tall, dark boy, his white shirt open at the neck and torn, his trousers dusty and shabby and held up with an old necktie, and he looked across the immeasurable, dreadful, breathing distance up to Gabriel, and began to walk down the long, bright aisle. Someone cried: "Oh, bless the Lord!" and tears filled Gabriel's eyes. The boy knelt, sobbing, at the mercy seat, and the church began to sing.

Then Gabriel turned away, knowing that this night he had run well, and that God had used him. The elders all were smiling, and one of them took him by the hand, and said: "That was mighty fine, boy. Mighty fine."

Then came the Sunday of the spectacular dinner that was to end the revival—for which dinner, Deborah and all the other women, had baked, roasted, fried, and boiled for many days beforehand. He jokingly suggested, to repay her a little for her contention that he was the best preacher of the revival, that she was the best cook among the women. She timidly suggested that he was here at a flattering disadvantage, for she had heard all of the preachers, but he had not, for a very long time, eaten another woman's cooking.

When the Sunday came, and he found himself once more among the elders, about to go to the table, Gabriel felt a drop in his happy, proud anticipation. He was not comfortable with these men—that was it—it was difficult for him to accept them as his elders and betters in the faith. They seemed to him so lax, so nearly worldly; they were not like those holy prophets of old who grew thin and naked in the service of the Lord. These, God's ministers, had indeed grown fat, and their dress was rich and various. They had been in the field so long that they did not tremble before God any more. They took God's power as their due, as something that made the more exciting their own assured, special atmosphere. They each had, it seemed, a bagful of sermons often preached; and knew, in the careless lifting of an eye, which sermon to bring to which congregation. Though they preached with great authority, and brought souls low before the altar—like so many ears of corn lopped off by the hired laborer in his daily work—they did not give God the glory, nor count it as glory at all; they might as easily have been, Gabriel thought, highly paid circus-performers, each with his own special dazzling gift. Gabriel discovered that they spoke, jokingly, of the comparative number of souls each of them had saved, as though they were keeping score in a poolroom. And this offended him and frightened him. He did not want, ever, to hold the gift of God so lightly.

They, the ministers, were being served alone in the upper room of the lodge hall—the less-specialized workers in Christ's vineyard were being fed at a table downstairs—and the women kept climbing up and down the stairs with loaded platters to see that they ate their fill. Deborah was one of the serving-women, and though she did not speak, and despite his discomfort, he nearly burst each time she entered the room, with the pride he knew she felt to see him sitting there, so serene and manly, among all these celebrated others, in the severe black and white that was his uniform. And if only, he felt, his mother could be there to see—her Gabriel, mounted so high!

But, near the end of the dinner, when the women had brought up the pies, and coffee, and cream, and when the talk around the table had become more jolly and more good-naturedly loose than ever, the door had but barely closed behind the women when one of the elders, a heavy, cheery, sandy-haired man, whose face, testifying no doubt to the violence of his beginnings, was splashed with freckles like dried blood, laughed and said, referring to Deborah, that there was a holy woman, all right! She had been choked so early on white men's milk, and it remained so sour in her belly yet, that she would never be able, now, to find a nigger who would let her taste his richer, sweeter substance. Everyone at the table roared, but Gabriel felt his blood turn cold that God's ministers should be guilty of such abominable levity, and that that woman sent by God to comfort him, and without whose support he might already have fallen by the wayside, should be held in such dishonor. They felt, he knew, that among themselves a little rude laughter could do no harm; they were too deeply rooted in the faith to be made to fall by such an insignificant tap from Satan's hammer. But he stared at their boisterous, laughing faces, and felt that they would have much to answer for on the day of judgment, for they were stumbling-stones in the path of the true believer.

Now the sandy-haired man, struck by Gabriel's bitter, astounded face, bit his laughter off, and said: "What's the matter, son? I hope I ain't said nothing to offend you?"

"She read the Bible for you the night you preached, didn't she?" asked another of the elders, in a conciliatory tone.

"That woman," said Gabriel, feeling a roaring in his head, "is my sister in the Lord."

"Well, Elder Peters here, he just didn't know that," said someone else. "He sure didn't mean no harm."

"Now, you ain't going to get mad?" asked Elder Peters, kindly—yet there remained, to Gabriel's fixed attention, something mocking in his face and voice. "You ain't going to spoil our little dinner?"

"I don't think it's right," said Gabriel, "to talk evil about *no*body. The Word tell me it ain't right to hold nobody up to scorn."

"Now you just remember," Elder Peters said, as kindly as before, "you's talking to your *elders.*"

"Then it seem to me," he said, astonished at his boldness, "that if I got to look to you for a example, you ought to *be* a example."

"Now, you know," said someone else, jovially, "you ain't fixing to make that woman your wife or nothing like that—so ain't no need to get all worked up and spoil our little gathering. Elder Peters didn't mean no harm. If *you* don't never say nothing worse than that, you can count yourself already up there in the Kingdom with the chosen."

And at this a small flurry of laughter swept over the table; they went back to their eating and drinking, as though the matter were finished.

Yet Gabriel felt that he had surprised them; he had found them out and they were a little ashamed and confounded before his purity. And he understood suddenly the words of Christ, where it was written: "Many are called but few are chosen." Yes, and he looked around the table, already jovial again, but rather watchful now, too, of him—and he wondered who, of all these, would sit in glory at the right hand of the Father?

And then, as he sat there, remembering again Elder Peters's boisterous, idle remark, this remark shook together in him all those shadowy doubts and fears, those hesitations and tendernesses, which were his in relation to Deborah, and the sum of which he now realized was his certainty that there was in that relationship something foreordained. It came to him that, as the Lord had given him Deborah, to help him to stand, so the Lord had sent him to her, to raise her up, to release her from that dishonor which was hers in the eyes of men. And this idea filled him, in a moment, wholly, with the intensity of a vision: What better woman could be found? *She* was not like the mincing daughters of Zion! She was not to be seen prancing lewdly through the streets, eyes sleepy and mouth half-open with lust, or to be found mewing under midnight fences, uncovered, uncovering some black boy's hanging curse! No, their married bed would be holy, and their children would continue the line of the faithful, a royal line. And, fired with this, a baser fire stirred in him also, rousing a slumbering fear, and he remembered (as the table, the ministers, the dinner, and the talk all burst in on him again) that Paul had written: "It is better to marry than to burn."

Yet, he thought, he would hold his peace awhile; he would seek to know more clearly the Lord's mind in this matter. For he remembered how much older she was than he—eight years; and he tried to imagine, for the first time in his life, that dishonor to which Deborah had been forced so many years ago by white men: her skirts above her head, her secrecy discovered—by white men. How many? How had she borne it? Had she screamed? Then he thought (but it did not really trouble him, for if Christ to save him could be crucified, he, for Christ's greater glory, could well be mocked) of what smiles would be occasioned, what filthy conjecture, barely sleeping now, would mushroom upward overnight like Jonah's gourd, when people heard that he and Deborah were going to be married. She, who had been the living proof and witness of their daily shame, and who had become their holy fool—and he, who had been the untamable despoiler of their daughters, and thief of their women, their walking prince of darkness! And he smiled, watching the elder's well-fed faces and their grinding jaws—unholy pastors all, unfaithful

stewards; he prayed that he would never be so fat, or so lascivious, but that God should work through him a mighty
work: to ring, it might be, through ages yet unborn, as sweet,
solemn, mighty proof of His everlasting love and mercy. He
trembled with the presence that surrounded him now; he
could scarcely keep his seat. He felt that light shone down on
him from Heaven, on him, the chosen; he felt as Christ must
have felt in the temple, facing His so utterly confounded elders; and he lifted up his eyes, not caring for their glances, or
their clearing of throats, and the silence that abruptly settled
over the table, thinking: "Yes. God works in many mysterious
ways His wonders to perform."

"Sister Deborah," he said, much later that night as he was
walking her to her door, "the Lord done laid something on
my heart and I want you to help me to pray over it and ask
Him to lead me right."

He wondered if she could divine what was in his mind. In
her face there was nothing but patience, as she turned to him,
and said: "I'm praying all the time. But I sure will pray extra
hard this week if you want me to."

And it was during this praying time that Gabriel had a
dream.

He could never afterwards remember how the dream began,
what had happened, or who he was with in the dream; or any
details at all. For there were really two dreams, the first like a
dim, blurred, infernal foreshadowing of the second. Of this
first dream, the overture, he remembered only the climate,
which had been like the climate of his day—heavy, with danger everywhere, Satan at his shoulder trying to bring him
down. That night as he tried to sleep, Satan sent demons to
his bedside—old friends he had had, but whom he saw no
more, and drinking and gambling scenes that he had thought
would never rise to haunt him again, and women he had
known. And the women were so real that he could nearly
touch them; and he heard again their laughter and their sighs,
and felt beneath his hands again their thighs and breasts.
Though he closed his eyes and called on Jesus—calling over
and over again the name of Jesus—his pagan body stiffened
and flamed and the women laughed. And they asked him why
he remained in this narrow bed alone when they waited for

him; why he had bound his body in the armor of chastity while they sighed and turned on their beds for him. And he sighed and turned, every movement torture, each touch of the sheets a lewd caress—and more abominable, then, in his imagination, than any caress he had received in life. And he clenched his fists and began to plead the blood, to exorcise the hosts of Hell, but even this motion was like another motion, and at length he fell on his knees to pray. By and by he fell into a troublous sleep—it seemed that he was going to be stoned, and then he was in battle, and then shipwrecked in the water—and suddenly he awoke, knowing that he must have dreamed, for his loins were covered with his own white seed.

Then, trembling, he got out of bed again and washed himself. It was a warning, and he knew it, and he seemed to see before him the pit dug by Satan—deep and silent, waiting for him. He thought of the dog returned to his vomit, of the man who had been cleansed, and who fell, and who was possessed by seven devils, the last state of that man being worse than his first. And he thought at last, kneeling by his cold bedside, but with the heart within him almost too sick for prayer, of Onan, who had scattered his seed on the ground rather than continue his brother's line. *Out of the house of David, the son of Abraham.* And he called again on the name of Jesus; and fell asleep again.

And he dreamed that he was in a cold, high place, like a mountain. He was high, so high that he walked in mist and cloud, but before him stretched the blank ascent, the steep side of the mountain. A voice said: "Come higher." And he began to climb. After a little, clinging to the rock, he found himself with only clouds above him and mist below—and he knew that beyond the wall of mist reigned fire. His feet began to slip; pebbles and rocks began ringing beneath his feet; he looked up, trembling, in terror of death, and he cried: "Lord, I can't come no higher." But the voice repeated after a moment, quiet and strong and impossible to deny: "Come on, son. Come higher." Then he knew that, if he would not fall to death, he must obey the voice. He began to climb again, and his feet slipped again; and when he thought that he would fall there suddenly appeared before him green, spiny leaves;

and he caught onto the leaves, which hurt his hand, and the voice said again: "Come higher." And so Gabriel climbed, the wind blowing through his clothes, and his feet began to bleed, and his hands were bleeding; and still he climbed, and he felt that his back was breaking; and his legs were growing numb and they were trembling, and he could not control them; and still before him there was only cloud, and below him the roaring mist. How long he climbed in this dream of his, he did not know. Then, of a sudden, the clouds parted, he felt the sun like a crown of glory, and he was in a peaceful field.

He began to walk. Now he was wearing long, white robes. He heard singing: "Walked in the valley, it looked so fine, I asked my Lord was all this mine." But he knew that it was his. A voice said: "Follow me." And he walked, and he was again on the edge of a high place, but bathed and blessed and glorified in the blazing sun, so that he stood like God, all golden, and looked down, down, at the long race he had run, at the steep side of the mountain he had climbed. And now up this mountain, in white robes, singing, the elect came. "Touch them not," the voice said, "my seal is on them." And Gabriel turned and fell on his face, and the voice said again: "So shall thy seed be." Then he awoke. Morning was at the window, and he blessed God, lying on his bed, tears running down his face, for the vision he had seen.

When he went to Deborah and told her that the Lord had led him to ask her to be his wife, his holy helpmeet, she looked at him for a moment in what seemed to be speechless terror. He had never seen such an expression on her face before. For the first time since he had known her he touched her, putting his hands on her shoulders, thinking what untender touch these shoulders had once known, and how she would be raised now in honor. And he asked: "You ain't scared, is you, Sister Deborah? You ain't got nothing to be scared of?"

Then she tried to smile, and began, instead, to weep. With a movement at once violent and hesitant, she let her head fall forward on his breast.

"No," she brought out, muffled in his arms, "I ain't scared." But she did not stop weeping.

He stroked her coarse, bowed head. "God bless you, little girl," he said, helplessly. "God bless you."

*   *   *

The silence in the church ended when Brother Elisha, kneeling near the piano, cried out and fell backward under the power of the Lord. Immediately, two or three others cried out also, and a wind, a foretaste of that great downpouring they awaited, swept the church. With this cry, and the echoing cries, the tarry service moved from its first stage of steady murmuring, broken by moans and now and again an isolated cry, into that stage of tears and groaning, of calling aloud and singing, which was like the labor of a woman about to be delivered of her child. On this threshing-floor the child was the soul that struggled to the light, and it was the church that was in labor, that did not cease to push and pull, calling on the name of Jesus. When Brother Elisha cried out and fell back, crying, Sister McCandless rose and stood over him to help him to pray. For the rebirth of the soul was perpetual; only rebirth every hour could stay the hand of Satan.

Sister Price began to sing:

> *"I want to go through, Lord,*
> *I want to go through.*
> *Take me through, Lord,*
> *Take me through."*

A lone voice, joined by others, among them, waveringly, the voice of John. Gabriel recognized the voice. When Elisha cried, Gabriel was brought back in an instant to this present time and place, fearing that it was John he heard, that it was John who lay astonished beneath the power of the Lord. He nearly looked up and turned around; but then he knew it was Elisha, and his fear departed.

> *"Have your way, Lord,*
> *Have your way."*

Neither of his sons was here tonight, had ever cried on the threshing-floor. One had been dead for nearly fourteen years—dead in a Chicago tavern, a knife kicking in his throat. And the living son, the child, Roy, was headlong already, and hardhearted: he lay at home, silent now, and bitter against his father, a bandage on his forehead. They were not here. Only the son of the bondwoman stood where the rightful heir should stand.

> *"I'll obey, Lord,*
> *I'll obey."*

He felt that he should rise and pray over Elisha—when a man cried out, it was right that another man should be his intercessor. And he thought how gladly he would rise, and with what power he would pray if it were only his son who lay crying on the floor tonight. But he remained, bowed low, on his knees. Each cry that came from the fallen Elisha tore through him. He heard the cry of his dead son and his living son; one who cried in the pit forever, beyond the hope of mercy; and one who would cry one day when mercy would be finished.

Now Gabriel tried, with the testimony he had held, with all the signs of His favor that God had shown him, to put himself between the living son and the darkness that waited to devour him. The living son had cursed him—*bastard*—and his heart was far from God; it could not be that the curse he had heard tonight falling from Roy's lips was but the curse repeated, so far, so long resounding, that the mother of his first son had uttered as she thrust the infant from her—herself immediately departing, this curse yet on her lips, into eternity. Her curse had devoured the first Royal; he had been begotten in sin, and he had perished in sin; it was God's punishment, and it was just. But Roy had been begotten in the marriage bed, the bed that Paul described as holy, and it was to him the Kingdom had been promised. It could not be that the living son was cursed for the sins of his father; for God, after much groaning, after many years, had given him a sign to make him know he was forgiven. And yet, it came to him that this living son, this headlong, living Royal, might be cursed for the sin of his mother, whose sin had never been truly repented; for that the living proof of her sin, he who knelt tonight, a very interloper among the saints, stood between her soul and God.

Yes, she was hardhearted, stiff-necked, and hard to bend, this Elizabeth whom he had married: she had not seemed so, years ago, when the Lord had moved in his heart to lift her up, she and her nameless child, who bore his name today. And he was exactly like her, silent, watching, full of evil pride—they would be cast out, one day, into the outer darkness.

Once he had asked Elizabeth—they had been married a long while, Roy was a baby, and she was big with Sarah—if she had truly repented of her sin.

And she had looked at him, and said: "You done asked me that before. And I done told you, yes."

But he did not believe her; and he asked: "You mean you wouldn't do it again? If you was back there, where you was, like you was then—would you do it again?"

She looked down; then, with impatience, she looked into his eyes again: "Well, if I was back there, Gabriel, and I was the same girl! . . ."

There was a long silence, while she waited. Then, almost unwillingly, he asked: "And . . . would you let *him* be born again?"

She answered, steadily: "I know you ain't asking me to say I'm sorry I brought Johnny in the world. Is you?" And when he did not answer: "And listen, Gabriel. I ain't going to let you *make* me sorry. Not you, nor nothing, nor nobody in this world. We is got *two* children, Gabriel, and soon we's going to have *three*; and I ain't going to make no difference amongst them and you ain't going to make none neither."

But how could there not be a difference between the son of a weak, proud woman and some careless boy, and the son that God had promised him, who would carry down the joyful line his father's name, and who would work until the day of the second coming to bring about His Father's Kingdom? For God had promised him this so many years ago, and he had lived only for this—forsaking the world and its pleasures, and the joys of his own life, he had tarried all these bitter years to see the promise of the Lord fulfilled. He had let Esther die, and Royal had died, and Deborah had died barren—but he had held on to the promise; he had walked before God in true repentance and waited on the promise. And the time of fulfillment was surely at hand. He had only to possess his soul in patience and wait before the Lord.

And his mind, dwelling bitterly on Elizabeth, yet moved backward to consider once again Esther, who had been the mother of the first Royal. And he saw her, with the dumb, pale, startled ghosts of joy and desire hovering in him yet, a thin, vivid, dark-eyed girl, with something Indian in her cheekbones and her carriage and her hair; looking at him with that look in which were blended mockery, affection, desire, impatience, and scorn; dressed in the flamelike colors that, in fact, she had seldom worn, but that he always thought of her as wearing. She was associated in his mind with flame; with fiery leaves in the autumn, and the fiery sun going down in the evening over the farthest hill, and with the eternal fires of Hell.

She had come to town very shortly after he and Deborah were married, and she took a job as serving-girl with the same white family for which he worked. He saw her, therefore, all the time. Young men were always waiting for her at the back door when her work was done: Gabriel used to watch her walk off in the dusk on a young man's arm, and their voices and their laughter floated back to him like a mockery of his condition. He knew that she lived with her mother and stepfather, sinful people, given to drinking and gambling and ragtime music and the blues, who never, except at Christmastime or Easter, appeared in church.

He began to pity her, and one day when he was to preach in the evening he invited her to come to church. This invitation marked the first time she ever really looked at him—he realized it then, and was to remember that look for many days and nights.

"You really going to preach tonight? A pretty man like you?"

"With the Lord's help," he said, with a gravity so extreme that it was almost hostility. At the same time, at her look and voice something leaped in him that he thought had been put down forever.

"Well, I be mighty delighted," she said after a moment, seeming to have briefly regretted the impetuosity that had led her to call him a "pretty" man.

"Can you make yourself free to come tonight?" he could not prevent himself from asking.

And she grinned, delighted at what she took to be an oblique compliment. "Well, I don't know, Reverend. But I'll try."

When the day was ended, she disappeared on the arm of yet another boy. He did not believe that she would come. And this so strangely depressed him that he could scarcely speak to Deborah at dinner, and they walked all the way to church in silence. Deborah watched him out of the corner of her eye, as was her silent and exasperating habit. It was her way of conveying respect for his calling; and she would have said, had it ever occurred to him to tax her with it, that she did not wish to distract him when the Lord had laid something on his heart. Tonight, since he was to preach, it could not be doubted that the Lord was speaking more than usual; and it behooved her, therefore, as the helpmeet of the Lord's anointed, as the caretaker, so to speak, of the sanctified temple, to keep silence. Yet, in fact, he would have liked to talk. He would have liked to ask her—so many things; to have listened to her voice, and watched her face while she told him of her day, her hopes, her doubts, her life, and her love. But he and Deborah never talked. The voice to which he listened in his mind, and the face he watched with so much love and care, belonged not to Deborah, but to Esther. Again he felt this strange chill in him, implying disaster and delight: and then he hoped that she would not come, that something would happen that would make it impossible for him ever to see her again.

She came, however; late, just before the pastor was about to present the speaker of the hour to the congregation. She did not come alone, but had brought her mother with her—promising what spectacle Gabriel could not imagine, nor could he imagine how she had escaped her young man of the evening. But she had; she was here; she preferred, then, to hear him preach the gospel than to linger with others in carnal delight. She was here, and his heart was uplifted; something exploded in his heart when the opening door revealed her, smiling faintly and with eyes downcast, moving directly to a seat in the back of the congregation. She did not look at him at all, and yet he knew immediately that she had seen him. And in a moment he imagined her, because of the sermon that he would preach, on her knees before the altar, and then her mother and that gambling, loud-talking stepfather of hers, brought by Esther into the service of the Lord. Heads turned when they came in, and a murmur, barely audible, of astonishment and pleasure swept over the church. Here were sinners, come to hear the Word of God.

And, indeed, from their apparel the sinfulness of their lives was evident: Esther wore a blue hat, trimmed with many ribbons, and a heavy, wine-red dress; and her mother, massive, and darker than Esther, wore great gold earrings in her pierced ears and had that air, vaguely disreputable, and hurriedly dressed, of women he had known in sporting-houses. They sat in the back, rigid and uncomfortable, like sisters of sin, like a living defiance of the drab sanctity of the saints. Deborah turned to look at them, and in that moment Gabriel saw, as though for the first time, how black and how bony was this wife of his, and how wholly undesirable. Deborah looked at him with a watchful silence in her look; he felt the hand that held his Bible begin to sweat and tremble; he thought of the joyless groaning of their marriage bed; and he hated her.

Then the pastor rose. While he spoke, Gabriel closed his eyes. He felt the words that he was about to speak fly from him; he felt the power of God go out of him. Then the voice of the pastor ceased, and Gabriel opened his eyes in the silence and found that all eyes were on him. And so he rose and faced the congregation.

"Dearly beloved in the Lord," he began—but her eyes were on him, that strange, that mocking light—"let us bow our heads in prayer." And he closed his eyes and bowed his head.

His later memory of this sermon was like the memory of a storm. From the moment that he raised his head and looked out over their faces again, his tongue was loosed and he was filled with the power of the Holy Ghost. Yes, the power of the Lord was on him that night, and he preached a sermon that was remembered in camp-meetings and in cabins, and that set a standard for visiting evangelists for a generation to come. Years later, when Esther and Royal and Deborah were dead, and Gabriel was leaving the South, people remembered this sermon and the gaunt, possessed young man who had preached it.

He took his text from the eighteenth chapter of the second book of Samuel, the story of the young Ahimaaz who ran too soon to bring the tidings of battle to King David. For, before he ran, he was asked by Joab: "Wherefore wilt thou run, my son, seeing that thou hast no tidings ready?" And when Ahimaaz reached King David, who yearned to know the fate of his headlong son, Absalom, he could only say: "I saw a great tumult but I knew not what it was."

And this was the story of all those who failed to wait on the counsel of the Lord; who made themselves wise in their own conceit and ran before they had the tidings ready. This was the story of innumerable shepherds who failed, in their arrogance, to feed the hungry sheep; of many a father and mother who gave to their children not bread but a stone, who offered not the truth of God but the tinsel of this world. This was not belief but unbelief, not humility but pride: there worked in the heart of such a one the same desire that had hurled the son of the morning from Heaven to the depths of Hell, the desire to overturn the appointed times of God, and to wrest from Him who held all power in His hands power not meet for men. Oh, yes, they had seen it, each brother and sister beneath the sound of his voice tonight, and they had seen the destruction caused by a so lamentable unripeness! Babies, bawling, fatherless, for bread, and girls in the gutters, sick with sin, and young men bleeding in the frosty fields. Yes, and there were those who cried—they had heard it, in their homes, and on the street corner, and from the very pulpit— that they should wait no longer, despised and rejected and spat on as they were, but should rise today and bring down the mighty, establishing the vengeance that God had claimed. But blood cried out for blood, as the blood of Abel cried out from the ground. Not for nothing was it written: "He that believeth will not make haste." Oh, but sometimes the road was rocky. Did they think sometimes that God forgot? Oh, fall on your knees and pray for patience; fall on your knees and pray for faith; fall on your knees and pray for overcoming power to be ready on the day of His soon appearing to receive the crown of life. For God did not forget, no word proceeding from his mouth could fail. Better to wait, like Job, through all the days of our appointed time until our change comes than to rise up, unready, before God speaks. For if we but wait humbly before Him, He will speak glad tidings to our souls; if we but wait our change will come, and that in an instant, in the twinkling of an eye—we will be changed one day from this corruption into incorruptibility forever, caught up with Him beyond the clouds. And these are the tidings we now must bear to all the nations: another son of David has hung from a tree, and he who knows not the meaning of that tumult shall be damned forever in Hell! Brother, sister, you may run, but the day is coming when the King will ask: "What are the tidings that you bear?" And what will you say on that great day if you know not of the death of His Son?

"Is there a soul here tonight"—tears were on his face and he stood above them with arms outstretched—"who knows not the meaning of that tumult? Is there a soul here tonight who wants to talk to Jesus? Who wants to wait before the Lord, amen, until He speaks? Until He makes to ring in your soul, amen, the glad tidings of salvation? Oh, brothers and sisters"—and still she did not rise; but only watched him from far away—"the time is running out. One day He's coming back to judge the nations, to take His children, hallelujah, to their rest. They tell me, bless God, that two shall be working in the fields, and one shall be taken and the other left. Two shall be lying, amen, in bed, and one shall be taken and the other left. He's coming, beloved, like a thief in the night, and no man knows the hour of His coming. It's going to be too late then to cry: 'Lord, have mercy.' Now is the time to make yourself ready, now, amen, tonight, before His altar. Won't somebody come tonight? Won't somebody say No to Satan and give their life to the Lord?"

But she did not rise, only looked at him and looked about her with a bright, pleased interest, as though she were at a theater and were waiting to see what improbable delights would next be offered her. He somehow knew that she would never rise and walk that long aisle to the mercy seat. And this filled him for a moment with a holy rage—that she stood, so brazen, in the congregation of the righteous and refused to bow her head.

He said amen, and blessed them, and turned away, and immediately the congregation began to sing. Now, again, he felt drained and sick; he was soaking wet and he smelled the odor of his own body. Deborah, singing and beating her tambourine in the front of the congregation, watched him. He felt suddenly like a helpless child. He wanted to hide himself forever and never cease from crying.

Esther and her mother left during the singing—they had come, then, only to hear him preach. He could not imagine what they were saying or thinking now. And he thought of tomorrow, when he would have to see her again.

"Ain't that the little girl what works at the same place with you?" Deborah asked him on the way home.

"Yes," he said. Now he did not feel like talking. He wanted to get home and take his wet clothes off and sleep.

"She mighty pretty," said Deborah. "I ain't never seen her in church before."

He said nothing.

"Was it you invited her to come out tonight?" she asked, after a bit.

"Yes," he said. "I didn't think the Word of God could do her no harm."

Deborah laughed. "Don't look like it, does it? She walked out just as cool and sinful as she come in—she and that mother of her'n. And you preached a mighty fine sermon. Look like she just ain't thinking about the Lord."

"Folks ain't got no time for the Lord," he said, "one day *He* ain't going to have no time for *them*."

When they got home she offered to make him a hot cup of tea, but he refused. He undressed in silence—which she again respected—and got into bed. At length, she lay beside him like a burden laid down at evening which must be picked up once more in the morning.

The next morning Esther said to him, coming into the yard while he was chopping wood for the woodpile: "Good morning, Reverend. I sure didn't look to see you today. I reckoned you'd be all wore out after *that* sermon—does you always preach as hard as that?"

He paused briefly with the axe in the air; then he turned again, bringing the axe down. "I preach the way the Lord leads me, sister," he said.

She retreated a little in the face of his hostility. "Well," she said in a different tone, "it was a mighty fine sermon. Me and Mama was mighty glad we come out."

He left the axe buried in the wood, for splinters flew and he was afraid one might strike her. "You and your ma—you don't get out to service much?"

"Lord, Reverend," she wailed, "look like we just ain't got the time. Mama work so hard all week she just want to lie up in bed on Sunday. And she like me," she added quickly, after a pause, "to keep her company."

Then he looked directly at her. "Does you really mean to say, sister, that you ain't got no time for the Lord? No time at all?"

"Reverend," she said, looking at him with the daring defiance of a threatened child, "I does my best. I really does. Ain't everybody got to have the same spirit."

And he laughed shortly. "Ain't but one spirit you got to have—and that's the spirit of the Lord."

"Well," she said, "that spirit ain't got to work in everybody the same, seems to me."

Then they were silent, each quite vividly aware that they had reached an impasse. After a moment he turned and picked up the axe again. "Well, you go along, sister. I'm praying for you."

Something struggled in her face then, as she stood for yet a moment more and watched him—a mixture of fury and amusement; it reminded him of the expression he had often found on the face of Florence. And it was like the look on the faces of the elders during that far-off and so momentous Sunday dinner. He was too angry, while she thus stared at him, to trust himself to speak. Then she shrugged, the mildest, most indifferent gesture he had ever seen, and smiled. "I'm mighty obliged to you, Reverend," she said. Then she went into the house.

This was the first time they spoke in the yard, a frosty morning. There was nothing in that morning to warn him of what was coming. She offended him because she was so brazen in her sins, that was all; and he prayed for her soul, which would one day find itself naked and speechless before the judgment bar of Christ. Later, she told him that he had pursued her, that his eyes had left her not a moment's peace. "That weren't no reverend looking at me them mornings in the yard," she had said. "You looked at me just like a man, like a man what hadn't never heard of the Holy Ghost." But he believed that the Lord had laid her like a burden on his heart. And he carried her in his heart; he prayed for her and exhorted her, while there was yet time to bring her soul to God.

But she had not been thinking about God; though she accused him of lusting after her in his heart, it was she who, when she looked at him, insisted on seeing not God's minister but a "pretty man." On her tongue the very title of his calling became a mark of disrespect.

It began on an evening when he was to preach, when they were alone in the house. The people of the house had gone away for three days to visit relatives; Gabriel had driven them to the railroad station after supper, leaving Esther clearing up the kitchen. When he came back to lock up the house, he found Esther waiting for him on the porch steps.

"I didn't think I'd better leave," she said, "till you got back. I ain't got no keys to lock up this house, and white folks is so funny. I don't want them blaming me if something's missing."

He realized immediately that she had been drinking—she was not drunk, but there was whisky on her breath. And this, for some reason, caused a strange excitement to stir in him.

"That was mighty thoughtful, sister," he said, staring hard at her to let her know that he knew she had been drinking. She met his stare with a calm, bold smile, a smile mocking innocence, so that her face was filled with the age-old cunning of a woman.

He started past her into the house; then, without thinking, and without looking at her, he offered: "If you ain't got nobody waiting for you I'll walk you a piece on your way home."

"No," she said, "ain't nobody waiting for me this evening, Reverend, thank you kindly."

He regretted making his offer almost as soon as it was made; he had been certain that she was about to rush off to some trysting-place or other, and he had merely wished to be corroborated. Now, as they walked together into the house, he became terribly aware of her youthful, vivid presence, of her lost condition; and at the same time the emptiness and silence of the house warned him that he was alone with danger.

"You just sit down in the kitchen," he said. "I be as quick as I can."

But his speech was harsh in his own ears, and he could not face her eyes. She sat down at the table, smiling, to wait for him. He tried to do everything as quickly as possible, the shuttering of windows, and locking of doors. But his fingers were stiff and slippery; his heart was in his mouth. And it came to him that he was barring every exit to this house, except the exit through the kitchen, where Esther sat.

When he entered the kitchen again she had moved, and now stood in the doorway, looking out, holding a glass in her hand. It was a moment before he realized that she had helped herself to more of the master's whisky.

She turned at his step, and he stared at her, and at the glass she held, with wrath and horror.

"I just thought," she said, almost entirely unabashed, "that I'd have me a little drink while I was waiting, Reverend. But I didn't figure on you catching me at it."

She swallowed the last of her drink and moved to the sink to rinse out the glass. She gave a little, ladylike cough as she swallowed—he could not be sure whether this cough was genuine or in mockery of him.

"I reckon," he said, malevolently, "you is just made up your mind to serve Satan all your days."

"I done made up my mind," she answered, "to live all I can *while* I can. If that's a sin, well, I'll go on down to Hell and pay for it. But don't *you* fret, Reverend—it ain't your soul."

He moved and stood next to her, full of anger.

"Girl," he said, "don't you believe God? God don't lie—and He says, plain as I'm talking to you, the soul that sinneth, it shall *die*."

She sighed. "Reverend, look like to me you'd get tired, all the time beating on poor little Esther, trying to make Esther something she ain't. I just don't feel it *here*," she said, and put one hand on her breast. "Now, what you going to do? Don't you know I'm a woman grown, and I ain't fixing to change?"

He wanted to weep. He wanted to reach out and hold her back from the destruction she so ardently pursued—to fold her in him, and hide her until the wrath of God was past. At the same time there rose to his nostrils again her whisky-laden breath, and beneath this, faint, intimate, the odor of her body. And he began to feel like a man in a nightmare, who stands in the path of oncoming destruction, who must move quickly—but who cannot move. "Jesus Jesus Jesus," rang over and over again in his mind, like a bell—as he moved closer to her, undone by her breath, and her wide, angry, mocking eyes.

"You know right well," he whispered, shaking with fury, "you know right well why I keep after you—why I keep after you like I do."

"No, I don't," she answered, refusing, with a small shake of the head, to credit his intensity. "I sure don't know why you can't let Esther have her little whisky, and have her little ways without all the time trying to make her miserable."

He sighed with exasperation, feeling himself begin to tremble. "I just don't want to see you go down, girl, I don't want you to wake up one fine morning sorry for all the sin you done, old, and all by yourself, with nobody to respect you."

But he heard himself speaking, and it made him ashamed. He wanted to have done with talking and leave this house—in a moment they would leave, and the nightmare would be over.

"Reverend," she said, "I ain't done nothing that I'm ashamed of, and I hope I *don't* do nothing I'm ashamed of, ever."

At the word "Reverend," he wanted to strike her; he reached out instead and took both her hands in his. And now they looked directly at each other. There was surprise in her look, and a guarded triumph; he was aware that their bodies were nearly touching and that he should move away. But he did not move—he could not move.

"But I can't help it," she said, after a moment, maliciously teasing, "if you done things that *you's* ashamed of, Reverend."

He held onto her hands as though he were in the middle of the sea and her hands were the lifeline that would drag him in to shore. "Jesus Jesus Jesus," he prayed, "oh, Jesus Jesus.

Help me to stand." He thought that he was pulling back against her hands—but he was pulling her to him. And he saw in her eyes now a look that he had not seen for many a long day and night, a look that was never in Deborah's eyes.

"*Yes*, you know," he said, "why I'm all the time worrying about you—why I'm all the time miserable when I look at you."

"But you ain't never told me none of this," she said.

One hand moved to her waist, and lingered there. The tips of her breasts touched his coat, burning in like acid and closing his throat. Soon it would be too late; he wanted it to be too late. That river, his infernal need, rose, flooded, sweeping him forward as though he were a long-drowned corpse.

"*You* know," he whispered, and touched her breasts and buried his face in her neck.

So he had fallen: for the first time since his conversion, for the last time in his life. Fallen: he and Esther in the white folks' kitchen, the light burning, the door half-open, grappling and burning beside the sink. Fallen indeed: time was no more, and sin, death, Hell, the judgment were blotted out. There was only Esther, who contained in her narrow body all mystery and all passion, and who answered all his need. Time, snarling so swiftly past, had caused him to forget the clumsiness, and sweat, and dirt of their first coupling; how his shaking hands undressed her, standing where they stood, how her dress fell at length like a snare about her feet; how his hands tore at her undergarments so that the naked, vivid flesh might meet his hands; how she protested: "Not here, not here"; how he worried, in some buried part of his mind, about the open door, about the sermon he was to preach, about his life, about Deborah; how the table got in their way, how his collar, until her fingers loosened it, threatened to choke him; how they found themselves on the floor at last, sweating and groaning and locked together; locked away from all others, all heavenly or human help. Only they could help each other. They were alone in the world.

Had Royal, his son, been conceived that night? Or the next night? Or the next? It had lasted only nine days. Then he had come to his senses—after nine days God gave him the power to tell her this thing could not be.

She took his decision with the same casualness, the same near-amusement, with which she had taken his fall. He understood about Esther, during those nine days: that she considered his fear and trembling fanciful and childish, a way of making life more complicated than it need be. She did not think life was like that; she wanted life to be simple. He understood that she was sorry for him because he was always worried. Sometimes, when they were together, he tried to tell her of what he felt, how the Lord would punish them for the sin they were committing. She would not listen: "You ain't in the pulpit now. You's here with me. Even a Reverend's got the right to take off his clothes *sometime* and act like a natural man." When he told her that he would not see her any more, she was angry, but she did not argue. Her eyes told him that she thought he was a fool; but that, even had she loved him ever so desperately, it would have been beneath her to argue about his decision—a large part of her simplicity consisted in determining not to want what she could not have with ease.

So it was over. Though it left him bruised and frightened, though he had lost the respect of Esther forever (he prayed that she would never again come to hear him preach) he thanked God that it had been no worse. He prayed that God would forgive him, and never let him fall again.

Yet what frightened him, and kept him more than ever on his knees, was the knowledge that, once having fallen, nothing would be easier than to fall again. Having possessed Esther, the carnal man awoke, seeing the possibility of conquest everywhere. He was made to remember that though he was holy he was yet young; the women who had wanted him wanted him still; he had but to stretch out his hand and take what he wanted—even sisters in the church. He struggled to wear out his visions in the marriage bed, he struggled to awaken Deborah, for whom daily his hatred grew.

He and Esther spoke in the yard again as spring was just beginning. The ground was wet still with melting snow and ice; the sun was everywhere; the naked branches of the trees seemed to be lifting themselves upward toward the pale sun, impatient to put forth leaf and flower. He was standing at the well in his shirtsleeves, singing softly to himself—praising God for the dangers he had passed. She came down the porch steps into the yard, and though he heard the soft step, and knew that it was she, it was a moment before he turned around.

He expected her to come up to him and ask for his help in something she was doing in the house. When she did not speak, he turned around. She was wearing a light, cotton dress of light-brown and dark-brown squares, and her hair was braided tightly all around her head. She looked like a little girl, and he almost smiled. Then: "What's the matter?" he asked her; and felt the heart within him sicken.

"Gabriel," she said, "I going to have a baby."

He stared at her; she began to cry. He put the two pails of water carefully on the ground. She put out her hands to reach him, but he moved away.

"Girl, stop that bellering. What you talking about?"

But, having allowed her tears to begin, she could not stop them at once. She continued to cry, weaving a little where she stood, and with her hands to her face. He looked in panic around the yard and toward the house. "Stop that," he cried again, not daring here and now to touch her, "and tell me what's the matter!"

"I told you," she moaned, "I done told you. I going to have a baby." She looked at him, her face broken up and the hot tears falling. "It's the Lord's truth. I ain't making up no story, it's the Lord's truth."

He could not take his eyes from her, though he hated what he saw. "And when you done find this out?"

"Not so long. I thought maybe I was mistook. But ain't no mistake. Gabriel, what we going to do?"

Then, as she watched his face, her tears began again.

"Hush," he said, with a calm that astonished him, "we *going* to do something, just you be quiet."

"What we going to do, Gabriel? *Tell* me—what you a-fixing in your mind to do?"

"You go on back in the house. Ain't no way for us to talk now."

"Gabriel—"

"Go on in the house, girl. Go *on*!" And when she did not move, but continued to stare at him: "We going to talk about it *tonight*. We going to get to the bottom of *this* thing tonight!"

She turned from him and started up the porch steps. "And dry your *face*," he whispered. She bent over, lifting the front of her dress to dry her eyes, and stood so for a moment on the bottom step while he watched her. Then she straightened and walked into the house, not looking back.

She was going to have his baby—*his* baby? While Deborah, despite their groaning, despite the humility with which she endured his body, yet failed to be quickened by any coming life. It was in the womb of Esther, who was no better than a harlot, that the seed of the prophet would be nourished.

And he moved from the well, picking up, like a man in a trance, the heavy pails of water. He moved toward the house, which now—high, gleaming roof, and spun-gold window—seemed to watch him and to listen; the very sun above his head and the earth beneath his feet had ceased their turning; the water, like a million warning voices, lapped in the buckets he carried on each side; and his mother, beneath the startled earth on which he moved, lifted up, endlessly, her eyes.

They talked in the kitchen as she was cleaning up.

"How come you"—it was his first question—"to be so sure this here's my baby?"

She was not crying now. "Don't you start a-talking that way," she said. "Esther ain't in the habit of lying to *no*body, and I ain't gone with so many men that I'm subject to get my mind confused."

She was very cold and deliberate, and moved about the kitchen with a furious concentration on her tasks, scarcely looking at him.

He did not know what to say, how to reach her.

"You tell your mother yet?" he asked, after a pause. "You been to see a doctor? How come you to be so sure?"

She sighed sharply. "No, I ain't told my mother, I ain't crazy. I ain't told nobody except you."

"How come you to be so sure?" he repeated. "If you ain't seen no doctor?"

"What doctor in this town you want me to go see? I go to see a doctor, I might as well get up and shout it from the housetops. No, I ain't seen no doctor, and I ain't fixing to see one in a hurry. I don't need no doctor to tell me what's happening in my belly."

"And how long you been knowing about this?"

"I been knowing this for maybe a month—maybe six weeks now."

"Six weeks? Why ain't you opened your mouth before?"

"Because I wasn't sure. I thought I'd wait and make sure. I didn't see no need for getting all up in the air before I *knew*. I didn't want to get you all upset and scared and evil, like you is now, if it weren't no need." She paused, watching him. Then: "And you said this morning we was going to do something. What we going to do? That's what we got to figure out now, Gabriel."

"What we going to do?" he repeated at last; and felt that the sustaining life had gone out of him. He sat down at the kitchen table and looked at the whirling pattern on the floor.

But the life had not gone out of her; she came to where he sat, speaking softly, with bitter eyes. "You sound mighty strange to me," she said. "Don't look to me like you thinking of nothing but how you can get shut of this—and me, too— quick as you know how. It wasn't like that always, was it, Reverend? Once upon a time you couldn't think of nothing and nobody *but* me. What you thinking about tonight? I be damned if I think it's *me* you thinking of."

"Girl," he said, wearily, "don't talk like you ain't got good sense. You know I got a wife to think about—" and he wanted to say more, but he could not find the words, and, helplessly, he stopped.

"I know that," she said with less heat, but watching him still with eyes from which the old, impatient mockery was not entirely gone, "but what I mean is, if you was able to forget her once you ought to be able to forget her twice."

He did not understand her at once; but then he sat straight up, his eyes wide and angry. "What you mean, girl? What you trying to say?"

She did not flinch—even in his despair and anger he recognized how far she was from being the frivolous child she had always seemed to him. Or was it that she had been, in so short a space of time, transformed? But he spoke to her at this disadvantage: that whereas he was unprepared for any change in her, she had apparently taken his measure from the first and could be surprised by no change in him.

"You know what I mean," she said. "You ain't never going to have no kind of life with that skinny, black woman—and you ain't never going to be able to make her happy—and she ain't never going to have no children. I be blessed, anyway, if I think you was in your right mind when you married her. And it's *me* that's going to have your baby!"

"You want me," he asked at last, "to leave my wife—and come with you?"

"*I* thought," she answered, "that you had done thought of that yourself, already, many and many a time."

"You know," he said, with a halting anger, "I ain't never said nothing like that. I ain't never told you I wanted to leave my wife."

"I ain't talking," she shouted, at the end of patience, "about nothing you done *said*!"

Immediately, they both looked toward the closed kitchen doors—for they were not alone in the house this time. She sighed, and smoothed her hair with her hand; and he saw then that her hand was trembling and that her calm deliberation was all a frenzied pose.

"Girl," he said, "does you reckon I'm going to run off and lead a life of sin with you somewhere, just because you tell me you got my baby kicking in your belly? How many kinds of a fool you think I am? I got God's work to do—my life don't belong to you. Nor to that baby, neither—if it *is* my baby."

"It's your baby," she said, coldly, "and ain't no way in the world to get around *that*. And it ain't been so very long ago, right here in this very *room*, when looked to me like a life of sin was all you was ready for."

"Yes," he answered, rising, and turning away, "Satan tempted me and I fell. I ain't the first man been made to fall on account of a wicked woman."

"You be careful," said Esther, "how you talk to me. I ain't the first girl's been ruined by a holy man, neither."

"Ruined?" he cried. "You? How you going to be ruined? When you been walking through this town just like a harlot, and a-kicking up your heels all over the pasture? How you going to stand there and tell me you been *ruined*? If it hadn't been me, it sure would have been somebody else."

"But it *was* you," she retorted, "and what I want to know is what we's going to do about it."

He looked at her. Her face was cold and hard—ugly; she had never been so ugly before.

"I don't know," he said, deliberately, "what *we* is going to do. But I tell you what I think *you* better do: you better go along and get one of these boys you been running around with to marry you. Because I can't go off with you nowhere."

She sat down at the table and stared at him with scorn and amazement; sat down heavily, as though she had been struck. He knew that she was gathering her forces; and now she said what he had dreaded to hear:

"And suppose I went through town and told your wife, and the churchfolks, and everybody—suppose I did that, Reverend?"

"And who you think," he asked—he felt himself enveloped by an awful, falling silence—"is going to believe you?"

She laughed. "Enough folks'd believe me to make it mighty hard on you." And she watched him. He walked up and down the kitchen, trying to avoid her eyes. "You just think back," she said, "to that first night, right here on this damn white folks' floor, and you'll see it's too late for you to talk to Esther about how holy you is. I don't care if you want to live a lie, but I don't see no reason for you to make me suffer on account of it."

"You can go around and tell folks if you want to," he said, boldly, "but it ain't going to look so good for you neither."

She laughed again. "But I ain't the holy one. You's a married man, and you's a preacher—and who you think folks is going to blame most?"

He watched her with a hatred that was mixed with his old desire, knowing that once more she had the victory.

"I can't marry you, you know that," he said. "Now, what you want me to do?"

"No," she said, "and I reckon you *wouldn't* marry me even if you *was* free. I reckon you don't want no whore like Esther for your wife. Esther's just for the night, for the dark, where won't nobody see you getting your holy self all dirtied up with Esther. Esther's just good enough to go out and have *your* bastard somewhere in the goddamn woods. Ain't that so, Reverend?"

He did not answer her. He could find no words. There was only silence in him, like the grave.

She rose, and moved to the open kitchen door, where she stood, her back to him, looking out into the yard and on the silent streets where the last, dead rays of the sun still lingered.

"But I reckon," she said slowly, "that I don't want to be with you no more'n you want to be with me. I don't want no man what's ashamed and scared. Can't do me no good, that kind of man." She turned in the door and faced him; this was the last time she really looked at him, and he would carry that look to his grave. "There's just one thing I want you to do," she said. "You do that, and we be all right."

"What you want me to do?" he asked, and felt ashamed.

"I *would* go through this town," she said, "and tell everybody about the Lord's anointed. Only reason I don't is because I don't want my mama and daddy to know what a fool I been. I ain't ashamed of *it*—I'm ashamed of *you*—you done made me feel a shame I ain't never felt before. I shamed before my *God*—to let somebody make me cheap, like you done done."

He said nothing. She turned her back to him again.

"I . . . just want to go somewhere," she said, "*go* somewhere, and *have* my baby, and think all this out of my mind. I want to go somewhere and get my mind straight. *That's* what I want you to do—and that's pretty cheap. I guess it takes a holy man to make a girl a real whore."

"Girl," he said, "I ain't got no *money*."

"Well," she said, coldly, "you damn well better find some."

Then she began to cry. He moved toward her, but she moved away.

"If I go out into the field," he said, helplessly, "I ought to be able to make enough money to send you away."

"How long that going to take?"

"A month maybe."

And she shook her head. "I ain't going to stay around here that long."

They stood in silence in the open kitchen door, she struggling against her tears, he struggling against his shame. He could only think: "Jesus Jesus Jesus. Jesus Jesus."

"Ain't you got nothing saved up?" she asked at last. "Look to me like you been married long enough to've saved something!"

Then he remembered that Deborah had been saving money since their wedding day. She kept it in a tin box at the top of the cupboard. He thought of how sin led to sin.

"Yes," he said, "a little. I don't know how much."

"You bring it tomorrow," she told him.

"Yes," he said.

He watched her as she moved from the door and went to the closet for her hat and coat. Then she came back, dressed for the street and, without a word, passed him, walking down the short steps into the yard. She opened the low gate and turned down the long, silent, flaming street. She walked slowly, head bowed, as though she were cold. He stood watching her, thinking of the many times he had watched her before, when her walk had been so different and her laughter had come ringing back to mock him.

He stole the money while Deborah slept. And he gave it to Esther in the morning. She gave notice that same day, and a week later she was gone—to Chicago, said her parents, to find a better job and to have a better life.

Deborah became more silent than ever in the weeks that followed. Sometimes he was certain she had discovered that the money was missing and knew that he had taken it—sometimes he was certain that she knew nothing. Sometimes he was certain that she knew everything: the theft, and the reason for the theft. But she did not speak. In the middle of the spring he went out into the field to preach, and was gone three months. When he came back he brought the money with him and put it in the box again. No money had been added in the meanwhile, so he still could not be certain whether Deborah knew or not.

He decided to let it all be forgotten, and begin his life again.

But the summer brought him a letter, with no return name or address, but postmarked from Chicago. Deborah gave it to him at breakfast, not seeming to have remarked the hand or the postmark, along with the bundle of tracts from a Bible house which they both distributed each week through the town. She had a letter, too, from Florence, and it was perhaps this novelty that distracted her attention.

Esther's letter ended:

What I think is, I made a mistake, that's true, and I'm paying for it now. But don't you think you ain't going to pay for it—I don't know when and I don't know how, but I know you going to be brought low one of these fine days. I ain't holy like you are, but I know right from wrong.

I'm going to have my baby and I'm going to bring him up to be a man. And I ain't going to read to him out of no Bibles and I ain't going to take him to hear no preaching. If he don't drink nothing but moonshine all his natural days he be a better man than his Daddy.

"What Florence got to say?" he asked dully, crumpling this letter in his fist.

Deborah looked up with a faint smile. "Nothing much, honey. But she sound like she going to get married."

Near the end of that summer he went out again into the field. He could not stand his home, his job, the town itself— he could not endure, day in, day out, facing the scenes and the people he had known all his life. They seemed suddenly to mock him, to stand in judgment on him; he saw his guilt in everybody's eyes. When he stood in the pulpit to preach they looked at him, he felt, as though he had no right to be there, as though they condemned him as he had once condemned the twenty-three elders. When souls came weeping to the altar he scarce dared to rejoice, remembering that soul who had not bowed, whose blood, it might be, would be required of him at judgment.

So he fled from these people, and from these silent witnesses, to tarry and preach elsewhere—to do, as it were, in secret, his first works over, seeking again the holy fire that had so transformed him once. But he was to find, as the prophets had found, that the whole earth became a prison for him who fled before the Lord. There was peace nowhere, and healing nowhere, and forgetfulness nowhere. In every church he entered, his sin had gone before him. It was in the strange, the welcoming faces, it cried up to him from the altar, it sat, as he mounted the pulpit steps, waiting for him in his seat. It stared upward from his Bible: there was no word in all that holy book which did not make him tremble. When he spoke of John on the isle of Patmos, taken up in the spirit on the Lord's day, to behold things past, present, and to come, saying: "he which is filthy, let him be filthy still," it was he who, crying these words in a loud voice, was utterly confounded; when he spoke of David, the shepherd boy, raised by God's power to be the King of Israel, it was he who, while they shouted: "Amen!" and: "Hallelujah!" struggled once more in his chains; when he spoke of the day of Pentecost when the Holy Ghost had come down on the apostles who tarried in the upper room, causing them to speak in tongues of fire, he thought of his own baptism and how he had offended the Holy Ghost. No: though his name was writ large on placards, though they praised him for the great work God worked through him, and though they came, day and night, before him to the altar, there was no word in the Book for him.

And he saw, in this wandering, how far his people had wandered from God. They had all turned aside, and gone out into the wilderness, to fall down before idols of gold and silver, and wood and stone, false gods that could not heal them. The music that filled any town or city he entered was not the music of the saints but another music, infernal, which glorified lust and held righteousness up to scorn. Women, some of whom should have been at home, teaching their grandchildren how to pray, stood, night after night, twisting their bodies into lewd hallelujahs in smoke-filled, gin-heavy dance halls, singing for their "loving man." And their loving man was any man, any morning, noon, or night—when one left town they got another—men could drown, it seemed, in their warm flesh and they would never know the difference. "It's here for you and if you don't get it it ain't no fault of mine." They laughed at him when they saw him—"a pretty man like you?"—and they told him that they knew a long brown girl who could make him lay his Bible down. He fled from them; they frightened him. He began to pray for Esther. He imagined her standing one day where these women stood today.

And blood, in all the cities through which he passed, ran down. There seemed no door, anywhere, behind which blood did not call out, unceasingly, for blood; no woman, whether singing before defiant trumpets or rejoicing before the Lord, who had not seen her father, her brother, her lover, or her son cut down without mercy; who had not seen her sister become part of the white man's great whorehouse, who had not, all too narrowly, escaped that house herself; no man, preaching, or cursing, strumming his guitar in the lone, blue evening, or blowing in fury and ecstasy his golden horn at night, who had not been made to bend his head and drink white men's muddy water; no man whose manhood had not been, at the root, sickened, whose loins had not been dishonored, whose seed had not been scattered into oblivion and worse than oblivion, into living shame and rage, and into endless battle. Yes, their parts were all cut off, they were dishonored, their very names were nothing more than dust blown disdainfully across the field of time—to fall where, to blossom where, bringing forth what fruit hereafter, where?—their very names were not their own. Behind them was the darkness, nothing but the darkness, and all around them destruction, and before them nothing but the fire—a bastard people, far from God, singing and crying in the wilderness!

Yet, most strangely, and from deeps not before discovered, his faith looked up; before the wickedness that he saw, the wickedness from which he fled, he yet beheld, like a flaming standard in the middle of the air, that power of redemption to which he must, till death, bear witness; which, though it crush him utterly, he could not deny; though none among the living might ever behold it, *he* had beheld it, and must keep the faith. He would not go back into Egypt for friend, or lover, or bastard son: he would not turn his face from God, no matter how deep might grow the darkness in which God hid His face from him. One day God would give him a sign, and the darkness would all be finished—one day God would raise him, who had suffered him to fall so low.

Hard on the heels of his return that winter, Esther came home too. Her mother and stepfather traveled North to claim her lifeless body and her living son. Soon after Christmas, on the last, dead days of the year, she was buried in the churchyard. It was bitterly cold and there was ice on the ground, as during the days when he had first possessed her. He stood next to Deborah, whose arm in his shivered incessantly with the cold, and watched while the long, plain box was lowered into the ground. Esther's mother stood in silence beside the deep hole, leaning on her husband, who held their grandchild in his arms. "Lord have mercy, have mercy, have mercy," someone began to chant; and the old mourning women clustered of a sudden around Esther's mother to hold her up. Then earth struck the coffin; the child awakened and began to scream.

Then Gabriel prayed to be delivered from blood-guiltiness. He prayed to God to give him a sign one day to make him know he was forgiven. But the child who screamed at that moment in the churchyard had cursed, and sung, and been silenced forever before God gave him a sign.

And he watched this son grow up, a stranger to his father and a stranger to God. Deborah, who became after the death of Esther more friendly with Esther's people, reported to him from the very beginning how shamefully Royal was being spoiled. He was, inevitably, the apple of their eye, a fact that, in operation, caused Deborah to frown, and sometimes, reluctantly, to smile; and, as they said, if there was any white blood in him, it didn't show—he was the spit and image of his mother.

The sun did not rise or set but that Gabriel saw his lost, his disinherited son, or heard of him; and he seemed with every passing day to carry more proudly the doom printed on his brow. Gabriel watched him run headlong, like David's headlong son, towards the disaster that had been waiting for him from the moment he had been conceived. It seemed that he had scarcely begun to walk before he swaggered; he had scarcely begun to talk before he cursed. Gabriel often saw him on the streets, playing on the curbstone with other boys his age. Once, when he passed, one of the boys had said: "Here comes Reverend Grimes," and nodded, in brief, respectful silence. But Royal had looked boldly up into the preacher's face. He had said: "How-de-do, Reverend?" and suddenly,

irrepressibly, laughed. Gabriel, wishing to smile down into the
boy's face, to pause and touch him on the forehead, did none
of these things, but walked on. Behind him, he heard Royal's
explosive whisper: "I bet he got a mighty big one!"—and
then all the children laughed. It came to Gabriel then how
his own mother must have suffered to watch him in the un-
redeemed innocence that so surely led to death and Hell.

"I wonder," said Deborah idly once, "why she called him
Royal? You reckon that's his daddy's name?"

He did not wonder. He had once told Esther that if the
Lord ever gave him a son he would call him Royal, because
the line of the faithful was a royal line—his son would be a
royal child. And this she had remembered as she thrust him
from her; with what had perhaps been her last breath she had
mocked him and his father with this name. She had died, then,
hating him; she had carried into eternity a curse on him and
his.

"I reckon," he said at last, "it *must* be his daddy's name—
less they just given him that name in the hospital up North
after . . . she was dead."

"His grandmama, Sister McDonald"—she was writing a
letter, and did not look at him as she spoke—"well, *she* think
it must've been one of them boys what's all time passing
through here, looking for work, on their way north—you
know? them real shiftless niggers—well, *she* think it must've
been one of them got Esther in trouble. She say Esther
wouldn't never've gone north if she hadn't been a-trying to
find that boy's daddy. Because she was in trouble when she
left here"—and she looked up from her letter a moment—
"*that's* for certain."

"I reckon," he said again, made uncomfortable by her unaccustomed chatter, but not daring, too sharply, to stop her.
He was thinking of Esther, lying cold and still in the ground,
who had been so vivid and shameless in his arms.

"And Sister McDonald say," she went on, "that she left
here with just a little *bit* of money; they had to keep a-sending
her money all the time she was up there almost, specially near
the end. We was just talking about it yesterday—she say, look
like Esther just decided over*night* she had to go, and couldn't
nothing stop her. And she say she didn't *want* to stand in the

girl's way—but if she'd've *known* something was the matter she wouldn't *never*'ve let that girl away from her."

"Seems funny to *me*," he muttered, scarcely knowing what he was saying, "that she didn't think *something*."

"Why she didn't think nothing, because Esther always *told* her mother everything—weren't no shame between them— they was just like two women together. She say she never *dreamed* that Esther would run away from her if she got herself in trouble." And she looked outward, past him, her eyes full of a strange, bitter pity. "That poor thing," she said, "she must have suffered *some*."

"I don't see no need for you and Sister McDonald to sit around and *talk* about it all the time," he said, then. "It all been a mighty long time ago; that boy is growing up already."

"That's true," she said, bending her head once more, "but some things, look like, ain't to be forgotten in a hurry."

"Who you writing to?" he asked, as oppressed suddenly by the silence as he had been by her talk.

She looked up. "I'm writing to your sister, Florence. You got anything you want me to say?"

"No," he said. "Just tell her I'm praying for her."

When Royal was sixteen the war came, and all the young men, first the sons of the mighty, and then the sons of his own people, were scattered into foreign lands. Gabriel fell on his knees each night to pray that Royal would not have to go. "But I hear he *want* to go," said Deborah. "His grandmama tell me he giving her a *time* because she won't let him go and sign up."

"Look like," he said sullenly, "that won't none of these young men be satisfied till they can go off and get themselves crippled or killed."

"Well, you know that's the way the young folks is," said Deborah, cheerfully. "You can't never tell them nothing—and when they find out it's too late then."

He discovered that whenever Deborah spoke of Royal, a fear deep within him listened and waited. Many times he had thought to unburden his heart to her. But she gave him no opportunity, never said anything that might allow him the healing humility of confession—or that might, for that matter, have permitted him at last to say how much he hated her for her barrenness. She demanded of him what she gave—nothing—nothing, at any rate, with which she could be reproached. She kept his house and shared his bed; she visited the sick, as she had always done, and she comforted the dying, as she had always done. The marriage for which he had once dreamed the world would mock him had so justified itself— in the eyes of the world—that no one now could imagine, for either of them, any other condition or alliance. Even Deborah's weakness, which grew more marked with the years, keeping her more frequently in her bed, and her barrenness, like her previous dishonor, had come to seem mysterious proofs of how completely she had surrendered herself to God.

He said: "Amen," cautiously, after her last remark, and cleared his throat.

"I declare," she said, with the same cheerfulness, "sometime he remind me of you when you was a young man."

And he did not look at her, though he felt her eyes on him; he reached for his Bible and opened it. "Young men," he said, "is all the same, don't Jesus change their hearts."

Royal did not go to war, but he went away that summer to work on the docks in another town. Gabriel did not see him any more until the war was over.

On that day, a day he was never to forget, he went when work was done to buy some medicine for Deborah, who was in bed with a misery in her back. Night had not yet fallen and the streets were gray and empty—save that here and there, polished in the light that spilled outward from a poolroom or a tavern, white men stood in groups of half a dozen. As he passed each group, silence fell, and they watched him insolently, itching to kill; but he said nothing, bowing his head, and they knew, anyway, that he was a preacher. There were no black men on the streets at all, save him. There had been found that morning, just outside of town, the dead body of a soldier, his uniform shredded where he had been flogged, and, turned upward through the black skin, raw, red meat. He lay face downward at the base of a tree, his fingernails digging into the scuffed earth. When he was turned over, his eyeballs stared upward in amazement and horror, his mouth was locked open wide; his trousers, soaked with blood, were torn open, and exposed to the cold, white air of morning the thick hairs of his groin, matted together, black and rust-red, and the wound that seemed to be throbbing still. He had been carried home in silence and lay now behind locked doors, with his living kinsmen, who sat, weeping, and praying, and dreaming of vengeance, and waiting for the next visitation. Now, someone spat on the sidewalk at Gabriel's feet, and he walked on, his face not changing, and he heard it reprovingly whispered behind him that he was a good nigger, surely up to no trouble. He hoped that he would not be spoken to, that he would not have to smile into any of these so well-known white faces. While he walked, held by his caution more rigid than an arrow, he prayed, as his mother had taught him to pray, for loving kindness; yet he dreamed of the feel of a white man's forehead against his shoe; again and again, until the head wobbled on the broken neck and his foot encountered nothing but the rushing blood. And he was thinking that it was only the hand of the Lord that had taken Royal away, because if he had stayed they would surely have killed him, when, turning a corner, he looked into Royal's face.

Royal was now as tall as Gabriel, broad-shouldered, and lean. He wore a new suit, blue, with broad, blue stripes, and carried, crooked under his arm, a brown-paper bundle tied with string. He and Gabriel stared at one another for a second with no recognition. Royal stared in blank hostility, before, seeming to remember Gabriel's face, he took a burning cigarette from between his lips, and said, with pained politeness: "How-de-do, sir." His voice was rough, and there was, faintly, the odor of whisky on his breath.

But Gabriel could not speak at once; he struggled to get his breath. Then: "How-de-do," he said. And they stood, each as though waiting for the other to say something of the greatest importance, on the deserted corner. Then, just as Royal was about to move, Gabriel remembered the white men all over town.

"Boy," he cried, "ain't you got good sense? Don't you know you ain't got no business to be out here, walking around like this?"

Royal stared at him, uncertain whether to laugh or to take offence, and Gabriel said, more gently: "I just mean you better be careful, son. Ain't nothing but white folks in town today. They done killed . . . last night . . ."

Then he could not go on. He saw, as though it were a vision, Royal's body, sprawled heavy and unmoving forever against the earth, and tears blinded his eyes.

Royal watched him, a distant and angry compassion in his face.

"I know," he said abruptly, "but they ain't going to bother me. They done got their nigger for this week. I ain't going far noway."

Then the corner on which they stood seemed suddenly to rock with the weight of mortal danger. It seemed for a moment, as they stood there, that death and destruction rushed towards them: two black men alone in the dark and silent town where white men prowled like lions—what mercy could they hope for, should they be found here, talking together? It would surely be believed that they were plotting vengeance. And Gabriel started to move away, thinking to save his son.

"God bless you, boy," said Gabriel. "You hurry along now."

"Yeah," said Royal, "thanks." He moved away, about to turn the corner. He looked back at Gabriel. "But you be careful, too," he said, and smiled.

He turned the corner and Gabriel listened as his footfalls moved away. They were swallowed up in silence; he heard no voices raised to cut down Royal as he went his way; soon there was silence everywhere.

Not quite two years later Deborah told him that his son was dead.

And now John tried to pray. There was a great noise of praying all around him, a great noise of weeping and of song. It was Sister McCandless who led the song, who sang it nearly alone, for the others did not cease to moan and cry. It was a song he had heard all his life:

> *"Lord, I'm traveling, Lord,*
> *I got on my traveling shoes."*

Without raising his eyes, he could see her standing in the holy place, pleading the blood over those who sought there, her head thrown back, eyes shut, foot pounding the floor. She did not look, then, like the Sister McCandless who sometimes came to visit them, like the woman who went out every day to work for the white people downtown, who came home at evening, climbing, with such weariness, the long, dark stairs. No: her face was transfigured now, her whole being was made new by the power of her salvation.

"Salvation is real," a voice said to him, "God is real. Death may come soon or late, why do you hesitate? Now is the time to seek and serve the Lord." Salvation was real for all these others, and it might be real for him. He had only to reach out and God would touch him; he had only to cry and God would hear. All these others, now, who cried so far beyond him with such joy, had once been in their sins, as he was now—and they had cried and God had heard them, and delivered them out of all their troubles. And what God had done for others, He could also do for him.

But—out of *all* their troubles? Why did his mother weep? Why did his father frown? If God's power was so great, why were their lives so troubled?

He had never tried to think of their trouble before; rather, he had never before confronted it in such a narrow place. It had always been there, at his back perhaps, all these years, but he had never turned to face it. Now it stood before him, staring, nevermore to be escaped, and its mouth was enlarged without any limit. It was ready to swallow him up. Only the hand of God could deliver him. Yet, in a moment, he somehow knew from the sound of that storm which rose so painfully in him now, which laid waste—forever?—the strange, yet comforting landscape of his mind, that the hand of God would surely lead him into this staring, waiting mouth, these distended jaws, this hot breath as of fire. He would be led into darkness, and in darkness would remain; until in some incalculable time to come the hand of God would reach down and raise him up; he, John, who having lain in darkness would no longer be himself but some other man. He would have been changed, as they said, forever; sown in dishonor, he would be raised in honor: he would have been born again.

Then he would no longer be the son of his father, but the son of his Heavenly Father, the King. Then he need no longer fear his father, for he could take, as it were, their quarrel over his father's head to Heaven—to the Father who loved him, who had come down in the flesh to die for him. Then he and his father would be equals, in the sight, and the sound, and the love of God. Then his father could not beat him any more, or despise him any more, or mock him any more—he, John, the Lord's anointed. He could speak to his father then as men spoke to one another—as sons spoke to their fathers, not in trembling but in sweet confidence, not in hatred but in love. His father could not cast him out, whom God had gathered in.

Yet, trembling, he knew that this was not what he wanted. He did not *want* to love his father; he wanted to hate him, to cherish that hatred, and give his hatred words one day. He did not want his father's kiss—not any more, he who had received so many blows. He could not imagine, on any day to come and no matter how greatly he might be changed, wanting to take his father's hand. The storm that raged in him tonight could not uproot this hatred, the mightiest tree in all John's country, all that remained tonight, in this, John's floodtime.

And he bowed his head yet lower before the altar in weariness and confusion. Oh, that his father would *die*!—and the road before John be open, as it must be open for others. Yet in the very grave he would hate him; his father would but have changed conditions, he would be John's father still. The grave was not enough for punishment, for justice, for revenge. Hell, everlasting, unceasing, perpetual, unquenched forever, should be his father's portion; with John there to watch, to linger, to smile, to laugh aloud, hearing, at last, his father's cries of torment.

And, even then, it would not be finished. *The everlasting father.*

Oh, but his thoughts were evil—but tonight he did not care. Somewhere, in all this whirlwind, in the darkness of his heart, in the storm—was something—something he must find. He could not pray. His mind was like the sea itself: troubled, and too deep for the bravest man's descent, throwing up now and again, for the naked eye to wonder at, treasure and debris long forgotten on the bottom—bones and jewels, fantastic shells, jelly that had once been flesh, pearls that had once been eyes. And he was at the mercy of this sea, hanging there with darkness all around him.

The morning of that day, as Gabriel rose and started out to work, the sky was low and nearly black and the air too thick to breathe. Late in the afternoon the wind rose, the skies opened, and the rain came. The rain came down as though once more in Heaven the Lord had been persuaded of the good uses of a flood. It drove before it the bowed wanderer, clapped children into houses, licked with fearful anger against the high, strong wall, and the wall of the lean-to, and the wall of the cabin, beat against the bark and the leaves of trees, trampled the broad grass, and broke the neck of the flower. The world turned dark, forever, everywhere, and windows ran as though their glass panes bore all the tears of eternity, threatening at every instant to shatter inward against this force, uncontrollable, so abruptly visited on the earth. Gabriel walked homeward through this wilderness of water (which had failed, however, to clear the air) to where Deborah waited for him in the bed she seldom, these days, attempted to leave.

And he had not been in the house five minutes before he was aware that a change had occurred in the quality of her silence: in the silence something waited, ready to spring.

He looked up at her from the table where he sat eating the meal that she had painfully prepared. He asked: "How you feel today, old lady?"

"I feel like about the way I always do," and she smiled. "I don't feel no better and I don't feel no worse."

"We going to get the church to pray for you," he said, "and get you on your feet again."

She said nothing and he turned his attention once more to his plate. But she was watching him; he looked up.

"I hear some mighty bad news today," she said slowly.

"What you hear?"

"Sister McDonald was over this afternoon, and Lord knows she was in a pitiful state." He sat stock-still, staring at her. "She done got a letter today what says her grandson—you know, that Royal—done got hisself killed in Chicago. It sure look like the Lord is put a curse on that family. First the mother, and now the son.''

For a moment he could only stare at her stupidly, while the food in his mouth slowly grew heavy and dry. Outside rushed the armies of the rain, and lightning flashed against the window. Then he tried to swallow, and his gorge rose. He began to tremble. "Yes," she said, not looking at him now, "he been living in Chicago about a year, just a-drinking and a-carrying on—and his grandmama, she tell me that look like he got to gambling one night with some of them northern niggers, and one of them got mad because he thought the boy was trying to cheat him, and took out his knife and stabbed him. Stabbed him in the throat, and she tell me he died right there on the floor in that barroom, didn't even have time to get him to no hospital." She turned in bed and looked at him. "The Lord sure give that poor woman a heavy cross to bear."

Then he tried to speak; he thought of the churchyard where Esther was buried, and Royal's first, thin cry. "She going to bring him back home?"

She stared. "Home? Honey, they done buried him already up there in the potter's field. Ain't nobody never going to look on that poor boy no more."

Then he began to cry, not making a sound, sitting at the table, and with his whole body shaking. She watched him for a long while and, finally, he put his head on the table, over-turning the coffee cup, and wept aloud. Then it seemed that there was weeping everywhere, waters of anguish riding the world; Gabriel weeping, and rain beating on the roof, and at the windows, and the coffee dripping from the end of the table. And she asked at last:

"Gabriel . . . that Royal . . . he were your flesh and blood, weren't he?''

"Yes," he said, glad even in his anguish to hear the words fall from his lips, "that was my son."

And there was silence again. Then: "And you sent that girl away, didn't you? With the money outen that box?''

"Yes," he said, "yes."

"Gabriel," she asked, "why did you do it? Why you let her go off and die, all by herself? Why ain't you never said nothing?''

And now he could not answer. He could not raise his head.

"Why?" she insisted. "Honey, I ain't never asked you. But I got a right to know—and when you wanted a son so bad?"

Then, shaking, he rose from the table and walked slowly to the window, looking out.

"I asked my God to forgive me," he said. "But I didn't want no harlot's son."

"Esther weren't no harlot," she said quietly.

"She weren't my wife. I couldn't make her my wife. I already had *you*"—and he said the last words with venom—"Esther's mind weren't on the Lord—she'd of dragged me right on down to Hell with her."

"She mighty near has," said Deborah.

"The Lord He held me back," he said, hearing the thunder, watching the lightning. "He put out His hand and held me back." Then, after a moment, turning back into the room: "I *couldn't* of done nothing else," he cried, "what else could I of done? Where could I of gone with Esther, and me a preacher, too? And what could I of done with you?" He looked at her, old and black and patient, smelling of sickness and age and death. "Ah," he said, his tears still falling, "I bet you was mighty happy today, old lady, weren't you? When she told you he, Royal, my son, was dead. *You* ain't never had no son." And he turned again to the window. Then: "How long you been knowing about this?"

"I been knowing," she said, "ever since that evening, way back there, when Esther come to church."

"You got a evil mind," he said. "I hadn't never touched her then."

"No," she said slowly, "but you had already done touched *me*."

He moved a little from the window and stood looking down at her from the foot of the bed.

"Gabriel," she said, "I been praying all these years that the Lord would touch my body, and make me like them women, all them women, you used to go with all the time." She was very calm; her face was very bitter and patient. "Look like it weren't His will. Look like I couldn't nohow forget . . . how they done me way back there when I weren't nothing but a girl." She paused and looked away. "But, Gabriel, if you'd said something even when that poor girl was buried, if you'd wanted to own that poor boy, I wouldn't nohow of cared what folks said, or where we might of had to go, or nothing. I'd have raised him like my own, I swear to my God I would have—and he might be living now."

"Deborah," he asked, "what you been thinking all this time?"

She smiled. "I been thinking," she said, "how you better commence to tremble when the Lord, He gives you your heart's desire." She paused. "I'd been wanting you since I wanted anything. And then I got you."

He walked back to the window, tears rolling down his face.

"Honey," she said, in another, stronger voice, "you better pray God to forgive you. You better not let go until He make you *know* you been forgiven."

"Yes," he sighed, "I'm waiting on the Lord."

Then there was only silence, except for the rain. The rain came down in buckets; it was raining, as they said, pitchforks and nigger babies. Lightning flashed again across the sky and thunder rolled.

"Listen," said Gabriel. "God is talking."

Slowly now, he rose from his knees, for half the church was standing: Sister Price, Sister McCandless, and Praying Mother Washington; and the young Ella Mae sat in her chair watching Elisha where he lay. Florence and Elizabeth were still on their knees; and John was on his knees.

And, rising, Gabriel thought of how the Lord had led him to this church so long ago, and how Elizabeth, one night after he had preached, had walked this long aisle to the altar, to repent before God her sin. And then they had married, for he believed her when she said that she was changed—and she was the sign, she and her nameless child, for which he had tarried so many dark years before the Lord. It was as though, when he saw them, the Lord had returned to him again that which was lost.

Then, as he stood with the others over the fallen Elisha, John rose from his knees. He bent a dazed, sleepy, frowning look on Elisha and the others, shivering a little as though he were cold; and then he felt his father's eyes and looked up at his father.

At the same moment, Elisha, from the floor, began to speak in a tongue of fire, under the power of the Holy Ghost. John and his father stared at each other, struck dumb and still and with something come to life between them—while the Holy Ghost spoke. Gabriel had never seen such a look on John's face before; Satan, at that moment, stared out of John's eyes while the Spirit spoke; and yet John's staring eyes tonight reminded Gabriel of other eyes: of his mother's eyes when she beat him, of Florence's eyes when she mocked him, of Deborah's eyes when she prayed for him, of Esther's eyes and Royal's eyes, and Elizabeth's eyes tonight before Roy cursed him, and of Roy's eyes when Roy said: "You black bastard." And John did not drop his eyes, but seemed to want to stare forever into the bottom of Gabriel's soul. And Gabriel, scarcely believing that John could have become so brazen, stared in wrath and horror at Elizabeth's presumptuous bastard boy, grown suddenly so old in evil. He nearly raised his hand to strike him, but did not move, for Elisha lay between them. Then he said, soundlessly, with his lips: "Kneel down." John turned suddenly, the movement like a curse, and knelt again before the altar.

THREE

Elizabeth's Prayer

Lord, I wish I had of died
In Egypt land!

W HILE Elisha was speaking, Elizabeth felt that the Lord was speaking a message to her heart, that this fiery visitation was meant for her; and that if she humbled herself to listen, God would give her the interpretation. This certainty did not fill her with exultation, but with fear. She was afraid of what God might say—of what displeasure, what condemnation, what prophesies of trials yet to be endured might issue from His mouth.

Now Elisha ceased to speak, and rose; now he sat at the piano. There was muted singing all around her; yet she waited. Before her mind's eyes wavered, in a light like the light from a fire, the face of John, whom she had brought so unwillingly into the world. It was for his deliverance that she wept tonight: that he might be carried, past wrath unspeakable, into a state of grace.

They were singing:

> *"Must Jesus bear the cross alone,*
> *And all the world go free?"*

Elisha picked out the song on the piano, his fingers seeming to hesitate, almost to be unwilling. She, too, strained against her great unwillingness, but forced her heart to say Amen, as the voice of Praying Mother Washington picked up the response:

> *"No, there's a cross for everyone,*
> *And there's a cross for me."*

She heard weeping near her—was it Ella Mae? or Florence? or the echo, magnified, of her own tears? The weeping was buried beneath the song. She had been hearing this song all her life, she had grown up with it, but she had never understood it as well as she understood it now. It filled the church, as though the church had merely become a hollow or a void, echoing with the voices that had driven her to this dark place. Her aunt had sung it always, harshly, under her breath, in a bitter pride:

> *"The consecrated cross I'll bear*
> *Till death shall set me free,*
> *And then go home, a crown to wear,*
> *For there's a crown for me."*

She was probably an old, old woman now, still in the same harshness of spirit, singing this song in the tiny house down home which she and Elizabeth had shared so long. And she did not know of Elizabeth's shame—Elizabeth had not written about John until long after she was married to Gabriel; and the Lord had never allowed her aunt to come to New York City. Her aunt had always prophesied that Elizabeth would come to no good end, proud, and vain, and foolish as she was, and having been allowed to run wild all her childhood days.

Her aunt had come second in the series of disasters that had ended Elizabeth's childhood. First, when she was eight, going on nine, her mother had died, an event not immediately recognized by Elizabeth as a disaster, since she had scarcely known her mother and had certainly never loved her. Her mother had been very fair, and beautiful, and delicate of health, so that she stayed in bed most of the time, reading spiritualist pamphlets concerning the benefits of disease and complaining to Elizabeth's father of how she suffered. Elizabeth remembered of her only that she wept very easily and that she smelled like stale milk—it was, perhaps, her mother's disquieting color that, whenever she was held in her mother's arms, made Elizabeth think of milk. Her mother did not, however, hold Elizabeth in her arms very often. Elizabeth very quickly suspected that this was because she was so very much darker than her mother and not nearly, of course, so beautiful. When she faced her mother she was shy, downcast, sullen. She did not know how to answer her mother's shrill, meaningless questions, put with the furious affectation of maternal concern; she could not pretend, when she kissed her mother, or submitted to her mother's kiss, that she was moved by anything more than an unpleasant sense of duty. This, of course, bred in her mother a kind of baffled fury, and she never tired of telling Elizabeth that she was an "unnatural" child.

But it was very different with her father; he was—and so Elizabeth never failed to think of him—young, and handsome, and kind, and generous; and he loved his daughter. He told her that she was the apple of his eye, that she was wound around his heartstrings, that she was surely the finest little lady in the land. When she was with her father she pranced and postured like a very queen: and she was not afraid of anything, save the moment when he would say that it was her bedtime, or that he had to be "getting along." He was always buying her things, things to wear and things to play with, and taking her on Sundays for long walks through the country, or to the circus, when the circus was in town, or to Punch and Judy shows. And he was dark, like Elizabeth, and gentle, and proud; he had never been angry with her, but she had seen him angry a few times with other people—her mother, for example, and later, of course, her aunt. Her mother was always angry and Elizabeth paid no attention; and, later, her aunt was perpetually angry and Elizabeth learned to bear it: but if her father had ever been angry with her—in those days—she would have wanted to die.

Neither had he ever learned of her disgrace; when it happened, she could not think how to tell him, how to bring such pain to him who had had such pain already. Later, when she would have told him, he was long past caring, in the silent ground.

She thought of him now, while the singing and weeping went on around her—and she thought how he would have loved his grandson, who was like him in so many ways. Perhaps she dreamed it, but she did not believe she dreamed when at moments she thought she heard in John echoes, curiously distant and distorted, of her father's gentleness, and the trick of his laugh—how he threw his head back and the years that marked his face fled away, and the soft eyes softened and the mouth turned upward at the corners like a little boy's mouth—and that deadly pride of her father's behind which he retired when confronted by the nastiness of other people. It was he who had told her to weep, when she wept, alone; never to let the world see, never to ask for mercy; if one had to die, to go ahead and die, but never to let oneself be beaten. He had said this to her on one of the last times she had seen him, when she was being carried miles away, to Maryland, to live with her aunt. She had reason, in the years that followed, to remember his saying this; and time, at last, to discover in herself the depths of bitterness in her father from which these words had come.

For when her mother died, the world fell down; her aunt, her mother's older sister, arrived, and stood appalled at Elizabeth's vanity and uselessness; and decided, immediately, that her father was no fit person to raise a child, especially, as she darkly said, an innocent little girl. And it was this decision on the part of her aunt, for which Elizabeth did not forgive her for many years, that precipitated the third disaster, the separation of herself from her father—from all that she loved on earth.

For her father ran what her aunt called a "house"—not the house where they lived, but another house, to which, as Elizabeth gathered, wicked people often came. And he had also, to Elizabeth's rather horrified confusion, a "stable." Low, common niggers, the lowest of the low, came from all over (and sometimes brought their women and sometimes found them there) to eat, and drink cheap moonshine, and play music all night long—and to do worse things, her aunt's dreadful silence then suggested, which were far better left unsaid. And she would, she swore, move Heaven and earth before she would let her sister's daughter grow up with such a man. Without, however, so much as looking at Heaven, and without troubling any more of the earth than that part of it which held the courthouse, she won the day: Like a clap of thunder, or like a magic spell, like light one moment and darkness the next, Elizabeth's life had changed. Her mother was dead, her father banished, and she lived in the shadow of her aunt.

Or, more exactly, as she thought now, the shadow in which she had lived was fear—fear made more dense by hatred. Not for a moment had she judged her father; it would have made no difference to her love for him had she been told, and even

seen it proved, that he was first cousin to the Devil. The proof
would not have existed for her, and if it had she would not
have regretted being his daughter, or have asked for anything
better than to suffer at his side in Hell. And when she had
been taken from him her imagination had been wholly unable
to lend reality to the wickedness of which he stood accused—*she*, certainly, did not accuse him. She screamed in
anguish when he put her from him and turned to go, and she
had to be carried to the train. And later, when she understood
perfectly all that had happened then, still in her heart she
could not accuse him. Perhaps his life had been wicked, but
he had been very good to her. His life had certainly cost him
enough in pain to make the world's judgment a thing of no
account. *They* had not known him as she had known him; *they*
did not care as she had cared! It only made her sad that he
never, as he had promised, came to take her away, and that
while she was growing up she saw him so seldom. When she
became a young woman she did not see him at all; but that
was her own fault.

No, she did not accuse him; but she accused her aunt, and
this from the moment she understood that her aunt had loved
her mother, but did not love *him*. This could only mean that
her aunt could not love *her*, either, and nothing in her life
with her aunt ever proved Elizabeth wrong. It was true that
her aunt was always talking of how much she loved her sister's
daughter, and what great sacrifices she had made on her account, and what great care she took to see to it that Elizabeth
should grow up a good, Christian girl. But Elizabeth was not
for a moment fooled, and did not, for as long as she lived
with her, fail to despise her aunt. She sensed that what her
aunt spoke of as love was something else—a bribe, a threat,
an indecent will to power. She knew that the kind of impris-
onment that love might impose was also, mysteriously, a freedom for the soul and spirit, was water in the dry place, and
had nothing to do with the prisons, churches, laws, rewards,
and punishments, that so positively cluttered the landscape of
her aunt's mind.

And yet, tonight, in her great confusion, she wondered if
she had not been wrong; if there had not been something
that she had overlooked, for which the Lord had made her

suffer. "You little miss great-I-am," her aunt had said to her in those days, "you better watch your step, you hear me? You go walking around with your nose in the air, the Lord's going to let you fall right on down to the bottom of the ground. *You* mark my words. You'll *see*."

To this perpetual accusation Elizabeth had never replied; she merely regarded her aunt with a wide-eyed, insolent stare, meant at once to register her disdain and to thwart any pretext for punishment. And this trick, which she had, unconsciously, picked up from her father, rarely failed to work. As the years went on, her aunt seemed to gauge in a look the icy distances that Elizabeth had put between them, and that would certainly never be conquered now. And she would add, looking down, and under her breath: " 'Cause God don't like it."

"I sure don't care what God don't like, or you, either," Elizabeth's heart replied. "I'm going away from here. He's going to come and get me, and I'm going away from here."

"He" was her father, who never came. As the years passed, she replied only: "I'm going away from here." And it hung, this determination, like a heavy jewel between her breasts; it was written in fire on the dark sky of her mind.

But, yes—there was something she had overlooked. *Pride goeth before destruction; and a haughty spirit before a fall.* She had not known this: she had not imagined that she could fall. She wondered, tonight, how she could give this knowledge to her son; if she could help him to endure what could now no longer be changed; if while life ran, he would forgive her—for her pride, her folly, and her bargaining with God! For, tonight, those years before her fall, in her aunt's dark house—that house which smelled always of clothes kept too long in closets, and of old women; which was redolent of their gossip, and was pervaded, somehow, by the odor of the lemon her aunt took in her tea, and by the odor of frying fish, and of the still that someone kept in the basement—came before her, entire and overwhelming; and she remembered herself, entering any room in which her aunt might be sitting, responding to anything her aunt might say, standing before her, as rigid as metal and cancerous with hate and fear, in battle every hour of every day, a battle that she continued in her dreams. She knew now of what it was that she had so silently and so early accused her aunt: it was of tearing a bewildered child away from the arms of the father she loved. And she knew now why she had sometimes, so dimly and so unwillingly, felt that her father had betrayed her: it was because he had not overturned the earth to take his daughter away from a woman who did not love her, and whom she did not love. Yet she knew tonight how difficult it was to overturn the earth, for she had tried once, and she had failed. And she knew, too—and it made the tears that touched her mouth more bitter than the most bitter herb—that without the pride and bitterness she had so long carried in her heart against her aunt she could never have endured her life with her.

And she thought of Richard. It was Richard who had taken her out of that house, and out of the South, and into the city of destruction. He had suddenly arrived—and from the moment he arrived until the moment of his death he had filled her life. Not even tonight, in the heart's nearly impenetrable secret place, where the truth is hidden and where only the truth can live, could she wish that she had not known him; nor deny that, so long as he was there, the rejoicing of Heaven could have meant nothing to her—that, being forced to choose between Richard and God, she could only, even with weeping, have turned away from God.

And this was why God had taken him from her. It was for all of this that she was paying now, and it was this pride, hatred, bitterness, lust—this folly, this corruption—of which her son was heir.

Richard had not been born in Maryland, but he was working there, the summer that she met him, as a grocery clerk. It was 1919, and she was one year younger than the century. He was twenty-two, which seemed a great age to her in those days. She noticed him at once because he was so sullen and only barely polite. He waited on folks, her aunt said, furiously, as though he hoped the food they bought would poison them. Elizabeth liked to watch him move; his body was very thin, and beautiful, and nervous—*high strung*, thought Elizabeth, wisely. He moved exactly like a cat, perpetually on the balls of his feet, and with a cat's impressive, indifferent aloofness, his face closed, in his eyes no light at all. He smoked all the time, a cigarette between his lips as he added up the figures, and sometimes left burning on the counter while he went to look for stock. When, as someone entered, he said good morning, or good day, he said it barely looking up, and with an indifference that fell just short of insolence. When, having bought what he wanted and counted his change, the customer turned to leave and Richard said: "Thank you," it sounded so much like a curse that people sometimes turned in surprise to stare.

"He sure don't like working in that store," Elizabeth once observed to her aunt.

"He don't like working," said her aunt, scornfully. "He just like you."

On a bright, summer day, bright in her memory forever, she came into the store alone, wearing her best white summer dress and with her hair, newly straightened and curled at the ends, tied with a scarlet ribbon. She was going to a great church picnic with her aunt, and had come in to buy some lemons. She passed the owner of the store, who was a very fat man, sitting out on the sidewalk, fanning himself; he asked her, as she passed, if it was hot enough for her, and she said something and walked into the dark, heavy-smelling store, where flies buzzed, and where Richard sat on the counter reading a book.

She felt immediately guilty about having disturbed him, and muttered apologetically that she only wanted to buy some lemons. She expected him to get them for her in his sullen fashion and go back to his book, but he smiled, and said:

"Is that all you want? You better think now. You sure you ain't forgot nothing?"

She had never seen him smile before, nor had she really, for that matter, ever heard his voice. Her heart gave a dreadful leap and then, as dreadfully, seemed to have stopped forever. She could only stand there, staring at him. If he had asked her to repeat what she wanted she could not possibly have remembered what it was. And she found that she was looking into his eyes and where she had thought there was no light at all she found a light she had never seen before—and he was smiling still, but there was something curiously urgent in his smile. Then he said: "How many lemons, little girl?"

"Six," she said at last, and discovered to her vast relief that nothing had happened: the sun was still shining, the fat man still sat at the door, her heart was beating as though it had never stopped. She was not, however, fooled; she remembered the instant at which her heart had stopped, and she knew that it beat now with a difference.

He put the lemons into a bag and, with a curious diffidence, she came closer to the counter to give him the money. She was in a terrible state, for she found that she could neither take her eyes off him nor look at him.

"Is that your mother you come in with all the time?" he asked.

"No," she said, "that's my aunt." She did not know why she said it, but she did: "My mother's dead."

"Oh," he said. Then: "Mine, too." They both looked thoughtfully at the money on the counter. He picked it up, but did not move. "I didn't think it was your mother," he said, finally.

"Why?"

"I don't know. She don't look like you."

He started to light a cigarette, and then looked at her and put the pack in his pocket again.

"Don't mind me," she said quickly. "Anyway, I got to go. She's waiting—we going out."

He turned and banged the cash register. She picked up her lemons. He gave her her change. She felt that she ought to say something else—it didn't seem right, somehow, just to walk out—but she could not think of anything. But he said:

"Then *that's* why you so dressed up today. Where you going to go?"

"We going to a picnic—a church picnic," she said, and suddenly, unaccountably, and for the first time, smiled.

And he smiled, too, and lit his cigarette, blowing the smoke carefully away from her. "You like picnics?"

"Sometimes," she said. She was not comfortable with him yet, and still she was beginning to feel that she would like to stand and talk to him all day. She wanted to ask him what he was reading, but she did not dare. Yet: "What's your name?" she abruptly brought out.

"Richard," he said.

"Oh," she said thoughtfully. Then: "Mine's Elizabeth."

"I know," he said. "I heard her call you one time."

"Well," she said helplessly, after a long pause, "good-bye."

"Good-*bye*? You ain't going away, is you?"

"Oh, no," she said, in confusion.

"Well," he said, and smiled and bowed, "good *day*."

"Yes," she said, "good day."

And she turned and walked out into the streets; not the same streets from which she had entered a moment ago. These streets, the sky above, the sun, the drifting people, all had, in a moment, changed, and would never be the same again.

"You remember that day," he asked much later, "when you come into the store?"

"Yes?"

"Well, you was mighty pretty."

"I didn't think you never looked at me."

"Well, I didn't think you never looked at me."

"You was reading a book."

"Yes."

"What book was it, Richard?"

"Oh, I don't remember. Just a book."

"You smiled."

"You did, too."

"No, I didn't. I remember."

"Yes, you did."

"No, I *didn't*. Not till you did."

"Well, anyway—you was mighty pretty."

She did not like to think of with what hardness of heart, what calculated weeping, what deceit, what cruelty she now went into battle with her aunt for her freedom. And she won it, even though on certain not-to-be-dismissed conditions. The principal condition was that she should put herself under the protection of a distant, unspeakably respectable female relative of her aunt's, who lived in New York City—for when the summer ended, Richard said that he was going there and he wanted her to come with him. They would get married there. Richard said that he hated the South, and this was perhaps the reason it did not occur to either of them to begin their married life there. And Elizabeth was checked by the fear that if her aunt should discover how things stood between her and Richard she would find, as she had found so many years before in the case of her father, some means of bringing about their separation. This, as Elizabeth later considered it, was the first in the sordid series of mistakes which was to cause her to fall so low.

But to look back from the stony plain along the road which led one to that place is not at all the same thing as walking on the road; the perspective, to say the very least, changes only with the journey; only when the road has, all abruptly and treacherously, and with an absoluteness that permits no argument, turned or dropped or risen is one able to see all that one could not have seen from any other place. In those days, had the Lord Himself descended from Heaven with trumpets telling her to turn back, she could scarcely have heard Him, and could certainly not have heeded. She lived, in those days, in a fiery storm, of which Richard was the center and the heart. And she fought only to reach him—only that; she was afraid only of what might happen if they were kept from one another; for what might come after she had no thoughts or fears to spare.

Her pretext for coming to New York was to take advantage of the greater opportunities the North offered colored people; to study in a Northern school, and to find a better job than any she was likely to be offered in the South. Her aunt, who listened to this with no diminution of her habitual scorn, was yet unable to deny that from generation to generation, things, as she grudgingly put it, were bound to change—and neither could she quite take the position of seeming to stand in Elizabeth's way. In the winter of 1920, as the year began, Elizabeth found herself in an ugly back room in Harlem in the home of her aunt's relative, a woman whose respectability was immediately evident from the incense she burned in her rooms and the spiritualist séances she held every Saturday night.

The house was still standing, not very far away; often she was forced to pass it. Without looking up, she was able to see the windows of the apartment in which she had lived, and the woman's sign, was in the window still: MADAME WILLIAMS, SPIRITUALIST.

She found a job as chambermaid in the same hotel in which Richard worked as elevator boy. Richard said that they would marry as soon as he had saved some money. But since he was going to school at night and made very little money, their marriage, which she had thought of as taking place almost as soon as she arrived, was planned for a future that grew ever more remote. And this presented her with a problem that she had refused, at home in Maryland, to think about, but from which, now, she could not escape: the problem of their life together. Reality, so to speak, burst in for the first time on her great dreaming, and she found occasion to wonder, ruefully, what had made her imagine that, once with Richard, she would have been able to withstand him. She had kept, precariously enough, what her aunt referred to as her pearl without price while she had been with Richard down home. This, which she had taken as witness to her own feminine moral strength, had been due to nothing more, it now developed, than her great fear of her aunt, and the lack, in that small town, of opportunity. Here, in this great city where no one cared, where people might live in the same building for years and never speak to one another, she found herself, when Richard took her in his arms, on the edge of a steep place: and down she rushed, on the descent uncaring, into the dreadful sea.

So it began. Had it been waiting for her since the day she had been taken from her father's arms? The world in which she now found herself was not unlike the world from which she had, so long ago, been rescued. Here were the women who had been the cause of her aunt's most passionate condemnation of her father—hard-drinking, hard-talking, with whisky- and cigarette-breath, and moving with the mystic authority of women who knew what sweet violence might be acted out under the moon and stars, or beneath the tigerish lights of the city, in the raucous hay or the singing bed. And was she, Elizabeth, so sweetly fallen, so tightly chained, one of these women now? And here were the men who had come day and night to visit her father's "stable"—with their sweet talk and their music, and their violence and their sex—black, brown, and beige, who looked on her with lewd, and lustful, and laughing eyes. And these were Richard's friends. Not one of them ever went to Church—one might scarcely have imagined that they knew that churches existed—they all, hourly, daily, in their speech, in their lives, and in their hearts, cursed God. They all seemed to be saying, as Richard, when she once timidly mentioned the love of Jesus, said: "You can tell that puking bastard to kiss my big black ass."

She, for very terror on hearing this, had wept; yet she could not deny that for such an abundance of bitterness there was a positive fountain of grief. There was not, after all, a great difference between the world of the North and that of the South which she had fled; there was only this difference: the North promised more. And this similarity: what it promised it did not give, and what it gave, at length and grudgingly with one hand, it took back with the other. Now she understood in this nervous, hollow, ringing city, that nervousness of Richard's which had so attracted her—a tension so total, and so without the hope, or possibility of release, or resolution, that she felt it in his muscles, and heard it in his breathing, even as on her breast he fell asleep.

And this was perhaps why she had never thought to leave him, frightened though she was during all that time, and in a world in which, had it not been for Richard, she could have found no place to put her feet. She did not leave him, because she was afraid of what might happen to him without her. She did not resist him, because he needed her. And she did not press about marriage because, upset as he was about everything, she was afraid of having him upset about her, too. She thought of herself as his strength; in a world of shadows, the indisputable reality to which he could always repair. And, again, for all that had come, she could not regret this. She had tried, but she had never been and was not now, even tonight, truly sorry. Where, then, was her repentance? And how could God hear her cry?

They had been very happy together, in the beginning; and until the very end he had been very good to her, had not ceased to love her, and tried always to make her know it. No more than she had been able to accuse her father had she ever been able to accuse him. His weakness she understood, and his terror, and even his bloody end. What life had made him bear, her lover, this wild, unhappy boy, many another stronger and more virtuous man might not have borne so well.

Saturday was their best day, for they only worked until one

o'clock. They had all the afternoon to be together, and nearly all of the night, since Madame Williams had her séances on Saturday night and preferred that Elizabeth, before whose silent skepticism departed spirits might find themselves reluctant to speak, should not be in the house. They met at the service entrance. Richard was always there before her, looking, oddly, much younger and less anonymous without the ugly, tight-fitting, black uniform that he had to wear when working. He would be talking, or laughing with some of the other boys, or shooting craps, and when he heard her step down the long, stone hall he would look up, laughing; and wickedly nudging one of the other boys, he would half shout, half sing: "He-y! Look-a-there, ain't she pretty?"

She never failed, at this—which was why he never failed to do it—to blush, half-smiling, half-frowning, and nervously to touch the collar of her dress.

"*Sweet* Georgia Brown!" somebody might say.

"*Miss* Brown to you," said Richard, then, and took her arm.

"Yeah, that's right," somebody else would say, "you *better* hold on to little Miss Bright-eyes, don't somebody sure going to take her away from you."

"Yeah," said another voice, "and it might be me."

"*Oh*, no," said Richard, moving with her towards the street, "ain't nobody going to take *my* little Little-bit away from *me*."

Little-bit: it had been his name for her. And sometimes he called her Sandwich Mouth, or Funnyface, or Frog-eyes. She would not, of course, have endured these names from anyone else, nor, had she not found herself, with joy and helplessness (and a sleeping panic), living it out, would she ever have suffered herself so publicly to become a man's property—"concubine," her aunt would have said, and at night, alone, she rolled the word, tart like lemon rind, on her tongue.

She was descending with Richard to the sea. She would have to climb back up alone, but she did not know this then. Leaving the boys in the hall, they gained the midtown New York streets.

"And what we going to do today, Little-bit?" With that smile of his, and those depthless eyes, beneath the towers of the white city, with people, white, hurrying all around them.

"I don't know, honey. What you want to do?"

"Well, maybe, we go to a *mu*seum."

The first time he suggested this, she demanded, in panic, if they would be allowed to enter.

"Sure, they let niggers in," Richard said. "Ain't we got to be educated, too—to live with the motherf——s?"

He never "watched" his language with her, which at first she took as evidence of his contempt because she had fallen so easily, and which later she took as evidence of his love.

And when he took her to the Museum of Natural History, or the Metropolitan Museum of Art, where they were almost certain to be the only black people, and he guided her through the halls, which never ceased in her imagination to be as cold as tombstones, it was then she saw another life in him. It never ceased to frighten her, this passion he brought to something she could not understand.

For she never grasped—not at any rate with her mind—what, with such incandescence, he tried to tell her on these Saturday afternoons. She could not find, between herself and the African statuette, or totem pole, on which he gazed with such melancholy wonder, any point of contact. She was only glad that she did not look that way. She preferred to look, in the other museum, at the paintings; but still she did not understand anything he said about them. She did not know why he so adored things that were so long dead; what sustenance they gave him, what secrets he hoped to wrest from them. But she understood, at least, that they *did* give him a kind of bitter nourishment, and that the secrets they held for him were a matter of his life and death. It frightened her because she felt that he was reaching for the moon and that he would, therefore, be dashed down against the rocks; but she did not say any of this. She only listened, and in her heart she prayed for him.

But on other Saturdays they went to see a movie; they went to see a play; they visited his friends; they walked through Central Park. She liked the park because, however spuriously, it recreated something of the landscape she had known. How many afternoons had they walked there! She had always, since, avoided it. They bought peanuts and for hours fed the animals at the zoo; they bought soda pop and drank it on the grass;

they walked along the reservoir and Richard explained how a city like New York found water to drink. Mixed with her fear for him was a total admiration: that he had learned so young, so much. People stared at them but she did not mind; he noticed, but he did not seem to notice. But sometimes he would ask, in the middle of a sentence—concerned, possibly, with ancient Rome:

"Little-bit—d'you love me?"

And she wondered how he could doubt it. She thought how infirm she must be not to have been able to make him know it; and she raised her eyes to his, and she said the only thing she could say:

"I wish to God I may die if I don't love you. There ain't no sky above us if I don't love you."

Then he would look ironically up at the sky, and take her arm with a firmer pressure, and they would walk on.

Once, she asked him:

"Richard, did you go to school much when you was little?"

And he looked at her a long moment. Then:

"Baby, I done told you, my mama died when I was born. And my daddy, he weren't nowhere to be found. Ain't nobody never took care of me. I just moved from one place to another. When one set of folks got tired of me they sent me down the line. I didn't hardly go to school at all."

"Then how come you got to be so smart? how come you got to know so much?"

And he smiled, pleased, but he said: "Little-bit, I don't know so much." Then he said, with a change in his face and voice which she had grown to know: "I just decided me one day that I was going to get to know everything them white bastards knew, and I was going to get to know it better than them, so could no white son-of-a-bitch *nowhere* never talk *me* down, and never make me feel like *I* was dirt, when I could read him the alphabet, back, front, and sideways. Shit—he weren't going to beat my ass, then. And if he tried to kill me, I'd take him with me, I swear to my mother I would." Then he looked at her again, and smiled and kissed her, and he said: "That's how I got to know so much, baby."

She asked: "And what you going to do, Richard? What you want to be?"

And his face clouded. "I don't know. I got to find out. Looks like I can't get my mind straight nohow."

She did not know *why* he couldn't—or she could only dimly face it—but she knew he spoke the truth.

She had made her great mistake with Richard in not telling him that she was going to have a child. Perhaps, she thought now, if she had told him everything might have been very different, and he would be living yet. But the circumstances under which she had discovered herself to be pregnant had been such to make her decide, for his sake, to hold her peace awhile. Frightened as she was, she dared not add to the panic that overtook him on the last summer of his life.

And yet perhaps it was, after all, this—this failure to demand of his strength what it might then, most miraculously, have been found able to bear; by which—indeed, how could she know?—his strength might have been strengthened, for which she prayed tonight to be forgiven. Perhaps she had lost her love because she had not, in the end, believed in it enough.

She lived quite a long way from Richard—four subway stops; and when it was time for her to go home, he always took the subway uptown with her and walked her to her door. On a Saturday when they had forgotten the time and stayed together later than usual, he left her at her door at two o'clock in the morning. They said good night hurriedly, for she was afraid of trouble when she got upstairs—though, in fact, Madame Williams seemed astonishingly indifferent to the hours Elizabeth kept—and he wanted to hurry back home and go to bed. Yet, as he hurried off down the dark, murmuring street, she had a sudden impulse to call him back, to ask him to take her with him and never let her go again. She hurried up the steps, smiling a little at this fancy: it was because he looked so young and defenseless as he walked away, and yet so jaunty and strong.

He was to come the next evening at suppertime, to make at last, at Elizabeth's urging, the acquaintance of Madame Williams. But he did not come. She drove Madame Williams wild with her sudden sensitivity to footsteps on the stairs. Having told Madame Williams that a gentleman was coming to visit her, she did not dare, of course, to leave the house and go out looking for him, thus giving Madame Williams the impression that she dragged men in off the streets. At ten o'clock, having eaten no supper, a detail unnoticed by her hostess, she went to bed, her head aching and her heart sick with fear; fear over what had happened to Richard, who had never kept her waiting before; and fear involving all that was beginning to happen in her body.

And on Monday morning he was not at work. She left during the lunch hour to go to his room. He was not there. His landlady said that he had not been there all weekend. While Elizabeth stood trembling and indecisive in the hall, two white policemen entered.

She knew the moment she saw them, and before they mentioned his name, that something terrible had happened to Richard. Her heart, as on that bright summer day when he had first spoken to her, gave a terrible bound and then was still, with an awful, wounded stillness. She put out one hand to touch the wall in order to keep standing.

"This here young lady was just looking for him," she heard the landlady say.

They all looked at her.

"You his girl?" one of the policemen asked.

She looked up at his sweating face, on which a lascivious smile had immediately appeared, and straightened, trying to control her trembling.

"Yes," she said. "Where is he?"

"He's in jail, honey," the other policeman said.

"What for?"

"For robbing a white man's store, black girl. That's what for."

She found, and thanked Heaven for it, that a cold, stony rage had entered her. She would, otherwise, certainly have fallen down, or began to weep. She looked at the smiling policeman.

"Richard ain't robbed no store," she said. "Tell me where he is."

"And *I* tell you," he said, not smiling, "that your boyfriend robbed a store and he's in jail for it. He's going to stay there, too—now, what you got to say to that?"

"And he probably did it for you, too," the other policeman said. "You look like a girl a man could rob a store for."

She said nothing; she was thinking how to get to see him, how to get him out.

One of them, the smiler, turned now to the landlady and said: "Let's have the key to his room. How long's he been living here?"

"About a year," the landlady said. She looked unhappily at Elizabeth. "He seemed like a real nice boy."

"Ah, yes," he said, mounting the steps, "they all seem like real nice boys when they pay their rent."

"You going to take me to see him?" she asked of the remaining policeman. She found herself fascinated by the gun in his holster, the club at his side. She wanted to take that pistol and empty it into his round, red face; to take that club and strike with all her strength against the base of his skull where his cap ended, until the ugly, silky, white man's hair was matted with blood and brains.

"Sure, girl," he said, "you're coming right along with us. The man at the stationhouse wants to ask you some questions."

The smiling policeman came down again. "Ain't nothing up there," he said. "Let's go."

She moved between them, out into the sun. She knew that there was nothing to be gained by talking to them any more. She was entirely in their power; she would have to think faster than they could think; she would have to contain her fear and her hatred, and find out what could be done. Not for anything short of Richard's life, and not, possibly, even for that, would she have wept before them, or asked of them a kindness.

A small crowd, children and curious passers-by, followed them as they walked the long, dusty, sunlit street. She hoped only that they would not pass anyone she knew; she kept her head high, looking straight ahead, and felt the skin settle over her bones as though she were wearing a mask.

And at the station she somehow got past their brutal laughter. (*What was he doing with you, girl, until two o'clock in the morning?—Next time you feel like* that, *girl, you come by here and talk to* me.) She felt that she was about to burst, or vomit, or die. Though the sweat stood out cruelly, like needles on her brow, and she felt herself, from every side, being covered with a stink and filth, she found out, in their own good time, what she wanted to know: He was being held in a prison downtown called the Tombs (the name made her heart turn over), and she could see him tomorrow. The state, or the prison, or someone, had already assigned him a lawyer; he would be brought to trial next week.

But the next day, when she saw him, she wept. He had been beaten, he whispered to her, and he could hardly walk. His body, she later discovered, bore almost no bruises, but was full of strange, painful swellings, and there was a welt above one eye.

He had not, of course, robbed the store, but, when he left her that Saturday night, had gone down into the subway station to wait for his train. It was late, and trains were slow; he was all alone on the platform, only half awake, thinking, he said, of her.

Then, from the far end of the platform, he heard a sound of running; and, looking up, he saw two colored boys come running down the steps. Their clothes were torn, and they were frightened; they came up the platform and stood near him, breathing hard. He was about to ask them what the trouble was when, running across the tracks towards them, and followed by a white man, he saw another colored boy; and at the same instant another white man came running down the subway steps.

Then he came full awake, in panic; he knew that whatever the trouble was, it was now his trouble also; for these white men would make no distinction between him and the three boys they were after: They were all colored, they were about the same age, and here they stood together on the subway platform. And they were all, with no questions asked, herded upstairs, and into the wagon and to the station house.

At the station Richard gave his name and address and age and occupation. Then for the first time he stated that he was not involved, and asked one of the other boys to corroborate his testimony. This they rather despairingly did. They might, Elizabeth felt, have done it sooner, but they probably also felt that it would be useless to speak. And they were not believed; the owner of the store was being brought there to make the identification. And Richard tried to relax: the man *could* not say that he had been there if he had never seen him before.

But when the owner came, a short man with a bloody shirt—for they had knifed him—in the company of yet another policeman, he looked at the four boys before him and said: "Yeah, that's them, all right."

Then Richard shouted: "But *I* wasn't there! Look at me, goddammit—I wasn't *there*!"

"You black bastards," the man said, looking at him, "you're all the same."

Then there was silence in the station, the eyes of the white men all watching. And Richard said, but quietly, knowing that he was lost: "But all the same, mister, I wasn't there." And he looked at the white man's bloody shirt and thought, he told Elizabeth, at the bottom of his heart: "I wish to God they'd killed you."

Then the questioning began. The three boys signed a confession at once, but Richard would not sign. He said at last that he would die before he signed a confession to something he hadn't done. "Well then," said one of them, hitting him suddenly across the head, "maybe you *will* die, you black son-of-a-bitch." And the beating began. He would not, then, talk to her about it; she found that, before the dread and the hatred that filled her mind, her imagination faltered and held its peace.

"What we going to do?" she asked at last.

He smiled a vicious smile—she had never seen such a smile on his face before. "Maybe you ought to pray to that Jesus of yours and get Him to come down and tell these white men something." He looked at her a long, dying moment. "Because I don't know nothing *else* to do," he said.

She suggested: "Richard, what about another lawyer?"

And he smiled again. "I declare," he said, "Little-bit's been holding out on me. She got a fortune tied up in a sock, and she ain't never told me nothing about it."

She had been trying to save money for a whole year, but she had only thirty dollars. She sat before him, going over in her mind all the things she might do to raise money, even to going on the streets. Then, for very helplessness, she began to shake with sobbing. At this, his face became Richard's face again. He said in a shaking voice: "Now, look here, Little-bit, don't you be like that. We going to work this out all right."

But she could not stop sobbing. "Elizabeth," he whispered, "Elizabeth, Elizabeth." Then the man came and said that it was time for her to go. And she rose. She had brought two packs of cigarettes for him, and they were still in her bag. Wholly ignorant of prison regulations, she did not dare to give them to him under the man's eyes. And, somehow, her failure to remember to give him the cigarettes, when she knew how much he smoked, made her weep the harder. She tried—and failed—to smile at him, and she was slowly led to the door. The sun nearly blinded her, and she heard him whisper behind her: "So long, baby. Be good."

In the streets she did not know what to do. She stood awhile before the dreadful gates, and then she walked and walked until she came to a coffee shop where taxi drivers and the people who worked in near-by offices hurried in and out all day. Usually she was afraid to go into downtown establishments, where only white people were, but today she did not care. She felt that if anyone said anything to her she would turn and curse him like the lowest bitch on the streets. If anyone touched her, she would do her best to send his soul to Hell.

But no one touched her; no one spoke. She drank her coffee, sitting in the strong sun that fell through the window. Now it came to her how alone, how frightened she was; she had never been so frightened in her life before. She knew that she was pregnant—knew it, as the old folks said, in her bones; and if Richard should be sent away, what, under Heaven, could she do? Two years, three years—she had no idea how long he might be sent away for—what would she do? And how could she keep her aunt from knowing? And if her aunt should find out, then her father would know, too. The tears welled up, and she drank her cold, tasteless coffee. And what would they do with Richard? And if they sent him away, what would he be like, then, when he returned? She looked out into the quiet, sunny streets, and for the first time in her life, she hated it all—the white city, the white world. She could not, that day, think of one decent white person in the whole world. She sat there, and she hoped that one day God, with tortures inconceivable, would grind them utterly into humility, and make them know that black boys and black girls, whom they treated with such condescension, such disdain, and such good humor, had hearts like human beings, too, more human hearts than theirs.

But Richard was not sent away. Against the testimony of the three robbers, and her own testimony, and, under oath, the storekeeper's indecision, there was no evidence on which to convict him. The courtroom seemed to feel, with some complacency and some disappointment, that it was his great good luck to be let off so easily. They went immediately to his room. And there—she was never all her life long to forget it—he threw himself, face downward, on his bed and wept.

She had only seen one other man weep before—her father—and it had not been like this. She touched him, but he did not stop. Her own tears fell on his dirty, uncombed hair. She tried to hold him, but for a long while he would not be held. His body was like iron; she could find no softness in it. She sat curled like a frightened child on the edge of the bed, her hand on his back, waiting for the storm to pass over. It was then that she decided not to tell him yet about the child.

By and by he called her name. And then he turned, and she held him against her breast, while he sighed and shook. He fell asleep at last, clinging to her as though he were going down into the water for the last time.

And it was the last time. That night he cut his wrists with his razor and he was found in the morning by his landlady, his eyes staring upward with no light, dead among the scarlet sheets.

And now they were singing:

> *"Somebody needs you, Lord,*
> *Come by here."*

At her back, above her, she heard Gabriel's voice. He had risen and was helping the others to pray through. She wondered if John were still on his knees, or had risen, with a child's impatience, and was staring around the church. There was a stiffness in him that would be hard to break, but that, nevertheless, would one day surely be broken. As hers had been, and Richard's—there was no escape for anyone. God was everywhere, terrible, the living God; and so high, the song said, you couldn't get over Him; so low you couldn't get under Him; so wide you couldn't get around Him; but must come in at the door.

And she, she knew today that door: a living, wrathful gate. She knew through what fires the soul must crawl, and with what weeping one passed over. Men spoke of how the heart broke up, but never spoke of how the soul hung speechless in the pause, the void, the terror between the living and the dead; how, all garments rent and cast aside, the naked soul passed over the very mouth of Hell. Once there, there was no turning back; once there, the soul remembered, though the heart sometimes forgot. For the world called to the heart, which stammered to reply; life, and love, and revelry, and, most falsely, hope, called the forgetful, the human heart. Only the soul, obsessed with the journey it had made, and had still to make, pursued its mysterious and dreadful end; and carried, heavy with weeping and bitterness, the heart along.

And, therefore, there was war in Heaven, and weeping before the throne: the heart chained to the soul, and the soul imprisoned within the flesh—a weeping, a confusion, and a weight unendurable filled all the earth. Only the love of God could establish order in this chaos; to Him the soul must turn to be delivered.

But what a turning! How could she fail to pray that He would have mercy on her son, and spare him the sin-born anguish of his father and his mother. And that his heart might know a little joy before the long bitterness descended.

Yet she knew that her weeping and her prayers were in vain. What was coming would surely come; nothing could stop it. She had tried, once, to protect someone and had only hurled him into prison. And she thought tonight, as she had thought so often, that it might have been better, after all, to have done what she had first determined in her heart to do—to have given her son away to strangers, who might have loved him more than Gabriel had ever loved him. She had believed him when he said that God had sent him to her for a sign. He had said that he would cherish her until the grave, and that he would love her nameless son as though he were his own flesh. And he had kept the letter of his promise: he had fed him and clothed him and taught him the Bible—but the spirit was not there. And he cherished—*if* he cherished her—only because she was the mother of his son, Roy. All of this she had through the painful years divined. He certainly did not know she knew it, and she wondered if he knew it himself.

She had met him through Florence. Florence and she had met at work in the middle of the summer, a year after Richard's death. John was then over six months old.

She was very lonely that summer, and beaten down. She was living alone with John in a furnished room even grimmer than the room that had been hers in Madame Williams's apartment. She had, of course, left Madame Williams's immediately upon the death of Richard, saying that she had found a sleep-in job in the country. She had been terribly grateful that summer for Madame Williams's indifference; the woman had simply not seemed to see that Elizabeth, overnight, had become an old woman and was half mad with fear and grief. She wrote her aunt the driest, and briefest, and coldest of notes, not wishing in any way to awaken whatever concern might yet slumber in her breast, telling her the same thing she had told Madame Williams, and telling her not to worry, she was in the hands of God. And she certainly was; through a bitterness that only the hand of God could have laid on her, this same hand brought her through.

Florence and Elizabeth worked as cleaning-women in a high, vast, stony office-building on Wall Street. They arrived in the evening and spent the night going through the great deserted halls and the silent offices with mops and pails and brooms. It was terrible work, and Elizabeth hated it; but it was at night, and she had taken it joyfully, since it meant that she could take care of John herself all day and not have to spend extra money to keep him in a nursery. She worried about him all night long, of course, but at least at night he was sleeping. She could only pray that the house would not burn down, that he would not fall out of bed or, in some mysterious way, turn on the gas-burner, and she had asked the woman next door, who unhappily drank too much, to keep an eye out for him. This woman, with whom she sometimes spent an hour or so in the afternoons, and her landlady, were the only people she saw. She had stopped seeing Richard's friends because, for some reason, she did not want them to know about Richard's child; and because, too, the moment that he was dead it became immediately apparent on both sides how little they had in common. And she did not seek new people; rather, she fled from them. She could not bear, in her changed and fallen state, to submit herself to the eyes of others. The Elizabeth that she had been was buried far away—with her lost and silent father, with her aunt, in Richard's grave—and the Elizabeth she had become she did not recognize, she did not want to know.

But one night, when work was ended, Florence invited her to share a cup of coffee in the all-night coffee shop near by. Elizabeth had, of course, been invited before by other people —the night watchman, for example—but she had always said no. She pleaded the excuse of her baby, whom she must rush home to feed. She was pretending in those days to be a young widow, and she wore a wedding ring. Very shortly, fewer people asked her, and she achieved the reputation of being "stuck up."

Florence had scarcely ever spoken to her before she arrived at this merciful unpopularity; but Elizabeth had noticed Florence. She moved in a silent ferocity of dignity which barely escaped being ludicrous. She was extremely unpopular also and she had nothing whatever to do with any of the women she worked with. She was, for one thing, a good deal older, and she seemed to have nothing to laugh or gossip about. She came to work, and she did her work, and she left. One could not imagine what she was thinking as she marched so grimly down the halls, her head tied up in a rag, a bucket and a mop in her hands. Elizabeth thought that she must once have been very rich, and had lost her money; and she felt for her, as one fallen woman for another, a certain kinship.

A cup of coffee together, as day was breaking, became in time their habit. They sat together in the coffee shop, which was always empty when they arrived and was crowded fifteen minutes later when they left, and had their coffee and dough- nuts before they took the subway uptown. While they had their coffee, and on the ride uptown, they talked, principally about Florence, how badly people treated her, and how empty her life was now that her husband was dead. He had adored her, she told Elizabeth, and satisfied her every whim, but he had tended to irresponsibility. If she had told him once, she had told him a hundred times: "Frank, you better take out life insurance." But he had thought—and wasn't it just like a man!—that he would live forever. Now here she was, a woman getting along in years, forced to make her living among all the black scum of this wicked city. Elizabeth, a little astonished at the need for confession betrayed by this proud woman, listened, nevertheless, with great sympathy. She was very grateful for Florence's interest. Florence was so much older and seemed so kind.

It was no doubt this, Florence's age and kindness, that led Elizabeth, with no premeditation, to take Florence into her confidence. Looking back, she found it hard to believe that she could have been so desperate, or so childish; though, again, on looking back, she was able to see clearly what she then so incoherently felt: how much she needed another human being, somewhere, who knew the truth about her.

Florence had often said how glad she would be to make the acquaintance of little Johnny; she was sure, she said, that any child of Elizabeth's must be a wonderful child. On a Sunday near the end of that summer, Elizabeth dressed him in his best clothes and took him to Florence's house. She was oddly and fearfully depressed that day; and John was not in a good mood. She found herself staring at him darkly, as though she were trying to read his future in his face. He would grow big one day, he would talk, and he would ask her questions. What questions would he ask her, what answers would she give? She surely would not be able to lie to him indefinitely about his father, for one day he would be old enough to realize that it was not his father's name he bore. Richard had been a fatherless child, she helplessly, bitterly remembered as she carried John through the busy, summer, Sunday streets. *When one set of folks got tired of me they sent me down the line.* Yes, down the line, through poverty, hunger, wandering, cruelty, fear, and trembling, to death. And she thought of the boys who had gone to prison. Were they there still? Would John be one of these boys one day? These boys, now, who stood before drugstore windows, before poolrooms, on every street corner, who whistled after her, whose lean bodies fairly rang, it seemed, with idleness, and malice, and frustration.

How could she hope, alone, and in famine as she was, to put herself between him and this so wide and raging destruction? And then, as though to confirm her in all her dark imaginings, he began, as she reached the subway steps, to whimper, and moan, and cry.

And he kept this up, too, all the way uptown—so that, what with the impossibility of pleasing him that day, no matter what she did, what with his restless weight, and the heat, and the smiling, staring people, and the strange dread that weighed on her so heavily, she was nearly ready to weep by the time she arrived at Florence's door.

He, at that moment, to her exasperated relief, became the most cheerful of infants. Florence was wearing a heavy, old-fashioned garnet brooch, which, as she opened the door, immediately attracted John's eye. He began reaching for the brooch and babbling and spitting at Florence as though he had known her all of his short life.

"Well!" said Florence, "when he get big enough to *really* go after the ladies you going to have your hands full, girl."

"That," said Elizabeth, grimly, "is the Lord's truth. He keep me so busy now I don't know half the time if I'm coming or going."

Florence, meanwhile, attempted to distract John's attention from the brooch by offering him an orange; but he had seen oranges before; he merely looked at it a moment before letting it fall to the floor. He began again, in his disturbingly fluid fashion, to quarrel about the brooch.

"He likes you," said Elizabeth, finally, calmed a little by watching him.

"You must be tired," said Florence, then. "Put him down there." And she dragged one large easy chair to the table so that John could watch them while they ate.

"I got a letter from my brother the other day," she said, bringing the food to the table. "His wife, poor ailing soul, done passed on, and he thinking about coming North."

"You ain't never told me," said Elizabeth, with a quick and rather false interest, "you had a brother! And he coming up here?"

"So he say. Ain't nothing, I reckon, to keep him down home no more—now Deborah's gone." She sat down opposite Elizabeth. "I ain't seen him," she said, musingly, "for more than twenty years."

"Then it'll be a great day," Elizabeth smiled, "when you two meet again."

Florence shook her head, and motioned for Elizabeth to start eating. "No," she said, "we ain't never got along, and I don't reckon he's changed."

"Twenty years is a mighty long time," Elizabeth said, "he's bound to have changed *some*."

"That man," said Florence, "would have to do a whole *lot* of changing before him and me hit it off. No,"—she paused, grimly, sadly—"I'm mighty sorry he's coming. I didn't look to see him no more in this world—or in the next one, neither."

This was not, Elizabeth felt, the way a sister ought to talk about her brother, especially to someone who knew him not at all, and who would, probably, eventually meet him. She asked, helplessly:

"What do he do—your brother?"

"He some kind of preacher," said Florence. "I ain't never heard him. When *I* was home he weren't doing nothing but chasing after women and lying in the ditches, drunk."

"I hope," laughed Elizabeth, "he done changed his *ways* at least."

"Folks," said Florence, "can change their ways much as they want to. But I don't care how many times you change your ways, what's in you is in you, and it's got to come out."

"Yes," said Elizabeth, thoughtfully. "But don't you think," she hesitantly asked, "that the Lord can change a person's heart?"

"I done heard it said often enough," said Florence, "but I got yet to see it. These niggers running around, talking about the Lord done changed their hearts—ain't nothing happened to them niggers. They got the same old black hearts they was born with. I reckon the Lord done give them *those* hearts—and, honey, the Lord don't give out no second helpings, *I'm* here to tell you."

"No," said Elizabeth heavily, after a long pause. She turned to look at John, who was grimly destroying the square, tasseled doilies that decorated Florence's easy chair. "I reckon that's the truth. Look like it go around once, and that's that. You miss it, and you's fixed for fair.''

"Now you sound," said Florence, "mighty sad all of a sudden. What's the matter with you?"

"Nothing," she said. She turned back to the table. Then, helplessly, and thinking that she must not say too much: "I was just thinking about this boy here, what's going to happen to him, how I'm going to raise him, in this awful city all by myself."

"But you ain't fixing, is you," asked Florence, "to stay single all your days? You's a right young girl, and a right pretty girl. I wouldn't be in no hurry if I was you to find no new husband. I don't believe the nigger's been born what knows how to treat a woman right. You got time, honey, so *take* your time."

"I ain't," said Elizabeth, quietly, "got so much time." She could not stop herself; though something warned her to hold her peace, the words poured out. "You see this wedding ring? Well, I bought this ring myself. This boy ain't got no daddy."

Now she had said it: the words could not be called back. And she felt, as she sat, trembling, at Florence's table, a reckless, pained relief.

Florence stared at her with a pity so intense that it resembled anger. She looked at John, and then back at Elizabeth.

"You poor thing," said Florence, leaning back in her chair, her face still filled with this strange, brooding fury, "you *is* had a time, ain't you?"

"I was *scared*," Elizabeth brought out, shivering, still compelled to speak.

"I ain't never," said Florence, "seen it to fail. Look like ain't no woman born what don't get walked over by some no-count man. Look like ain't no woman nowhere but ain't been dragged down in the dirt by some man, and left there, too, while he go on about his business."

Elizabeth sat at the table, numb, with nothing more to say.

"What he do," asked Florence, finally, "run off and leave you?"

"Oh, no," cried Elizabeth, quickly, and the tears sprang to her eyes, "he weren't like that! He died, just like I say—he got in trouble, and he died—a long time before this boy was born." She began to weep with the same helplessness with which she had been speaking. Florence rose and came over to Elizabeth, holding Elizabeth's head against her breast. "He wouldn't never of left me," said Elizabeth, "but he *died*."

And now she wept, after her long austerity, as though she would never be able to stop.

"Hush now," said Florence, gently, "hush now. You going to frighten the little fellow. He don't want to see his mama cry. All right," she whispered to John, who had ceased his attempts at destruction, and stared now at the two women, "all right. Everything's all right."

Elizabeth sat up and reached in her handbag for a handkerchief, and began to dry her eyes.

"Yes," said Florence, moving to the window, "the menfolk, they die, all right. And it's us women who walk around, like the Bible says, and mourn. The menfolk, they die, and it's over for them, but we women, we have to keep on living and try to forget what they done to us. Yes, Lord—" and she paused; she turned and came back to Elizabeth. "Yes, Lord," she repeated, "don't *I* know."

"I'm mighty sorry," said Elizabeth, "to upset your nice dinner this way."

"Girl," said Florence, "don't you say a word about being sorry, or I'll show you to this door. You pick up that boy and sit down there in that easy chair and pull yourself together. I'm going out in the kitchen and make us something cold to drink. You try not to fret, honey. The Lord, He ain't going to let you fall but so low."

Then she met Gabriel, two or three weeks later, at Florence's house on a Sunday.

Nothing Florence had said had prepared her for him. She had expected him to be older than Florence, and bald, or gray. But he seemed considerably younger than his sister, with all his teeth and hair. There he sat, that Sunday, in Florence's tiny, fragile parlor, a very rock, it seemed to the eye of her confusion, in her so weary land.

She remembered that as she mounted the stairs with John's heavy weight in her arms, and as she entered the door, she heard music, which became perceptibly fainter as Florence closed the door behind her. John had heard it, too, and had responded by wriggling, and moving his hands in the air, and making noises, meant, she supposed, to be taken for a song. "You's a nigger, all right," she thought with amusement and impatience—for it was someone's gramophone, on a lower floor, filling the air with the slow, high, measured wailing of the blues.

Gabriel rose, it seemed to her, with a speed and eagerness that were not merely polite. She wondered immediately if Florence had told him about her. And this caused her to stiffen with a tentative anger against Florence, and with pride and fear. Yet when she looked into his eyes she found there a strange humility, an altogether unexpected kindness. She felt the anger go out of her, and her defensive pride; but somewhere, crouching, the fear remained.

Then Florence introduced them, saying: "Elizabeth, this here's my brother I been telling you so much about. He's a preacher, honey—so we got to be mighty careful what we talk about when *he's* around."

Then he said, with a smile less barbed and ambiguous than his sister's remark: "Ain't no need to be afraid of me, sister. I ain't nothing but a poor, weak vessel in the hands of the Lord."

"You *see!*" said Florence, grimly. She took John from his mother's arms. "And this here's little Johnny," she said, "shake hands with the preacher, Johnny."

But John was staring at the door that held back the music; towards which, with an insistence at once furious and feeble, his hands were still outstretched. He looked questioningly, reproachfully, at his mother; who laughed, watching him, and said, "Johnny want to hear some more of that music. He like to started dancing when we was coming up the stairs."

Gabriel laughed, and said, circling around Florence to look into John's face: "Got a man in the Bible, son, who liked music, too. He used to play on his harp before the king, and he got to dancing one day before the Lord. You reckon you going to dance for the Lord one of these days?"

John looked with a child's impenetrable gravity into the preacher's face, as though he were turning this question over in his mind and would answer when he had thought it out. Gabriel smiled at him, a strange smile—strangely, she thought, loving—and touched him on the crown of the head.

"He a mighty fine boy," said Gabriel. "With them big eyes he ought to see everything *in* the Bible."

And they all laughed. Florence moved to deposit John in the easy chair that was his Sunday throne. And Elizabeth found that she was watching Gabriel, unable to find in the man before her the brother whom Florence so despised.

They sat down at the table, John placed between herself and Florence and opposite Gabriel.

"So," Elizabeth said, with a nervous pleasantness, it being necessary, she felt, to say something, "you just getting to this big city? It must seem mighty strange to you."

His eyes were still on John, whose eyes had not left him. Then he looked again at Elizabeth. She felt that the air between them was beginning to be charged, and she could find no name, or reason, for the secret excitement that moved in her.

"It's mighty big," he said, "and looks to me—and *sounds* to me—like the Devil's working every day."

This was in reference to the music, which had not ceased, but she felt, immediately, that it included her; this, and something else in Gabriel's eyes, made her look down quickly to her plate.

"He ain't," said Florence, briskly, "working no harder up here than he worked down home. Them niggers down home," she said to Elizabeth, "they think New York ain't nothing but one long, Sunday drunk. They don't *know*. Somebody better tell them—they can get better moonshine right there where they is than they likely to here—and cheaper, too."

"But I *do* hope," he said, with a smile, "that you ain't taken to drinking moonshine, sister."

"It wasn't never *me*," she said, promptly, "had *that* habit."

"Don't know," he persisted, still smiling, and still looking at Elizabeth, "tell me folks do things up North they wouldn't think about doing down home."

"Folks got their dirt to do," said Florence. "They going to

do it, no matter where they is. Folks do lots of things down home they don't want nobody to know about."

"Like my aunt used to say," Elizabeth said, smiling timidly, "she used to say, folks sure better not do in the dark what they's scared to look at in the light."

She had meant it as a kind of joke; but the words were not out of her mouth before she longed for the power to call them back. They rang in her own ears like a confession.

"That's the Lord's truth," he said, after the briefest pause. "Does you really believe that?"

She forced herself to look up at him, and felt at that moment the intensity of the attention that Florence fixed on her, as though she were trying to shout a warning. She knew that it was something in Gabriel's voice that had caused Florence, suddenly, to be so wary and so tense. But she did not drop her eyes from Gabriel's eyes. She answered him: "Yes. That's the way I want to live."

"Then the Lord's going to bless you," he said, "and open up the windows of Heaven for you—for you, and that boy. He going to pour down blessings on you till you won't know where to put them. You mark my words."

"Yes," said Florence, mildly, "you *mark* his words."

But neither of them looked at her. It came into Elizabeth's mind, filling her mind: *All things work together for good to them that love the Lord*. She tried to obliterate this burning phrase, and what it made her feel. What it made her feel, for the first time since the death of Richard, was hope; his voice had made her feel that she was not altogether cast down, that God might raise her again in honor; his eyes had made her know that she could be—again, this time in honor—a woman. Then, from what seemed to be a great, cloudy distance, he smiled at her—and she smiled.

The distant gramophone stuck now, suddenly, on a grinding, wailing, sardonic trumpet-note; this blind, ugly crying swelled the moment and filled the room. She looked down at John. A hand somewhere struck the gramophone arm and sent the silver needle on its way through the whirling, black grooves, like something bobbing, anchorless, in the middle of the sea.

"Johnny's done fell asleep," she said.

She, who had descended with such joy and pain, had begun her upward climb—upward, with her baby, on the steep, steep side of the mountain.

She felt a great commotion in the air around her—a great excitement, muted, waiting on the Lord. And the air seemed to tremble, as before a storm. A light seemed to hang—just above, and all around them—about to burst into revelation. In the great crying, the great singing all around her, in the wind that gathered to fill the church, she did not hear her husband; and she thought of John as sitting, silent now and sleepy, far in the back of the church—watching, with that wonder and that terror in his eyes. She did not raise her head. She wished to tarry yet a little longer, that God might speak to her.

It had been before this very altar that she had come to kneel, so many years ago, to be forgiven. When the fall came, and the air was dry and sharp, and the wind high, she was always with Gabriel. Florence did not approve of this, and Florence said so often; but she never said more than this, for the reason, Elizabeth decided, that she had no evil to report— it was only that she was not fond of her brother. But even had Florence been able to find a language unmistakable in which to convey her prophecies, Elizabeth could not have heeded her because Gabriel had become her strength. He watched over her and her baby as though it had become his calling; he was very good to John, and played with him, and bought him things, as though John were his own. She knew that his wife had died childless, and that he had always wanted a son— he was praying still, he told her, that God would bless him with a son. She thought sometimes, lying on her bed alone, and thinking of all his kindness, that perhaps John was that son, and that he would grow one day to comfort and bless them both. Then she thought how, now, she would embrace again the faith she had abandoned, and walk again in the light from which, with Richard, she had so far fled. Sometimes, thinking of Gabriel, she remembered Richard—his voice, his breath, his arms—with a terrible pain; and then she felt herself shrinking from Gabriel's anticipated touch. But this shrinking she would not countenance. She told herself that it was foolish and sinful to look backward when her safety lay before her, like a hiding-place hewn in the side of the mountain.

"Sister," he asked one night, "don't you reckon you ought to give your heart to the Lord?"

They were in the dark streets, walking to church. He had asked her this question before, but never in such a tone; she had never before felt so compelling a need to reply.

"I reckon," she said.

"If you call on the Lord," he said, "He'll lift you up, He'll give you your heart's desire. I'm a witness," he said, and smiled at her, "you call on the Lord, you wait on the Lord, He'll answer. God's promises don't never fail."

Her arm was in his, and she felt him trembling with his passion.

"Till you come," she said, in a low, trembling voice, "I didn't never hardly go to church at all, Reverend. Look like I couldn't see my way nohow—I was all bowed down with shame . . . and sin."

She could hardly bring the last words out, and as she spoke tears were in her eyes. She had told him that John was name-less; and she had tried to tell him something of her suffering, too. In those days he had seemed to understand, and he had not stood in judgment on her. When had he so greatly changed? Or was it that he had not changed, but that her eyes had been opened through the pain he had caused her?

"Well," he said, "I done come, and it was the hand of the Lord what sent me. He brought us together for a sign. You fall on your knees and see if that ain't so—you fall down and ask Him to speak to you tonight."

Yes, a sign, she thought, a sign of His mercy, a sign of His forgiveness.

When they reached the church doors he paused, and looked at her and made his promise.

"Sister Elizabeth," he said, "when you go down on your knees tonight, I want you to ask the Lord to speak to your heart, and tell you how to answer what I'm going to say."

She stood a little below him, one foot lifted to the short, stone step that led to the church entrance, and looked up into his face. And looking into his face, which burned—in the dim, yellow light that hung about them there—like the face of a man who has wrestled with angels and demons and looked on the face of God, it came to her, oddly, and all at once, that she had become a woman.

"Sister Elizabeth," he said, "the Lord's been speaking to my heart, and I believe it's His will that you and me should be man and wife."

And he paused; she said nothing. His eyes moved over her body.

"I know," he said, trying to smile, and in a lower voice, "I'm a lot older than you. But that don't make no difference. I'm a mighty strong man yet. I done been down the line, Sister Elizabeth, and maybe I can keep you from making . . . some of my mistakes, bless the Lord . . . maybe I can help keep your foot from stumbling . . . again . . . girl . . . for as long as we's in this world."

Still she waited.

"And I'll love you," he said, "and I'll honor you . . . until the day God calls me home."

Slow tears rose to her eyes; of joy, for what she had come to; of anguish, for the road that had brought her here.

"And I'll love your son, your little boy," he said at last, "just like he was my own. He won't never have to fret or worry about nothing; he won't never be cold or hungry as long as I'm alive and I got my two hands to work with. I swear this before my God," he said, "because He done give me back something I thought was lost."

Yes, she thought, a sign—a sign that He is mighty to save. Then she moved and stood on the short step, next to him, before the doors.

"Sister Elizabeth," he said—and she would carry to the grave the memory of his grace and humility at that moment, "will you pray?"

"Yes," she said. "I been praying. I'm going to pray."

They had entered this church, these doors; and when the pastor made the altar call, she rose, while she heard them praising God, and walked down the long church aisle; down this aisle, to this altar, before this golden cross; to these tears, into this battle—would the battle end one day? When she rose, and as they walked once more through the streets, he had called her God's daughter, handmaiden to God's minister. He had kissed her on the brow, with tears, and said that God had brought them together to be each other's deliverance. And she had wept, in her great joy that the hand of God had changed her life, had lifted her up and set her on the solid rock, alone.

She thought of that far-off day when John had come into the world—that moment, the beginning of her life and death. Down she had gone that day, alone, a heaviness intolerable at her waist, a secret in her loins, down into the darkness, weeping and groaning and cursing God. How long she had bled, and sweated, and cried, no language on earth could tell—how long she had crawled through darkness she would never, never know. There, her beginning, and she fought through darkness still; toward that moment when she would make her peace with God, when she would hear Him speak, and He would wipe all tears from her eyes; as, in that other darkness, after eternity, she had heard John cry.

As now, in the sudden silence, she heard him cry: not the cry of the child, newborn, before the common light of earth; but the cry of the man-child, bestial, before the light that comes down from Heaven. She opened her eyes and stood straight up; all of the saints surrounded her; Gabriel stood staring, struck rigid as a pillar in the temple. On the threshing-floor, in the center of the crying, singing saints, John lay astonished beneath the power of the Lord.

PART THREE

THE THRESHING-FLOOR

Then said I, Woe is me! for I am undone; because I am a man of unclean lips, and I dwell in the midst of a people of unclean lips; for mine eyes have seen the King, the Lord of hosts.

Then I buckled up my shoes,
And I started.

H E KNEW, without knowing how it had happened, that he lay on the floor, in the dusty space before the altar which he and Elisha had cleaned; and knew that above him burned the yellow light which he had himself switched on. Dust was in his nostrils, sharp and terrible, and the feet of the saints, shaking the floor beneath him, raised small clouds of dust that filmed his mouth. He heard their cries, so far, so high above him—he could never rise that far. He was like a rock, a dead man's body, a dying bird, fallen from an awful height; something that had no power of itself, any more, to turn.

And something moved in John's body which was not John. He was invaded, set at naught, possessed. This power had struck John, in the head or in the heart; and, in a moment, wholly, filling him with an anguish that he could never in his life have imagined, that he surely could not endure, that even now he could not believe, had opened him up; had cracked him open, as wood beneath the axe cracks down the middle, as rocks break up; had ripped him and felled him in a moment, so that John had not felt the wound, but only the agony, had not felt the fall, but only the fear; and lay here, now, helpless, screaming, at the very bottom of darkness.

He wanted to rise—a malicious, ironic voice insisted that he rise—and, at once, to leave this temple and go out into the world.

He wanted to obey the voice, which was the only voice that spoke to him; he tried to assure the voice that he would do his best to rise; he would only lie here a moment, after his dreadful fall, and catch his breath. It was at this moment, precisely, that he found he could not rise; something had happened to his arms, his legs, his feet—ah, something had happened to John! And he began to scream again in his great, bewildered terror, and felt himself, indeed, begin to move—not upward, toward the light, but down again, a sickness in his bowels, a tightening in his loin-strings; he felt himself

187

turning, again and again, across the dusty floor, as though God's toe had touched him lightly. And the dust made him cough and retch; in his turning the center of the whole earth shifted, making of space a sheer void and a mockery of order, and balance, and time. Nothing remained: all was swallowed up in chaos. And: *Is this it?* John's terrified soul inquired— *What is it?*—to no purpose, receiving no answer. Only the ironic voice insisted yet once more that he rise from that filthy floor if he did not want to become like all the other niggers.

Then the anguish subsided for a moment, as water withdraws briefly to dash itself once more against the rocks: he knew that it subsided only to return. And he coughed and sobbed in the dusty space before the altar, lying on his face. And still he was going down, farther and farther from the joy, the singing, and the light above him.

He tried, but in such despair!—the utter darkness does not present any point of departure, contains no beginning, and no end—to rediscover, and, as it were, to trap and hold tightly in the palm of his hand, the moment preceding his fall, his change. But that moment was also locked in darkness, was wordless, and would not come forth. He remembered only the cross: he had turned again to kneel at the altar, and had faced the golden cross. And the Holy Ghost was speaking— seeming to say, as John spelled out the so abruptly present and gigantic legend adorning the cross: *Jesus Saves.* He had stared at this, an awful bitterness in his heart, wanting to curse—and the Spirit spoke, and spoke in him. Yes: there was Elisha, speaking from the floor, and his father, silent, at his back. In his heart there was a sudden yearning tenderness for holy Elisha; desire, sharp and awful as a reflecting knife, to usurp the body of Elisha, and lie where Elisha lay; to speak in tongues, as Elisha spoke, and, with that authority, to confound his father. Yet this had not been the moment; it was as far back as he could go, but the secret, the turning, the abysmal drop was farther back, in darkness. As he cursed his father, as he loved Elisha, he had, even then, been weeping; he had already passed his moment, was already under the power, had been struck, and was going down.

Ah, down!—and to what purpose, where? To the bottom of the sea, the bowels of the earth, to the heart of the fiery

furnace? Into a dungeon deeper than Hell, into a madness
louder than the grave? What trumpet sound would awaken
him, what hand would lift him up? For he knew, as he was
struck again, and screamed again, his throat like burning
ashes, and as he turned again, his body hanging from him like
a useless weight, a heavy, rotting carcass, that if he were not
lifted he would never rise.

His father, his mother, his aunt, Elisha—all were far above
him, waiting, watching his torment in the pit. They hung over
the golden barrier, singing behind them, light around their
heads, weeping, perhaps, for John, struck down so early. And,
no, they could not help him any more—nothing could help
him any more. He struggled, struggled to rise up, and meet
them—he wanted wings to fly upward and meet them in that
morning, that morning where they were. But his struggles
only thrust him downward, his cries did not go upward, but
rang in his own skull.

Yet, though he scarcely saw their faces, he knew that they
were there. He felt them move, every movement causing a
trembling, an astonishment, a horror in the heart of darkness
where he lay. He could not know if they wished him to come
to them as passionately as he wished to rise. Perhaps they did
not help him because they did not care—because they did not
love him.

Then his father returned to him, in John's changed and low
condition; and John thought, but for a moment only, that his
father had come to help him. In the silence, then, that filled
the void, John looked on his father. His father's face was
black—like a sad, eternal night; yet in his father's face there
burned a fire—a fire eternal in an eternal night. John trembled
where he lay, feeling no warmth for him from this fire, trembled, and could not take his eyes away. A wind blew over him,
saying: "Whosoever loveth and maketh a lie." Only: "Whosoever loveth and maketh a lie." And he knew that he had
been thrust out of the holy, the joyful, the blood-washed
community, that his father had thrust him out. His father's
will was stronger than John's own. His power was greater
because he belonged to God. Now, John felt no hatred, nothing, only a bitter, unbelieving despair: all prophecies were
true, salvation was finished, damnation was real!

Then Death is real, John's soul said, and Death will have his moment.

"Set thine house in order," said his father, "for thou shalt die and not live."

And then the ironic voice spoke again, saying: "Get up, John. Get up, boy. Don't let him keep you here. You got everything your daddy got."

John tried to laugh—John thought that he was laughing—but found, instead, that his mouth was filled with salt, his ears were full of burning water. Whatever was happening in his distant body now, he could not change or stop; his chest heaved, his laughter rose and bubbled at his mouth, like blood.

And his father looked on him. His father's eyes looked down on him, and John began to scream. His father's eyes stripped him naked, and hated what they saw. And as he turned, screaming, in the dust again, trying to escape his father's eyes, those eyes, that face, and all their faces, and the far-off yellow light, all departed from his vision as though he had gone blind. He was going down again. There is, his soul cried out again, no bottom to the darkness!

He did not know where he was. There was silence everywhere—only a perpetual, distant, faint trembling far beneath him—the roaring, perhaps, of the fires of Hell, over which he was suspended, or the echo, persistent, invincible still, of the moving feet of the saints. He thought of the mountaintop, where he longed to be, where the sun would cover him like a cloth of gold, would cover his head like a crown of fire, and in his hands he would hold a living rod. But this was no mountain where John lay, here, no robe, no crown. And the living rod was uplifted in other hands.

"I'm going to beat sin out of him. I'm going to beat it out."

Yes, he had sinned, and his father was looking for him. Now, John did not make a sound, and did not move at all, hoping that his father would pass him by.

"Leave him be. Leave him alone. Let him pray to the Lord."

"Yes, Mama. I'm going to try to love the Lord."

"He done run off somewhere. I'm going to find him. I'm going to beat it out."

Yes, he had sinned: one morning, alone, in the dirty bathroom, in the square, dirt-gray cupboard room that was filled with the stink of his father. Sometimes, leaning over the cracked, "tattle-tale gray" bathtub, he scrubbed his father's back; and looked, as the accursed son of Noah had looked, on his father's hideous nakedness. It was secret, like sin, and slimy, like the serpent, and heavy, like the rod. Then he hated his father, and longed for the power to cut his father down.

Was this why he lay here, thrust out from all human or heavenly help tonight? This, and not that other, his deadly sin, having looked on his father's nakedness and mocked and cursed him in his heart? Ah, that son of Noah's had been cursed, down to the present groaning generation: *A servant of servants shall he be unto his brethren.*

Then the ironic voice, terrified, it seemed, of no depth, no darkness, demanded of John, scornfully, if he believed that he was cursed. All niggers had been cursed, the ironic voice reminded him, all niggers had come from this most undutiful of Noah's sons. How could John be cursed for having seen in a bathtub what another man—*if* that other man had ever lived—had seen ten thousand years ago, lying in an open tent? Could a curse come down so many ages? Did it live in time, or in the moment? But John found no answer for this voice, for he was in the moment, and out of time.

And his father approached. "I'm going to beat sin out of him. I'm going to beat it out." All the darkness rocked and wailed as his father's feet came closer; feet whose tread resounded like God's tread in the garden of Eden, searching the covered Adam and Eve. Then his father stood just above him, looking down. Then John knew that a curse was renewed from moment to moment, from father to son. Time was indifferent, like snow and ice; but the heart, crazed wanderer in the driving waste, carried the curse forever.

"John," said his father, "come with me."

Then they were in a straight street, a narrow, narrow way. They had been walking for many days. The street stretched before them, long, and silent, going down, and whiter than the snow. There was no one on the street, and John was frightened. The buildings on this street, so near that John could touch them on either side, were narrow, also, rising like spears into the sky, and they were made of beaten gold and silver. John knew that these buildings were not for him—not today—*no, nor tomorrow, either!* Then, coming up this straight and silent street, he saw a woman, very old and black, coming toward them, staggering on the crooked stones. She was drunk, and dirty, and very old, and her mouth was bigger than his mother's mouth, or his own; her mouth was loose and wet, and he had *never* seen anyone so black. His father was astonished to see her, and beside himself with anger; but John was glad. He clapped his hands, and cried:

"See! She's uglier than Mama! She's uglier than me!"

"You mighty proud, ain't you," his father said, "to be the Devil's son?"

But John did not listen to his father. He turned to watch the woman pass. His father grabbed his arm.

"You see that? That's sin. That's what the Devil's son runs after."

"Whose son are you?" John asked.

His father slapped him. John laughed, and moved a little away.

"I seen it. I seen it. I ain't the Devil's son for nothing."

His father reached for him, but John was faster. He moved backward down the shining street, looking at his father—his father who moved toward him, one hand outstretched in fury.

"And I *heard* you—all the nighttime long. I know what you do in the dark, black man, when you think the Devil's son's asleep. I heard you, spitting, and groaning, and choking—and I *seen* you, riding up and down, and going in and out. I ain't the Devil's son for nothing."

The listening buildings, rising upward yet, leaned, closing out the sky. John's feet began to slip; tears and sweat were in his eyes; still moving backward before his father, he looked about him for deliverance; but there was no deliverance in this street for him.

"And I hate you. I hate you. I don't care about your golden crown. I don't care about your long white robe. I seen you under the robe, I seen you!"

Then his father was upon him; at his touch there was singing, and fire. John lay on his back in the narrow street, looking
up at his father, that burning face beneath the burning towers.

"I'm going to beat it out of you. I'm going to beat it out."

His father raised his hand. The knife came down. John
rolled away, down the white, descending street, screaming:

"Father! Father!"

These were the first words he uttered. In a moment there
was silence, and his father was gone. Again, he felt the saints
above him—and dust was in his mouth. There was singing
somewhere; far away, above him; singing slow and mournful.
He lay silent, racked beyond endurance, salt drying on his
face, with nothing in him any more, no lust, no fear, no
shame, no hope. And yet he knew that it would come
again—the darkness was full of demons crouching, waiting to
worry him with their teeth again.

Then I looked in the grave and I wondered.

Ah, down!—what was he searching here, all alone in darkness? But now he knew, for irony had left him, that he was
searching something, hidden in the darkness, that must be
found. He would die if it was not found; or, he was dead
already, and would never again be joined to the living, if it
was not found.

And the grave looked so sad and lonesome.

In the grave where he now wandered—he knew it was the
grave, it was so cold and silent, and he moved in icy mist—
he found his mother and his father, his mother dressed in
scarlet, his father dressed in white. They did not see him: they
looked backward, over their shoulders, at a cloud of witnesses.
And there was his Aunt Florence, gold and silver flashing on
her fingers, brazen earrings dangling from her ears; and there
was another woman, whom he took to be that wife of his
father's, called Deborah—who had, as he had once believed,
so much to tell him. But she, alone, of all that company,
looked at him and signified that there was no speech in the
grave. He was a stranger there—they did not see him pass,
they did not know what he was looking for, they could not
help him search. He wanted to find Elisha, who knew, perhaps, who would help him—but Elisha was not there. There
was Roy: Roy also might have helped him, but he had been

stabbed with a knife, and lay now, brown and silent, at his father's feet.

Then there began to flood John's soul the waters of despair. *Love is as strong as death, as deep as the grave.* But love, which had, perhaps, like a benevolent monarch, swelled the population of his neighboring kingdom, Death, had not himself descended: they owed him no allegiance here. Here there was no speech or language, and there was no love; no one to say: You are beautiful, John; no one to forgive him, no matter what his sin; no one to heal him, and lift him up. No one: father and mother looked backward, Roy was bloody, Elisha was not here.

Then the darkness began to murmur—a terrible sound—and John's ears trembled. In this murmur that filled the grave, like a thousand wings beating on the air, he recognized a sound that he had always heard. He began, for terror, to weep and moan—and this sound was swallowed up, and yet was magnified by the echoes that filled the darkness.

This sound had filled John's life, so it now seemed, from the moment he had first drawn breath. He had heard it everywhere, in prayer and in daily speech, and wherever the saints were gathered, and in the unbelieving streets. It was in his father's anger, and in his mother's calm insistence, and in the vehement mockery of his aunt; it had rung, so oddly, in Roy's voice this afternoon, and when Elisha played the piano it was there; it was in the beat and jangle of Sister McCandless's tambourine, it was in the very cadence of her testimony, and invested that testimony with a matchless, unimpeachable authority. Yes, he had heard it all his life, but it was only now that his ears were opened to this sound that came from darkness, that could only come from darkness, that yet bore such sure witness to the glory of the light. And now in his moaning, and so far from any help, he heard it in himself—it rose from his bleeding, his cracked-open heart. It was a sound of rage and weeping which filled the grave, rage and weeping from time set free, but bound now in eternity; rage that had no language, weeping with no voice—which yet spoke now, to John's startled soul, of boundless melancholy, of the bitterest patience, and the longest night; of the deepest water, the strongest chains, the most cruel lash; of humility most wretched, the dungeon most absolute, of love's bed defiled, and birth dishonored, and most bloody, unspeakable, sudden death. Yes, the darkness hummed with murder: the body in the water, the body in the fire, the body on the tree. John looked down the line of these armies of darkness, army upon army, and his soul whispered: *Who are these? Who are they?* And wondered: *Where shall I go?*

There was no answer. There was no help or healing in the grave, no answer in the darkness, no speech from all that company. They looked backward. And John looked back, seeing no deliverance.

I, John, saw the future, way up in the middle of the air.

Were the lash, the dungeon, and the night for him? And the sea for him? And the grave for him?

I, John, saw a number, way in the middle of the air.

And he struggled to flee—out of this darkness, out of this company—into the land of the living, so high, so far away. Fear was upon him, a more deadly fear than he had ever known, as he turned and turned in the darkness, as he moaned, and stumbled, and crawled through darkness, finding no hand, no voice, finding no door. *Who are these? Who are they?* They were the despised and rejected, the wretched and the spat upon, the earth's offscouring; and he was in their company, and they would swallow up his soul. The stripes they had endured would scar his back, their punishment would be his, their portion his, his their humiliation, anguish, chains, their dungeon his, their death his. *Thrice was I beaten with rods, once I was stoned, thrice I suffered shipwreck, a night and a day I have been in the deep.*

And their dread testimony would be his!

In journeyings often, in perils of waters, in perils of robbers, in perils by mine own countrymen, in perils by the heathen, in perils in the city, in perils in the wilderness, in perils in the sea, in perils among false brethren.

And their desolation, his:

In weariness and painfulness, in watchings often, in hunger and thirst, in fastings often, in cold and nakedness.

And he began to shout for help, seeing before him the lash, the fire, and the depthless water, seeing his head bowed down forever, he, John, the lowest among these lowly. And he looked for his mother, but her eyes were fixed on this dark army—she was claimed by this army. And his father would not help him, his father did not see him, and Roy lay dead.

Then he whispered, not knowing that he whispered: "Oh, Lord, have mercy on me. Have mercy on me."

And a voice, for the first time in all his terrible journey, spoke to John, through the rage and weeping, and fire, and darkness, and flood:

"Yes," said the voice, "go through. Go through."

"Lift me up," whispered John, "lift me up. I can't go through."

"Go through," said the voice, "go through."

Then there was silence. The murmuring ceased. There was only this trembling beneath him. And he knew there was a light somewhere.

"Go through."

"Ask Him to take you through."

But he could never go through this darkness, through this fire and this wrath. He never could go through. His strength was finished, and he could not move. He belonged to the darkness—the darkness from which he had thought to flee had claimed him. And he moaned again, weeping, and lifted up his hands.

"Call on Him. Call on Him."

"Ask Him to take you through."

Dust rose again in his nostrils, sharp as the fumes of Hell. And he turned again in the darkness, trying to remember something he had heard, something he had read.

Jesus saves.

And he saw before him the fire, red and gold, and waiting for him—yellow, and red, and gold, and burning in a night eternal, and waiting for him. He must go through this fire, and into this night.

Jesus saves.

Call on Him.

Ask Him to take you through.

He could not call, for his tongue would not unlock, and his heart was silent, and great with fear. In the darkness, how to move?—with death's ten thousand jaws agape, and waiting in the darkness. On any turning whatsoever the beast may spring—to move in the darkness is to move into the waiting jaws of death. And yet, it came to him that he must move; for there was a light somewhere, and life, and joy, and singing—somewhere, somewhere above him.

And he moaned again: "Oh, Lord, have mercy. Have mercy, Lord."

There came to him again the communion service at which Elisha had knelt at his father's feet. Now this service was in a great, high room, a room made golden by the light of the sun; and the room was filled with a multitude of people, all in long, white robes, the women with covered heads. They sat at a long, bare, wooden table. They broke at this table flat, unsalted bread, which was the body of the Lord, and drank from a heavy silver cup the scarlet wine of His blood. Then he saw that they were barefoot, and that their feet were stained with this same blood. And a sound of weeping filled the room as they broke the bread and drank the wine.

Then they rose, to come together over a great basin filled with water. And they divided into four groups, two of women and two of men; and they began, woman before woman, and man before man, to wash each other's feet. But the blood would not wash off; many washings only turned the crystal water red; and someone cried: *"Have you been to the river?"*

Then John saw the river, and the multitude was there. And now they had undergone a change; their robes were ragged, and stained with the road they had traveled, and stained with unholy blood; the robes of some barely covered their nakedness; and some indeed were naked. And some stumbled on the smooth stones at the river's edge, for they were blind; and some crawled with a terrible wailing, for they were lame; some did not cease to pluck at their flesh, which was rotten with running sores. All struggled to get to the river, in a dreadful hardness of heart: the strong struck down the weak, the ragged spat on the naked, the naked cursed the blind, the blind crawled over the lame. And someone cried: *"Sinner, do you love my Lord?"*

Then John saw the Lord—for a moment only; and the darkness, for a moment only, was filled with a light he could not bear. Then, in a moment, he was set free; his tears sprang as from a fountain; his heart, like a fountain of waters, burst.

Then he cried: "Oh, blessed Jesus! Oh, Lord Jesus! Take me through!"

Of tears there was, yes, a very fountain—springing from a depth never sounded before, from depths John had not known were in him. And he wanted to rise up, singing, singing in that great morning, the morning of his new life. Ah, how his tears ran down, how they blessed his soul!—as he felt himself, out of the darkness, and the fire, and the terrors of death, rising upward to meet the saints.

"Oh, yes!" cried the voice of Elisha. "Bless our God forever!"

And a sweetness filled John as he heard this voice, and heard the sound of singing: the singing was for him. For his drifting soul was anchored in the love of God; in the rock that endured forever. The light and the darkness had kissed each other, and were married now, forever, in the life and the vision of John's soul.

> *I, John, saw a city, way in the middle of the air,*
> *Waiting, waiting, waiting up there.*

He opened his eyes on the morning, and found them, in the light of the morning, rejoicing for him. The trembling he had known in darkness had been the echo of their joyful feet—these feet, bloodstained forever, and washed in many rivers—they moved on the bloody road forever, with no continuing city, but seeking one to come: a city out of time, not made with hands, but eternal in the heavens. No power could hold this army back, no water disperse them, no fire consume them. One day they would compel the earth to heave upward, and surrender the waiting dead. They sang, where the darkness gathered, where the lion waited, where the fire cried, and where blood ran down:

My soul, don't you be uneasy!

They wandered in the valley forever; and they smote the rock, forever; and the waters sprang, perpetually, in the perpetual desert. They cried unto the Lord forever, and lifted up their eyes forever, they were cast down forever, and He lifted them up forever. No, the fire could not hurt them, and yes, the lion's jaws were stopped; the serpent was not their master, the grave was not their resting-place, the earth was not their home. Job bore them witness, and Abraham was their father, Moses had elected to suffer with them rather than glory in sin for a season. Shadrach, Meshach, and Abednego had gone before them into the fire, their grief had been sung by David, and Jeremiah had wept for them. Ezekiel had prophesied upon them, these scattered bones, these slain, and, in the fulness of time, the prophet, John, had come out of the wilderness, crying that the promise was for them. They were encompassed with a very cloud of witnesses: Judas, who had betrayed the Lord; Thomas, who had doubted Him; Peter, who had trembled at the crowing of a cock; Stephen, who had been stoned; Paul, who had been bound; the blind man crying in the dusty road, the dead man rising from the grave. And they looked unto Jesus, the author and the finisher of their faith, running with patience the race He had set before them; they endured the cross, and they despised the shame, and waited to join Him, one day, in glory, at the right hand of the Father.

My soul! don't you be uneasy!
Jesus going to make up my dying bed!

"Rise up, rise up, Brother Johnny, and talk about the Lord's deliverance."

It was Elisha who had spoken; he stood just above John, smiling; and behind him were the saints—Praying Mother Washington, and Sister McCandless, and Sister Price. Behind these, he saw his mother, and his aunt; his father, for the moment, was hidden from his view.

"Amen!" cried Sister McCandless, "rise up, and praise the Lord!"

He tried to speak, and could not, for the joy that rang in him this morning. He smiled up at Elisha, and his tears ran down; and Sister McCandless began to sing:

> *"Lord, I ain't*
> *No stranger now!"*

"Rise up, Johnny," said Elisha, again. "Are you saved, boy?"

"Yes," said John, "oh, yes!" And the words came upward, it seemed, of themselves, in the new voice God had given him. Elisha stretched out his hand, and John took the hand, and

stood—so suddenly, and so strangely, and with such wonder!
—once more on his feet.

> *"Lord, I ain't*
> *No stranger now!"*

Yes, the night had passed, the powers of darkness had been
beaten back. He moved among the saints, he, John, who had
come home, who was one of their company now; weeping,
he yet could find no words to speak of his great gladness; and
he scarcely knew how he moved, for his hands were new, and
his feet were new, and he moved in a new and Heaven-bright
air. Praying Mother Washington took him in her arms, and
kissed him, and their tears, his tears and the tears of the old,
black woman, mingled.

"God bless you, son. Run on, honey, and don't get weary!"

> *"Lord, I been introduced*
> *To the Father and the Son,*
> *And I ain't*
> *No stranger now!"*

Yet, as he moved among them, their hands touching, and
tears falling, and the music rising—as though he moved down
a great hall, full of a splendid company—something began to
knock in that listening, astonished, newborn, and fragile heart
of his; something recalling the terrors of the night, which were
not finished, his heart seemed to say; which, in this company,
were now to begin. And, while his heart was speaking, he
found himself before his mother. Her face was full of tears,
and for a long while they looked at each other, saying nothing.
And once again, he tried to read the mystery of that face—
which, as it had never before been so bright and pained with
love, had never seemed before so far from him, so wholly in
communion with a life beyond his life. He wanted to comfort
her, but the night had given him no language, no second
sight, no power to see into the heart of any other. He knew
only—and now, looking at his mother, he knew that he could
never tell it—that the heart was a fearful place. She kissed him,
and she said: "I'm mighty proud, Johnny. You keep the faith.
I'm going to be praying for you till the Lord puts me in my
grave."

Then he stood before his father. In the moment that he forced himself to raise his eyes and look into his father's face, he felt in himself a stiffening, and a panic, and a blind rebellion, and a hope for peace. The tears still on his face, and smiling still, he said: "Praise the Lord."

"Praise the Lord," said his father. He did not move to touch him, did not kiss him, did not smile. They stood before each other in silence, while the saints rejoiced; and John struggled to speak the authoritative, the living word that would conquer the great division between his father and himself. But it did not come, the living word; in the silence something died in John, and something came alive. It came to him that he must testify: his tongue only could bear witness to the wonders he had seen. And he remembered, suddenly, the text of a sermon he had once heard his father preach. And he opened his mouth, feeling, as he watched his father, the darkness roar behind him, and the very earth beneath him seem to shake; yet he gave to his father their common testimony. "I'm saved," he said, "and I know I'm saved." And then, as his father did not speak, he repeated his father's text: "My witness is in Heaven and my record is on high."

"It come from your mouth," said his father then. "I want to see you live it. It's more than a notion."

"I'm going to pray God," said John—and his voice shook, whether with joy or grief he could not say—"to keep me, and make me strong . . . to stand . . . to stand against the enemy . . . and against everything and everybody . . . that wants to cut down my soul."

Then his tears came down again, like a wall between him and his father. His Aunt Florence came and took him in her arms. Her eyes were dry, and her face was old in the savage, morning light. But her voice, when she spoke, was gentler than he had ever known it to be before.

"You fight the good fight," she said, "you hear? Don't you get weary, and don't you get scared. Because I *know* the Lord's done laid His hands on you."

"Yes," he said, weeping, "yes. I'm going to serve the Lord."

"Amen!" cried Elisha. "Bless our God!"

*   *   *

The filthy streets rang with the early-morning light as they came out of the temple.

They were all there, save young Ella Mae, who had departed while John was still on the floor—she had a bad cold, said Praying Mother Washington, and needed to have her rest. Now, in three groups, they walked the long, gray, silent avenue: Praying Mother Washington with Elizabeth and Sister McCandless and Sister Price, and before them Gabriel and Florence, and Elisha and John ahead.

"You know, the Lord is a wonder," said the praying mother. "Don't you know, all this week He just burdened my soul, and kept me a-praying and a-weeping before Him? Look like I just couldn't get no ease nohow—and I *know* He had me a-tarrying for that boy's soul."

"Well, amen," said Sister Price. "Look like the Lord just wanted this church to *rock*. You remember how He spoke through Sister McCandless Friday night, and told us to pray, and He'd work a mighty wonder in our midst? And He done *moved*—hallelujah—He done troubled *everybody's* mind."

"I just tell you," said Sister McCandless, "all you got to do is *listen* to the Lord; He'll lead you right every *time*; He'll move every *time*. Can't nobody tell me *my* God ain't real."

"And you see the way the Lord worked with young Elisha there?" said Praying Mother Washington, with a calm, sweet smile. "Had that boy down there on the floor a-prophesying in *tongues*, amen, just the very *minute* before Johnny fell out a-screaming, and a-crying before the Lord. Look like the Lord was using Elisha to say: 'It's time, boy, come on home.' "

"Well, He *is* a wonder," said Sister Price. "And Johnny's got *two* brothers now."

Elizabeth said nothing. She walked with her head bowed, hands clasped lightly before her. Sister Price turned to look at her, and smiled.

"I know," she said, "you's a mighty happy woman this morning."

Elizabeth smiled and raised her head, but did not look directly at Sister Price. She looked ahead, down the long avenue, where Gabriel walked with Florence, where John walked with Elisha.

"Yes," she said, at last, "I been praying. And I ain't stopped praying yet."

"Yes, Lord," said Sister Price, "can't none of us stop praying till we see His blessed face."

"But I bet you didn't never think," said Sister McCandless, with a laugh, "that little Johnny was going to jump up so soon, and get religion. *Bless* our God!"

"The Lord's going to bless that boy, you mark my words," said Praying Mother Washington.

"Shake hands with the preacher, Johnny."

"Got a man in the Bible, son, who liked music, too. And he got to dancing one day before the Lord. You reckon you going to dance before the Lord one of these days?"

"Yes, Lord," said Sister Price, "the Lord done raised you up a holy son. He going to comfort your gray hairs."

Elizabeth found that her tears were falling, slowly, bitterly, in the morning light. "I pray the Lord," she said, "to bear him up on every side."

"Yes," said Sister McCandless, gravely, "it's more than a notion. The Devil rises on every hand."

Then, in silence, they came to the wide crossing where the streetcar line ran. A lean cat stalked the gutter and fled as they approached; turned to watch them, with yellow, malevolent eyes, from the ambush of a garbage can. A gray bird flew above them, above the electric wires for the streetcar line, and perched on the metal cornice of a roof. Then, far down the avenue, they heard a siren, and the clanging of a bell, and looked up to see the ambulance speed past them on the way to the hospital that was near the church.

"Another soul struck down," murmured Sister Mc-Candless. "Lord have mercy."

"He said in the last days evil would abound," said Sister Price.

"Well, yes, He *did* say it," said Praying Mother Washington, "and I'm so glad He told us He wouldn't leave us comfortless."

"When ye see all these things, know that your salvation is at hand," said Sister McCandless. "A thousand shall fall at thy side, and ten thousand at thy right hand—but it ain't going to come nigh thee. So glad, amen, this morning, bless my Redeemer."

"You remember that day when you come into the store?"

"I didn't think you never looked at me."

"Well—you was mighty pretty."

"Didn't little Johnny never say nothing," asked Praying Mother Washington, "to make you think the Lord was working in his heart?"

"He always kind of quiet," said Elizabeth. "He don't say much."

"No," said Sister McCandless, "he ain't like all these rough young ones nowadays—*he* got some respect for his elders. You done raised him mighty well, Sister Grimes."

"It was his birthday yesterday," Elizabeth said.

"No!" cried Sister Price. "How old he got to be yesterday?"

"He done made fourteen," she said.

"You hear that?" said Sister Price, with wonder. "The Lord done saved that boy's soul on his birthday!"

"Well, he got two birthdays now," smiled Sister McCandless, "just like he got two brothers—one in the flesh, and one in the Spirit."

"Amen, bless the Lord!" cried Praying Mother Washington.

"What book was it, Richard?"

"Oh, I don't remember. Just a book."

"You smiled."

"You was mighty pretty."

She took her sodden handkerchief out of her bag, and dried her eyes; and dried her eyes again, looking down the avenue.

"Yes," said Sister Price, gently, "you just *thank* the Lord. You just *let* the tears fall. I know your heart is full this morning."

"The Lord's done give you," said Praying Mother Washington, "a mighty blessing—and what the Lord gives, can't no man take away."

"I open," said Sister McCandless, "and no man can shut. I shut, and no man can open."

"Amen," said Sister Price. "Amen."

"Well, I reckon," Florence said, "your soul is praising God this morning."

He looked straight ahead, saying nothing, holding his body more rigid than an arrow.

"You always been saying," Florence said, "how the Lord would answer prayer." And she looked sideways at him, with a little smile.

"He going to learn," he said at last, "that it ain't all in the singing and the shouting—the way of holiness is a hard way. He got the steep side of the mountain to climb."

"But he got you there," she said, "ain't he, to help him when he stumbles, and to be a good example?"

"I'm going to see to it," he said, "that he walks right before the Lord. The Lord's done put his soul in *my* charge—and I ain't going to have that boy's blood on my hands."

"No," she said, mildly, "I reckon you don't want that."

Then they heard the siren, and the headlong, warning bell. She watched his face as he looked outward at the silent avenue and at the ambulance that raced to carry someone to healing, or to death.

"Yes," she said, "that wagon's coming, ain't it, one day for everybody?"

"I pray," he said, "it finds you ready, sister."

"Is it going to find you ready?" she asked.

"I know my name is written in the Book of Life," he said. "I know I'm going to look on my Saviour's face in glory."

"Yes," she said, slowly, "we's all going to be together there. Mama, and you, and me, and Deborah—and what was the name of that little girl who died not long after I left home?"

"What little girl who died?" he asked. "A *lot* of folks died after *you* left home—you left your *mother* on her dying bed."

"This girl was a mother, too," she said. "Look like she went north all by herself, and had her baby, and died—weren't nobody to help her. Deborah wrote me about it. Sure, you ain't forgotten that girl's name, Gabriel!"

Then his step faltered—seemed, for a moment, to drag. And he looked at her. She smiled, and lightly touched his arm.

"You ain't forgotten her name," she said. "You can't tell me you done forgot her name. Is you going to look on her face, too? Is her name written in the Book of Life?"

In utter silence they walked together, her hand still under his trembling arm.

"Deborah didn't never write," she at last pursued, "about what happened to the baby. Did you ever see him? You going to meet him in Heaven, too?"

"The Word tell us," he said, "to let the dead bury the dead. Why you want to go rummaging around back there, digging up things what's all forgotten now? The Lord, He knows my life—He done forgive me a long time ago."

"Look like," she said, "you think the Lord's a man like you; you think you can fool Him like you fool men, and you think He forgets, like men. But God don't forget nothing, Gabriel—if your name's down there in the Book, like you say, it's got all what you done right down there with it. And you going to answer for it, too."

"I done answered," he said, "already before my God. I ain't got to answer now, in front of you."

She opened her handbag, and took out the letter.

"I been carrying this letter now," she said, "for more than thirty years. And I been wondering all that time if I'd ever talk to you about it."

And she looked at him. He was looking, unwillingly, at the letter, which she held tightly in one hand. It was old, and dirty, and brown, and torn; he recognized Deborah's uncertain, trembling hand, and he could see her again in the cabin, bending over the table, laboriously trusting to paper the bitterness she had not spoken. It had lived in her silence, then, all of those years? He could not believe it. She had been praying for him as she died—she had sworn to meet him in glory. And yet, this letter, her witness, spoke, breaking her long silence, now that she was beyond his reach forever.

"Yes," said Florence, watching his face, "you didn't give her no bed of roses to sleep on, did you?—poor, simple, ugly, black girl. And you didn't treat that other one no better. Who is you met, Gabriel, all your holy life long, you ain't made to drink a cup of sorrow? And you doing it still—you going to be doing it till the Lord puts you in your grave."

"God's way," he said, and his speech was thick, his face was slick with sweat, "ain't man's way. I been doing the will of the Lord, and can't nobody sit in judgment on me but the Lord. The Lord called me out, He chose *me*, and I been running with Him ever since I made a start. You can't keep your eyes on all this foolishness here below, all this wickedness here below—you got to lift up your eyes to the hills and run from the destruction falling on the earth, you got to put your hand in Jesus' hand, and go where *He* says go."

"And if you been but a stumbling-stone here below?" she said. "If you done caused souls right and left to stumble and fall, and lose their happiness, and lose their souls? What then, prophet? What then, the Lord's anointed? Ain't no reckoning going to be called of *you*? What you going to say when the wagon comes?"

He lifted up his head, and she saw tears mingled with his sweat. "The Lord," he said, "He sees the heart—He sees the heart."

"Yes," she said, "but I done read the Bible, too, and it tells me you going to know the tree by its fruit. What fruit I seen from you if it ain't been just sin and sorrow and shame?"

"You be careful," he said, "how you talk to the Lord's anointed. 'Cause my life ain't in that letter—you don't know my life."

"Where *is* your life, Gabriel?" she asked, after a despairing pause. "Where *is* it? Ain't it all done gone for nothing? Where's your branches? Where's your fruit?"

He said nothing; insistently, she tapped the letter with her thumbnail. They were approaching the corner where she must leave him, turning westward to take her subway home. In the light that filled the streets, the light that the sun was now beginning to corrupt with fire, she watched John and Elisha just before them, John's listening head bent, Elisha's arm about his shoulder.

"I got a son," he said at last, "and the Lord's going to raise him up. I know—the Lord has promised—His word is true."

And then she laughed. "*That* son," she said, "that Roy. You going to weep for many a eternity before you see him crying in front of the altar like Johnny was crying tonight."

"God sees the heart," he repeated, "He sees the heart."

"Well, He ought to see it," she cried, "He made it! But don't nobody else see it, not even your own self! *Let* God see it—He sees it all right, and He don't say nothing."

"He speaks," he said, "He speaks. All you got to do is listen."

"I been listening many a nighttime long," said Florence, then, "and He ain't never spoke to me."

"He ain't never spoke," said Gabriel, "because you ain't never wanted to hear. You just wanted Him to tell you your way was right. And that ain't no way to wait on God."

"Then tell me," said Florence, "what He done said to you—that you didn't want to hear?"

And there was silence again. Now they both watched John and Elisha.

"I going to tell you something, Gabriel," she said. "I know you thinking at the bottom of your heart that if you just make *her*, her and her bastard boy, pay enough for her sin, *your* son won't have to pay for yours. But I ain't going to let you do that. You done made enough folks pay for sin, it's time you started paying."

"What you think," he asked, "you going to be able to do—against me?"

"Maybe," she said, "I ain't long for this world, but I got this letter, and I'm sure going to give it to Elizabeth before I go, and if she don't want it, I'm going to find *some* way—some way, I don't know how—to rise up and tell it, tell *everybody*, about the blood the Lord's anointed is got on his hands."

"I done told you," he said, "that's all done and finished; the Lord done give me a sign to make me know I been forgiven. What good you think it's going to do to start talking about it now?"

"It'll make Elizabeth to know," she said, "that she ain't the only sinner . . . in your holy house. And little Johnny, there—he'll know he ain't the only bastard."

Then he turned again, and looked at her with hatred in his eyes.

"You ain't never changed," he said. "You still waiting to see my downfall. You just as wicked now as you was when you was young."

She put the letter in her bag again.

"No," she said, "I ain't changed. You ain't changed neither. You still promising the Lord you going to do better—and you think whatever you done already, whatever you doing right at that *minute*, don't count. Of all the men I *ever* knew,

you's the man who ought to be hoping the Bible's all a lie—
'cause if that trumpet ever sounds, you going to spend eternity talking."

They had reached her corner. She stopped, and he stopped
with her, and she stared into his haggard, burning face.

"I got to take my subway," she said. "You got anything
you want to say to me?"

"I been living a long time," he said, "and I ain't never seen
nothing but evil overtake the enemies of the Lord. You think
you going to use that letter to hurt me—but the Lord ain't
going to let it come to pass. You going to be cut down."

The praying women approached them, Elizabeth in the
middle.

"Deborah," Florence said, "was cut down—but she left
word. She weren't no enemy of *nobody*—and she didn't see
nothing but evil. When I go, brother, you better tremble,
'cause I ain't going to go in silence."

And, while they stared at each other, saying nothing more,
the praying women were upon them.

Now the long, the silent avenue stretched before them like
some gray country of the dead. It scarcely seemed that he had
walked this avenue only (as time was reckoned up by men)
some few hours ago; that he had known this avenue since his
eyes had opened on the dangerous world; that he had played
here, wept here, fled, fallen down, and been bruised here—in
that time, so far behind him, of his innocence and anger.

Yes, on the evening of the seventh day, when, raging, he
had walked out of his father's house, this avenue had been
filled with shouting people. The light of the day had begun
to fail—the wind was high, and the tall lights, one by one,
and then all together, had lifted up their heads against the
darkness—while he hurried to the temple. Had he been
mocked, had anyone spoken, or laughed, or called? He could
not remember. He had been walking in a storm.

Now the storm was over. And the avenue, like any landscape
that has endured a storm, lay changed under Heaven, exhausted and clean, and new. Not again, forever, could it return
to the avenue it once had been. Fire, or lightning, or the latter
rain, coming down from these skies which moved with such

pale secrecy above him now, had laid yesterday's avenue waste, had changed it in a moment, in the twinkling of an eye, as all would be changed on the last day, when the skies would open up once more to gather up the saints.

Yet the houses were there, as they had been; the windows, like a thousand, blinded eyes, stared outward at the morning—at the morning that was the same for them as the mornings of John's innocence, and the mornings before his birth. The water ran in the gutters with a small, discontented sound; on the water traveled paper, burnt matches, sodden cigarette-ends; gobs of spittle, green-yellow, brown, and pearly; the leavings of a dog, the vomit of a drunken man, the dead sperm, trapped in rubber, of one abandoned to his lust. All moved slowly to the black grating where down it rushed, to be carried to the river, which would hurl it into the sea.

Where houses were, where windows stared, where gutters ran, were people—sleeping now, invisible, private, in the heavy darknesses of these houses, while the Lord's day broke outside. When John should walk these streets again, they would be shouting here again; the roar of children's roller skates would bear down on him from behind; little girls in pigtails, skipping rope, would establish on the sidewalk a barricade through which he must stumble as best he might. Boys would be throwing ball in these streets again—they would look at him, and call:

"Hey, Frog-eyes!"

Men would be standing on corners again, watching him pass, girls would be sitting on stoops again, mocking his walk. Grandmothers would stare out of windows, saying:

"That sure is a sorry little boy."

He would weep again, his heart insisted, for now his weeping had begun; he would rage again, said the shifting air, for the lions of rage had been unloosed; he would be in darkness again, in fire again, now that he had seen the fire and the darkness. He was free—*whom the Son sets free is free indeed*—he had only to stand fast in his liberty. He was in battle no longer, this unfolding Lord's day, with this avenue, these houses, the sleeping, staring, shouting people, but had entered into battle with Jacob's angel, *with the princes and the powers of the air*. And he was filled with a joy, a joy unspeakable, whose roots, though he would not trace them on this new day of his life, were nourished by the wellspring of a despair not yet discovered. *The joy of the Lord is the strength of His people*. Where joy was, there strength followed; where strength was, sorrow came—forever? Forever and forever, said the arm of Elisha, heavy on his shoulder. And John tried to see through the morning wall, to stare past the bitter houses, to tear the thousand gray veils of the sky away, and look into the heart—that monstrous heart which beat forever, turning the astounded universe, commanding the stars to flee away before the sun's red sandal, bidding the moon to wax and wane, and disappear, and come again; with a silver net holding back the sea, and, out of mysteries abysmal, recreating, each day, the earth. That heart, that breath, without which *was not anything made which was made*. Tears came into his eyes again, making the avenue shiver, causing the houses to shake—his heart swelled, lifted up, faltered, and was dumb. Out of joy strength came, strength that was fashioned to bear sorrow: sorrow brought forth joy. Forever? This was Ezekiel's wheel, in the middle of the burning air forever—and the little wheel ran by faith, and the big wheel ran by the grace of God.

"Elisha?" he said.

"If you ask Him to bear you up," said Elisha, as though he had read his thoughts, "He won't never let you fall."

"It was you," he said, "wasn't it, who prayed me through?"

"We was all praying, little brother," said Elisha, with a smile, "but yes, I was right over you the whole time. Look like the Lord had put you like a burden on my soul."

"Was I praying long?" he asked.

Elisha laughed. "Well, you started praying when it was night and you ain't stopped praying till it was morning. That's a right smart time, it seems to me."

John smiled, too, observing with some wonder that a saint of God could laugh.

"Was you glad," he asked, "to see me at the altar?"

Then he wondered why he had asked this, and hoped Elisha would not think him foolish.

"I was mighty glad," said Elisha soberly, "to see little Johnny lay his sins on the altar, lay his *life* on the altar and rise up, praising God."

Something shivered in him as the word *sin* was spoken. Tears sprang to his eyes again. "Oh," he said, "I pray God, I *pray* the Lord . . . to make me strong . . . to sanctify me wholly . . . and keep me saved!"

"Yes," said Elisha, "you keep that spirit, and I know the Lord's going to see to it that you get home all right."

"It's a long way," John said slowly, "ain't it? It's a hard way. It's uphill all the way."

"You remember Jesus," Elisha said. "You keep your mind on Jesus. *He* went that way—up the steep side of the mountain—and He was carrying the cross, and didn't nobody help Him. He went that way for us. He carried that cross for us."

"But He was the Son of God," said John, "and He knew it."

"He knew it," said Elisha, "because He was willing to pay the price. Don't you know it, Johnny? Ain't you willing to pay the price?"

"That song they sing," said John, finally, "*if it costs my life*—is that the price?"

"Yes," said Elisha, "that's the price."

Then John was silent, wanting to put the question another way. And the silence was cracked, suddenly, by an ambulance siren, and a crying bell. And they both looked up as the ambulance raced past them on the avenue on which no creature moved, save for the saints of God behind them.

"But that's the Devil's price, too," said Elisha, as silence came again. "The Devil, he don't ask for nothing less than your life. And he take it, too, and it's lost forever. Forever, Johnny. You in darkness while you living and you in darkness when you dead. Ain't nothing but the love of God can make the darkness light."

"Yes," said John, "I remember. I remember."

"Yes," said Elisha, "but you got to remember when the evil day comes, when the flood rises, boy, and look like your soul is going under. You got to remember when the Devil's doing all he can to make you forget."

"The Devil," he said, frowning and staring, "the Devil. How many faces is the Devil got?"

"He got as many faces," Elisha said, "as you going to see between now and the time you lay your burden down. And he got a lot more than that, but ain't nobody seen them all."

"Except Jesus," John said then. "Only Jesus."

"Yes," said Elisha, with a grave, sweet smile, "that's the Man you got to call on. That's the Man who knows."

They were approaching his house—his father's house. In a moment he must leave Elisha, step out from under his protecting arm, and walk alone into the house—alone with his mother and his father. And he was afraid. He wanted to stop and turn to Elisha, and tell him . . . something for which he found no words.

"Elisha—" he began, and looked into Elisha's face. Then: "You pray for me? Please pray for me?"

"I been praying, little brother," Elisha said, "and I sure ain't going to stop praying now."

"For me," persisted John, his tears falling, "for *me*."

"You know right well," said Elisha, looking at him, "I ain't going to stop praying for the brother what the Lord done give me."

Then they reached the house, and paused, looking at each other, waiting. John saw that the sun was beginning to stir, somewhere in the sky; the silence of the dawn would soon give way to the trumpets of the morning. Elisha took his arm from John's shoulder and stood beside him, looking backward. And John looked back, seeing the saints approach.

"Service is going to be mighty late *this* morning," Elisha said, and suddenly grinned and yawned.

And John laughed. "But you be there," he asked, "won't you? This morning?"

"Yes, little brother," Elisha laughed, "I'm going to be there. I see I'm going to have to do some running to keep up with *you*."

And they watched the saints. Now they all stood on the corner, where his Aunt Florence had stopped to say goodbye. All the women talked together, while his father stood a little apart. His aunt and his mother kissed each other, as he had seen them do a hundred times, and then his aunt turned to look for them, and waved.

They waved back, and she started slowly across the street, moving, he thought with wonder, like an old woman.

"Well, *she* ain't going to be out to service this morning, I tell you that," said Elisha, and yawned again.

"And look like *you* going to be half asleep," John said.

"Now don't you *mess* with me this morning," Elisha said, "because you ain't *got* so holy I can't turn you over my knee. I's your *big* brother in the Lord—you just remember *that*."

Now they were on the near corner. His father and mother were saying good-bye to Praying Mother Washington, and Sister McCandless, and Sister Price. The praying woman waved to them, and they waved back. Then his mother and his father were alone, coming toward them.

"Elisha," said John, "Elisha."

"Yes," said Elisha, "what you want now?"

John, staring at Elisha, struggled to tell him something more—struggled to say—all that could never be said. Yet: "I was down in the valley," he dared, "I was by myself down there. I won't never forget. May God forget me if I forget."

Then his mother and his father were before them. His mother smiled, and took Elisha's outstretched hand.

"Praise the Lord this morning," said Elisha. "He done give us something to praise Him for."

"Amen," said his mother, "praise the Lord!"

John moved up to the short, stone step, smiling a little, looking down on them. His mother passed him, and started into the house.

"You better come on upstairs," she said, still smiling, "and take off them wet clothes. Don't want you catching cold."

And her smile remained unreadable; he could not tell what it hid. And to escape her eyes, he kissed her, saying: "Yes, Mama. I'm coming."

She stood behind him, in the doorway, waiting.

"Praise the Lord, Deacon," Elisha said. "See you at the morning service, Lord willing."

"Amen," said his father, "praise the Lord." He started up the stone steps, staring at John, who blocked the way. "Go on upstairs, boy," he said, "like your mother told you."

John looked at his father and moved from his path, stepping down into the street again. He put his hand on Elisha's arm, feeling himself trembling, and his father at his back.

"Elisha," he said, "no matter what happens to me, where

I go, what folks say about me, no matter what *any*body says, you remember—please remember—I was saved. I was *there*."

Elisha grinned, and looked up at his father.

"He come through," cried Elisha, "didn't he, Deacon Grimes? The Lord done laid him out, and turned him around and wrote his *new* name down in glory. Bless our God!"

And he kissed John on the forehead, a holy kiss.

"Run on, little brother," Elisha said. "Don't you get weary. God won't forget you. You won't forget."

Then he turned away, down the long avenue, home. John stood still, watching him walk away. The sun had come full awake. It was waking the streets, and the houses, and crying at the windows. It fell over Elisha like a golden robe, and struck John's forehead, where Elisha had kissed him, like a seal ineffaceable forever.

And he felt his father behind him. And he felt the March wind rise, striking through his damp clothes, against his salty body. He turned to face his father—he found himself smiling, but his father did not smile.

They looked at each other a moment. His mother stood in the doorway, in the long shadows of the hall.

"I'm ready," John said, "I'm coming. I'm on my way."

GIOVANNI'S ROOM

For LUCIEN

I am the man, I suffered, I was there.
　　　　　　　　　　—WHITMAN

I

I STAND at the window of this great house in the south of France as night falls, the night which is leading me to the most terrible morning of my life. I have a drink in my hand, there is a bottle at my elbow. I watch my reflection in the darkening gleam of the window pane. My reflection is tall, perhaps rather like an arrow, my blond hair gleams. My face is like a face you have seen many times. My ancestors conquered a continent, pushing across death-laden plains, until they came to an ocean which faced away from Europe into a darker past.

I may be drunk by morning but that will not do any good. I shall take the train to Paris anyway. The train will be the same, the people, struggling for comfort and, even, dignity on the straight-backed, wooden, third-class seats will be the same, and I will be the same. We will ride through the same changing countryside northward, leaving behind the olive trees and the sea and all of the glory of the stormy southern sky, into the mist and rain of Paris. Someone will offer to share a sandwich with me, someone will offer me a sip of wine, someone will ask me for a match. People will be roaming the corridors outside, looking out of windows, looking in at us. At each stop, recruits in their baggy brown uniforms and colored hats will open the compartment door to ask *Complet?* We will all nod Yes, like conspirators, smiling faintly at each other as they continue through the train. Two or three of them will end up before our compartment door, shouting at each other in their heavy, ribald voices, smoking their dreadful army cigarettes. There will be a girl sitting opposite me who will wonder why I have not been flirting with her, who will be set on edge by the presence of the recruits. It will all be the same, only I will be stiller.

And the countryside is still tonight, this countryside reflected through my image in the pane. This house is just outside a small summer resort—which is still empty, the season has not yet begun. It is on a small hill, one can look down on the lights of the town and hear the thud of the sea. My girl, Hella, and I rented it in Paris, from photographs, some months ago. Now she has been gone a week. She is on the high seas now, on her way back to America.

I can see her, very elegant, tense, and glittering, surrounded by the light which fills the salon of the ocean liner, drinking rather too fast, and laughing, and watching the men. That was how I met her, in a bar in St. Germain des Pres, she was drinking and watching, and that was why I liked her, I thought she would be fun to have fun with. That was how it began, that was all it meant to me; I am not sure now, in spite of everything, that it ever really meant more than that to me. And I don't think it ever really meant more than that to her—at least not until she made that trip to Spain and, finding herself there, alone, began to wonder, perhaps, if a lifetime of drinking and watching the men was exactly what she wanted. But it was too late by that time. I was already with Giovanni. I had asked her to marry me before she went away to Spain; and she laughed and I laughed but that, somehow, all the same, made it more serious for me, and I persisted; and then she said she would have to go away and think about it. And the very last night she was here, the very last time I saw her, as she was packing her bag, I told her that I had loved her once and I made myself believe it. But I wonder if I had. I was thinking, no doubt, of our nights in bed, of the peculiar innocence and confidence which will never come again which had made those nights so delightful, so unrelated to past, present, or anything to come, so unrelated, finally, to my life since it was not necessary for me to take any but the most mechanical responsibility for them. And these nights were being acted out under a foreign sky, with no-one to watch, no penalties attached—it was this last fact which was our undoing, for nothing is more unbearable, once one has it, than freedom. I suppose this was why I asked her to marry me: to give myself something to be moored to. Perhaps this was why, in Spain, she decided that she wanted to marry me. But people can't, unhappily, invent their mooring posts, their lovers and their friends, anymore than they can invent their parents. Life gives these and also takes them away and the great difficulty is to say Yes to life.

I was thinking, when I told Hella that I had loved her, of those days before anything awful, irrevocable, had happened to me, when an affair was nothing more than an affair. Now, from this night, this coming morning, no matter how many beds I find myself in between now and my final bed, I shall never be able to have any more of those boyish, zestful affairs—which are, really, when one thinks of it, a kind of higher, or, anyway, more pretentious masturbation. People are too various to be treated so lightly. I am too various to be trusted. If this were not so I would not be alone in this house tonight. Hella would not be on the high seas. And Giovanni would not be about to perish, sometime between this night and this morning, on the guillotine.

I repent now—for all the good it does—one particular lie among the many lies I've told, told, lived, and believed. This is the lie which I told to Giovanni, but never succeeded in making him believe, that I had never slept with a boy before. I had. I had decided that I never would again. There is something fantastic in the spectacle I now present to myself of having run so far, so hard, across the ocean even, only to find myself brought up short once more before the bulldog in my own backyard—the yard, in the meantime, having grown smaller and the bulldog bigger.

I have not thought of that boy—Joey—for many years; but I see him quite clearly tonight. It was several years ago, I was still in my teens, he was about my age, give or take a year. He was a very nice boy, too, very quick and dark, and always laughing. For a while he was my best friend. Later, the idea that such a person *could* have been my best friend was proof of some horrifying taint in me. So I forgot him. But I see him very well tonight.

It was in the summer, there was no school. His parents had gone someplace for the weekend and I was spending the weekend at his house, which was near Coney Island, in Brooklyn. We lived in Brooklyn too, in those days, but in a better neighborhood than Joey's. I think we had been lying around the beach, swimming a little and watching the near-naked girls pass, whistling at them, and laughing. I am sure that if any of the girls we whistled at that day had shown any signs of re-

sponding the ocean would not have been deep enough to
drown our shame and terror. But the girls, no doubt, had
some intimation of this, possibly from the way we whistled,
and they ignored us. As the sun was setting we started up the
boardwalk towards his house, with our wet bathing trunks on
under our trousers.

And I think it began in the shower. I know that I felt something—as we were horsing around in that small, steamy room,
stinging each other with wet towels—which I had not felt
before, which mysteriously, and yet aimlessly, included him. I
remember in myself a heavy reluctance to get dressed: I
blamed it on the heat. But we did get dressed, sort of, and
we ate cold things out of his icebox and drank a lot of beer.
We must have gone to the movies. I can't think of any other
reason for our going out and I remember walking down the
dark, tropical Brooklyn streets with heat coming up from the
pavements and banging from the walls of houses with enough
force to kill a man, with all the world's grownups, it seemed,
sitting shrill and dishevelled on the stoops and all the world's
children on the sidewalks or in the gutters or hanging from
fire-escapes, with my arm around Joey's shoulder. I was
proud, I think, because his head came just below my ear. We
were walking along and Joey was making dirty wisecracks and
we were laughing. Odd to remember, for the first time in so
long, how good I felt that night, how fond of Joey.

When we came back along those streets it was quiet; we
were quiet too. We were very quiet in the apartment and
sleepily got undressed in Joey's bedroom and went to bed. I
fell asleep—for quite awhile, I think. But I woke up to find
the light on and Joey examining the pillow with great, ferocious care.

'What's the matter?'

'I think a bedbug bit me.'

'You slob. You got bedbugs?'

'I think one bit me.'

'You ever have a bedbug bite you before?'

'No.'

'Well, go back to sleep. You're dreaming.'

He looked at me with his mouth open and his dark eyes
very big. It was as though he had just discovered that I was

an expert on bedbugs. I laughed and grabbed his head as I had done God knows how many times before, when I was playing with him or when he had annoyed me. But this time when I touched him something happened in him and in me which made this touch different from any touch either of us had ever known. And he did not resist, as he usually did, but lay where I had pulled him, against my chest. And I realized that my heart was beating in an awful way and that Joey was trembling against me and the light in the room was very bright and hot. I started to move and to make some kind of joke but Joey mumbled something and I put my head down to hear. Joey raised his head as I lowered mine and we kissed, as it were, by accident. Then, for the first time in my life, I was really aware of another person's body, of another person's smell. We had our arms around each other. It was like holding in my hand some rare, exhausted, nearly doomed bird which I had miraculously happened to find. I was very frightened, I am sure he was frightened too, and we shut our eyes. To remember it so clearly, so painfully tonight tells me that I have never for an instant truly forgotten it. I feel in myself now a faint, a dreadful stirring of what so overwhelmingly stirred in me then, great thirsty heat, and trembling, and tenderness so painful I thought my heart would burst. But out of this astounding, intolerable pain came joy, we gave each other joy that night. It seemed, then, that a lifetime would not be long enough for me to act with Joey the act of love.

But that lifetime was short, was bounded by that night—it ended in the morning. I awoke while Joey was still sleeping, curled like a baby on his side, toward me. He looked like a baby, his mouth half open, his cheek flushed, his curly hair darkening the pillow and half hiding his damp round forehead and his long eyelashes glinting slightly in the summer sun. We were both naked and the sheet we had used as a cover was tangled around our feet. Joey's body was brown, was sweaty, the most beautiful creation I had ever seen till then. I would have touched him to wake him up but something stopped me. I was suddenly afraid. Perhaps it was because he looked so innocent lying there, with such perfect trust; perhaps it was because he was so much smaller than me; my own body suddenly seemed gross and crushing and the desire which was rising in me seemed monstrous. But, above all, I was suddenly afraid. It was borne in on me: *But Joey is a boy.* I saw suddenly the power in his thighs, in his arms, and in his loosely curled fists. The power and the promise and the mystery of that body made me suddenly afraid. That body suddenly seemed the black opening of a cavern in which I would be tortured till madness came, in which I would lose my manhood. Precisely, I wanted to know that mystery and feel that power and have that promise fulfilled through me. The sweat on my back grew cold. I was ashamed. The very bed, in its sweet disorder, testified to vileness. I wondered what Joey's mother would say when she saw the sheets. Then I thought of my father, who had no one in the world but me, my mother having died when I was little. A cavern opened in my mind, black, full of rumor, suggestion, of half-heard, half-forgotten, half-understood stories, full of dirty words. I thought I saw my future in that cavern. I was afraid. I could have cried, cried for shame and terror, cried for not understanding how this could have happened to me, how this could have happened *in* me. And I made my decision. I got out of bed and took a shower and was dressed and had breakfast ready when Joey woke up.

I did not tell him my decision, that would have broken my will. I did not wait to have breakfast with him but only drank some coffee and made an excuse to go home. I knew the excuse did not fool Joey; but he did not know how to protest or insist; he did not know that this was all he needed to have done. Then I, who had seen him that summer nearly every day till then, no longer went to see him. He did not come to see me. I would have been very happy to see him if he had, but the manner of my leavetaking had begun a constriction which neither of us knew how to arrest. When I finally did see him, more or less by accident, near the end of the summer, I made up a long and totally untrue story about a girl I was going with and when school began again I picked up with a rougher, older crowd and was very nasty to Joey. And the sadder this made him, the nastier I became. He moved away at last, out of the neighborhood, away from our school, and I never saw him again.

I began, perhaps, to be lonely that summer and began, that

summer, the flight which has brought me to this darkening window.

And yet—when one begins to search for the crucial, the definitive moment, the moment which changed all others, one finds oneself pressing, in great pain, through a maze of false signals and abruptly locking doors. My flight may, indeed, have begun that summer—which does not tell me where to find the germ of the dilemma which resolved itself, that summer, into flight. Of course, it is somewhere before me, locked in that reflection I am watching in the window as the night comes down outside. It is trapped in the room with me, always has been, and always will be, and it is yet more foreign to me than those foreign hills outside.

We lived in Brooklyn then, as I say; we had also lived in San Francisco, where I was born, and where my mother lies buried, and we lived for awhile in Seattle, and then in New York—for me, New York is Manhattan. Later on, then, we moved from Brooklyn back to New York and by the time I came to France my father and his new wife had graduated to Connecticut. I had long been on my own by then, of course, and had been living in an apartment in the east sixties.

We, in the days when I was growing up, were my father and his unmarried sister and myself. My mother had been carried to the graveyard when I was five. I scarcely remember her at all, yet she figured in my nightmares, blind with worms, her hair as dry as metal and brittle as a twig, straining to press me against her body; that body so putrescent, so sickening soft, that it opened, as I clawed and cried, into a breach so enormous as to swallow me alive. But when my father or my aunt came rushing into my room to find out what had frightened me I did not dare describe this dream, which seemed disloyal to my mother. I said that I had dreamed about a graveyard. They concluded that the death of my mother had had this unsettling effect on my imagination and perhaps they thought that I was grieving for her. And I may have been, but if that is so, then I am grieving still.

My father and my aunt got on very badly and, without ever knowing how or why I felt it, I felt that their long battle had everything to do with my dead mother. I remember when I was very young how, in the big living room of the house in San Francisco, my mother's photograph, which stood all by itself on the mantelpiece, seemed to rule the room. It was as though her photograph proved how her spirit dominated that air and controlled us all. I remember the shadows gathering in the far corners of that room, in which I never felt at home, and my father washed in the gold light which spilled down on him from the tall lamp which stood beside his easy chair. He would be reading his newspaper, hidden from me behind his newspaper, so that, desperate to conquer his attention, I sometimes so annoyed him that our duel ended with me being carried from the room in tears. Or I remember him sitting bent forward, his elbows on his knees, staring towards the great window which held back the inky night. I used to wonder what he was thinking. In the eye of my memory he always wears a grey, sleeveless sweater and he has loosened his tie, and his sandy hair falls forward over a square, ruddy face. He was one of those people who, quick to laugh, are slow to anger; so that their anger, when it comes, is all the more impressive, seeming to leap from some unsuspected crevice like a fire which will bring the whole house down.

And his sister, Ellen, a little older than he, a little darker, always over-dressed, over made-up, with a face and figure beginning to harden, and with too much jewelry everywhere, clanging and banging in the light, sits on the sofa, reading; she read a lot, all the new books, and she used to go to the movies a great deal. Or she knits. It seems to me that she was always carrying a great bag full of dangerous looking knitting needles, or a book, or both. And I don't know what she knitted, though I suppose she must, at least occasionally, have knitted something for my father, or me. But I don't remember it, anymore than I remember the books she read. It might always have been the same book and she might have been working on the same scarf, or sweater, or God knows what, all the years I knew her. Sometimes she and my father played cards—this was rare; sometimes they talked together in friendly, teasing tones, but this was dangerous. Their banter nearly always ended in a fight. Sometimes there was company and I was often allowed to watch them drink their cocktails. Then my father was at his best, boyish and expansive, moving about through the crowded room with a glass in his hand, refilling people's drinks, laughing a lot, handling all the men as though they were his brothers, and flirting with the women. Or no, not flirting with them, strutting like a cock before them. Ellen always seemed to be watching him as though she were afraid he would do something awful, watched him and watched the women and, yes, she flirted with the men in a strange, nerve-wracking kind of way. There she was, dressed, as they say, to kill, with her mouth redder than any blood, dressed in something which was either the wrong color, or too tight, or too young, the cocktail glass in her hand threatening, at any instant, to be reduced to shards, to splinters, and that voice going on and on like a razor blade on glass. When I was a little boy and I watched her in company, she frightened me.

But no matter what was happening in that room, my mother was watching it. She looked out of the photograph frame, a pale, blonde woman, delicately put together, dark-eyed, and straight-browed, with a nervous, gentle mouth. But something about the way the eyes were set in the head and stared straight out, something very faintly sardonic and knowing in the set of the mouth suggested that, somewhere beneath this tense fragility was a strength as various as it was unyielding and, like my father's wrath, dangerous because it was so entirely unexpected. My father rarely spoke of her and when he did he covered, by some mysterious means, his face; he spoke of her only as my mother and, in fact, as he spoke of her, he might have been speaking of his own. Ellen spoke of my mother often, saying what a remarkable woman she had been but she made me uncomfortable. I felt that I had no right to be the son of such a mother.

Years later, when I had become a man, I tried to get my father to talk about my mother. But Ellen was dead, he was about to marry again. He spoke of my mother, then, as Ellen had spoken of her and he might, indeed, have been speaking of Ellen.

They had a fight one night when I was about thirteen. They had a great many fights, of course; but perhaps I remember this one so clearly because it seemed to be about me.

I was in bed upstairs, asleep. It was quite late. I was suddenly awakened by the sound of my father's footfalls on the walk beneath my window. I could tell by the sound and the rhythm that he was a little drunk and I remember that at that moment a certain disappointment, an unprecedented sorrow entered into me. I had seen him drunk many times and had never felt this way—on the contrary, my father sometimes had great charm when he was drunk—but that night I suddenly felt that there was something in it, in him, to be despised.

I heard him come in. Then, at once, I heard Ellen's voice.

'Aren't you in bed yet?' my father asked. He was trying to be pleasant and trying to avoid a scene, but there was no cordiality in his voice, only strain and exasperation.

'I thought,' said Ellen, coldly, 'that someone ought to tell you what you're doing to your son.'

'What I'm doing to my son?' And he was about to say something more, something awful; but he caught himself and only said, with a resigned, drunken, despairing calm: 'What are you talking about, Ellen?'

'Do you really think,' she asked—I was certain that she was standing in the center of the room, with her hands folded before her, standing very straight and still—'that you're the kind of man he ought to be when he grows up?' And, as my father said nothing: 'He *is* growing up, you know.' And then, spitefully, 'Which is more than I can say for you.'

'Go to bed, Ellen,' said my father—sounding very weary.

I had the feeling, since they were talking about me, that I ought to go downstairs and tell Ellen that whatever was wrong between my father and myself we could work out between us without her help. And, perhaps—which seems odd—I felt that she was disrespectful of *me*. For I had certainly never said a word to her about my father.

I heard his heavy, uneven footfalls as he moved across the room, towards the stairs.

'Don't think,' said Ellen, 'that I don't know where you've been.'

'I've been out—drinking—' said my father, 'and now I'd like to get a little sleep. Do you mind?'

'You've been with that girl, Beatrice,' said Ellen. 'That's where you always are and that's where all your money goes and all your manhood and self-respect, too.'

She had succeeded in making him angry. He began to stammer. 'If you think—if you *think*—that I'm going to stand—stand—stand here—and argue with *you* about my private life—*my* private life!—if you think I'm going to argue with *you* about it, why, you're out of your mind.'

'I certainly don't care,' said Ellen, 'what you do with yourself. It isn't *you* I'm worried about. It's only that you're the only person who has any authority over David. I don't. And he hasn't got any mother. And he only listens to me when he thinks it pleases you. Do you really think it's a good idea for David to see you staggering home drunk all the time? And don't fool yourself,' she added, after a moment, in a voice thick with passion, 'don't fool yourself that he doesn't know where you're coming from, don't think he doesn't know about your women!'

She was wrong. I don't think I did know about them—or I had never thought about them. But from that evening, I thought about them all the time. I could scarcely ever face a woman without wondering whether or not my father had, in Ellen's phrase, been 'interfering' with her.

'I think it barely possible,' said my father, 'that David has a cleaner mind than yours.'

The silence, then, in which my father climbed the stairs was by far the worst silence my life had ever known. I was wondering what they were thinking—each of them. I wondered how they looked. I wondered what I would see when I saw them in the morning.

'And listen,' said my father suddenly, from the middle of the staircase, in a voice which frightened me, 'all I want for David is that he grow up to be a man. And when I say a man, Ellen, I don't mean a Sunday school teacher.'

'A man,' said Ellen, shortly, 'is not the same thing as a bull. Good-night.'

'Good-night,' he said, after a moment.

And I heard him stagger past my door.

From that time on, with the mysterious, cunning, and dreadful intensity of the very young, I despised my father and I hated Ellen. It is hard to say why. I don't know why. But it allowed all of Ellen's prophecies about me to come true. She had said that there would come a time when nothing and nobody would be able to rule me, not even my father. And that time certainly came.

It was after Joey. The incident with Joey had shaken me profoundly and its effect was to make me secretive and cruel. I could not discuss what had happened to me with anyone, I could not even admit it to myself; and, while I never thought about it, it remained, nevertheless, at the bottom of my mind, as still and as awful as a decomposing corpse. And it changed, it thickened, it soured the atmosphere of my mind. Soon it was I who came staggering home late at night, it was I who found Ellen waiting up for me, Ellen and I who wrangled night in and night out.

My father's attitude was that this was but an inevitable phase of my growing up and he affected to take it lightly. But beneath his jocular, boys-together air, he was at a loss, he was frightened. Perhaps he had supposed that my growing up would bring us closer together—whereas, now that he was trying to find out something about me, I was in full flight from him. I did not *want* him to know me. I did not want anyone to know me. And then, again, I was undergoing with my father what the very young inevitably undergo with their elders: I was beginning to judge him. And the very harshness of this judgment, which broke my heart, revealed, though I could not have said it then, how much I had loved him, how that love, along with my innocence, was dying.

My poor father was baffled and afraid. He was unable to believe that there could be anything seriously wrong between us. And this was not only because he would not then have known what to do about it; it was mainly because he would then have had to face the knowledge that he had left something, somewhere, undone, something of the utmost importance. And since neither of us had any idea of what this so significant omission could have been, and since we were forced to remain in tacit league against Ellen, we took refuge in being hearty with each other. We were not like father and son, my father sometimes proudly said, we were like buddies. I think my father sometimes actually believed this. I never did. I did not want to be his buddy, I wanted to be his son. What passed between us as masculine candor exhausted and appalled me. Fathers ought to avoid utter nakedness before their sons.

I did not want to know—not, anyway, from his mouth—that his flesh was as unregenerate as my own. The knowledge did not make me feel more like his son—or buddy—it only made me feel like an interloper, and a frightened one at that. He thought we were alike. I did not want to think so. I did not want to think that my life would be like his, or that my mind would ever grow so pale, so without hard places and sharp, sheer drops. He wanted no distance between us, he wanted me to look on him as a man like myself. But I wanted the merciful distance of father and son, which would have permitted me to love him.

One night, drunk, with several other people on the way back from an out of town party, the car I was driving smashed up. It was entirely my fault. I was almost too drunk to walk and had no business driving; but the others did not know this, since I am one of those people who can look and sound sober while practically in a state of collapse. On a straight, level piece of highway something weird happened to all my reactions and the car sprang suddenly out of my control. And a telephone pole, foam white, came crying at me out of the pitch darkness; I heard screams and then a heavy, roaring, tearing sound. Then everything turned absolutely scarlet and then as bright as day and I went into a darkness I had never known before.

I must have begun to wake up as we were being moved to the hospital. I dimly remember movement and voices, but they seemed very far away, they seemed to have nothing to do with me. Then, later, I woke up in a spot which seemed to be the very heart of winter, a high, white ceiling and white walls, and a hard, glacial window, bent, as it seemed, over me. I must have tried to rise, for I remember an awful roaring in my head, and then a weight on my chest and a huge face over me. And as this weight, this face, began to push me under again, I screamed for my mother. Then it was dark again.

When I came to myself at last, my father was standing over my bed. I knew he was there before I saw him, before my eyes focussed and I carefully turned my head. When he saw that I was awake, he carefully stepped closer to the bed, motioning to me to be still. And he looked very old. I wanted to cry. For a moment we just stared at each other.

'How do you feel?' he whispered, finally.

It was when I tried to speak that I realized I was in pain and immediately I was frightened. He must have seen this in my eyes, for he said in a low voice, with a pained, a marvellous intensity, 'Don't worry, David. You're going to be alright. You're going to be alright.'

I still could not say anything. I simply watched his face.

'You kids were mighty lucky,' he said, trying to smile. 'You're the one got smashed up the most.'

'I was drunk,' I said at last. I wanted to tell him everything—but speaking was such agony.

'Don't you know,' he asked, with an air of extreme bafflement—for this was something he could allow himself to be baffled about—'better than to go driving around like that when you're drunk? You know better than that,' he said, severely, and pursed his lips. 'Why you could all have been killed.' And his voice shook.

'I'm sorry,' I said, suddenly. 'I'm sorry.' I did not know how to say what it was I was sorry for.

'Don't be sorry,' he said. 'Just be careful next time.' He had been patting his handkerchief between his palms; now he opened this handkerchief and reached out and wiped my forehead. 'You're all I've got,' he said then, with a shy, pained grin. 'Be careful.'

'Daddy,' I said. And began to cry. And if speaking had been agony, this was worse and yet I could not stop.

And my father's face changed. It became terribly old and at the same time absolutely, helplessly young. I remember being absolutely astonished, at the still, cold center of the storm which was occurring in me, to realize that my father had been suffering, was suffering still.

'Don't cry,' he said, 'don't cry.' He stroked my forehead with that absurd handkerchief as though it possessed some healing charm. 'There's nothing to cry about. Everything's going to be all right.' He was almost weeping himself. 'There's nothing wrong, is there? I haven't done anything wrong, have I?' And all the time he was stroking my face with that handkerchief, smothering me.

'We were drunk,' I said. 'We were drunk.' For this seemed, somehow, to explain everything.

'Your aunt Ellen says it's my fault,' he said. 'She says I never

raised you right.' He put away, thank heaven, that handkerchief, and weakly straightened his shoulders. 'You got nothing
against me, have you? Tell me if you have?'

My tears began to dry, on my face and in my breast. 'No,'
I said, 'no. Nothing. Honest.'

'I did the best I could,' he said. 'I really did the best I
could.' I looked at him. And at last he grinned and said,
'You're going to be on your back for awhile but when you
come home, while you're lying around the house, we'll talk,
huh? and try to figure out what the hell we're going to do
with you when you get on your feet. OK?'

'OK,' I said.

For I understood, at the bottom of my heart, that we had
never talked, that now we never would. I understood that he
must never know this. When I came home he talked with me
about my future but I had made up my mind. I was not going
to go to college, I was not going to remain in that house with
him and Ellen. And I maneuvered my father so well that he
actually began to believe that my finding a job and being on
my own was the direct result of his advice and a tribute to the
way he had raised me. Once I was out of the house, of course,
it became much easier to deal with him and he never had any
reason to feel shut out of my life for I was always able, when
talking about it, to tell him what he wished to hear. And we
got on quite well, really, for the vision I gave my father of my
life was exactly the vision in which I myself most desperately
needed to believe.

For I am—or I was—one of those people who pride themselves on their willpower, on their ability to make a decision
and carry it through. This virtue, like most virtues, is ambi-
guity itself. People who believe that they are strong-willed and
the masters of their destiny can only continue to believe this
by becoming specialists in self-deception. Their decisions are
not really decisions at all—a real decision makes one humble,
one knows that it is at the mercy of more things than can be
named—but elaborate systems of evasion, of illusion, designed
to make themselves and the world appear to be what they and
the world are not. This is certainly what my decision, made
so long ago in Joey's bed, came to. I had decided to allow no
room in the universe for something which shamed and fright-

ened me. I succeeded very well—by not looking at the universe, by not looking at myself, by remaining, in effect, in constant motion. Even constant motion, of course, does not prevent an occasional mysterious drag, a drop, like an airplane hitting an air pocket. And there were a number of those, all drunken, all sordid, one very frightening such drop while I was in the Army which involved a fairy who was later court-martialed out. The panic his punishment caused in me was as close as I ever came to facing in myself the terrors I sometimes saw clouding another man's eyes.

What happened was that, all unconscious of what this ennui meant, I wearied of the motion, wearied of the joyless seas of alcohol, wearied of the blunt, bluff, hearty, and totally meaningless friendships, wearied of wandering through the forests of desperate women, wearied of the work which fed me only in the most brutally literal sense. Perhaps, as we say in America, I wanted to find myself. This is an interesting phrase, not current as far as I know in the language of any other people, which certainly does not mean what it says but betrays a nagging suspicion that something has been misplaced. I think now that if I had had any intimation that the self I was going to find would turn out to be only the same self from which I had spent so much time in flight, I would have stayed at home. But, again, I think I knew, at the very bottom of my heart, exactly what I was doing when I took the boat for France.

2

I MET Giovanni during my second year in Paris, when I had no money. On the morning of the evening that we met I had been turned out of my room. I did not owe an awful lot of money, only around six thousand francs, but Parisian hotel-keepers have a way of smelling poverty and then they do what anybody does who is aware of a bad smell, they throw whatever stinks outside.

My father had money in his account which belonged to me but he was very reluctant to send it because he wanted me to come home—to come home, as he said, and settle down, and whenever he said that I thought of the sediment at the bottom of a stagnant pond. I did not, then, know many people in Paris and Hella was in Spain. Most of the people I knew in Paris were, as Parisians sometimes put it, of *le milieu* and, while this milieu was certainly anxious enough to claim me, I was intent on proving, to them and to myself, that I was not of their company. I did this by being in their company a great deal and manifesting toward all of them a tolerance which placed me, I believed, above suspicion. I had written to friends for money, of course, but the Atlantic Ocean is deep and wide and money doesn't hurry from the other side.

So I went through my address book, sitting over a tepid coffee in a boulevard cafe, and decided to call up an old acquaintance who was always asking me to call, an aging, Belgian-born, American businessman, named Jacques. He had a big, comfortable apartment and lots of things to drink and lots of money. He was, as I knew he would be, surprised to hear from me and before the surprise and the charm wore off, giving him time to become wary, he had invited me for supper. He may have been cursing as he hung up, and reaching for his wallet but it was too late. Jacques is not too bad. Perhaps he is a fool and a coward but almost everybody is one or the other and most people are both. In some ways I liked him. He was silly but he was so lonely; anyway, I understand now that the contempt I felt for him involved my self-contempt. He could be unbelievably generous, he could be unspeakably stingy. Though he wanted to trust everybody, he was incapable of trusting a living soul; to make up for this, he threw his money away on people; inevitably, then, he was abused. Then he buttoned his wallet, locked his door, and retired into that strong self-pity which was, perhaps, the only thing he had which really belonged to him. I thought for a long while that he, with his big apartment, his well-meant promises, his whiskey, his marijuana, his orgies, had helped to kill Giovanni. As, indeed, perhaps he had. But Jacques' hands are certainly no bloodier than mine.

I saw Jacques, as a matter of fact, just after Giovanni was sentenced. He was sitting bundled up in his greatcoat on the terrace of a cafe, drinking a *vin chaud*. He was alone on the terrace. He called me as I passed.

He did not look well, his face was mottled, his eyes, behind his glasses, were like the eyes of a dying man who looks everywhere for healing.

'You've heard,' he whispered, as I joined him, 'about Giovanni?'

I nodded yes. I remember the winter sun was shining and I felt as cold and distant as the sun.

'It's terrible, terrible, terrible,' Jacques moaned. 'Terrible.'

'Yes,' I said. I could not say anything more.

'I wonder why he did it,' Jacques pursued, 'why he didn't ask his friends to help him.' He looked at me. We both knew that the last time Giovanni had asked Jacques for money, Jacques had refused. I said nothing. 'They say he had started taking opium,' Jacques said, 'that he needed the money for opium. Did you hear that?'

I had heard it. It was a newspaper speculation which, however, I had reasons of my own for believing, remembering the extent of Giovanni's desperation, knowing how far this terror which was so vast that it had simply become a void had driven him. 'Me, I want to escape,' he had told me, '*je veux m'evader*—this dirty world, this dirty body. I never wish to make love again with anything more than the body.'

Jacques waited for me to answer. I stared out into the street. I was beginning to think of Giovanni dying—where Giovanni had been there would be nothing, nothing forever.

'I hope it's not my fault,' Jacques said at last. 'I didn't give

him the money. If I'd known—I would have given him everything I had.'

But we both knew this was not true.

'You two together,' Jacques suggested, 'you weren't happy
together?'

'No,' I said. I stood up. 'It might have been better,' I said,
'if he'd stayed down there in that village of his in Italy and
planted his olive trees and had a lot of children and beaten
his wife. He used to love to sing,' I remembered suddenly,
'maybe he could have stayed down there and sung his life
away and died in bed.'

Then Jacques said something that surprised me. People are
full of surprises, even for themselves, if they have been stirred
enough. 'Nobody can stay in the garden of Eden,' Jacques
said. And then: 'I wonder why.'

I said nothing. I said goodbye and left him. Hella had long
since returned from Spain and we were already arranging to
rent this house and I had a date to meet her.

I have thought about Jacques' question since. The question
is banal but one of the real troubles with living is that living
is so banal. Everyone, after all, goes the same dark road—and
the road has a trick of being most dark, most treacherous,
when it seems most bright—and it's true that nobody stays in
the garden of Eden. Jacques' garden was not the same as
Giovanni's, of course. Jacques' garden was involved with football players and Giovanni's was involved with maidens—but
that seems to have made so little difference. Perhaps everybody has a garden of Eden, I don't know; but they have
scarcely seen their garden before they see the flaming sword.
Then, perhaps, life only offers the choice of remembering the
garden or forgetting it. Either, or: it takes strength to remember, it takes another kind of strength to forget, it takes a hero
to do both. People who remember court madness through
pain, the pain of the perpetually recurring death of their innocence; people who forget court another kind of madness,
the madness of the denial of pain and the hatred of innocence;
and the world is mostly divided between madmen who remember and madmen who forget. Heroes are rare.

Jacques had not wanted to have supper in his apartment
because his cook had run away. His cooks were always running

away. He was always getting young boys from the provinces, God knows how, to come up and be cooks; and they, of course, as soon as they were able to find their way around the capital, decided that cooking was the last thing they wanted to do. They usually ended up going back to the provinces, those, that is, who did not end up on the streets, or in jail, or in Indo-China.

I met him at a rather nice restaurant on the rue de Grenelle and arranged to borrow ten thousand francs from him before we had finished our aperitifs. He was in a good mood and I, of course, was in a good mood too, and this meant that we would end up drinking in Jacques' favorite bar, a noisy, crowded, ill-lit sort of tunnel, of dubious—or perhaps not dubious at all, of rather too emphatic—reputation. Every once in a while it was raided by the police, apparently with the connivance of Guillaume, the *patron*, who always managed, on the particular evening, to warn his favorite customers that if they were not armed with identification papers they might be better off elsewhere.

I remember that the bar, that night, was more than ordinarily crowded and noisy. All of the habitues were there and many strangers, some looking, some just staring. There were three or four very chic Parisian ladies sitting at a table with their gigolos or their lovers or perhaps simply their country cousins, God knows; the ladies seemed extremely animated, their males seemed rather stiff; the ladies seemed to be doing most of the drinking. There were the usual paunchy, bespectacled gentlemen with avid, sometimes despairing eyes, the usual, knife-blade lean, tight-trousered boys. One could never be sure, as concerns these latter, whether they were after money or blood or love. They moved about the bar incessantly, cadging cigarettes and drinks, with something behind their eyes at once terribly vulnerable and terribly hard. There were, of course, *les folles*, always dressed in the most improbable combinations, screaming like parrots the details of their latest love-affairs—their love-affairs always seemed to be hilarious. Occasionally one would swoop in, quite late in the evening, to convey the news that he—but they always called each other 'she'—had just spent time with a celebrated movie star, or boxer. Then all of the others closed in on this newcomer and they looked like a peacock garden and sounded like a barnyard. I always found it difficult to believe that they ever went to bed with anybody for a man who wanted a woman would certainly have rather had a real one and a man who wanted a man would certainly not want one of *them*. Perhaps, indeed, that was why they screamed so loud. There was the boy who worked all day, it was said, in the post-office, who came out at night wearing makeup and ear-rings and with his heavy blond hair piled high. Sometimes he actually wore a skirt and high heels. He usually stood alone unless Guillaume walked over to tease him. People said that he was very nice but I confess that his utter grotesqueness made me uneasy; perhaps in the same way that the sight of monkeys eating their own excrement turns some people's stomachs. They might not mind so much if monkeys did not—so grotesquely—re-semble human beings.

This bar was practically in my *quartier* and I had many times had breakfast in the nearby working man's cafe to which all the nightbirds of the neighborhood retired when the bars closed. Sometimes I was with Hella, sometimes I was alone. And I had been in this bar, too, two or three times; once very drunk, I had been accused of causing a minor sensation by flirting with a soldier. My memory of that night was, happily, very dim, and I took the attitude that no matter how drunk I may have been I could not possibly have done such a thing. But my face was known and I had the feeling that people were taking bets about me. Or, it was as though they were the elders of some strange and austere holy order and were watch-ing me in order to discover, by means of signs I made but which only they could read, whether or not I had a true vocation.

Jacques was aware, I was aware, as we pushed our way to the bar—it was like moving into the field of a magnet or like approaching a small circle of heat—of the presence of a new bar-man. He stood, insolent and dark and leonine, his elbow leaning on the cash-register, his fingers playing with his chin, looking out at the crowd. It was as though his station were a promontory and we were the sea.

Jacques was immediately attracted. I felt him, so to speak, preparing himself for conquest. I felt the necessity for tolerance.

'I'm sure,' I said, 'that you'll want to get to know the barman. So I'll vanish any time you like.'

There was, in this tolerance of mine, a fund, by no means meagre, of malicious knowledge—I had drawn on it when I called him up to borrow money. I knew that Jacques could only hope to conquer the boy before us if the boy was, in effect, for sale; and if he stood with such arrogance on an auction block he could certainly find bidders richer and more attractive than Jacques. I knew that Jacques knew this. I knew something else: that Jacques' vaunted affection for me was involved with desire, the desire, in fact, to be rid of me, to be able, soon, to despise me as he now despised that army of boys who had come, without love, to his bed. I held my own against this desire by pretending that Jacques and I were friends, by forcing Jacques, on pain of humiliation, to pretend this. I pretended not to see, although I exploited it, the lust not quite sleeping in his bright, bitter eyes and, by means of the rough, male candor with which I conveyed to him his case was hopeless, I compelled him, endlessly, to hope. And I knew, finally, that in bars such as these I was Jacques' protection. As long as I was there the world could see and he could believe that he was out with me, his friend, he was not there out of desperation, he was not at the mercy of whatever adventurer chance, cruelty, or the laws of actual and emotional poverty might throw his way.

'You stay right here,' said Jacques. 'I'll look at him from time to time and talk to you and that way I'll save money—and stay happy, too.'

'I wonder where Guillaume found him,' I said.

For he was so exactly the kind of boy that Guillaume always dreamed of that it scarcely seemed possible that Guillaume could have found him.

'What will you have?' he now asked us. His tone conveyed that, though he spoke no English, he knew that we had been speaking about him and hoped we were through.

'*Une fine a l'eau,*' I said; and '*un cognac sec,*' said Jacques, both speaking too quickly, so that I blushed and realized by a faint merriment on Giovanni's face as he served us that he had seen it.

Jacques, wilfully misinterpreting Giovanni's nuance of a smile, made of it an opportunity. 'You're new here?' he asked in English.

Giovanni almost certainly understood the question but it suited him better to look blankly from Jacques to me and then back again at Jacques. Jacques translated his question.

Giovanni shrugged. 'I have been here a month,' he said.

I knew where the conversation was going and I kept my eyes down and sipped my drink.

'It must,' Jacques suggested, with a sort of bludgeoning insistence on the light touch, 'seem very strange to you.'

'Strange?' asked Giovanni. 'Why?'

And Jacques giggled. I was suddenly ashamed that I was with him. 'All these men'—and I knew that voice, breathless, insinuating, high as no girl's had ever been, and hot, suggesting, somehow, the absolutely motionless, deadly heat which hangs over swamp ground in July—'all these men,' he gasped, 'and so few women. Doesn't that seem strange to you?'

'Ah,' said Giovanni, and turned away to serve another customer, 'no doubt the women are waiting at home.'

'I'm sure one's waiting for you,' insisted Jacques, to which Giovanni did not respond.

'Well. That didn't take long,' said Jacques, half to me, half to the space which had just held Giovanni. 'Aren't you glad you stayed? You've got me all to yourself.'

'Oh, you're handling it all wrong,' I said. 'He's mad for you. He just doesn't want to seem too anxious. Order him a drink. Find out where he likes to buy his clothes. Tell him about that cunning little Alfa Romeo you're just dying to give away to some deserving bartender.'

'*Very* funny,' said Jacques.

'Well,' I said, 'faint heart never won fair athlete, that's for sure.'

'Anyway, I'm sure he sleeps with girls. They always do, you know.'

'I've heard about boys who do that. Nasty little beasts.'

We stood in silence for awhile.

'Why don't *you* invite him to have a drink with us?' Jacques suggested.

I looked at him.

'Why don't *I*? Well, you may find this hard to believe, but, actually, I'm sort of queer for girls myself. If that was his sister looking so good, I'd invite *her* to have a drink with us. I don't spend money on men.'

I could see Jacques struggling not to say that I didn't have any objection to allowing men to spend money on *me*; I watched his brief struggle with a slight smile, for I knew he couldn't say it; then he said, with that cheery, brave smile of his:

'I was not suggesting that you jeopardize, even for a moment, that'—he paused—'that *immaculate* manhood which is your pride and joy. I only suggested that *you* invite him because he will almost certainly refuse if *I* invite him.'

'But man,' I said, grinning, 'think of the confusion. He'll think that *I'm* the one who's lusting for his body. How do we get out of that?'

'If there should be any confusion,' said Jacques, with dignity, 'I will be happy to clear it up.'

We measured each other for a moment. Then I laughed. 'Wait till he comes back this way. I hope he orders a magnum of the most expensive champagne in France.'

I turned, leaning on the bar. I felt, somehow, elated. Jacques, beside me, was very quiet, suddenly very frail and old, and I felt a quick, sharp, rather frightened pity for him. Giovanni had been out on the floor, serving the people at tables, and he now returned with a rather grim smile on his face, carrying a loaded tray.

'Maybe,' I said, 'it would look better if our glasses were empty.'

We finished our drinks. I set down my glass.

'Barman?' I called.

'The same?'

'Yes.' He started to turn away. 'Barman,' I said, quickly, 'we would like to offer you a drink, if we may.'

'*Eh, bien!*' said a voice behind us, '*c'est fort ca!* Not only have you finally—thank heaven!—corrupted this great Amer-

ican football player, you use him now to corrupt *my* barman.
Vraiment, Jacques! At your age!'

It was Guillaume standing behind us, grinning like a movie
star, and waving that long white handkerchief which he was
never, in the bar at any rate, to be seen without. Jacques
turned, hugely delighted to be accused of such rare seduc-
tiveness, and he and Guillaume fell into each others arms like
old theatrical sisters.

'*Eh bien, ma cheri, comment vas tu?* I have not seen you for
a long time.'

'But I have been awfully busy,' said Jacques.

'I don't doubt it! Aren't you ashamed, *veille folle*?'

'*Et toi?* You certainly don't seem to have been wasting your
time.'

And Jacques threw a delighted look in the direction of Giovanni, rather as though Giovanni were a valuable race horse
or a rare bit of china. Guillaume followed the look and his
voice dropped.

'*Ah, ca, mon cher, c'est strictement du* business, *comprends-
tu?*'

They moved a little away. This left me surrounded,
abruptly, with an awful silence. At last I raised my eyes and
looked at Giovanni, who was watching me.

'I think you offered me a drink,' he said.

'Yes,' I said. 'I offered you a drink.'

'I drink no alcohol while I work, but I will take a Coca-
Cola.' He picked up my glass. 'And for you—it is the same?'

'The same.' I realized that I was quite happy to be talking
with him and this realization made me shy. And I felt menaced
since Jacques was no longer at my side. Then I realized that
I would have to pay, for this round anyway; it was impossible
to tug Jacques' sleeve for the money as though I were his
ward. I coughed and put my ten thousand franc note on the
bar.

'You are rich,' said Giovanni, and set my drink before
me.

'But no. No. I simply have no change.'

He grinned. I could not tell whether he grinned because
he thought I was lying or because he knew I was telling the

truth. In silence he took the bill and rang it up and carefully counted out my change on the bar before me. Then he filled his glass and went back to his original position at the cash-register. I felt a tightening in my chest.

'*A la votre,*' he said.

'*A la votre.*' We drank.

'You are an American?' he asked at last.

'Yes,' I said. 'From New York.'

'Ah! I am told that New York is very beautiful. Is it more beautiful than Paris?'

'Oh, no,' I said, '*no* city is more beautiful than Paris—'

'It seems the very suggestion that one *could* be is enough to make you very angry,' grinned Giovanni. 'Forgive me. I was not trying to be heretical.' Then, more soberly and as though to appease me, 'You must like Paris very much.'

'I like New York, too,' I said, uncomfortably aware that my voice had a defensive ring, 'but New York is very beautiful in a very different way.'

He frowned. 'In what way?'

'No one,' I said, 'who has never seen it can possibly imagine it. It's very high and new and electric—exciting.' I paused. 'It's hard to describe. It's very—twentieth century.'

'You find that Paris is *not* of this century?' he asked with a smile.

His smile made me feel a little foolish. 'Well,' I said, 'Paris is *old*, is many centuries. You feel, in Paris, all the time gone by. That isn't what you feel in New York—' He was smiling. I stopped.

'What do you feel in New York?' he asked.

'Perhaps you feel,' I told him, 'all the time to come. There's such power there, everything is in such movement. You can't help wondering—*I* can't help wondering—what it will all be like—many years from now.'

'Many years from now? When we are dead and New York is old?'

'Yes,' I said. 'When everyone is tired, when the world—for Americans—is not so new.'

'I don't see why the world is so new for Americans,' said Giovanni. 'After all, you are all merely emigrants. And you did not leave Europe so very long ago.'

'The ocean is very wide,' I said. 'We have led different lives than you, things have happened to us there which have never happened here. Surely you can understand that this would make us a different people?'

'Ah! If it had only made you a different people!' he laughed. 'But it seems to have turned you into another species. You are not, are you, on another planet? For I suppose that would explain everything.'

'I admit,' I said with some heat—for I do not like to be laughed at—'that we may sometimes give the impression that we think we are. But we are not on another planet, no. And neither, my friend, are you.'

He grinned again. 'I will not,' he said, 'argue that most unlucky fact.'

We were silent for a moment. Giovanni moved to serve several people at either end of the bar. Guillaume and Jacques were still talking. Guillaume seemed to be recounting one of his interminable anecdotes, anecdotes which invariably pivoted on the hazards of business or the hazards of love, and Jacques' mouth was stretched in a rather painful grin. I knew that he was dying to get back to the bar.

Giovanni placed himself before me again and began wiping the bar with a damp cloth. 'The Americans are funny. You have a funny sense of time—or perhaps you have no sense of time at all, I can't tell. Time always sounds like a parade *chez vous*—a *triumphant* parade, like armies with banners entering a town. As though, with enough time, and that would not need to be so very much for Americans, *n'est-ce pas?*' and he smiled, giving me a mocking look, but I said nothing. 'Well then,' he continued, 'as though with enough time and all that fearful energy and virtue you people have, everything will be settled, solved, put in its place. And when I say everything,' he added, grimly, 'I mean all the serious, dreadful things, like pain and death and love, in which you Americans do not believe.'

'What makes you think we don't? And what do you believe?'

'I don't believe in this nonsense about time. Time is just common, it's like water for a fish. Everybody's in this water, nobody gets out of it, or if he does the same thing happens to him that happens to the fish, he dies. And you know what happens in this water, time? The big fish eat the little fish. That's all. The big fish eat the little fish and the ocean doesn't care.'

'Oh, please,' I said. 'I don't believe *that*. Time's not water and we're not fish and you can choose to be eaten and also not to eat—not to eat,' I added quickly, turning a little red before his delighted and sardonic smile, 'the little fish, of course.'

'To choose!' cried Giovanni, turning his face away from me and speaking, it appeared, to an invisible ally who had been eavesdropping on this conversation all along. 'To *choose!*' He turned to me again. 'Ah, you are really an American. *J'adore votre enthousiasme!*'

'I adore yours,' I said, politely, 'though it seems to be a blacker brand than mine.'

'Anyway,' he said mildly, 'I don't see what you can do with little fish except eat them. What else are they good for?'

'In my country,' I said, feeling a subtle war within me as I said it, 'the little fish seem to have gotten together and are nibbling at the body of the whale.'

'That will not make them whales,' said Giovanni. 'The only result of all that nibbling will be that there will no longer be any grandeur anywhere, not even at the bottom of the sea.'

'Is *that* what you have against us? That we're not grand?'

He smiled—smiled like someone who, faced with the total inadequacy of the opposition, is prepared to drop the argument. *'Peut-etre.'*

'You people are impossible,' I said. 'You're the ones who killed grandeur off, right here in this city, with paving stones. Talk about little fish—!' He was grinning. I stopped.

'Don't stop,' he said, still grinning. 'I am listening.'

I finished my drink. 'You people dumped all this *merde* on us,' I said, sullenly, 'and now you say we're barbaric because we stink.'

My sullenness delighted him. 'You're charming,' he said. 'Do you always speak like this?'

'No,' I said, and looked down. 'Almost never.'

There was something in him of the coquette. 'I am flattered

then,' he said, with a sudden, disconcerting gravity, which contained, nevertheless, the very faintest hint of mockery.

'And you,' I said, finally, 'have you been here long? Do you like Paris?'

He hesitated a moment and then grinned, suddenly looking rather boyish and shy. 'It's cold in the winter,' he said. 'I don't like that. And Parisians—I do not find them so very friendly, do you?' He did not wait for my answer. 'They are not like the people I knew when I was younger. In Italy we are friendly, we dance and sing and make love—but these people,' and he looked out over the bar, and then at me, and finished his Coca-Cola, 'these people, they are cold, I do not understand them.'

'But the French say,' I teased, 'that the Italians are too fluid, too volatile, have no sense of measure—'

'Measure!' cried Giovanni, 'ah, these people and their measure! They measure the gram, the centimetre, these people, and they keep piling all the little scraps they save, one on top of the other, year in and year out, all in the stocking or under the bed—and what do they get out of all this measure? A country which is falling to pieces, measure by measure, before their eyes. Measure. I do not like to offend your ears by saying all the things I am sure these people measure before they permit themselves any act whatever. May I offer you a drink now,' he asked suddenly, 'before the old man comes back? Who is he? Is he your uncle?'

I did not know whether the word 'uncle' was being used euphemistically or not. I felt a very urgent desire to make my position clear but I did not know how to go about it. I laughed. 'No,' I said, 'he is not my uncle. He is just somebody I know.'

Giovanni looked at me. And this look made me feel that no one in my life had ever looked at me directly before. 'I hope he is not very dear to you,' he said, with a smile, 'because I think he is silly. Not a bad man, you understand—just a little silly.'

'Perhaps,' I said, and at once felt like a traitor. 'He's not bad,' I added quickly, 'he's really a pretty nice guy.' That's not true, either, I thought, he's far from being a nice guy. 'Anyway,' I said, 'he's certainly not very dear to me,' and felt again, at once, this strange tightening in my chest and wondered at the sound of my voice.

Carefully now, Giovanni poured my drink. *'Vive l'amerique,'* he said.

'Thank you,' I said, and lifted my glass, *'vive le vieux continent.'*

We were silent for a moment.

'Do you come in here often?' asked Giovanni suddenly.

'No,' I said, 'not very often.'

'But you will come,' he teased, with a wonderful, mocking light on his face, 'more often *now*?'

I stammered: 'Why?'

'Ah!' cried Giovanni. 'Don't you know when you have made a friend?'

I knew I must look foolish and that my question was foolish too: 'So soon?'

'Why no,' he said, reasonably, and looked at his watch, 'we can wait another hour if you like. We can become friends then. Or we can wait until closing time. We can become friends *then*. Or we can wait until tomorrow, only that means that you must come in here tomorrow and perhaps you have something else to do.' He put his watch away and leaned both elbows on the bar. 'Tell me,' he said, 'what is this thing about time? Why is it better to be late than early? People are always saying, we must wait, we must wait. What are they waiting for?'

'Well,' I said, feeling myself being led by Giovanni into deep and dangerous water, 'I guess people wait in order to make sure of what they feel.'

'In order to make *sure*!' He turned again to that invisible ally and laughed again. I was beginning, perhaps, to find his phantom a little unnerving but the sound of his laughter in that airless tunnel was the most incredible sound. 'It's clear that you are a true philosopher.' He pointed a finger at my heart. 'And when you have waited—has it made you sure?'

For this I could simply summon no answer. From the dark, crowded center of the bar someone called *'Garçon!'* and he moved away from me, smiling. 'You can wait now. And tell me how sure you have become when I return.'

And he took his round metal tray and moved out into the

crowd. I watched him as he moved. And then I watched their faces, watching him. And then I was afraid. I knew that they were watching, had been watching both of us. They knew that they had witnessed a beginning and now they would not cease to watch until they saw the end. It had taken some time but the tables had been turned, now I was in the zoo, and they were watching.

I stood at the bar for quite a while alone, for Jacques had escaped from Guillaume but was now involved, poor man, with two of the knife-blade boys. Giovanni came back for an instant and winked.

'Are you sure?'

'You win. You're the philosopher.'

'Oh, you must wait some more. You do not yet know me well enough to say such a thing.'

And he filled his tray and disappeared again.

Now someone whom I had never seen before came out of the shadows toward me. It looked like a mummy or a zombie—this was the first, overwhelming impression—of something walking after it had been put to death. And it walked, really, like someone who might be sleepwalking or like those figures in slow motion one sometimes sees on the screen. It carried a glass, it walked on its toes, the flat hips moved with a dead, horrifying lasciviousness. It seemed to make no sound; this was due to the roar of the bar, which was like the roaring of the sea, heard at night, from far away. It glittered in the dim light; the thin, black hair was violent with oil, combed forward, hanging in bangs; the eyelids gleamed with mascara, the mouth raged with lipstick. The face was white and thoroughly bloodless with some kind of foundation cream; it stank of powder and a gardenia-like perfume. The shirt, open coquettishly to the navel, revealed a hairless chest and a silver crucifix; the shirt was covered with round, paper thin wafers, red and green and orange and yellow and blue, which stormed in the light and made one feel that the mummy might, at any moment, disappear in flame. A red sash was around the waist, the clinging pants were a surprisingly sombre grey. He wore buckles on his shoes.

I was not sure that he was coming towards me but I could not take my eyes away. He stopped before me, one hand on his hip, looked me up and down, and smiled. He had been eating garlic and his teeth were very bad. His hands, I noticed, with an unbelieving shock, were very large and strong.

'*Eh bien,*' he said, '*il te plaît?*'

'*Comment?*' I said.

I really was not sure I had heard him right, though the bright, bright eyes, looking, it seemed, at something amusing within the recess of my skull, did not leave much room for doubt.

'You like him—the barman?'

I did not know what to do or say. It seemed impossible to hit him, it seemed impossible to get angry. It did not seem real, he did not seem real. Besides—no matter what I said, those eyes would mock me with it. I said, as drily as I could:

'How does that concern you?'

'But it concerns me not at all, darling. *Je m'en fou.*'

'Then please get the hell away from me.'

He did not move at once, but smiled at me again. '*Il est dangereux, tu sais.* And for a boy like you—he is *very* dangerous.'

I looked at him. I almost asked him what he meant. 'Go to hell,' I said, and turned my back.

'Oh, no,' he said—and I looked at him again. He was laughing, showing all his teeth—there were not many. 'Oh, no,' he said, 'I go not to hell,' and he clutched his crucifix with one large hand. 'But you, my dear friend—I fear that you shall burn in a very hot fire.' He laughed again. 'Oh, such fire!' He touched his head. 'Here.' And he writhed, as though in torment. 'Every*where.*' And he touched his heart. 'And here.' And he looked at me with malice and mockery and something else; he looked at me as though I were very far away. 'Oh, my poor friend, so young, so strong, so handsome—will you not buy me a drink?'

'*Va te faire foutre.*'

His face crumpled in the sorrow of infants and of very old men—the sorrow, also, of certain, aging actresses who were renowned in their youth for their fragile, child-like beauty. The dark eyes narrowed in spite and fury and the scarlet mouth turned down like the mask of tragedy. '*T'aura du chagrin,'* he said. 'You will be very unhappy. Remember that I told you so.'

And he straightened, as though he were a princess and moved, flaming, away through the crowd.

Then Jacques spoke, at my elbow. 'Everyone in the bar,' he said, 'is talking about how beautifully you and the barman have hit it off.' He gave me a radiant and vindictive smile. 'I trust there has been no confusion?'

I looked down at him. I wanted to do something to his cheerful, hideous, worldly face which would make it impossible for him ever again to smile at anyone the way he was smiling at me. Then I wanted to get out of this bar, out into the air, perhaps to find Hella, my suddenly so sorely menaced girl.

'There's been no confusion,' I snapped. 'Don't you go getting confused, either.'

'I think I can safely say,' said Jacques, 'that I have scarcely ever been less confused than I am at this moment.' He had stopped smiling; he gave me a look which was dry, bitter, and impersonal. 'And, at the risk of losing forever your so remarkably candid friendship, let me tell you something. Confusion is a luxury which only the very, very young can possibly afford and you are not that young anymore.'

'I don't know what you're talking about,' I said. 'Let's have another drink.'

I felt that I had better get drunk. Now Giovanni went behind the bar again and winked at me. Jacques' eyes never left my face. I turned rudely from him and faced the bar again. He followed me.

'The same,' said Jacques.

'Certainly,' said Giovanni, 'that's the way to do it.' He fixed our drinks. Jacques paid. I suppose I did not look too well, for Giovanni shouted at me playfully, 'Eh? Are you drunk already?'

I looked up and smiled. 'You know how Americans drink,' I said. 'I haven't even started yet.'

'David is far from drunk,' said Jacques. 'He is only reflecting bitterly that he must get a new pair of suspenders.'

I could have killed Jacques. Yet it was only with difficulty that I kept myself from laughing. I made a face to signify to

Giovanni that the old man was making a private joke, and he disappeared again. That time of evening had come when great batches of people were leaving and great batches were coming in. They would all encounter each other later anyway, in the last bar, all those, that is, unlucky enough to be searching still at such an advanced hour.

I could not look at Jacques; which he knew. He stood beside me, smiling at nothing, humming a tune. There was nothing I could say. I did not dare to mention Hella. I could not even pretend to myself that I was sorry she was in Spain. I was glad. I was utterly, hopelessly, horribly glad. I knew I could do nothing whatever to stop the ferocious excitement which had burst in me like a storm. I could only drink, in the faint hope that the storm might thus spend itself without doing any more damage to my land. But I was glad. I was only sorry that Jacques had been a witness. He made me ashamed. I hated him because he had now seen all that he had waited, often scarcely hoping, so many months to see. We had, in effect, been playing a deadly game and he was the winner. He was the winner in spite of the fact that I had cheated to win.

I wished, nevertheless, standing there at the bar, that I had been able to find in myself the force to turn and walk out—to have gone over to Montparnasse perhaps and picked up a girl. Any girl. I could not do it. I told myself all sorts of lies, standing there at the bar, but I could not move. And this was partly because I knew that it did not really matter anymore; it did not even matter if I never spoke to Giovanni again; for they had become visible, as visible as the wafers on the shirt of the flaming princess, they stormed all over me, my awakening, my insistent possibilities.

That was how I met Giovanni. I think we connected the instant that we met. And remain connected still, in spite of our later *separation de corps*, despite the fact that Giovanni will be rotting soon in unhallowed ground near Paris. Until I die there will be those moments, moments seeming to rise up out of the ground like Macbeth's witches, when his face will come before me, that face in all its changes, when the exact timbre of his voice and tricks of his speech will nearly burst my ears, when his smell will overpower my nostrils. Sometimes, in the days which are coming—God grant me the grace to live them: in the glare of the grey morning, sour-mouthed, eyelids raw and red, hair tangled and damp from my stormy sleep, facing, over coffee and cigarette smoke, last night's impenetrable, meaningless boy who will shortly rise and vanish like the smoke, I will see Giovanni again, as he was that night, so vivid, so winning, all of the light of that gloomy tunnel trapped around his head.

3

At five o'clock in the morning Guillaume locked the door of the bar behind us. The streets were empty and grey. On a corner near the bar a butcher had already opened his shop and one could see him within, already bloody, hacking at the meat. One of the great, green Paris buses lumbered past, nearly empty, its bright electric flag waving fiercely to indicate a turn. A *garcon de cafe* spilled water on the sidewalk before his establishment and swept it into the gutter. At the end of the long, curving street which faced us were the trees of the boulevard and straw chairs piled high before cafes and the great stone spire of St. Germain des Pres—the most magnificent spire, as Hella and I believed, in Paris. The street beyond the *place* stretched before us to the river and, hidden beside and behind us, meandered to Montparnasse. It was named for an adventurer who sowed a crop in Europe which is being harvested until today. I had often walked this street, sometimes, with Hella, towards the river, often, without her, towards the girls of Montparnasse. Not very long ago either, though it seemed, that morning, to have occurred in another life.

We were going to Les Halles for breakfast. We piled into a taxi, the four of us, unpleasantly crowded together, a circumstance which elicited from Jacques and Guillaume a series of lewd speculations. This lewdness was particularly revolting in that it not only failed of wit, it was so clearly an expression of contempt and self-contempt; it bubbled upward out of them like a fountain of black water. It was clear that they were tantalizing themselves with Giovanni and me and this set my teeth on edge. But Giovanni leaned back against the taxi window, allowing his arm to press my shoulder lightly, seeming to say that we should soon be rid of these old men and should not be distressed that their dirty water splashed—we would have no trouble washing it away.

'Look,' said Giovanni, as we crossed the river. 'This old whore, Paris, as she turns in bed, is very moving.'

I looked out, beyond his heavy profile, which was grey—

from fatigue and from the light of the sky above us. The river was swollen and yellow. Nothing moved on the river. Barges were tied up along the banks. The island of the city widened away from us, bearing the weight of the cathedral; beyond this, dimly, through speed and mist, one made out the individual roofs of Paris, their myriad, squat chimney stacks very beautiful and vari-colored under the pearly sky. Mist clung to the river, softening that army of trees, softening those stones, hiding the city's dreadful corkscrew alleys and dead-end streets, clinging like a curse to the men who slept beneath the bridges—one of whom flashed by beneath us, very black and lone, walking along the river.

'Some rats have gone in,' said Giovanni, 'and now other rats come out.' He smiled bleakly and looked at me; to my surprise, he took my hand and held it. 'Have you ever slept under a bridge?' he asked. 'Or perhaps they have soft beds with warm blankets under the bridges in your country?'

I did not know what to do about my hand; it seemed better to do nothing. 'Not yet,' I said, 'but I may. My hotel wants to throw me out.'

I had said it lightly, with a smile, out of a desire to put myself, in terms of an acquaintance with wintry things, on an equal footing with him. But the fact that I had said it as he held my hand made it sound to me unutterably helpless and soft and coy. But I could not say anything to counteract this impression: to say anything more would confirm it. I pulled my hand away, pretending that I had done so in order to search for a cigarette.

Jacques lit it for me.

'Where do you live?' he asked Giovanni.

'Oh,' said Giovanni, 'out. Far out. It is almost not Paris.'

'He lives in a dreadful street, near *Nation*,' said Guillaume, 'among all the dreadful bourgeoisie and their pig-like children.'

'You failed to catch the children at the right age,' said Jacques. 'They go through a period, all too brief, *helas!* when a pig is perhaps the *only* animal they do not call to mind.' And, again to Giovanni: 'In a hotel?'

'No,' said Giovanni, and for the first time he seemed slightly uncomfortable. 'I live in a maid's room.'

'With the maid?'

'No,' said Giovanni, and smiled, 'the maid is I don't know where. You could certainly tell that there was no maid if you ever saw my room.'

'I would love to,' said Jacques.

'Then we will give a party for you one day,' said Giovanni.

This, too courteous and too bald to permit any further questioning, nearly forced, nevertheless, a question from my lips. Guillaume looked briefly at Giovanni, who did not look at him but out into the morning, whistling. I had been making resolutions for the last six hours and now I made another one: to have this whole thing 'out' with Giovanni as soon as I got him alone at Les Halles. I was going to have to tell him that he had made a mistake but that we could still be friends. But I could not be certain, really, that it might not be I who was making a mistake, blindly misreading everything—and out of necessities, then, too shameful to be uttered. I was in a box for I could see that, no matter how I turned, the hour of confession was upon me and could scarcely be averted; unless, of course, I leaped out of the cab, which would be the most terrible confession of all.

Now the cab-driver asked us where we wanted to go, for we had arrived at the choked boulevards and impassable side-streets of Les Halles. Leeks, onions, cabbages, oranges, apples, potatoes, cauliflowers, stood gleaming in mounds all over, on the sidewalks, in the streets, before great metal sheds. The sheds were blocks long and within the sheds were piled more fruit, more vegetables, in some sheds, fish, in some sheds, cheese, in some whole animals, lately slaughtered. It scarcely seemed possible that all of this could ever be eaten. But in a few hours it would all be gone and trucks would be arriving from all corners of France—and making their way, to the great profit of a beehive of middlemen, across the city of Paris—to feed the roaring multitude. Who were roaring now, at once wounding and charming the ear, before and behind, and on either side of our taxi—our taxi driver, and Giovanni, too, roared back. The multitude of Paris seems to be dressed in blue every day but Sunday, when, for the most part, they put on an unbelievably festive black. Here they were now, in blue, disputing, every inch, our passage, with their wagons, hand-trucks, camions, their bursting baskets carried at an angle steeply self-confident, on the back. A red-faced woman, burdened with fruit, shouted—to Giovanni, the driver, to the world—a particularly vivid *cochonnerie*, to which the driver and Giovanni, at once, at the top of their lungs, responded, though the fruit lady had already passed beyond our sight and perhaps no longer even remembered her precisely obscene conjectures. We crawled along, for no one had yet told the driver where to stop, and Giovanni and the driver, who had, it appeared, immediately upon entering Les Halles, been transformed into brothers, exchanged speculations, unflattering in the extreme, concerning the hygiene, language, private parts, and habits, of the citizens of Paris. (Jacques and Guillaume were exchanging speculations, unspeakably less good-natured, concerning every passing male.) The pavements were slick with leavings, mainly cast-off, rotten leaves, flowers, fruit and vegetables which had met with disaster natural and slow, or abrupt. And the walls and corners were combed with *pissoirs*, dull-burning, make-shift braziers, cafes, restaurants, and smoky yellow bistros—of these last, some so small that they were little more than diamond shaped, enclosed corners holding bottles and a zinc-covered counter. At all these points, men, young, old, middle-aged, powerful, powerful even in the various fashions in which they had met, or were meeting, their various ruin; and women, more than making up, in shrewdness and patience, in an ability to count and weigh—and shout—whatever they might lack in muscle; though they did not, really, seem to lack much. Nothing here reminded me of home, though Giovanni recognized, revelled in it all.

'I know a place,' he told the driver, *'tres bon marche'*—and told the driver where it was. It developed that it was one of the driver's favorite rendezvous.

'Where is this place?' asked Jacques, petulantly. 'I thought we were going to'—and he named another place.

'You are joking,' said Giovanni, with contempt. 'That place is *very* bad and *very* expensive, it is only for tourists. We are not tourists,' and he added, to me, 'When I first came to Paris I worked in Les Halles—a long time, too. *Nom de Dieu, quelle boulot!* I pray always never to do that again.' And he regarded the streets through which we passed with a sadness which was not less real for being a little theatrical and self-mocking.

Guillaume said, from his corner of the cab: 'Tell him who rescued you.'

'Ah, yes,' said Giovanni, 'behold my saviour, my *patron.*' He was silent a moment. Then: 'You do not regret it, do you? I have not done you any harm? You are pleased with my work?'

'Mais oui,' said Guillaume.

Giovanni sighed. *'Bien sûr.'* He looked out of the window again, again whistling. We came to a corner remarkably clear. The taxi stopped.

'Ici,' said the driver.

'Ici,' Giovanni echoed.

I reached for my wallet but Giovanni sharply caught my hand, conveying to me with an angry flick of his eyelash the intelligence that the least these dirty old men could do was *pay.* He opened the door and stepped out into the street. Guillaume had not reached for his wallet and Jacques paid for the cab.

'Ugh,' said Guillaume, staring at the door of the cafe before which we stood, 'I am sure this place is infested with vermin. Do you want to poison us?'

'It's not the outside you're going to eat,' said Giovanni. 'You are in much more danger of being poisoned in those dreadful, chic places you always go to, where they always have the face clean, *mais, mon Dieu, les fesses!*' He grinned. '*Fais-moi confiance.* Why would I want to poison you? Then I would have no job and I have only just found out that I want to live.'

He and Guillaume, Giovanni still smiling, exchanged a look which I would not have been able to read even if I had dared to try; and Jacques, pushing all of us before him as though we were his chickens, said, with that grin: 'We can't stand here in the cold and argue. If we can't eat inside, we can drink. Alcohol kills all microbes.'

And Guillaume brightened suddenly—he was really remarkable, as though he carried, hidden somewhere on his person, a needle filled with vitamins, which, automatically, at the blackening hour, discharged itself into his veins. '*Il y a les jeunes dedans,*' he said, and we went in.

Indeed there were young people, half a dozen at the zinc counter before glasses of red and white wine, along with others, not young at all. A pockmarked boy and a very rough looking girl were playing the pinball machine near the window. There were a few people sitting at the tables in the back, served by an astonishingly clean looking waiter. In the gloom, the dirty walls, the sawdust covered floor, his white jacket gleamed like snow. Behind these tables one caught a glimpse of the kitchen and the surly, obese cook. He lumbered about like one of those overloaded trucks outside, wearing one of those high, white hats, and with a dead cigar stuck between his lips.

Behind the counter sat one of those absolutely inimitable and indomitable ladies, produced only in the city of Paris, but produced there in great numbers, who would be as outrageous and unsettling in any other city as a mermaid on a mountaintop. All over Paris they sit behind their counters like a mother bird in a nest and brood over the cash-register as though it were an egg. Nothing occurring under the circle of heaven where they sit escapes their eye, if they have ever been surprised by anything, it was only in a dream—a dream they long ago ceased having. They are neither ill- nor good-natured, though they have their days and styles, and they know, in the way, apparently, that other people know when they have to go to the bathroom, everything about everyone who enters their domain. Though some are white-haired and some not, some fat, some thin, some grandmothers and some but lately virgins, they all have exactly the same, shrewd, vacant, all-registering eye; it is difficult to believe that they ever cried for milk, or looked at the sun; it seems they must have come into the world hungry for banknotes, and squinting helplessly, unable to focus their eyes until they came to rest on a cash-register.

This one's hair is black and grey and she has a face which comes from Brittany; and she, like almost everyone else standing at the bar, knows Giovanni and, after her fashion, likes him. She has a big, deep bosom and she clasps Giovanni to it; and a big, deep voice.

'*Ah, mon pote!*' she cries. '*Tu es revenu!* You have come back at last! *Salaud!* Now that you are rich and have found rich friends you never come to see us anymore! *Canaille!*'

And she beams at us, the 'rich' friends, with a friendliness deliciously, deliberately vague; she would have no trouble reconstructing every instant of our biographies from the moment we were born until this morning. She knows exactly who is rich—and how rich—and she knows it isn't me. For this reason, perhaps, there was a click of speculation infinitesimally double behind her eyes when she looked at me. In a moment, however, she knows that she will understand it all.

'You know how it is,' says Giovanni, extricating himself and throwing back his hair, 'when you work, when you become serious, you have no time to play.'

'*Tiens,*' says she, with mockery. '*Sans blague?*'

'But I assure you,' says Giovanni, 'even when you are a young man like me, you get very tired'—she laughs—'and you go to sleep early'—she laughs again—'and *alone,*' says Giovanni, as though this proved everything, and she clicks her teeth in sympathy and laughs again.

'And now,' she says, 'are you coming or going? Have you come for breakfast or have you come for a nightcap? *Nom de Dieu,* you do not *look* very serious, I believe you need a drink.'

'*Bien sûr,*' says someone at the bar, 'after such hard work he needs a bottle of white wine—and perhaps a few dozen oysters.'

Everybody laughs. Everybody, without seeming to, is looking at us and I am beginning to feel like part of a travelling circus. Everybody, also, seems very proud of Giovanni.

Giovanni turns to the voice at the bar. 'An excellent idea, friend,' he says, 'and exactly what I had in mind.' Now he turns to us. 'You have not met my friends,' he says, looking at me, then at the woman. 'This is Monsieur Guillaume,' he tells her, and with the most subtle flattening of his voice, 'my *patron.* He can tell you if I am serious.'

'Ah,' she dares to say, 'but I cannot tell if *he* is,' and covers this daring with a laugh.

Guillaume, raising his eyes with difficulty from the young men at the bar, stretches out his hand and smiles. 'But you are right, Madame,' he says. 'He is so much more serious than I am that I fear he will own my bar one day.'

He will when lions fly, she is thinking, but professes herself enchanted by him and shakes his hand with energy.

'And Monsieur Jacques,' says Giovanni, 'one of our finest customers.'

'*Enchante, Madame,*' says Jacques, with his most dazzling smile, of which she, in responding, produces the most artless parody.

'And this is *monsieur l'americain,*' says Giovanni, 'otherwise known as: *Monsieur David. Madame Clothilde.*'

And he stands back slightly. Something is burning in his eyes and it lights up all his face, it is joy and pride.

'*Je suis ravi, monsieur,*' she tells me and looks at me and shakes my hand and smiles.

I am smiling too, I scarcely know why; everything in me is jumping up and down. Giovanni carelessly puts an arm around my shoulder. 'What have you got good to eat?' he cried. 'We are hungry.'

'But we must have a drink first!' cried Jacques.

'But we can drink sitting down,' said Giovanni, 'no?'

'No,' said Guillaume, to whom leaving the bar, at the moment, would have seemed like being driven from the promised land, 'let us first have a drink, here at the bar, with Madame.'

Guillaume's suggestion had the effect—but subtly, as though a wind had blown over everything or a light been imperceptibly intensified—of creating among the people at the bar, a *troupe*, who would now play various roles in a play they knew very well. Madame Clothilde would demur, as, indeed, she instantly did, but only for a moment; then she would accept, it would be something expensive; it turned out to be champagne. She would sip it, making the most noncommittal conversation, so that she could vanish out of it a split-second before Guillaume had established contact with one of the boys at the bar. As for the boys at the bar, they were each invisibly preening, having already calculated how much money he and his *copain* would need for the next few days, having already appraised Guillaume to within a decimal of that figure, and having already estimated how long

Guillaume, as a fountainhead, would last, and also how long they would be able to endure him. The only question left was whether they would be *vache* with him, or *chic*, but they knew that they would probably be *vache*. There was also Jacques, who might turn out to be a bonus, or merely a consolation prize. There was me, of course, another matter altogether, innocent of apartments, soft beds, or food, a candidate, therefore, for affection, but, as Giovanni's *môme*, out of honorable reach. Their only means, practically at least, of conveying their affection for Giovanni and me was to relieve us of these two old men. So that there was added, to the roles they were about to play, a certain, jolly aura of conviction and, to self-interest, an altruistic glow.

I ordered black coffee and a cognac, a large one. Giovanni was far from me, drinking *marc* between an old man who looked like a receptacle of all the world's dirt and disease and a young boy, a redhead, who would look like that man one day, if one could read, in the dullness of his eye, anything so real as a future. Now, however, he had something of a horse's dreadful beauty; some suggestion, too, of the storm trooper; covertly, he was watching Guillaume; he knew that both Guillaume and Jacques were watching him. Guillaume chatted, meanwhile, with Madame Clothilde, they were agreeing that business was awful, that all standards had been debased by the *nouveau riche*, and that the country needed DeGaulle. Luckily, they had both had this conversation so many times before that it ran, so to speak, all by itself, demanding of them nothing in the way of concentration. Jacques would, shortly, offer one of the boys a drink but, for the moment, he wished to play uncle to me.

'How do you feel?' he asked me. 'This is a very important day for you.'

'I feel fine,' I said. 'How do you feel?'

'Like a man,' he said, 'who has seen a vision.'

'Yes?' I said. 'Tell me about this vision.'

'I am not joking,' he said. 'I am talking about you. *You* were the vision. You should have seen yourself tonight. You should see yourself now.'

I looked at him and said nothing.

'You are—how old? Twenty-six or seven? I am nearly twice

that and, let me tell you, you are lucky. You are lucky that what is happening to you now is happening *now* and not when you are forty, or something like that, when there would be no hope for you and you would simply be destroyed.'

'What is happening to me?' I asked. I had meant to sound sardonic but I did not sound sardonic at all.

He did not answer this, but sighed, looking briefly in the direction of the redhead. Then he turned to me. 'Are you going to write to Hella?'

'I very often do,' I said. 'I suppose I will again.'

'That does not answer my question.'

'Oh. I was under the impression that you had asked me if I was going to write to Hella.'

'Well. Let's put it another way. Are you going to write to Hella about this night and this morning?'

'I really don't see what there is to write about. But what's it to you if I do or I don't?'

He gave me a look full of a certain despair which I had not, till that moment, known was in him. It frightened me. 'It's not,' he said, 'what it is to *me*. It's what it is to *you*. And to her. And to that poor boy, yonder, who doesn't know that when he looks at you the way he does, he is simply putting his head in the lion's mouth. Are you going to treat them as you've treated me?'

'*You?* What have *you* to do with all this? How have I treated *you?*'

'You have been very unfair to me,' he said. 'You have been very dishonest.'

This time I did sound sardonic. 'I suppose you mean that I would have been fair, I would have been honest if I had— if—'

'I mean you could have been fair to me by despising me a little less.'

'I'm sorry. But I think, since you bring it up, that a lot of your life *is* despicable.'

'I could say the same about yours,' said Jacques. 'There are so many ways of being despicable it quite makes one's head spin. But the way to be really despicable is to be contemptuous of other people's pain. You ought to have some apprehension that the man you see before you was once even

younger than you are now and arrived at his present wretchedness by imperceptible degrees.'

There was silence for a moment, threatened, from a distance, by that laugh of Giovanni's.

'Tell me,' I said at last, 'is there really no other way for you
but this? To kneel down forever before an army of boys for
just five dirty minutes in the dark?'

'Think,' said Jacques, 'of the men who have kneeled before
you while you thought of something else and pretended that
nothing was happening down there in the dark between your
legs.'

I stared at the amber cognac and at the wet rings on the
metal. Deep below, trapped in the metal, the outline of my
own face looked upward hopelessly at me.

'You think,' he persisted, 'that my life is shameful because
my encounters are. And they are. But you should ask yourself
why they are.'

'Why are they—shameful?' I asked him.

'Because there is no affection in them, and no joy. It's like
putting an electric plug in a dead socket. Touch, but no contact. All touch, but no contact and no light.'

I asked him: 'Why?'

'That you must ask yourself,' he told me, 'and perhaps one
day this morning will not be ashes in your mouth.'

I looked over at Giovanni, who now had one arm around
the ruined looking girl, who could have once been very beautiful but who never would be now.

Jacques followed my look. 'He is very fond of you,' he said,
'already. But this doesn't make you happy or proud, as it
should. It makes you frightened and ashamed. Why?'

'I don't understand him,' I said at last. 'I don't know what
his friendship means, I don't know what he means by friendship.'

Jacques laughed. 'You don't know what he means by
friendship but you have the feeling it may not be safe. You
are afraid it may change you. What kind of friendships have
you had?'

I said nothing.

'Or for that matter,' he continued, 'what kind of love affairs?'

I was silent for so long that he teased me, saying, 'Come out, come out, wherever you are!'

And I grinned, feeling chilled.

'Love him,' said Jacques, with vehemence, 'love him and let him love you. Do you think anything else under heaven really matters? And how long, at the best, can it last? since you are both men and still have everywhere to go? Only five minutes, I assure you, only five minutes, and most of that, *helas!* in the dark. And if you think of them as dirty, then they *will* be dirty—they will be dirty because you will be giving nothing, you will be despising your flesh and his. But you can make your time together anything but dirty, you can give each other something which will make both of you better—forever—if you will *not* be ashamed, if you will only *not* play it safe.' He paused, watching me, and then looked down to his cognac. 'You play it safe long enough,' he said, in a different tone, 'and you'll end up trapped in your own dirty body, forever and forever and forever—like me.' And he finished his cognac, ringing his glass slightly on the bar to attract the attention of Madame Clothilde.

She came at once, beaming; and in that moment Guillaume dared to smile at the redhead. Mme. Clothilde poured Jacques a fresh cognac and looked questioningly at me, the bottle poised over my half full glass. I hesitated.

'*Et pourquoi pas?*' she asked, with a smile.

So I finished my glass and she filled it. Then, for the briefest of seconds, she glanced at Guillaume; who cried, '*Et le rouquin la!* What's the redhead drinking?'

Mme. Clothilde turned with the air of an actress about to deliver the severely restrained last lines of an exhausting and mighty part. '*On t'offre, Pierre,*' she said, majestically. 'What will you have?'—holding slightly aloft meanwhile the bottle containing the most expensive cognac in the house.

'*Je prendrai un petit cognac,*' Pierre mumbled after a moment and, oddly enough, he blushed, which made him, in the light of the pale, just rising sun, resemble a freshly fallen angel.

Mme. Clothilde filled Pierre's glass and, amid a beautifully resolving tension, as of slowly dimming lights, replaced the bottle on the shelf and walked back to the cash-register; off-stage, in effect, into the wings, where she began to recover herself by finishing the last of the champagne. She sighed and sipped and looked outward contentedly into the slowly rising morning. Guillaume had murmured a *'Je m'excuse un instant, Madame,'* and now passed behind us on his way to the red-head.

I smiled. 'Things my father never told me.'

'Somebody,' said Jacques, 'your father or mine, should have told us that not many people have ever died of love. But multitudes have perished, and are perishing every hour—and in the oddest places!—for the lack of it.' And then: 'Here comes your baby. *Sois sage. Sois chic.'*

He moved slightly away and began talking to the boy next to him.

And here my baby came indeed, through all that sunlight, his face flushed and his hair flying, his eyes, unbelievably, like morning stars. 'It was not very nice of me to go off for so long,' he said, 'I hope you have not been too bored.'

'You certainly haven't been,' I told him. 'You look like a kid about five years old waking up on Christmas morning.'

This delighted, even flattered him, as I could see from the way he now humorously pursed his lips. 'I am sure I cannot look like that,' he said. 'I was always disappointed on Christmas morning.'

'Well, I mean very *early* on Christmas morning, before you saw what was under the tree.' But his eyes have somehow made of my last statement a *double entendre*, and we are both laughing.

'Are you hungry?' he asked.

'Perhaps I would be if I were alive and sober. I don't know. Are you?'

'I think we should eat,' he said, with no conviction whatever, and we began to laugh again.

'Well,' I said, 'what shall we eat?'

'I scarcely dare suggest white wine and oysters,' said Giovanni, 'but that is really the best thing after such a night.'

'Well, let's do that,' I said, 'while we can still walk to the dining room.' I looked beyond him to Guillaume and the redhead, they had apparently found something to talk about, I could not imagine what it was; and Jacques was deep in conversation with the tall, very young, pockmarked boy, whose turtleneck black sweater made him seem even paler and thinner than he actually was. He had been playing the pinball machine when we came in, his name appeared to be Yves. 'Are they going to eat now?' I asked Giovanni.

'Perhaps not now,' said Giovanni, 'but they are certainly going to eat. Everyone is very hungry.' I took this to refer more to the boys than to our friends, and we passed into the dining room, which was now empty, the waiter nowhere in sight.

'Mme. Clothilde!' shouted Giovanni, *'on mange ici, non?'*

This shout produced an answering shout from Mme. Clothilde and also produced the waiter, whose jacket was less spotless, seen in closeup, than it had seemed from a distance. It also officially announced our presence in the dining room to Jacques and Guillaume and must have definitely increased, in the eyes of the boys they were talking to, a certain tigerish intensity of affection.

'We'll eat quickly and go,' said Giovanni. 'After all, I have to work tonight.'

'Did you meet Guillaume here?' I asked him.

He grimaced, looking down. 'No. That is a long story.' He grinned. 'No, I did not meet him here. I met him'—he laughed—'in a cinema!' We both laughed. *'C'etait un film du far west, avec Gary Cooper.'* This seemed terribly funny, too, we kept laughing until the waiter came with our bottle of white wine.

'Well,' said Giovanni, sipping the wine, his eyes damp, 'after the last gun-shot had been fired and all the music came up to celebrate the triumph of goodness and I came up the aisle, I bumped into this man—Guillaume—and I excused myself and walked into the lobby. Then here he came, after me, with a long story about leaving his scarf in *my* seat because, it appeared, he had been sitting *behind* me, you understand, with his coat and his scarf on the seat *before* him and when I sat down I pulled his scarf down with me. Well, I told him I didn't work for the cinema and I told him what he could do with his scarf—but I did not really get angry because he made me want to laugh. He said that all the people who worked for the cinema were thieves and he was sure that they would keep it if they so much as laid eyes on it, and it was very expensive, and a gift from his mother and—oh, I assure you, not even Garbo ever gave such a performance. So I went back and of course there was no scarf there and when I told him this it seemed he would fall dead right there in the lobby. And by this time, you understand, everybody thought we were to-gether and I didn't know whether to kick him or the people who were looking at us; but he was very well dressed, of course, and I was not and so I thought, well, we had better get out of this lobby. So we went to a cafe and sat on the terrace and when he had got over his grief about the scarf and what his mother would say and so on and so on, he asked me to have supper with him. Well, naturally, I said no, I had certainly had enough of him by that time, but the only way I could prevent another scene, right there on the terrace, was to promise to have supper with him a few days later—I did not intend to go,' he said, with a shy grin, 'but when the day came I had not eaten for a long time and I was very hungry.' He looked at me and I saw in his face again something which I have fleetingly seen there during these hours: under his beauty and his bravado, terror, and a terrible desire to please; dreadfully, dreadfully moving, and it made me want, in an-guish, to reach out and comfort him.

Our oysters came and we began to eat. Giovanni sat in the sun, his black hair gathering to itself the yellow glow of the wine and the many dull colors of the oyster where the sun struck it.

'Well'—with his mouth turned down—'dinner was awful, of course, since he can make scenes in his apartment, too. But by this time I knew he owned a bar and was a French citizen. I am not and I had no job and no *carte de travail*. So I saw that he could be useful if I could only find some way to make him keep his hands off me. I did not, I must say'—this with that look at me—'altogether succeed in remaining untouched by him, he has more hands than an octopus, and no dignity whatever, *but*'—grimly throwing down another oyster and re-filling our glasses of wine—'I *do* now have a *carte de travail* and I have a job. Which pays very well,' he grinned, 'it appears that I am good for business. For this reason, he leaves me mostly alone.' He looked out into the bar. 'He is really not a man at all,' he said, with a sorrow and bewilderment at once childlike and ancient, 'I do not know what he is, he is horrible. But I will keep my *carte de travail*. The job is another matter, but'—he knocked wood—'we have had no trouble now for nearly three weeks.'

'But you think that trouble is coming,' I said.

'Oh, yes,' said Giovanni, with a quick, startled look at me, as if he were wondering if I had understood a word of what he had said, 'we are certainly going to have a little trouble soon again. Not right away, of course, that is not his style. But he will invent something to be angry at me about.'

Then we sat in silence for awhile, smoking cigarettes, surrounded by oyster shells, and finishing the wine. I was all at once very tired. I looked out into the narrow street, this strange, crooked corner where we sat, which was brazen now with the sunlight and heavy with people—people I would never understand. I ached abruptly, intolerably, with a longing to go home; not to that hotel, in one of the alleys of Paris, where the concierge barred the way with my unpaid bill; but home, home across the ocean, to things and people I knew and understood; to those things, those places, those people which I would always, helplessly, and in whatever bitterness of spirit, love above all else. I had never realized such a sentiment in myself before, and it frightened me. I saw myself, sharply, as a wanderer, an adventurer, rocking through the world, unanchored. I looked at Giovanni's face, which did not help me. He belonged to this strange city, which did not belong to me. I began to see that, while what was happening to me was not so strange as it would have comforted me to believe, yet it was strange beyond belief. It was not really so strange, so unprecedented, though voices deep within me boomed, For shame! For shame! that I should be so abruptly, so hideously entangled with a boy; what was strange was that this was but one tiny aspect of the dreadful human tangle, occurring everywhere, without end, forever.

'*Viens,*' said Giovanni.

We rose and walked back into the bar and Giovanni paid our bill. Another bottle of champagne had been opened and Jacques and Guillaume were now really beginning to be drunk. It was going to be ghastly and I wondered if those poor, patient boys were ever going to get anything to eat.

Giovanni talked to Guillaume for a moment, agreeing to open up the bar; Jacques was too busy with the pale, tall boy to have much time for me; we said good-morning and left them.

'I must go home,' I said to Giovanni when we were in the street. 'I must pay my hotel bill.'

Giovanni stared. *'Mais tu es fou,'* he said, mildly. 'There is certainly no point in going home now, to face an ugly concierge and then go to sleep in that room all by yourself and then wake up later, with a terrible stomach and a sour mouth, wanting to commit suicide. Come with me, we will rise at a civilized hour, and have a gentle aperitif somewhere and then a little dinner. It will be much more cheerful like that,' he said, with a smile, 'you will see.'

'But I must get my clothes,' I said.

He took my arm. *'Bien sûr.* But you do not have to get them *now.'* I held back. He stopped. 'Come. I am sure that I am much prettier than your wall-paper—or your concierge. I will smile at you when you wake up. They will not.'

'Ah,' I could only say, *'tu es vache.'*

'It is you who are *vache,'* he said, 'to want to leave me alone in this lonely place when you know that I am far too drunk to reach my home unaided.'

We laughed together, both caught up in a stinging, teasing sort of game. We reached the Boulevard Sebastopol. 'But we will not any longer discuss the painful subject of how you desired to desert Giovanni, at so dangerous an hour, in the middle of a hostile city.' I began to realize that he, too, was nervous. Far down the boulevard a cab meandered toward us, and he put up his hand. 'I will show you my room,' he said, 'it is perfectly clear that you would have to see it one of these days, anyway.' The taxi stopped beside us, and Giovanni, as though he were suddenly afraid that I would really turn and run, pushed me in before him. He got in beside me and told the driver: *'Nation.'*

The street he lived on was wide, respectable rather than elegant, and massive with fairly recent apartment buildings; the street ended in a small park. His room was in the back, on the ground floor of the last building on this street. We passed the vestibule and the elevator into a short, dark corridor which led to his room. The room was small, I only made out the outlines of clutter and disorder, there was the smell of the alcohol he burned in his stove. He locked the door behind us, and then for a moment, in the gloom, we simply stared at each other—with dismay, with relief, and breathing hard. I was trembling. I thought, if I do not open the door at once and get out of here, I am lost. But I knew I could not open the door, I knew it was too late; soon it was too late to do anything but moan. He pulled me against him, putting himself into my arms as though he were giving me himself to carry, and slowly pulled me down with him to that bed. With everything in me screaming *No!* yet the sum of me sighed *Yes.*

Here in the south of France it does not often snow; but snowflakes, in the beginning rather gently and now with more force, have been falling for the last half hour. It falls as though it might quite possibly decide to turn into a blizzard. It has been cold down here this winter, though the people of the region seem to take it as a mark of ill-breeding in a foreigner if he makes any reference to this fact. They themselves, even when their faces are burning in that wind which seems to blow from everywhere at once, and which penetrates everything, are as radiantly cheerful as children at the sea-shore. *'Il fait beau bien?'*—throwing their faces toward the lowering sky in which the celebrated southern sun has not made an appearance in days.

I leave the window of the big room and walk through the house. While I am in the kitchen, staring into the mirror—I have decided to shave before all the water turns cold—I hear a knocking at the door. Some vague, wild hope leaps in me for a second and then I realize that it is only the caretaker from across the road, come to make certain that I have not stolen the silver, or smashed the dishes or chopped up the furniture for firewood. And, indeed, she rattles the door and I hear her voice out there, cracking, *'M'sieu! M'sieu! M'sieu, l'americain!'* I wonder, with annoyance, why on earth she should sound so worried.

But she smiles at once when I open the door, a smile which weds the coquette and the mother. She is quite old and not really French; she came many years ago, 'when I was a very

young girl, sir,' from just across the border, out of Italy. She
seems, like most of the women down here, to have gone into
mourning directly the last child moved out of childhood.
Hella thought that they were all widows, but, it turned out,
most of them had husbands living yet. These husbands might
have been their sons. They sometimes played *belote* in the sunshine in a flat field near our house, and their eyes, when they
looked at Hella, contained the proud watchfulness of a father
and the watchful speculation of a man. I sometimes played
billiards with them, and drank red wine, in the *tabac*. But they
made me tense—with their ribaldries, their good-nature, their
fellowship, the life written on their hands and in their faces
and in their eyes. They treated me as the son who has but
lately been initiated into manhood; but at the same time, with
great distance, for I did not really belong to any of them; and
they also sensed (or I felt they did) something else about me,
something which it was no longer worth their while to pursue.
This seemed to be in their eyes when I walked with Hella and
they passed us on the road, saying, very respectfully, *Salut,
Monsieur-dame.* They might have been the sons of these
women in black, come home after a lifetime of storming and
conquering the world, home, to rest and be scolded and wait
for death, home to those breasts, now dry, which had nourished them in their beginnings.

Flakes of snow have drifted across the shawl which covers
her head; and hang on her eyelashes and on the wisps of black
and white hair not covered by the shawl. She is very strong
yet, though, now, a little bent, a little breathless.

'*Bonsoir, monsieur. Vous n'etes pas malade?*'

'No,' I say, 'I have not been sick. Come in.'

She comes in, closing the door behind her, and allowing
the shawl to fall from her head. I still have my drink in my
hand and she notices this, in silence.

'*Eh bien,*' she says. '*Tant mieux.* But we have not seen you
for several days. You have been staying in the house?'

And her eyes search my face.

I am embarrassed and resentful; yet it is impossible to rebuff
something at once shrewd and gentle in her eyes and voice.
'Yes,' I say, 'the weather has been bad.'

'It is not the middle of August, to be sure,' says she, 'but you do not have the air of an invalid. It is not good to sit in the house alone.'

'I am leaving in the morning,' I say, desperately. 'Did you want to take the inventory?'

'Yes,' she says, and produces from one of her pockets the list of household goods I signed upon arrival. 'It will not be long. Let me start from the back.'

We start toward the kitchen. On the way I put my drink down on the night table in my bedroom.

'It doesn't matter to me if you drink,' she says, not turning around. But I leave my drink behind anyway.

We walk into the kitchen. The kitchen is suspiciously clean and neat. 'Where have you been eating?' she asks, sharply. 'They tell me at the *tabac* you have not been seen for days. Have you been going to town?'

'Yes,' I say, lamely, 'sometimes.'

'On foot?' she inquires. 'Because the bus driver, he has not seen you, either.' All this time she is not looking at me but around the kitchen, checking off the list in her hand with a short, yellow pencil.

I can make no answer to her last, sardonic thrust, having forgotten that in a small village almost every move is made under the village's collective eye and ear.

She looks briefly in the bathroom. 'I'm going to clean that tonight,' I say.

'I should hope so,' she says. 'Everything was clean when you moved in.' We walk back through the kitchen. She has failed to notice that two glasses are missing, broken by me, and I have not the energy to tell her. I will leave some money in the cupboard. She turns on the light in the guest-room. My dirty clothes are lying all over.

'Those go with me,' I say, trying to smile.

'You could have come just across the road,' she says. 'I would have been glad to give you something to eat. A little soup, something nourishing. I cook every day for my husband, what difference does one more make?'

This touches me, but I do not know how to indicate it, and I cannot say, of course, that eating with her and her husband would have stretched my nerves to the breaking point.

She is examining a decorative pillow. 'Are you going to join your fiancée?' she asks.

I know I ought to lie, but, somehow, I cannot. I am afraid of her eyes. I wish, now, that I had my drink with me. 'No,' I say, flatly, 'she has gone to America.'

'*Tiens!*' she says. 'And you—do you stay in France?' She looks directly at me.

'For awhile,' I say. I am beginning to sweat. It has come to me that this woman, a peasant from Italy, must resemble, in so many ways, the mother of Giovanni. I keep trying not to hear her howls of anguish, I keep trying not to see in her eyes what would surely be there if she knew that her son would be dead by morning, if she knew what I had done to her son.

But, of course, she is not Giovanni's mother.

'It is not good,' she says, 'it is not right for a young man like you to be sitting alone in a great big house with no woman.' She looks, for a moment, very sad; starts to say something more and thinks better of it. I know she wants to say something about Hella, whom neither she, nor any of the other women here had liked. But she turns out the light in the guest room and we go into the big bedroom, the master bedroom, which Hella and I had used, not the one in which I have left my drink. This, too, is very clean and orderly. She looks about the room and looks at me, and smiles.

'You have not been using this room lately,' she says.

I feel myself blushing painfully. She laughs.

'But you will be happy again,' she says. 'You must go and find yourself another woman, a *good* woman, and get married, and have babies. *Yes,* that is what you ought to do,' she says, as though I had contradicted her, and before I can say anything, 'Where is your *maman?*'

'She is dead.'

'Ah!' She clicks her teeth in sympathy. 'That is sad. And your Papa—is he dead, too?'

'No. He is in America.'

'*Pauvre bambino!*' She looks at my face. I am really helpless in front of her and if she does not leave soon she will reduce me to tears or curses. 'But you do not have the intention of just wandering through the world like a sailor? I am sure that would make your mother very unhappy. You will make a home someday?'

'Yes, surely. Someday.'

She puts her strong hand on my arm. 'Even if your *maman*, she is dead—that is very sad!—your Papa will be very happy to see bambinos from you.' She pauses, her black eyes soften; she is looking at me, but she is looking beyond me, too. 'We had three sons. Two of them were killed in the war. In the war, too, we lost all our money. It is sad, is it not, to have worked so hard all one's life in order to have a little peace in one's old age and then to have it all taken away? It almost killed my husband, he has never been the same since.' Then I see that her eyes are not merely shrewd, they are also bitter and very sad. She shrugs her shoulders. 'Ah! What can one do? It is better not to think about it.' Then she smiles. 'But our last son, he lives in the north, he came to see us two years ago, and he brought with him his little boy. His little boy, he was only four years old then. He was so beautiful! Mario, he is called.' She gestures. 'It is my husband's name. They stayed about ten days and we felt young again.'' She smiles again. 'Especially my husband.' And she stands there a moment with this smile on her face. Then she asks, abruptly, 'Do you pray?'

I wonder if I can stand this another moment. 'No,' I stammer. 'No. Not often.'

'But you are a believer?'

I smile. It is not even a patronizing smile, though, perhaps, I wish it could be. 'Yes.'

But I wonder what my smile could have looked like. It did not reassure her. 'You must pray,' she says, very soberly. 'I assure you. Even just a little prayer, from time to time. Light a little candle. If it were not for the prayers of the blessed saints one could not live in this world at all. I speak to you,' she says, drawing herself up slightly, 'as though I were your *maman*. Do not be offended.'

'But I am not offended. You are very nice. You are very nice to speak to me this way.'

She smiles a satisfied smile. 'Men—not just babies like you, but old men, too—they always need a woman to tell them the truth. *Les hommes, ils sont impossible.*' And she smiles, and forces me to smile at the cunning of this universal joke, and turns out the light in the master bedroom. We go down the hall again, thank heaven, to my drink. This bedroom, of course, is quite untidy, the light burning, my bathrobe, books, dirty socks, and a couple of dirty glasses, and a coffee cup half full of stale coffee—lying around, all over the place; and the sheets on the bed a tangled mess.

'I'll fix this up before morning,' I say.

'*Bien sûr.*' She sighs. 'You really must take my advice, monsieur, and get married.' At this, suddenly, we both laugh. Then I finish my drink.

The inventory is almost done. We go into the last room, the big room, where the bottle is, before the window. She looks at the bottle, then at me. 'But you will be drunk by morning,' she says.

'Oh, no! I'm taking the bottle *with* me.'

It is quite clear that she knows this is not true. But she shrugs her shoulders again. Then she becomes, by the act of wrapping the shawl around her head, very formal, even a little shy. Now that I see she is about to leave I wish I could think of something to make her stay. When she has gone back across the road, the night will be blacker and longer than ever. I have something to say to her—to her?—but of course it will never be said. I feel that I want to be forgiven, I want *her* to forgive me. But I do not know how to state my crime. My crime, in some odd way, is in being a man and she knows all about this already. It is terrible how naked she makes me feel, like a half grown boy, naked before his mother.

She puts out her hand. I take it, awkwardly.

'*Bon voyage, monsieur.* I hope that you were happy while you were here and that, perhaps, one day, you will visit us again.' She is smiling and her eyes are kind but now the smile is purely social, it is the graceful termination of a business deal.

'Thank you,' I say. 'Perhaps I will be back next year.' She releases my hand and we walk to the door.

'Oh!' she says, at the door, 'please do not wake me up in the morning. Put the keys in my mailbox. I do not, any more, have any reason to get up so early.'

'Surely.' I smile and open the door. 'Goodnight, Madame.'

'*Bonsoir, Monsieur. Adieu!*' She steps out into the darkness. But there is a light coming from my house and from her house across the road. The town lights glimmer beneath us and I hear, briefly, the sea again.

She walks a little away from me, and turns. *'Souvenez-vous,'* she tells me. 'One must make a little prayer from time to time.'

And I close the door.

She has made me realize that I have much to do before morning. I decide to clean the bathroom before I allow myself another drink. And I begin to do this, first scrubbing out the tub, then running water into the pail to mop the floor. The bathroom is tiny and square, with one frosted window. It reminds me of that claustrophobic room in Paris. Giovanni had had great plans for remodelling the room and there was a time, when he had actually begun to do this, when we lived with plaster all over everything and bricks piled on the floor. We took packages of bricks out of the house at night and left them in the streets.

I suppose they will come for him early in the morning, perhaps just before dawn, so that the last thing Giovanni will ever see will be that grey, lightless sky over Paris, beneath which we stumbled homeward together so many desperate and drunken mornings.

I REMEMBER that life in that room seemed to be occurring beneath the sea, time flowed past indifferently above us, hours and days had no meaning. In the beginning our life together held a joy and amazement which was new-born every day. Beneath the joy, of course, was anguish and beneath the amazement was fear; but they did not work themselves to the beginning until our high beginning was aloes on our tongues. By then anguish and fear had become the surface on which we slipped and slid, losing balance, dignity, and pride. Giovanni's face, which I had memorized so many mornings, noons, and nights, hardened before my eyes, began to give in secret places, began to crack. The light in the eyes became a glitter, the wide and beautiful brow began to suggest the skull beneath. The sensual lips turned inward, busy with the sorrow overflowing from his heart. It became a stranger's face—or it made me so guilty to look on him that I wished it were a stranger's face. Not all my memorizing had prepared me for the metamorphosis which my memorizing had helped to bring about.

Our day began before daybreak, when I drifted over to Guillaume's bar in time for a pre-closing drink. Sometimes, when Guillaume had closed the bar to the public, a few friends and Giovanni and myself stayed behind for breakfast and music. Sometimes Jacques was there—from the time of our meeting with Giovanni he seemed to come out more and more. If we had breakfast with Guillaume, we usually left around seven o'clock in the morning. Sometimes, when Jacques was there, he offered to drive us home in the car which he had suddenly and inexplicably bought, but we almost always walked the long way home along the river.

Spring was approaching Paris. Walking up and down this house tonight, I see again the river, the cobblestoned *quais*, the bridges. Low boats passed beneath the bridges and on those boats one sometimes saw women hanging washing out to dry. Sometimes we saw a young man in a canoe, energetically rowing, looking rather helpless, and, also, rather silly. There were yachts tied up along the banks from time to time, and house-boats, and barges; we passed the firehouse so often on our way home that the firemen got to know us. When winter came again and Giovanni found himself in hiding in one of these barges, it was a fireman, who, seeing him crawl back into hiding with a loaf of bread one night, tipped off the police.

The trees grew green those mornings, the river dropped, and the brown winter smoke dropped downward out of it, and fishermen appeared. Giovanni was right about the fishermen, they certainly never seemed to catch anything, but it gave them something to do. Along the *quais* the bookstalls seemed to become almost festive, awaiting the weather which would allow the passerby to leaf idly through the dog-eared books, and which would inform the tourist with a passionate desire to carry off to the United States, or Denmark, more colored prints than he could afford, or, when he got home, know what to do with. Also, the girls appeared on their bicycles, along with boys similarly equipped, and we sometimes saw them along the river, as the light began to fade, their bicycles put away until the morrow. This was after Giovanni had lost his job and we walked around in the evenings. Those evenings were bitter. Giovanni knew that I was going to leave him but he did not dare accuse me for fear of being corroborated. I did not dare to tell him. Hella was on her way back from Spain and my father had agreed to send me money, which I was not going to use to help Giovanni, who had done so much to help me. I was going to use it to escape his room.

Every morning the sky and the sun seemed to be a little higher and the river stretched before us with a greater haze of promise. Every day the book-stall keepers seemed to have taken off another garment, so that the shape of their bodies appeared to be undergoing a most striking and continual metamorphosis. One began to wonder what the final shape would be. It was observable, through open windows on the *quais* and sidestreets, that *hoteliers* had called in painters to paint the rooms; the women in the dairies had taken off their blue sweaters and rolled up the sleeves of their dresses, so that one saw their powerful arms; the bread seemed warmer and fresher in the bakeries. The small school children had taken off their capes and their knees were no longer scarlet with the cold. There seemed to be more chatter—in that curiously measured and vehement language, which sometimes reminds me of stiffening egg white and sometimes of stringed instruments but always of the underside and aftermath of passion.

But we did not often have breakfast in Guillaume's bar because Guillaume did not like me. Usually I simply waited around, as inconspicuously as possible, until Giovanni had finished cleaning up the bar and had changed his clothes. Then we said good-night and left. The habitues had evolved toward us a curious attitude, composed of an unpleasant maternalism, and envy, and disguised dislike. They could not, somehow, speak to us as they spoke to one another and they resented the strain we imposed on them of speaking in any other way. And it made them furious that the dead center of their lives was, in this instance, none of their business. It made them feel their poverty again, through the narcotics of chatter, and dreams of conquest, and mutual contempt.

Wherever we ate breakfast, and wherever we walked, when we got home we were always too tired to sleep right away. We made coffee and sometimes drank cognac with it; we sat on the bed and talked and smoked. We seemed to have a great deal to tell—or Giovanni did. Even at my most candid, even when I tried hardest to give myself to him as he gave himself to me, I was holding something back. I did not, for example, really tell him about Hella until I had been living in the room a month. I told him about her then because her letters had begun to sound as though she would be coming back to Paris very soon.

'What is she doing, wandering around through Spain alone?' asked Giovanni.

'She likes to travel,' I said.

'Oh,' said Giovanni, 'nobody likes to travel, especially not women. There must be some other reason.' He raised his eyebrows suggestively. 'Perhaps she has a Spanish lover and is afraid to tell you—? Perhaps she is with a *torero*.'

Perhaps she is, I thought. 'But she wouldn't be afraid to tell me.'

Giovanni laughed. 'I do not understand Americans at all,' he said.

'I don't see that there's anything very hard to understand. We aren't married, you know.'

'But she is your mistress, no?' asked Giovanni.

'Yes.'

'And she is still your mistress?'

I stared at him. 'Of course,' I said.

'Well then,' said Giovanni, 'I do not understand what she is doing in Spain while you are in Paris.' Another thought struck him. 'How old is she?'

'She's two years younger than I am.' I watched him. 'What's that got to do with it?'

'Is she married? I mean to somebody else, naturally.'

I laughed. He laughed too. 'Of course not.'

'Well, I thought she might be an older woman,' said Giovanni, 'with a husband somewhere and perhaps she had to go away with him from time to time in order to be able to continue her affair with you. That would be a nice arrangement. Those women are sometimes *very* interesting and they usually have a little money. If *that* woman was in Spain, she would bring back a wonderful gift for you. But a young girl, bouncing around in a foreign country by herself—I do not like that at all. You should find another mistress.'

It all seemed very funny. I could not stop laughing. 'Do *you* have a mistress?' I asked him.

'Not now,' he said, 'but perhaps I will again one day.' He half frowned, half smiled. 'I don't seem to be very interested in women right now—I don't know why. I used to be. Perhaps I will be again.' He shrugged. 'Perhaps it is because women are just a little more trouble than I can afford right now. *Et puis*'— He stopped.

I wanted to say that it seemed to me that he had taken a most peculiar road out of his trouble; but I only said, after a moment, cautiously: 'You don't seem to have a very high opinion of women.'

'Oh, women! There is no need, thank heaven, to have an opinion about *women*. Women are like water. They are tempting like that, and they can be that treacherous, and they can seem to be that bottomless, you know?—and they can be that shallow. And that dirty.' He stopped. 'I perhaps don't like women very much, that's true. That hasn't stopped me from making love to many and loving one or two. But most of the time—most of the time I made love only with the body.'

'That can make one very lonely,' I said. I had not expected to say it.

He had not expected to hear it. He looked at me and reached out and touched me on the cheek. 'Yes,' he said. Then: 'I am not trying to be *méchant* when I talk about women. I respect women—very much—for their inside life, which is not like the life of a man.'

'Women don't seem to like that idea,' I said.

'Oh, well,' said Giovanni, 'these absurd women running around today, full of ideas and nonsense, and thinking themselves equal to men—*quelle rigolade!*—they need to be beaten half to death so that they can find out who rules the world.'

I laughed. 'Did the women you knew like to get beaten?'

He smiled. 'I don't know if they liked it. But a beating never made them go away.' We both laughed. 'They were not, anyway, like that silly little girl of yours, wandering all over Spain and sending postcards back to Paris. What does she think she is doing? Does she want you or does she not want you?'

'She went to Spain,' I said, 'to find out.'

Giovanni opened his eyes wide. He was indignant. 'To Spain? Why not to China? What is she doing, testing all the Spaniards and comparing them with you?'

I was a little annoyed. 'You don't understand,' I said. 'She is a very intelligent, very complex girl, she wanted to go away and think.'

'What is there to think about? She sounds rather silly, I must say. She just can't make up her mind what bed to sleep in. She wants to eat her cake and she wants to have it all.'

'If she were in Paris now,' I said, abruptly, 'then I would not be in this room with you.'

'You would possibly not be living here,' he conceded, 'but we would certainly be seeing each other, why not?'

'Why *not*? Suppose she found out?'

'Found *out*? Found out what?'

'Oh, stop it,' I said. 'You know what there is to find out.'

He looked at me very soberly. 'She sounds more and more impossible, this little girl of yours. What does she do, follow you everywhere? Or will she hire detectives to sleep under our bed? And what business is it of hers, anyway?'

'You can't possibly be serious,' I said.

'I certainly can be,' he retorted, 'and I am. You are the incomprehensible one.' He groaned and poured more coffee and picked up our cognac from the floor. '*Chez toi* everything sounds extremely feverish and complicated, like one of those English murder mysteries. To find out, to find out, you keep saying, as though we were accomplices in a crime. We have not committed any crime.' He poured the cognac.

'It's just that she'll be terribly hurt if she does find out, that's all. People have very dirty words for—for this situation.' I stopped. His face suggested that my reasoning was flimsy. I added, defensively, 'Besides, it *is* a crime—in my country and, after all, I didn't grow up here, I grew up *there*.'

'If dirty words frighten you,' said Giovanni, 'I really do not know how you have managed to live so long. People are full of dirty words. The only time they do not use them, most people I mean, is when they are describing something dirty.' He paused and we watched each other. In spite of what he was saying he looked rather frightened himself. 'If your countrymen think that privacy is a crime, so much the worse for your country. And as for this girl of yours—are you always at her side when she is here? I mean, all day, every day? You go out sometimes to have a drink alone, no? Maybe you sometimes take a walk without her—to think, as you say. The Americans seem to do a great deal of thinking. And perhaps while you are thinking and having that drink, you look at another girl who passes, no? Maybe you even look up at that sky and feel your own blood in you? Or does everything stop when Hella comes? No drinks alone, no looks at other girls, no sky? Eh? Answer me.'

'I've told you already that we're not married. But I don't seem to be able to make you understand anything at all this morning.'

'But anyway—when Hella is here you do sometimes see other people—without Hella?'

'Of course.'

'And does she make you tell her everything you have done while you were not with her?'

I sighed. I had lost control of the conversation somewhere along the line and I simply wanted it to end. I drank my cognac too fast and it burned my throat. 'Of course not.'

'Well. You are a very charming and good-looking and civilized boy and, unless you are impotent, I do not see what she has to complain about, or what you have to worry about. To arrange, *mon cher, la vie pratique,* is very simple—it only has to be done.' He reflected. 'Sometimes things go wrong, I agree, then you have to arrange it another way. But it is certainly not the English melodrama you make it. Why, that way, life would simply be unbearable.' He poured more cognac and grinned at me, as though he had solved all my problems. And there was something so artless in this smile that I had to smile back. Giovanni liked to believe that he was hard-headed and that I was not and that he was teaching me the stony facts of life. It was very important for him to feel this: it was because he knew, unwillingly, at the very bottom of his heart, that I, helplessly, at the very bottom of mine, resisted him with all my strength.

Eventually we grew still, we fell silent, and we slept. We awoke around three or four in the afternoon, when the dull sun was prying at odd corners of the cluttered room. We arose and washed and shaved, bumping into each other and making jokes and furious with the unstated desire to escape the room. Then we danced out into the streets, into Paris, and ate quickly somewhere, and I left Giovanni at the door to Guillaume's bar.

Then I, alone, and relieved to be alone, perhaps went to a movie, or walked, or returned home and read, or sat in a park and read, or sat on a cafe terrace, or talked to people, or wrote letters. I wrote to Hella, telling her nothing, or I wrote to my father asking for money. And no matter what I was doing, another me sat in my belly, absolutely cold with terror over the question of my life.

Giovanni had awakened an itch, had released a gnaw in me. I realized it one afternoon, when I was taking him to work via the boulevard Montparnasse. We had bought a kilo of cherries and we were eating them as we walked along. We

were both insufferably childish and high-spirited that afternoon and the spectacle we presented, two grown men, jostling
each other on the wide sidewalk, and aiming the cherry-pits,
as though they were spitballs, into each other's faces, must
have been outrageous. And I realized that such childishness
was fantastic at my age and the happiness out of which it
sprang yet more so; for that moment I really loved Giovanni,
who had never seemed more beautiful than he was that afternoon. And, watching his face, I realized that it meant much
to me that I could make his face so bright. I saw that I might
be willing to give a great deal not to lose that power. And I
felt myself flow toward him, as a river rushes when the ice
breaks up. Yet, at that very moment, there passed between us
on the pavement another boy, a stranger, and I invested him
at once with Giovanni's beauty and what I felt for Giovanni
I also felt for him. Giovanni saw this and saw my face and it
made him laugh the more. I blushed and he kept laughing
and then the boulevard, the light, the sound of his laughter
turned into a scene from a nightmare. I kept looking at the
trees, the light falling through the leaves. I felt sorrow and
shame and panic and great bitterness. At the same time—it
was part of my turmoil and also outside it—I felt the muscles
in my neck tighten with the effort I was making not to turn
my head and watch that boy diminish down the bright avenue.
The beast which Giovanni had awakened in me would never
go to sleep again; but one day I would not be with Giovanni
anymore. And would I then, like all the others, find myself
turning and following all kinds of boys down God knows what
dark avenues, into what dark places?

With this fearful intimation there opened in me a hatred for
Giovanni which was as powerful as my love and which was
nourished by the same roots.

2

I SCARCELY know how to describe that room. It became, in a way, every room I had ever been in and every room I find myself in hereafter will remind me of Giovanni's room. I did not really stay there very long—we met before the spring began and I left there during the summer—but it still seems to me that I spent a lifetime there. Life in that room seemed to be occurring underwater, as I say, and it is certain that I underwent a sea-change there.

To begin with, the room was not large enough for two, it looked out on a small courtyard. 'Looked out' means only that the room had two windows, against which the courtyard malevolently pressed, encroaching day by day, as though it had confused itself with a jungle. We, or rather Giovanni kept the windows closed most of the time; he had never bought any curtains, neither did we buy any while I was in the room; to insure privacy, Giovanni had obscured the window panes with a heavy, white cleaning polish. We sometimes heard children playing outside our window, sometimes strange shapes loomed against it. At such moments, Giovanni, working in the room, or lying in bed, would stiffen like a hunting dog and remain perfectly silent until whatever seemed to threaten our safety had moved away.

He had always had great plans for remodelling this room and before I arrived he had already begun. One of the walls was a dirty, streaked white where he had torn off the wallpaper. The wall facing it was destined never to be uncovered and on this wall a lady in a hoop skirt and a man in knee breeches perpetually walked together, hemmed in by roses. The wall paper lay on the floor, in great sheets and scrolls, in dust. On the floor also, lay our dirty laundry, along with Giovanni's tools and the paint brushes and the bottles of oil and turpentine. Our suitcases teetered on top of something, so that we dreaded ever having to open them and sometimes went without some minor necessity, such as clean socks, for days.

No one ever came to see us, except Jacques, and he did not

come often. We were far from the center of the city and we had no phone.

I remember the first afternoon I woke up there, with Giovanni fast asleep beside me, heavy as a fallen rock. The sun filtered through the room so faintly that I was worried about the time. I stealthily lit a cigarette, for I did not want to wake Giovanni. I did not yet know how I would face his eyes. I looked about me. Giovanni had said something in the taxi about his room being very dirty. 'I'm sure it is,' I had said lightly, and turned away from him, looking out of the window. Then we had both been silent. When I woke up in his room, I remembered that there had been something strained and painful in the quality of that silence; which had been broken when Giovanni said, with a shy, bitter smile: 'I must find some poetic figure.'

And he spread his heavy fingers in the air, as though a metaphor were tangible. I watched him.

'Look at the garbage of this city,' he said, finally, and his fingers indicated the flying street, 'all of the garbage of this city? Where do they take it? I don't know where they take it— but it might very well be my room.'

'It's much more likely,' I said, 'that they dump it into the Seine.'

But I sensed, when I woke up and looked around the room, the bravado and the cowardice of his figure of speech. This was not the garbage of Paris, which would have been anonymous: this was Giovanni's regurgitated life.

Before and beside me and all over the room, towering like a wall, were boxes of cardboard and leather, some tied with string, some locked, some bursting, and out of the topmost box before me spilled down sheets of violin music. There was a violin in the room, lying on the table in its warped, cracked case—it was impossible to guess from looking at it whether it had been laid to rest there yesterday or a hundred years before. The table was loaded with yellowing newspapers and empty bottles and it held a single brown and wrinkled potato in which even the sprouting eyes were rotten. Red wine had been spilled on the floor, it had been allowed to dry and it made the air in the room sweet and heavy. But it was not the room's disorder which was frightening; it was the fact that when one began searching for the key to this disorder one realized that it was not to be found in any of the usual places. For this was not a matter of habit or circumstance or temperament; it was a matter of punishment and grief. I do not know how I knew this, but I knew it at once; perhaps I knew it because I wanted to live. And I stared at the room with the same, nervous, calculating extension of the intelligence and of all one's forces which occurs when gauging a mortal and unavoidable danger: at the silent walls of the room with its distant, archaic lovers trapped in an interminable rose garden, and the staring windows, staring like two great eyes of ice and fire, and the ceiling which lowered like those clouds out of which fiends have sometimes spoken and which obscured but failed to soften its malevolence behind the yellow light which hung like a diseased and undefinable sex in its center. Under this blunted arrow, this smashed flower of light lay the terrors which encompassed Giovanni's soul. I understood why Giovanni had wanted me and had brought me to his last retreat. I was to destroy this room and give to Giovanni a new and better life. This life could only be my own, which, in order to transform Giovanni's, must first become a part of Giovanni's room.

In the beginning, because the motives which led me to Giovanni's room were so mixed; had so little to do with his hopes and desires and were so deeply a part of my own desperation, I invented in myself a kind of pleasure in playing the housewife after Giovanni had gone to work. I threw out the paper, the bottles, the fantastic accumulation of trash, I examined the contents of the innumerable boxes and suitcases and disposed of them. But I am not a housewife—men never can be housewives. And the pleasure was never real or deep, though Giovanni smiled his humble, grateful smile and told me in as many ways as he could find how wonderful it was to have me there, how I stood, with my love and my ingenuity, between him and the dark. Each day he invited me to witness how he had changed, how love had changed him, how he worked and sang and cherished me. I was in a terrible confusion. Sometimes I thought, but this *is* your life. Stop fighting it. Stop fighting. Or I thought, but I am happy. And he loves me. I am safe. Sometimes, when he was not near me, I thought, I will never let him touch me again. Then, when he touched me, I thought, it doesn't matter, it is only the body, it will soon be over. When it was over I lay in the dark and listened to his breathing and dreamed of the touch of hands, of Giovanni's hands, or anybody's hands, hands which would have the power to crush me and make me whole again.

Sometimes I left Giovanni over our afternoon breakfast, blue smoke from a cigarette circling around his head, and went off to the American Express office at Opera, where my mail would be, if I had any. Sometimes, but rarely, Giovanni came with me; he said that he could not endure being surrounded by so many Americans. He said they all looked alike—as I am sure they did, to him. But they didn't look alike to me. I was aware that they all had in common something that made them Americans but I could never put my finger on what it was. I knew that whatever this common quality was, I shared it. And I knew that Giovanni had been attracted to me partly because of it. When Giovanni wanted me to know that he was displeased with me, he said I was a *'vrai americain'*; conversely, when delighted, he said that I was not an American at all; and on both occasions he was striking, deep in me, a nerve which did not throb in him. And I resented this: resented being called an American (and resented resenting it) because it seemed to make me nothing more than that, whatever that was; and I resented being called *not* an American because it seemed to make me nothing.

Yet, walking into the American Express Office one harshly bright, midsummer afternoon, I was forced to admit that this active, so disquietingly cheerful horde struck the eye, at once, as a unit. At home, I could have distinguished patterns, habits, accents of speech—with no effort whatever: now everybody sounded, unless I listened hard, as though they had just arrived from Nebraska. At home I could have seen the clothes they were wearing, but here I only saw bags, cameras, belts and hats, all, clearly, from the same department store. At home I would have had some sense of the individual womanhood of the woman I faced: here the most ferociously accomplished seemed to be involved in some ice cold or sun-dried travesty of sex, and even grandmothers seemed to have had no traffic with the flesh. And what distinguished the men was that they seemed incapable of age; they smelled of soap, which seemed indeed to be their preservative against the dangers and exigencies of any more intimate odor; the boy he had been shone, somehow, unsoiled, untouched, unchanged, through the eyes of the man of sixty, booking passage, with his smiling wife, to Rome. His wife might have been his mother, forcing more oatmeal down his throat, and Rome might have been the movie she had promised to allow him to see. Yet I also suspected that what I was seeing was but a part of the truth and perhaps not even the most important part; beneath these faces, these clothes, accents, rudenesses, was power and sorrow, both unadmitted, unrealized, the power of inventors, the sorrow of the disconnected.

I took my place in the mail line behind two girls who had decided that they wanted to stay on in Europe and who were hoping to find jobs with the American government in Germany. One of them had fallen in love with a Swiss boy; so I gathered, from the low, intense, and troubled conversation she was having with her friend. The friend was urging her to 'put her foot down'—on what principle I could not discover; and the girl in love kept nodding her head, but more in perplexity than agreement. She had the choked and halting air of someone who has something more to say but finds no way of saying it. 'You mustn't be a fool about this,' the friend was saying. 'I know, I know,' said the girl. One had the impression that, though she certainly did not wish to be a fool, she had lost one definition of the word and might never be able to find another.

There were two letters for me, one from my father and one from Hella. Hella had been sending me only postcards for quite awhile. I was afraid her letter might be important and I did not want to read it. I opened the letter from my father first. I read it, standing just beyond reach of the sunlight, beside the endlessly swinging double doors.

'Dear Butch,' my father said, *'aren't you ever coming home? Don't think I'm only being selfish but it's true I'd like to see you. I think you have been away long enough, God knows I don't know what you're doing over there, and you don't write enough for me even to guess. But my guess is you're going to be sorry one of these fine days that you stayed over there, looking at your*

navel, and let the world pass you by. There's nothing over there for you. You're as American as pork and beans, though maybe you don't want to think so anymore. And maybe you won't mind my saying that you're getting a little old for studying, after all, if that's what you're doing. You're pushing thirty. I'm getting along, too, and you're all I've got. I'd like to see you.

'You keep asking me to send you your money and I guess you think I'm being a bastard about it. I'm not trying to starve you out and you know if you really need anything, I'll be the first to help you but I really don't think I'd be doing you a favor by letting you spend what little money you've got over there and then coming home to nothing. What the hell are you doing? Let your old man in on the secret, can't you? You may not believe this, but once I was a young man, too.'

And then he went on about my stepmother and how she wanted to see me, and about some of our friends and what they were doing. It was clear that my absence was beginning to frighten him. He did not know what it meant. But he was living, obviously, in a pit of suspicions which daily became blacker and vaguer—he would not have known how to put them into words, even if he had dared. The question he longed to ask was not in the letter and neither was the offer: *Is it a woman, David? Bring her on home. I don't care who she is. Bring her on home and I'll help you get set up.* He could not risk this question because he could not have endured an answer in the negative. An answer in the negative would have revealed what strangers we had become. I folded the letter and put it in my back pocket and looked out for a moment at the wide, sunlit foreign avenue.

There was a sailor, dressed all in white, coming across the boulevard, walking with that funny roll sailors have and with that aura, hopeful and hard, of having to make a great deal happen in a hurry. I was staring at him, though I did not know it, and wishing I were he. He seemed—somehow—younger than I had ever been, and blonder and more beautiful, and he wore his masculinity as unequivocally as he wore his skin. He made me think of home—perhaps home is not a place but simply an irrevocable condition. I knew how he drank and how he was with his friends and how pain and women baffled him. I wondered if my father had ever been like that, if I had ever been like that—though it was hard to imagine, for this boy, striding across the avenue like light itself, any antecedents, any connections at all. We came abreast and, as though he had seen some all-revealing panic in my eyes, he gave me a look contemptuously lewd and knowing; just such a look as he might have given, but a few hours ago, to the desperately well-dressed nymphomaniac or trollop who was trying to make him believe she was a lady. And in another second, had our contact lasted, I was certain that there would erupt into speech, out of all that light and beauty, some brutal variation of *Look, baby. I know you.* I felt my face flame, I felt my heart harden and shake as I hurried past him, trying to look stonily beyond him. He had caught me by surprise, for I had, somehow, not really been thinking of him but of the letter in my pocket, of Hella and Giovanni. I got to the other side of the boulevard, not daring to look back, and I wondered what he had seen in me to elicit such instantaneous contempt. I was too old to suppose that it had anything to do with my walk, or the way I held my hands, or my voice— which, anyway, he had not heard. It was something else and I would never see it. I would never dare to see it. It would be like looking at the naked sun. But, hurrying, and not daring now to look at anyone, male or female, who passed me on the wide sidewalks, I knew that what the sailor had seen in my unguarded eyes was envy and desire: I had seen it often in Jacques' eyes and my reaction and the sailor's had been the same. But if I were still able to feel affection and if he had seen it in my eyes, it would not have helped, for affection, for the boys I was doomed to look at, was vastly more frightening than lust.

I walked further than I had intended, for I did not dare to stop while the sailor might still be watching. Near the river, on rue des Pyramides, I sat down at a cafe table and opened Hella's letter.

Mon cher, she began, *Spain is my favorite country* mais ca n'empêche que Paris est toujours ma ville preferé. *I long to be again among all those foolish people, running for metros and jumping off of buses and dodging motorcycles and having traffic jams and admiring all that crazy statuary in all those absurd parks. I weep for the fishy ladies in the place de la Concorde.*

Spain is not like that at all. Whatever else Spain is, it is not frivolous. I think, really, that I would stay in Spain forever—if I had never been to Paris. Spain is very beautiful, stony and sunny and lonely. But by and by you get tired of olive oil and fish and castanets and tambourines—or, anyway, I do. I want to come home, to come home to Paris. It's funny, I've never felt anyplace was home before.

Nothing has happened to me here—I suppose that pleases you, I confess it rather pleases me. The Spaniards are nice, but, of course, most of them are terribly poor, the ones who aren't are impossible, I don't like the tourists, mainly English and American dipsomaniacs, paid, my dear, by their families to stay away. (I wish I had a family.) I'm on Mallorca now and it would be a pretty place if you could dump all the pensioned widows into the sea and make dry-martini drinking illegal. I've never seen anything like it! The way these old hags guzzle and make eyes at anything in pants, especially anything about eighteen—well, I said to myself, Hella, my girl, take a good look. You may be looking at your future. The trouble is that I love myself too much. And so I've decided to let two try it, this business of loving me, I mean, and see how that works out. (I feel fine, now that I've made the decision, I hope you'll feel fine, too, dear knight in Gimble's armor.)

I've been trapped into some dreary expedition to Seville with an English family I met in Barcelona. They adore Spain and they want to take me to see a bull-fight—I never have, you know, all the time I've been wandering around here. They're really quite nice, he's some kind of poet with the B.B.C. and she's his efficient and adoring spouse. Quite nice, really. They do *have an impossibly lunatick* son *who imagines himself mad about me, but he's much too English and much, much too young. I leave tomorrow and shall be gone ten days. Then, they to England and I—to you!*

I folded this letter, which I now realized I had been awaiting for many days and nights, and the waiter came and asked me what I wanted to drink. I had meant to order an aperitif but now, in some grotesque spirit of celebration, ordered a Scotch and soda. And over this drink, which had never seemed more American than it did at that moment, I stared at absurd Paris, which was as cluttered now, under the scalding sun, as the landscape of my heart. I wondered what I was going to do.

I cannot say that I was frightened. Or, it would be better to say that I did not feel any fear—the way men who are shot do not, I am told, feel any pain for awhile. I felt a certain relief. It seemed that the necessity for decision had been taken from my hands. I told myself that we both had always known, Giovanni and myself, that our idyll could not last forever. And it was not as though I had not been honest with him—he knew all about Hella. He knew that she would be returning to Paris one day. Now she would be coming back and my life with Giovanni would be finished. It would be something that had happened to me once—it would be something that had happened to many men once. I paid for my drink and got up and walked across the river to Montparnasse.

I felt elated—yet, as I walked down Raspail toward the cafes of Montparnasse, I could not fail to remember that Hella and I had walked here, Giovanni and I had walked here. And, with each step, the face that glowed insistently before me was not her face, but his. I was beginning to wonder how he would take my news. I did not think he would fight me but I was afraid of what I would see in his face. I was afraid of the pain I would see there. But even this was not my real fear. My real fear was buried and was driving me to Montparnasse. I wanted to find a girl, any girl at all.

But the terraces seemed oddly deserted. I walked along slowly, on both sides of the street, looking at the tables. I saw no one I knew. I walked down as far as the *Closerie des Lilas* and I had a solitary drink there. I read my letters again. I thought of finding Giovanni at once and telling him I was leaving him but I knew he would not yet have opened the bar and he might be almost anywhere in Paris at this hour. I walked slowly back up the boulevard. Then I saw a couple of girls, French whores, but they were not very attractive. I told myself that I could do better than *that*. I got to the *Select* and sat down. I watched the people pass, and I drank. No one I knew appeared on the boulevard for the longest while.

The person who appeared, and whom I did not know very well, was a girl named Sue, blonde, and rather puffy, with the quality, in spite of the fact that she was not pretty, of the girls who are selected each year to be Miss Rheingold. She wore her curly blonde hair cut very short, she had small breasts and a big behind, and, in order, no doubt, to indicate to the world how little she cared for appearance or sensuality, she almost always wore tight blue jeans. I think she came from Philadelphia and her family was very rich. Sometimes, when she was drunk, she reviled them, and, sometimes, drunk in another way, she extolled their virtues of thrift and fidelity. I was both dismayed and relieved to see her. The moment she appeared I began, mentally, to take off all her clothes.

'Sit down,' I said. 'Have a drink.'

'I'm glad to *see* you,' she cried, sitting down, and looking about for the waiter. 'You'd rather dropped out of sight. How've you been?'—abandoning her search for the waiter and leaning forward to me with a friendly grin.

'I've been fine,' I told her. 'And you?'

'Oh, *me!* Nothing ever happens to me.' And she turned down the corners of her rather predatory and also vulnerable mouth to indicate that she was both joking and not joking. 'I'm built like a brick stonewall.' We both laughed. She peered at me. 'They tell me you're living way out at the end of Paris, near the zoo.'

'I found a maid's room out there. Very cheap.'

'Are you living alone?'

I did not know whether she knew about Giovanni or not. I felt a hint of sweat on my forehead. 'Sort of,' I said.

'Sort of? What the hell does *that* mean? Do you have a monkey with you, or something?'

I grinned. 'No. But this French kid I know, he lives with his mistress, but they fight a lot and it's really *his* room so sometimes, when his mistress throws him out, he bunks with me for a couple of days.'

'Ah!' she sighed. *'Chagrin d'amour!'*

'He's having a good time,' I said. 'He loves it.' I looked at her. 'Aren't you?'

'Stone walls,' she said, 'are impenetrable.'

The waiter arrived. 'Doesn't it,' I dared, 'depend on the weapon?'

'What are you buying me to drink?' she asked.

'What do you want?' We were both grinning. The waiter stood above us, manifesting a kind of surly *joie de vivre*.

'I believe I'll have'—she batted the eyelashes of her tight blue eyes—'*un ricard*. With a hell of a lot of ice.'

'*Deux ricards,*' I said to the waiter, '*avec beaucoup de la glace.*'

'*Oui, monsieur.*' I was sure he despised us both. I thought of Giovanni and of how many times in an evening the phrase, *Oui, monsieur* fell from his lips. With this fleeting thought there came another, equally fleeting: a new sense of Giovanni, his private life and pain, and all that moved like a flood in him when we lay together at night.

'To continue,' I said.

'To continue?' She made her eyes very wide and blank. 'Where were we?' She was trying to be coquettish and she was trying to be hard-headed. I felt that I was doing something very cruel.

But I could not stop. 'We were talking about stonewalls and how they could be entered.'

'I never knew,' she simpered, 'that you had any interest in stone walls.'

'There's a lot about me you don't know.' The waiter returned with our drinks. 'Don't you think discoveries are fun?'

She stared discontentedly at her drink. 'Frankly,' she said, turning toward me again, with those eyes, 'no.'

'Oh, you're much too young for that,' I said. '*Everything* should be a discovery.'

She was silent for a moment. She sipped her drink. 'I've made,' she said, finally, 'all the discoveries that I can stand.' But I watched the way her thighs moved against the cloth of her jeans.

'But you can't just go on being a brick stonewall forever.'

'I don't see why not,' she said. 'Nor do I see *how* not.'

'Baby,' I said, 'I'm making you a proposition.'

She picked up her glass again and sipped it, staring straight outward at the boulevard. 'And what's the proposition?'

'Invite me for a drink. *Chez toi.*'

'I don't believe,' she said, turning to me, 'that I've got anything in the house.'

'We can pick up something on the way,' I said.

She stared at me for a long time. I forced myself not to drop my eyes. 'I'm sure that I shouldn't,' she said at last.

'Why not?'

She made a small, helpless movement in the wicker chair. 'I don't know. I don't know what you want.'

I laughed. 'If you invite me home for a drink,' I said, 'I'll show you.'

'I think you're being impossible,' she said, and for the first time there was something genuine in her eyes and voice.

'Well,' I said, 'I think *you* are.' I looked at her with a smile which was, I hoped, both boyish and insistent. 'I don't know what I've said that's so impossible. I've put all my cards on the table. But you're still holding yours. I don't know why you should think a man's being impossible when he declares himself attracted to you.'

'Oh, please,' she said, and finished her drink, 'I'm sure it's just the summer sun.'

'The summer sun,' I said, 'has nothing to do with it.' And when she still made no answer, 'All you've got to do,' I said, desperately, 'is decide whether we'll have another drink here or at your place.'

She snapped her fingers abruptly but did not succeed in appearing jaunty. 'Come along,' she said. 'I'm certain to regret it. But you really will have to buy something to drink. There *isn't* anything in the house. And that way,' she added, after a moment, 'I'll be sure to get something out of the deal.'

It was I, then, who felt a dreadful holding back. To avoid looking at her, I made a great show of getting the waiter. And he came, as surly as ever, and I paid him, and we rose and started walking towards the rue de Sevres, where Sue had a small apartment.

Her apartment was dark and full of furniture. 'None of it is mine,' she said. 'It all belongs to the French lady of a certain age from whom I rented it, who is now in Monte Carlo for her nerves.' She was very nervous, too, and I saw that this nervousness could be, for a little while, a great help to me. I had bought a small bottle of cognac and I put it down on her marble-topped table and took her in my arms. For some reason I was terribly aware that it was after seven in the evening, that soon the sun would have disappeared from the river, that all the Paris night was about to begin, and that Giovanni was now at work.

She was very big and she was disquietingly fluid—fluid, without, however, being able to flow. I felt a hardness and a constriction in her, a grave distrust, created already by too many men like me, ever to be conquered now. What we were about to do would not be pretty.

And, as though she felt this, she moved away from me. 'Let's have a drink,' she said. 'Unless, of course, you're in a hurry. I'll try not to keep you any longer than absolutely necessary.'

She smiled and I smiled, too. We were as close in that instant as we would ever get—like two thieves. 'Let's have several drinks,' I said.

'But not *too* many,' she said, and simpered again, suggestively, like a broken down movie queen facing the cruel cameras again after a long eclipse.

She took the cognac and disappeared into her corner of a kitchen. 'Make yourself comfortable,' she shouted out to me. 'Take off your shoes. Take off your socks. Look at my books— I often wonder what I'd do if there weren't any books in the world.'

I took off my shoes and lay back on her sofa. I tried not to think. But I was thinking that what I did with Giovanni could not possibly be more immoral than what I was about to do with Sue.

She came back with two great brandy snifters. She came close to me on the sofa and we touched glasses. We drank a little, she watching me all the while, and then I touched her breasts. Her lips parted and she put her glass down with extraordinary clumsiness and lay against me. It was a gesture of great despair and I knew that she was giving herself, not to me, but to that lover who would never come.

And I—I thought of many things, lying coupled with Sue in that dark place. I wondered if she had done anything to prevent herself from becoming pregnant; and the thought of a child belonging to Sue and me, of my being trapped that way—in the very act, so to speak, of trying to escape—almost precipitated a laughing jag. I wondered if her blue jeans had been thrown on top of the cigarette she had been smoking. I wondered if anyone else had a key to her apartment, if we could be heard through the inadequate walls, how much, in a few moments, we would hate each other. I also approached Sue as though she were a job of work, a job which it was necessary to do in an unforgettable manner. Somewhere, at the very bottom of myself, I realized that I was doing something awful to her and it became a matter of my honor not to let this fact become too obvious. I tried to convey, through this grisly act of love, the intelligence, at least, that it was not her, not *her* flesh, that I despised—it would not be her I could not face when we became vertical again. Again, somewhere at the bottom of me, I realized that my fears had been excessive and groundless and, in effect, a lie: it became clearer every instant that what I had been afraid of had nothing to do with my body. Sue was not Hella and she did not lessen my terror of what would happen when Hella came: she increased it, she made it more real than it had been before. At the same time, I realized that my performance with Sue was succeeding even too well, and I tried not to despise her for feeling so little what her laborer felt. I travelled through a network of Sue's cries, of Sue's tom-tom fists on my back, and judged, by means of her thighs, by means of her legs, how soon I could be free. Then I thought, *The end is coming soon,* her sobs became even higher and harsher, I was terribly aware of the small of my back and the cold sweat there, I thought, *Well, let her have it for Christ sake, get it over with,* then it was ending and I hated her and me, then it was over, and the dark, tiny room rushed back. And I wanted only to get out of there.

She lay still for a long time. I felt the night outside and it was calling me. I leaned up at last and found a cigarette.

'Perhaps,' she said, 'we should finish our drinks.'

She sat up and switched on the lamp which stood beside her bed. I had been dreading this moment. But she saw nothing in my eyes—she stared at me as though I had made a long journey on a white charger all the way to her prison house. She lifted her glass.

'*A la votre,*' I said.

'*A la votre?*' She giggled. '*A la tienne, cheri!*' She leaned over and kissed me on the mouth. Then, for a moment, she felt something; she leaned back and stared at me, her eyes not quite tightening yet; and she said, lightly, 'Do you suppose we could do this again sometime?'

'I don't see why not,' I told her, trying to laugh. 'We carry our own equipment.'

She was silent. Then: 'Could we have supper together—tonight?'

'I'm sorry,' I said. 'I'm really sorry, Sue, but I've got a date.'

'Oh. Tomorrow, maybe?'

'Look, Sue. I hate to make dates. I'll just surprise you.'

She finished her drink. 'I doubt that,' she said. She got up and walked away from me. 'I'll just put on some clothes and come down with you.'

She disappeared and I heard the water running. I sat there, still naked, but with my socks on, and poured myself another brandy. Now I was afraid to go out into that night which had seemed to be calling me only a few moments before.

When she came back she was wearing a dress and some real shoes, and she had sort of fluffed up her hair. I had to admit she looked better that way, really more like a girl, like a school-girl. I rose and started putting on my clothes. 'You look nice,' I said.

There were a great many things she wanted to say, but she forced herself to say nothing. I could scarcely bear to watch the struggle occurring in her face, it made me so ashamed. 'Maybe you'll be lonely again,' she said, finally. 'I guess I won't mind if you come looking for me.' She wore the strangest smile I had ever seen. It was pained and vindictive and humiliated but she inexpertly smeared across this grimace a bright, girlish gaiety—as rigid as the skeleton beneath her flabby body. If fate ever allowed Sue to reach me, she would kill me with just that smile.

'Keep a candle,' I said, 'in the window'—and she opened her door and we passed out into the streets.

3

I LEFT HER at the nearest corner, mumbling some school boy excuse, and watched her stolid figure cross the boulevard towards the cafes.

I did not know what to do or where to go. I found myself at last along the river, slowly going home.

And this was perhaps the first time in my life that death occurred to me as a reality. I thought of the people before me who had looked down at the river and gone to sleep beneath it. I wondered about them. I wondered how they had done it—it, the physical act. I had thought of suicide when I was much younger, as, possibly, we all have, but then it would have been for revenge, it would have been my way of informing the world how awfully it had made me suffer. But the silence of the evening, as I wandered home, had nothing to do with that storm, that far-off boy. I simply wondered about the dead because their days had ended and I did not know how I would get through mine.

The city, Paris, which I loved so much, was absolutely silent. There seemed to be almost no one on the streets, although it was still very early in the evening. Nevertheless, beneath me—along the river bank, beneath the bridges, in the shadow of the walls, I could almost hear the collective, shivering sigh—were lovers and ruins, sleeping, embracing, coupling, drinking, staring out at the descending night. Behind the walls of the houses I passed, the French nation was clearing away the dishes, putting little Jean Pierre and Marie to bed, scowling over the eternal problems of the sou, the shop, the church, the unsteady State. Those walls, those shuttered windows, held them in and protected them against the darkness and the long moan of this long night. Ten years hence, little Jean Pierre or Marie might find themselves out here beside the river and wonder, like me, how they had fallen out of the web of safety. What a long way, I thought, I've come—to be destroyed!

Yet it was true, I recalled, turning away from the river down the long street home, I wanted children. I wanted to be inside

again, with the light and safety, with my manhood unques-
tioned, watching my woman put my children to bed. I wanted
the same bed at night and the same arms and I wanted to rise
in the morning, knowing where I was. I wanted a woman to
be for me a steady ground, like the earth itself, where I could
always be renewed. It had been so once; it had almost been
so once. I could make it so again, I could make it real. It only
demanded a short, hard strength for me to become myself
again.

I saw a light burning beneath our door as I walked down
the corridor. Before I put my key in the lock the door was
opened from within. Giovanni stood there, his hair in his eyes,
laughing. He held a glass of cognac in his hand. I was struck
at first by what seemed to be the merriment on his face. Then
I saw that it was not merriment but hysteria and despair.

I started to ask him what he was doing home, but he pulled
me into the room, holding me around the neck tightly, with
one hand. He was shaking. 'Where have you been?' I looked
into his face, pulling slightly away from him. 'I have looked
for you everywhere.'

'Didn't you go to work?' I asked him.

'No,' he said. 'Have a drink. I have bought a bottle of
cognac to celebrate my freedom.' He poured me a cognac. I
did not seem to be able to move. He came toward me again,
thrusting the glass into my hand.

'Giovanni—what happened?'

He did not answer. He suddenly sat down on the edge of
the bed, bent over. I saw then that he was also in a state of
rage. *'Ils sont sale, les gens, tu sais?'* He looked up at me. His
eyes were full of tears. 'They are just dirty, all of them, low
and cheap and dirty.' He stretched out his hand and pulled
me down to the floor beside him. 'All except you. *Tous, sauf
toi.'* He held my face between his hands and I suppose such
tenderness has scarcely ever produced such terror as I then
felt. *'Ne me laisse pas tomber, je t'en prie,'* he said, and kissed
me, with a strange insistent gentleness on the mouth.

His touch could never fail to make me feel desire; yet his
hot, sweet breath also made me want to vomit. I pulled away
as gently as I could and drank my cognac. 'Giovanni,' I said,
'please tell me what happened. What's the matter?'

'He fired me,' he said. 'Guillaume. *Il m'a mis a la porte.*'
He laughed and rose and began walking up and down the
tiny room. 'He told me never to come to his bar anymore.
He said I was a gangster and a thief and a dirty little street
boy and the only reason I ran after him—*I* ran after *him*—
was because I intended to rob him one night. *Apres l'amour.*
Merde!' He laughed again.

I could not say anything. I felt that the walls of the room
were closing in on me.

Giovanni stood in front of our whitewashed windows, his
back to me. 'He said all these things in front of many people,
right downstairs in the bar. He waited until people came. I
wanted to kill him, I wanted to kill them all.' He turned back
into the center of the room and poured himself another cognac. He drank it at a breath, then suddenly took his glass
and hurled it with all his strength against the wall. It rang
briefly and fell in a thousand pieces all over our bed, all over
the floor. I could not move at once; then, feeling that my feet
were being held back by water but also watching myself move
very fast, I grabbed him by the shoulders. He began to cry. I
held him. And, while I felt his anguish entering into me, like
acid in his sweat, and felt that my heart would burst for him,
I also wondered, with an unwilling, unbelieving contempt,
why I had ever thought him strong.

He pulled away from me and sat against the wall which had
been uncovered. I sat facing him.

'I arrived at the usual time,' he said. 'I felt very good today.
He was not there when I arrived and I cleaned the bar as
usual and had a little drink and a little something to eat.
Then he came and I could see at once that he was in a dangerous mood—perhaps he had just been humiliated by some
young boy. It is funny'—and he smiled—'you can tell when
Guillaume is in a dangerous mood because he then becomes
so respectable. When something has happened to humiliate
him and make him see, even for a moment, how disgusting
he is, and how alone, then he remembers that he is a member
of one of the best and oldest families in France. But maybe,
then, he remembers that his name is going to die with him.
Then he has to do something, quick, to make the feeling go
away. He has to make much noise or have some *very* pretty

boy or get drunk or have a fight or look at his dirty pictures.'
He paused and stood up and began walking up and down
again. 'I do not know what happened to him today, but when
he came in he tried at first to be very business-like—he was
trying to find fault with my work. But there was nothing
wrong and he went upstairs. Then, by and by, he called me.
I hate going up to that little *pied-a-terre* he has up there over
the bar, it always means a scene. But I had to go and I found
him in his dressing gown, covered with perfume. I do not
know why, but the moment I saw him like that, I began to
be angry. He looked at me as though he were some fabulous
coquette—and he is ugly, ugly, he has a body just like sour
milk!—and then he asked me how you were. I was a little
astonished, for he never mentions you. I said you were fine.
He asked me if we still lived together. I think perhaps I should
have lied to him but I did not see any reason to lie to such a
disgusting old fairy, so I said, *Bien sûr*. I was trying to be
calm. Then he asked me terrible questions and I began to get
sick watching him and listening to him. I thought it was best
to be very quick with him and I said that such questions were
not asked, even by a priest or a doctor, and I said he should
be ashamed. Maybe he had been waiting for me to say something like that, for then he became angry and he reminded
me that he had taken me out of the streets, *et il a fait ceci et
il a fait cela*, everything for me because he thought I was
adorable, *parcequ'il m'adorait*—and on and on and that I had
no gratitude and no decency. I maybe handled it all very
badly, I know how I would have done it even a few months
ago, I would have made him scream, I would have made him
kiss my feet, *je te jure!*—but I did not want to do that, I really
did not want to be dirty with him. I tried to be serious. I told
him that I had never told him any lies and I had always said
that I did not want to be lovers with him—and—he had given
me the job all the same. I said I worked very hard and was
very honest with him and that it was not my fault if—if—if I
did not feel for him as he felt for me. Then he reminded me
that once—one time—and I did not want to say yes, but I
was weak from hunger and had had trouble not to vomit. I
was still trying to be calm and trying to handle it right. So I
said, *Mais a ce moment là je n'avais pas un copain*. I am not

alone anymore, *je suis avec un gars maintenant.* I thought he
would understand that, he is very fond of romance and the
dream of fidelity. But not this time. He laughed and said a
few more awful things about you, and he said that you were
just an American boy, after all, doing things in France which
you would not dare to do at home, and that you would leave
me very soon. Then, at last, I got angry and I said that he did
not pay me a salary for listening to slander and then I heard
someone come into the bar downstairs so I turned around
without saying anything more and walked out.'

He stopped in front of me. 'Can I have some more cognac?'
he asked, with a smile. 'I won't break the glass this time.'

I gave him my glass. He emptied it and handed it back. He
watched my face. 'Don't be afraid,' he said. 'We will be alright. I am not afraid.' Then his eyes darkened, he looked
again toward the windows.

'Well,' he said, 'I hoped that that would be the end of it.
I worked in the bar and tried not to think of Guillaume or of
what he was thinking or doing upstairs. It was apéritif time,
you know? and I was very busy. Then, suddenly, I heard the
door slam upstairs and the moment I heard that I knew that
it had happened, the awful thing had happened. He came into
the bar, all dressed now, like a French business man, and came
straight to me. He did not speak to anyone as he came in,
and he looked white and angry and, naturally, this attracted
attention. Everyone was waiting to see what he would do.
And, I must say, I thought he was going to strike me, or he
had maybe gone mad and had a pistol in his pocket. So I am
sure I looked frightened and this did not help matters, either.
He came behind the bar and began saying that I was a *tapette*
and a thief and told me to leave at once or he would call the
police and have me put behind bars. I was so astonished I
could not say anything and all the time his voice was rising
and people were beginning to listen and, suddenly, *mon cher*,
I felt that I was falling, falling from a great, high place. For a
long while I could not get angry and I could feel the tears,
like fire, coming up. I could not get my breath, I could not
believe that he was really doing this to me. I kept saying, what
have I done? What have I *done*? And he would not answer

and then he shouted, very loud, it was like a gun going off, '*Mais tu le sais, salop!* You know very well!' And nobody knew what he meant, but it was just as though we were back in that theatre lobby again, where we met, you remember? Everybody knew that Guillaume was right and I was wrong, that I had done something awful. And he went to the cash-register and took out some money—but I knew that he knew that there was not much money *in* the cash-register at such an hour—and pushed it at me and said, 'Take it! Take it! Better to give it to you than have you steal it from me at night! Now go!' And, oh, the faces in that bar, you should have seen them, they were so wise and tragic and they knew that *now* they knew everything, that they had always known it, and they were so glad that they had never had anything to do with me. 'Ah! *Les encules!* The dirty sons-of-bitches! *Les gonzesses!*' He was weeping again, with rage this time. 'Then, at last, I struck him and then many hands grabbed me and now I hardly know what happened but by and by I was in the street, with all these torn bills in my hand and everybody staring at me. I did not know what to do, I hated to walk away but I knew if anything more happened the police would come and Guillaume would have me put in jail. But I will see him again, I swear it, and on that day—!'

He stopped and sat down, staring at the wall. Then he turned to me. He watched me for a long time, in silence. Then, 'If you were not here,' he said, very slowly, 'this would be the end of Giovanni.'

I stood up. 'Don't be silly,' I said. 'It's not so tragic as all that.' I paused. 'Guillaume's disgusting. They all are. But it's not the worst thing that ever happened to you. Is it?'

'Maybe everything bad that happens to you makes you weaker,' said Giovanni, as though he had not heard me, 'and so you can stand less and less.' Then, looking up at me, 'No. The worst thing happened to me long ago and my life has been awful since that day. You are not going to leave me, are you?'

I laughed, 'Of course not.' I started shaking the broken glass off our blanket onto the floor.

'I do not know what I would do if you left me.' For the

first time I felt the suggestion of a threat in his voice—or I put it there. 'I have been alone so long—I do not think I would be able to live if I had to be alone again.'

'You aren't alone now,' I said. And then, quickly, for I could not, at that moment, have endured his touch: 'Shall we go for a walk? Come—out of this room for a minute.' I grinned and cuffed him roughly, football fashion, on the neck. Then we clung together for an instant. I pushed him away. 'I'll buy you a drink,' I said.

'And will you bring me home again?' he asked.

'Yes. I'll bring you home again.'

Je t'aime, tu sais?'

Je le sais, mon vieux.'

He went to the sink and started washing his face. He combed his hair. I watched him. He grinned at me in the mirror, looking, suddenly, beautiful and happy. And young—I had never in my life before felt so helpless or so old.

'But we will be alright!' he cried. *'N'est-ce pas?'*

'Certainly,' I said.

He turned from the mirror. He was serious again. 'But you know—I do not know how long it will be before I find another job. And we have almost no money. Do you have any money? Did any money come from New York for you today?'

'No money came from New York today,' I said, calmly, 'but I have a little money in my pocket.' I took it all out and put it on the table. 'About four thousand francs.'

'And I'—he went through his pockets, scattering bills and change. He shrugged and smiled at me, that fantastically sweet and helpless and moving smile. *'Je m'excuse.* I went a little mad.' He went down on his hands and knees and gathered it up and put it on the table beside the money I had placed there. About three thousand francs worth of bills had to be pasted together and we put those aside until later. The rest of the money on the table totalled about nine thousand francs.

'We are not rich,' said Giovanni, grimly, 'but we will eat tomorrow.'

I somehow did not want him to be worried. I could not endure that look on his face. 'I'll write my father again tomorrow,' I said. 'I'll tell him some kind of lie, some kind of lie that he'll believe and I'll *make* him send me some money.'

And I moved toward him as though I were driven, putting my hands on his shoulders, and forcing myself to look into his eyes. I smiled and I really felt at that moment that Judas and the Saviour had met in me. 'Don't be frightened. Don't worry.'

And I also felt, standing so close to him, feeling such a passion to keep him from terror, that a decision—once again!—had been taken from my hands. For neither my father, nor Hella, was real at that moment. And yet even this was not as real as my despairing sense that nothing was real for me, nothing would ever be real for me again—unless, indeed, this sensation of falling was reality.

The hours of this night begin to dwindle and now, with every second that passes on the clock, the blood at the bottom of my heart begins to boil, to bubble, and I know that no matter what I do anguish is about to overtake me in this house, as naked and silver as that great knife which Giovanni will be facing very soon. My executioners are here with me, walking up and down with me, washing things, and packing, and drinking from my bottle. They are everywhere I turn. Walls, windows, mirrors, water, the night outside—they are everywhere. I might call—as Giovanni, at this moment, lying in his cell, might call. But no one will hear. I might try to explain. Giovanni tried to explain. I might ask to be forgiven—if I could name and face my crime, if there were anything, or anybody, anywhere, with the power to forgive.

No. It would help if I were able to feel guilty. But the end of innocence is also the end of guilt.

No matter how it seems now, I must confess: I loved him. I do not think that I will ever love anyone like that again. And this might be a great relief if I did not also know that, when the knife has fallen, Giovanni, if he feels anything will feel relief.

I walk up and down this house—up and down this house. I think of prison. Long ago, before I had ever met Giovanni, I met a man at a party at Jacques' house who was celebrated because he had spent half his life in prison. He had then written a book about it which displeased the prison authorities and won a literary prize. But this man's life was over. He was fond of saying that, since to be in prison was simply not to live, the death penalty was the only merciful verdict any jury could deliver. I remember thinking that, in effect, he had never left prison, prison was all that was real to him, he could speak of nothing else. All his movements, even to the lighting of a cigarette, were stealthy, wherever his eyes focussed one saw a wall rise up. His face, the color of his face, brought to mind darkness and dampness, I felt that if one cut him his flesh would be the flesh of mushrooms. And he described to us, in avid, nostalgic detail, the barred windows, the barred doors, the judas, the guards standing at far ends of corridors, under the light. It is three tiers high inside the prison and everything is the color of gunmetal. Everything is dark and cold, except for those patches of light, where authority stands. There is on the air, perpetually, the memory of fists against the metal, a dull, booming tom-tom possibility, like the possibility of madness. The guards move and mutter and pace the corridors and boom dully up and down the stairs. They are in black, they carry guns, they are always afraid, they scarcely dare be kind. Three tiers down, in the prison's center, in the prison's great, cold heart, there is always activity: trusted prisoners wheeling things about, going in and out of the offices, ingratiating themselves with the guards for privileges of cigarettes, alcohol, and sex. The night deepens in the prison, there is muttering everywhere, and everybody knows—somehow—that death will be entering the prison courtyard early in the morning. Very early in the morning, before the trusties begin wheeling great garbage cans of food along the corridors, three men in black will come noiselessly down the corridor, one of them will turn the key in the lock. They will lay hands on someone and rush him down the corridor, first to the priest and then to a door which will open only for him, which will allow him, perhaps, one glimpse of the morning before he is thrown forward on his belly on a board and the knife falls on his neck.

I wonder about the size of Giovanni's cell. I wonder if it is bigger than his room. I know that it is colder. I wonder if he is alone or with two or three others; if he is perhaps playing cards, or smoking, or talking, or writing a letter—to whom would he be writing a letter?—or walking up and down. I

wonder if he knows that the approaching morning is the last
morning of his life. (For the prisoner, usually, does not know:
the lawyer knows and tells the family or friends but does not
tell the prisoner.) I wonder if he cares. Whether he knows or
not, cares or not, he is certainly afraid. Whether he is with
others or not, he is certainly alone. I try to see him, his back
to me, standing at the window of his cell. From where he is
perhaps he can only see the opposite wing of the prison; perhaps, by straining a little, just over the high wall, a patch of
the street outside. I do not know if his hair has been cut, or
is long—I should think it would have been cut. I wonder if
he is shaven. And now a million details, proof and fruit of
intimacy, flood my mind. I wonder, for example, if he feels
the need to go to the bathroom, if he has been able to eat
today, if he is sweating, or dry. I wonder if anyone has made
love to him in prison. And then something shakes me, I feel
shaken hard and dry, like some dead thing in the desert, and
I know that I am hoping that Giovanni is being sheltered in
someone's arms tonight. I wish that someone were here with
me. I would make love to whoever was here all night long, I
would labor with Giovanni all night long.

Those days after Giovanni had lost his job, we dawdled;
dawdled as doomed mountain climbers may be said to dawdle
above the chasm, held only by a snapping rope. I did not write
my father—I put it off from day to day. It would have been
too definitive an act. I knew which lie I would tell him and I
knew the lie would work—only—I was not sure that it would
be a lie. Day after day we lingered in that room and Giovanni
began to work on it again. He had some weird idea that it
would be nice to have a bookcase sunk in the wall and he
chipped through the wall until he came to the brick and began
pounding away at the brick. It was hard work, it was insane
work, but I did not have the energy or the heart to stop him.
In a way he was doing it for me, to prove his love for me. He
wanted me to stay in the room with him. Perhaps he was
trying, with his own strength, to push back the encroaching
walls, without, however, having the walls fall down.
   Now—now, of course, I see something very beautiful in
those days, which were such torture then. I felt, then, that

Giovanni was dragging me with him to the bottom of the sea. He could not find a job. I knew that he was not really looking for one, that he could not. He had been bruised, so to speak, so badly that the eyes of strangers lacerated him like salt. He could not endure being very far from me for very long. I was the only person on God's cold, green earth who cared about him, who knew his speech and silence, knew his arms, and did not carry a knife. The burden of his salvation seemed to be on me and I could not endure it.

And the money dwindled—it went, it did not dwindle, very fast. Giovanni tried to keep panic out of his voice when he asked me, each morning, 'Are you going to American Express today?'

'Certainly,' I would answer.

'Do you think your money will be there today?'

'I don't know.'

'What are they *doing* with your money in New York?'

Still, still, I could not act. I went to Jacques and borrowed ten thousand francs from him again. I told him that Giovanni and I were going through a difficult time but that it would be over soon.

'He was very nice about it,' said Giovanni.

'He *can*, sometimes, be a very nice man.' We were sitting on a terrace near Odeon. I looked at Giovanni and thought, for a moment, how nice it would be if Jacques would take him off my hands.

'What are you thinking?' asked Giovanni.

For a moment I was frightened and I was also ashamed. 'I was thinking,' I said, 'that I'd like to get out of Paris.'

'Where would you like to go?' he asked.

'Oh, I don't know. Anywhere. I'm sick of this city,' I said suddenly, with a violence that surprised us both. 'I'm tired of this ancient pile of stone and all these goddam, smug people. Everything you put your hands on here comes to pieces in your hands.'

'That,' said Giovanni, gravely, 'is true.' He was watching me with a terrible intensity. I forced myself to look at him and smile.

'Wouldn't you like to get out of here for awhile?' I asked.

'Ah!' he said, and raised both hands, briefly, palms outward, in a kind of mock resignation. 'I would like to go wherever you go. I do not feel so strongly about Paris as you do, suddenly. I have never liked Paris very much.'

'Perhaps,' I said—I scarcely knew what I was saying—'we could go to the country. Or to Spain.'

'Ah,' he said, lightly, 'you are lonely for your mistress.'

I was guilty and irritated and full of love and pain. I wanted to kick him and I wanted to take him in my arms. 'That's no reason to go to Spain,' I said, sullenly. 'I'd just like to see it, that's all. This city is expensive.'

'Well,' he said, brightly, 'let us go to Spain. Perhaps it will remind me of Italy.'

'Would you rather go to Italy? Would you rather visit your home?'

He smiled. 'I do not think I have a home there anymore.' And then: 'No. I would not like to go to Italy—perhaps, after all, for the same reason you do not want to go to the United States.'

'But I *am* going to the United States,' I said, quickly. And he looked at me. 'I mean, I'm certainly going to go back there one of these days.'

'One of these days,' he said. 'Everything bad will happen—one of these days.'

'Why is it bad?'

He smiled, 'Why, you will go home and then you will find that home is not home anymore. Then you will really be in trouble. As long as you stay here, you can always think: One day I will go home.' He played with my thumb and grinned. '*N'est-ce pas?*'

'Beautiful logic,' I said. 'You mean I have a home to go to as long as I don't go there?'

He laughed. 'Well, isn't it true? You don't have a home until you leave it and then, when you have left it, you never can go back.'

'I seem,' I said, 'to have heard this song before.'

'Ah, *yes*,' said Giovanni, 'and you will certainly hear it again. It is one of those songs that somebody, somewhere, will always be singing.'

We rose and started walking. 'And what would happen,' I asked, idly, 'if I shut my ears?'

He was silent for a long while. Then: 'You do, sometimes, remind me of the kind of man who is tempted to put himself in prison in order to avoid being hit by a car.'

'That,' I said, sharply, 'would seem to apply much more to you than to me.'

'What do you mean?' he asked.

'I'm talking about that room, that hideous room. Why have you buried yourself there so long?'

'Buried myself? Forgive me, *mon cher Americain*, but Paris is not like New York, it is not full of palaces for boys like me. Do you think I should be living in Versailles instead?'

'There must—there must,' I said, 'be other rooms.'

'*Ca ne manque pas, les chambres.* The world is full of rooms—big rooms, little rooms, round rooms, square ones, rooms high up, rooms low down—all kinds of rooms! What kind of room do you think Giovanni should be living in? How long do you think it took me to find the room I have? And since when, since when'—he stopped and beat with his fore-finger on my chest—'have you so hated the room? Since when? Since yesterday, since always? *Dis-moi.*'

Facing him, I faltered. 'I don't hate it. I—I didn't mean to hurt your feelings.'

His hands dropped to his sides. His eyes grew big. He laughed. 'Hurt my *feelings*! Am I now a stranger that you speak to me like that, with such an American politeness?'

'All I mean, baby, is that I wish we could move.'

'We can move. Tomorrow! Let us go to a hotel. Is that what you want? *Le Crillon peut-etre?*'

I sighed, speechless, and we started walking again.

'I know,' he burst out, after a moment, 'I know! You want to leave Paris, you want to leave the room—ah! you are wicked. *Comme tu es méchant!*'

'You misunderstand me,' I said. 'You misunderstand me.'

He smiled grimly, to himself. '*J'espère bien.*'

Later, when we were back in the room, putting the loose bricks Giovanni had taken out of the wall into a sack, he asked me, 'This girl of yours—have you heard from her lately?'

'Not lately,' I said. I did not look up. 'But I expect her to turn up in Paris almost any day now.'

He stood up, standing in the center of the room, under the

light, looking at me. I stood up, too, half smiling, but also, in some strange, dim way, a little frightened.

'*Viens m'embrasser,*' he said.

I was vividly aware that he held a brick in his hand, I held a brick in mine. It really seemed for an instant that if I did not go to him, we would use these bricks to beat each other to death.

Yet, I could not move at once. We stared at each other across a narrow space that was full of danger, that almost seemed to roar, like flame.

'Come,' he said.

I dropped my brick and went to him. In a moment I heard his fall. And at moments like this I felt that we were merely enduring and committing the longer and lesser and more perpetual murder.

4

At LAST there came the note which I had been waiting for, from Hella, telling me what day and hour she would arrive in Paris. I did not tell this to Giovanni, but walked out alone that day and went to the station to meet her.

I had hoped that when I saw her something instantaneous, definitive, would have happened in me, something to make me know where I should be and where I was. But nothing happened. I recognized her at once, before she saw me, she was wearing green, her hair was a little shorter, and her face was tan, and she wore the same brilliant smile. I loved her as much as ever and I still did not know how much that was.

When she saw me she stood stock-still on the platform, her hands clasped in front of her, with her wide-legged, boyish stance, smiling. For a moment we simply stared at each other.

'Eh bien,' she said, 't'embrasse pas ta femme?'

Then I took her in my arms and something happened then. I was terribly glad to see her. It really seemed, with Hella in the circle of my arms, that my arms were home and I was welcoming her back there. She fitted in my arms, she always had, and the shock of holding her caused me to feel that my arms had been empty since she had been away.

I held her very close in that high, dark shed, with a great confusion of people all about us, just beside the breathing train. She smelled of the wind and the sea and of space and I felt in her marvellously living body the possibility of legitimate surrender.

Then she pulled away. Her eyes were damp. 'Let me look at you,' she said. She held me at arm's length, searching my face. 'Ah. You look wonderful. I'm so happy to see you again.'

I kissed her lightly on the nose and felt that I had passed the first inspection. I picked up her bags and we started towards the exit. 'Did you have a good trip? And how was Seville? And how do you like bull-fights? Did you meet any bull-fighters? Tell me everything.'

She laughed. 'Everything is a very tall order. I had a terrible trip, I hate trains, I wish I'd flown but I've been in one Spanish airplane and I swore never, never again. It rattled, my dear, in the middle of the air just like a model T Ford—it had probably *been* a model T Ford at one time—and I just sat there, praying and drinking brandy. I was sure I'd never see land again.' We passed through the barrier, into the streets. Hella looked about delightedly at all of it, the cafés, the self-contained people, the violent snarl of the traffic, the blue-caped traffic policeman and his white, gleaming club. 'Coming back to Paris,' she said, after a moment, 'is always so lovely, no matter where you've been.' We got into a cab and our driver made a wide, reckless circle into the stream of traffic. 'I should think that even if you returned here in some awful sorrow, you might—well, you might find it possible here to begin to be reconciled.'

'Let's hope,' I said, 'that we never have to put Paris to that test.'

Her smile was at once bright and melancholy. 'Let's hope.' Then she suddenly took my face between her hands and kissed me. There was a great question in her eyes and I knew that she burned to have this question answered at once. But I could not do it yet. I held her close and kissed her, closing my eyes. Everything was as it had been between us and at the same time everything was different.

I told myself I would not think about Giovanni yet, I would not worry about him yet; for tonight, anyway, Hella and I should be together with nothing to divide us. Still, I knew very well that this was not really possible: he had already divided us. I tried not to think of him sitting alone in that room, wondering why I stayed away so long.

Then we were sitting together in Hella's room on the rue de Tournon, sampling Fundador. 'It's much too sweet,' I said. 'Is this what they drink in Spain?'

'I never saw any Spaniards drinking it,' she said, and laughed. '*They* drink wine. *I* drank gin-fizz—in Spain I somehow had the feeling that it was healthy,' and she laughed again.

I kept kissing her and holding her, trying to find my way in her again, as though she were a familiar, darkened room in which I fumbled to find the light. And, with my kisses, I was trying also to delay the moment which would commit me to her, or fail to commit me to her. But I think she felt that the indefinitive constraint between us was of her doing and all on her side. She was remembering that I had written her less and less often while she had been away. In Spain, until near the end, this had probably not worried her; not until she herself had come to a decision did she begin to be afraid that I might also have arrived at a decision, opposite to hers. Perhaps she had kept me dangling too long.

She was by nature forthright and impatient; she suffered when things were not clear; yet she forced herself to wait for some word or sign from me and held the reins of her strong desire tightly in her hands.

I wanted to force her to relinquish reins. Somehow, I would be tongue-tied until I took her again. I hoped to burn out, through Hella, my image of Giovanni and the reality of his touch—I hoped to drive out fire with fire. Yet, my sense of what I was doing made me double-minded. And at last she asked me, with a smile, 'Have I been away too long?'

'I don't know,' I said. 'It's been a long time.'

'It was a very lonely time,' she said, unexpectedly. She turned slightly away from me, lying on her side, looking toward the window. 'I felt so aimless—like a tennis ball, bouncing, bouncing—I began to wonder where I'd land. I began to feel that I'd, somewhere, missed the boat.' She looked at me. 'You know the boat I'm talking about. They make movies about it where I come from. It's the boat that, when you miss it, it's a boat, but when it comes in, it's a ship.' I watched her face. It was stiller than I had ever known it to be before.

'Didn't you like Spain,' I asked, nervously, 'at all?'

She ran one hand, impatiently, through her hair. 'Oh. Of course, I liked Spain, why not? it's very beautiful. I just didn't know what I was doing there. And I'm beginning to be tired of being in places for no particular reason.'

I lit a cigarette and smiled. 'But you went to Spain to get away from me—remember?'

She smiled and stroked my cheek. 'I haven't been very nice to you, have I?'

'You've been very honest.' I stood up and walked a little away from her. 'Did you get much thinking done, Hella?'

'I told you in my letter—don't *you* remember?'

For a moment everything seemed perfectly still. Even the faint street noises died. I had my back to her but I felt her eyes. I felt her waiting—everything seemed to be waiting.

'I wasn't sure about that letter.' I was thinking, *Perhaps I can get out of it without having to tell her anything.* 'You were so sort of—offhand—I couldn't be sure whether you were glad or sorry to be throwing in with me.'

'Oh,' she said, 'but we've always been offhand, it's the only way I could have said it. I was afraid of embarrassing you— don't you understand that?'

What I wanted to suggest was that she was taking me out of desperation, less because she wanted me than because I was there. But I could not say it. I sensed that, though it might be true, she no longer knew it.

'But, perhaps,' she said, carefully, 'you feel differently now. Please say so if you do.' She waited for my answer for a moment. Then: 'You know, I'm not really the emancipated girl I try to be at all. I guess I just want a man to come home to me every night. I want to be able to sleep with a man without being afraid he's going to knock me up. Hell, I want to be knocked up. I want to start having babies. In a way, it's really all I'm good for.' There was silence again. 'Is that what you want?'

'Yes,' I said, 'I've always wanted that.'

I turned to face her, very quickly, or as though strong hands on my shoulders had turned me around. The room was darkening. She lay on the bed, watching me, her mouth slightly open, and her eyes like lights. I was terribly aware of her body, and of mine. I walked over to her and put my head on her breast. I wanted to lie there, hidden and still. But then, deep within, I felt her moving, rushing to open the gates of her strong, walled city and let the king of glory come in.

Dear Dad, I wrote, *I won't keep any secrets from you any-more, I found a girl and I want to marry her and it wasn't that I was keeping secrets from you, I just wasn't sure she wanted to marry me. But she's finally agreed to risk it, poor soft-headed thing that she is, and we're planning to tie the knot while we're still over here and make our way home by easy stages. She's not French, in case you're worried (I know you don't dislike the*

French, it's just that you don't think they have our virtues—I might add, they don't). Anyway, Hella—her name is Hella Lincoln, she comes from Minneapolis, her father and mother still live there, he's a corporation lawyer, she's just the little woman— Hella would like us to honeymoon here and it goes without saying that I like anything she likes. So. Now will you send your loving son some of his hard-earned money. Tout de suite. That's French for pronto.

Hella—the photo doesn't really do her justice—came over here a couple of years ago to study painting. Then she discovered she wasn't a painter and just about the time she was ready to throw herself into the Seine, we met, and the rest, as they say, is history. I know you'll love her, Dad, and she'll love you. She's already made me a very happy man.

Hella and Giovanni met by accident, after Hella had been in Paris for three days. During those three days I had not seen him and I had not mentioned his name.

We had been wandering about the city all day and all day Hella had been full of a subject which I had never heard her discuss at such length before: women. She claimed it was hard to be one.

'I don't see what's so hard about being a woman. At least, not as long as she's got a man.'

'That's just it,' said she. 'Hasn't it ever struck you that that's a sort of humiliating necessity?'

'Oh, please,' I said. 'It never seemed to humiliate any of the women I knew.'

'Well,' she said, 'I'm sure you never thought about any of them—in that way.'

'I certainly didn't. I hope they didn't, either. And why are *you*? What's *your* beef?'

'I've got no *beef*,' she said. She hummed, low in her throat, a kind of playful, Mozart tune. 'I've got no beef at all. But it does seem—well, difficult—to be at the mercy of some gross, unshaven stranger before you can begin to be yourself.'

'I don't know if I like *that*,' I said. 'Since when have I been gross? or a stranger? It may be true that I need a shave but that's *your* fault, I haven't been able to tear myself away from you.' And I grinned and kissed her.

'Well,' she said, 'you may not be a stranger *now*. But you were once and I'm sure you will be again—many times.'

'If it comes to that,' I said, 'so will you be, for me.'

She looked at me with a quick, bright smile. 'Will I?' Then: 'But what I mean about being a woman is, we might get married now and stay married for fifty years and I might be a stranger to you every instant of that time and you might never know it.'

'But if *I* were a stranger—*you* would know it?'

'For a woman,' she said, 'I think a man is always a stranger. And there's something awful about being at the mercy of a stranger.'

'But men are at the mercy of women, too. Have you never thought of that?'

'Ah!' she said, 'men may be at the mercy of women—I think men like that idea, it strokes the misogynist in them. But if a particular *man* is ever at the mercy of a particular *woman*—why, he's somehow stopped being a man. And the lady, then, is more neatly trapped than ever.'

'You mean, I can't be at your mercy? But you can be at mine?' I laughed. 'I'd like to see you at *anybody's* mercy, Hella.'

'You may laugh,' she said, humorously, 'but there is something in what I say. I began to realize it in Spain—that I wasn't free, that I couldn't be free until I was attached—no, *committed*—to someone.'

'To someone? Not *something*?'

She was silent. 'I don't know,' she said at last, 'but I'm beginning to think that women get attached to some*thing* really by default. They'd give it up, if they could, anytime, for a man. Of course they can't admit this, and neither can most of them let go of what they have. But I think it kills them—perhaps I only mean,' she added, after a moment, 'that it would have killed *me*.'

'What do you want, Hella? What have you got now that makes such a difference?'

She laughed. 'It isn't what I've *got*. It isn't even what I *want.* It's that *you've* got *me.* So now I can be—your obedient and most loving servant.'

I felt cold. I shook my head in mock confusion. 'I don't know what you're talking about.'

'Why,' she said, 'I'm talking about my life. I've got you to take care of and feed and torment and trick and love—I've got you to put up with. From now on, I can have a wonderful time complaining about being a woman. But I won't be terrified that I'm *not* one.' She looked at my face, and laughed. 'Oh, I'll be doing other *things,*' she cried. 'I won't stop being intelligent. I'll read and argue and *think* and all that—and I'll make a great point of not thinking *your* thoughts—and you'll be pleased because I'm sure the resulting confusion will cause you to see that I've only got a finite woman's mind, after all. And, if God is good, you'll love me more and more and we'll be quite happy.' She laughed again. 'Don't bother your head about it, sweetheart. Leave it to me.'

Her amusement was contagious and I shook my head again, laughing with her. 'You're adorable,' I said. 'I don't understand you at all.'

She laughed again. 'There,' she said, 'that's fine. We're both taking to it like ducks to water.'

We were passing a book-store and she stopped. 'Can we go in for just a minute?' she asked. 'There's a book I'd like to get. Quite,' she added, as we entered the shop, 'a trivial book.'

I watched her with amusement as she went over to speak to the woman who ran the shop. I wandered idly over to the farthest book shelf, where a man stood, his back to me, leafing through a magazine. As I stood beside him, he closed the magazine and put it down, and turned. We recognized each other at once. It was Jacques.

'*Tiens!*' he cried. 'Here you are! We were beginning to think that you had gone back to America.'

'Me?' I laughed. 'No, I'm still in Paris. I've just been busy.' Then, with a terrible suspicion, I asked, 'Who's *we?*'

'Why,' said Jacques, with a hard, insistent smile, 'your baby. It seems you left him alone in that room without any food, without any money, without, even, any cigarettes. He finally persuaded his concierge to allow him to put a phone call on his bill and called me. The poor boy sounded as though he would have put his head in the gas oven. If,' he laughed, 'he had *had* a gas oven.'

We stared at each other. He, deliberately, said nothing. I did not know what to say.

'I threw a few provisions in my car,' said Jacques, 'and hurried out to get him. He thought we should drag the river for you. But I assured him that he did not know Americans as well as I and that you had not drowned yourself. You had only disappeared in order—to think. And I see that I was right. You have thought so much that now you must find what others have thought before you. One book,' he said, finally, 'that you can surely spare yourself the trouble of reading is the Marquis de Sade.'

'Where is Giovanni now?' I asked.

'I finally remembered the name of Hella's hotel,' said Jacques. 'Giovanni said that you were more or less expecting her and so I gave him the bright idea of calling you there. He has stepped out for an instant to do just that. He'll be along presently.'

Hella had returned, with her book.

'You two have met before,' I said, awkwardly. 'Hella, you remember Jacques.'

She remembered him and also remembered that she disliked him. She smiled politely and held out her hand. 'How are you?'

'Je suis ravi, mademoiselle,' said Jacques. He knew that Hella disliked him and this amused him. And, to corroborate her dislike, and also because at that moment he really hated me, he bowed low over her outstretched hand and became, in an instant, outrageously and offensively effeminate. I watched him as though I were watching an imminent disaster from many miles away. He turned playfully to me. 'David has been hiding from us,' he murmured, 'now that you are back.'

'Oh?' said Hella, and moved closer to me, taking my hand, 'that was very naughty of him. I'd never have allowed it—if I'd known we were hiding.' She grinned. 'But, then, he never tells me anything.'

Jacques looked at her. 'No doubt,' he said, 'he finds more fascinating topics when you are together than why he hides from old friends.'

I felt a great need to get out of there before Giovanni arrived. 'We haven't eaten supper yet,' I said, trying to smile, 'perhaps we can meet you later?' I knew that my smile was begging him to be kind to me.

But at that moment the tiny bell which announced every entry into the shop rang, and Jacques said, 'Ah. Here is Giovanni.' And, indeed, I felt him behind me, standing stockstill, staring, and felt in Hella's clasp, in her entire body, a kind of wild shrinking and not all of her composure kept this from showing in her face. When Giovanni spoke his voice was thick with fury and relief and unshed tears.

'Where have you been?' he cried. 'I thought you were dead! I thought you had been knocked down by a car or thrown into the river—what have you been doing all these days?'

I was able, oddly enough, to smile. And I was astonished at my calm. 'Giovanni,' I said, 'I want you to meet my fiancée. Mlle. Hella. Monsieur Giovanni.'

He had seen her before his outburst ended and now he touched her hand with a still, astounded politeness and stared at her with black, steady eyes as though he had never seen a woman before.

'Enchanté, mademoiselle,' he said. And his voice was dead and cold. He looked briefly at me, then back at Hella. For a moment we, all four, stood there as though we were posing for a tableau.

'Really,' said Jacques, 'now that we are all together, I think we should have one drink together. A very short one,' he said to Hella, cutting off her attempt at polite refusal, and taking her arm. 'It's not every day,' he said, 'that old friends get together.' He forced us to move, Hella and he together, Giovanni and I ahead. The bell rang viciously as Giovanni opened the door. The evening air hit us like a blaze. We started walking away from the river, toward the boulevard.

'When I decide to leave a place,' said Giovanni, 'I tell the concierge, so that at least she will know where to forward my mail.'

I flared briefly, unhappily. I had noticed that he was shaven and wore a clean, white shirt and tie—a tie which surely belonged to Jacques. 'I don't see what you've got to complain about,' I said. 'You sure knew where to go.'

But with the look he gave me then my anger left me and I wanted to cry. 'You are not nice,' he said. *'Tu n'est pas chic du tout.'* Then he said no more and we walked to the boulevard in silence. Behind us I could hear the murmur of Jacques' voice. On the corner we stood and waited for them to catch up with us.

'Darling,' said Hella, as she reached me, 'you stay and have a drink if you want to, I can't, I really can't, I don't feel well at all.' She turned to Giovanni. 'Please forgive me,' she said, 'but I've just come back from Spain and I've hardly sat down a moment since I got off the train. Another time, truly—but I *must* get some sleep tonight.' She smiled and held out her hand but he did not seem to see it.

'I'll walk Hella home,' I said, 'and then I'll come back. If you'll tell me where you're going to be.'

Giovanni laughed, abruptly. 'Why, we will be in the quarter,' he said. 'We will not be difficult to find.'

'I am sorry,' said Jacques, to Hella, 'that you do not feel well. Perhaps another time.' And Hella's hand, which was still uncertainly outstretched, he bowed over and kissed a second time. He straightened and looked at me. 'You must bring Hella to dinner at my house one night.' He made a face. 'There is no need to hide your fiancée from us.'

'No need whatever,' said Giovanni. 'She is very charming. And we'—with a grin, to Hella—'will try to be charming, too.'

'Well,' I said, and took Hella by the arm, 'I'll see you later.'

'If I am not here,' said Giovanni, both vindictive and near tears, 'by the time you come back again, I will be at home. You remember where that is—? it is near a zoo.'

'I remember,' I said. I started backing away, as though I were backing out of a cage, 'I'll see you later. *A tout à l'heure.*'

'A la prochaine,' said Giovanni.

I felt their eyes on our backs as we walked away from them. For a long while Hella was silent—possibly because, like me, she was afraid to say anything. Then: 'I really can't stand that man. He gives me the creeps.' After a moment: 'I didn't know you'd seen so much of him while I was away.'

'I didn't,' I said. To do something with my hands, to give myself a moment of privacy, I stopped and lit a cigarette. I felt her eyes. But she was not suspicious; she was only troubled.

'And who is Giovanni?' she asked, when we started walking again. She gave a little laugh. 'I just realized that I haven't even asked you where you were living. Are you living with him?'

'We've been sharing a maid's room out at the end of Paris,' I said.

'Then it wasn't very nice of you,' said Hella, 'to go off for so long, without any warning.'

'Well, my God,' I said, 'he's only my room-mate. How was I to know he'd start dragging the river just because I stayed out a couple of nights?'

'Jacques said you left him there without any money, without any cigarettes, or anything, and you didn't even tell him you were going to be with me.'

'There are lots of things I didn't tell Giovanni. But he's never made any kind of scene before—I guess he must be drunk. I'll talk to him later.'

'Are you going to go back there later?'

'Well,' I said, 'if I don't go back there later, I'll go on over to the room. I've been meaning to do that, anyway.' I grinned. 'I have to get shaved.'

Hella sighed. 'I didn't mean to get your friends mad at you,' she said. 'You ought to go back and have a drink with them. You said you were going to.'

'Well, I may, I may not. I'm not married to them, you know.'

'Well, the fact that you're going to be married to *me* doesn't mean you have to break your word to your friends. It doesn't even mean,' she added, shortly, 'that I have to *like* your friends.'

'Hella,' I said, 'I am perfectly aware of that.'

We turned off the boulevard, toward her hotel.

'He's very intense, isn't he?' she said. I was staring at the dark mound of the Senate, which ended our dark, slightly uphill street.

'Who is?'

'Giovanni. He's certainly very fond of you.'

'He's Italian,' I said. 'Italians are theatrical.'

'Well, this one,' she laughed, 'must be special, even in Italy! How long have you been living with him?'

'A couple of months.' I threw away my cigarette. 'I ran out of money while you were away—you know, I'm still waiting for money—and I moved in with him because it was cheaper. At that time he had a job and was living with his mistress most of the time.'

'Oh?' she said. 'He has a mistress?'

'He had a mistress,' I said. 'He also had a job. He's lost both.'

'Poor boy,' she said. 'No wonder he looks so lost.'

'He'll be alright,' I said, briefly. We were before her door. She pressed the night-bell.

'Is he a very good friend of Jacques?' she asked.

'Perhaps,' I said, 'not quite good enough to please Jacques.'

She laughed. 'I always feel a cold wind go over me,' she said, 'when I find myself in the presence of a man who dislikes women as much as Jacques does.'

'Well, then,' I said, 'we'll just keep him away from you. We don't want no cold winds blowing over this girl.' I kissed her on the tip of her nose. At the same moment there was a rumble from deep within the hotel and the door unlocked itself with a small, violent shudder. Hella looked humorously into the blackness. 'I always wonder,' she said, 'if I *dare* go in.' Then she looked up at me. 'Well? Do you want to have a drink upstairs before you go back to join your friends?'

'Sure,' I said. We tiptoed into the hotel, closing the door gently behind us. My fingers finally found the *minuterie* and the weak, yellow light spilled over us. A voice, completely unintelligible, shouted out at us and Hella shouted back her name, which she tried to pronounce with a French accent. As we started up the stairs, the light went out and Hella and I began to giggle like two children. We were unable to find the minute-switch on any of the landings—I don't know why we both found this so hilarious, but we did, and we held on to each other, giggling, all the way to Hella's top-floor room.

'Tell me about Giovanni,' she asked, much later, while we lay in bed and watched the black night tease her stiff, white curtains. 'He interests me.'

'That's a pretty tactless thing to say at this moment,' I told her. 'What the hell do you mean, he interests you?'

'I mean who he is, what he thinks about. How he got that face.'

'What's the matter with his face?'

'Nothing. He's very beautiful, as a matter of fact. But there's something in that face—so old-fashioned.'

'Go to sleep,' I said. 'You're babbling.'

'How did you meet him?'

'Oh. In a bar one drunken night, with lots of other people.'

'Was Jacques there?'

'I don't remember. Yes, I guess so. I guess he met Giovanni at the same time I did.'

'What made you go to live with him?'

'I told you. I was broke and he had this room—'

'But that can't have been the *only* reason.'

'Oh, well,' I said, 'I liked him.'

'And don't you like him any more?'

'I'm very fond of Giovanni. You didn't see him at his best tonight, but he's a very nice man.' I laughed; covered by the night, emboldened by Hella's body and my own, and protected by the tone of my voice, I found great relief in adding: 'I love him, in a way. I really do.'

'He seems to feel that you have a funny way of showing it.'

'Oh, well,' I said, 'these people have another style from us. They're much more demonstrative. I can't help it. I just can't—do all that.'

'Yes,' she said, thoughtfully, 'I've noticed that.'

'You've noticed what?'

'Kids here—they think nothing of showing a lot of affection for each other. It's sort of a shock at first. Then you begin to think it's sort of nice.'

'It *is* sort of nice,' I said.

'Well,' said Hella, 'I think we ought to take Giovanni out to dinner or something one of these days. After all, he did sort of rescue you.'

'That's a good idea,' I said. 'I don't know what he's doing these days but I imagine he'll have a free evening.'

'Does he hang around with Jacques much?'

'No, I don't think so. I think he just ran into Jacques tonight.' I paused. 'I'm beginning to see,' I said, carefully, 'that kids like Giovanni are in a difficult position. This isn't, you know, the land of opportunity—there's no provision made for them. Giovanni's poor, I mean he comes from poor folks, and there isn't really much that he can do. And for what he *can* do, there's terrific competition. And, at that, very little money, not enough for them to be able to think of building any kind of future. That's why so many of them wander the streets and turn into gigolos and gangsters and God knows what.'

'It's cold,' she said, 'out here in the Old World.'

'Well, it's pretty cold out there in the New One, too,' I said. 'It's cold out here, period.'

She laughed. 'But we—we have our love to keep us warm.'

'We're not the first people who thought that as they lay in bed.' Nevertheless, we lay silent and still in each other's arms for awhile. 'Hella,' I said at last.

'Yes?'

'Hella, when the money gets here, let's take it and get out of Paris.'

'Get out of Paris? Where do you want to go?'

'I don't care. Just out. I'm sick of Paris. I want to leave it for awhile. Let's go south. Maybe there'll be some sun.'

'Shall we get married in the south?'

'Hella,' I said, 'you have to believe me, I can't do anything or decide anything, I can't even see straight until we get out of this town. I don't want to get married here, I don't even want to think about getting married here. Let's just get out.'

'I didn't know you felt this way,' she said.

'I've been living in Giovanni's room for months,' I said, 'and I just can't stand it anymore. I have to get out of there. Please.'

She laughed nervously and moved slightly away from me. 'Well, I really don't see why getting out of Giovanni's room means getting out of Paris.'

I sighed. 'Please, Hella. I don't feel like going into long explanations now. Maybe it's just that if I stay in Paris I'll keep running into Giovanni and . . .' I stopped.

'Why should that disturb you?'

'Well—I can't do anything to help him and I can't stand having him watch me—as though—I'm an American, Hella, he thinks I'm *rich*.' I paused and sat up, looking outward. She watched me. 'He's a very nice man, as I say, but he's very persistent—and he's got this *thing* about me, he thinks I'm God. And that room is so stinking and dirty. And soon winter'll be here and it's going to be cold . . .' I turned to her again and took her in my arms. 'Look. Let's just go. I'll explain a lot of things to you later—later—when we get out.'

There was a long silence.

'And you want to leave right away?' she said.

'Yes. As soon as that money comes, let's rent a house.'

'You're sure,' she said, 'that you don't just want to go back to the States?'

I groaned. 'No. Not yet. That isn't what I mean.'

She kissed me. 'I don't care where we go,' she said, 'as long as we're together.' Then she pushed me away. 'It's almost morning,' she said. 'We'd better get some sleep.'

I got to Giovanni's room very late the next evening. I had been walking by the river with Hella and, later, I drank too much in several bistros. The light crashed on as I came into the room and Giovanni sat up in bed, crying out in a voice of terror, *'Qui est là? Qui est là?'*

I stopped in the doorway, weaving a little in the light, and I said, 'It's me, Giovanni. Shut up.'

Giovanni stared at me and turned on his side, facing the wall, and began to cry.

I thought, *Sweet Jesus!* and I carefully closed the door. I took my cigarettes out of my jacket pocket and hung my jacket over the chair. With my cigarettes in my hand I went to the bed and leaned over Giovanni. I said, 'Baby, stop crying. Please stop crying.'

Giovanni turned and looked at me. His eyes were red and wet, but he wore a strange smile, it was composed of cruelty and shame and delight. He held out his arms and I leaned down, brushing his hair from his eyes.

'You smell of wine,' said Giovanni, then.

'I haven't been drinking wine. Is that what frightened you? Is that why you are crying?'

'No.'

'What is the matter?'

'Why have you gone away from me?'

I did not know what to say. Giovanni turned to the wall again. I had hoped, I had supposed that I would feel nothing: but I felt a tightening in a far corner of my heart, as though a finger had touched me there.

'I have never reached you,' said Giovanni. 'You have never really been here. I do not think you have ever lied to me but I know that you have never told me the truth—why? Sometimes you were here all day long and you read or you opened the window or you cooked something—and I watched you— and you never said anything—and you looked at me with such eyes, as though you did not see me. All day, while I worked, to make this room for you.'

I said nothing. I looked beyond Giovanni's head at the square windows which held back the feeble moonlight.

'What are you doing all the time? And why do you say nothing? You are evil, you know, and sometimes when you smiled at me I hated you. I wanted to strike you. I wanted to make you bleed. You smiled at me the way you smiled at everyone, you told me what you told everyone—and you tell nothing but lies. What are you always hiding? And do you think I did not know when you made love to me, you were making love to no one? *No one!* Or everyone—but not *me*, certainly. I am nothing to you, nothing, and you bring me fever but no delight."

I moved, looking for a cigarette. They were in my hand. I lit one. In a moment, I thought, I will say something. I will say something and then I will walk out of this room forever.

'You know I cannot be alone. I have told you. What is the matter? Can we never have a life together?'

He began to cry again. I watched the hot tears roll from the corners of his eyes onto the dirty pillow.

'If you cannot love me, I will die. Before you came I wanted to die, I have told you many times. It is cruel to have made me want to live only to make my death more bloody.'

I wanted to say so many things. Yet, when I opened my mouth, I made no sound. And yet—I do not know what I felt for Giovanni. I felt nothing for Giovanni. I felt terror and pity and a rising lust.

He took my cigarette from my lips and puffed on it, sitting up in bed, his hair in his eyes again.

'I have never known anyone like you before. I was never like this before you came. Listen. In Italy I had a woman and she was very good to me. She loved me, she loved *me*, and she took care of me and she was always there when I came in from work, in from the vineyards, and there was never any trouble between us, never. I was young then and did not know the things I learned later or the terrible things you have taught me. I thought all women were like that. I thought all men were like me—I thought I was like all other men. I was not unhappy then and I was not lonely—for she was there— and I did not want to die. I wanted to stay forever in our village and work in the vineyards and drink the wine we made and make love to my girl. I have told you about my village—? It is very old and in the south, it is on a hill. At night, when we walked by the wall, the world seemed to fall down before us, the whole, far-off, dirty world. I did not ever want to see it. Once we made love under the wall.

'Yes, I wanted to stay there forever and eat much spaghetti and drink much wine and make many babies and grow fat. You would not have liked me if I had stayed. I can see you, many years from now, coming through our village in the ugly, fat, American motor car you will surely have by then and looking at me and looking at all of us and tasting our wine and shitting on us with those empty smiles Americans wear everywhere and which you wear all the time and driving off with a great roar of the motors and a great sound of tires and telling all the other Americans you meet that they must come and see our village because it is so picturesque. And you will have no idea of the life there, dripping and bursting and beautiful and terrible, as you have no idea of my life now. But I think I would have been happier there and I would not have minded your smiles. I would have had my life. I have lain here many nights, waiting for you to come home, and thought how far away is my village and how terrible it is to be in this cold city, among people whom I hate, where it is cold and wet and never dry and hot as it was there, and where Giovanni has no one to talk to, and no one to be with, and where he has found a lover who is neither man nor woman, nothing that I can know or touch. You do not know, do you, what it is like to lie awake at night and wait for someone to come home? But I am sure you do not know. You do not know anything. You do not know any of the terrible things—that is why you smile and dance the way you do and you think that the comedy you are playing with the short-haired, moon-faced little girl is love.'

He dropped the cigarette to the floor, where it lay burning faintly. He began to cry again. I looked at the room, thinking: I cannot bear it.

'I left my village one wild, sweet day. I will never forget that day. It was the day of my death—I wish it had been the day of my death. I remember the sun was hot and scratchy on the back of my neck as I walked the road away from my village and the road went upward and I walked bent over. I remember everything, the brown dust at my feet, and the little pebbles which rushed before me, and the short trees along the road and all the flat houses and all their colors under the sun. I remember I was weeping, but not as I am weeping now, much worse, more terrible—since I am with you, I cannot even cry as I cried then. That was the first time in my life that I wanted to die. I had just buried my baby in the churchyard where my father and my father's fathers were and I had left my girl screaming in my mother's house. Yes, I had made a baby but it was born dead. It was all grey and twisted when I saw it and it made no sound—and we spanked it on the buttocks and we sprinkled it with holy water and we prayed but it never made a sound, it was dead. It was a little boy, it would have been a wonderful, strong man, perhaps even the kind of man *you* and Jacques and Guillaume and all your disgusting band of fairies spend all your days and nights looking for, and dreaming of—but it was dead, it was my baby and we had made it, my girl and I, and it was dead. When I knew that it was dead I took our crucifix off the wall and I spat on it and I threw it on the floor and my mother and my girl screamed and I went out. We buried it right away, the next day, and then I left my village and I came to this city where surely God has punished me for all my sins and for spitting on His holy Son, and where I will surely die. I do not think that I will ever see my village again.'

I stood up. My head was turning. Salt was in my mouth. The room seemed to rock, as it had the first time I had come here, so many lifetimes ago. I heard Giovanni's moan behind me. '*Cheri. Mon tres cher*. Don't leave me. Please don't leave me.' I turned and held him in my arms, staring above his head at the wall, at the man and woman on the wall who walked together among roses. He was sobbing, it would have been said, as though his heart would break. But I felt that it was my heart which was broken. Something had broken in me to make me so cold and so perfectly still and far away.

Still, I had to speak.

'Giovanni,' I said. 'Giovanni.'

He began to be still, he was listening; I felt, unwillingly, not for the first time, the cunning of the desperate.

'Giovanni,' I said, 'you always knew that I would leave one day. You knew my fiancée was coming back to Paris.'

'You are not leaving me for her,' he said. 'You are leaving me for some other reason. You lie so much, you have come to believe all your own lies. But I, *I* have senses. You are not leaving me for a *woman*. If you were really in love with this little girl, you would not have had to be so cruel to me.'

'She's not a little girl,' I said. 'She's a woman and no matter what you think, I *do* love her . . .'

'You do not,' cried Giovanni, sitting up, 'love anyone! You never have loved anyone, I am sure you never will! You love your purity, you love your mirror—you are just like a little virgin, you walk around with your hands in front of you as though you had some precious metal, gold, silver, rubies, maybe *diamonds* down there between your legs! You will never give it to anybody, you will never let anybody *touch* it— man *or* woman. You want to be *clean*. You think you came here covered with soap and you think you will go out covered with soap—and you do not want to *stink*, not even for five minutes, in the meantime.' He grasped me by the collar, wrestling and caressing at once, fluid and iron at once: saliva spraying from his lips and his eyes full of tears, but with the bones of his face showing and the muscles leaping in his arms and neck. 'You want to leave Giovanni because he makes you stink. You want to despise Giovanni because he is not afraid of the stink of love. You want to *kill* him in the name of all your lying little moralities. And you—you are *immoral.* You are, by far, the most immoral man I have met in all my life. Look, *look* what you have done to me. Do you think you could have done this if I did not love you? Is *this* what you should do to love?'

'Giovanni, stop it! For God's sake, *stop* it! What in the world do you want me to do? I can't *help* the way I feel.'

'Do you *know* how you feel? *Do* you feel? *What* do you feel?'

'I feel nothing now,' I said, 'nothing. I want to get out of this room, I want to get away from you, I want to end this terrible scene.'

'You want to get away from me.' He laughed; he watched me; the look in his eyes was so bottomlessly bitter it was almost benevolent. 'At last you are beginning to be honest. And do you know *why* you want to get away from me?'

Inside me something locked. 'I—I cannot have a life with you,' I said.

'But you can have a life with Hella. With that moon-faced little girl who thinks babies come out of cabbages—or frigidaires, I am not acquainted with the mythology of your country. You can have a life with her.'

'Yes,' I said, wearily, 'I can have a life with her.' I stood up. I was shaking. 'What kind of life can we have in this room?—this filthy little room. What kind of life can two men have together, anyway? All this love you talk about—isn't it just that you want to be made to feel strong? You want to go out and be the big laborer and bring home the money and you want me to stay here and wash the dishes and cook the food and clean this miserable closet of a room and kiss you when you come in through that door and lie with you at night and be your little *girl.* That's what you want. That's what you mean and that's *all* you mean when you say you love me. You say I want to kill *you.* What do you think you've been doing to me?'

'I am not trying to make you a little girl. If I wanted a little girl, I would be *with* a little girl.'

'Why aren't you? Isn't it just that you're afraid? And you take *me* because you haven't got the guts to go after a woman, which is what you *really* want?'

He was pale. 'You are the one who keeps talking about *what* I want. But I have only been talking about *who* I want.'

'But I'm a man,' I cried, 'a man! What do you think can *happen* between us?'

'You know very well,' said Giovanni, slowly, 'what can happen between us. It is for that reason you are leaving me.' He got up and walked to the window and opened it. *'Bon,'* he said. He struck his fist once against the window sill. '*If* I could make you stay, I would,' he shouted. 'If I had to beat you, chain you, starve you—*if* I could make you stay, I would.' He turned back into the room; the wind blew his hair. He shook his finger at me, grotesquely playful. 'One day, perhaps, you will wish I had.'

'It's cold,' I said. 'Close the window.'

He smiled. 'Now that you are leaving—you want the windows closed. *Bien sûr.*' He closed the window and we stood staring at each other in the center of the room. 'We will not fight any more,' he said. 'Fighting will not make you stay. In French we have what is called *une separation de corps*—not a divorce, you understand, just a separation. Well. We will separate. But I know you belong with me. I believe, I must believe—that you will come back.'

'Giovanni,' I said, 'I'll not be coming back. You know I won't be back.'

He waved his hand. 'I said we would not fight any more. The Americans have no sense of doom, none whatever. They do not recognize doom when they see it.' He produced a bottle from beneath the sink. 'Jacques left a bottle of cognac here. Let us have a little drink—for the road, as I believe you people say sometimes.'

I watched him. He carefully poured two drinks. I saw that he was shaking—with rage, or pain, or both.

He handed me my glass.

'A la tienne,' he said.

'A la tienne.'

We drank. I could not keep myself from asking: 'Giovanni. What are you going to do now?'

'Oh,' he said, 'I have friends. I will think of things to do. Tonight, for example, I shall have supper with Jacques. No doubt, tomorrow night I shall also have supper with Jacques.

He has become very fond of me. He thinks you are a monster.'

'Giovanni,' I said, helplessly, 'be careful. Please be careful.'

He gave me an ironical smile. 'Thank you,' he said. 'You should have given me that advice the night we met.'

That was the last time we really spoke to one another. I stayed with him until morning and then I threw my things into a bag and took them away with me, to Hella's place.

I will not forget the last time he looked at me. The morning light filled the room, reminding me of so many mornings and of the morning I had first come there. Giovanni sat on the bed, completely naked, holding a glass of cognac between his hands. His body was dead white, his face was wet and grey. I was at the door with my suitcase. With my hand on the knob, I looked at him. Then I wanted to beg him to forgive me. But this would have been too great a confession; any yielding at that moment would have locked me forever in that room with him. And in a way this was exactly what I wanted. I felt a tremor go through me, like the beginning of an earthquake, and felt, for an instant, that I was drowning in his eyes. His body, which I had come to know so well, glowed in the light and charged and thickened the air between us. Then something opened in my brain, a secret, noiseless door swung open, frightening me: it had not occurred to me until that instant that, in fleeing from his body, I confirmed and perpetuated his body's power over me. Now, as though I had been branded, his body was burned into my mind, into my dreams. And all this time he did not take his eyes from me. He seemed to find my face more transparent than a shop-window. He did not smile, he was neither grave, nor vindictive, nor sad; he was still. He was waiting, I think, for me to cross that space and take him in my arms again—waiting, as one waits at a death-bed for the miracle one dare not disbelieve, which will not happen. I had to get out of there for my face showed too much, the war in my body was dragging me down. My feet refused to carry me over to him again. The wind of my life was blowing me away.

'*Au revoir, Giovanni.*'

'*Au revoir, mon cher.*'

I turned from him, unlocked the door. The weary exhale

of his breath seemed to ruffle my hair and brush my brow like the very wind of madness. I walked down the short corridor, expecting every instant to hear his voice behind me, passed through the vestibule, passed the *loge* of the still sleeping concierge, into the morning streets. And with every step I took it became more impossible for me to turn back. And my mind was empty—or it was as though my mind had become one enormous, anaesthetized wound. I thought only, *One day I'll weep for this. One of these days I'll start to cry.*

At the corner, in a faint patch of the morning sun, I looked in my wallet to count my bus tickets. In the wallet I found three hundred francs, taken from Hella, my *carte d'identité*, my address in the United States, and paper, paper, scraps of paper, cards, photographs. On each piece of paper I found addresses, telephone numbers, memos of various rendezvous made and kept—or perhaps not kept—people met and remembered, or perhaps not remembered, hopes probably not fulfilled: certainly not fulfilled, or I would not have been standing on that street corner.

I found four bus tickets in my wallet and I walked to the *arret*. There was a policeman standing there, his blue hood, weighted, hanging down behind, his white club gleaming. He looked at me and smiled and cried, *'Ca va?'*

'*Oui, merci.* And you?'

'*Toujours.* It's a nice day, no?'

'Yes.' But my voice trembled. 'The autumn is beginning.'

'*C'est ca.*' And he turned away, back to his contemplation of the boulevard. I smoothed my hair with my hand, feeling foolish for feeling shaken. I watched a woman pass, coming from the market, her string bag full; at the top, precariously, a litre of red wine. She was not young but she was clear-faced and bold, she had a strong, thick body and strong, thick hands. The policeman shouted something to her and she shouted back—something bawdy and good-natured. The policeman laughed; but refused to look at me again. I watched the woman continue down the street—home, I thought, to her husband, dressed in blue working clothes, dirty, and to her children. She passed the corner where the patch of sunlight fell and crossed the street. The bus came and the policeman and I, the only people waiting, got on—he stood on the platform, far from me. The policeman was not young, either, but he had a gusto which I admired. I looked out of the window and the streets rolled by. Ages ago, in another city, on another bus, I sat so at the windows, looking outward, inventing for each flying face which trapped my brief attention some life, some destiny, in which I played a part. I was looking for some whisper, or promise, of my possible salvation. But it seemed to me that morning that my ancient self had been dreaming the most dangerous dream of all.

The days that followed seemed to fly. It seemed to turn cold overnight. The tourists in their thousands disappeared, conjured away by time-tables. When one walked through the gardens, leaves fell about one's head and sighed and crashed beneath one's feet. The stone of the city, which had been luminous and changing, faded slowly, but with no hesitation, into simple grey stone again. It was apparent that the stone was hard. Daily, fishermen disappeared from the river until, one day, the river banks were clear. The bodies of young boys and girls began to be compromised by heavy underwear, by sweaters and mufflers, hoods and capes. Old men seemed older, old women slower. The colors on the river faded, the rain began, and the river began to rise. It was apparent that the sun would soon give up the tremendous struggle it cost her to get to Paris for a few hours every day.

'But it will be warm in the south,' I said.

The money had come. Hella and I were busy every day, on the track of a house in Eze, in Cagnes-sur-mer, in Vence, in Monte Carlo, in Antibes, in Grasse. We were scarcely ever seen in the quarter. We stayed in her room, we made love a lot, we went to the movies, and had long, frequently rather melancholy dinners in strange restaurants on the right bank. It is hard to say what produced this melancholy, which sometimes settled over us like the shadow of some vast, some predatory, waiting bird. I do not think that Hella was unhappy, for I had never before clung to her as I clung to her during that time. But perhaps she sensed, from time to time, that my clutch was too insistent to be trusted, certainly too insistent to last.

And from time to time, around the quarter, I ran into Giovanni. I dreaded seeing him, not only because he was almost always with Jacques, but also because, though he was often rather better dressed, he did not look well. I could not endure something at once abject and vicious which I began to see in his eyes, nor the way he giggled at Jacques' jokes, nor the mannerisms, a fairy's mannerisms, which he was beginning, sometimes, to affect. I did not want to know what his status was with Jacques; yet the day came when it was revealed to me in Jacques' spiteful and triumphant eyes. And Giovanni, during this short encounter, in the middle of the boulevard as dusk fell, with people hurrying all about us, was really amazingly giddy and girlish, and very drunk—it was as though he were forcing me to taste the cup of his humiliation. And I hated him for this.

The next time I saw him it was in the morning. He was buying a newspaper. He looked up at me insolently, into my eyes, and looked away. I watched him diminish down the boulevard. When I got home, I told Hella about it, trying to laugh.

Then I began to see him around the quarter without Jacques, with the street-boys of the quarter, whom he had once described to me as 'lamentable.' He was no longer so well dressed, he was beginning to look like one of them. His special friend among them seemed to be the same, tall, pock-marked boy, named Yves, whom I remembered having seen briefly, playing the pinball machine, and, later, talking to Jacques on that first morning in Les Halles. One night, quite drunk myself, and wandering about the quarter alone, I ran into this boy and bought him a drink. I did not mention Giovanni but Yves volunteered the information that he was not with Jacques anymore. But it seemed that he might be able to get back his old job in Guillaume's bar. It was certainly not more than a week after this that Guillaume was found dead in the private quarters above his bar, strangled with the sash of his dressing gown.

5

It was a terrific scandal, if you were in Paris at the time you certainly heard of it, and saw the picture printed in all the newspapers, of Giovanni, just after he was captured. Editorials were written and speeches were made, and many bars of the genre of Guillaume's bar were closed. (But they did not stay closed long.) Plain-clothes policemen descended on the quarter, asking to see everyone's papers, and the bars were emptied of *tapettes*. Giovanni was nowhere to be found. All of the evidence, above all, of course, his disappearance, pointed to him as the murderer. Such a scandal always threatens, before its reverberations cease, to rock the very foundations of the state. It is necessary to find an explanation, a solution, and a victim with the utmost possible speed. Most of the men picked up in connection with this crime were not picked up on suspicion of murder. They were picked up on suspicion of having what the French, with a delicacy I take to be sardonic, call *les goûts particuliers*. These 'tastes,' which do not constitute a crime in France, are nevertheless regarded with extreme disapprobation by the bulk of the populace, which also looks on its rulers and 'betters' with a stony lack of affection. When Guillaume's corpse was discovered it was not only the boys of the street who were frightened; they, in fact, were a good deal less frightened than the men who roamed the streets to buy them, whose careers, positions, aspirations, could never have survived such notoriety. Fathers of families, sons of great houses, and itching adventurers from Belleville were all desperately anxious that the case be closed, so that things might, in effect, go back to normal and the dreadful whiplash of public morality not fall on their backs. Until the case was closed they could not be certain which way to jump, whether they should cry out that they were martyrs, or remain what, at heart, of course, they were, simple citizens, bitter against outrage and anxious to see justice done and the health of the state preserved.

It was fortunate, therefore, that Giovanni was a foreigner. As though by some magnificently tacit agreement, with every day that he was at large, the press became more vituperative against him and more gentle towards Guillaume. It was remembered that there perished with Guillaume one of the oldest names in France. Sunday supplements were run on the history of his family; and his old, aristocratic mother, who did not survive the trial of his murderer, testified to the sterling qualities of her son and regretted that corruption had become so vast in France that such a crime could go so long unpunished. With this sentiment the populace was, of course, more than ready to agree. It is perhaps not as incredible as it certainly seemed to me, but Guillaume's name became fantastically entangled with French history, French honor, and French glory, and very nearly became, indeed, a symbol of French manhood.

'But listen,' I said to Hella, 'he was just a disgusting old fairy. That's *all* he was!'

'Well, how in the world do you expect the people who read newspapers to know that? *If* that's what he was, I'm sure he didn't advertise it—and he must have moved in a pretty limited circle.'

'Well—*somebody* knows it. Some of the people who write this drivel know it.'

'There doesn't seem to be much point,' she said, quietly, 'in defaming the dead.'

'But isn't there some point in telling the truth?'

'They're telling the truth. He's a member of a very important family and he's been murdered. I know what *you* mean. There's another truth they're *not* telling. But newspapers never do, that's not what they're for.'

I sighed. 'Poor, poor, poor Giovanni.'

'Do you believe he did it?'

'I don't know. It certainly *looks* as though he did it. He was there that night. People saw him go upstairs before the bar closed and they don't remember seeing him come down.'

'Was he working there that night?'

'Apparently not. He was just drinking. He and Guillaume seemed to have become friendly again.'

'You certainly made some peculiar friends while I was away.'

'They wouldn't seem so damn peculiar if one of them

hadn't got murdered. Anyway, none of them were my friends—except Giovanni.'

'You lived with him. Can't you tell whether he'd commit murder or not?'

'How? You live with me. Can I commit a murder?'

'You? Of course not.'

'How do you *know* that? You don't know that. How do you know I'm what you see?'

'Because'—she leaned over and kissed me—'I love you.'

'Ah! I loved Giovanni—'

'Not as I love you,' said Hella.

'I might have committed murder already, for all you know. How do you know?'

'Why are you so upset?'

'Wouldn't *you* be upset if a friend of yours was accused of murder and was hiding somewhere? What do you mean, why am I so upset? What do you want me to do, sing Christmas carols?'

'Don't shout. It's just that I never realized he meant so much to you.'

'He was a nice man,' I said, finally. 'I just hate to see him in trouble.'

She came to me and put her hand lightly on my arm. 'We'll leave this city soon, David. You won't have to think about it anymore. People get into trouble, David. But don't act as though it were, somehow, your fault. It's not your fault.'

'*I* know it's not my fault!' But my voice, and Hella's eyes, astounded me into silence. I felt, with terror, that I was about to cry.

Giovanni stayed at large nearly a week. As I watched, from Hella's window, each night creeping over Paris, I thought of Giovanni somewhere outside, perhaps under one of those bridges, frightened and cold and not knowing where to go. I wondered if he had, perhaps, found friends to hide him—it was astonishing that in so small and policed a city he should prove so hard to find. I feared, sometimes, that he might come to find me—to beg me to help him, or to kill me. Then I thought that he probably considered it beneath him to ask me for help; he, no doubt, felt by now that I was not worth killing. I looked to Hella for help. I tried to bury each night, in her, all my guilt and terror. The need to act was like a fever in me, the only act possible was the act of love.

He was finally caught, very early one morning, in a barge tied up along the river. Newspaper speculation had already placed him in Argentina, so it was a great shock to discover that he had got no farther than the Seine. This lack, on his part, of 'dash' did nothing to endear him to the public. He was a criminal, Giovanni, of the dullest kind, a bungler; robbery, for example, had been insisted on as the motive for Guillaume's murder; but, though Giovanni had taken all the money Guillaume had in his pockets, he had not touched the cash-register and had not even suspected, apparently, that Guillaume had over one hundred thousand francs hidden in another wallet at the bottom of his closet. The money he had taken from Guillaume was still in his pockets when he was caught; he had not been able to spend it. He had not eaten for two or three days and was weak and pale and unattractive. His face was on news-stands all over Paris. He looked young, bewildered, terrified, depraved; as though he could not believe that he, Giovanni, had come to this; had come to this and would go no further, his short road ending in a common knife. He seemed already to be rearing back, every inch of his flesh revolting before that icy vision. And it seemed, as it had seemed so many times, that he looked to me for help. The newsprint told the unforgiving world how Giovanni repented, cried for mercy, called on God, wept that he had not meant to do it. And told us, too, in delicious detail, *how* he had done it: but not why. Why was too black for the newsprint to carry and too deep for Giovanni to tell.

I may have been the only man in Paris who knew that he had not meant to do it, who could read *why* he had done it beneath the details printed in the newspapers. I remembered again the evening I had found him at home and he told me how Guillaume had fired him. I heard his voice again and saw the vehemence of his body and saw his tears. I knew his bravado, how he liked to feel himself *debrouillard*, more than equal to any challenge, and saw him swagger into Guillaume's bar. He must have felt that, having surrendered to Jacques, his apprenticeship was over, love was over, and he could do with Guillaume anything he liked. He could, indeed, have done with Guillaume anything at all—but he could not do anything about being Giovanni. Guillaume certainly knew, Jacques would have lost no time in telling him, that Giovanni was no longer with *le jeune Americain*; perhaps Guillaume had even attended one or two of Jacques' parties, armed with his own entourage; and he certainly knew, all his circle knew, that Giovanni's new freedom, his loverless state, would turn into license, into riot—it had happened to every one of them. It must have been a great evening for the bar when Giovanni swaggered in alone.

I could hear the conversation:

'*Alors, tu es revenu?*' This from Guillaume, with a seductive, sardonic, speaking look.

Giovanni sees that he does not wish to be reminded of his last, disastrous tantrum, that he wishes to be friendly. At the same moment Guillaume's face, voice, manner, smell, hit him; he is actually facing Guillaume, not conjuring him up in his mind; the smile with which he responds to Guillaume almost causes him to vomit. But Guillaume does not see this, of course, and offers Giovanni a drink.

'I thought you might need a bar-man,' Giovanni says.

'But are you looking for work? I thought your American would have bought you an oil-well in Texas by now.'

'No. My American'—he makes a gesture—'has flown!' They both laugh.

'The Americans always fly. They are not serious,' says Guillaume.

'*C'est vrai,*' says Giovanni. He finishes his drink, looking away from Guillaume, looking dreadfully self-conscious, per-haps almost unconsciously, whistling. Guillaume, now, can hardly keep his eyes off him, or control his hands.

'Come back, later, at closing, and we will talk about this job,' he says at last.

And Giovanni nods and leaves. I can imagine him, then, finding some of his street-cronies, drinking with them, and laughing, stiffening up his courage as the hours tick by. He is dying for someone to tell him not to go back to Guillaume, not to let Guillaume touch him. But his friends tell him how rich Guillaume is, how he is a silly old queen, how much he can get out of Guillaume if he will only be smart.

No one appears on the boulevards to speak to him, to save him. He feels that he is dying.

Then the hour comes when he must go back to Guillaume's bar. He walks there alone. He stands outside awhile. He wants to turn away, to run away. But there is no place to run. He looks up the long, dark, curving street as though he were looking for someone. But there is no one there. He goes into the bar. Guillaume sees him at once and discreetly motions him upstairs. He climbs the stairs. His legs are weak. He finds himself in Guillaume's rooms, surrounded by Guillaume's silks, colors, perfumes, staring at Guillaume's bed.

Then Guillaume enters and Giovanni tries to smile. They have a drink. Guillaume is precipitate, flabby, and moist, and, with each touch of his hand, Giovanni shrinks further and more furiously away. Guillaume disappears to change his clothes and comes back in his theatrical dressing gown. He wants Giovanni to undress. . . .

Perhaps at this moment Giovanni realizes that he cannot go through with it, that his will cannot carry him through. He remembers the job. He tries to talk, to be practical, to be reasonable, but, of course, it is too late. Guillaume seems to surround him like the sea itself. And I think that Giovanni, tortured into a state like madness, feels himself going under, is overcome, and Guillaume has his will. I think if this had not happened, Giovanni would not have killed him.

For, with his pleasure taken, and while Giovanni still lies suffocating, Guillaume becomes a business man once more and, walking up and down, gives excellent reasons why Giovanni cannot work for him anymore. Beneath whatever reasons Guillaume invents the real one lies hidden and they both, dimly, in their different fashions, see it: Giovanni, like a falling movie star, has lost his drawing power. Everything is known about him, his secrecy has been discovered. Giovanni certainly feels this and the rage which has been building in him for many months begins to be swollen now with the memory of Guillaume's hands and mouth. He stares at Guillaume in silence for a moment and then begins to shout. And Guillaume answers him. With every word exchanged Giovanni's head begins to roar and a blackness comes and goes before his eyes. And Guillaume is in seventh heaven and begins to prance about the room—he has scarcely ever gotten so much for so little before. He plays this scene for all it's worth, deeply rejoicing in the fact that Giovanni's face grows scarlet, and his voice thick, watching, with pure delight, the bone-hard muscles in his neck. And he says something, for he thinks the tables have been turned; he says something, one phrase, one insult, one mockery too many; and in a split-second, in his own shocked silence, in Giovanni's eyes, he realizes that he has unleashed something he cannot turn back.

Giovanni certainly did not mean to do it. But he grabbed him, he struck him. And with that touch, and with each blow, the intolerable weight at the bottom of his heart began to lift: now it was Giovanni's turn to be delighted. The room was overturned, the fabrics were shredded, the odor of perfume was thick. Guillaume struggled to get out of the room, but Giovanni followed him everywhere: now it was Guillaume's turn to be surrounded. And perhaps at the very moment Guillaume thought he had broken free, when he had reached the door perhaps, Giovanni lunged after him and caught him by the sash of the dressing gown and wrapped the sash around his neck. Then he simply held on, sobbing, becoming lighter every moment as Guillaume grew heavier, tightening the sash and cursing. Then Guillaume fell. And Giovanni fell—back into the room, the streets, the world, into the presence and the shadow of death.

By the time we found this great house it was clear that I had no right to come here. By the time we found it, I did not even want to see it. But by this time, also, there was nothing else to do. There was nothing else I wanted to do. I thought, it is true, of remaining in Paris in order to be close to the trial, perhaps to visit him in prison. But I knew there was no reason to do this. Jacques, who was in constant touch with Giovanni's lawyer, and in constant touch with me, had seen Giovanni once. He told me what I knew already, that there was nothing I, or anyone, could do for Giovanni anymore.

Perhaps he wanted to die. He pleaded guilty, with robbery as the motive. The circumstances under which Guillaume had fired him received great play in the press. And, from the press, one received the impression that Guillaume had been a good-hearted, a perhaps somewhat erratic philanthropist who had had the bad judgment to befriend the hardened and ungrateful adventurer, Giovanni. Then the case drifted downward from the headlines. Giovanni was taken to prison to await trial.

And Hella and I came here. I may have thought—I am sure I thought, in the beginning—that, though I could do nothing for Giovanni, I might, perhaps, be able to do something for Hella. I must have hoped that there would be something Hella could do for me. And this might have been possible if the days had not dragged by, for me, like days in prison. I could not get Giovanni out of my mind, I was at the mercy of the bulletins which sporadically arrived from Jacques. All that I remember of the autumn is waiting for Giovanni to come to trial. Then, at last, he came to trial, was found guilty, and placed under sentence of death. All winter long I counted the days. And the nightmare of this house began.

Much has been written of love turning to hatred, of the heart growing cold with the death of love. It is a remarkable process. It is far more terrible than anything I have ever read about it, more terrible than anything I will ever be able to say.

I don't know, now, when I first looked at Hella and found her stale, found her body uninteresting, her presence grating. It seemed to happen all at once—I suppose that only means that it had been happening for a long time. I trace it to something as fleeting as the tip of her breast lightly touching my forearm as she leaned over me to serve my supper. I felt my flesh recoil. Her underclothes, drying in the bathroom, which I had often thought of as smelling even rather improbably sweet and as being washed much too often, now began to seem unaesthetic and unclean. A body which had to be covered with such crazy, catty-cornered bits of stuff began to seem grotesque. I sometimes watched her naked body move and wished that it were harder and firmer, I was fantastically intimidated by her breasts, and when I entered her I began to feel that I would never get out alive. All that had once delighted me seemed to have turned sour on my stomach.

I think—I think that I have never been more frightened in my life. When my fingers began, involuntarily, to loose their hold on Hella, I realized that I was dangling from a high place and that I had been clinging to her for my very life. With each moment, as my fingers slipped, I felt the roaring air beneath me and felt everything in me bitterly contracting, crawling furiously upward against that long fall.

I thought that it was only, perhaps, that we were alone too much and so, for a while, we were always going out. We made expeditions to Nice and Monte Carlo and Cannes and Antibes. But we were not rich and the south of France, in the winter-time, is a playground for the rich. Hella and I went to a lot of movies and found ourselves, very often, sitting in empty, fifth-rate bars. We walked a lot, in silence. We no longer seemed to see things to point out to each other. We drank too much, especially me. Hella, who had been so brown and confident and glowing on her return from Spain, began to lose all this, she began to be pale and watchful and uncertain. She ceased to ask me what the matter was, for it was borne in on her that I either did not know, or would not say. She watched me. I felt her watching and it made me wary and it made me hate her. My guilt, when I looked into her closing face, was more than I could bear.

We were at the mercy of bus schedules and often found ourselves, in the wintry dawn, huddled sleepily together in a waiting room or freezing on the street-corner of some totally deserted town. We arrived home in the grey morning, crippled with weariness, and went straight to bed.

I was able, for some reason, to make love in the mornings. It may have been due to nervous exhaustion; or wandering about at night engendered in me a curious, irrepressible excitement. But it was not the same, something was gone; the astonishment, the power, and the joy were gone, the peace was gone.

I had nightmares and sometimes my own cries woke me up and sometimes my moaning made Hella shake me awake.

'I wish,' she said, one day, 'you'd tell me what it is. Tell me what it is, let me help you.'

I shook my head in bewilderment and sorrow and sighed. We were sitting in the big room, where I am standing now. She was sitting in the easy chair, under the lamp, with a book open on her lap.

'You're sweet,' I said. Then: 'It's nothing. It'll go away. It's probably just nerves.'

'It's Giovanni,' she said.

I watched her.

'Isn't it,' she asked, carefully, 'that you think you've done something awful to him by leaving him in that room? I think you blame yourself for what happened to him. But, darling, nothing you could have done would have helped him. Stop torturing yourself.'

'He was so beautiful,' I said. I had not meant to say it. I felt myself beginning to shake. She watched me while I walked to the table—there was a bottle there then, as now—and poured myself a drink.

I could not stop talking, though I feared at every instant that I would say too much. Perhaps I wanted to say too much.

'I can't help feeling that I placed him in the shadow of the knife. He wanted me to stay in that room with him, he begged me to stay. I didn't tell you—we had an awful fight the night I went there, to get my things.' I paused. I sipped my drink. 'He cried.'

'He was in love with you,' said Hella. 'Why didn't you tell me that? Or didn't you know it?'

I turned away, feeling my face flame.

'It's not your fault,' she said. 'Don't you understand that? You couldn't keep him from falling in love with you. You couldn't have kept him from—from killing that awful man.'

'You don't know anything about it,' I muttered. 'You don't know anything about it.'

'I know how you feel—'

'You *don't* know how I feel.'

'David. Don't shut me out. Please don't shut me out. Let me help you.'

'Hella. Baby. I know you want to help me. But just let me be for awhile. I'll be all right.'

'You've been saying that now,' she said, wearily, 'for a long time.' She looked at me steadily for awhile and then she said, 'David. Don't you think we ought to go home?'

'Go home? What for?'

'What are we staying here for? How long do you want to

sit in this house, eating your heart out? And what do you think it's doing to me?' She rose and came to me. 'Please. I want to go home. I want to get married. I want to start having kids. I want us to live someplace, I want *you*. Please David. What are we marking time over here for?'

I moved away from her, quickly. At my back she stood perfectly still.

'What's the *matter*, David? What do you *want*?'

'I don't know. I don't *know*.'

'What is it you're not telling me? Why don't you tell me the truth? Tell me the *truth*.'

I turned and faced her. 'Hella—bear with me, *bear* with me—a little while.'

'I want to,' she cried, 'but where *are* you? You've gone away somewhere and I can't find you. If you'd only let me *reach* you—!'

She began to cry. I held her in my arms. I felt nothing at all.

I kissed her salty tears and murmured, murmured I don't know what. I felt her body straining, straining to meet mine and I felt my own contracting and drawing away and I knew that I had begun the long fall down. I stepped away from her. She swayed, where I had left her, like a puppet dangling from a string.

'David, please let me be a woman. I don't care what you do to me. I don't care what it costs. I'll wear my hair long, I'll give up cigarettes, I'll throw away the books.' She tried to smile; my heart turned over. 'Just let me be a woman, take me. It's what I want. It's *all* I want. I don't care about anything else.' She moved toward me. I stood perfectly still. She touched me, raising her face, with a desperate and terribly moving trust, to mine. 'Don't throw me back into the sea, David. Let me stay here with you.' Then she kissed me, watching my face. My lips were cold. I felt nothing on my lips. She kissed me again and I closed my eyes, feeling that strong chains were dragging me to fire. It seemed that my body, next to her warmth, her insistence, under her hands, would never awaken. But when it awakened, I had moved out of it. From a great height, where the air all around me was colder than ice, I watched my body in a stranger's arms.

It was that evening, or an evening very soon thereafter, that I left her sleeping in the bedroom and went, alone, to Nice.

I roamed all the bars of that glittering town and at the end of the first night, blind with alcohol and grim with lust, I climbed the stairs of a dark hotel, in company with a sailor. It turned out, late the next day, that the sailor's leave was not yet ended and that the sailor had friends. We went to visit them. We stayed the night. We spent the next day together, and the next. On the final night of the sailor's leave, we stood drinking together in a crowded bar. We faced the mirror. I was very drunk. I was almost penniless. In the mirror, suddenly, I saw Hella's face. I thought for a moment that I had gone mad, and I turned. She looked very tired and drab and small.

For a long time we said nothing to each other. I felt the sailor staring at both of us.

'Hasn't she got the wrong bar?' he asked me, finally.

Hella looked at him. She smiled.

'It's not the only thing I got wrong,' she said.

Now the sailor stared at me.

'Well,' I said to Hella, 'now you know.'

'I think I've known it for a long time,' she said. She turned and started away from me. I moved to follow her. The sailor grabbed me.

'Are you—is she—?'

I nodded. His face, open-mouthed, was comical. He let me go and I passed him and, as I reached the doors, I heard his laughter.

We walked for a long time in the stone-cold streets, in silence. There seemed to be no one on the streets at all. It seemed inconceivable that the day would ever break.

'Well,' said Hella, 'I'm going home. I wish I'd never left it.'

'If I stay here much longer,' she said, later that same morning, as she packed her bag, 'I'll forget what it's like to be a woman.'

She was extremely cold, she was very bitterly handsome.

'I'm not sure any woman *can* forget that,' I said.

'There are women who have forgotten that to be a woman doesn't simply mean humiliation, doesn't simply mean bitter-

ness. I haven't forgotten it yet,' she added, 'in spite of you.
I'm not going to forget it. I'm getting out of this house, away
from you, just as fast as taxis, trains, and boats will carry me.'

And in the room which had been our bedroom in the beginning of our life in this house, she moved with the desperate
haste of someone about to flee—from the open suitcase on
the bed, to the chest of drawers, to the closet. I stood in the
doorway, watching her. I stood there the way a small boy who
has wet his pants stands before his teacher. All the words I
wanted to say closed my throat, like weeds, and stopped my
mouth.

'I wish, anyway,' I said at last, 'that you'd believe me when
I say that, if I was lying, I wasn't lying to *you*.'

She turned toward me with a terrible face. '*I* was the one
you were talking to. *I* was the one you wanted to come with
you, to this terrible house in the middle of nowhere. *I* was
the one you said you wanted to marry!'

'I mean,' I said, 'I was lying to myself.'

'Oh,' said Hella, 'I see. That makes everything different, of
course.'

'I only mean to say,' I shouted, 'that whatever I've done to
hurt you, I didn't mean to do!'

'Don't shout,' said Hella. 'I'll soon be gone. Then you can
shout it to those hills out there, shout it to the peasants, how
guilty you are, how you love to be guilty!'

She started moving back and forth again, more slowly, from
the suitcase to the chest of drawers. Her hair was damp and
fell over her forehead, and her face was damp. I longed to
reach out and take her in my arms and comfort her. But that
would not be comfort anymore, only torture, for both of us.

She did not look at me as she moved, but kept looking at
the clothes she was packing, as though she were not sure they
were hers.

'But I *knew*,' she said, 'I knew. This is what makes me so
ashamed. I knew it every time you looked at me. I knew it
every time we went to bed. If only you had told me the truth
then. Don't you see how unjust it was to wait for *me* to find
it out? To put all the burden on *me*? I had the *right* to expect
to hear from you—women are always waiting for the *man* to
speak. Or hadn't you heard?'

I said nothing.

'I wouldn't have had to spend all this time in this *house*, I wouldn't be wondering how in the name of God I'm going to stand that long trip back. I'd *be* home by now, dancing with some man who wanted to make me. And I'd *let* him make me, too, why not?' And she smiled bewilderedly at a crowd of nylon stockings in her hand and carefully crushed them in the suitcase.

'Perhaps *I* didn't know it then. I only knew I had to get out of Giovanni's room.'

'Well,' she said, 'you're out. And now I'm getting out. It's only poor Giovanni who's—lost his head.'

It was an ugly joke and made with the intention of wounding me; yet she couldn't quite manage the sardonic smile she tried to wear.

'I'll never understand it,' she said at last, and she raised her eyes to mine as though I could help her to understand. 'That sordid little gangster has wrecked your life. I think he's wrecked mine, too. Americans should never come to Europe,' she said, and tried to laugh and began to cry, 'it means they never can be happy again. What's the good of an American who isn't happy? Happiness was all we had.' And she fell forward into my arms, into my arms for the last time, sobbing.

'Don't believe it,' I muttered, 'don't believe it. We've got much more than that, we've always had much more than that. Only—only—it's sometimes hard to bear.'

'Oh, God, I wanted you,' she said. 'Every man I come across will make me think of you.' She tried to laugh again. 'Poor man! Poor men! Poor *me*!'

'Hella. Hella. One day, when you're happy, try to forgive me.'

She moved away. 'Ah. I don't know anything about happiness anymore. I don't know anything about forgiveness. But if women are supposed to be led by men and there aren't any men to lead them, what happens then? What happens then?' She went to the closet and got her coat; dug in her handbag and found her compact and, looking into the tiny mirror, carefully dried her eyes and began to apply her lipstick. 'There's a difference between little boys and little girls, just like they say in those little blue books. Little girls want little boys. But little boys—!' She snapped her compact shut. 'I'll never again, as long as I live, know *what* they want. And now I know they'll never tell me. I don't think they know how.' She ran her fingers through her hair, brushing it back from her forehead, and, now, with the lipstick, and in the heavy, black coat, she looked, again, cold, brilliant, and bitterly helpless, a terrifying woman. 'Mix me a drink,' she said, 'we can drink to old time's sake before the taxi comes. No, I don't want you to come to the station with me. I wish I could drink all the way to Paris and all the way across that criminal ocean.'

We drank in silence, waiting to hear the sound of tires on gravel. Then we heard it, saw the lights, and the driver began honking his horn. Hella put down her drink and wrapped her coat around her and started for the door. I picked up her bags and followed. The driver and I arranged the baggage in the car; all the time I was trying to think of some last thing to say to Hella, something to help wipe away the bitterness. But I could not think of anything. She said nothing to me. She stood very erect beneath the dark, winter sky, looking far out. And when all was ready, I turned to her.

'Are you sure you wouldn't like me to come with you as far as the station, Hella?'

She looked at me and held out her hand.

'Good-bye, David.'

I took her hand. It was cold and dry, like her lips.

'Good-bye, Hella.'

She got into the taxi. I watched it back down the drive, onto the road. I waved one last time, but Hella did not wave back.

Outside my window the horizon begins to lighten, turning the grey sky a purplish blue.

I have packed my bags and I have cleaned the house. The keys to the house are on the table before me. I have only to change my clothes. When the horizon has become a little lighter the bus which will take me to town, to the station, to the train which will take me to Paris, will appear at the bend of the highway. Still, I cannot move.

On the table, also, is a small, blue envelope, the note from Jacques informing me of the date of Giovanni's execution.

I pour myself a very little drink, watching, in the window pane, my reflection, which steadily becomes more faint. I seem to be fading away before my eyes—this fancy amuses me, and I laugh to myself.

It should be now that gates are opening before Giovanni and clanging shut behind him, never, for him, to be opened or shut anymore. Or perhaps it is already over. Perhaps it is only beginning. Perhaps he still sits in his cell, watching, with me, the arrival of the morning. Perhaps now there are whispers at the end of the corridor, three heavy men in black taking off their shoes, one of them holding the ring of keys, all of the prison silent, waiting, charged with dread. Three tiers down, the activity on the stone floor has become silent, is suspended, someone lights a cigarette. Will he die alone? I do not know if death, in this country, is a solitary or a mass produced affair. And what will he say to the priest?

Take off your clothes, something tells me, *it's getting late.*

I walk into the bedroom where the clothes I will wear are lying on the bed and my bag lies open and ready. I begin to undress. There is a mirror in this room, a large mirror. I am terribly aware of the mirror.

Giovanni's face swings before me like an unexpected lantern on a dark, dark night. His eyes—his eyes, they glow like a tiger's eyes, they stare straight out, watching the approach of his last enemy, the hair of his flesh stands up. I cannot read what is in his eyes: if it is terror, then I have never seen terror, if it is anguish, then anguish has never laid hands on me. Now they approach, now the key turns in the lock, now they have him. He cries out, once. They look at him from far away. They pull him to the door of his cell, the corridor stretches before him like the graveyard of his past, the prison spins around him. Perhaps he begins to moan, perhaps he makes no sound. The journey begins. Or, perhaps, when he cries out, he does not stop crying, perhaps his voice is crying now, in all that stone and iron. I see his legs buckle, his thighs jelly, the buttocks quiver, the secret hammer there begins to knock. He is sweating, or he is dry. They drag him, or he walks. Their grip is terrible, his arms are not his own anymore.

Down that long corridor, down those metal stairs, into the

heart of the prison and out of it, into the office of the priest. He kneels. A candle burns, the Virgin watches him.

Mary, blessed mother of God.

My own hands are clammy, my body is dull and white and dry. I see it in the mirror, out of the corner of my eye.

Mary, blessed mother of God.

He kisses the cross and clings to it. The priest gently lifts the cross away. Then they lift Giovanni. The journey begins. They move off, toward another door. He moans. He wants to spit, but his mouth is dry. He cannot ask that they let him pause for a moment to urinate—all that, in a moment, will take care of itself. He knows that beyond the door which comes so deliberately closer, the knife is waiting. That door is the gateway he has sought so long out of this dirty world, this dirty body.

It's getting late.

The body in the mirror forces me to turn and face it. And I look at my body, which is under sentence of death. It is lean, hard, and cold, the incarnation of a mystery. And I do not know what moves in this body, what this body is searching. It is trapped in my mirror as it is trapped in time and it hurries toward revelation.

When I was a child, I spake as a child, I understood as a child, I thought as a child: but when I became a man, I put away childish things.

I long to make this prophecy come true. I long to crack that mirror and be free. I look at my sex, my troubling sex, and wonder how it can be redeemed, how I can save it from the knife. The journey to the grave is already begun, the journey to corruption is, always, already, half over. Yet, the key to my salvation, which cannot save my body, is hidden in my flesh.

Then the door is before him. There is darkness all around him, there is silence in him. Then the door opens and he stands alone, the whole world falling away from him. And the brief corner of the sky seems to be shrieking, though he does not hear a sound. Then the earth tilts, he is thrown forward on his face in darkness, and his journey begins.

I move at last from the mirror and begin to cover that

nakedness which I must hold sacred, though it be never so vile, which must be scoured perpetually with the salt of my life. I must believe, I must believe, that the heavy grace of God, which has brought me to this place, is all that can carry me out of it.

And at last I step out into the morning and I lock the door behind me. I cross the road and drop the keys into the old lady's mailbox. And I look up the road, where a few people stand, men and women, waiting for the morning bus. They are very vivid beneath the awakening sky, and the horizon beyond them is beginning to flame. The morning weighs on my shoulders with the dreadful weight of hope and I take the blue envelope which Jacques has sent me and tear it slowly into many pieces, watching them dance in the wind, watching the wind carry them away. Yet, as I turn and begin walking toward the waiting people, the wind blows some of them back on me.

ANOTHER COUNTRY

For Mary S. Painter

They strike one, above all, as giving no account of themselves in any terms already consecrated by human use; to this inarticulate state they probably form, collectively, the most unprecedented of monuments; abysmal the mystery of what they think, what they feel, what they want, what they suppose themselves to be saying.

HENRY JAMES

BOOK ONE:

EASY RIDER

*I told him, easy riders
Got to stay away,
So he had to vamp it,
But the hike ain't far.*
                    W. C. HANDY

HE WAS FACING Seventh Avenue, at Times Square. It was past midnight and he had been sitting in the movies, in the top row of the balcony, since two o'clock in the afternoon. Twice he had been awakened by the violent accents of the Italian film, once the usher had awakened him, and twice he had been awakened by caterpillar fingers between his thighs. He was so tired, he had fallen so low, that he scarcely had the energy to be angry; nothing of his belonged to him anymore—*you took the best, so why not take the rest?*—but he had growled in his sleep and bared the white teeth in his dark face and crossed his legs. Then the balcony was nearly empty, the Italian film was approaching a climax; he stumbled down the endless stairs into the street. He was hungry, his mouth felt filthy. He realized too late, as he passed through the doors, that he wanted to urinate. And he was broke. And he had nowhere to go.

The policeman passed him, giving him a look. Rufus turned, pulling up the collar of his leather jacket while the wind nibbled delightedly at him through his summer slacks, and started north on Seventh Avenue. He had been thinking of going downtown and waking up Vivaldo—the only friend he had left in the city, or maybe in the world—but now he decided to walk up as far as a certain jazz bar and night club and look in. Maybe somebody would see him and recognize him, maybe one of the guys would lay enough bread on him for a meal or at least subway fare. At the same time, he hoped that he would not be recognized.

The Avenue was quiet, too, most of its bright lights out. Here and there a woman passed, here and there a man; rarely, a couple. At corners, under the lights, near drugstores, small knots of white, bright, chattering people showed teeth to each other, pawed each other, whistled for taxis, were whirled away in them, vanished through the doors of drugstores or into the blackness of side streets. Newsstands, like small black blocks on a board, held down corners of the pavements and policemen and taxi drivers and others, harder to place, stomped their feet before them and exchanged such words as they both knew with the muffled vendor within. A sign advertised the chewing gum which would help one to relax and keep smiling. A hotel's enormous neon name challenged the starless sky. So did the names of movie stars and people currently appearing or scheduled to appear on Broadway, along with the mile-high names of the vehicles which would carry them into immortality. The great buildings, unlit, blunt like the phallus or sharp like the spear, guarded the city which never slept.

Beneath them Rufus walked, one of the fallen—for the weight of this city was murderous—one of those who had been crushed on the day, which was every day, these towers fell. Entirely alone, and dying of it, he was part of an unprecedented multitude. There were boys and girls drinking coffee at the drugstore counters who were held back from his condition by barriers as perishable as their dwindling cigarettes. They could scarcely bear their knowledge, nor could they have borne the sight of Rufus, but they knew why he was in the streets tonight, why he rode subways all night long, why his stomach growled, why his hair was nappy, his armpits funky, his pants and shoes too thin, and why he did not dare to stop and take a leak.

Now he stood before the misty doors of the jazz joint, peering in, sensing rather than seeing the frantic black people on the stand and the oblivious, mixed crowd at the bar. The music was loud and empty, no one was doing anything at all, and it was being hurled at the crowd like a malediction in which not even those who hated most deeply any longer believed. They knew that no one heard, that bloodless people cannot be made to bleed. So they blew what everyone had heard before, they reassured everyone that nothing terrible was happening, and the people at the tables found it pleasant to shout over this stunning corroboration and the people at the bar, under cover of the noise they could scarcely have lived without, pursued whatever it was they were after. He wanted to go in and use the bathroom but he was ashamed of the way he looked. He had been in hiding, really, for nearly a month. And he saw himself now, in his mind's eye, shambling through this crowd to the bathroom and crawling out again while everyone watched him with pitying or scornful or mocking eyes. Or, someone would be certain to whisper *Isn't that Rufus Scott?* Someone would look at him with horror, then turn back to his business with a long-drawn-out, pitying, *Man!* He could not do it—and he danced on one foot and then the other and tears came to his eyes.

A white couple, laughing, came through the doors, giving him barely a glance as they passed. The warmth, the smell of people, whiskey, beer, and smoke which came out to hit him as the doors opened almost made him cry for fair and it made his empty stomach growl again.

It made him remember days and nights, days and nights, when he had been inside, on the stand or in the crowd, sharp, beloved, making it with any chick he wanted, making it to parties and getting high and getting drunk and fooling around with the musicians, who were his friends, who respected him. Then, going home to his own pad, locking his door and taking off his shoes, maybe making himself a drink, maybe listening to some records, stretching out on the bed, maybe calling up some girl. And changing his underwear and his socks and his shirt, shaving, and taking a shower, and making it to Harlem to the barber shop, then seeing his mother and his father and teasing his sister, Ida, and eating: spareribs or pork chops or chicken or greens or cornbread or yams or biscuits. For a moment he thought he would faint with hunger and he moved to a wall of the building and leaned there. His forehead was freezing with sweat. He thought: this is got to stop, Rufus. This shit is got to stop. Then, in weariness and recklessness, seeing no one on the streets and hoping that no one would come through the doors, leaning with one hand against the wall he sent his urine splashing against the stone-cold pavement, watching the faint steam rise.

He remembered Leona. Or a sudden, cold, familiar sickness filled him and he knew he was remembering Leona. And he began to walk, very slowly now, away from the music, with his hands in his pockets and his head down. He no longer felt the cold.

For to remember Leona was also—somehow—to remember the eyes of his mother, the rage of his father, the beauty of his sister. It was to remember the streets of Harlem, the boys on the stoops, the girls behind the stairs and on the roofs, the

white policeman who had taught him how to hate, the stickball games in the streets, the women leaning out of windows
and the numbers they played daily, hoping for the hit his father never made. It was to remember the juke box, the teasing, the dancing, the hard-on, the gang fights and gang bangs,
his first set of drums—bought him by his father—his first taste
of marijuana, his first snort of horse. Yes: and the boys too far
out, jackknifed on the stoops, the boy dead from an overdose
on a rooftop in the snow. It was to remember the beat: *A
nigger*, said his father, *lives his whole life, lives and dies according to a beat. Shit, he humps to that beat and the baby he throws
up in there, well, he jumps to it and comes out nine months later
like a goddamn tambourine*. The beat: hands, feet, tambourines, drums, pianos, laughter, curses, razor blades; the man
stiffening with a laugh and a growl and a purr and the woman
moistening and softening with a whisper and a sigh and a cry.
The beat—in Harlem in the summertime one could almost
see it, shaking above the pavements and the roof.

And he had fled, so he had thought, from the beat of Harlem, which was simply the beat of his own heart. Into a boot
camp in the South, and onto the pounding sea.

While he had still been in the Navy, he had brought back
from one of his voyages an Indian shawl for Ida. He had
picked it up someplace in England. On the day that he gave
it to her and she tried it on, something shook in him which
had never been touched before. He had never seen the beauty
of black people before. But, staring at Ida, who stood before
the window of the Harlem kitchen, seeing that she was no
longer merely his younger sister but a girl who would soon
be a woman, she became associated with the colors of the
shawl, the colors of the sun, and with a splendor incalculably
older than the gray stone of the island on which they had
been born. He thought that perhaps this splendor would
come into the world again one day, into the world they knew.
Ages and ages ago, Ida had not been merely the descendant
of slaves. Watching her dark face in the sunlight, softened and
shadowed by the glorious shawl, it could be seen that she had
once been a monarch. Then he looked out of the window, at
the air shaft, and thought of the whores on Seventh Avenue.

He thought of the white policemen and the money they made on black flesh, the money the whole world made.

He looked back at his sister, who was smiling at him. On her long little finger she twisted the ruby-eyed snake ring which he had brought her from another voyage.

"You keep this up," she said, "and you'll make me the best-dressed girl on the block."

He was glad Ida could not see him now. She would have said, My Lord, Rufus, you got no right to walk around like this. Don't you know we're counting on you?

Seven months ago, a lifetime ago, he had been playing a gig in one of the new Harlem spots owned and operated by a Negro. It was their last night. It had been a good night, everybody was feeling good. Most of them, after the set, were going to make it to the home of a famous Negro singer who had just scored in his first movie. Because the joint was new, it was packed. Lately, he had heard, it hadn't been doing so well. All kinds of people had been there that night, white and black, high and low, people who came for the music and people who spent their lives in joints for other reasons. There were a couple of minks and a few near-minks and a lot of God-knows-what shining at wrists and ears and necks and in the hair. The colored people were having a good time because they sensed that, for whatever reason, this crowd was solidly with them; and the white people were having a good time because nobody was putting them down for being white. The joint, as Fats Waller would have said, was jumping.

There was some pot on the scene and he was a little high. He was feeling great. And, during the last set, he came doubly alive because the saxophone player, who had been way out all night, took off on a terrific solo. He was a kid of about the same age as Rufus, from some insane place like Jersey City or Syracuse, but somewhere along the line he had discovered that he could say it with a saxophone. He had a lot to say. He stood there, wide-legged, humping the air, filling his barrel chest, shivering in the rags of his twenty-odd years, and screaming through the horn *Do you love me? Do you love me? Do you love me?* And, again, Do *you* love *me? Do you* love *me?*

Do you love me? This, anyway, was the question Rufus heard, the same phrase, unbearably, endlessly, and variously repeated, with all of the force the boy had. The silence of the listeners became strict with abruptly focused attention, cigarettes were unlit, and drinks stayed on the tables; and in all of the faces, even the most ruined and most dull, a curious, wary light appeared. They were being assaulted by the saxophonist who perhaps no longer wanted their love and merely hurled his outrage at them with the same contemptuous, pagan pride with which he humped the air. And yet the question was terrible and real; the boy was blowing with his lungs and guts out of his own short past; somewhere in that past, in the gutters or gang fights or gang shags; in the acrid room, on the sperm-stiffened blanket, behind marijuana or the needle, under the smell of piss in the precinct basement, he had received the blow from which he never would recover and this no one wanted to believe. *Do you love me? Do you love me? Do you love* me? The men on the stand stayed with him, cool and at a little distance, adding and questioning and corroborating, holding it down as well as they could with an ironical self-mockery; but each man knew that the boy was blowing for every one of them. When the set ended they were all soaking. Rufus smelled his odor and the odor of the men around him and "Well, that's it," said the bass man. The crowd was yelling for more but they did their theme song and the lights came on. And he had played the last set of his last gig.

He was going to leave his traps there until Monday afternoon. When he stepped down from the stand there was this blonde girl, very plainly dressed, standing looking at him.

"What's on your mind, baby?" he asked her. Everybody was busy all around them, preparing to make it to the party. It was spring and the air was charged.

"What's on *your* mind?" she countered, but it was clear that she simply had not known what else to say.

She had said enough. She was from the South. And something leaped in Rufus as he stared at her damp, colorless face, the face of the Southern poor white, and her straight, pale hair. She was considerably older than he, over thirty probably, and her body was too thin. Just the same, it abruptly became the most exciting body he had gazed on in a long time.

"Honeychild," he said and gave her his crooked grin, "ain't you a long ways from home?"

"I sure am," she said, "and I ain't never going back there."

He laughed and she laughed. "Well, Miss Anne," he said, "if we both got the same thing on our mind, let's make it to that party."

And he took her arm, deliberately allowing the back of his hand to touch one of her breasts, and he said, "Your name's not really Anne, is it?"

"No," she said, "it's Leona."

"Leona?" And he smiled again. His smile could be very effective. "That's a pretty name."

"What's yours?"

"Me? I'm Rufus Scott."

He wondered what she was doing in this joint, in Harlem. She didn't seem at all the type to be interested in jazz, still less did she seem to be in the habit of going to strange bars alone. She carried a light spring coat, her long hair was simply brushed back and held with some pins, she wore very little lipstick and no other make-up at all.

"Come on," he said. "We'll pile into a cab."

"Are you sure it's all right if I come?"

He sucked his teeth. "If it wasn't all right, I wouldn't ask you. If I say it's all right, it's all *right*."

"Well," she said with a short laugh, "all right, then."

They moved with the crowd, which, with many interruptions, much talking and laughing and much erotic confusion, poured into the streets. It was three o'clock in the morning and gala people all around them were glittering and whistling and using up all the taxicabs. Others, considerably less gala—they were on the western edge of 125th Street—stood in knots along the street, switched or swaggered or dawdled by, with glances, sidelong or full face, which were more calculating than curious. The policemen strolled by, carefully, and in fact rather mysteriously conveying their awareness that these particular Negroes, though they were out so late, and mostly drunk, were not to be treated in the usual fashion; and neither were the white people with them. But Rufus suddenly realized that Leona would soon be the only white person left. This made him uneasy and his uneasiness made him angry. Leona spotted an empty cab and hailed it.

The taxi driver, who was white, seemed to have no hesitation in stopping for them, nor, once having stopped, did he seem to have any regrets.

"You going to work tomorrow?" he asked Leona. Now that they were alone together, he felt a little shy.

"No," she said, "tomorrow's Sunday."

"That's right." He felt very pleased and free. He had planned to visit his family but he thought of what a ball it would be to spend the day in bed with Leona. He glanced over at her, noting that, though she was tiny, she seemed very well put together. He wondered what she was thinking. He offered her a cigarette, putting his hand on hers briefly, and she refused it. "You don't smoke?"

"Sometimes. When I drink."

"Is that often?"

She laughed. "No. I don't like to drink alone."

"Well," he said, "you ain't *going* to be drinking alone for awhile."

She said nothing but she seemed, in the darkness, to tense and blush. She looked out of the window on her side. "I'm glad I ain't got to worry none about getting you home early tonight."

"You ain't got to worry about that, nohow. I'm a big girl."

"Honey," he said, "you ain't no bigger than a minute."

She sighed. "Sometimes a minute can be a mighty powerful thing."

He decided against asking what she meant by this. He said, giving her a significant look, "That's true," but she did not seem to take his meaning.

They were on Riverside Drive and nearing their destination. To the left of them, pale, unlovely lights emphasized the blackness of the Jersey shore. He leaned back, leaning a little against Leona, watching the blackness and the lights roll by. Then the cab turned; he glimpsed, briefly, the distant bridge which glowed like something written in the sky. The cab slowed down, looking for the house number. A taxi ahead of them had just discharged a crowd of people and was disappearing down the block. "Here we are," said Rufus; "Looks like a real fine party," the taxi driver said, and winked. Rufus said nothing. He paid the man and they got out and walked into the lobby, which was large and hideous, with mirrors and chairs. The elevator had just started upward; they could hear the crowd.

"What were you doing in that club all by yourself, Leona?" he asked.

She looked at him, a little startled. Then, "I don't know. I just wanted to see Harlem and so I went up there tonight to look around. And I just happened to pass that club and I heard the music and I went in and I *stayed*. I liked the music." She gave him a mocking look. "Is that all right?"

He laughed and said nothing.

She turned from him as they heard the sound of the closing elevator door reverberate down the shaft. Then they heard the drone of the cables as the elevator began to descend. She watched the closed doors as though her life depended on it.

"This your first time in New York?"

Yes, it was, she told him, but she had been dreaming about it all her life—half-facing him again, with a little smile. There was something halting in her manner which he found very moving. She was like a wild animal who didn't know whether to come to the outstretched hand or to flee and kept making startled little rushes, first in one direction and then in the other.

"I was born here," he said, watching her.

"I know," she said, "so it can't seem as wonderful to you as it does to me."

He laughed again. He remembered, suddenly, his days in boot camp in the South and felt again the shoe of a white officer against his mouth. He was in his white uniform, on the ground, against the red, dusty clay. Some of his colored buddies were holding him, were shouting in his ear, helping him to rise. The white officer, with a curse, had vanished, had gone forever beyond the reach of vengeance. His face was full of clay and tears and blood; he spat red blood into the red dust.

The elevator came and the doors opened. He took her arm as they entered and held it close against his chest. "I think you're a real sweet girl."

"You're nice, too," she said. In the closed, rising elevator her voice had a strange trembling in it and her body was also trembling—very faintly, as though it were being handled by the soft spring wind outside.

He tightened his pressure on her arm. "Didn't they warn you down home about the darkies you'd find up North?"

She caught her breath. "They didn't never worry me none. People's just people as far as I'm concerned."

And pussy's just pussy as far as I'm concerned, he thought—but was grateful, just the same, for her tone. It gave him an instant to locate himself. For he, too, was trembling slightly.

"What made you come North?" he asked.

He wondered if he should proposition her or wait for her to proposition him. He couldn't beg. But perhaps she could. The hairs of his groin began to itch slightly. The terrible muscle at the base of his belly began to grow hot and hard.

The elevator came to a halt, the doors opened, and they walked a long corridor toward a half-open door.

She said, "I guess I just couldn't take it down there any more. I was married but then I broke up with my husband and they took away my kid—they wouldn't even let me see him—and I got to thinking that rather than sit down there and go crazy, I'd try to make a new life for myself up here."

Something touched his imagination for a moment, suggesting that Leona was a person and had her story and that all stories were trouble. But he shook the suggestion off. He wouldn't be around long enough to be bugged by her story. He just wanted her for tonight.

He knocked on the door and walked in without waiting for an answer. Straight ahead of them, in the large living room which ended in open French doors and a balcony, more than a hundred people milled about, some in evening dress, some in slacks and sweaters. High above their heads hung an enormous silver ball which reflected unexpected parts of the room and managed its own unloving comment on the people in it. The room was so active with coming and going, so bright with jewelry and glasses and cigarettes, that the heavy ball seemed almost to be alive.

His host—whom he did not really know very well—was nowhere in sight. To the right of them were three rooms, the first of which was piled high with wraps and overcoats.

The horn of Charlie Parker, coming over the hi-fi, dominated all the voices in the room.

"Put your coat down," he told Leona, "and I'll try to find out if I know anybody in this joint."

"Oh," she said, "I'm sure you know them all."

"Go on, now," he said, smiling, and pushing her gently into the room, "do like I tell you."

While she was putting away her coat—and powdering her nose, probably—he remembered that he had promised to call Vivaldo. He wandered through the house, looking for a relatively isolated telephone, and found one in the kitchen.

He dialed Vivaldo's number.

"Hello, baby. How're you?"

"Oh, all right, I guess. What's happening? I thought you were going to call me sooner. I'd just about given you up."

"Well, I only just made it up here." He dropped his voice, for a couple had entered the kitchen, a blonde girl with a disarrayed Dutch bob and a tall Negro. The girl leaned against the sink, the boy stood before her, rubbing his hands slowly along the outside of her thighs. They barely glanced at Rufus. "A whole lot of elegant squares around, you dig?"

"Yeah," said Vivaldo. There was a pause. "You think it's worthwhile making it up there?"

"Well, hell, I don't know. If you got something *better* to do——"

"Jane's here," Vivaldo said, quickly. Rufus realized that Jane was probably lying on the bed, listening.

"Oh, you got your grandmother with you, you don't need nothing up here then." He did not like Jane, who was somewhat older than Vivaldo, with prematurely gray hair. "Ain't nothing up here old enough for you."

"That's enough, you bastard." He heard Jane's voice and Vivaldo's, murmuring; he could not make out what was being said. Then Vivaldo's voice was at his ear again. "I think I'll skip it."

"I guess you better. I'll see you tomorrow."

"Maybe I'll come by your pad—?"

"Okay. Don't let grandma wear you out now; they tell me women get real ferocious when they get as old as she is."

"They can't get too ferocious for me, dad!"

Rufus laughed. "You better *quit* trying to compete with me. *You* ain't never going to make it. So long."

"So long."

He hung up, smiling, and went to find Leona. She stood helplessly in the foyer, watching the host and hostess saying good night to several people.

"Think I'd deserted you?"

"No. I knew you wouldn't do that."

He smiled at her and touched her on the chin with his fist. The host turned away from the door and came over to them.

"You kids go on inside and get yourselves a drink," he said. "Go on in and get with it." He was a big, handsome, expansive man, older and more ruthless than he looked, who had fought his way to the top in show business via several of the rougher professions, including boxing and pimping. He owed his present eminence more to his vitality and his looks than he did to his voice, and he knew it. He was not the kind of man who fooled himself and Rufus liked him because he was rough and good-natured and generous. But Rufus was also a little afraid of him; there was that about him, in spite of his charm, which did not encourage intimacy. He was a great success with women, whom he treated with a large, affectionate contempt, and he was now on his fourth wife.

He took Leona and Rufus by the arm and walked them to the edge of the party. "We might have us some real doings if these squares ever get out of here," he said. "Stick around."

"How does it feel to be respectable?" Rufus grinned.

"Shit. I been respectable all my life. It's these *respectable* motherfuckers been doing all the dirt. They been stealing the colored folks blind, man. And niggers helping them do it." He laughed. "You know, every time they give me one of them great big checks I think to myself, they just giving me back a *little* bit of what they been stealing all these years, you know what I mean?" He clapped Rufus on the back. "See that Little Eva has a good time."

The crowd was already thinning, most of the squares were

beginning to drift away. Once they were gone, the party would change character and become very pleasant and quiet and private. The lights would go down, the music become softer, the talk more sporadic and more sincere. Somebody might sing or play the piano. They might swap stories of the laughs they'd had, gigs they'd played, riffs they remembered, or the trouble they'd seen. Somebody might break out with some pot and pass it slowly around, like the pipe of peace. Somebody, curled on a rug in a far corner of the room, would begin to snore. Whoever danced would dance more languorously, holding tight. The shadows of the room would be alive. Toward the very end, as morning and the brutal sounds of the city began their invasion through the wide French doors, somebody would go into the kitchen and break out with some coffee. Then they would raid the icebox and go home. The host and hostess would finally make it between their sheets and stay in bed all day.

From time to time Rufus found himself glancing upward at the silver ball in the ceiling, always just failing to find himself and Leona reflected there.

"Let's go out to the balcony," he said to her.

She held out her glass. "Freshen my drink first?" Her eyes were now very bright and mischievous and she looked like a little girl.

He walked to the table and poured two very powerful drinks. He went back to her. "Ready?"

She took her glass and they stepped through the French doors.

"Don't let Little Eva catch cold!" the host called.

He called back. "She may burn, baby, but she sure won't freeze!"

Directly before and beneath them stretched the lights of the Jersey shore. He seemed, from where he stood, to hear a faint murmur coming from the water.

When a child he had lived on the eastern edge of Harlem, a block from the Harlem River. He and other children had waded into the water from the garbage-heavy bank or dived from occasional rotting promontories. One summer a boy had drowned there. From the stoop of his house Rufus had watched as a small group of people crossed Park Avenue, beneath the heavy shadow of the railroad tracks, and come into the sun, one man in the middle, the boy's father, carrying the boy's unbelievably heavy, covered weight. He had never forgotten the bend of the man's shoulders or the stunned angle of his head. A great screaming began from the other end of the block and the boy's mother, her head tied up, wearing her bathrobe, stumbling like a drunken woman, began running toward the silent people.

He threw back his shoulders, as though he were casting off a burden, and walked to the edge of the balcony where Leona stood. She was staring up the river, toward the George Washington Bridge.

"It's real beautiful," she said, "it's just so beautiful."

"You seem to like New York," he said.

She turned and looked at him and sipped her drink. "Oh, I do. Can I trouble you for a cigarette now?"

He gave her a cigarette and lit it for her, then lit one for himself. "How're you making it up here?"

"Oh, I'm doing just fine," she said. "I'm waiting tables in a restaurant way downtown, near Wall Street, that's a real pretty part of town, and I'm rooming with two other girls"—they couldn't go to *her* place, anyway!—"and, oh, I'm doing just fine." And she looked up at him with her sad-sweet, poor-white smile.

Again something warned him to stop, to leave this poor little girl alone; and at the same time the fact that he thought of her as a poor little girl caused him to smile with real affection, and he said, "You've got a lot of guts, Leona."

"Got to, the way I look at it," she said. "Sometimes I think I'll just give up. But—*how* do you give up?"

She looked so lost and comical that he laughed out loud and, after a moment, she laughed too.

"If my husband could see me now," and she giggled, "my, my, my!"

"Why, what would your husband say?" he asked her.

"Why—I don't know." But her laugh didn't come this time. She looked at him as though she were slowly coming out of a dream. "Say—do you think I could have another drink?"

"Sure, Leona," and he took her glass and their hands and

their bodies touched for a moment. She dropped her eyes. "Be right back," he said, and dropped back into the room, in which the lights now were dim. Someone was playing the piano.

"Say, man, how you coming with Eva?" the host asked.

"Fine, fine, we lushing it up."

"That ain't nowhere. Blast Little Eva with some pot. Let her get her kicks."

"I'll see to it that she gets her kicks," he said.

"Old Rufus left her out there digging the Empire State building, man," said the young saxophonist, and laughed.

"Give me some of that," Rufus said, and somebody handed him a stick and he took a few drags.

"Keep it, man. It's choice."

He made a couple of drinks and stood in the room for a moment, finishing the pot and digging the piano. He felt fine, clean, on top of everything, and he had a mild buzz on when he got back to the balcony.

"Is everybody gone home?" she asked, anxiously. "It's so quiet in there."

"No," he said, "they just sitting around." She seemed prettier suddenly, and softer, and the river lights fell behind her like a curtain. This curtain seemed to move as she moved, heavy and priceless and dazzling. "I didn't know," he said, "that you were a princess."

He gave her her drink and their hands touched again. "I know you must be drunk," she said, happily, and now, over her drink, her eyes unmistakably called him.

He waited. Everything seemed very simple now. He played with her fingers. "You seen anything you want since you been in New York?"

"Oh," she said, "I want it all!"

"You see anything you want right now?"

Her fingers stiffened slightly but he held on. "Go ahead. Tell me. You ain't got to be afraid." These words then echoed in his head. He had said this before, years ago, to someone else. The wind grew cold for an instant, blowing around his body and ruffling her hair. Then it died down.

"Do *you*?" she asked faintly.

"Do I what?"

"See anything you want?"

He realized that he was high from the way his fingers seemed hung up in hers and from the way he was staring at her throat. He wanted to put his mouth there and nibble it slowly, leaving it black and blue. At the same time he realized how far they were above the city and the lights below seemed to be calling him. He walked to the balcony's edge and looked over. Looking straight down, he seemed to be standing on a cliff in the wilderness, seeing a kingdom and a river which had not been seen before. He could make it his, every inch of the territory which stretched beneath and around him now, and, unconsciously, he began whistling a tune and his foot moved to find the pedal of his drum. He put his drink down carefully on the balcony floor and beat a riff with his fingers on the stone parapet.

"You never answered my question."

"What?"

He turned to face Leona, who held her drink cupped in both her hands and whose brow was quizzically lifted over her despairing eyes and her sweet smile.

"You never answered mine."

"Yes, I did." She sounded more plaintive than ever. "I said I wanted it all."

He took her drink from her and drank half of it, then gave the glass back, moving into the darkest part of the balcony.

"Well, then," he whispered, "come and get it."

She came toward him, holding her glass against her breasts. At the very last moment, standing directly before him, she whispered in bafflement and rage, "What are you trying to do to me?"

"Honey," he answered, "I'm doing it," and he pulled her to him as roughly as he could. He had expected her to resist and she did, holding the glass between them and frantically trying to pull her body away from his body's touch. He knocked the glass out of her hand and it fell dully to the balcony floor, rolling away from them. Go ahead, he thought humorously; if I was to let you go now you'd be so hung up you'd go flying over this balcony, most likely. He whispered, "Go ahead, fight. I like it. Is this the way they do down home?"

"Oh God," she murmured, and began to cry. At the same time, she ceased struggling. Her hands came up and touched his face as though she were blind. Then she put her arms around his neck and clung to him, still shaking. His lips and his teeth touched her ears and her neck and he told her, "Honey, you ain't got nothing to cry about yet."

Yes, he was high; everything he did he watched himself doing, and he began to feel a tenderness for Leona which he had not expected to feel. He tried, with himself, to make amends for what he was doing—for what he was doing to her. Everything seemed to take a very long time. He got hung up on her breasts, standing out like mounds of yellow cream, and the tough, brown, tasty nipples, playing and nuzzling and nibbling while she moaned and whimpered and her knees sagged. He gently lowered them to the floor, pulling her on top of him. He held her tightly at the hip and the shoulder. Part of him was worried about the host and hostess and the other people in the room but another part of him could not stop the crazy thing which had begun. Her fingers opened his shirt to the navel, her tongue burned his neck and his chest; and his hands pushed up her skirt and caressed the inside of her thighs. Then, after a long, high time, while he shook beneath every accelerating tremor of her body, he forced her beneath him and he entered her. For a moment he thought she was going to scream, she was so tight and caught her breath so sharply, and stiffened so. But then she moaned, she moved beneath him. Then, from the center of his rising storm, very slowly and deliberately, he began the slow ride home.

And she carried him, as the sea will carry a boat: with a slow, rocking and rising and falling motion, barely suggestive of the violence of the deep. They murmured and sobbed on this journey, he softly, insistently cursed. Each labored to reach a harbor: there could be no rest until this motion became unbearably accelerated by the power that was rising in them both. Rufus opened his eyes for a moment and watched her face, which was transfigured with agony and gleamed in the darkness like alabaster. Tears hung in the corners of her eyes and the hair at her brow was wet. Her breath came with moaning and short cries, with words he couldn't understand, and in spite of himself he began moving faster and thrusting deeper. He wanted her to remember him the longest day she lived. And, shortly, nothing could have stopped him, not the white God himself nor a lynch mob arriving on wings. Under his breath he cursed the milk-white bitch and groaned and rode his weapon between her thighs. She began to cry. *I told you*, he moaned, *I'd give you something to cry about*, and, at once, he felt himself strangling, about to explode or die. A moan and a curse tore through him while he beat her with all the strength he had and felt the venom shoot out of him, enough for a hundred black-white babies.

He lay on his back, breathing hard. He heard music coming from the room inside, and a whistle on the river. He was frightened and his throat was dry. The air was chilly where he was wet.

She touched him and he jumped. Then he forced himself to turn to her, looking into her eyes. Her eyes were wet still, deep and dark, her trembling lips curved slightly in a shy, triumphant smile. He pulled her to him, wishing he could rest. He hoped she would say nothing but, "It was so wonderful," she said, and kissed him. And these words, though they caused him to feel no tenderness and did not take away his dull, mysterious dread, began to call desire back again.

He sat up. "You're a funny little cracker," he said. He watched her. "I don't know what you going to say to your husband when you come home with a little black baby."

"I ain't going to be having no more babies," she said, "you ain't got to worry about that." She said nothing more; but she had much more to say. "He beat that out of me, too," she said finally.

He wanted to hear her story. And he wanted to know nothing more about her.

"Let's go inside and wash up," he said.

She put her head against his chest. "I'm afraid to go in there now."

He laughed and stroked her hair. He began to feel affection for her again. "You ain't fixing to stay here all night, are you?"

"What are your friends going to think?"

"Well, one thing, Leona, they ain't going to call the law." He kissed her. "They ain't going to think nothing, honey."

"You coming in with me?"

"Sure, I'm coming in with you." He held her away from him. "All you got to do is sort of straighten your clothes"—he stroked her body, looking into her eyes—"and sort of run your hand through your hair, like this"—and he brushed her hair back from her forehead. She watched him. He heard himself ask, "Do you like me?"

She swallowed. He watched the vein in her neck throb. She seemed very fragile. "Yes," she said. She looked down. "Rufus," she said, "I really do like you. Please don't hurt me."

"Why should I want to hurt you, Leona?" He stroked her neck with one hand, looking at her gravely. "What makes you think I want to hurt you?"

"People *do*," she said, finally, "hurt each other."

"Is somebody been hurting you, Leona?"

She was silent, her face leaning into his palm. "My husband," she said, faintly. "I thought he loved me, but he didn't—oh, I knew he was rough but I didn't think he was *mean*. And he couldn't of loved me because he took away my kid, he's off someplace where I can't never see him." She looked up at Rufus with her eyes full of tears. "He said I wasn't a fit mother because—I—drank too much. I *did* drink too much, it was the only way I could stand living with him. But I would of died for my kid, I wouldn't never of let anything happen to him."

He was silent. Her tears fell on his dark fist. "He's still down there," she said, "my husband, I mean. Him and my mother and my brother is as thick as thieves. They think I ain't never been no good. Well, hell, if people keep telling you you ain't no good"—she tried to laugh—"you bound to turn out pretty bad."

He pushed out of his mind all of the questions he wanted to ask her. It was beginning to be chilly on the balcony; he was hungry and he wanted a drink and he wanted to get home to bed. "Well," he said, at last, "I ain't going to hurt you," and he rose, walking to the edge of the balcony. His shorts were like a rope between his legs, he pulled them up, and felt that he was glued inside them. He zipped up his fly, holding his legs wide apart. The sky had faded down to purple. The stars were gone and the lights on the Jersey shore were out. A coal barge traveled slowly down the river.

"How do I look?" she asked him.

"Fine," he said, and she did. She looked like a tired child. "You want to come down to my place?"

"If you want me to," she said.

"Well, yes, that's what I want." But he wondered why he was holding on to her.

Vivaldo came by late the next afternoon to find Rufus still in bed and Leona in the kitchen making breakfast.

It was Leona who opened the door. And Rufus watched with delight the slow shock on Vivaldo's face as he looked from Leona, muffled in Rufus' bathrobe, to Rufus, sitting up in bed, and naked except for the blankets.

Let the liberal white bastard squirm, he thought.

"Hi, baby," he called, "come on in. You just in time for breakfast."

"I've *had* my breakfast," Vivaldo said, "but you people aren't even decent yet. I'll come back later."

"Shit, man, come on in. That's Leona. Leona, this here's a friend of mine, Vivaldo. For short. His real name is Daniel Vivaldo Moore. He's an Irish wop."

"Rufus is just full of prejudice against everybody," said Leona, and smiled. "Come on in."

Vivaldo closed the door behind him awkwardly and sat down on the edge of the bed. Whenever he was uncomfortable—which was often—his arms and legs seemed to stretch to monstrous proportions and he handled them with bewildered loathing, as though he had been afflicted with them only a few moments before.

"I hope you can eat *something*," Leona said. "There's plenty and it'll be ready in just a second."

"I'll have a cup of coffee with you," Vivaldo said, "unless you happen to have some beer." Then he looked over at Rufus. "I guess it was quite a party."

Rufus grinned. "Not bad, not bad."

Leona opened some beer and poured it into a tumbler and brought it to Vivaldo. He took it, looking up at her with his quick, gypsy smile, and spilled some on one foot.

"You want some, Rufus?"

"No, honey, not yet. I'll eat first."

Leona walked back into the kitchen.

"Ain't she a splendid specimen of Southern womanhood?" Rufus asked. "Down yonder, they teach their womenfolks to *serve.*"

From the kitchen came Leona's laugh. "They sure don't teach us nothing else."

"Honey, as long as you know how to make a man as happy as you making me, you don't *need* to know nothing else."

Rufus and Vivaldo looked at each other a moment. Then Vivaldo grinned. "How about it, Rufus. You going to get your ass up out of that bed?"

Rufus threw back the covers and jumped out of bed. He raised his arms high and yawned and stretched.

"You're giving quite a show this afternoon," Vivaldo said, and threw him a pair of shorts.

Rufus put on the shorts and an old pair of gray slacks and a faded green sport shirt. "You should have made it to that party," he said, "after all. There was some pot on the scene that wouldn't wait."

"Well. I had my troubles last night."

"You and Jane? As usual?"

"Oh, she got drunk and pulled some shit. You know. She's sick, she can't help it."

"I know *she's* sick. But what's wrong with you?"

"I guess I just like to get beaten over the head." They walked to the table. "This your first time in the Village, Leona?"

"No, I've walked around here some. But you don't really know a place unless you know some of the people."

"You know us now," said Vivaldo, "and between us we must know everybody else. We'll show you around."

Something in the way Vivaldo said this irritated Rufus. His buoyancy evaporated; sour suspicions filled him. He stole a look at Vivaldo, who was sipping his beer and watching Leona with an impenetrable smile—impenetrable exactly because it seemed so open and good-natured. He looked at Leona, who, this afternoon anyway, drowning in his bathrobe, her hair piled on top of her head and her face innocent of make-up, couldn't really be called a pretty girl. Perhaps Vivaldo was contemptuous of her because she was so plain—which meant that Vivaldo was contemptuous of *him.* Or perhaps he was flirting with her because she seemed so simple and available: the proof of her availability being her presence in Rufus' house.

Then Leona looked across the table and smiled at him. His heart and his bowels shook; he remembered their violence and their tenderness together; and he thought, To hell with Vivaldo. He had something Vivaldo would never be able to touch.

He leaned across the table and kissed her.

"Can I have some more beer?" asked Vivaldo, smiling.

"You know where it is," Rufus said.

Leona took his glass and went to the kitchen. Rufus stuck out his tongue at Vivaldo, who was watching him with a faintly quizzical frown.

Leona returned and set a fresh beer before Vivaldo and said, "You boys finish up now, I'm going to get dressed." She gathered her clothes together and vanished into the bathroom.

There was silence at the table for a moment.

"She going to stay here with you?" Vivaldo asked.

"I don't know yet. Nothing's been decided yet. But I think she wants to—"

"Oh, that's obvious. But isn't this place a little small for two?"

"Maybe we'll find a bigger place. Anyway—you know—I'm not home a hell of a lot."

Vivaldo seemed to consider this. Then, "I hope you know what you're doing, baby. I know it's none of my business, but——"

Rufus looked at him. "Don't you like her?"

"Sure, I like her. She's a sweet girl." He took a swallow of his beer. "The question is—how much do *you* like her?"

"Can't you tell?" And Rufus grinned.

"Well, no, frankly—I can't. I mean, sure you like her. But—oh, I don't know."

There was silence again. Vivaldo dropped his eyes.

"There's nothing to worry about," said Rufus. "I'm a big boy, you know."

Vivaldo raised his eyes and said, "It's a pretty big world, too, baby. I hope you've thought of that."

"I've thought of that."

"Trouble is, I feel too paternal towards you, you son of a bitch."

"That's the trouble with all you white bastards."

They encountered the big world when they went out into the Sunday streets. It stared unsympathetically out at them from the eyes of the passing people; and Rufus realized that he had not thought at all about this world and its power to hate and destroy. He had not thought at all about his future with Leona, for the reason that he had never considered that they had one. Yet, here she was, clearly intending to stay if he would have her. But the price was high: trouble with the land-lord, with the neighbors, with all the adolescents in the Village and all those who descended during the week ends. And his family would have a fit. It didn't matter so very much about his father and mother—their fit, having lasted a lifetime, was now not much more than reflex action. But he knew that Ida would instantly hate Leona. She had always expected a great deal from Rufus, and she was very race-conscious. She would say, You'd never even have looked at that girl, Rufus, if she'd been black. But you'll pick up any white trash just because she's white. What's the matter—you ashamed of being black?

Then, for the first time in his life, he wondered about that— or, rather, the question bumped against his mind for an instant and then speedily, apologetically, withdrew. He looked sideways at Leona. Now she was quite pretty. She had plaited her hair and pinned the braids up, so that she looked very old-fashioned and much younger than her age.

A young couple came toward them, carrying the Sunday papers. Rufus watched the eyes of the man as the man looked at Leona; and then both the man and the woman looked swiftly from Vivaldo to Rufus as though to decide which of the two was her lover. And, since this was the Village—the place of liberation—Rufus guessed, from the swift, nearly sheepish glance the man gave them as they passed, that he had decided that Rufus and Leona formed the couple. The face of his wife, however, simply closed tight, like a gate.

They reached the park. Old, slatternly women from the slums and from the East Side sat on benches, usually alone, sometimes sitting with gray-haired, matchstick men. Ladies from the big apartment buildings on Fifth Avenue, vaguely and desperately elegant, were also in the park, walking their dogs; and Negro nursemaids, turning a stony face on the grown-up world, crooned anxiously into baby carriages. The Italian laborers and small-business men strolled with their families or sat beneath the trees, talking to each other; some played chess or read *L'Espresso*. The other Villagers sat on benches, reading—Kierkegaard was the name shouting from the paper-covered volume held by a short-cropped girl in blue jeans—or talking distractedly of abstract matters, or gossiping or laughing; or sitting still, either with an immense, invisible effort which all but shattered the benches and the trees, or else with a limpness which indicated that they would never move again.

Rufus and Vivaldo—but especially Vivaldo—had known or been intimate with many of these people, so long ago, it now seemed, that it might have occurred in another life. There was something frightening about the aspect of old friends, old lovers, who had, mysteriously, come to nothing. It argued the presence of some cancer which had been operating in them, invisibly, all along and which might, now, be operating in oneself. Many people had vanished, of course, had returned to the havens from which they had fled. But many others were still visible, had turned into lushes or junkies or had embarked on a nerve-rattling pursuit of the perfect psychiatrist; were vindictively married and progenitive and fat; were dreaming the same dreams they had dreamed ten years before, clothed these in the same arguments, quoted the same masters; and dispensed, as they hideously imagined, the same charm they had possessed before their teeth began to fail and their hair began to fall. They were more hostile now than they had been, this was the loud, inescapable change in their tone and the only vitality left in their eyes.

Then Vivaldo was stopped on the path by a large, good-natured girl, who was not sober. Rufus and Leona paused, waiting for him.

"Your friend's real nice," said Leona. "He's real natural. I feel like we known each other for years."

Without Vivaldo, there was a difference in the eyes which

watched them. Villagers, both bound and free, looked them over as though where they stood were an auction block or a stud farm. The pale spring sun seemed very hot on the back of his neck and on his forehead. Leona gleamed before him and seemed to be oblivious of everything and everyone but him. And if there had been any doubt concerning their relationship, her eyes were enough to dispel it. Then he thought, If she could take it so calmly, if she noticed nothing, what was the matter with him? Maybe he was making it all up, maybe nobody gave a damn. Then he raised his eyes and met the eyes of an Italian adolescent. The boy was splashed by the sun falling through the trees. The boy looked at him with hatred; his glance flicked over Leona as though she were a whore; he dropped his eyes slowly and swaggered on—having registered his protest, his backside seemed to snarl, having made his point.

"Cock sucker," Rufus muttered.

Then Leona surprised him. "You talking about that boy? He's just bored and lonely, don't know no better. You could probably make friends with him real easy if you tried."

He laughed.

"Well, that's what's the matter with most people," Leona insisted, plaintively, "ain't got nobody to be with. That's what makes them so evil. I'm telling you, boy, I know."

"Don't call me *boy*," he said.

"Well," she said, looking startled, "I didn't mean nothing by it, honey." She took his arm and they turned to look for Vivaldo. The large girl had him by the collar and he was struggling to get away, and laughing.

"That Vivaldo," said Rufus, amused, "he has more trouble with women."

"He's sure enjoying it," Leona said. "Look like she's enjoying it, too."

For now the large girl had let him go and seemed about to collapse on the path with laughter. People, with a tolerant smile, looked up from the benches or the grass or their books, recognizing two Village characters.

Then Rufus resented all of them. He wondered if he and Leona would dare to make such a scene in public, if such a day could ever come for them. No one dared to look at

Vivaldo, out with any girl whatever, the way they looked at Rufus now; nor would they ever look at the girl the way they looked at Leona. The lowest whore in Manhattan would be protected as long as she had Vivaldo on her arm. This was because Vivaldo was white.

He remembered a rainy night last winter, when he had just come in from a gig in Boston, and he and Vivaldo had gone out with Jane. He had never really understood what Vivaldo saw in Jane, who was too old for him, and combative and dirty; her gray hair was never combed, her sweaters, of which she seemed to possess thousands, were all equally raveled and shapeless; and her blue jeans were baggy and covered with paint. "She dresses like a goddamn bull dagger," Rufus had told Vivaldo once, and then laughed at Vivaldo's horrified expression. His face had puckered as though someone had just cracked a rotten egg. But he had never really hated Jane until this rainy night.

It had been a terrible night, with rain pouring down like great tin buckets, filling the air with a roaring, whining clatter, and making lights and streets and buildings as fluid as itself. It battered and streamed against the windows of the fetid, poor-man's bar Jane had brought them to, a bar where they knew no one. It was filled with shapeless, filthy women with whom Jane drank, apparently, sometimes, during the day; and pale, untidy, sullen men, who worked on the docks, and resented seeing him there. He wanted to go, but he was trying to wait for the rain to let up a little. He was bored speechless with Jane's chatter about her paintings, and he was ashamed of Vivaldo for putting up with it. How had the fight begun? He had always blamed it on Jane. Finally, in order not to go to sleep, he had begun to tease Jane a little; but this teasing revealed, of course, how he really felt about her, and she was not slow to realize it. Vivaldo watched them with a faint, wary smile. He, too, was bored, and found Jane's pretensions intolerable.

"Anyway," Jane said, "you aren't an artist and so I don't see how you can possibly judge the work I do—"

"Oh, stop it," said Vivaldo. "Do you know how silly you sound? You mean you just paint for this half-assed gang of painters down here?"

"Oh, let her swing, man," Rufus said, beginning to enjoy himself. He leaned forward, grinning at Jane in a way at once lewd and sardonic. "This chick's too deep for us, man, we can't dig that shit she's putting down."

"You're the snobs," she said, "not I. I bet you I've reached more people, honest, hard-working, ignorant people, right here in his bar, than either of you ever reach. Those people you hang out with are *dead*, man—at least, these people are *alive*."

Rufus laughed. "I thought it smelled funny in here. So that's it. Shit. It's life, huh?" And he laughed again.

But he was also aware that they were beginning to attract attention, and he glanced at the windows where the rain streamed down, saying to himself, Okay, Rufus, behave yourself. And he leaned back in the booth, where he sat facing Jane and Vivaldo.

He had reached her, and she struck back with the only weapon she had, a shapeless instrument which might once have been fury. "It doesn't smell any worse in here than it does where you come from, baby."

Vivaldo and Rufus looked at each other. Vivaldo's lips turned white. He said, "You say another word, baby, and I'm going to knock your teeth, both of them, right down your throat."

This profoundly delighted her. She became Bette Davis at once, and shouted at the top of her voice, "Are you threatening me?"

Everyone turned to look at them.

"Oh, shit," said Rufus, "let's go."

"Yes," said Vivaldo, "let's get out of here." He looked at Jane. "Move. You filthy bitch."

And now she was contrite. She leaned forward and grabbed Rufus' hand. "I didn't mean it the way it sounded." He tried to pull his hand away; she held on. He relaxed, not wanting to seem to struggle with her. Now she was being Joan Fontaine. "Please, you *must* believe me, Rufus!"

"I believe you," he said, and rose; to find a heavy Irishman standing in his way. They stared at each other for a moment and then the man spit in his face. He heard Jane scream, but he was already far away. He struck, or thought he struck; a

fist slammed into his face and something hit him at the back
of the head. The world, the air, went red and black, then
roared in at him with faces and fists. The small of his back
slammed against something cold, hard, and straight; he supposed it was the end of the bar, and he wondered how he had
got there. From far away, he saw a barstool poised above
Vivaldo's head, and he heard Jane screaming, keening like all
of Ireland. He had not known there were so many men in the
bar. He struck a face, he felt bone beneath the bone of his
fist, and weak green eyes, glaring into his like headlights at
the moment of collision, shuttered in distress. Someone had
reached him in the belly, someone else in the head. He was
being spun about and he could no longer strike, he could only
defend. He kept his head down, bobbing and shifting, pushed
and pulled, and he crouched, trying to protect his private
parts. He heard the crash of glass. For an instant he saw
Vivaldo, at the far end of the bar, blood streaming down from
his nose and his forehead, surrounded by three or four men,
and he saw the back of a hand send Jane spinning half across
the room. Her face was white and terrified. *Good*, he thought,
and felt himself in the air, going over the bar. Glass crashed
again, and wood was splintered. There was a foot on his shoulder and a foot on one ankle. He pressed his buttocks against
the floor and drew his free leg in as far as he could; and with
one arm he tried to hold back the fist which crashed down
again and again into his face. Far behind the fist was the face
of the Irishman, with the green eyes ablaze. Then he saw
nothing, heard nothing, felt nothing. Then he heard running
feet. He was on his back behind the bar. There was no one
near him. He pulled himself up and half-crawled out. The
bartender was at the door, shooing his customers out; an old
woman sat at the bar, tranquilly sipping gin; Vivaldo lay on
his face in a pool of blood. Jane stood helplessly over him.
And the sound of the rain came back.

"I think he's dead," Jane said.

He looked at her, hating her with all his heart. He said, "I
wish to God it was you, you cunt." She began to cry.

He leaned down and helped Vivaldo to rise. Half-leaning
on, half-supporting each other, they made it to the door. Jane
came behind them. "Let me help you."

Vivaldo stopped and tried to straighten. They leaned, half-in, half-out of the door. The bartender watched them. Vivaldo looked at the bartender, then at Jane. He and Rufus stumbled together into the blinding rain.

"Let me *help* you," Jane cried again. But she stopped in the doorway long enough to say to the bartender, whose face held no expression whatever, "You're going to hear about this, believe me. I'm going to close this bar and have your job, if it's the last thing I ever do." Then she ran into the rain, and tried to help Rufus support Vivaldo.

Vivaldo pulled away from her touch, and slipped and almost fell. "Get away from me. Get away from me. You've been enough help for one night."

"You've got to get in somewhere!" Jane cried.

"Don't you *worry* about it. Don't worry about it. Drop dead, get lost, go fuck yourself. We're going to the hospital."

Rufus looked into Vivaldo's face and became frightened. Both his eyes were closing and the blood poured down from some wound in his scalp. And he was crying.

"What a way to talk to my buddy, man," he said, over and over. "Wow! What a way to talk to my *buddy!*"

"Let's go to her place," Rufus whispered. "It's closer." Vivaldo did not seem to hear him. "Come on, baby, let's go on over to Jane's, it don't matter."

He was afraid that Vivaldo had been badly hurt, and he knew what would happen at the hospital if two fays and a spade came bleeding in. For the doctors and nurses were, first of all, upright, clean-living white citizens. And he was not really afraid for himself, but for Vivaldo, who knew so little about his countrymen.

So, slipping and sliding, with Jane now circling helplessly around them and now leading the way, like a big-assed Joan of Arc, they reached Jane's pad. He carried Vivaldo into the bathroom and sat him down. He looked in the mirror. His face looked like jam, but the scars would probably heal, and only one eye was closed; but when he began washing Vivaldo, he found a great gash in his skull, and this frightened him.

"Man," he whispered, "you got to go to the hospital."

"That's what I said. All right. Let's go."

And he tried to rise.

"No, man. Listen. If I go with you, it's going to be a whole lot of who shot John because I'm black and you're white. You dig? I'm telling it to you like it is."

Vivaldo said, "I really don't want to hear all that shit, Rufus."

"Well, it's true, whether you want to hear it or not. Jane's got to take you to the hospital, I can't come with you." Vivaldo's eyes were closed and his face was white. "Vivaldo?"

He opened his eyes. "Are you mad at me, Rufus?"

"Shit, no, baby, why should I be mad with you?" But he knew what was bothering Vivaldo. He leaned down and whispered, "Don't you worry, baby, everything's cool. I know you're my friend."

"I love you, you shithead, I really do."

"I love you, too. Now, get on to that hospital, I don't want you to drop dead in this phony white chick's bathroom. I'll wait here for you. I'll be all right." Then he walked quickly out of the bathroom. He said to Jane, "Take him to the hospital, he's hurt worse than I am. I'll wait here."

She had the sense, then, to say nothing. Vivaldo remained in the hospital for ten days and had three stitches taken in his scalp. In the morning Rufus went uptown to see a doctor and stayed in bed for a week. He and Vivaldo never spoke of this night, and though he knew that Vivaldo had finally begun seeing her again, they never spoke of Jane. But from that time on, Rufus had depended on and trusted Vivaldo—depended on him even now, as he bitterly watched him horsing around with the large girl on the path. He did not know why this was so; he scarcely knew that it was so. Vivaldo was unlike everyone else that he knew in that they, all the others, could only astonish him by kindness or fidelity; it was only Vivaldo who had the power to astonish him by treachery. Even his affair with Jane was evidence in his favor, for if he were really likely to betray his friend for a woman, as most white men seemed to do, especially if the friend were black, then he would have found himself a smoother chick, with the manners of a lady and the soul of a whore. But Jane seemed to be exactly what she was, a monstrous slut, and she thus, without knowing it, kept Rufus and Vivaldo equal to one another.

At last Vivaldo was free and hurried toward them on the

path still grinning, and now waving to someone behind them.

"Look," he cried, "there's Cass!"

Rufus turned and there she was, sitting alone on the rim of the circle, frail and fair. For him, she was thoroughly mysterious. He could never quite place her in the white world to which she seemed to belong. She came from New England, of plain old American stock—so she put it; she was very fond of remembering that one of her ancestors had been burned as a witch. She had married Richard, who was Polish, and they had two children. Richard had been Vivaldo's English instructor in high school, years ago. They had known him as a brat, they said—not that he had changed much; they were his oldest friends.

With Leona between them, Rufus and Vivaldo crossed the road.

Cass looked up at them with that smile which was at once chilling and warm. It was warm because it was affectionate; it chilled Rufus because it was amused. "Well, I'm not sure I'm speaking to either of you. You've been neglecting us shamefully. Richard has crossed you *off* his list." She looked at Leona and smiled. "I'm Cass Silenski."

"This is Leona," Rufus said, putting one hand on Leona's shoulder.

Cass looked more amused than ever, and at the same time more affectionate. "I'm very happy to meet you."

"I'm glad to meet *you*," said Leona.

They sat down on the stone rim of the fountain, in the center of which a little water played, enough for small children to wade in.

"Give an account of yourselves," Cass said. "*Why* haven't you come to see us?"

"Oh," said Vivaldo, "I've been busy. I've been working on my novel."

"He's been working on a novel," said Cass to Leona, "ever since we've known him. Then he was seventeen and now he's nearly thirty."

"That's unkind," said Vivaldo, looking amused at the same time that he looked ashamed and annoyed.

"Well, Richard was working on one, too. Then he was

twenty-five and now he's close to forty. So—" She considered
Vivaldo a moment. "Only, he's had a brand-new inspiration
and he's been working on it like a madman. I think that's one
of the reasons he's been rather hoping you'd come by—he
may have wanted to discuss it with you."

"What is this new inspiration?" Vivaldo asked. "Off-hand,
it sounds unfair."

"Ah!"—she shrugged merrily, and took a deep drag on her
cigarette—"I wasn't consulted, and I'm kept in the dark. You
know Richard. He gets up at some predawn hour and goes
straight to his study and stays there until it's time to go to
work; comes home, goes straight to his study and stays there
until it's time to go to bed. I hardly ever see him. The children
no longer have a father, I no longer have a husband." She
laughed. "He did manage to grunt something the other
morning about it's going very well."

"It certainly *sounds* as though it's going well." Vivaldo
looked at Cass enviously. "And you say it's new?—it's not the
same novel he was working on before?"

"I gather not. But I really know nothing about it." She
dragged on her cigarette again, crushed it under her heel,
immediately began searching in her bag for another.

"Well, I'll certainly have to come by and check on all this
for myself," said Vivaldo. "At this rate, he'll be famous before
I am."

"Oh, I've always known that," said Cass, and lit another
cigarette.

Rufus watched the pigeons strutting along the walks and
the gangs of adolescents roaming up and down. He wanted
to get away from this place and this danger. Leona put her
hand on his. He grabbed one of her fingers and held it.

Cass turned to Rufus. "Now, *you* haven't been working on
a novel, why haven't *you* come by?"

"I've been working uptown. *You* promised to come and
hear *me*. Remember?"

"We've been terribly broke, Rufus——"

"When I'm working in a joint, you haven't got to worry
about being broke, I told you that before."

"He's a great musician," Leona said. "I heard him for the
first time last night."

Rufus looked annoyed. "That gig ended last night. I ain't got nothing to do for awhile except take care of my old lady." And he laughed.

Cass and Leona looked briefly at each other and smiled.

"How long have you been up here, Leona?" Cass asked.

"Oh, just a little over a month."

"Do you like it?"

"Oh, I love it. It's just as different as night from day, I can't tell you."

Cass looked briefly at Rufus. "That's wonderful," she said, gravely. "I'm very glad for you."

"Yes, I can feel that," said Leona. "You seem to be a very nice woman."

"Thank you," said Cass, and blushed.

"*How*'re you going to take care of your old lady," Vivaldo asked, "if you're not working?"

"Oh, I've got a couple of record dates coming up; don't you worry about old Rufus."

Vivaldo sighed. "I'm worried about *me*. I'm in the wrong profession—or, rather, I'm not. *In* it, I mean. Nobody wants to hear my story."

Rufus looked at him. "Don't let me start talking to you about *my* profession."

"Things are tough all over," said Vivaldo.

Rufus looked out over the sun-filled park.

"Nobody ever has to take up a collection to bury managers or agents," Rufus said. "But they sweeping musicians up off the streets every day."

"Never mind," said Leona, gently, "they ain't never going to sweep you up off the streets."

She put her hand on his head and stroked it. He reached up and took her hand away.

There was a silence. Then Cass rose. "I hate to break this up, but I must go home. One of my neighbors took the kids to the zoo, but they're probably getting back by now. I'd better rescue Richard."

"How *are* your kids, Cass?" Rufus asked.

"Much *you* care. It would serve you right if they'd forgotten all about you. They're fine. They've got much more energy than their parents."

Vivaldo said, "I'm going to walk Cass home. What do you think you'll be doing later?"

He felt a dull fear and a dull resentment, almost as though Vivaldo were deserting him. "Oh, I don't know. I guess we'll go along home——"

"I got to go uptown later, Rufus," said Leona. "I ain't got nothing to go to work in tomorrow."

Cass held out her hand to Leona. "It was nice meeting you. Make Rufus bring you by to see us one day."

"Well, it was sure nice meeting you. I been meeting some real nice people lately."

"Next time," said Cass, "we'll go off and have a drink by ourselves someplace, without all these *men*."

They laughed together. "I *really* would like that."

"Suppose I pick you up at Benno's," Rufus said to Vivaldo, "around ten-thirty?"

"Good enough. Maybe we'll go across town and pick up on some jazz?"

"Good."

"So long, Leona. Glad to have met you."

"Me, too. Be seeing you real soon."

"Give my regards," said Rufus, "to Richard and the kids, and tell them I'm coming by."

"I'll do that. Make sure you *do* come by, we'd dearly love to see you."

Cass and Vivaldo started slowly in the direction of the arch. The bright-red, setting sun burned their silhouettes against the air and crowned the dark head and the golden one. Rufus and Leona stood and watched them; when they were under the arch, they turned and waved.

"We better be making tracks," said Rufus.

"I guess so." They started back through the park. "You got some real nice friends, Rufus. You're lucky. They're real fond of you. They think you're somebody."

"You think they do?"

"I know they do. I can tell by the way they talk to you, the way they treat you."

"I guess they *are* pretty nice," he said, "at that."

She laughed. "*You're* a funny boy"—she corrected herself—"a funny *person*. You act like you don't know who you are."

"I know who I am, all right," he said, aware of the eyes that watched them pass, the nearly inaudible murmur that came from the benches or the trees. He squeezed her thin hand between his elbow and his side. "I'm your boy. You know what that means?"

"What does it mean?"

"It means you've got to be good to me."

"Well, Rufus, I sure am going to try."

Now, bowed down with the memory of all that had happened since that day, he wandered helplessly back to Forty-second Street and stopped before the large bar and grill on the corner. Near him, just beyond the plate glass, stood the sandwich man behind his counter, the meat arrayed on the steam table beneath him. Bread and rolls, mustard, relish, salt and pepper, stood at the level of his chest. He was a big man, wearing white, with a blank, red, brutal face. From time to time he expertly knifed off a sandwich for one of the derelicts within. The old seemed reconciled to being there, to having no teeth, no hair, having no life. Some laughed together, the young, with dead eyes set in yellow faces, the slackness of their bodies making vivid the history of their degradation. They were the prey that was no longer hunted, though they were scarcely aware of this new condition and could not bear to leave the place where they had first been spoiled. And the hunters were there, far more assured and patient than the prey. In any of the world's cities, on a winter night, a boy can be bought for the price of a beer and the promise of warm blankets.

Rufus shivered, his hands in his pockets, looking through the window and wondering what to do. He thought of walking to Harlem but he was afraid of the police he would encounter in his passage through the city; and he did not see how he could face his parents or his sister. When he had last seen Ida, he had told her that he and Leona were about to make it to Mexico, where, he said, people would leave them alone. But no one had heard from him since then.

Now a big, rough-looking man, well dressed, white, with black-and-gray hair, came out of the bar. He paused next to Rufus, looking up and down the street. Rufus did not move, though he wanted to; his mind began to race, painfully, and his empty stomach turned over. Once again, sweat broke out on his forehead. Something in him knew what was about to happen; something in him died in the freezing second before the man walked over to him and said:

"It's cold out here. Wouldn't you like to come in and have a drink with me?"

"I'd rather have a sandwich," Rufus muttered, and thought *You've really hit the bottom now.*

"Well, you can have a sandwich, too. There's no law that says you can't."

Rufus looked up and down the street, then looked into the man's ice-cold, ice-white face. He reminded himself that he knew the score, he'd been around; neither was this the first time during his wanderings that he had consented to the bleakly physical exchange; and yet he felt that he would never be able to endure the touch of this man. They entered the bar and grill.

"What kind of sandwich would you like?"

"Corned beef," Rufus whispered, "on rye."

They watched while the meat was hacked off, slammed on bread, and placed on the counter. The man paid and Rufus took his sandwich over to the bar. He felt that everyone in the place knew what was going on, knew that Rufus was peddling his ass. But nobody seemed to care. Nobody looked at them. The noise at the bar continued, the radio continued to blare. The bartender served up a beer for Rufus and a whiskey for the man and rang up the money on the cash register. Rufus tried to turn his mind away from what was happening to him. He wolfed down his sandwich. But the heavy bread, the tepid meat, made him begin to feel nauseous; everything wavered before his eyes for a moment; he sipped his beer, trying to hold the sandwich down.

"You were hungry."

Rufus, he thought, you can't make this scene. There's no way in the world you can make it. Don't come on with the man. Just get out of here.

"Would you like another sandwich?"

The first sandwich was still threatening to come up. The bar stank of stale beer and piss and stale meat and unwashed bodies.

Suddenly he felt that he was going to cry.

"No, thank you," he said, "I'm all right now."

The man watched him for a moment.

"Then have another beer."

"No, thank you." But he leaned his head on the bar, trembling.

"Hey!"

Lights roared around his head, the whole bar lurched, righted itself, faces weaved around him, the music from the radio pounded in his skull. The man's face was very close to his: hard eyes and a cruel nose and flabby, brutal lips. He smelled the man's odor. He pulled away.

"I'm all right."

"You almost blacked out there for a minute."

The bartender watched them.

"You better have a drink. Hey, Mac, give the kid a drink."

"You sure he's all right?"

"Yeah, he's all right, I know him. Give him a drink."

The bartender filled a shot glass and placed it in front of Rufus. And Rufus stared into the gleaming cup, praying, Lord, don't let it happen. Don't let me go home with this man.

I've got so little left, Lord, don't let me lose it all.

"Drink. It'll do you good. Then you can come on over to my place and get some sleep."

He drank the whiskey, which first made him feel even sicker, then warmed him. He straightened up.

"You live around here?" he asked the man. If you touch me, he thought, still with these strange tears threatening to boil over at any moment, I'll beat the living shit out of you. I don't want no more hands on me, no more, no more, no more.

"Not very far. Forty-sixth Street."

They walked out of the bar, into the streets again.

"It's a lonely city," the man said as they walked. "I'm lonely. Aren't you lonely, too?"

Rufus said nothing.

"Maybe we can comfort each other for a night."

Rufus watched the traffic lights, the black, nearly deserted streets, the silent black buildings, the deep shadows of doorways.

"Do you know what I mean?"

"I'm not the boy you want, mister," he said at last, and suddenly remembered having said exactly these words to Eric—long ago.

"How do you mean, you're not the boy I want?" And the man tried to laugh. "Shouldn't I be the best judge of that?"

Rufus said, "I don't have a thing to give you. I don't have nothing to give nobody. Don't make me go through with this. Please."

They stopped on the silent Avenue, facing each other. The man's eyes hardened and narrowed.

"Didn't you know what was going on—back there?"

Rufus said, "I was hungry."

"What are you, anyway—just a cock teaser?"

"I was hungry," Rufus repeated; "I was hungry."

"Don't you have any family—any friends?"

Rufus looked down. He did not answer right away. Then, "I don't want to die, mister. I don't want to kill you. Let me go—to my friends."

"Do you know where to find them?"

"I know where to find—one of them."

There was a silence. Rufus stared at the sidewalk and, very slowly, the tears filled his eyes and began trickling down his nose.

The man took his arm. "Come on—come on to my place."

But now the moment, the possibility, had passed; both of them felt it. The man dropped his arm.

"You're a good-looking boy," he said.

Rufus moved away. "So long, mister. Thanks."

The man said nothing. Rufus watched him walk away.

Then he, too, turned and began walking downtown. He thought of Eric for the first time in years, and wondered if he were prowling foreign streets tonight. He glimpsed, for the first time, the extent, the nature, of Eric's loneliness, and the

danger in which this placed him; and wished that he had been
nicer to him. Eric had always been very nice to Rufus. He had
had a pair of cufflinks made for Rufus, for Rufus' birthday,
with the money which was to have bought his wedding rings:
and this gift, this confession, delivered him into Rufus' hands.
Rufus had despised him because he came from Alabama; perhaps he had allowed Eric to make love to him in order to
despise him more completely. Eric had finally understood this,
and had fled from Rufus, all the way to Paris. But his stormy
blue eyes, his bright red hair, his halting drawl, all returned
very painfully to Rufus now.

Go ahead and tell me. You ain't got to be afraid.

And, as Eric hesitated, Rufus added—slyly, grinning, watching him:

"You act like a little girl—or something."

And even now there was something heady and almost sweet
in the memory of the ease with which he had handled Eric,
and elicited his confession. When Eric had finished speaking,
he said, slowly;

"I'm not the boy for you. I don't go that way."

Eric had placed their hands together, and he stared down
at them, the red and the brown.

"I know," he said.

He moved to the center of his room.

"But I can't help wishing you did. I wish you'd try."

Then, with a terrible effort, Rufus heard it in his voice, his
breath:

"I'd do anything. I'd try anything. To please you."

Then, with a smile, "I'm almost as young as you are. I don't
know—much—about it."

Rufus had watched him, smiling. He felt a flood of affection
for Eric. And he felt his own power.

He walked over to Eric and put his hands on Eric's shoulders. He did not know what he was going to say or do. But
with his hands on Eric's shoulders, affection, power, and curiosity all knotted together in him—with a hidden, unforeseen
violence which frightened him a little; the hands that were
meant to hold Eric at arm's length seemed to draw Eric to
him; the current that had begun flowing he did not know
how to stop.

At last, he said in a low voice, smiling, "I'll try anything once, old buddy."

Those cufflinks were now in Harlem, in Ida's bureau drawer. And when Eric was gone, Rufus forgot their battles and the unspeakable physical awkwardness, and the ways in which he had made Eric pay for such pleasure as Eric gave, or got. He remembered only that Eric had loved him; as he now remembered that Leona had loved him. He had despised Eric's manhood by treating him as a woman, by telling him how inferior he was to a woman, by treating him as nothing more than a hideous sexual deformity. But Leona had not been a deformity. And he had used against her the very epithets he had used against Eric, and in the very same way, with the same roaring in his head and the same intolerable pressure in his chest.

Vivaldo lived alone in a first-floor apartment on Bank Street. He was home, Rufus saw the light in the window. He slowed down a little but the cold air refused to let him hesitate; he hurried through the open street door, thinking, Well, I might as well get it over with. And he knocked quickly on Vivaldo's door.

There had been the sound of a typewriter; now it stopped. Rufus knocked again.

"Who is it?" called Vivaldo, sounding extremely annoyed.

"It's me. It's me. Rufus."

The sudden light, when Vivaldo opened the door, was a great shock, as was Vivaldo's face.

"My God," said Vivaldo.

He grabbed Rufus around the neck, pulling him inside and holding him. They both leaned for a moment against Vivaldo's door.

"My God," Vivaldo said again, "where've you been? Don't you know you shouldn't do things like that? You've had all of us scared to death, baby. We've been looking for you everywhere."

It was a great shock and it weakened Rufus, exactly as though he had been struck in the belly. He clung to Vivaldo as though he were on the ropes. Then he pulled away.

Vivaldo looked at him, looked hard at him, up and down.

And Vivaldo's face told him how he looked. He moved away from the door, away from Vivaldo's scrutiny.

"Ida's been here; she's half crazy. Do you realize you dropped out of sight almost a month ago?"

"Yes," he said, and sat down heavily in Vivaldo's easy chair—which sagged beneath him almost to the floor. He looked around the room, which had once been so familiar, which now seemed so strange.

He leaned back, his hands over his eyes.

"Take off your jacket," Vivaldo said. "I'll see if I can scare up something for you to eat—are you hungry?"

"No, not now. Tell me, how is Ida?"

"Well, she's *worried*, you know, but there's nothing wrong with her. Rufus, you want me to fix you a drink?"

"When was she here?"

"Yesterday. And she called me tonight. And she's been to the police. Everybody's been worried, Cass, Richard, everybody——"

He sat up. "The police are looking for me?"

"Well, hell, yes, baby, people aren't supposed to just disappear." He walked into his small, cluttered kitchen and opened his refrigerator, which contained a quart of milk and half a grapefruit. He stared at them helplessly. "I'll have to take you out, I haven't got anything to eat in this joint." He closed the refrigerator door. "You can have a drink, though, I've got some bourbon."

Vivaldo made two drinks, gave one to Rufus and sat down on the other, straight-backed, chair.

"Well, let's have it. What've you been doing, where've you been?"

"I've just been wandering the streets."

"My God, Rufus, in this weather? Where've you been sleeping?"

"Oh. Subways, hallways. Movies sometimes."

"And how'd you eat?"

He took a swallow of his drink. Perhaps it was a mistake to have come. "Oh," he said, astonished to hear the truth come out, "sometimes I sort of peddled my ass."

Vivaldo looked at him. "I guess you had pretty rough competition." He lit a cigarette and threw the pack and the matches to Rufus. "You should have got in touch with some-body, you should have let somebody know what was hap-pening."

"I—couldn't. I just couldn't."

"We're supposed to be friends, you and me."

He stood up, holding an unlit cigarette, and walked around the small room, touching things. "I don't know. I don't know what I was thinking." He lit the cigarette. "I know what I did to Leona. I'm not dumb."

"So do I know what you did to Leona. Neither am I dumb."

"I guess I just didn't think—"

"What?"

"That anyone would care."

In the silence that hung in the room then, Vivaldo rose and went to his phonograph. "You didn't think Ida would care? You didn't think I would care?"

He felt as though he were smothering. "I don't know. I don't know what I thought."

Vivaldo said nothing. His face was pale and angry and he concentrated on looking through his records. Finally he put one on the machine; it was James Pete Johnson and Bessie Smith batting out *Backwater Blues*.

"Well," said Vivaldo, helplessly, and sat down again.

Besides Vivaldo's phonograph, there wasn't much else in his apartment. There was a homemade lamp, brick-supported bookshelves, records, a sagging bed, the sprung easy chair, and the straight-backed chair. There was a high stool before Vivaldo's worktable on which Vivaldo teetered now, his coarse, curly black hair hanging forward, his eyes somber, and his mouth turned down. The table held his pencils, papers, his typewriter, and the telephone. In a small alcove was the kitchen in which the overhead light was burning. The sink was full of dirty dishes, topped by a jaggedly empty and open tin can. A paper sack of garbage leaned against one of the kitchen table's uncertain legs.

There's thousands of people, Bessie now sang, *ain't got no place to go,* and for the first time Rufus began to hear, in the severely understated monotony of this blues, something which spoke to his troubled mind. The piano bore the singer witness, stoic and ironic. Now that Rufus himself had no place to go—*'cause my house fell down and I can't live there no mo'*, sang Bessie—he heard the line and the tone of the singer, and he wondered how others had moved beyond the emptiness and horror which faced him now.

Vivaldo was watching him. Now he cleared his throat and said, "Maybe it would be a good idea for you to make a change of scene, Rufus. Everything around here will just keep reminding you—sometimes it's better just to wipe the slate clean and take off. Maybe you should go to the Coast."

"There's nothing happening on the Coast."

"A lot of musicians have gone out there."

"They're on their ass out there, too. It's no different from New York."

"No, they're working. You might feel differently out there, with all the sunshine and oranges and all." He smiled. "Make a new man of you, baby."

"I guess you think," said Rufus, malevolently, "that it's time I started trying to be a new man."

There was a silence. Then Vivaldo said, "It's not so much what *I* think. It's what *you* think."

Rufus watched the tall, lean, clumsy white boy who was his best friend, and felt himself nearly strangling with the desire to hurt him.

"Rufus," said Vivaldo, suddenly, "believe me, I know, I know—a lot of things hurt you that I can't really understand." He played with the keys of his typewriter. "A lot of things hurt me that *I* can't really understand."

Rufus sat on the edge of the sprung easy chair, watching Vivaldo gravely.

"Do you blame me for what happened to Leona?"

"Rufus, what good would it do if I *did* blame you? You blame yourself enough already, that's what's wrong with you, what's the good of *my* blaming you?"

He could see, though, that Vivaldo had also hoped to be able to avoid this question.

"Do you blame me or don't you? Tell the truth."

"Rufus, if I wasn't your friend, I think I'd blame you, sure. You acted like a bastard. But I understand that, I think I do, I'm trying to. But, anyway, since you *are* my friend, and, after all, let's face it, you mean much more to me than Leona ever did, well, I don't think I should put you down just because you acted like a bastard. We're *all* bastards. That's why we need our friends."

"I wish I could tell you what it was like," Rufus said, after a long silence. "I wish I could undo it."

"Well, you can't. So please start trying to forget it."

Rufus thought, But it's not possible to forget anybody you were that hung up on, who was that hung up on you. You can't forget anything that hurt so badly, went so deep, and changed the world forever. It's not possible to forget anybody you've destroyed.

He took a great swallow of his bourbon, holding it in his mouth, then allowing it to trickle down his throat. He would never be able to forget Leona's pale, startled eyes, her sweet smile, her plaintive drawl, her thin, insatiable body.

He choked slightly, put down his drink, and ground out his cigarette in the spilling ashtray.

"I bet you won't believe this," he said, "but I loved Leona. I did."

"Oh," said Vivaldo, "believe you! Of course I believe you. That's what all the bleeding was *about.*"

He got up and turned the record over. Then there was silence, except for the voice of Bessie Smith.

When my bed get empty, make me feel awful mean and blue,

"Oh, sing it, Bessie," Vivaldo muttered.

My springs is getting rusty, sleeping single like I do.

Rufus picked up his drink and finished it.

"Did you ever have the feeling," he asked, "that a woman was eating you up? I mean—no matter what she was like or what else she was doing—that that's what she was *really* doing?"

"Yes," said Vivaldo.

Rufus stood. He walked up and down.

"She can't help it. And you can't help it. And there you are." He paused. "Of course, with Leona and me—there was lots of other things, too——"

Then there was a long silence. They listened to Bessie.

"Have you ever wished you were queer?" Rufus asked, suddenly.

Vivaldo smiled, looking into his glass. "I used to think maybe I was. Hell, I think I even *wished* I was." He laughed. "But I'm not. So I'm stuck."

Rufus walked to Vivaldo's window. "So you been all up and down that street, too," he said.

"We've all been up the same streets. There aren't a hell of a lot of streets. Only, we've been taught to lie so much, about so many things, that we hardly ever know *where* we are."

Rufus said nothing. He walked up and down.

Vivaldo said, "Maybe you should stay here, Rufus, for a couple of days, until you decide what you want to do."

"I don't want to bug you, Vivaldo."

Vivaldo picked up Rufus' empty glass and paused in the archway which led into his kitchen. "You can lie here in the mornings and look at my ceiling. It's full of cracks, it makes all kinds of pictures. Maybe it'll tell you things it hasn't told me. I'll fix us another drink."

Again he felt that he was smothering. "Thanks, Vivaldo."

Vivaldo dragged his ice out and poured two drinks. He came back into the room. "Here. To all the things we don't know."

They drank.

"You had me worried," said Vivaldo. "I'm glad you're back."

"I'm glad to see you," said Rufus.

"Your sister left me a phone number to call in case I saw you. It's the lady who lives next door to you. I guess maybe I should call her now."

"No," said Rufus, after a moment, "it's too late. I'll go on up there in the morning." And this thought, the thought of seeing his parents and his sister in the morning, checked and chilled him. He sat down again in the easy chair and leaned back with his hands over his eyes.

"Rufus," Leona had said—time and again—"ain't nothing wrong in being colored."

Sometimes, when she said this, he simply looked at her coldly, from a great distance, as though he wondered what on earth she was trying to say. His look seemed to accuse her of ignorance and indifference. And, as she watched his face, her eyes became more despairing than ever but at the same time filled with some immense sexual secret which tormented her.

He had put off going back to work until he began to be afraid to go to work.

Sometimes, when she said that there was nothing wrong in being colored, he answered,

"Not if you a hard-up white lady."

The first time he said this, she winced and said nothing. The second time she slapped him. And he slapped her. They fought all the time. They fought each other with their hands and their voices and then with their bodies: and the one storm was like the other. Many times—and now Rufus sat very still, pressing darkness against his eyes, listening to the music—he had, suddenly, without knowing that he was going to, thrown the whimpering, terrified Leona onto the bed, the floor, pinned her against a table or a wall; she beat at him, weakly, moaning, unutterably abject; he twisted his fingers in her long pale hair and used her in whatever way he felt would humiliate her most. It was not love he felt during these acts of love: drained and shaking, utterly unsatisfied, he fled from the raped white woman into the bars. In these bars no one applauded his triumph or condemned his guilt. He began to pick fights with white men. He was thrown out of bars. The eyes of his friends told him that he was falling. His own heart told him so. But the air through which he rushed was his prison and he could not even summon the breath to call for help.

Perhaps now, though, he had hit bottom. One thing about the bottom, he told himself, you can't fall any farther. He tried to take comfort from this thought. Yet there knocked in his heart the suspicion that the bottom did not really exist.

"I don't want to die," he heard himself say, and he began to cry.

The music went on, far from him, terribly loud. The lights were very bright and hot. He was sweating and he itched, he stank. Vivaldo was close to him, stroking his head; the stuff of Vivaldo's sweater stifled him. He wanted to stop crying, stand up, breathe, but he could only sit there with his face in his hands. Vivaldo murmured, "Go ahead, baby, let it out, let it all out." He wanted to stand up, breathe, and at the same time he wanted to lie flat on the floor and to be swallowed into whatever would stop this pain.

Yet, he was aware, perhaps for the first time in his life, that nothing would stop it, nothing: this was himself. Rufus was aware of every inch of Rufus. He was flesh: flesh, bone, muscle, fluid, orifices, hair, and skin. His body was controlled by laws he did not understand. Nor did he understand what force within this body had driven him into such a desolate place. The most impenetrable of mysteries moved in this darkness for less than a second, hinting of reconciliation. And still the music continued, Bessie was saying that she wouldn't mind being in jail but she had to stay there so long.

"I'm sorry," he said, and raised his head.

Vivaldo gave him a handkerchief and he dried his eyes and blew his nose.

"Don't be sorry," said Vivaldo. "Be glad." He stood over Rufus for yet another moment, then he said, "I'm going to take you out and buy you a pizza. You hungry, child, that's why you carrying on like that." He went into the kitchen and began to wash his face. Rufus smiled, watching him, bent over the sink, under the hideous light.

It was like the kitchen in St. James Slip. He and Leona had ended their life together there, on the very edge of the island. When Rufus had ceased working and when all his money was gone, and there was nothing left to pawn, they were wholly dependent on the money Leona brought home from the restaurant. Then she lost this job. Their domestic life, which involved a hideous amount of drinking, made it difficult for her to get there on time and also caused her to look more and more disreputable. One evening, half-drunk, Rufus had gone to the restaurant to pick her up. The next day she was fired. She never held a steady job again.

One evening Vivaldo came to visit them in their last apartment. They heard the whistles of tugboats all day and all night long. Vivaldo found Leona sitting on the bathroom floor, her hair in her eyes, her face swollen and dirty with weeping. Rufus had been beating her. He sat silently on the bed.

"Why?" cried Vivaldo.

"I don't know," Leona sobbed, "it can't be for nothing I did. He's always beating me, for nothing, for nothing!" She gasped for breath, opening her mouth like an infant, and in that instant Vivaldo really hated Rufus and Rufus knew it. "He says I'm sleeping with other colored boys behind his back and it's not true, God knows it's not true!"

"Rufus knows it isn't true," Vivaldo said. He looked over at Rufus, who said nothing. He turned back to Leona. "Get up, Leona. Stand up. Wash your face."

He went into the bathroom and helped her to her feet and turned the water on. "Come on, Leona. Pull yourself together, like a good girl."

She tried to stop sobbing, and splashed water on her face. Vivaldo patted her on the shoulder, astonished all over again to realize how frail she was. He walked into the bedroom.

Rufus looked up at him. "This is my house," he said, "and that's my girl. You ain't got nothing to do with this. Get your ass out of here."

"You could be killed for this," said Vivaldo. "All she has to do is yell. All *I* have to do is walk down to the corner and get a cop."

"You trying to scare me? Go *get* a cop."

"You must be out of your mind. They'd take one look at this situation and put you *under* the jailhouse." He walked to the bathroom door. "Come on, Leona. Get your coat. I'm taking you out of here."

"I'm not out of *my* mind," Rufus said, "but *you* are. Where you think you taking Leona?"

"I got no place to go," Leona muttered.

"Well, you can stay at my place until you *find* some place to go. I'm not leaving you here."

Rufus threw back his head and laughed. Vivaldo and Leona both turned to watch him. Rufus cried to the ceiling, "He's going to come to *my* house and walk out with *my* girl and he thinks this poor nigger's just going to sit and let him do it. Ain't this a bitch?"

He fell over on his side, still laughing.

Vivaldo shouted, "For Christ's sake, Rufus! *Rufus!*"

Rufus stopped laughing and sat straight up. "What? Who the hell do you think you're kidding? I know you only got one bed in your place!"

"Oh, Rufus," Leona wailed, "Vivaldo's only trying to help."

"You shut up," he said instantly, and looked at her.

"Everybody ain't a animal," she muttered.

"You mean, like me?"

She said nothing. Vivaldo watched them both.

"You mean, like me, bitch? Or you mean, like you?"

"If I'm a animal," she flared—perhaps she was emboldened by the presence of Vivaldo—"I'd like you to tell me who made me one. Just tell me that?"

"Why, your husband did, you bitch. You told me yourself he had a thing on him like a horse. You told me yourself how he did you—he kept telling you how he had the biggest thing in Dixie, black *or* white. And you said you couldn't stand it. Ha-*ha*. *That's* one of the funniest things I *ever* heard."

"I guess," she said, wearily, after a silence, "I told you a lot of things I shouldn't have."

Rufus snorted. "I guess you did." He said—to Vivaldo, the room, the river—"it was her husband ruined this bitch. Your husband and all them funky niggers screwed you in the Georgia bushes. That's why your husband threw you out. Why don't you tell the truth? I wouldn't have to beat you if you'd tell the truth." He grinned at Vivaldo. "Man, this chick can't get enough"—and he broke off, staring at Leona.

"Rufus," said Vivaldo, trying to be calm, "I don't know what you're putting down. I think you must be crazy. You got a great chick, who'd go all the way for you—and you know it—and you keep coming on with this *Gone with the Wind* crap. What's the matter with your head, baby?" He tried to smile. "Baby, please don't do this. Please?"

Rufus said nothing. He sat down on the bed, in the position in which he had been sitting when Vivaldo arrived.

"Come on, Leona," said Vivaldo at last and Rufus stood up, looking at them both with a little smile, with hatred.

"I'm just going to take her away for a few days, so you can both cool down. There's no point in going on like this."

"Sir Walter Raleigh—with a hard on," Rufus sneered.

"Look," said Vivaldo, "if you don't trust me, man, I'll get

a room at the Y. I'll come back here. Goddammit," he
shouted, "I'm not trying to steal your girl. You know me
better than that."

Rufus said, with an astonishing and a menacing humility,
"I guess you don't think she's good enough for you."

"Oh, shit. You don't think she's good enough for *you*."

"No," said Leona, and both men turned to watch her,
"ain't neither one of you got it right. Rufus don't think he's
good enough for *me*."

She and Rufus stared at each other. A tugboat whistled, far
away. Rufus smiled.

"You see? *You* bring it up all the time. *You* the one who
brings it up. Now, how you expect me to make it with a bitch
like you?"

"It's the way you was raised," she said, "and I guess you
just can't help it."

Again, there was a silence. Leona pressed her lips together
and her eyes filled with tears. She seemed to wish to call the
words back, to call time back, and begin everything over
again. But she could not think of anything to say and the
silence stretched. Rufus pursed his lips.

"Go on, you slut," he said, "go on and make it with your
wop lover. He ain't going to be able to do you no good. Not
now. You be back. You can't do without me now." And he
lay face downward on the bed. "Me, I'll get me a good night's
sleep for a change."

Vivaldo pushed Leona to the door, backing out of the
room, watching Rufus.

"I'll be back," he said.

"No, you won't," said Rufus. "I'll kill you if you come
back."

Leona looked at him quickly, bidding him to be silent, and
Vivaldo closed the door behind them.

"Leona," he asked, when they were in the streets, "how
long have things been like this? Why do you take it?"

"Why," asked Leona, wearily, "do people take anything?
Because they can't help it, I guess. Well, that's me. Before
God, I don't know what to do." She began to cry again. The
streets were very dark and empty. "I know he's sick and I
keep hoping he'll get well and I can't make him see a doctor.

He knows I'm not doing none of those things he says, he knows it!"

"But you can't go on like this, Leona. He can get both of you killed."

"He says it's me trying to get us killed." She tried to laugh. "He had a fight last week with some guy in the subway, some real, ignorant, unhappy man just didn't like the idea of our being together, you know? and, well, you know, he blamed that fight on me. He said I was encouraging the man. Why, Viv, I didn't even *see* the man until he opened his mouth. But, Rufus, he's all the time looking for it, he sees it where it ain't, he don't see nothing else no more. He says I ruined his life. Well, he sure ain't done mine much good."

She tried to dry her eyes. Vivaldo gave her his handkerchief and put one arm around her shoulders.

"You know, the world is hard enough and people is evil enough without all the time looking for it and stirring it up and making it worse. I keep telling him, I know a lot of people don't like what I'm doing. But I don't care, let them go their way, I'll go mine."

A policeman passed them, giving them a look. Vivaldo felt a chill go through Leona's body. Then a chill went through his own. He had never been afraid of policemen before; he had merely despised them. But now he felt the impersonality of the uniform, the emptiness of the streets. He felt what the policeman might say and do if he had been Rufus, walking here with his arm around Leona.

He said, nevertheless, after a moment, "You ought to leave him. You ought to leave town."

"I tell you, Viv, I keep hoping—it'll all come all right somehow. He wasn't like this when I met him, he's not really like this at all. I *know* he's not. Something's got all twisted up in his mind and he can't help it."

They were standing under a street lamp. Her face was hideous, was unutterably beautiful with grief. Tears rolled down her thin cheeks and she made doomed, sporadic efforts to control the trembling of her little-girl's mouth.

"I love him," she said, helplessly, "I love him, I can't help it. No matter what he does to me. He's just lost and he beats me because he can't find nothing else to hit."

He pulled her against him while she wept, a thin, tired girl, unwitting heiress of generations of bitterness. He could think of nothing to say. A light was slowly turning on inside him, a dreadful light. He saw—dimly—dangers, mysteries, chasms which he had never dreamed existed.

"Here comes a taxi," he said.

She straightened and tried to dry her eyes again.

"I'll come with you," he said, "and come right back."

"No," she said, "just give me the keys. I'll be all right. You go on back to Rufus."

"Rufus said he'd kill me," he said, half-smiling.

The taxi stopped beside them. He gave her his keys. She opened the door, keeping her face away from the driver.

"Rufus ain't going to kill nobody but himself," she said, "if he don't find a friend to help him." She paused, half-in, half-out of the cab. "You the only friend he's got in the world, Vivaldo."

He gave her some money for the fare, looking at her with something, after all these months, explicit at last between them. They both loved Rufus. And they were both white. Now that it stared them so hideously in the face, each could see how desperately the other had been trying to avoid this confrontation.

"You'll *go* there now?" he asked. "You'll *go* to my place?"

"Yes. I'll go. You go on back to Rufus. Maybe you can help him. He needs somebody to help him."

Vivaldo gave the driver his address and watched the taxi roll away. He turned and started back the way they had come.

The way seemed longer, now that he was alone, and darker. His awareness of the policeman, prowling somewhere in the darkness near him, made the silence ominous. He felt threatened. He felt totally estranged from the city in which he had been born; this city for which he sometimes felt a kind of stony affection because it was all he knew of home. Yet he had no home here—the hovel on Bank Street was not a home. He had always supposed that he would, one day, make a home here for himself. Now he began to wonder if anyone could ever put down roots in this rock; or, rather, he began to be aware of the shapes acquired by those who had. He began to wonder about his own shape.

He had often thought of his loneliness, for example, as a condition which testified to his superiority. But people who were not superior were, nevertheless, extremely lonely—and unable to break out of their solitude precisely because they had no equipment with which to enter it. His own loneliness, magnified so many million times, made the night air colder. He remembered to what excesses, into what traps and night-mares, his loneliness had driven him; and he wondered where such a violent emptiness might drive an entire city.

At the same time, as he came closer to Rufus' building, he was trying very hard not to think about Rufus.

He was in a section of warehouses. Very few people lived down here. By day, trucks choked the streets, laborers stood on these ghostly platforms, moving great weights, and curs-ing. As he had once; for a long time, he had been one of them. He had been proud of his skill and his muscles and happy to be accepted as a man among men. Only—it was they who saw something in him which they could not accept, which made them uneasy. Every once in a while, a man, light-ing his cigarette, would look at him quizzically, with a little smile. The smile masked an unwilling, defensive hostility. They said he was a "bright kid," that he would "go places"; and they made it clear that they expected him to go, to which places did not matter—he did not belong to them.

But at the bottom of his mind the question of Rufus nagged and stung. There had been a few colored boys in his high school but they had mainly stayed together, as far as he re-membered. He had known boys who got a bang out of going out and beating up niggers. It scarcely seemed possible—it scarcely, even, seemed fair—that colored boys who were beaten up in high school could grow up into colored men who wanted to beat up everyone in sight, including, or per-haps especially, people who had never, one way or another, given them a thought.

He watched the light in Rufus' window, the only light on down here.

Then he remembered something that had happened to him a long time ago, two years or three. It was when he had been spending a lot of time in Harlem, running after the whores up there. One night, as a light rain fell, he was walking uptown on Seventh Avenue. He walked very briskly, for it was very late and this section of the Avenue was almost entirely deserted and he was afraid of being stopped by a prowl car. At 116th Street he stopped in a bar, deliberately choosing a bar he did not know. Since he did not know the bar he felt an unaccustomed uneasiness and wondered what the faces around him hid. Whatever it was, they hid it very well. They went on drinking and talking to each other and putting coins in the juke box. It certainly didn't seem that his presence caused anyone to become wary, or to curb their tongues. Nevertheless, no one made any effort to talk to him and an almost imperceptible glaze came over their eyes whenever they looked in his direction. This glaze remained, even when they smiled. The barman, for example, smiled at something Vivaldo said and yet made it clear, as he pushed his drink across the bar, that the width of the bar was but a weak representation of the great gulf fixed between them.

This was the night that he saw the eyes unglaze. Later, a girl came over to him. They went around the corner to her room. There they were; he had his tie loosened and his trousers off and they had been just about to begin when the door opened and in walked her "husband." He was one of the smooth-faced, laughing men who had been in the bar. The girl squealed, rather prettily, and then calmly began to get dressed again. Vivaldo had first been so disappointed that he wanted to cry, then so angry that he wanted to kill. Not until he looked into the man's eyes did he begin to be afraid.

The man looked down at him and smiled.

"Where was you thinking of putting that, white boy?"

Vivaldo said nothing. He slowly began pulling on his trousers. The man was very dark and very big, nearly as big as Vivaldo, and, of course, at that moment, in much better fighting condition.

The girl sat on the edge of the bed, putting on her shoes. There was silence in the room except for her low, disjointed, intermittent humming. He couldn't quite make out the tune she was humming and this, for some insane reason, drove him wild.

"You might at least have waited a couple of minutes," Vivaldo said. "I never even got it in."

He said this as he was buckling his belt, idly, out of some dim notion that he might thus, in effect, reduce the fine. The words were hardly out of his mouth before the man had struck him, twice, palm open, across the face. Vivaldo staggered backward from the bed into the corner which held the sink and a water glass went crashing to the floor.

"Goddamnit," said the girl, sharply, "ain't no need to wreck the joint." And she bent down to pick up the bits of glass. But it also seemed to Vivaldo that she was a little frightened and a little ashamed. "Do what you going to do," she said, from her knees, "and get him out of here."

Vivaldo and the man stared at each other and terror began draining Vivaldo's rage out of him. It was not merely the situation which frightened him: it was the man's eyes. They stared at Vivaldo with a calm, steady hatred, as remote and unanswerable as madness.

"You goddamn lucky you *didn't* get it in," he said. "You'd be a mighty sorry white boy if you had. You wouldn't be putting that white prick in no more black pussy, I can guarantee you that."

Well, if that's the way you feel, Vivaldo wanted to say, why the hell don't you keep her off the streets? But it really seemed better—and it seemed, weirdly enough, that the girl was silently trying to convey this to him—to say as little as possible.

So he only said, after a moment, as mildly as he could, "Look. I fell for the oldest gag in the business. Here I am. Okay. What do you want?"

And what the man wanted was more than he knew how to say. He watched Vivaldo, waiting for Vivaldo to speak again. Vivaldo's mind was filled suddenly with the image of a movie he had seen long ago. He saw a bird dog, tense, pointing, absolutely silent, waiting for a covey of quail to surrender to panic and fly upward, where they could be picked off by the guns of the hunters. So it was in the room while the man waited for Vivaldo to speak. Whatever Vivaldo might say would be turned into an opportunity for slaughter. Vivaldo held his breath, hoping that his panic did not show in his eyes, and felt his flesh begin to crawl. Then the man looked over at the girl, who stood near the bed, watching him, and then he slowly moved closer to Vivaldo. When he stood directly before Vivaldo, his eyes still driving, it seemed, into Vivaldo's as though he would pierce the skull and the brain and possess it all, he abruptly held out his hand.

Vivaldo handed him the wallet.

The man lit a cigarette which he held in the corner of his mouth as he deliberately, insolently, began looking through the wallet. "What I don't understand," he said, with a fearful laziness, "is why you white boys always come uptown, sniffing around our black girls. You don't see none of us spooks downtown, sniffing around your white girls." He looked up. "Do you?"

Don't be so sure, Vivaldo thought, but said nothing. But this had struck some nerve in him and he felt himself beginning to be angry again.

"Suppose I told you that that was my sister," the man said, gesturing toward the girl. "What would *you* do if you found me with your sister?"

I wouldn't give a damn if you split her in two, Vivaldo thought, promptly. At the same time this question made him tremble with rage and he realized, with another part of his mind, that this was exactly what the man wanted.

There remained at the bottom of his mind, nevertheless, a numb speculation as to why *this* question should make him angry.

"I mean, what would you do to me?" the man persisted, still holding Vivaldo's wallet and looking at him with a smile. "I want you to name your own punishment." He waited. Then: "Come on. You know what *you* guys do." And then the man seemed, oddly, a little ashamed, and at the same time more dangerous than ever.

Vivaldo said at last, tightly, "*I* haven't got a sister" and straightened his tie, willing his hands to be steady, and began looking around for his jacket.

The man considered him a moment more, looked at the girl, then looked down to the wallet again. He took out all the money. "This all you got."

In those days Vivaldo had been working steadily and his wallet had contained nearly sixty dollars. "Yes," Vivaldo said.

"Nothing in your pockets?"

Vivaldo emptied his pockets of bills and change, perhaps five dollars in all. The man took it all.

"I need something to get home on, mister," Vivaldo said.

The man gave him his wallet. "Walk," he said. "You lucky that you can. If I catch your ass up here again, I'll show you what happened to a nigger I know when Mr. Charlie caught him with Miss Anne."

He put his wallet in his back pocket and picked up his jacket from the floor. The man watched him, the girl watched the man. He got to the door and opened it and realized that his legs were weak.

"Well," he said, "thanks for the buggy ride," and stumbled down the stairs. He had reached the first landing when he heard a door above him open and quick, stealthy footsteps descending. Then the girl stood above him, stretching her hand over the banister.

"Here," she whispered, "take this," and leaned dangerously far over the banister and stuffed a dollar into his breast pocket. "Go along home now," she said, "hurry!" and rushed back up the stairs.

The man's eyes remained with him for a long time after the rage and the shame and terror of that evening. And were with him now, as he climbed the stairs to Rufus' apartment. He walked in without knocking. Rufus was standing near the door, holding a knife.

"Is that for me or for you? Or were you planning to cut yourself a hunk of salami?"

He forced himself to stand where he was and to look directly at Rufus.

"I was thinking about putting it into you, motherfucker."

But he had not moved. Vivaldo slowly let out his breath.

"Well, put it down. If I ever saw a poor bastard who needed his friends, you're it."

They watched each other for what seemed like a very long time and neither of them moved. They stared into each other's eyes, each, perhaps, searching for the friend each remembered. Vivaldo knew the face before him so well that he had ceased, in a way, to look at it and now his heart turned over to see what time had done to Rufus. He had not seen before the fine lines in the forehead, the deep, crooked line between the brows, the tension which soured the lips. He wondered what the eyes were seeing—they had not been seeing it years before. He had never associated Rufus with violence, for his walk was always deliberate and slow, his tone mocking and gentle: but now he remembered how Rufus played the drums.

He moved one short step closer, watching Rufus, watching the knife.

"Don't kill me, Rufus," he heard himself say. "I'm not trying to hurt you. I'm only trying to help."

The bathroom door was still open and the light still burned. The bald kitchen light burned mercilessly down on the two orange crates and the board which formed the kitchen table, and on the uncovered wash and bathtub. Dirty clothes lay flung in a corner. Beyond them, in the dim bedroom, two suitcases, Rufus' and Leona's, lay open in the middle of the floor. On the bed was a twisted gray sheet and a thin blanket.

Rufus stared at him. He seemed not to believe Vivaldo; he seemed to long to believe him. His face twisted, he dropped the knife, and fell against Vivaldo, throwing his arms around him, trembling.

Vivaldo led him into the bedroom and they sat down on the bed.

"Somebody's got to help me," said Rufus at last, "somebody's got to help me. This shit has got to stop."

"Can't you tell me about it? You're screwing up your life. And I don't know why."

Rufus sighed and fell back, his arms beneath his head, staring at the ceiling. "I don't know, either. I don't know up from down. I don't know what I'm doing no more."

The entire building was silent. The room in which they sat seemed very far from the life breathing all around them, all over the island.

Vivaldo said, gently, "You know, what you're doing to Leona—that's not right. Even if she were doing what you say she's doing—it's not right. If all you can do is beat her, well, then, you ought to leave her."

Rufus seemed to smile. "I guess there *is* something the matter with my head."

Then he was silent again; he twisted his body on the bed; he looked over at Vivaldo.

"You put her in a cab?"

"Yes," Vivaldo said.

"She's gone to your place?"

"Yes."

"You going back there?"

"I thought, maybe, I'd stay here with you for awhile—if you don't mind."

"What're you trying to do—be a warden or something?"

He said it with a smile, but there was no smile in his voice.

"I just thought maybe you wanted company," said Vivaldo.

Rufus rose from the bed and walked restlessly up and down the two rooms.

"I don't need no company. I done had enough company to last me the rest of my life." He walked to the window and stood there, his back to Vivaldo. "How I hate them—all those white sons of bitches out there. They're trying to kill me, you think I don't know? They got the world on a string, man, the miserable white cock suckers, and they tying that string around my neck, they killing *me*." He turned into the room again; he did not look at Vivaldo. "Sometimes I lie here and I listen—just listen. They out there, scuffling, making that change, they think it's going to last forever. Sometimes I lie here and listen, listen for a bomb, man, to fall on this city and make all that noise stop. I listen to hear them moan, I want them to bleed and choke, I want to hear them *crying*, man, for somebody to come help them. They'll cry a long time before *I* come down there." He paused, his eyes glittering with tears and with hate. "It's going to happen one of these days, it's got to happen. I sure would like to see it." He walked back to the window. "Sometimes I listen to those boats on the river—I listen to those whistles—and I think wouldn't it be nice to get on a boat again and go someplace away from all these nowhere people, where a man could be treated like a man." He wiped his eyes with the back of his hand and then suddenly brought his fist down on the window sill. "You got to fight with the landlord because the landlord's *white*! You got to fight with the elevator boy because the motherfucker's *white*. Any bum on the Bowery can shit all over you because maybe he can't hear, can't see, can't walk, can't fuck—but he's *white!*"

"Rufus. Rufus. What about——" He wanted to say, What about me, Rufus? I'm white. He said, "Rufus, not everybody's like that."

"No? That's news to me."

"Leona loves you—"

"She loves the colored folks so *much,*" said Rufus, "sometimes I just can't stand it. You know all that chick knows about me? The *only* thing she knows?" He put his hand on his sex, brutally, as though he would tear it out, and seemed pleased to see Vivaldo wince. He sat down on the bed again. "That's all."

"I think you're out of your mind," said Vivaldo. But fear drained his voice of conviction.

"But she's the only chick in the world for me," Rufus added, after a moment, "ain't that a bitch?"

"You're destroying that girl. Is that what you want?"

"She's destroying me, too," said Rufus.

"Well. Is *that* what you want?"

"What *do* two people want from each other," asked Rufus, "when they get together? Do *you* know?"

"Well, they don't want to drive each other crazy, man. I know that."

"You know more than I do," Rufus said, sardonically. "What do *you* want—when you get together with a girl?"

"What do I *want?*"

"Yeah, what do you *want?*"

"Well," said Vivaldo, fighting panic, trying to smile, "I just want to get laid, man." But he stared at Rufus, feeling terrible things stir inside him.

"Yeah?" And Rufus looked at him curiously, as though he were thinking, *So that's the way white boys make it.* "Is that all?"

"Well"—he looked down—"I want the chick to love me. I want to make her love me. I want to be loved."

There was silence. Then Rufus asked, "Has it ever happened?"

"No," said Vivaldo, thinking of Catholic girls, and whores, "I guess not."

"How do you *make* it happen?" Rufus whispered. "What do you *do?*" He looked over at Vivaldo. He half-smiled. "What do *you* do?"

"What do you mean, what do I do?" He tried to smile; but he knew what Rufus meant.

"You just do it like you was told?" He tugged at Vivaldo's sleeve; his voice dropped. "That white chick—Jane—of yours—she ever give you a blow job?"

Oh, Rufus, he wanted to cry, *stop this crap!* and he felt tears well up behind his eyes. At the same time his heart lunged in terror and he felt the blood leave his face. "I haven't had a chick that great," he said, briefly, thinking again of the dreadful Catholic girls with whom he had grown up, of his sister and his mother and father. He tried to force his mind back through the beds he had been in—his mind grew as blank as a wall. "Except," he said, suddenly, "with whores," and felt in the silence that then fell that murder was sitting on the bed beside them. He stared at Rufus.

Rufus laughed. He lay back on the bed and laughed until tears began running from the corners of his eyes. It was the worst laugh Vivaldo had ever heard and he wanted to shake Rufus or slap him, anything to make him stop. But he did nothing; he lit a cigarette; the palms of his hands were wet. Rufus choked, sputtered, and sat up. He turned his agonized face to Vivaldo for an instant. Then: "Whores!" he shouted and began to laugh again.

"What's so funny?" Vivaldo asked, quietly.

"If you don't see it, I can't tell you," Rufus said. He had stopped laughing, was very sober and still. "Everybody's on the A train—you take it uptown, I take it downtown—it's crazy." Then, again, he looked at Vivaldo with hatred. He said, "Me and Leona—she's the greatest lay I ever had. Ain't nothing we don't do."

"Crazy," said Vivaldo. He crushed out his cigarette on the floor. He was beginning to be angry. At the same time he wanted to laugh.

"But it ain't going to work," said Rufus. "It ain't going to work." They heard the whistles on the river; he walked to the window again. "I ought to get out of here. I better get out of here."

"Well, then, *go.* Don't hang around, waiting—just *go.*"

"I'm *going* to go," said Rufus. "I'm going to go. I just want to see Leona one more time." He stared at Vivaldo. "I just want to get laid—get blowed—loved—one more time."

"You know," said Vivaldo, "I'm not really interested in the details of your sex life."

Rufus smiled. "No? I thought all you white boys had a big thing about how us spooks was making out."

"Well," said Vivaldo, "I'm different."

"Yeah," said Rufus, "I bet you are."

"I just want to be your friend," said Vivaldo. "That's all. But you don't want any friends, do you?"

"Yes, I do," said Rufus, quietly. "Yes, I do." He paused; then, slowly, with difficulty, "Don't mind me. I know you're the only friend I've got left in the world, Vivaldo."

And that's why you hate me, Vivaldo thought, feeling still and helpless and sad.

Now Vivaldo and Rufus sat together in silence, near the window of the pizzeria. There was little left for them to say. They had said it all—or Rufus had; and Vivaldo had listened. Music from a nearby night club came at them, faintly, through the windows, along with the grinding, unconquerable hum of the streets. And Rufus watched the streets with a helpless, sad intensity, as though he were waiting for Leona. These streets had claimed her. She had been found, Rufus said, one freezing night, half-naked, looking for her baby. She knew where it was, where they had hidden her baby, she knew the house; only she could not remember the address.

And then, Rufus said, she had been taken to Bellevue, and he had been unable to get her out. The doctors had felt that it would be criminal to release her into the custody of the man who was the principal reason for her breakdown, and who had, moreover, no legal claim on her. They had notified Leona's family, and her brother had come from the South and carried Leona back with him. Now she sat somewhere in Georgia, staring at the walls of a narrow room; and she would remain there forever.

Vivaldo yawned and felt guilty. He was tired—tired of Rufus' story, tired of the strain of attending, tired of friendship.

He wanted to go home and lock his door and sleep. He was tired of the troubles of real people. He wanted to get back to the people he was inventing, whose troubles he could bear.

But he was restless, too, and unwilling, now that he was out, to go home right away.

"Let's have a nightcap at Benno's," he said. And then, because he knew Rufus did not really want to go there, he added, "All right?"

Rufus nodded, feeling a little frightened. Vivaldo watched him, feeling it all come back, his love for Rufus, and his grief for him. He leaned across the table and tapped him on the cheek. "Come on," he said, "you haven't got to be afraid of anybody."

With these words, at which Rufus looked even more frightened, though a small smile played around the corners of his mouth, Vivaldo felt that whatever was coming had already begun, that the master switch had been thrown. He sighed, relieved, also wishing to call the words back. The waiter came. Vivaldo paid the check and they walked out into the streets.

"It's almost Thanksgiving," said Rufus, suddenly. "I didn't realize that." He laughed. "It'll soon be Christmas, the year will soon be over—" He broke off, raising his head to look over the cold streets.

A policeman, standing under the light on the corner, was phoning in. On the opposite pavement a young man walked his dog. The music from the night club dwindled as they walked away from it, toward Benno's. A heavy Negro girl, plain, carrying packages, and a surly, bespectacled white boy ran together toward a taxi. The yellow light on the roof went out, the doors slammed. The cab turned, came toward Rufus and Vivaldo, and the street lights blazed for an instant on the faces of the silent couple within.

Vivaldo put one arm around Rufus and pushed him ahead of him into Benno's Bar.

The bar was terribly crowded. Advertising men were there, drinking double shots of bourbon or vodka, on the rocks; college boys were there, their wet fingers slippery on the beer bottles; lone men stood near the doors or in corners, watching the drifting women. The college boys, gleaming with ignorance and mad with chastity, made terrified efforts to attract the feminine attention, but succeeded only in attracting each other. Some of the men were buying drinks for some of the women—who wandered incessantly from the juke box to the bar—and they faced each other over smiles which were pitched, with an eerie precision, between longing and contempt. Black-and-white couples were together here—closer together now than they would be later, when they got home. These several histories were camouflaged in the jargon which, wave upon wave, rolled through the bar; were locked in a silence like the silence of glaciers. Only the juke box spoke, grinding out each evening, all evening long, syncopated, synthetic laments for love.

Rufus' eyes had trouble adjusting to the yellow light, the smoke, the movement. The place seemed terribly strange to him, as though he remembered it from a dream. He recognized faces, gestures, voices—from this same dream; and, as in a dream, no one looked his way, no one seemed to remember him. Just next to him, at a table, sat a girl he had balled once or twice, whose name was Belle. She was talking to her boy friend, Lorenzo. She brushed her long black hair out of her eyes and looked directly at him for a moment, but she did not seem to recognize him.

A voice spoke at his ear: "Hey! Rufus! When did they let you out, man?"

He turned to face a grinning chocolate face, topped by processed hair casually falling forward. He could not remember the name which went with the face. He could not remember what his connection with the face had been. He said, "Yeah, I'm straight, how you been making it?"

"Oh, I'm scuffling, man, got to keep scuffling, you know"—eyes seeming to press forward like two malevolent insects, hair flying, lips and forehead wet. The voice dropped to a whisper. "I was kind of strung out there for awhile, but I'm straight now. I heard you got busted, man."

"Busted? No, I've just been making the uptown scene."

"Yeah? Well, crazy." He jerked his head around to the door in response to a summons Rufus had not heard. "I got to split, my boy's waiting for me. See you around, man."

Cold air swept into the bar for a moment, then steam and smoke settled again over everything.

Then, while they stood there, not yet having been able to order anything to drink and undecided as to whether or not they would stay, Cass appeared out of the gloom and noise. She was very elegant, in black, her golden hair pulled carefully back and up. She held a drink and a cigarette in one hand and looked at once like the rather weary matron she actually was and the mischievous girl she once had been.

"What are you doing here?" asked Vivaldo. "And all dressed up, too. What's happening?"

"I'm tired of my husband. I'm looking for a new man. But I guess I came to the wrong store."

"You may have to wait for a fire sale," said Vivaldo.

Cass turned to Rufus and put her hand on his arm.

"It's nice to have you back," she said. Her large brown eyes looked directly into his. "Are you all right? We've all missed you."

He shrank involuntarily from her touch and her tone. He wanted to thank her; he said, nodding and trying to smile, "I'm fine, Cass." And then: "It's kind of nice to be back."

She grinned. "Do you know what I realize every time I see you? That we're very much alike." She turned back to Vivaldo. "I don't see your aging mistress anywhere. Are you looking for a new woman? If so, you too have come to the wrong store."

"I haven't seen Jane for a hell of a long time," said Vivaldo, "and it might be a good idea for us never to see each other again." But he looked troubled.

"Poor Vivaldo," Cass said. After a moment they both laughed. "Come on in the back with me. Richard's there. He'll be very glad to see you."

"I didn't know you people ever set foot in this joint. Can't you bear domestic bliss any longer?"

"We're celebrating tonight. Richard just sold his novel."

"*No!*"

"Yes. *Yes.* Isn't that marvelous?"

"Well, I'll be damned," said Vivaldo, looking a little dazed.

"Come on," Cass said. She took Rufus by the hand and, with Vivaldo ahead of them, they began pushing their way to the back. They stumbled down the steps into the back room.

Richard sat alone at a table, smoking his pipe. "Richard," Cass cried, "look what I brought back from the dead!"

"You should have let them rot there," Richard grinned. "Come on in, sit down. I'm glad to see you."

"I'm glad to see *you*," said Vivaldo, and sat down. He and Richard grinned at each other. Then Richard looked at Rufus, briefly and sharply, and looked away. Perhaps Richard had never liked Rufus as much as the others had and now, perhaps, he was blaming him for Leona.

The air in the back room was close, he was aware of his odor, he wished he had taken a shower at Vivaldo's house. He sat down.

"So!" said Vivaldo, "you sold it!" He threw back his head and gave a high, whinnying laugh. "You sold it. That's just great, baby. How does it feel?"

"I held off as long as I could," Richard said. "I kept telling them that my good friend, Vivaldo, was going to come by and look it over for me. They said, 'That Vivaldo? He's a poet, man, he's *bohemian*! He wouldn't read a murder novel, not if it was written by God almighty.' So, when you didn't come by, baby, I figured they were right and I just had to let them have it."

"Shit, Richard, I'm sorry about that. I've just been so hung up—"

"Yeah, I know. Let's have a drink. You, Rufus. What're you doing with yourself these days?"

"I'm just pulling myself together," said Rufus, with a smile. Richard was being kind, he told himself, but in his heart he accused him of cowardice.

"Don't be self-conscious," Cass said. "We've been trying to pull ourselves together for years. You can see what progress we've made. You're in very good company." She leaned her head against Richard's shoulder. Richard stroked her hair and picked up his pipe from the ashtray.

"I don't think it's just a murder story," he said, gesturing with the pipe. "I mean, I don't see why you can't do something fairly serious within the limits of the form. I've always been fascinated by it, really."

"You didn't think much of them when you were teaching me English in high school," said Vivaldo, with a smile.

"Well, I was younger then than you are now. We change, boy, we grow——!" The waiter entered the room, looking as though he wondered where on earth he could be, and Richard called him. "Hey! We're dying of thirst over here!" He turned to Cass. "You want another drink?"

"Oh, yes," she said, "now that our friends are here. I might as well make the most of my night out. Except I'm a kind of dreamy drunk. Do you mind my head on your shoulder?"

"Mind?" He laughed. He looked at Vivaldo. "*Mind!* Why do you think I've been knocking myself out, trying to be a success?" He bent down and kissed her and something appeared in his boyish face, a single-mindedness of tenderness and passion, which made him very gallant. "You can put your head on my shoulder anytime. Anytime, baby. That's what my shoulders are for." And he stroked her hair again, proudly, as the waiter vanished with the empty glasses.

Vivaldo turned to Richard. "When can I read your book? I'm jealous. I want to find out if I should be."

"Well, if you take that tone, you bastard, you can buy it at the bookstore when it comes out."

"Or borrow it from the library," Cass suggested.

"No, really, when can I read it? Tonight? Tomorrow? How long is it?"

"It's over three hundred pages," Richard said. "Come by tomorrow, you can look at it then." He said to Cass, "It's one way of getting him to the house." Then: "You really don't come to see us like you used to—is anything the matter? Because we still love *you*."

"No, nothing's the matter," Vivaldo said. He hesitated. "I had this thing with Jane and then we broke up—and—oh, I don't know. Work wasn't going well, and"—he looked at Rufus—"all kinds of things. I was drinking too much and running around whoring when I should have been—being serious, like you, and getting my novel finished."

"How's it coming—your novel?"

"Oh"—he looked down and sipped his drink—"slow. I'm really not a very good writer."

"Bullshit," said Richard, cheerfully.

He almost looked again like the English instructor Vivaldo

had idolized, who had been the first person to tell him things he needed to hear, the first person to take Vivaldo seriously.

"I'm very glad," Vivaldo said, "seriously, *very* glad that you got the damn thing done and that it worked so well. And I hope you make a fortune."

Rufus thought of afternoons and evenings on the stand when people had come up to him to bawl their appreciation and to prophesy that he would do great things. They had bugged him then. Yet how he wished now to be back there, to have someone looking at him as Vivaldo now looked at Richard. And he looked at Vivaldo's face, in which affection and something coldly speculative battled. He was happy for Richard's triumph but perhaps he wished it were his own; and at the same time he wondered what order of triumph it was. And the way the people had looked at Rufus was not unlike this look. They wondered where it came from, this force that they admired. Dimly, they wondered how he stood it, wondered if perhaps it would not kill him soon.

Vivaldo looked away, down into his drink, and lit a cigarette. Richard suddenly looked very tired.

A tall girl, very pretty, carefully dressed—she looked like an uptown model—came into the room, looked about her, peered sharply at their table. She paused, then started out.

"I wish you were looking for me?" Vivaldo called.

She turned and laughed. "You're lucky I'm *not* looking for you!" She had a very attractive laugh and a slight Southern accent. Rufus turned to watch her move daintily up the steps and disappear into the crowded bar.

"Well, you scored, old buddy," Rufus said, "go get her."

"No," said Vivaldo, smiling, "better leave well enough alone." He stared at the door where the girl had vanished. "She's pretty, isn't she?" he said partly to himself, partly to the table. He looked at the door again, shifting slightly in his seat, then threw down the last of his drink.

Rufus wanted to say, *Don't let me stop you, man,* but he said nothing. He felt black, filthy, foolish. He wished he were miles away, or dead. He kept thinking of Leona; it came in waves, like the pain of a toothache or a festering wound.

Cass left her seat and came over and sat beside him. She stared at him and he was frightened by the sympathy on her face. He wondered why she should look like that, what her memories or experience could be. She could only look at him this way because she knew things he had never imagined a girl like Cass could know.

"How is Leona?" she asked. "Where is she now?" and did not take her eyes from his face.

He did not want to answer. He did not want to talk about Leona—and yet there was nothing else that he could possibly talk about. For a moment he almost hated Cass; and then he said:

"She's in a home—down South somewhere. They come and took her out of Bellevue. I don't even know where she is."

She said nothing. She offered him a cigarette, lit it, and lit one for herself.

"I saw her brother once. I had to see him, I made him see me. He spit in my face, he said he would have killed me had we been down home."

He wiped his face now with the handkerchief Vivaldo had lent him.

"But I felt like I was already dead. They wouldn't let me see her. I wasn't a relative, I didn't have no right to see her."

There was silence. He remembered the walls of the hospital: white; and the uniforms and the faces of the doctors and nurses, white on white. And the face of Leona's brother, white, with the blood beneath it rushing thickly, bitterly, to the skin's surface, summoned by his mortal enemy. Had they been down home, his blood and the blood of his enemy would have rushed out to mingle together over the uncaring earth, under the uncaring sky.

"At least," Cass said, finally, "you didn't have any children. Thank God for that."

"She did," he said, "down South. They took the kid away from her." He added, "That's why she come North." And he thought of the night they had met.

"She was a nice girl," Cass said. "I liked her."

He said nothing. He heard Vivaldo say, "—but I never know what to do when I'm *not* working."

"You know what to do, all right. You just don't have anybody to do it with."

He listened to their laughter, which seemed to shake him as though it were a drill.

"Just the same," said Richard, in a preoccupied tone, "nobody can work all the time."

Out of the corner of his eye, Rufus watched him stabbing the table with his stir-stick.

"I hope," Cass said, "that you won't sit around blaming yourself too much. Or too long. That won't undo anything." She put her hand on his. He stared at her. She smiled. "When you're older you'll see, I think, that we all commit our crimes. The thing is not to lie about them—to try to understand what you have done, why you have done it." She leaned closer to him, her brown eyes popping and her blonde hair, in the heat, in the gloom, forming a damp fringe about her brow. "That way, you can begin to forgive yourself. That's very important. If you don't forgive yourself you'll never be able to forgive anybody else and you'll go on committing the same crimes forever."

"I know," Rufus muttered, not looking at her, bent over the table with his fists clenched together. From far away, from the juke box, he heard a melody he had often played. He thought of Leona. Her face would not leave him. "I know," he repeated, though in fact he did not know. He did not know why this woman was talking to him as she was, what she was trying to tell him.

"What," she asked him, carefully, "are you going to do now?"

"I'm going to try to pull myself together," he said, "and get back to work."

But he found it unimaginable that he would ever work again, that he would ever play drums again.

"Have you seen your family? I think Vivaldo's seen your sister a couple of times. She's very worried about you."

"I'm going up there," he said. "I haven't wanted to go—looking this way."

"They don't care how you look," she said, shortly. "*I* don't care how you look. I'm just glad to see you're all right—and I'm not even related to you."

He thought, with a great deal of wonder, That's true, and

turned to stare at her again, smiling a little and very close to tears.

"I've always thought of you," she said, "as a very nice person." She gave his arm a little tap and pushed a crumpled bill into his hand. "It might help if you thought of yourself that way."

"Hey, old lady," Richard called, "want to make it in?"

"I guess so," she said, and yawned. "I suppose we've celebrated enough for one night, one book."

She rose and returned to her side of the table and began to gather her things together. Rufus was suddenly afraid to see her go.

"Can I come to see you soon?" he asked, with a smile.

She stared at him across the width of the table. "Please do," she said. "Soon."

Richard knocked his pipe out and put it in his pocket, looking around for the waiter. Vivaldo was staring at something, at someone, just behind Rufus and suddenly seemed about to spring out of his seat. "Well," he said, faintly, "here's Jane," and Jane walked over to the table. Her short, graying hair was carefully combed, which was unusual, and she was wearing a dark dress, which was also unusual. Perhaps Vivaldo was the only person there who had ever seen her out of blue jeans and sweaters. "Hi, everybody," she said, and smiled her bright, hostile smile. She sat down. "Haven't seen any of you for months."

"Still painting?" Cass asked. "Or have you given that up?"

"I've been working like a dog," Jane said, continuing to look around her and avoiding Vivaldo's eyes.

"Seems to suit you," Cass muttered, and put on her coat.

Jane looked at Rufus, beginning, it seemed, to recover her self-possession. "How've you been, Rufus?"

"Just fine," he said.

"We've all been dissipating," said Richard, "but you look like you've been being a good girl and getting your beauty sleep every night."

"You look great," said Vivaldo, briefly.

For the first time she looked directly at him. "Do I? I guess I've been feeling pretty well. I've cut down on my drinking," and she laughed a little too loudly and looked down. Richard was paying the waiter and had stood up, his trench coat over his arm. "Are you all leaving?"

"We've got to," said Cass, "we're just dull, untalented, old married people."

Cass glanced over at Rufus, saying, "Be good now; get some rest." She smiled at him. He longed to do something to prolong that smile, that moment, but he did not smile back, only nodded his head. She turned to Jane and Vivaldo. "So long, kids. See you soon."

"Sure," Jane said.

"I'll be over tomorrow," said Vivaldo.

"I'm expecting you," Richard said, "don't fail me. So long, Jane."

"So long."

"So long."

Everyone was gone except Jane and Rufus and Vivaldo.

I wouldn't mind being in jail but I've got to stay there so long. . . .

The seats the others had occupied were like a chasm now between Rufus and the white boy and the white girl.

"Let's have another drink," Vivaldo said.

So long. . . .

"Let me buy," Jane said. "I sold a painting."

"Did you now? For a lot of money?"

"Quite a lot of money. That's probably why I was in such a stinking mood the last time you saw me—it wasn't going well."

"You were in a stinking mood, all right."

Wouldn't mind being in jail. . . .

"What're you having, Rufus?"

"I'll stick to Scotch, I guess."

But I've got to stay there. . . .

"I'm sorry," she said, "I don't know what makes me such a bitch."

"You drink too much. Let's just have one drink here. Then I'll walk you home."

They both looked quickly at Rufus.

So long. . . .

"I'm going to the head," Rufus said. "Order me a Scotch with water."

He walked out of the back room into the roaring bar. He

stood at the door for a moment, watching the boys and girls, men and women, their wet mouths opening and closing, their faces damp and pale, their hands grim on the glass or the bottle or clutching a sleeve, an elbow, clutching the air. Small flames flared incessantly here and there and they moved through shifting layers of smoke. The cash register rang and rang. One enormous bouncer stood at the door, watching everything, and another moved about, clearing tables and re-arranging chairs. Two boys, one Spanish-looking in a red shirt, one Danish-looking in brown, stood at the juke box, talking about Frank Sinatra.

Rufus stared at a small blonde girl who was wearing a striped open blouse and a wide skirt with a big leather belt and a bright brass buckle. She wore low shoes and black knee socks. Her blouse was low enough for him to see the beginnings of her breasts; his eye followed the line down to the full nipples, which pushed aggressively forward; his hand encircled her waist, caressed the belly button and slowly forced the thighs apart. She was talking to another girl. She felt his eyes on her and looked his way. Their eyes met. He turned and walked into the head.

It smelled of thousands of travelers, oceans of piss, tons of bile and vomit and shit. He added his stream to the ocean, holding that most despised part of himself loosely between two fingers of one hand. *But I've got to stay there so long. . . .* He looked at the horrible history splashed furiously on the walls—telephone numbers, cocks, breasts, balls, cunts, etched into these walls with hatred. *Suck my cock. I like to get whipped. I want a hot stiff prick up my ass. Down with Jews. Kill the niggers. I suck cocks.*

He washed his hands very carefully and dried them on the filthy roller towel and walked out into the bar. The two boys were still at the juke box, the girl with the striped blouse was still talking to her friend. He walked through the bar to the door and into the street. Only then did he reach in his pocket to see what Cass had pushed into his palm.

Five dollars. Well, that would take care of him until morning. He would get a room at the Y.

He crossed Sheridan Square and walked slowly along West Fourth Street. The bars were beginning to close. People stood before bar doors, trying vainly to get in, or simply delaying going home; and in spite of the cold there were loiterers under street lamps. He felt as removed from them, as he walked slowly along, as he might have felt from a fence, a farmhouse, a tree, seen from a train window: coming closer and closer, the details changing every instant as the eye picked them out; then pressing against the window with the urgency of a messenger or a child; then dropping away, diminishing, vanished, gone forever. *That fence is falling down,* he might have thought as the train rushed toward it, or *That house needs paint,* or *The tree is dead.* In an instant, gone in an instant— it was not his fence, his farmhouse, or his tree. As now, passing, he recognized faces, bodies, postures, and thought *That's Ruth.* Or *There's old Lennie. Son of a bitch is stoned again.* It was very silent.

He passed Cornelia Street. Eric had once lived there. He saw again the apartment, the lamplight in the corners, Eric under the light, books falling over everything, and the bed unmade. Eric——and he was on Sixth Avenue, traffic lights and the lights of taxis blazing around him. Two girls and two boys, white, stood on the opposite corner, waiting for the lights to change. Half a dozen men, in a heavy gleaming car, rolled by and shouted at them. Then there was someone at his shoulder, a young white boy in a vaguely military cap and a black leather jacket. He looked at Rufus with the greatest hostility, then started slowly down the Avenue away from him, waving his rump like a flag. He looked back, stopped beneath the marquee of a movie theater. The lights changed. Rufus and the two couples started toward each other, came abreast in the middle of the avenue, passed—only, one of the girls looked at him with a kind of pitying wonder in her eyes. *All right, bitch.* He started toward Eighth Street, for no reason; he was simply putting off his subway ride.

Then he stood at the subway steps, looking down. For a wonder, especially at this hour, there was no one on the steps, the steps were empty. He wondered if the man in the booth would change his five-dollar bill. He started down.

Then, as the man gave him change and he moved toward the turnstile, other people came, rushing and loud, pushing past him as though they were swimmers and he nothing but an upright pole in the water. Then something began to awaken in him, something new; it increased his distance; it increased his pain. They were rushing—to the platform, to the tracks. Something he had not thought of for many years, something he had never ceased to think of, came back to him as he walked behind the crowd. The subway platform was a dangerous place—so he had always thought; it sloped downward toward the waiting tracks; and when he had been a little boy and stood on the platform beside his mother he had not dared let go her hand. He stood on the platform now, alone with all these people, who were each of them alone, and waited in acquired calmness, for the train.

But suppose something, somewhere, failed, and the yellow lights went out and no one could see, any longer, the platform's edge? Suppose these beams fell down? He saw the train in the tunnel, rushing under water, the motorman gone mad, gone blind, unable to decipher the lights, and the tracks gleaming and snarling senselessly upward forever, the train never stopping and the people screaming at windows and doors and turning on each other with all the accumulated fury of their blasphemed lives, everything gone out of them but murder, breaking limb from limb and splashing in blood, with joy—for the first time, joy, joy, after such a long sentence in chains, leaping out to astound the world, to astound the world again. Or, the train in the tunnel, the water outside, the power failing, the walls coming in, and the water not rising like a flood but breaking like a wave over the heads of these people, filling their crying mouths, filling their eyes, their hair, tearing away their clothes and discovering the secrecy which only the water, by now, could use. It could happen. It could happen; and he would have loved to see it happen, even if he perished, too. The train came in, filling the great scar of the tracks. They all got on, sitting in the lighted car which was far from empty, which would be choked with people before they got very far uptown, and stood or sat in the isolation cell into which they transformed every inch of space they held.

The train stopped at Fourteenth Street. He was sitting at the window and he watched a few people get on. There was a colored girl among them who looked a little like his sister, but she looked at him and looked away and sat down as far from him as she could. The train rolled on through the tunnel. The next stop was Thirty-fourth Street, his stop. People got on; he watched the stop roll by. Forty-second Street. This time a crowd got on, some of them carrying papers, and there were no seats left. A white man leaned on a strap near him. Rufus felt his gorge rise.

At Fifty-ninth Street many came on board and many rushed across the platform to the waiting local. Many white people and many black people, chained together in time and in space, and by history, and all of them in a hurry. In a hurry to get away from each other, he thought, but we ain't never going to make it. We been fucked for fair.

Then the doors slammed, a loud sound, and it made him jump. The train, as though protesting its heavier burden, as though protesting the proximity of white buttock to black knee, groaned, lurched, the wheels seemed to scrape the track, making a tearing sound. Then it began to move uptown, where the masses would divide and the load become lighter. Lights flared and teetered by, they passed other platforms where people waited for other trains. Then they had the tunnel to themselves. The train rushed into the blackness with a phallic abandon, into the blackness which opened to receive it, opened, opened, the whole world shook with their coupling. Then, when it seemed that the roar and the movement would never cease, they came into the bright lights of 125th Street. The train gasped and moaned to a halt. He had thought that he would get off here, but he watched the people move toward the doors, watched the doors open, watched them leave. It was mainly black people who left. He had thought that he would get off here and go home; but he watched the girl who reminded him of his sister as she moved sullenly past white people and stood for a moment on the platform before walking toward the steps. Suddenly he knew that he was never going home any more.

The train began to move, half-empty now; and with each stop it became lighter; soon the white people who were left looked at him oddly. He felt their stares but he felt far away from them. *You took the best. So why not take the rest?* He got off at the station named for the bridge built to honor the father of his country.

And walked up the steps, into the streets, which were empty. Tall apartment buildings, lightless, loomed against the dark sky and seemed to be watching him, seemed to be pressing down on him. The bridge was nearly over his head, intolerably high; but he did not yet see the water. He felt it, he smelled it. He thought how he had never before understood how an animal could smell water. But it was over there, past the highway, where he could see the speeding cars.

Then he stood on the bridge, looking over, looking down. Now the lights of the cars on the highway seemed to be writing an endless message, writing with awful speed in a fine, unreadable script. There were muted lights on the Jersey shore and here and there a neon flame advertising something somebody had for sale. He began to walk slowly to the center of the bridge, observing that, from this height, the city which had been so dark as he walked through it seemed to be on fire.

He stood at the center of the bridge and it was freezing cold. He raised his eyes to heaven. He thought, You bastard, you motherfucking bastard. Ain't I your baby, too? He began to cry. Something in Rufus which could not break shook him like a rag doll and splashed salt water all over his face and filled his throat and his nostrils with anguish. He knew the pain would never stop. He could never go down into the city again. He dropped his head as though someone had struck him and looked down at the water. It was cold and the water would be cold.

He was black and the water was black.

He lifted himself by his hands on the rail, lifted himself as high as he could, and leaned far out. The wind tore at him, at his head and shoulders, while something in him screamed, Why? Why? He thought of Eric. His straining arms threatened to break. *I can't make it this way.* He thought of Ida. He whispered, *I'm sorry, Leona,* and then the wind took him, he felt himself going over, head down, the wind, the stars, the lights, the water, all rolled together, *all right.* He felt a shoe fly off behind him, there was nothing around him, only the wind, *all right, you motherfucking Godalmighty bastard, I'm coming to you.*

IT WAS RAINING. Cass sat on her living-room floor with the Sunday papers and a cup of coffee. She was trying to decide which photograph of Richard would look best on the front page of the book-review section. The telephone rang.

"Hello?"

She heard an intake of breath and a low, vaguely familiar voice:

"Is this Cass Silenski?"

"Yes."

She looked at the clock, wondering who this could be. It was ten-thirty and she was the only person awake in her house.

"Well"—swiftly—"I don't know if you remember me, but we met once, downtown, in a night club where Rufus was working. I'm his sister—Ida? Ida Scott——"

She remembered a very young, striking, dark girl who wore a ruby-eyed snake ring. "Why, yes, I remember you very well. How are you?"

"I'm fine. Well"—with a small, dry laugh—"maybe I'm not so fine. I'm trying to locate my brother. I been calling Vivaldo's house all morning, but he's not home"—the voice was making an effort not to tremble, not to break—"and so I called you because I thought maybe you'd seen him, Vivaldo, I mean, or maybe you could tell me how to reach him." And now the girl was crying. "You haven't seen him, have you? Or my brother?"

She heard sounds coming from the children's bedroom. "Please," she said, "try not to be so upset. I don't know where Vivaldo is this morning but I saw your brother last night. And he was fine."

"You saw him *last night*?"

"Yes."

"Where'd you see him? Where was he?"

"We had a couple of drinks together in Benno's." Then she remembered Rufus' face and felt a dim, unwilling alarm. "We talked for a while. He seemed fine."

"Oh!"—the voice was flooded with relief and made Cass remember the girl's smile—"wait till I get my hands on him!" Then: "Do you know where he went? Where's he staying?"

The sounds from the bedroom suggested that Paul and Michael were having a fight. "I don't know." I should have asked him, she thought. "Vivaldo would know, they were together, I left them together—look—" Michael screamed and then began to cry, they were going to awaken Richard— "Vivaldo is coming by here this afternoon; why don't you come, too?"

"What time?"

"Oh. Three-thirty, four. Do you know where we live?"

"Yes. Yes, I'll be there. Thank you."

"Please don't be so upset. I'm sure everything will be all right."

"Yes. I'm glad I called you."

"Till later, then."

"Yes. Good-bye."

"Good-bye."

Cass ran into the children's bedroom and found Paul and Michael rolling furiously about on the floor. Michael was on top. She dragged him to his feet. Paul rose slowly, looking defiant and ashamed. He was eleven, after all, and Michael was only eight. "What's all this noise about?"

"He was trying to take my chess set," Michael said.

The box, the board, and broken chessmen were scattered on both beds and all over the room.

"I was not," Paul said, and looked at his mother. "I was only trying to teach him how to play."

"You don't know *how* to play," said Michael; now that his mother was in the room, he sniffed loudly once or twice and began collecting his property.

Paul *did* know how to play—or knew, anyway, that chess was a game with rules that had to be learned. He played with his father from time to time. But he also loved to torment his brother, who preferred to make up stories about his various chessmen as he moved them about. For this, of course, he did not need a partner. Watching Michael manipulate Richard's old, broken chess set always made Paul very indignant.

"Never mind that," Cass said, "you know that's Michael's chess set and he can do whatever he wants with it. Now, come on, wash up, and get your clothes on."

She went into the bathroom to supervise their washing and get them dressed.

"Is Daddy up yet?" Paul wanted to know.

"No. He's sleeping. He's tired."

"Can't I go in and wake him?"

"No. Not this morning. Stand still."

"What about his breakfast?" Michael asked.

"He'll have his breakfast when he gets up," she said.

"We never have breakfast together any more," said Paul. "Why can't I go and wake him?"

"Because I told you not to," she said. They walked into the kitchen. "*We* can have breakfast together now, but your father needs his sleep."

"He's always sleeping," said Paul.

"You were out real late last night," said Michael, shyly.

She was a fairly impartial mother, or tried to be; but sometimes Michael's shy, grave charm moved her as Paul's more direct, more calculating presence seldom could.

"What do you care?" she said, and ruffled his reddish blond hair. "And, anyway, how do you know?" She looked at Paul. "I bet that woman let you stay up until all hours. What time did you go to bed last night?"

Her tone, however, had immediately allied them against her. She was their common property; but they had more in common with each other than they had with her.

"Not so late," Paul said, judiciously. He winked at his brother and began to eat his breakfast.

She held back a smile. "What time was it, Michael?"

"I don't know," Michael said, "but it was *real* early."

"If that woman let you stay up one minute past ten o'clock—"

"Oh, it wasn't *that* late," said Paul.

She gave up, poured herself another cup of coffee, and watched them eat. Then she remembered Ida's call. She dialed Vivaldo's number. There was no answer. He was probably at Jane's, she thought, but she did not know Jane's address, or her last name.

She heard Richard moving about in the bedroom and eventually watched him stumble into the shower.

When he came out, she watched him eat a while before she said,

"Richard—? Rufus's sister just called."

"His sister? Oh, yes, I remember her, we met her once. What did she want?"

"She wanted to know where Rufus was."

"Well, if she doesn't know, how the hell does she expect us to know?"

"She sounded very worried. She hasn't seen him, you know—in a long time."

"She's complaining? Bastard's probably found some other defenseless little girl to beat up."

"Oh—that hasn't got anything to do with it. She's worried about her brother, she wants to know where he is."

"Well, she hasn't got a very nice *brother*, she'll probably run into him someplace one of these days." He looked into her worried face. "Hell, Cass, we saw him last night, there's nothing wrong with him."

"Yes," she said. Then: "She's coming here this afternoon."

"Oh, Christ. What time?"

"I told her about three or four. I thought Vivaldo would be here by then."

"Well, good." He stood up. They walked into the living room. Paul stood at the window, looking out at the wet streets. Michael was on the floor, scribbling in his notebook. He had a great many notebooks, all of them filled with trees and houses and monsters and entirely cryptic anecdotes.

Paul moved from the window to come and stand beside his father.

"Are we going to go now?" he asked. "It's getting late."

For Paul never forgot a promise or an appointment.

Richard winked at Paul and reached down to cuff Michael lightly on the head. Michael always reacted to this with a kind of surly, withdrawn delight; seeming to say to himself, each time, that he loved his father enough to overlook an occasional lapse of dignity.

"Come on, now," Richard said. "You want me to walk you to the movies, you got to get a move on."

Then she stood at the window and watched the three of them, under Richard's umbrella, walking away from her.

Twelve years. She had been twenty-one, he had been twenty-five; it was the middle of the war. She eventually ended up in San Francisco and got paid for hanging around a shipyard. She could have done better, but she hadn't cared. She was simply waiting for the war to be over and for Richard to be home. He ended up in a quartermaster depot in North Africa where he had spent most of his time, as far as she could gather, defending Arab shoeshine boys and beggars against the cynical and malicious French.

She was in the kitchen, mixing batter for a cake, when Richard came back. He put his head in the kitchen door, water running from the end of his nose.

"How're you feeling now?"

She laughed. "Gloomier than ever. I'm baking a cake."

"That's a terrible sign. I can see there's not much hope for you." He grabbed one of the dish towels and mopped his face.

"What happened to the umbrella?"

"I left it with the boys."

"Oh, Richard, it's so big. Can Paul handle that?"

"No, of course not," he said. "The umbrella's going to get caught in a high wind and they'll be carried away over the rooftops and we'll never see them again." He winked. "That's why I gave it to them. I'm not so dumb." He walked into his study and closed the door.

She put the cake in the oven, peeled potatoes and carrots and left them in the water and calculated the time it would take for the roast beef. She had changed her clothes and set the cake out to cool when the bell rang.

It was Vivaldo. He was wearing a black raincoat and his hair was wild and dripping from the rain. His eyes seemed blacker than ever, and his face paler.

"Heathcliff!" she cried, "how nice you could come!"—and pulled him into the apartment, for it did not seem that he was going to move. "Put those wet things in the bathroom and I'll make you a drink."

"What a bright girl you are," he said, barely smiling.

"Christ, it's pissing out there!" He took off his coat and disappeared into the bathroom.

She went to the study door and knocked on it. "Richard. Vivaldo's here."

"Okay. I'll be right out."

She made two drinks and brought them into the living room. Vivaldo sat on the sofa, his long legs stretched before him, staring at the carpet.

She handed him his drink. "How are you?"

"All right. Where're the kids?" He put his drink down carefully on the low table near him.

"They're at the movies." She considered him a moment. "You may be all right but I've seen you look better."

"Well"—again that bleak smile—"I haven't really sobered up yet. I got real drunk last night with Jane. She can't screw if she's sober." He picked up his drink and took a swallow of it, dragged a bent cigarette from one of his pockets and lit it. He looked so sad and beaten for a moment, hunched over the flame of the cigarette, that she did not speak. "Where's Richard?"

"He'll be out. He's in his study."

He sipped his drink, obviously trying to think of something to say, and not succeeding.

"Vivaldo?"

"Yeah?"

"Did Rufus stay at your place last night?"

"Rufus?" He looked frightened. "No. Why?"

"His sister called up to find out where he was."

They stared at each other and his face made her frightened all over again.

"Where did he go?" she asked.

"I don't know. I figured he'd gone to Harlem. He just disappeared."

"Vivaldo, she's coming here this afternoon."

"Who is?"

"His sister, Ida. I told her that I left him with you and that you would be here this afternoon."

"But I don't know where he *is*. I was in the back, talking to Jane—and he said he was going to the head or something—

and he never came back." He stared at her, then at the window. "I wonder where he went."

"Maybe," she said, "he met a friend."

He did not trouble to respond to this. "He should have known I wasn't just going to dump him. He could have stayed at my place, I ended up at Jane's place, anyway."

Cass watched him as he banged his cigarette out in the ashtray.

"I have never," she said, mildly, "understood what Jane wanted from you. Or, for that matter, what you wanted from her."

He examined his fingernails, they were jagged and in mourning. "I don't know. I just wanted a girl, I guess, someone to share those long winter evenings."

"But she's so much older than you are." She picked up his empty glass. "She's older than *I* am."

"That hasn't got anything to do with it," he said, sullenly. "Anyway, I wanted a girl who—sort of knows the score."

She considered him. "Yes," she said, with a sigh, "that girl certainly knows how to keep score."

"I needed a woman," Vivaldo said, "she needed a man. What's wrong with that?"

"Nothing," she said. "If that's really what both of you needed."

"What do *you* think I was doing?"

"Oh, I don't know," she said. "I really don't know. Only, I've told you, you always seem to get involved with impossible women—whores, nymphomaniacs, drunks—and I think you do it in order to protect yourself—from anything serious. Permanent."

He sighed, smiled. "Hell, I just want to be friends."

She laughed. "Oh, Vivaldo."

"You and I are friends," he said.

"Well—yes. But I've always been the wife of a friend of yours. So you never thought of me—"

"Sexually," he said. Then he grinned. "Don't be so sure."

She flushed, at once annoyed and pleased. "I'm not talking about your fantasies."

"I've always admired you," he said soberly, "and envied Richard."

"Well," she said, "you'd better get over that."

He said nothing. She rattled the ice around in his empty glass.

"Well," he said, "what am I going to do with it? I'm not a monk, I'm tired of running uptown and paying for it——"

"For it's uptown that you run," she said, with a smile. "What a good American you are."

This angered him. "I haven't said they were any better than white chicks." Then he laughed. "Maybe I better cut the damn thing off."

"Don't be such a baby. Really. You should hear yourself."

"You're telling me someone's going to come along who needs it? Needs me?"

"I'm not telling you anything," she said, shortly, "that you don't already know." They heard Richard's study door open. "I'll fix you another drink; you might as well get *good* and drunk." She bumped into Richard in the hall. He was carrying the manuscript. "Do you want a drink now?"

"Love one," he said, and walked into the living room. From the kitchen she heard their voices, a little too loud, a little too friendly. When she came back into the living room, Vivaldo was leafing through the manuscript. Richard stood by the window.

"Just read it," he was saying, "don't go thinking about Dostoievski and all that. It's just a book—a pretty good book."

She handed Richard his drink. "It's a *very* good book," she said. She put Vivaldo's drink on the table beside him. She was surprised and yet not surprised to realize that she was worried about the effect on Richard of Vivaldo's opinion.

"The next book, though, will be better," Richard said. "And very different."

Vivaldo put the manuscript down and sipped his drink. "Well," he said, with a grin, "I'll read it just as soon as I sober up. Whenever," he added, grimly, "that may be."

"And tell me the truth, you hear? You bastard."

Vivaldo looked at him. "I'll tell you the truth."

Years ago, Vivaldo had brought his manuscripts to Richard with almost exactly the same words. She moved away from them both and lit a cigarette. Then she heard the elevator door open and close and she looked at the clock. It was four. She looked at Vivaldo. The bell rang.

"There she is," said Cass.

She and Vivaldo stared at each other.

"Take it easy," Richard said. "What're you looking so tragic about?"

"Richard," she said, "that must be Rufus's sister."

"Well, go let her in. Don't leave her waiting in the hall." As he spoke, the bell rang again.

"Oh my God," said Vivaldo, and he stood up, looking very tall and helpless. She put down her drink and went to the door.

The girl who faced her was fairly tall, sturdy, very carefully dressed, and somewhat darker than Rufus. She wore a raincoat, with a hood, and carried an umbrella; and beneath the hood, in the shadows of the hall, the dark eyes in the dark face considered Cass intently. There was a hint of Rufus in the eyes—large, intelligent, wary—and in her smile.

"Cass Silenski?"

Cass put out her hand. "Come in. I *do* remember you." She closed the door behind them. "I thought you were one of the most beautiful women I'd ever seen."

The girl looked at her and Cass realized, for the first time, that a Negro girl could blush. "Oh, come on, now, Mrs. Silenski—"

"Give me your things. And please call me Cass."

"Then you call me Ida."

She put the things away. "Shall I make you a drink?"

"Yes, I think I need one," Ida said. "I been scouring this city, I don't know how long, looking for that no-good brother of mine——"

"Vivaldo's inside," Cass said, quickly, wishing to say something to prepare the girl but not knowing what to say. "Will you have bourbon or Scotch or rye? and I think we've got a little vodka—"

"I'll have bourbon." She sounded a little breathless; she followed Cass into the kitchen and stood watching her while she made the drink. Cass handed her the glass and looked into Ida's eyes. "Vivaldo hasn't seen him since last night," she said. Ida's eyes widened, and she thrust out her lower lip, which trembled slightly. Cass touched her elbow. "Come on in. Try not to worry." They walked into the living room.

Vivaldo was standing exactly as she had left him, as though he had not moved at all. Richard rose from the hassock; he had been clipping his nails. "This is my husband, Richard," Cass said, "and you know Vivaldo."

They shook hands and murmured salutations in a silence that began to stiffen like the beaten white of an egg. They sat down.

"Well!" Ida said, shakily, "it's been a long time."

"Over two years," Richard said. "Rufus let us see you a couple of times and then he hustled you out of sight somewhere. Very wise of him, too."

Vivaldo said nothing. His eyes, his eyebrows, and his hair looked like so many streaks of charcoal on a dead white surface.

"But none of you," said Ida, "know where my brother is now?" And she looked around the room.

"He was with me last night," Vivaldo said. His voice was too low; Ida strained forward to hear. He cleared his throat.

"We all saw him," Richard said, "he was fine."

"He was supposed to stay at my place," said Vivaldo, "but we—I—got talking to somebody—and then, when I looked up, he was gone." He seemed to feel that this was not the best way to put it. "There were lots of his friends around; I figured he had a drink with some of them and then maybe went off and decided to stay the night."

"Do you know these friends?" Ida asked.

"Well, I know them when I see them. I don't know—all their *names*."

The silence stretched. Vivaldo dropped his eyes.

"Did he have any money?"

"Well"—he looked to Richard and Cass—"I don't *know*."

"How did he look?"

They stared at each other. "All right. Tired, maybe."

"I'll bet." She sipped her drink; her hand shook a little. "I don't want to make a big fuss over nothing. I'm sure he's all right, wherever he is. I'd just like to *know*. Our Mama and Daddy are having a fit, and," she laughed, catching her breath roughly, "I guess I am, too." She was silent. Then: "He's the only big brother I got." She sipped her drink, then she put it on the floor beside her chair. She played with the ruby-eyed snake ring on her long little finger.

"I'm sure he's all right," Cass said, miserably aware of the empty sound of the words, "it's just that—well, Rufus is like a lot of people I know. When something goes wrong, when he gets hurt, he just wants to go and hide until it's over. He licks his wounds. Then he comes back." She looked to Richard for help.

He did his best. "I think Cass may be right," he murmured.

"I've been everywhere," said Ida, "everywhere he ever played, I been talking to everybody I could find who ever worked with him, anybody I could find he'd even ever said hello to—I even tried relatives in Brooklyn—" She stopped and turned to Vivaldo. "When you saw him—where did he say he'd been?"

"He didn't say."

"Didn't you ask him?"

"Yes. He wouldn't say."

"I gave you a phone number to call the minute you saw him. Why didn't you call me?"

"It was late when he came to my house, he asked me not to call, he said he was coming to see you in the morning!"

He sounded helpless and close to tears. She stared at him, then dropped her eyes. The silence began to crawl with an acrid, banked hostility emanating from the girl who sat alone, in the round chair, in the center of the room. She looked in turn at each of her brother's friends. "It's funny he didn't make it, then," she said.

"Well, Rufus doesn't talk much," said Richard. "You must know how hard it is to get anything out of him."

"Well," she said, shortly, "*I* would have got it out of him."

"You're his sister," Cass said, gently.

"Yes," Ida said, and looked down at her hands.

"Have you been to the police?" Richard asked.

"Yes." She made a gesture of disgust and rose and walked to the window. "They said it happens all the time—colored men running off from their families. They said they'd try to find him. But they don't care. They don't care what happens—to a black man!"

"Oh, well, now," cried Richard, his face red, "is that fair? I mean, hell, I'm sure they'll look for him just like they look for any other citizen of this city."

She looked at him. "How would you know? I *do* know— know what I'm talking about. I say they don't care—and they *don't* care."

"I don't think you should look at it like that."

She was staring out of the window. "Goddamnit. He's out there somewhere. I've got to find him." Her back was to the room. Cass watched her shoulders begin to shake. She went to the window and put her hand on Ida's arm. "I'm all right," Ida said, moving slightly away. She fumbled in the pocket of her suit, then crossed to where she had been sitting and pulled Kleenex out of her handbag. She dried her eyes and blew her nose and picked up her drink.

Cass stared at her helplessly. "Let me freshen it for you," she said, and took the glass into the kitchen.

"Ida," Vivaldo was saying as she re-entered, "if there's anything I can do to help you find him—anything at all—" He stopped. "Hell," he said, "I love him, too, I want to find him, too. I've been kicking myself all day for letting him get away last night."

When Vivaldo said, "I love him, too," Ida looked over at him, her eyes very big, as though she were, now, really meeting him for the first time. Then she dropped her eyes. "I don't really know anything you *can* do," she said.

"Well—I could come with you while you look. We could look together."

She considered this; she considered him. "Well," she said, finally, "maybe you could come with me to a couple of places in the Village——"

"All right."

"I can't help it. I have the feeling they think I'm just being hysterical."

"I'll come with you. They won't think *I'm* hysterical."

Richard grinned. "Vivaldo's never hysterical, we all know that." Then he said, "I really don't see the point of all this. Rufus is probably just sleeping it off somewhere."

"Nobody's seen him," Ida cried, "for nearly six *weeks*! Until last night! I *know* my brother, he doesn't do things like this.

He always come by the house, no matter where he'd been, or what was happening, just so we wouldn't worry. He used to bring money and things—but even when he was broke, he come anyway. Don't tell me he's just sleeping it off somewhere. Six weeks is a long time." She subsided a little, subsided to a venomous murmur. "And you know what happened—between him and that damn crazy little cracker bitch he got hung up with."

"All right," Richard said, helplessly, after a considerable silence, "have it your own way."

Cass said, "But there's no need to go rushing off in the rain right away. Rufus knows Vivaldo is going to be here. He may come by. I was hoping you would all stay for supper." She smiled at Ida. "Won't you, please? I'm sure you'll feel better. It may all be cleared up by this evening."

Ida and Vivaldo stared at each other, having, it seemed, become allies in the course of the afternoon. "Well?" asked Vivaldo.

"I don't know. I'm so tired and evil I don't seem to be able to think straight."

Richard looked as though he thoroughly agreed with this; and he said, "Look. You've been to the police. You've told everyone you could. You've checked the hospitals, and"—he looked at her questioningly—"the morgue"—and she nodded, not dropping her eyes. "Well. I don't see any point in rushing out in this damn Sunday-afternoon rain, when you hardly even know where you're going. And we all saw him last night. So we know he's around. So why not relax for a couple of hours? Hell, in a couple of hours you may find out you haven't got to go anywhere, he'll turn up."

"Really," said Cass, "there's a very good chance he'll turn up here today." Ida looked at Cass. Then Cass realized that something in Ida was enjoying this—the attention, the power she held for this moment. This made Cass angry, but then she thought: Good. It means that whatever's coming, she'll be able to get through it. Without quite knowing it, from the moment Ida stepped through the door, she was preparing herself for the worst.

"Well," said Ida, looking at Vivaldo, "I asked Mama to call me here—just in case."

"Well, then," said Cass, "it seems to me it's settled." She looked at the clock. "The boys should be home in about another hour. I think what I'll do is fix us all a fresh drink."

Ida grinned. "That's a very friendly idea."

She was terribly attractive when she grinned. Her face, then, made one think of a mischievous street boy. And at the same time there glowed in her eyes a marvelously feminine mockery. Vivaldo kept watching her, a small smile playing around the corners of his mouth.

The snow which had been predicted for the day before Thanksgiving did not begin to fall until late in the evening—slow, halfhearted flakes, spinning and gleaming in the darkness, melting on the ground.

All day long a cold sun glared down on Manhattan, giving no heat.

Cass woke a little earlier than usual, and fed the children and sent them off to school. Richard ate his breakfast and retired into his study—he was not in a good mood. Cass cleaned the house, thinking of tomorrow's dinner, and went out in the early afternoon to shop and to walk for a little while alone.

She was gone longer than she had intended, for she loved to walk around this city. She was chilled when at last she started home.

They lived just below Twenty-third Street, on the West Side, in a neighborhood that had lately acquired many Puerto Ricans. For this reason it was said that the neighborhood was declining; from what previous height it would have been hard to say. It seemed to Cass very much as it always had, run-down, and with a preponderance of very rough-looking people. As for the Puerto Ricans, she rather liked them. They did not impress her as being rough; they seemed, on the contrary, rather too gentle for their brutal environment. She liked the sound of their talk, soft and laughing, or else violently, clearly, brilliantly hostile; she liked the life in their eyes and the way they treated their children, as though all children were naturally the responsibility of all grownups. Even when the adolescents whistled after her, or said lewd things as she passed and laughed among themselves, she did not become resentful or afraid; she did not feel in it the tense New York hostility. They were not cursing something they longed for and feared, they were joking about something they longed for and loved.

Now, as she labored up the outside steps of the building, one of the Puerto Rican boys she had seen everywhere in the neighborhood opened the door for her with a small, half-smile. She smiled at him and thanked him as forthrightly as she could, and stepped into the elevator.

There was something in Richard's face as he closed the door behind her, and in the loud silence of the apartment. She looked at him and started to ask about the children—but then she heard them in the living room. Richard followed her into the kitchen and she put down her packages. She looked into his face.

"What is it?" she asked. Then, after the instant in which she checked off all the things it wasn't, "Rufus," she said, suddenly, "you've got news about Rufus."

"Yes." She watched the way a small vein in his forehead fluttered. "He's dead, Cass. They found his body floating in the river."

She sat down at the kitchen table.

"When?"

"Sometime this morning."

"How long—how long ago—?"

"A few days. They figured he must have jumped off the George Washington Bridge."

"My God," she said. Then: "Who—?"

"Vivaldo. He called. Just after you went out. Ida had called him."

"My God," she said, again, "it's going to kill that poor girl."

He paused. "Vivaldo sounded as though he'd just been kicked in the belly by a horse."

"Where is he?"

"I tried to make him come here. But he was going uptown to the girl—Ida—I don't know what good he can do."

"Well. He was much closer to Rufus than we were."

"Would you like a drink?"

"Yes," she said, "I think I'd like a drink." She sat staring at the table. "I wonder if there was anything—we—anyone—could have done."

"No," he said, pouring a little whiskey in a glass and setting it before her, "there was nothing anyone could have done. It was too late. He wanted to die."

She was silent, sipping the whiskey. She watched the way the sunlight fell on the table.

Richard put his hand on her shoulder. "Don't take it too hard, Cass. After all——"

She remembered his face as it had been the last time she talked to him, the look in his eyes, and his smile when he asked *Can I come to see you soon?* How she wished, now, that she had stayed and talked to him a little longer. Perhaps—she sipped the whiskey, marveling that the children were so quiet. Tears filled her eyes and dropped slowly down her face, onto the table.

"It's a dirty, rotten shame," she said. "It's a terrible, terrible, terrible thing."

"He was heading that way," said Richard, mildly, "nothing, no one, could have stopped him."

"How do we know that?" Cass asked.

"Oh, honey, you know what he's been like these last few months. We hardly ever saw him but everybody knew."

Knew what? she wanted to ask. Just what in hell did everybody know? But she dried her eyes and stood up.

"Vivaldo tried like hell to stop what he was doing to Leona. And if he could have stopped him from doing *that*—well, then, maybe he could have stopped this, too."

That's true, she thought, and looked at Richard, who, under stress, could always surprise her into taking his measure again.

"I was very fond of him," she said, helplessly. "There was something very sweet in him."

He looked at her with a faint smile. "Well, I guess you're just naturally nicer than I am. I didn't think that. I thought he was a pretty self-centered character, if you want the truth."

"Oh, well," she said, "self-centered—! We don't know a soul who isn't."

"You're not," he said. "You think of other people and you

try to treat them right. You spend your life trying to take care of the children—and me—"

"Oh, but you *are* my life—you and the children. What would I do, what would I be, without you? I'm just as self-centered as anybody else. Can't you see that?"

He grinned and rubbed his hand roughly over her head. "No. And I'm not going to argue about it any more." But, after a moment, he persisted. "I didn't love Rufus, not the way you did, the way all of you did. I couldn't help feeling, anyway, that one of the reasons all of you made such a kind of—*fuss*—over him was partly just because he was colored. Which is a hell of a reason to love anybody. I just had to look on him as another guy. And I couldn't forgive him for what he did to Leona. You once said you couldn't, either."

"I've had to think about it since then. I've thought about it since then."

"And what have you thought? You find a way to justify it?"

"No. I wasn't trying to justify it. It can't be justified. But now I think—oh, I just don't know enough to be able to judge him. He must—he must have been in great pain. He must have loved her." She turned to him, searching his face. "I'm sure he loved her."

"Some love," he said.

"Richard," she said, "you and I have hurt each other—many times. Sometimes we didn't mean to and sometimes we did. And wasn't it because—just *because*—we loved—love—each other?"

He looked at her oddly, head to one side. "Cass," he said, "how can you compare it? We've never tried to destroy each other—have we?"

They watched each other. She said nothing.

"I've never tried to destroy you. Have you ever tried to destroy me?"

She thought of his face as it had been when they met; and watched it now. She thought of all they had discovered together and meant to each other, and of how many small lies had gone into the making of their one, particular truth: this love, which bound them to one another. She had said No, many times, to many things, when she knew she might have said Yes, because of Richard; believed many things, because of Richard, which she was not sure she really believed. He had been absolutely necessary to her—or so she had believed; it came to the same thing—and so she had attached herself to him and her life had taken shape around him. She did not regret this for herself. I want him, something in her had said, years ago. And she had bound him to her; he had been her salvation; and here he was. She did not regret it for herself and yet she began to wonder if there were not something in it to be regretted, something she had done to Richard which Richard did not see.

"No," she said, faintly. And then, irrepressibly, "But I wouldn't have had to try."

"What do you mean by that?"

"I mean"—he was watching her; she sat down again, playing with the glass of whiskey—"a man meets a woman. And he needs her. But she uses this need against him, she uses it to undermine him. And it's easy. Women don't see men the way men want to be seen. They see all the tender places, all the places where blood could flow." She finished the whiskey. "Do you see what I mean?"

"No," he said, frankly, "I don't. I don't believe all this female intuition shit. It's something women have dreamed up."

"You can *say* that—and in such a tone!" She mimicked him: "Something women have dreamed up. But *I* can't say that— what men have 'dreamed up' is all there is, the world they've dreamed up *is* the world." He laughed. She subsided. "Well. It's true."

"What a funny girl you are," he said. "You've got a bad case of penis envy."

"So do most men," she said, sharply, and he laughed. "All I meant, anyway," she said, soberly, "is that I had to try to fit myself around you and not try to make you fit around me. That's all. And it hasn't been easy."

"No."

"No. Because I love you."

"Ah!" he said, and laughed aloud, "you *are* a funny girl. I love you, too, you know that."

"I hope you do," she said.

"You know me so well and you don't know that? What

happened to all that intuition, all that—*specialized*—point of view?"

"Beyond a certain point," she said, with a sullen smile, "it doesn't seem to work so well."

He pulled her up from the table and put both arms around her, bending his cheek to her hair. "What point is that, my darling?"

Everything, his breath in her hair, his arms, his chest, his odor—was familiar, confining, unutterably dear. She turned her head slightly to look out of the kitchen window. "Love," she said, and watched the cold sunlight. She thought of the cold river and of the dead black boy, their friend. She closed her eyes. "Love," she said, again, "love."

Richard stayed with the children Saturday, while Cass and Vivaldo went uptown to Rufus' funeral. She did not want to go but she could not refuse Vivaldo, who knew that he had to be there but dreaded being there alone.

It was a morning funeral, and Rufus was to be driven to the graveyard immediately afterward. Early on that cold, dry Saturday, Vivaldo arrived, emphatically in black and white: white shirt, black tie, black suit, black shoes, black coat; and black hair, eyes, and eyebrows, and a dead-white, bone-dry face. She was struck by his panic and sorrow; without a word, she put on her dark coat and put her hand in his; and they rode down in the elevator in silence. She watched him in the elevator mirror. Sorrow became him. He was reduced to his beauty and elegance—as bones, after a long illness, come forward through the flesh.

They got into a taxi and started uptown. Vivaldo sat beside her, his hands on his knees, staring straight ahead. She watched the streets. Traffic was heavy, but rolling; the cab kept swerving and jerking, slowing down and speeding up but managing not to stop. Then, at Thirty-fourth Street, the red light brought it to a halt. They were surrounded by a violence of cars, great trucks, green buses lumbering across town, and boys, dark boys, pushing wooden wagons full of clothes. The people on the sidewalks overflowed into the streets. Women in heavy coats moved heavily, carrying large packages and enormous handbags—for Thanksgiving was over but signs proclaimed the dwindling number of shopping days to Christmas. Men, relatively unburdened, pursuing the money which Christmas cost, hurried around and past the women; boys in ducktail haircuts swung over the cold black asphalt as though it were a dance floor. Outside the window, as close to her as Vivaldo, one of the colored boys stopped his wagon, lit a cigarette, and laughed. The taxi could not move and the driver began cursing. Cass lit a cigarette and handed it to Vivaldo. She lit another for herself. Then, abruptly, the taxi jerked forward.

The driver turned on his radio and the car was filled suddenly with the sound of a guitar, a high, neighing voice, and a chorus, crying, *"love me!"* The other words were swallowed in the guttural moans of the singer, which were nearly as obscene as the driver's curses had been, but these two words kept recurring.

"My whole family thinks I'm a bum," said Vivaldo. "I'd say they've given me up, except I know they're scared to death of what I'll do next."

She said nothing. He looked out of the cab window. They were crossing Columbus Circle.

"Sometimes—like today," he said, "I think they're probably right and I've just been kidding myself. About everything."

The walls of the park now closed on either side of them and beyond these walls, through speed and barren trees, the walls of hotels and apartment buildings.

"*My* family thinks I married beneath me," she said. "Beneath *them*." And she smiled at him and crushed out her cigarette on the floor.

"I don't think I ever saw my father sober," he said, "not in all these years. He used to say, 'I want you to tell me the truth now, always tell me the truth.' And then, if I told him the truth, he'd slap me up against the wall. So, naturally, I didn't tell him the truth, I'd just tell him any old lie, I didn't give a shit. The last time I went over to the house to see them I was wearing my red shirt, and he said, 'What's the matter, you turned queer?' Jesus."

She lit another cigarette and she listened. There was a horseback rider on the bridle path, a pale girl with a haughty, bewildered face. Cass had time to think, unwillingly, as the rider vanished forever from sight, that it might have been herself, many years ago, in New England.

"That neighborhood was terrific," Vivaldo said, "you had to be tough, they'd kill you if you weren't, people were dying around us all the time, for nothing. I wasn't really much interested in hanging out with most of those kids, they bored me. But they scared me, too. I couldn't stand watching my father. He's such an awful coward. He spent all his time pretending—well, I don't know *what* he was pretending, that everything was great, I guess—while his wife was going crazy in the hardware store we've got. And he knew that neither me nor my brother had any respect for him. And his daughter was turning into the biggest cock teaser going. She finally got married, I hate to think what her husband must have to promise her each time she lets him have a little bit."

He was silent for a moment. Then, "Of course, he's an asshole, too. Lord. I used to like to just get on a bus and go to some strange part of town by myself and just walk around or go to the movies by myself or just read or just goof. But, no. You had to be a man where I come from, and you had to prove it, prove it all the time. But I could tell you things"— He sighed. "Well, my Dad's still there, sort of helping to keep the liquor industry going. Most of the kids I knew are dead or in jail or on junk. I'm just a bum; I'm lucky."

She listened because she knew that he was going back over it, looking at it, trying to put it all together, to understand it, to express it. But he had not expressed it. He had left something of himself back there on the streets of Brooklyn which he was afraid to look at again.

"One time," he said, "we got into a car and drove over to the Village and we picked up this queer, a young guy, and we drove him back to Brooklyn. Poor guy, he was scared green before we got halfway there but he couldn't jump out of the car. We drove into this garage, there were seven of us, and we made him go down on all of us and then we beat the piss out of him and took all his money and took his clothes and left him lying on that cement floor, and, you know, it was winter." He looked over at her, looked directly at her for the first time that morning. "Sometimes I still wonder if they found him in time, or if he died, or what." He put his hands together and looked out of the window. "Sometimes I wonder if I'm still the same person who did those things—so long ago."

No. It was not expressed. She wondered why. Perhaps it was because Vivaldo's recollections in no sense freed him from the things recalled. He had not gone back into it—that time, that boy; he regarded it with a fascinated, even romantic horror, and he was looking for a way to deny it.

Perhaps such secrets, the secrets of everyone, were only expressed when the person laboriously dragged them into the light of the world, imposed them on the world, and made them a part of the world's experience. Without this effort, the secret place was merely a dungeon in which the person perished; without this effort, indeed, the entire world would be an uninhabitable darkness; and she saw, with a dreadful reluctance, why this effort was so rare. Reluctantly, because she then realized that Richard had bitterly disappointed her by writing a book in which he did not believe. In that moment she knew, and she knew that Richard would never face it, that the book he had written to make money represented the absolute limit of his talent. It had not really been written to make money—if only it had been! It had been written because he was afraid, afraid of things dark, strange, dangerous, difficult, and deep.

I don't care, she told herself, quickly. And: It's not his fault if he's not Dostoievski, I don't care. But whether or not she cared didn't matter. *He* cared, cared tremendously, and he was dependent on her faith in him.

"Isn't it strange," she said, suddenly, "that you should be remembering all these things now!"

"Maybe," he said, after a moment, "it's because of her. When I went up there, the day she called me to say Rufus was dead—I don't know—I walked through that block and I walked in that house and it all seemed—I don't know—*familiar*." He turned his pale, troubled face toward her but she felt that he was staring at the high, hard wall which stood between himself and his past. "I don't just mean that I used to spend a lot of time in Harlem," and he looked away, nervously, "I was hardly ever there in the daytime anyway. I mean, there were the same kids on the block that used to be on my block—they were colored but they were the same, really the same—and, hell, the hallways have the same stink, and everybody's, well, trying to make it but they know they haven't got much of a chance. The same old women, the same old men—maybe they're a little bit more *alive*—and I walked into that house and they were just sitting there, Ida and her mother and her father, and there were some other people there, relatives, maybe, and friends. I don't know, no one really spoke to me except Ida and she didn't say much. And they all looked at me as though—well, as though I had *done* it—and, oh, I wanted so bad to take that girl in my arms and kiss that look off her face and make her know that I didn't do it, *I* wouldn't do it, whoever was doing it was doing it to me, too." He was crying, silently, and he bent forward, hiding his face with one long hand. "I know I failed him, but I loved him, too, and nobody there wanted to know that. I kept thinking, They're colored and I'm white but the same things have happened, really the *same* things, and how can I make them know that?"

"But they didn't," she said, "happen to you *because* you were white. They just happened. But what happens up here"—and the cab came out of the park; she stretched her hands, inviting him to look—"happens *because* they are colored. And that makes a difference." And, after a moment, she dared to add, "You'll be kissing a long time, my friend, before you kiss any of this away."

He looked out of the window, drying his eyes. They had come out on Lenox Avenue, though their destination was on Seventh; and nothing they passed was unfamiliar because everything they passed was wretched. It was not hard to imagine that horse carriages had once paraded proudly up this wide avenue and ladies and gentlemen, ribboned, beflowered, brocaded, plumed, had stepped down from their carriages to enter these houses which time and folly had so blasted and darkened. The cornices had once been new, had once gleamed as brightly as now they sulked in shame, all tarnished and despised. The windows had not always been blind. The doors had not always brought to mind the distrust and secrecy of a city long besieged. At one time people had cared about these houses—that was the difference; they had been proud to walk on this Avenue; it had once been home, whereas now it was prison.

Now, no one cared: this indifference was all that joined this ghetto to the mainland. Now, everything was falling down and the owners didn't care; no one cared. The beautiful children in the street, black-blue, brown, and copper, all with a gray ash on their faces and legs from the cold wind, like the faint coating of frost on a window or a flower, didn't seem to care, that no one saw their beauty. Their elders, great, trudging, black women, lean, shuffling men, had taught them, by precept or example, what it meant to care or not to care: whatever precepts were daily being lost, the examples remained, all up and down the street. The trudging women trudged, paused, came in and out of dark doors, talked to each other, to the men, to policemen, stared into shop windows, shouted at the children, laughed, stopped to caress them. All the faces, even those of the children, held a sweet or poisonous disenchantment which made their faces extraordinarily definite, as though they had been struck out of stone. The cab sped uptown, past men in front of barber shops, in front of barbeque joints, in front of bars; sped past side streets, long, dark, noisome, with gray houses leaning forward to cut out the sky; and in the shadow of these houses, children buzzed and boomed, as thick as flies on flypaper. Then they turned off the Avenue, west, crawled up a long, gray street. They had to crawl, for the street was choked with unhurrying people and children kept darting out from between the cars which were parked, for the length of the street, on either side. There were people on the stoops, people shouting out of windows, and young men peered indifferently into the slow-moving cab, their faces set ironically and their eyes unreadable.

"Did Rufus ever have you up here?" she asked. "To visit his family, I mean."

"Yes," said Vivaldo. "A long time ago. I had almost forgotten it. I *had* forgotten it until Ida reminded me. She was in pigtails then, the cutest little colored girl you ever saw. She was about fifteen. Rufus and I took her to Radio City."

She smiled at his description of Ida, and at his tone, which was unconsciously erotic. The cab crossed the Avenue and stopped on the far corner of the block they had come through, where the chapel stood. Two women stood on the steps of the chapel, talking together in low tones. As Cass watched and Vivaldo paid the driver, a young man joined them and they went inside.

Suddenly, with a curse, she put her hand on her uncovered head.

"Vivaldo," she said, "I can't go in there."

He stared at her blankly, while the taxi driver paused in the act of handing him his change.

"What're you talking about?" he asked. "What's the matter with you?"

"Nothing. Nothing. But a woman's head has to be *covered*. I can't go in there without a hat."

"Of course you can!" But at the same moment he remembered that he had never in his life seen a bareheaded woman in a church.

"No, no, I *can't*. They're all wearing hats, all of them. It would be an insult if I didn't, it would be like coming here in slacks." She paused. "It's a *church*, Vivaldo, it's a funeral, it would be an insult."

He had already conceded her point and he stared at her helplessly. The cab driver still held the change and watched Vivaldo with a careful lack of expression.

"Well, haven't you got a scarf, or something?"

"No." She dug in her handbag, the pockets of her coat, close to tears. "No. Nothing."

"Listen, buddy," the driver said.

Vivaldo's face lightened. "What about your belt? Can't you tie that around your head? It's black."

"Oh, no. That'll never work. Besides—they'd *know* it was my belt."

"Try it."

To end the argument and prove her point, she took off her belt and tied it around her head. "You see? It'll never work."

"What're you people going to do?" the driver asked. "I ain't got all day."

"I'll have to buy something," Cass said.

"We'll be late."

"Well, you go on in. I'll just drive to a store somewhere and I'll come right back."

"Ain't no stores around here, lady," the driver said.

"Of course there are stores somewhere near here," Cass said, sharply. "You go on in, Vivaldo; I'll come right back. What's the address here?"

Vivaldo gave her the address and said, "You'll have to go to 125th Street, that's the only place I know where there are any stores." Then he took his change from the driver and tipped him. "The lady wants to go to 125th street," he said.

The driver turned in his seat resignedly, and turned on his meter. "You go on in, Vivaldo," Cass said again. "I'm sorry. I'll be right back."

"You have enough money on you?"

"Yes. Go on in."

He got out of the cab, looking helpless and annoyed, and turned into the chapel as the cab pulled away. The driver left her at the corner of 125th Street and Eighth Avenue and she realized, as she hurried down the wide, crowded street, that she was in a strange, unnameable state, neither rage nor tears but close to both. One small, lone, white woman hurrying along 125th Street on a Saturday morning was apparently a very common sight, for no one looked at her at all. She did not see any stores with ladies' hats in the window. But she was hurrying too fast and looking too hard. If she did not pull herself together, she might very well spend the day wandering up and down this street. For a moment she thought to stop one of the women—one of the women whose faces she watched as though they contained something it was necessary for her to learn—to ask directions. Then she realized that she was mysteriously afraid: afraid of these people, these streets, the chapel to which she must return. She forced herself to walk more slowly. She saw a store and entered it.

A Negro girl came toward her, a girl with red, loosely waved hair, who wore a violently green dress and whose skin was a kind of dusty copper.

"Can I help you?"

The girl was smiling, the same smile—as Cass insisted to herself—that all salesgirls, everywhere, have always worn. This smile made Cass feel poor and shabby indeed. But now she felt it more vehemently than she had ever felt it before. And though she was beginning to shake with a thoroughly mysterious anger, she knew that her dry, aristocratic sharpness, however well it had always worked downtown, would fail of its usual effect here.

"I want," she stammered, "to see a hat."

Then she remembered that she hated hats and never wore them. The girl, whose smile had clearly been taught her by masters, looked as though she sold at least one hat, every Saturday morning, to a strange, breathless, white woman.

"Will you come with me?" she asked.

"Well—no," Cass said, suddenly—and the girl turned, impeccably made up eyebrows arched—"I mean, I don't really want a hat." Cass tried to smile; she wanted to run. Silence had fallen over the shop. "I think I'd just like to get a scarf. Black"—and how the word seemed to roll through the shop!—"for my head," she added, and felt that in another moment they would call the police. And she had no way of identifying herself.

"Oh," said the girl. Cass had managed to wipe away the smile. "Marie!" she called, sharply, "will you take care of this lady?"

She walked away and another, older and plainer girl, who was also, however, very carefully dressed and made-up, came over to Cass, wearing a very different smile: a bawdy, amused smile, full of complicity and contempt. Cass felt herself blushing. The girl pulled out boxes of scarves. They all seemed sleazy and expensive, but she was in no position to complain. She took one, paid for it, tied it around her head, and left. Her knees were shaking. She managed to find a cab at the corner and, after fighting a small duel with herself, gave the driver the address of the chapel: she had really wanted to tell him to take her home.

The chapel was small and there were not many people in it. She entered as silently as she could, but heads turned at her entrance. An elderly man, probably an usher, hurried silently toward her, but she sat down in the first seat she saw, in the very last row, near the door. Vivaldo was sitting further up, near the middle; the only other white person, as far as she could tell, in the place. People sat rather scattered from each other—in the same way, perhaps, that the elements of Rufus' life had been scattered—and this made the chapel seem emptier than it was. There were many young people there, Rufus' friends, she supposed, the boys and girls who had grown up with him. In the front row sat six figures, the family: no amount of mourning could make Ida's proud back less proud. Just before the family, just below the altar, stood the bier, dominating the place, mother of pearl, closed.

Someone had been speaking as she came in, who now sat down. He was very young and he was dressed in the black robes of an evangelist. She wondered if he could be an evangelist, he did not seem to be much more than a boy. But he moved with great authority, the authority indeed of someone who has found his place and made his peace with it. As he sat down, a very thin girl walked up the aisle and the boy in black robes moved to the piano at the side of the altar.

"I remember Rufus," the girl said, "from when he was a big boy and I was just a little girl—" and she tried to smile at the front-row mourners. Cass watched her, seeing that the girl was doing her best not to cry. "—me and his sister used to sit around trying to console each other when Rufus went off with the big boys and wouldn't let us play with him." There was a murmur of amusement and sorrow and heads in the front row nodded. "We lived right next door to each other, he was like a brother to me." Then she dropped her head and twisted a white handkerchief, the whitest handkerchief Cass had ever seen, between her two dark hands. She was silent for several seconds and, once again, a kind of wind seemed to whisper through the chapel as though everyone there shared the girl's memories and her agony and were willing her through it. The boy at the piano struck a chord. "Sometimes Rufus used to like me to sing this song," the girl said, abruptly. "I'll sing it for him now."

The boy played the opening chord. The girl sang in a rough, untrained, astonishingly powerful voice:

> *I'm a stranger, don't drive me away.*
> *I'm a stranger, don't drive me away.*
> *If you drive me away, you may need me some day,*
> *I'm a stranger, don't drive me away.*

When she finished she walked over to the bier and stood there for a moment, touching it lightly with both hands. Then she walked back to her seat.

There was weeping in the front row. She watched as Ida rocked an older, heavier woman in her arms. One of the men blew his nose loudly. The air was heavy. She wished it were over.

Vivaldo sat very still and alone, looking straight ahead.

Now, a gray-haired man stepped forward from behind the altar. He stood watching them for a moment and the black-robed boy strummed a mournful hymn.

"Some of you know me," he said, finally, "and some of you don't. My name is Reverend Foster." He paused. "And I know some of your faces and some of you are strangers to me." He made a brief bow, first toward Cass, then toward Vivaldo. "But ain't none of us really strangers. We all here for the same reason. Someone we loved is dead." He paused again and looked down at the bier. "Someone we loved and laughed with and talked with—and got mad at—and prayed over—is gone. He ain't with us no more. He's gone someplace where the wicked cease from troubling." He looked down at the bier again. "We ain't going to look on his face again—no more. He had a hard time getting through this world and he had a rough time getting out of it. When he stand before his Maker he going to look like a lot of us looked when we first got here—like he had a rough time getting through the passage. It was *narrow*." He cleared his throat and blew his nose. "I ain't going to stand here and tell you all a whole lot of lies about Rufus. I don't believe in that. I used to know Rufus, I knew him all his life. He was a bright kid and he was full of the devil and weren't no way in the world of keeping up with him. He got into a lot of trouble, all of you know that. A lot of our boys get into a lot of trouble and some of you know why. We used to talk about it sometimes, him and me—we was always pretty good friends, Rufus and me, even after he jumped up and went off from here and even though he didn't never attend church service like I—we—all wanted him to do." He paused again. "He had to go his way. He had his trouble and he's gone. He was young, he was bright, he was beautiful, we expected great things from him—but he's gone away from us now and it's us will have to make the great things happen. I believe I know how terrible some of you feel. I know how terrible I feel—ain't nothing I can say going to take away that ache, not right away. But that boy was one of the best men I ever met, and I been around awhile. I ain't going to try to judge him. That ain't for us to do. You know, a lot of people say that a man who takes his own life oughtn't to be buried in holy ground. I don't know nothing about that. All *I* know, God made every bit of ground I ever walked on and everything God made is *holy*. And don't none of us know what goes on in the heart of someone, don't many of us know what's going on in our own hearts for the matter of that, and so can't none of us say why he did what he did. Ain't none of us been there and so don't none of us know. We got to pray that the Lord will receive him like we pray that the Lord's going to receive us. That's all. That's *all*. And I tell you something else, don't none of you forget it: I know a lot of people done took their own lives and they're walking up and down the streets today and some of them is preaching the gospel and some is sitting in the seats of the mighty. Now, you remember that. If the world wasn't so full of dead folks maybe those of us that's trying to live wouldn't have to suffer so bad."

He walked up and down behind the altar, behind the bier.

"I know there ain't nothing I can say to you that sit before me—his mother and father, his sister, his kinfolks, his friends—to bring him back or to keep you from grieving that he's gone. I know that. Ain't nothing I can say will make his life different, make it the life that maybe some other man might have lived. It's all been done, it's all written down on high. But don't lose heart, dear ones—don't lose heart. Don't let it make you bitter. Try to understand. Try to understand. The world's already bitter enough, we got to try to be better than the world."

He looked down, then over to the front row.

"You got to remember," he said, gently, "he was *trying*. Ain't many trying and all that tries must suffer. Be proud of him. You got a right to be proud. And that's all he ever wanted in this world."

Except for someone—a man—weeping in the front row,

there was silence all over the chapel. Cass thought that the man must be Rufus' father and she wondered if he believed what the preacher said. What had Rufus been to him?—a troublesome son, a stranger while living and now a stranger forever in death. And now nothing else would ever be known. Whatever else had been, or might have been, locked in Rufus' heart or in the heart of his father, had gone into oblivion with Rufus. It would never be expressed now. It was over.

"There're some friends of Rufus's here," said Reverend Foster, "and they going to play something for us and then we going to go."

Two young men walked up the aisle, one carrying a guitar, one carrying a bass fiddle. The thin dark girl followed them. The black-robed boy at the piano flexed his fingers. The two boys stood directly in front of the covered corpse, the girl stood a little away from them, near the piano. They began playing something Cass did not recognize, something very slow, and more like the blues than a hymn. Then it began to be more tense and more bitter and more swift. The people in the chapel hummed low in their throats and tapped their feet. Then the girl stepped forward. She threw back her head and closed her eyes and that voice rang out again:

> *Oh, that great getting-up morning,*
> *Fare thee well, fare thee well!*

Reverend Foster, standing on a height behind her, raised both hands and mingled his voice with hers:

> *We'll be coming from every nation,*
> *Fare thee well, fare thee well!*

The chapel joined them, but the girl ended the song alone:

> *Oh, on that great getting-up morning,*
> *Fare thee well, fare thee well!*

Then Reverend Foster prayed a brief prayer for the safe journey of the soul that had left them and the safe journey, throughout their lives and after death, of all the souls under the sound of his voice. It was over.

The pallbearers, two of the men in the front row, and the two musicians, lifted the mother-of-pearl casket to their shoulders and started down the aisle. The mourners followed.

Cass was standing near the door. The four still faces passed her with their burden and did not look at her. Directly behind them came Ida and her mother. Ida paused for a moment and looked at her—looked directly, unreadably, at her from beneath her heavy veil. Then she seemed to smile. Then she passed. And the others passed. Vivaldo joined her and they walked out of the chapel.

For the first time she saw the hearse, which stood on the Avenue, facing downtown.

"Vivaldo," she asked, "are we going to the cemetery?"

"No," he said, "they don't have enough cars. I think only the family's going."

He was watching the car behind the hearse. Ida's parents had already entered the car. She stood on the sidewalk. She looked around her, then walked swiftly over to them. She took each of them by one hand.

"I just wanted to thank you," she said, quickly, "for coming." Her voice was rough from weeping and Cass could not see her face behind the veil. "You don't know what it means to me—to us."

Cass pressed Ida's hand, not knowing what to say. Vivaldo said, "Ida, anything we can do—anything *I* can do—*anything*—!"

"You've done wonders. You been wonderful. I'll never forget it."

She pressed their hands again and turned away. She got into the car and the door closed behind her. The hearse slowly moved out from the curb, and the car, then a second car, followed. Others who had been at the funeral service looked briefly at Cass and Vivaldo, stood together a few moments, and then began to disperse. Cass and Vivaldo started down the Avenue.

"Shall we take a subway?" Vivaldo asked.

"I don't," she said, "think I could face that now."

They continued to walk, nevertheless, aimlessly, in silence. Cass walked with her hands deep in her pockets, staring down at the cracks in the sidewalk.

"I hate funerals," she said, finally, "they never seem to have anything to do with the person who died."

"No," he said, "funerals are for the living."

They passed a stoop where a handful of adolescents stood, who looked at them curiously.

"Yes," she said. And they kept walking, neither seeming to have the energy it would have demanded to stop and hail a cab. They could not talk about the funeral now; there was too much to say; perhaps each had too much to hide. They walked down the wide, crowded Avenue, surrounded, it seemed, by an atmosphere which prevented others from jostling them or looking at them too directly or for too long a time. They reached the mouth of the subway at 125th Street. People climbed up from the darkness and a group of people stood on the corner, waiting for the bus.

"Let's get that cab," she said.

Vivaldo hailed a cab and they got in—as, she could not help feeling they had been expected to do—and they began to roll away from the dark, the violent scene, over which, now, a pale sun fell.

"I wonder," he said. "I wonder."

"Yes? What do you wonder?"

Her tone was sharper than she had intended, she could not have said why.

"What she means when she says she'll never forget it."

Something was going on in her mind, something she could not name or stop; but it was almost as though she were her mind's prisoner, as though the jaws of her mind had closed on her.

"Well, at least that proves that you're intelligent," she said. "Much good may it do you." She watched the cab roll down the Avenue which would eventually turn into the Avenue she knew.

"I'd like to prove to her—one day," he said; and paused. He looked out of the window. "I'd like to make her know that the world's not as black as she thinks it is."

"Or," she said, dryly, after a moment, "as white."

"Or as white," he said, mildly. She sensed that he was refusing to react to her tone. Then he said, "You don't like her—Ida."

"I like her well enough. I don't know her."

"I guess that proves my point," he said. "You don't know her and you don't want to know her."

"It doesn't matter whether I like Ida or not," she said. "The point is, you like her. Well, that's fine. I don't know why you want me to object. I *don't* object. But what difference would it make if I did?"

"None," he said, promptly. Then, "Well, some. I'd worry about my judgment."

"Judgment," she said. "has nothing to do with love."

He looked at her sharply, but with gratitude, too. "For it's love we're talking about—?"

"For what you seem to be trying to prove," she said, "it had better be." She was silent. Then she said, "Of course, she may also have something to prove."

"I think she has something to forget," he said. "I think I can help her forget it."

She said nothing. She watched the cold trees and the cold park. She wondered how Richard's work had gone that morning; she wondered about the children. It seemed, suddenly, that she had been away a long time, had failed very great obligations. And all she wanted in the world right now was to get home safely and find everything as she had left it—as she had left it so long ago, this morning.

"You're so juvenile," she heard herself saying. She was using her most matronly tone. "You know so little"—she smiled—"about life. About women."

He smiled, too, a pale, weary smile. "All right. But I want something real to happen to me. I do. How do you find out about"—he grinned, mocking her—"life? About women? Do you know a lot about men?"

The great numbers above faraway Columbus Circle glowed in the gray sky and said that it was twelve twenty-seven. She would get home just in time to make lunch.

Then the depression she had been battling came down again, as though the sky had descended and turned into fog.

"Once I thought I did," she said. "Once I thought I knew. Once I was even younger than you are now."

Again he stared at her but this time said nothing. For a moment, as the road swerved, the skyline of New York rose

before them like a jagged wall. Then it was gone. She lit a
cigarette and wondered why, in that moment, she had so
hated the proud towers, the grasping antennae. She had never
hated the city before. Why did everything seem so pale and
so profitless: and why did she feel so cold, as though nothing
and no one could ever warm her again?

Low in his throat Vivaldo hummed the blues they had
heard at the funeral. He was thinking of Ida, dreaming of Ida,
rushing ahead to what awaited him with Ida. For a moment
she hated his youth, his expectations, possibilities, she hated
his masculinity. She envied Ida. She listened to Vivaldo hum
the blues.

3

O N A SATURDAY in early March, Vivaldo stood at his window and watched the morning rise. The wind blew through the empty streets with a kind of dispirited moan; had been blowing all night long, while Vivaldo sat at his worktable, struggling with a chapter which was not going well. He was terribly weary—he had worked in the bookstore all day and then come downtown to do a moving job—but this was not the reason for his paralysis. He did not seem to know enough about the people in his novel. They did not seem to trust him. They were all named, more or less, all more or less destined, the pattern he wished them to describe was clear to him. But it did not seem clear to them. He could move them about but they themselves did not move. He put words in their mouths which they uttered sullenly, unconvinced. With the same agony, or greater, with which he attempted to seduce a woman, he was trying to seduce his people: he begged them to surrender up to him their privacy. And they refused—without, for all their ugly intransigence, showing the faintest desire to leave him. They were waiting for him to find the key, press the nerve, tell the truth. *Then*, they seemed to be complaining, they would give him all he wished for and much more than he was now willing to imagine. All night long, in an increasing rage and helplessness, he had walked from his worktable to his window and back again. He made himself coffee, he smoked cigarettes, he looked at the clock—and the night wore on, but his chapter didn't and he kept feeling that he ought to get some sleep because today, for the first time in several weeks, he was seeing Ida. This was her Saturday off, but she was having a cup of coffee with one of her girl friends in the restaurant where she worked. He was to meet her there, and then they were to visit Richard and Cass.

Richard's novel was about to be published, and it promised to be very successful. Vivaldo, to his confusion and relief, had not found it very remarkable. But he had not had the courage to say this to Richard or to admit to himself that he would never have read the novel if Richard had not written it.

All the street sounds eventually ceased—motors, and the silky sound of tires, footfalls, curses, pieces of songs, and loud and prolonged good nights; the last door in his building slammed, the last murmurs, rustling, and creaking ended. The night grew still around him and his apartment grew cold. He lit the oven. They swarmed, then, in the bottom of his mind, his cloud of witnesses, in an air as heavy as the oven heat, clustering, really, around the desired and unknown Ida. Perhaps it was she who caused them to be so silent.

He stared into the streets and thought—bitterly, but also with a chilling, stunned sobriety—that, though he had been seeing them so long, perhaps he had never known them at all. The occurrence of an event is not the same thing as knowing what it is that one has lived through. Most people had not lived—nor could it, for that matter, be said that they had died—through any of their terrible events. They had simply been stunned by the hammer. They passed their lives thereafter in a kind of limbo of denied and unexamined pain. The great question that faced him this morning was whether or not he had ever, really, been present at his life. For if he had ever been present, then he was present still, and his world would open up before him.

Now the girl who lived across the street, whose name, he knew, was Nancy, but who reminded him of Jane—which was certainly why he never spoke to her—came in from her round of the bars and the coffee houses with yet another boneless young man. They were everywhere, which explained how she met them, but why she brought them home with her was a somewhat more sinister question. Those who wore their hair long wore beards; those who wore theirs short felt free to dispense with this useful but somewhat uneasy emphasis. They read poetry or they wrote it, furiously, as though to prove that they had been cut out for more masculine pursuits. This morning's specimen wore white trousers and a yachting cap, and a paranoiac little beard jutted out from the bottom half of his face. This beard was his most aggressive feature, his only suggestion of hardness or tension. The girl, on the other hand, was all angles, bone, muscle, jaw; even her breasts seemed stony. They walked down the street, hand in hand, but not together. They paused before her stoop and the girl staggered. She leaned against him in an agony of loathing, belching alcohol; his rigidity suggested that her weight was onerous; and they climbed the short steps to the door. Here she paused and smiled at him, coquettishly raising those stony breasts as she pulled back her hair with her hands. The boy seemed to find this delay intolerable. He muttered something about the cold, pushing the girl in before him.

Well, now, they would make it—make what? not love, certainly—and should he be standing at this window twenty-four hours hence, he would see the same scene repeated with another boy.

How could they endure it? Well, he had been there. How had he endured it? Whiskey and marijuana had helped; he was a pretty good liar and that had helped; and most women inspired great contempt in him and that had helped. But there was more to it than that. After all, the country, the world— this city—was full of people who got up in the morning and went to bed at night and, mainly, throughout their lives, to the same bed. They did whatever it was they were supposed to do, and they raised their children. And perhaps he didn't like these people very much, but, then, he didn't, on the other hand, know them. He supposed that they existed because he had been told that they did; presumably, the faces he saw on subways and in the streets belonged to these people, who were admirable because they were numerous. His mother and father and his married sister and her husband and their friends were part of this multitude, and his younger brother would belong to them soon. And what did he know about them, really, except that they were ashamed of him? They didn't know that he was real. It seemed that they didn't, for that matter, know that *they* were real, but he was insufficiently simple to find this notion comforting.

He watched a lone man come up the street, his tight black overcoat buttoned to the neck, looking back from time to time as though he hoped he were being followed. Then the garbage truck came up the street, like a gray brainless insect. He watched the garbage being loaded. Then there was nothing, no one. The light was growing stronger. Soon, alarm clocks would begin to ring and the houses would expel the morning people. Then he thought of the scene which would now be occurring between the boy and the girl in the room.

The yellow electric light, self-consciously indirect, would by now have been discovered to be useless and would have been turned off. The girl would have taken off her shoes and turned on her radio or her hi-fi set and would be lying on the bed. The gray light, coming in through the monk's-cloth blinds, would, with the malice of the noncommittal, be examining every surface, corner, angle, of the unloved room. The music would not be loud. They would have poured drinks by now and the girl's drink would be on the table. The boy's would be between his hands. He would be sitting on the bed, turned a little away from the girl, staring at the floor. His cap would have been pushed further back. And the silence, beneath the music, would be tremendous with their fear. Presently, one of them would make a move to conquer this. If it were the girl, the movement would be sighing and halting—sighing because of need, halting because of hostility. If it were the boy, the movement would be harshly or softly brutal: he would lunge over the girl as though rape were in his mind, or he would try to arouse her lust by means of feathery kisses, meant to be burning, which he had seen in the movies. Friction and fantasy could not fail to produce a physiological heat and hardness; and this sheathed pressure between her thighs would be the girl's signal to moan. She would toss her head a little and hold the boy more tightly and they would begin their descent into confusion. Off would come the cap—as the bed sighed and the gray light stared. Then his jacket would come off. His hands would push up the sweater and unlock the brassière. Perhaps both might wish to pause here and begin a discovery of each other, but neither would dare. She moaned and clung to darkness, he removed the sweater. He struggled unlovingly with her breasts; the sound of her gasps foreshadowed his failure. Then the record on the hi-fi came to an end, or, on the radio, a commercial replaced the love song. He pulled up her skirt. Then the half-naked girl, with a small, apologetic murmur, rose from the bed, switched off the machine. Standing in the center of the room, she might mock her nakedness with a small, cruel joke. Then she would vanish into the john.

The boy would finish his drink and take off everything except his undershorts. When the girl reappeared, both would be ready.

Yes, he had been there: chafing and pushing and pounding, trying to awaken a frozen girl. The battle was awful because the girl wished to be awakened but was terrified of the unknown. Every movement that seemed to bring her closer to him, to bring them closer together, had its violent recoil, driving them farther apart. Both clung to a fantasy rather than to each other, tried to suck pleasure from the crannies of the mind, rather than surrender the secrets of the body. The tendrils of shame clutched at them, however they turned, all the dirty words they knew commented on all they did. These words sometimes brought on the climax—joylessly, with loathing, and too soon. The best that he had ever managed in bed, so far, had been the maximum of relief with the minimum of hostility.

In Harlem, however, he had merely dropped his load and marked the spot with silver. It had seemed much simpler for a time. But even simple pleasure, bought and paid for, did not take long to fail—pleasure, as it turned out, was not simple. When, wandering about Harlem, he came across a girl he liked, he could not fail to wish that he had met her somewhere else, under different circumstances. He could not fail to disapprove of her situation and to demand of her more than any girl in such a situation could give. If he did not like her, then he despised her and it was very painful for him to despise a colored girl, it increased his self-contempt. So that, by and by, however pressing may have been the load he carried uptown, he returned home with a greater one, not to be so easily discharged.

For several years it had been his fancy that he belonged in those dark streets uptown precisely because the history written in the color of his skin contested his right to be there. He enjoyed this, his right to *be* being everywhere contested; uptown, his alienation had been made visible and, therefore, almost bearable. It had been his fancy that danger, there, was more real, more open, than danger was downtown and that he, having chosen to run these dangers, was snatching his manhood from the lukewarm waters of mediocrity and testing it in the fire. He had felt more alive in Harlem, for he had moved in a blaze of rage and self-congratulation and sexual excitement, with danger, like a promise, waiting for him everywhere. And, nevertheless, in spite of all this daring, this running of risks, the misadventures which had actually befallen him had been banal indeed and might have befallen him anywhere. His dangerous, overwhelming lust for life had failed to involve him in anything deeper than perhaps half a dozen extremely casual acquaintanceships in about as many bars. For memories, he had one or two marijuana parties, one or two community debauches, one or two girls whose names he had forgotten, one or two addresses which he had lost. He knew that Harlem was a battlefield and that a war was being waged there day and night—but of the war aims he knew nothing.

And this was due not only to the silence of the warriors—their silence being, anyway, spectacular in that it rang so loud: it was due to the fact that one knew of battles only what one had accepted of one's own. He was forced, little by little, against his will, to realize that in running the dangers of Harlem he had not been testing his manhood or heightening his sense of life. He had merely been taking refuge in the outward adventure in order to avoid the clash and tension of the adventure proceeding inexorably within. Perhaps this was why he sometimes seemed to surprise in the dark faces which watched him a hint of amused and not entirely unkind contempt. He must be poor indeed, they seemed to say, to have been driven here. They knew that he was driven, in flight: the liberal, even revolutionary sentiments of which he was so proud meant nothing to them whatever. He was just a poor white boy in trouble and it was not in the least original of him to come running to the niggers.

This sentiment had sometimes seemed to stare out at him from the eyes of Rufus. He had refused to see it, for he had insisted that he and Rufus were equals. They were friends, far beyond the reach of anything so banal and corny as color. They had slept together, got drunk together, balled chicks together, cursed each other out, and loaned each other money. And yet how much, as it turned out, had each kept hidden in his heart from the other! It had all been a game, a game in which Rufus had lost his life. All of the pressures that each had denied had gathered together and killed him. Why had it been necessary to deny anything? What had been the point of the game? He turned into the room again and lit a cigarette and walked up and down. Well, perhaps they had been afraid that if they looked too closely into one another each would have found——he looked out of the window, feeling damp and frightened. Each would have found the abyss. Somewhere in his heart the black boy hated the white boy because he was white. Somewhere in his heart Vivaldo had feared and hated Rufus because he was black. They had balled chicks together, once or twice the same chick—why? And what had it done to them? And then they never saw the girl again. And they never really talked about it.

Once, while he was in the service, he and a colored buddy had been drunk, and on leave, in Munich. They were in a cellar someplace, it was very late at night, there were candles on the tables. There was one girl sitting near them. Who had dared whom? Laughing, they had opened their trousers and shown themselves to the girl. To the girl, but also to each other. The girl had calmly moved away, saying that she did not understand Americans. But perhaps she had understood them well enough. She had understood that their by-play had had very little to do with her. But neither could it be said that they had been trying to attract each other—they would never, certainly, have dreamed of doing it that way. Perhaps they had merely been trying to set their minds at ease; at ease as to which of them was the better man. And what had the black boy thought then? But the question was, What had *he* thought? He had thought, Hell, I'm doing all right. There might have been the faintest pang caused by the awareness that his colored buddy was doing possibly a little better than that, but, indeed, in the main, he had been relieved. It was out in the open, practically on the goddamn table, and it was just like his, there was nothing frightening about it.

He smiled—*I bet mine's bigger than yours is*—but remembered occasional nightmares in which this same vanished buddy pursued him through impenetrable forests, came at him with a knife on the edge of precipices, threatened to hurl him down steep stairs to the sea. In each of the nightmares he wanted revenge. Revenge for what?

He sat down again at his worktable. The page on the type-writer stared up at him, full of hieroglyphics. He read it over. It meant nothing whatever. Nothing was happening on that page. He walked back to the window. It was daylight now, and there were people on the streets, the expected, daytime people. The tall girl, with the bobbed hair and spectacles, wearing a long, loose coat, walked swiftly down the street. The grocery store was open. The old Rumanian who ran it carried in the case of milk which had been deposited on the sidewalk. He thought again that he had better get some sleep. He was seeing Ida today, they were having lunch with Richard and Cass. It was eight o'clock.

He stretched out on the bed and stared up at the cracks in the ceiling. He thought of Ida. He had seen her for the first time about seven years ago. She had been about fourteen. It was a holiday of some kind and Rufus had promised to take her out. And perhaps the reason he had asked Vivaldo to come with him was because Vivaldo had had to loan him the money. *Because I can't disappoint my sister, man.*

It had been a day rather like today, bright, cold, and hard. Rufus had been unusually silent and he, too, had been un-comfortable. He felt that he was forcing himself in where he did not belong. But Rufus had made the invitation and he had accepted; neither of them could get out of it now.

They had reached the house around one o'clock in the af-ternoon. Mrs. Scott had opened the door. She was dressed as though she, too, were going out, in a dark gray dress a little too short for her. Her hair was short but had lately been treated with the curling iron. She kissed Rufus lightly on the cheek.

"Hey, there," she said, "how's my bad boy?"

"Hey, yourself," said Rufus, grinning. There was an ex-pression on his face which Vivaldo had never seen before. It was a kind of teasing flush of amusement and pleasure; as though his mother, standing there in her high heels, her gray dress, and with her hair all curled, had just done something extraordinarily winning. And this flush was repeated in his mother's darker face as she smiled—gravely—back at him. She seemed to take him in from top to toe and to know exactly how he had been getting along with the world.

"This here's a friend of mine," Rufus said, "Vivaldo."

"How do you do?" She gave him her hand, briefly. The brevity was not due to discourtesy or coldness, simply to lack of habit. Insofar as she saw him at all, she saw him as Rufus' friend, one of the inhabitants of the world in which her son had chosen to live. "Sit down, do. Ida'll be right out."

"She ready?"

"Lord, she been getting ready for days. Done drove me nearly wild." They sat down. Vivaldo sat near the window which looked out on a dirty back yard and the back fire escape of other buildings. Across the way, a dark man sat in front of his half-open window, staring out. In spite of the cold, he wore nothing but an undershirt. There was nothing in the yard except cans, bottles, papers, filth, and a single tree. "If anything had happened and you hadn't showed up, I hate to think of the weeping and wailing that would have gone on in this house." She paused and looked toward the door which led to the rest of the apartment. "Maybe you boys like a little beer while you waiting?"

"That all you got to offer us?" Rufus asked, with a smile. "Where's Bert?"

"Bert's down to the store and he ain't back yet. You know how your father is. He going to be sorry he missed you." She turned to Vivaldo. "Would you like a glass of beer, son? I'm sorry we ain't got nothing else——"

"Oh, beer's fine," said Vivaldo, looking at Rufus, "I'd love a glass of beer."

She rose and walked into the kitchen. "What your friend do? He a musician?"

"Naw," said Rufus, "he ain't got no talent."

Vivaldo blushed. Mrs. Scott returned with a quart bottle of beer and three glasses. She had a remarkably authoritative and graceful walk. "Don't you mind my boy," she said, "he's just full of the devil, he can't help it. I been trying to knock it out of him, but I ain't had much luck." She smiled at Vivaldo as she poured his beer. "You look kind of shy. Don't you be shy. You just feel as welcome here as if you was in your own house, you hear?" And she handed him his glass.

"Thank you," said Vivaldo. He took a swallow of the beer, thinking she'd probably be surprised to know how unwelcome

ANOTHER COUNTRY

he felt in his own house. And then, again, perhaps she
wouldn't be surprised at all.

"You look as though you dressed up to go out someplace,
too, old lady."

"Oh," she said, deprecatingly, "I'm just going down the
block to see Mrs. Braithwaite. You remember her girl, Vickie?
Well, she done had her baby. We going to the hospital to visit
her."

"Vickie got a baby? *Already?*"

"Well, the young folks don't wait these days, you know
that." She laughed and sipped her beer.

Rufus looked over at Vivaldo with a frown. "Damn," he
said. "How's she doing?"

"Pretty well—under the *circumstances.*" Her pause suggested that the circumstances were grim. "She had a right fine
boy, weighed seven pounds." She was about to say more; but
Ida entered.

She was already quite tall, nearly as tall as she was going to
be. She, too, had been dealing in hot combs and curling irons,
Vivaldo's later impression that she had been in pigtails was
due to the fact that her hair had been curled tightly all over
her head. The dress she wore was long and blue and full, of
some rustling material which billowed above her long legs.

She came into the room, looking only at her brother, with
an enormous, childlike smile. He and Rufus stood up.

"You see, I got here," said Rufus, smiling, and he and his
sister kissed each other on the cheek. Their mother stood
watching them with a proud, frowning smile.

"I see you did," said Ida, moving a little away from him,
and laughing. Her delight in seeing her brother was so real
that Vivaldo felt a kind of anguish, thinking of his own house,
his own sister. "I been *wondering* if you'd make it—you keep
so *busy* all the time."

She said the last with a wry, proud, grown-up exasperation,
as one submitting to the penalties imposed by her brother's
power and glory. She had not looked at Vivaldo, though she
was vividly aware of him. But Vivaldo would not exist until
Rufus permitted it.

He permitted it now, tentatively, with one hand on his

sister's neck. He turned her toward Vivaldo. "I brought a friend of mine along, Vivaldo Moore. This is my sister, Ida."

They shook hands. Her handshake was as brief as her mother's had been, but stronger. And she looked at Vivaldo differently, as though he were a glamorous stranger, glamorous not only in himself and his color but in his scarcely to-be-imagined relation to her brother.

"Well, now, where," asked Rufus, teasingly, "do you think you'd like to go, young lady?"

And he watched her, grinning. But there was a constraint in the room now, too, which had not been there before, which had entered with the girl who would soon be a woman. She stood there like a target and a prize, the natural prey of someone—somewhere—who would soon be on her trail.

"Oh, I don't care," she said. "Anywhere you-all want to go."

"But you so dressed up—you sure you ain't ashamed to be seen with us?"

He was also dressed up, in his best dark suit and a shirt and tie he had borrowed from Vivaldo.

Ida and her mother laughed. "Boy, you stop teasing your sister," said Mrs. Scott.

"Well, go on, get your coat," Rufus said, "and we'll make tracks."

"We going *far?*"

"We going far enough for you to have to wear a *coat.*"

"She don't mean is you going far," said Mrs. Scott. "She trying to find out *where* you going and what time you coming back."

Ida had moved to the door by which she had entered and stood there, hesitating. "Go on," her mother said, "get your coat and mine, too. I'm going to walk down the block with you."

Ida left and Mrs. Scott smiled and said, "If she thought I was coming with you today, she be *highly* displeased. She want you all to herself today."

She picked up the empty beer glasses and carried them into the kitchen. "When they were younger," she said to Vivaldo, "Rufus just couldn't do no wrong, far as Ida was concerned."

She ran water to rinse out the glasses. "She always been real afraid of the dark, you know? but, shucks, honey, many's the time Ida used to crawl out of her bed, middle of the night, and go running through this dark house to get in bed with Rufus. Look like she just felt *safe* with him. I don't know why, Rufus sure didn't pay her much mind."

"That's not true," said Rufus, "I was always real sweet to my little sister."

She put the glasses down to drain and dried her hands. She peered into a hand mirror and patted her hair and then carefully put on her hat. "You used to tease her something awful," she said.

Ida returned, wearing a coat trimmed with fur, and with her mother's coat over her arm.

"Ah!" cried Rufus, "she's glamorous!"

"She's beautiful," said Vivaldo.

"Now, if you-all going to make fun of me," said Ida, "I ain't going to come with you nowhere."

Mrs. Scott put on her coat and looked critically at her bareheaded daughter. "If she don't stop being so glamorous, she going to end up with the flu." She pulled Ida's collar up higher and buttoned it. "Can't get nobody in this family to wear a hat," she said, "and then they wonder why they always full of cold." Ida made an impatient gesture. "She afraid a hat going to mess up her hair. But she ain't afraid of the wind doing nothing to it." They laughed, Ida a little unwillingly, as though she were embarrassed that the joke was being shared with Vivaldo.

They walked down the wintry block. Children were playing stickball in the streets, but it was otherwise nearly empty. A couple of boys were standing on a nearby stoop and they greeted Ida and Rufus and Mrs. Scott and looked with interest at Vivaldo; looked at him as though he were a member of an enemy gang, which, indeed, he had been, not very long before. An elderly woman slowly climbed the brownstone steps of a run-down building. A black sign jutted out from the building, saying, in white letters, MOUNT OLIVE APOSTOLIC FAITH CHURCH.

"I don't know where your father done got to," said Mrs. Scott.

"He right around the corner, in Jimmy's Bar," said Ida, shortly. "I doubt if he be home by the time I get back."

"Because I know you ain't intending to be home before four in the morning," said Mrs. Scott, smiling.

"Well, he ain't going to be home by *then*," said Ida, "and you know it well as I do."

A girl came toward them now, narrow-hipped, swift, and rough-looking. She, too, was bareheaded, with short, dirty, broken-off hair. She wore a man's suede jacket, too large for her, and she held it at the neck with her hand. Vivaldo watched Ida watching the girl approach.

"Here come Willa Mae," said Mrs. Scott. "Poor little thing."

Then the girl stood before them, and she smiled. When she smiled her face was very different. She was very young.

"How you-all today?" she asked. "Rufus, I ain't seen you for the longest time."

"Just fine," Rufus said. "How you making it?" He held his head very high and his eyes were expressionless. Ida looked down at the ground and held on to her mother.

"Oh"—she laughed—"I can't complain. Wouldn't do no good nohow."

"You still at the same place?"

"Sure. Where you think I'm going to move to?"

There was a pause. The girl looked at Vivaldo, looked away. "Well, I got to be going," she said. "Nice running into you." She was no longer smiling.

"Nice seeing you," said Rufus.

After the girl had gone, Ida, said disapprovingly, "She used to be your girl friend, too."

Rufus ignored this. He said to Vivaldo, "She used to be a nice girl. Some cat turned her on, and then he split." He spat on the sidewalk. "Man, what a scene."

Mrs. Scott halted before steps leading up into a tenement. Ida took Rufus by the arm. "I got to leave you children here," said Mrs. Scott. She looked at Rufus. "What time you going to bring this girl home?"

"Oh, I don't know. It won't be late. I know she want to go out night-clubbing but I ain't going to let her get *too drunk*."

Mrs. Scott smiled and held out her hand to Vivaldo.

"Nice meeting you, son," she said. "You make Rufus bring you by again, you hear? Don't you be a stranger."

"No ma'am. Thank you, I'll come up again real soon."

But he never did see her again, not until Rufus was dead. Rufus had never invited him home again.

"I'll be seeing *you* later, young lady," she said. She started up the steps. "You children have a good time."

She had been fourteen or fifteen that day. She would be twenty-one or twenty-two now. She had told him that she remembered that day; but he wondered *how* she remembered it. He had not seen her again until she had become a woman and at that time he had not remembered their first meeting. But he remembered it now. He remembered delight and discomfort. What did she remember?

He thought, "I've got to get some sleep." *I've got to get some sleep.* But the people in his novel massed against him. They seemed to watch him with a kind of despairing, beseeching reproach. His typewriter, a dark shapeless presence, accused him, reminding him of the days and nights, the weeks, the months, the years by now, that he had spent without sleep, pursuing easier and less honorable seductions. Then he turned on his belly and his sex accused him, his sex immediately filled with blood. He turned on his back with a furious sigh. He thought, *I'm twenty-eight years old. I'm too old for this bit.* He closed his eyes and he groaned. He thought, *I've got to finish that damn novel,* and he thought, *Oh, God, make her love me, oh God, let me love.*

"What a wonderful day!" cried Ida.

He watched her face for a moment, looking extremely pleased himself, and then delicately increased his pressure on her elbow, more for the pleasure this gave him than to hurry them across the broad, impatient, startling Avenue.

"Yes," he said, "it's a great day."

They had just come up from the subway and it was perhaps this ascent from darkness to day which made the streets so dazzling. They were on Broadway at Seventy-second Street, walking uptown—for Cass and Richard had moved, they were climbing that well-known ladder, Cass said. The light seemed to fall with an increased hardness, examining and inciting the city with an unsparing violence, like the violence of love, and striking from the city's grays and blacks a splendor as of steel on steel. In the windows of tall buildings flame wavered, alive, in ice.

There was a high, driving wind which brightened the eyes and the faces of the people and forced their lips slightly apart, so that they all seemed to be carrying, to some immense encounter, the bright, fragile bubble of a lifetime of expectation. Bright boys in windbreakers, some of them with girls whose hair, whose fingertips, caught the light, looked into polished delicatessen windows, the windows of shops, paused at the entrances of movie theatres to look at the gleaming stills; and their voices, which shared the harsh quality of the light which covered them, seemed breaking on the air like glass splinters.

Children, in great gangs and clouds, erupted out of side streets with the sound of roller skates and came roaring down on their elders like vengeance long prepared, or the arrow released from the bow.

"I've never *seen* such a day," he said to Ida, and it was true. Everything seemed to be swollen, thrusting and shifting and changing, about to burst into music or into flame or revelation.

Ida said nothing. He felt, rather then saw her smile, and he was delighted all over again by her beauty. It was as though she were wearing it especially for him. She was more friendly with him today than she had ever been. He did not feel today, as he had felt for so long, that she was evading him, locking herself away from him, forcing him to remain a stranger in her life. Today she was gayer and more natural, as though she had at last decided to come out of mourning. There was in her aspect the flavor of something won, the atmosphere of hard decisions past. She had come up from the valley.

She moved with a wonderful, long-legged stride and she carried her head high, as though it had borne, but only yesterday, the weight of an African water jar. Her mother's head had borne the weight of white folk's washing, and it was because Ida had never known what to make of this fact—should she be ashamed of it, or proud?—that there mingled in her regal beauty something of the too-quick, diffident, plebeian disdain. She was working now as a waitress in a chain restaurant on the eastern edge of the Village and her confusion revealed itself in her attitude toward her customers, an attitude which was at once haughty and free. He had often watched her as she crossed the floor in her checkered apron, her face a dark mask behind which belligerence battled with humility. This was in her eyes which never for an instant lost their wariness and which were always ready, within a split second, to turn black and lightless with contempt. Even when she was being friendly there was something in her manner, in her voice, which carried a warning; she was always waiting for the veiled insult or the lewd suggestion. And she had good reason for it, she was not being fantastical or perverse. It was the way the world treated girls with bad reputations and every colored girl had been born with one.

Now, as she walked beside him, trim and oddly elegant in a heavy, dark blue coat, and with her head covered by an old-fashioned and rather theatrical shawl, he saw that both her vanity and her contempt were being swollen by the glances which rested on her as briefly and unforgettably as the touch of a whip. She was very, very dark, she was beautiful; and he was proud to be with her, artlessly proud, in the shining, overt, male way; but the eyes they passed accused him, enviously, of a sniggering, back-alley conquest. White men looked at her, then looked at him. They looked at her as though she were no better, though more lascivious and rare, than a whore. And then the eyes of the men sought his, inviting a wet complicity.

The women, too. They saw Ida first and might have been happy to admire her if she had been walking alone. But she was with Vivaldo, which gave her the status of a thief. The means that she had used to accomplish this abduction were beneath or perhaps beyond them, but their eyes briefly accused Vivaldo of betrayal, then narrowed against a dream or a nightmare, and turned away.

Ida strode past, seeming not to see them. She conveyed with this stride and her bright, noncommittal face how far she felt them to be beneath her. She had the great advantage of being extraordinary—however she might bear this distinction, or however others might wish to deny it; whereas, her smile suggested, these people, the citizens of the world's most be-wildered city, were so common that they were all but invisible. Nothing was simpler for her than to ignore, or to seem to ignore, these people: nothing was farther beyond them than the possibility of ignoring her. And the disadvantage at which they thus were placed, for which, after all, they had only them-selves to blame, said something which Vivaldo could scarcely believe concerning the poverty of their lives.

So their passage raised small clouds of male and female hos-tility which blew into their faces like dust. And Ida accepted this spiteful tribute with a spiteful pride.

"What are you humming?" he asked. She had been hum-ming to herself for a block or so.

She continued humming for another second, coming to the end of a phrase. Then she said, smiling. "You wouldn't know it. It's an old church song. I woke up with it this morning and it's been with me all day."

"What is it?" he asked. "Won't you sing it for me?"

"You not about to get religion, are you?" She looked at him sideways, grinning. "I used to have religion, did you know that? A long time ago, when I was a little girl."

"No," he said, "there's a whole lot about you I don't know. Sing your song."

She bent her head toward him, leaning more heavily on his arm, as though they were two children. The colors of the shawl flashed.

She sang, in her low, slightly rough voice, whispering the words to him:

> *I woke up this morning with my mind*
> *Stayed on Jesus.*
> *I woke up this morning with my mind*
> *Stayed on Jesus.*

"That's a great way to wake up," he said.
And she continued:

> *I stayed all day with my mind*
> *Stayed on Jesus.*
> *Hallelu, Hallelu*
> *Hallelujah!*

"That's a great song," he said. "That's tremendous. You've got a wonderful voice, you know that?"

"I just woke up with it—and it made me feel, I don't know—different than I've felt for months. It was just as though a burden had been taken off me."

"You still *do* have religion," he said.

"You know, I think I do? It's funny, I haven't thought of church or any of that type stuff for years. But it's still there, I guess." She smiled and sighed. "Nothing ever goes away." And then she smiled again, looking into his eyes. This shy, confiding smile made his heart move up until it hung like a Ferris wheel at its zenith, looking down at the fair. "It seems to go away," she said in a wondering tone, "but it doesn't, it all comes back." And his heart plunged; he watched her face, framed by the brilliant shawl. "I guess it's true, what they used to tell me—if you can get through the worst, you'll see the best."

They turned off the Avenue, toward Cass' house.

"What a beautiful girl you are," he said. She turned from him, irrepressibly humming her song. "You are, you know."

"Well," she said, and turned toward him again, "I don't know if I'm beautiful or not. But I know you're crazy."

"I'm crazy about *you*. I hope you know *that*."

He said it lightly and did not know if he should curse himself for his cowardice or congratulate himself on his restraint.

"I don't know what I'd have done without you," she said, "these last few months. I know I didn't see much of you, but I knew you were there, I felt it, and it helped—oh, more than I'll ever be able to tell you."

"I had the feeling sometimes," he said, "that you thought I was just being a pest." And now he did curse himself for not saying more precisely what he felt and for sounding so much like a child.

But this was his day, apparently—he seemed to be coming to the end of the tunnel in which he had been traveling so long. "A pest!" she cried, and laughed. "If you aren't the cutest thing." Then, soberly, "I was the one who was the *pest*—but I just couldn't help it."

They turned into a gray, anonymous building which had two functionless pillars on either side of the door and an immense plain of imitation marble and leather beyond it. And he suddenly remembered—it had gone entirely out of his mind—that this lunch was for the purpose of celebrating the publication of Richard's first novel. He said to Ida, "You know, this lunch is a celebration and I forgot to bring anything."

The elevator man rose from his chair, looking at them dubiously, and Vivaldo gave him the floor number and then, as the man still seemed to hesitate, the number of the apartment. He closed the door and the elevator began to move upward.

"What are we celebrating?" Ida asked.

"You and me. We finally have a real date together. You didn't call to break it at the last minute and you haven't said you've got to rush right home after just *one* drink." He grinned at Ida, but he was aware that he was speaking partly for the benefit of the elevator man, whom he had never noticed before. But he disliked him intensely now.

"No, come on, now, what are we *really* celebrating? Or maybe I should say what are Richard and Cass celebrating?"

"Richard's novel. It's published. It'll be in all the bookstores Monday."

"Oh, Vivaldo," she said, "that's wonderful. He must feel *wonderful.* A real, honest-to-God published writer."

"Yes," he said, "one of our boys made it." He was touched by her enthusiasm. And he was aware, at the same time, that she had also been speaking for the benefit of the elevator man.

"It must be wonderful for Cass, too," she said. "And for *you*, he's your friend." She looked at him. "When are you going to bring out *your* novel?"

This question, and even more her way of asking it, seemed to contain implications he scarcely dared to trust. "One of these days," he muttered; and he blushed. The elevator stopped and they walked into a corridor. Richard's door was to the left of them. "It looks like I've got my hands full right now."

"What do you mean? It's not working the way you want it to?"

"The novel, you mean?"

"Yes." Then, as they faced each other before the door, "What did you think I meant?"

"Oh, that's what I thought you meant, all right." He thought, *Now listen, don't spoil it, don't rush it, you stupid bastard, don't spoil it.* "It's just that it's not exactly what *I* meant."

"What *did* you mean?" She was smiling.

"I meant—I hoped I'm going to have my hands full now, with you." She called part of her smile back, but she still looked amused. She watched him. "You know—dinners and lunches and—walks—and movies and things—with you. With you." He dropped his eyes. "You know what I mean?" Then, in the warm, electrical silence, he raised his eyes to hers, and he said, "You know what I mean."

"Well," she said, "let's talk about it after lunch, okay?" She turned from him and faced the door. He did not move. She looked at him with her eyes very wide. "Aren't you going to ring the bell?"

"Sure." They watched each other. Ida reached out and touched him on the cheek. He grabbed her hand and held it for a moment against his face. Very gently, she pulled her hand away. "You are the cutest thing I've ever seen," she said, "you *are*. Go on and ring that bell, I'm hungry."

He laughed and pressed the button. They heard the sour buzzing inside the apartment, then confusion, a slammed door, and footsteps. He took one of Ida's hands in both of his. "I want to be with you," he said. "I want you to be with me. I want that more than I've ever wanted anything in the world."

Then the door opened and Cass stood before them, dressed in a rusty orange frock, her hair pulled back and falling around her shoulders. She held a cigarette in one hand, with which she made a gesture of exaggerated welcome.

"Come in, children," she said, "I'm delighted to see you, but there's absolute chaos in this house today. Everything's gone wrong." She closed the door behind them. They heard a child screaming somewhere in the apartment, and Richard's voice raised in anger. Cass listened for a moment, her forehead wrinkled with worry. "That's Michael," she said, helplessly. "He's been impossible all day—fighting with his brother, with his father, with me. Richard finally gave him a spanking and I guess he's going to leave him in his room." Michael's screams diminished and they heard the voices of Michael and his father working out, apparently, the terms of a truce. Cass lifted her head. "Well. I'm sorry to keep you standing in the hall. Take off your things, I'll show you into the living room and give you things to drink and to nibble on—you'll need them, lunch is going to be late, of course. Ida, how are you? I haven't seen you in God knows when." She took Ida's coat and shawl. "Do you mind if I don't hang them up? I'll just dump them in the bedroom, other people are coming over after lunch." They followed her into the large bedroom. Ida immediately walked over to the large, full-length mirror and worriedly patted her hair and applied new lipstick.

"I'm just fine, Cass," she said, "but you're the one—! You got a famous husband all of a sudden. How does it feel?"

"He's not even famous *yet*," said Cass, "and, already I can't stand it. Somehow, it just seems to reduce itself to having drinks and dinners with lots of people you certainly wouldn't be talking to if they weren't"—she coughed—"in the *profession*. God, what a profession. I had no idea." Then she laughed. They started toward the living room. "Try to persuade Vivaldo to become a plumber."

"No, dear," said Ida, "I wouldn't trust Vivaldo with no tools whatever. This boy is just as clumsy as they come. I'm always expecting him to fall over those front feet he's got. Never saw anybody with so *many* front feet." The living room was down two steps and the wide windows opened on a view of the river. Ida seemed checked, but only for an instant by the view of the river. She walked into the center of the room. "This is wonderful. You people have really got some space."

"We were really very lucky," Cass said. "The people who had it had been here for years and years and they finally decided to move to Connecticut—or someplace like that. I don't remember. Anyway, since they'd been here so long the rent hadn't gone up much, you know? So it's really a lot cheaper than most things like this in the city." She looked over at Ida. "You know, you look wonderful, you really do. I'm so glad to see you."

"I'm glad to see you," said Ida, "and I feel fine, I feel better than I've felt, oh, in years." She crossed to the bar, and stood facing Cass. "Look like you people done got serious about your drinking, too," she said, in a raucous, whiskey voice. "Let me have a taste of that there Cutty Sark."

Cass laughed, "I thought you were a bourbon woman." She dropped some ice in a glass.

"When it comes to liquor," Ida said, "I's *anybody's* woman." And she laughed, looking exactly like a little girl. "Let me have some water in that, sugar, I don't want to get carried away here this afternoon." She looked toward Vivaldo, who stood on the steps, watching her. She leaned toward Cass. "Honey, who's that funny-looking number standing in the do'way?"

"Oh, he drops by from time to time. He always looks that way. He's harmless."

"I'll have the same thing the lady's drinking," said Vivaldo, and joined them at the bar.

"Well, I'm glad you told me he's harmless," Ida said, and winked at him, and drummed her long fingernails on the bar.

"I'll have a short drink with you," said Cass, "and then I'm simply going to have to vanish. I've got to finish fixing lunch—and we have to *eat* it—and I'm not even dressed yet."

"Well, I'll help you in the kitchen," Ida said. "What time are all these other people coming over?"

"About five, I guess. There's this TV producer coming, he's supposed to be very bright and liberal—Steve Ellis, does that sound right?—"

"Oh, yes," said Ida, "he's supposed to be very good, that man. He's *very* well known." She mentioned a show of his she had seen some months ago, which utilized Negroes, and which had won a great many awards. "Wow." She wiggled her shoulders. "Who else is coming?"

"Well. Ellis. And Richard's editor. And some other writer whose name I can't remember. And I guess they're bringing their wives." She sipped her drink, looking rather weary. "I can't imagine why we're doing this. I guess it's mainly on account of the TV man. But Richard's publishers are giving Richard a small party Monday—in their offices—and he could just as well see all those people then."

"Buck up, old girl," said Vivaldo. "You're just going to have to get used to it."

"I expect so." She gave them a quick, mischievous grin,

and whispered, "But they seem so silly—! those I've met. And they're so *serious*, they just *shine* with it."

Vivaldo laughed. "That's treason, Cass. Be careful."

"I know. They really are getting behind the book, though; they have great hopes for it. You haven't seen it yet, have you?" She walked over to the sofa, where books and papers were scattered and picked the book up, thoughtfully. She crossed the room again. "Here it is."

She put the book down on the bar between Ida and Vivaldo. "It's had great advance notices. You know, 'literate,' 'adult,' 'thrilling'—that sort of thing. Richard'll show them to you. It's even been compared to *Crime and Punishment* —because they both have such a simple story line, I guess." Vivaldo looked at her sharply. "Well. I'm only quoting."

The sun broke free of a passing cloud and filled the room. They squinted down at the book on the bar. Cass stood quietly behind them.

The book jacket was very simple, jagged red letters on a dark blue ground: *The Strangled Men. A novel of murder, by Richard Silenski*. He looked at the jacket flap which described the story and then turned the book over to find himself looking into Richard's open, good-natured face. The paragraph beneath the picture summed up Richard's life, from his birth to the present: *Mr. Silenski is married and is the father of two sons, Paul (11) and Michael (8). He makes his home in New York City.*

He put the book down. Ida picked it up.

"It's wonderful," he said to Cass. "You must be proud." He took her face between his hands and kissed her on the forehead. He picked up his drink. "There's always something wonderful about a book, you know?—when it's really, all of a sudden, a book, and it's there between covers. And there's your name on it. It must be a great feeling."

"Yes," said Cass.

"You'll know that feeling soon," said Ida. She was examining the book intently. She looked up with a grin. "I bet I just found out something you never knew," she said to Vivaldo.

"Impossible," said Vivaldo. "I'm sure I know everything Richard knows."

"*I* wouldn't be so sure," said Cass.

"I bet you don't know Cass's real name."

Cass laughed. "He does, but he's forgotten it."

He looked at her. "That's true, I have. What *is* your real name—? I know you hate it, that's why nobody ever uses it."

"Richard just did," she said. "I think he did it just to tease me."

Ida showed him the book's dedication page, which read *for Clarissa, my wife.* "That's cute, isn't it?" She looked at Cass. "You sure had me fooled, baby; you just don't seem to be the Clarissa *type.*"

"As it turned out," said Cass, with a smile. Then she looked at Vivaldo. "Ah," she said, "did you happen to note a very small note in today's theatrical section?" She went to the sofa and picked up one of the newspapers and returned to Vivaldo. "Look. Eric's coming home."

"Who's Eric?" Ida asked.

"Eric Jones," Cass said. "He's an actor friend of ours who's been living in France for the last couple of years. But he's been signed to do a play on Broadway this fall."

Vivaldo read. *Lee Bronson has signed Eric Jones, who last appeared locally three seasons ago in the short-lived* Kingdom of the Blind, *for the role of the elder son in the Lane Smith drama,* Happy Hunting Ground, *which opens here in November.*

"Son of a bitch," said Vivaldo, looking very pleased. He turned to Cass. "Have you heard from him?"

"Oh, no," said Cass, "not for a very long time."

"It'll be nice to see him again," Vivaldo said. He looked at Ida. "You'll like him. Rufus knew him, we were all very good friends." He folded the paper and dropped it on the bar. "Everybody's famous, goddamnit, except me."

Richard came into the room, looking harried and boyish, wearing an old gray sweater over a white T-shirt and carrying his belt in his hands.

"It's easy to see what you've been doing," said Vivaldo, smiling. "We heard it all the way in here."

Richard looked at the belt shamefacedly and threw it on the sofa. "I didn't really use it on him. I just made believe I was going to. I probably should have whaled the daylights out of him." He said to Cass, "What's the matter with him all of a sudden? He's never acted like this before."

"I've already told you what I think it is. It's the new house and kind of new excitement, and he doesn't see as much of you as he's used to, and he's reacted to all of this very badly. He'll get over it, but it's going to take a little time."

"Paul's not like that. Hell, he's gone out and made friends already. He's having a ball."

"Richard, Paul and Michael are not at all *alike*."

He stared at her and shook his head. "That's true. Sorry." He turned to Ida and Vivaldo. "Excuse us. We're fascinated by our offspring. We sometimes sit around and talk about them for hours. Ida, you look wonderful, it's great to see you." He took her hand in his, looking into her eyes. "Are you all right?"

"I'm fine, Richard. And it's wonderful to see *you*. Especially now that you're such a success."

"Ah, you mustn't listen to my wife," he said. He went behind the bar. "Everybody's got a drink except me, I guess. And *I*'—he looked very boyish, very secure and happy—"am going to have a dry martini on the rocks." He opened the ice bucket. "Only, there aren't any rocks."

"I'll get you some ice," Cass said. She put her drink on the bar and picked up the ice bucket. "You know, I think we're going to have to buy some ice from the delicatessen."

"Well, I'll go down and do that later, chicken." He pinched her cheek. "Don't worry."

Cass left the room. Richard grinned at Vivaldo. "If you hadn't got here today, I swore I was just going to cut you out of my heart forever."

"You knew I'd be here." He raised his glass. "Congratulations." Then, "What's this I hear about all the TV networks just crying for you?"

"Don't exaggerate. There's just *one* producer who's got some project he wants to talk to me about, I don't even know what it is. But my agent thinks I should see him."

Vivaldo laughed. "Don't sound so defensive. I *like* TV."

"You're a liar. You haven't even got a TV set."

"Well, that's just because I'm *poor*. When I get to be a success like you, I'll go out and buy me the biggest screen on the market." He watched Richard's face and laughed again. "I'm just teasing you."

"Yeah. Ida, see what you can do to civilize this character. He's a barbarian."

"I know," Ida said, sadly, "but I hardly know what to do about it. Of course," she added, "if you were to offer me an autographed copy of your book, I might come up with an inspiration."

"It's a deal," Richard said. Cass came back with the ice bucket and Richard took it from her and set it on the bar. He mixed his drink. Then he joined them on the other side of the bar and put his arm around Cass' shoulders. "To the best Saturday we've ever had," he said, and raised his glass. "May there be many more." He took a large swallow of his drink. "I love you all," he said.

"We love you, too," said Vivaldo.

Cass kissed Richard on the cheek. "Before I go and try to salvage lunch—tell me, just what kind of arrangement *did* you make with Michael? Just so I'll know."

"He's taking a nap. I promised to wake him in time for cocktails. We have to buy him some ginger ale."

"And Paul?"

"Oh, Paul. He'll tear himself away from his cronies in time to come upstairs and get washed and meet the people. Wild horses wouldn't keep him away." He turned to Vivaldo. "He's been bragging about me all over the house."

Cass watched him for a moment. "Very well managed. And now I leave you."

Ida picked up her glass. "Wait a minute. I'm coming with you."

"You don't have to, Ida. I can do it."

"These men can get drunk, too, if we keep them waiting too long. I'll help you, we can get it done in no time." She followed Cass to the doorway. With one foot on the step, she turned. "Now, I'm going to hold you to your promise, Richard. About that book, I mean."

"I'm going to hold you to yours. You're the one who got the dirty end of *this* deal."

She looked at Vivaldo. "Oh, I don't know. I might think of something."

"I hope you know what you're getting into," Cass said. "I don't like that look on Vivaldo's face at *all*."

Ida laughed. "He *is* kind of simple-looking, I declare. Come on. I'll tell you about it in the kitchen."

"Don't believe a word Cass says about me," Vivaldo called.

"Oh, you mean she *knows* something about you? Come on, Cass, honey, we going to get down to the knitty-gritty *this* afternoon." And they disappeared.

"You've always had a thing about colored girls, haven't you?" Richard asked, after a moment. There was something curiously wistful in his voice.

Vivaldo looked at him. "No. I've never been involved with a colored girl."

"No. But you used to do a lot of tomcatting up in Harlem. And it's so logical, somehow, that you should be trying to make it with a colored girl now—you certainly scraped the bottom of the white barrel."

Against his will, Vivaldo was forced to laugh. "Well. I don't think Ida's color has a damn thing to do with it, one way or the other."

"Are you sure? Isn't she just another in your long line of waifs and strays and unfortunates?"

"Richard," Vivaldo said, and he put his glass down on the bar, "are you trying to bug me? What is it?"

"Of course I'm not trying to bug you," Richard said. "I just think that maybe it's time you straightened out—settled down—time you figured out what you want to do and started doing it instead of bouncing around like a kid. You're not a kid."

"Well, I think it's time you stopped treating me like one. I know what I want to do and I *am* doing it. All right? And I've got to do it my own way. So get off my back." He smiled, but it was too late.

"I didn't think I was on your back," said Richard. "I'm sorry."

"I didn't mean it the way it sounded, you know that."

"Let's just forget it, okay?"

"Well, hell, I don't want you mad at me."

"I'm *not* mad at you." He walked to the window and stood there, looking out. With his back to Vivaldo, he said, "You didn't really like my book much, did you?"

"So that's it."

"What?" Richard turned, the sunlight full on his face, revealing the lines in his forehead, around and under his eyes, and around his mouth and chin. The face was full of lines; it was a tough face, a good face, and Vivaldo had loved it for a long time. Yet, the face lacked something, he could not have said what the something was, and he knew his helpless judgment was unjust.

He felt tears spring to his eyes. "Richard, we talked about the book and I told you what I thought, I told you that it was a brilliant idea and wonderfully organized and beautifully written and—" He stopped. He had not liked the book. He could not take it seriously. It was an able, intelligent, mildly perceptive *tour de force* and it would never mean anything to anyone. In the place in Vivaldo's mind in which books lived, whether they were great, mangled, mutilated, or mad, Richard's book did not exist. There was nothing he could do about it. "And you yourself said that the next book would be better."

"What are you crying about?"

"What?" He wiped his eyes with the back of his hand. "Nothing." He walked over to the bar and leaned on it. Some deep and curious cunning made him add, "You talk as though you didn't want us to be friends any more."

"Oh, crap. Is that what you think? Of course we're friends, we'll be friends till we die." He walked to the bar and put his hand on Vivaldo's shoulder, leaning down to look into his face. "Honest. Okay?"

They shook hands. "Okay. Don't bug me any more."

Richard laughed. "I *won't* bug you any more, you stupid bastard."

Ida came to the doorway. "Lunch is on the table. Come on, now, hurry, before it gets cold."

They were all a little drunk by the time lunch was over, having drunk with it two bottles of champagne; and eventually they sat in the living room again as the sun began to grow fiery, preparing to go down. Paul arrived, dirty, breathless, and cheerful. His mother sent him into the bathroom to wash and change his clothes. Richard remembered the ice that had to be bought for the party and the ginger ale that he had promised Michael, and he went downstairs to buy them. Cass decided that she had better change her clothes and put up her hair.

Ida and Vivaldo had the living room to themselves for a short time. Ida put on an old Billie Holiday record and she and Vivaldo danced.

There was a hammer knocking in his throat as she stepped into his arms with a friendly smile, one hand in his hand, one hand resting lightly on his arm. He held her lightly at the waist. His fingers, at her waist, seemed to have become abnormally and dangerously sensitive, and he prayed that his face did not show the enormous, illicit pleasure which entered him through his fingertips. He seemed to feel, beneath the heavy fabric of the suit she wore, the texture of the cloth of her blouse, the delicate obstruction which was the fastening of her skirt, the slick material of her slip which seemed to purr and crackle under his fingers, against her smooth, warm skin. She seemed to be unaware of the liberties being taken by his stiff, unmoving fingers. She moved with him, both guiding and being guided by him, effortlessly keeping her feet out of the path of his great shoes. Their bodies barely touched but her hair tickled his chin and gave off a sweet, dry odor and suggested, as did everything about this girl, a deep, slow-burning, carnal heat. He wanted to hold her closer to him. Perhaps, now, at this very moment, as she looked up at him, smiling, he would lower his head and wipe that smile from her face, placing his unsmiling mouth on hers.

"Your hands are cold," he said, for the hand which held his was very dry, and the fingertips were cool.

"That's supposed to mean that I've got a warm heart," said Ida, "but what it really means is poor circulation."

"I prefer," he said, "to believe that you've got a warm heart."

"I was counting on that," she said, with a laugh, "but when you get to know me better you'll find out that I'm the one who's right. I'm afraid," she said, with a teasing, frowning smile, "that I'm usually right." She added, "About me."

"I wish I knew you better," he said.

"So," she said, with a short, light laugh, "do I!"

Richard returned. Michael, grave and shy, came out of his exile and he and Paul were given ginger ales on the rocks.

Cass appeared in a high-necked, old-fashioned, burgundy-colored dress, and with her hair up. Richard put on a sport shirt and a more respectable-looking sweater, and Ida vanished to put on her face. The people began to arrive.

The first to arrive was Richard's editor, Loring Montgomery, a chunky, spectacled man, with smooth, graying hair, who was younger than he looked—nearly ten years younger, in fact, than Richard. He had a diffident manner and a nervous giggle. With him was Richard's agent, a dark-haired, dark-eyed young woman, who wore much silver and a little gold, and whose name was Barbara Wales. She, too, had a giggle but it was not nervous, and a great deal of manner but it was not diffident. She apparently felt that her status as Richard's agent created a bond of intimacy between herself and Cass; who, helplessly and miserably mesmerized, and handicapped by the volume of Miss Wales' voice and the razorlike distinctness of her syllables, trotted obediently behind her into the bedroom where coats and hats were to be deposited and where the women could repair their make-up.

"The bar is over here," Richard called, "whatever you're drinking, come and get it."

"I could stand another drink," Vivaldo said. "I've been drinking all day and I can't get drunk."

"Are you trying to?" asked Ida.

He looked at her and smiled. "No," he said, "no, I'm not trying to. But if I were, I couldn't make it, not today." They stood facing the window. "You're going to have supper with me, aren't you?"

"You're not hungry, *already*?"

"No. But I'm going to be hungry around suppertime."

"Well," she said, "ask me around suppertime."

"You're not suddenly going to decide you have to go home, or anything? You're not going to run out on me?"

"No," she said, "I'm going to stick with you until the bitter end. You've got to talk to that agent, you know."

"Do I have to?" He looked in the direction of the glittering Miss Wales.

"Of course you do. I'm sure it's one of the reasons Richard wanted you here this afternoon. And you have to talk to the editor, too."

"Why? I haven't got anything to show him."

"Well, you *will*. I'm sure Richard arranged all this partly for you. Now, you've got to cooperate."

"And what are you going to be doing while I'm having all these conferences?"

"I'll talk to Cass. Nobody's really interested in us; we don't write."

He kissed her hair. "You *are* the cutest thing," he said.

The doorbell rang. This time it was Steve Ellis, who had come with his wife. Ellis was a short, square man with curly hair and a boyish face. The face was just beginning, as is the way with boyish faces, not so much to harden as to congeal. He had a reputation as the champion of doomed causes, reaction's intrepid foe; and he walked into the drawing rooms of the world as though he expected to find the enemy ambushed there. His wife wore a mink coat and a flowered hat, seemed somewhat older than he, and was inclined to be talkative.

"Great meeting you, Silenski," he said. Though he was compelled to look up to Richard, he did so with his head at an odd and belligerent angle, as though he were looking up in order more clearly to sight down. The hand he extended to Richard with a bulletlike directness suggested also the arrogant limpness of hands which have the power to make or break: only custom prevented the hand from being kissed. "I've been hearing tremendous things about you. Maybe we can have a chat a little later."

And his smile was good-natured, open, and boyish. When he was introduced to Ida, he stood stock-still, throwing out his arms as though he were a little boy.

"You're an actress," he said. "You've *got* to be an actress."

"No," said Ida, "I'm not."

"But you *must* be. I've been looking for you for years. You're sensational!"

"Thank you, Mr. Ellis," she said, laughing, "but I am not an actress." Her laugh was a little strained but Vivaldo could not know whether this was due to nerves or displeasure. People stood in smiling groups around them. Cass stood behind the bar, watching.

Ellis smiled conspiratorially and pushed his head a little forward. "What do you *do*, then? Come on, tell me."

"Well, at the moment," Ida said, rather pulling herself to-gether, "I work as a waitress."

"A waitress. Well, my wife's here, so I won't ask you where you work." He stepped a little closer to Ida. "But what do you think about while you walk around waiting on tables?" Ida hesitated, and he smiled again, coaxing and tender. "Come *on*. You can't tell me that all you want is to get to be head waitress."

Ida laughed. Her lips curved rather bitterly, and she said, "No." She hesitated and looked toward Vivaldo, and Ellis followed her look. "I've sometimes thought of singing. That's what I'd like to do."

"Aha!" he cried, triumphantly, "I knew I'd get it out of you." He pulled a card out of his breast pocket. "When you get ready to make the break, and let it be soon, you come and see me. Don't you forget."

"You won't remember my name, Mr. Ellis." She said it lightly and the look with which she measured Ellis gave Vivaldo no clue as to what was going on in her mind.

"Your name," he said, "is Ida Scott. Right?"

"Right."

"Well, I never forget names or faces. Try me."

"That's true," said his wife, "he never forgets a name or a face. I don't know how he does it."

"I," said Vivaldo, "am not an actress."

Ellis looked startled, then he laughed. "You could have fooled me," he said. He took Vivaldo by the elbow. "Come and have a drink with me. Please."

"I don't know why I said that. I was half-kidding."

"But only half. What's your name?"

"Vivaldo. Vivaldo Moore."

"And you're not an actress—?"

"I'm a writer. Unpublished."

"A*ha*! You're working on something?"

"A novel."

"What's it about?"

"My novel's about Brooklyn."

"The tree? Or the kids or the murderers or the junkies?"

Vivaldo swallowed. "All of them."

"That's quite an assignment. And if you don't mind my

saying so, it sounds just a little bit old-fashioned." He put his hand before his mouth and burped. "Brooklyn's been done. *And* done."

No it hasn't, Vivaldo thought. "You mean," he said, with a smile, "that it doesn't have any TV possibilities?"

"It might have, who knows?" He looked at Vivaldo with friendly interest. "You really have a sneer in your voice when you say TV, you know that? What are you so afraid of?" He tapped Vivaldo on the chest. "Art doesn't exist in a vacuum; it isn't just for you and your handful of friends. Christ, if you knew how sick I am of this sensitive-young-man horseshit!"

"I'm sick of it, too," said Vivaldo. "I don't think of myself as a sensitive young man."

"No? You sound like one and you act like one. You look down your nose at everybody. Yes," he insisted, for Vivaldo looked at him in some surprise, "you think that most people are shit and you'd rather die than get yourself dirtied up in any of the *popular* arts." Then he gave Vivaldo a deliberate, insolent once-over. "And here you are, in your best suit, and I bet you live in some dingy, ice-water apartment and you can't even take your girl out to a night club." His voice dropped. "The colored girl, Miss Scott, you see I do remember names, she's your girl, isn't she? That's why you got pissed off at me. Man, you're too touchy."

"I thought you were too free."

"I bet you wouldn't have felt that if she were a white girl."

"I'd have felt that about any girl who happened to be with me."

But he wondered if Ellis were right. And he realized that he would never know, there would never be any way for him to know. He felt that Ellis had treated Ida with a subtle lack of respect. But he had spoken to her in the only way he could, and it was the way he spoke to everyone. All of the people in Ellis' world approached each other under cover of a manner designed to hide whatever they might really be feeling, about each other or about themselves. When confronted with Ida, who was so visibly rejected from the only world they knew, this manner was forced to become relatively personal, self-conscious, and tense. It became entangled with an effort to avoid being called into judgment; with a fear that their spiritual and social promissory notes might suddenly be called up. By being pressed into the service of an impulse that was real, the manner revealed itself as totally false and because it was false, it was sinister.

Then, as Ellis poured himself another applejack and he poured himself another Scotch, he realized that the things which Ellis had, and the things which Richard was now going to have, were things that he wanted very much. Ellis could get anything he wanted by simply lifting up a phone; head-waiters were delighted to see him; his signature on a bill or a check was simply not to be questioned. If he needed a suit, he bought it; he was certainly never behind in his rent; if he decided to fly to Istanbul tomorrow, he had only to call his travel agent. He was famous, he was powerful, and he was not really much older than Vivaldo, and he worked very hard.

Also, he could get the highest-grade stuff going; he had only to give the girl his card. And then Vivaldo realized why he hated him. He wondered what he would have to go through to achieve a comparable eminence. He wondered how much he was willing to give—to be powerful, to be adored, to be able to make it with any girl he wanted, to be sure of holding any girl he had. And he looked around for Ida. At the same time, it occurred to him that the question was not really what he was going to "get" but how he was to discover his possibilities and become reconciled to them.

Richard, now, was talking, or, rather, listening to Mrs. Ellis; Ida was listening to Loring; Cass sat on the sofa, listening to Miss Wales. Paul stood near her, looking about the room; Cass held him absently and yet rather desperately by the elbow.

"Anyway—I'd like to keep in touch with you, maybe you've got something." And Ellis handed him his card. "Why don't you give me a ring sometime? and I meant what I said to Miss Scott, too. I produce pretty good shows, you know." He grinned and punched Vivaldo on the shoulder. "You won't have to lower your *artistic* standards."

Vivaldo looked at the card, then looked at Ellis. "Thanks," he said. "I'll bear it in mind."

Ellis smiled. "I like you," he said. "I'm even willing to suggest an analyst for you. Let's join the party."

He walked over to Richard and Mrs. Ellis. Vivaldo walked over to Ida.

"I've been trying to find out about your novel," Loring said, "but your young lady here is *most* cagey. She won't give me a clue."

"I keep telling him that I don't know anything about it," Ida said, "but he won't believe me."

"She doesn't know much about it," Vivaldo said. "I'm not sure I know an awful lot about it myself." Abruptly, he felt himself beginning to tremble with weariness. He wanted to take Ida and go home. But she seemed pleased enough to stay; it was not really late; the last rays of the setting sun were fading beyond the river.

"Well," said Loring, "as soon as you *do* have something, I hope you'll get in touch with me. Richard thinks you're tremendously talented and I'd certainly trust his judgment."

He knew that Ida was puzzled and irritated by the mediocrity of his response. He tried to pump up enthusiasm, and watching Ida's face helped. He could not imagine what she thought of Ellis, and rage at himself, his jealousy, his fear, and his confusion, contributed a saving intensity to his evasive reply. Loring seemed more certain than ever that he was a diamond in the rough, and Ida more certain than ever that he was in need of hands to push him.

And he himself felt, in a way he had not felt before, that it was time for him to take the plunge. This was the water, the people in this room; it impressed him, certainly, as far from fine, but it was the only water there was.

Miss Wales now looked over toward him, but he avoided her eyes, giving all of his attention to Ida.

"Let's go," he said, in a low voice, "let's get out of here. I've had it."

"You want to go *now*? You haven't talked to Miss Wales." But he watched her eyes flicker toward the bar, where Ellis stood. And there was something in her face which he could not read, something speculative and hard.

"I don't *want* to talk to Miss Wales."

"Why on earth *not*? You're being silly."

"Look," he said, "is there someone here *you* want to talk

to?" *Oh, you idiot!* he groaned to himself. But the words were said.

She looked at him. "I don't know what you mean. What are you talking about?"

"Nothing," he said, sullenly. "I'm just crazy. Don't mind me."

"You were thinking something. What were you thinking?"

"Nothing," he said, "really nothing." He smiled. "I don't care. We can stay if you want to."

"I was only staying," she said, "on account of you."

He was about to say, Well then, we can *go,* but decided that it would be smarter not to. The doorbell rang. He said, "I just wanted to avoid getting involved in a supper deal with any of these people, that's all."

"But *who,*" she persisted, "did you think I wanted to talk to?"

"Oh," he said, "I thought if you were really serious about that singing business, you might have wanted to make an appointment with Ellis. I imagine he could be helpful."

She looked at him wearily, with mockery and pity. "Oh, Vivaldo," she said, "what a busy little mind you've got." Then her manner changed, and she said, very coldly, "You don't really have the right, you know, to worry about who I talk to. And what you're suggesting doesn't flatter me at *all.*" She kept her voice low, but it had begun to shake. "Maybe, now, I'll behave like what you think I am!" She walked over to the bar and stepped between Richard and Ellis. She was smiling. Ellis put one hand on her elbow and his face changed as he spoke to her, becoming greedier and more vulnerable. Richard went behind the bar to pour Ida a drink.

Vivaldo could have joined them, but he did not dare. Her outburst had come so mysteriously, and with such speed, that he was afraid to think of what might happen if he walked over to the bar. And she was right; he was wrong. Who she talked to was none of his business.

But her reaction had been so swift and terrible! Now, his advantage was gone. His patiently amassed and hoarded capital—of understanding and gallantry—had vanished in the twinkling of an eye.

"I'd like you to meet Sydney Ingram. This is Vivaldo Moore."

Cass was at his shoulder, presenting the newcomer, of whose arrival he had been vaguely aware. He had come alone. Vivaldo recognized his name because the boy's first novel had just been published and he wanted to read it. He was tall, nearly as tall as Vivaldo, with a pleasant, heavy-featured face and a great deal of black hair and, like Vivaldo, was dressed in a dark suit, probably his best one.

"I'm delighted to meet you," Vivaldo said—sincerely, for the first time that evening.

"I've read his novel," Cass said, "it's wonderful, you must read it."

"I want to," said Vivaldo. Ingram smiled, looking uncomfortable, and stared into his glass as though he wished he could drown in it.

"I've circulated enough for the time being," Cass said. "Let me stay with you two for a while." She led them slowly toward the big window. It was twilight, the sun was gone, soon the street lamps would be turned on. "Somehow, I don't think I'm cut out to be a literary hostess."

"You looked fine to me," said Vivaldo.

"You weren't trying to keep up a conversation with me. My attention just keeps wandering, I can't help it. I might as well be in a room full of physicists."

"What are they talking about over at the bar?" Vivaldo asked.

"Steve Ellis's responsibility to the televiewers of America," Ingram said. They laughed. "Don't laugh," said Ingram, "he, too, can become President. At least, he can read and write."

"I should think," said Cass, "that that would disqualify him."

She took each of them by one arm and they stood together in the darkening window, staring out at the highway and the shining water. "What a great difference there is," she said, "between dreaming of something and dealing with it!" Neither Vivaldo nor Ingram spoke. Cass turned to Ingram and, in a voice he had never heard her use before, wistful and desirous, she asked, "Are you working on something new, Mr. Ingram? I hope you are."

And his voice seemed, oddly, to respond to hers. They might have been calling each other across that breadth of water, seeking for each other as the darkness relentlessly fell. "Yes," he said, "I am, it's a new novel, it's a love story."

"A love story!" she said. Then, "And where does it take place?"

"Oh, here in the city. Now."

There was a silence. Vivaldo felt her small hand, under his elbow, tighten. "I'm looking forward to reading it," she said, "very much."

"Not more," he said, "than I am looking forward to finishing it and having it read, especially, if I may say so, by you."

She turned her face to Ingram, and he could not see her smile but he could feel it. "Thank you," she said. She turned to the window again and she sighed. "I suppose I must get back to my physicists."

They watched the street lamps click on.

"I'm going to have a drink," Cass said. "Will anyone join me?"

"Sure," said Vivaldo. They walked to the bar. Richard, Ellis, and Loring were sitting on the sofa. Miss Wales and Mrs. Ellis were standing at the bar. Ida was not in the room.

"Excuse me," said Vivaldo.

"I think somebody's in there!" cried Miss Wales.

He walked down the hall, but did not reach the bathroom. She was sitting in the bedroom, among all the coats and hats, perfectly still.

"Ida—?"

Her hands were folded in her lap and she was staring at the floor.

"Ida, why are you mad at me? I didn't mean anything."

She looked up at him. Her eyes were full of tears.

"Why did you have to say what you said? Everything was fine and I was so happy until you said that. You think I'm nothing but a whore. That's the only reason you want to see me." The tears dripped down her face. "All you white bastards are the same."

"Ida, I swear that isn't true. I swear that isn't true." He dropped to one knee beside the bed and tried to take her hands in his. She turned her face away. "Honey, I'm in love with you. I got scared and I got jealous, but I swear I didn't mean what you thought I meant, I didn't, I couldn't, I love you. Ida, please believe me. I love you."

Her body kept shaking and he felt her tears on his hands. He raised her hands to his lips and kissed them. He tried to look into her face, but she kept her face turned away. "Ida. Ida, please."

"I don't know any of these people," she said, "I don't care about them. They think I'm just another colored girl, and they trying to be nice, but they don't care. They don't want to talk to me. I only stayed because you asked me, and you've been so nice, and I was so proud of you, and now you've spoiled it all."

"Ida," he said, "if I've spoiled things between you and me, I don't know how I'm going to live. You can't say that. You've got to take it back, you've got to forgive me and give me another chance. Ida." He put one hand to her face and slowly turned it toward him. "Ida, I love you, I do, more than anything in this world. You've got to believe me. I'd rather die than hurt you." She was silent. "I was jealous and I was scared and that was a very dumb thing I said. But I was just afraid you didn't care about me. That's all. I didn't mean anything bad about you."

She sighed and reached for her purse. He gave her a handkerchief. She dried her eyes and blew her nose. She looked very tired and helpless.

He moved and sat beside her on the bed. She avoided looking at him but she did not move.

"Ida—" and he was shocked by the sound of his voice, it contained such misery. It did not seem to be his voice, it did not seem to be under his control. "I told you, I love you. Do you care about me?" She rose and walked to the mirror. He watched her. "Please tell me."

She looked into the mirror, then picked up her handbag from the bed. She opened it, closed it, then looked in the mirror again. Then she looked at him, "Yes," she said, helplessly, "yes, I do."

He took her face between his hands and kissed her. At first she did not answer him, seemed merely to be enduring him, seemed suspended, hanging, waiting. She was trembling and he tried to control her trembling with the force of his arms and hands. Then something seemed to bend in her, to give, and she put her arms around him, clinging to him. Finally, he whispered in her ear, "Let's get out of here. Let's go."

"Yes," she said, after a moment, "I guess it's time to go." But she did not step out of his arms at once. She looked at him and she said, "I'm sorry I was so silly. I know you didn't mean it."

"I'm sorry, too. I'm just a jealous, no-good bastard, I can't help it, I'm crazy about you."

And he kissed her again.

"——leaving so soon!" said Miss Wales. "And we never got a chance to talk!"

"Vivaldo," said Cass, "I'll call you this week. Ida, I can't call you, will you call me? Let's get together."

"I'm waiting for a script from you, you bum," said Ellis, "just as soon as you climb down out of that makeshift ivory tower. Nice meeting you, Miss Scott."

"He means it," said Mrs. Ellis. "He really means it."

"I was happy to meet you both," said Ingram, "very happy. Good luck with your novel."

Richard walked them to the door. "Are we still friends?"

"Are you kidding? Of course, we're still friends."

But he wondered if they were.

The door closed behind them and they stood in the corridor, staring at each other.

"Shall we go home?" he asked.

She watched him, her eyes very large and dark. "You got anything to eat down there?"

"No. But the stores are still open. We can get something."

She took his arm and they walked to the elevator. He rang the bell. He stared at her as though he could not believe his eyes.

"Good," she said. "We'll get something and I'll cook you a decent supper."

"I'm not very hungry," he said.

They heard the elevator door slam beneath them and the elevator began to rise.

The smell of the chicken she had fried the night before still hung in the room, and the dishes were still in the sink. The wishbone lay drying on the table, surrounded by the sticky glasses out of which they had drunk beer, and by their sticky coffee cups. Her clothes were thrown over a chair, his were mainly on the floor. He had awakened, she was asleep. She slept on her side, her dark head turned away from him, making no sound.

He leaned up a little and watched her face. Her face would now be, forever, more mysterious and impenetrable than the face of any stranger. Strangers' faces hold no secrets because the imagination does not invest them with any. But the face of a lover is an unknown precisely because it is invested with so much of oneself. It is a mystery, containing, like all mysteries, the possibility of torment.

She slept. He felt that she was sleeping partly in order to avoid him. He fell back on his pillow, staring up at the cracks in the ceiling. She was in his bed but she was far from him; she was with him and yet she was not with him. In some deep, secret place she watched herself, she held herself in check, she fought him. He felt that she had decided, long ago, precisely where the limits were, how much she could afford to give, and he had not been able to make her give a penny more. She made love to him as though it were a technique of pacification, a means to some other end. However she might wish to delight him, she seemed principally to wish to exhaust him; and to remain, above all, herself on the banks of pleasure the while she labored mightily to drown him in the tide. *His* pleasure was enough for her, she seemed to say, his pleasure was hers. But he wanted her pleasure to be his, for them to drown in the tide together.

He had slept, but badly, aware of Ida's body next to his, and aware of a failure more subtle than any he had known before.

And his mind was troubled with questions which he had not before permitted to enter but whose hour, now, had struck. He wondered who had been with her before him; how many, how often, how long; what he, or they before him, had meant to her; and he wondered if her lover, or lovers, had been white or black. What difference does it make? he asked himself. What difference does any of it make? One or more, white or black—she would tell him one of these days. They would learn everything about each other, they had time, she would tell him. Would she? Or would she merely accept his secrets as she accepted his body, happy to be the vehicle of his relief? While offering in return (for she knew the rules) revelations intended to pacify and also intended to frustrate him; to frustrate, that is, any attempt on his part to strike deeper into that incredible country in which, like the princess of fairy tales, sealed in a high tower and guarded by beasts, bewitched and exiled, she paced her secret round of secret days.

It was early in the morning, around seven, and there was no sound anywhere. The girl beside him stirred silently in her sleep and threw one hand up, as though she had been frightened. The scarlet eye on her little finger flashed. Her heavy hair was wild and tangled and the face she wore in sleep was not the face she wore when awake. She had taken off all her make-up, so that she had scarcely any eyebrows, and her un-painted lips were softer now, and defenseless. Her skin was darker than it was in the daytime and the round, rather high forehead held a dull, mahogany sheen. She looked like a little girl as she slept, but she was not a very trusting little girl; one hand half-covered her face and the other was hidden between her thighs. It made him think, somehow, of all the sleeping children of the poor. He touched her forehead lightly with his lips, then eased himself quietly out of bed and went into the bathroom. When he came out he stood staring for a moment at the kitchen, then lit a cigarette, and brought an ash-tray back to the bed with him. He lay on his belly, smoking, his long arms dangling to the floor, where he had placed the ashtray.

"What time is it?"

He leaned up, smiling, "I didn't know you were awake." And, strangely, he suddenly felt terribly shy, as though this was his first time to awaken, naked, next to a naked girl.

"Oh," she said, "I like to watch people when they think I'm asleep."

"That's good to know. How long have you been watching me?"

"Not long. Just when you came out of the bathroom. I saw your face and I wondered what you were thinking about."

"I was thinking about you." Then he kissed her. "Good morning. It's seven-thirty."

"My Lord. Do you always wake up so early?" And she yawned and grinned.

"No. But I guess I couldn't wait to see you again."

"Now, I'm going to remember that," she said, "when you start waking up at noon and even later and act like you don't want to get up out of the bed."

"Well, I may not be so anxious to jump right out of *bed*." She motioned for his cigarette and he held it for her while she took a drag or two. Then he put the cigarette out in the ashtray. He leaned over her. "How about you?"

"You're sweet," she said, and, after a moment, "you're a deep-sea diver." Each of them blushed. He put his hands on her breasts, which were heavy and wide apart, with reddish-brown nipples. Her large shoulders quivered a little, a pulse beat in her neck. She watched him with a face at once troubled and detached, calm, and, at the same time, frightened.

"Love me," he said. "I want you to love me."

She caught one of his hands as it moved along her belly.

"You think I'm one of those just-love-to-love girls."

"Baby," he said, "I sure hope so; we're going to be great, let me tell you. We haven't even started yet." His voice had dropped to a whisper and their two hands knotted together in a teasing tug of war.

She smiled. "How many times have you said *that*?"

He paused, looking over her head at the blinds which held back the morning. "I don't believe I've ever said it. I've never felt this way before." He looked down at her again and kissed her again. "Never."

After a moment she said, "Neither have I." She said it quickly, as though she had just popped a pill into her mouth and were surprised at its taste and apprehensive about its effects.

He looked into her eyes. "Is that true?"

"Yes." Then she dropped her eyes. "I've got to watch my step with you."

"Why? Don't you trust me?"

"It's maybe that I don't trust myself."

"Maybe you've never loved a man before," he said.

"I've never loved a white man, that's the truth."

"Oh, well," he said, smiling, trying to empty his mind of the doubts and fears which filled it, "be my guest." He kissed her again, a little drunk with her heat, her taste, her smell. "Never," he said, gravely, "never anyone like you." Her hand relaxed a little and he guided it down. He kissed her neck and shoulders. "I love your colors. You're so many different, crazy colors."

"Lord," she said, and laughed, sharply, nervously, and tried to move her hand away but he held it: the tug of war began again. "I'm the same old color all over."

"You can't see yourself all over. But I can. Part of you is honey, part of you is copper, some of you is gold—"

"Lord. What're we going to do with you this morning?"

"I'll show you. Part of you is black, too, like the entrance to a tunnel—"

"Vivaldo." Her head hit the pillow from side to side in a kind of torment which had nothing to do with him, but for which, just the same, he was responsible. He put his hand on her forehead, already beginning to be damp, and was struck by the way she then looked at him; looked at him as though she were, indeed, a virgin, promised at her birth to him, the bridegroom; whose face she now saw for the first time, in the darkened bridal chamber, after all the wedding guests had gone. There was no sound of revelry anywhere, only silence, no help anywhere if not in this bed, violation by the bridegroom's body her only hope. Yet she tried to smile. "I've never met a man like you before." She said this in a low voice, in a tone that mixed hostility with wonder.

"Well, I told you—I've never met a girl like you before, either." But he wondered what kind of men she *had* known. Gently, he forced her thighs open; she allowed him to place her hand on his sex. He felt that, for the first time, his body presented itself to her as a mystery and that, immediately, therefore, he, Vivaldo, became totally mysterious in her eyes. She touched him for the first time with wonder and terror, realizing that she did not know how to caress him. It was being borne in on her that he wanted *her*: this meant that she no longer knew what he wanted. "You've slept with lots of girls like me before, haven't you? With colored girls."

"I've slept with lots of all kinds of girls." There was no laughter between them now; they whispered, and the heat between them rose. Her odor rose to meet him, it mingled with his own, sharper sweat. He was between her thighs and in her hands, her eyes stared fearfully into his.

"But with colored girls, too?"

"Yes."

There was a long pause, she sighed a long, shuddering sigh. She arched her head upward, away from him. "Were they friends of my brother's?"

"No. No. I paid them."

"Oh." Her head dropped, she closed her eyes, she brought her thighs together, then opened them. The covers were in his way and he threw them off and then for a moment, half-kneeling, he stared at the honey and the copper and the gold and the black of her. Her breath came in short, sharp, trembling gasps. He wanted her to turn her face to him and open her eyes.

"Ida. Look at me."

She made a sound, a kind of moan, and turned her face toward him but kept her eyes closed. He took her hand again.

"Come on. Help me."

Her eyes opened for a second, veiled, but she smiled. He lowered himself down upon her, slowly, allowing her hands to guide him, and kissed her on the mouth. They locked together, shaking, her hands fluttered upward and settled on his back. *I paid them.* She sighed again, a different sigh, long and surrendering, and the struggle began.

It was not like the thrashing of the night before, when she bucked beneath him like an infuriated horse or a beached fish. Now she was attentive to the point of trembling and because he felt that one thoughtless moment would send her slipping and sliding away from him, he was very attentive, too. Her hands moved along his back, up and down, sometimes seeming to wish to bring him closer, sometimes being tempted to push him away, moved in a terrible, a beautiful indecision, and caused him, brokenly, deep in his throat, to moan. She opened up before him, yet fell back before him, too, he felt that he was traveling up a savage, jungle river, looking for the source which remained hidden just beyond the black, dan-

gerous, dripping foliage. Then, for a moment, they seemed to
be breaking through. Her hands broke free, her thighs inexorably loosened, their bellies ground cruelly together, and a
curious, low whistle forced itself up through her throat, past
her bared teeth. Then she was checked, her hands flew up to
his neck, the moment passed. He rested. Then he began
again. He had never been so patient, so determined, or so
cruel before. Last night she had watched him; this morning
he watched her; he was determined to bring her over the edge
and into his possession, even, if at the moment she finally
called his name, the heart within him burst. This, anyway,
seemed more imminent than the spilling of his seed. He was
aching in a way he had never ached before, was congested in
a new way, and wherever her hands had touched him and then
fled, he was cold. Her hands clung to his neck as though she
were drowning and she was absolutely silent, silent as a child
is silent before it finally summons enough breath to scream,
before the blow lands, before the long fall begins. And, ruth-
lessly, viciously, he pushed her to the edge. He did not know
whether her body moved with his or not, her body was so
nearly his. He felt the bed throbbing beneath them, and heard
it sing. Her hands went wild, flying from his neck to his throat
to his shoulders, his chest, she began to thrash beneath him,
trying to get away and trying to come closer. Her hands, at
last, had their own way and grasped his friendly body, caressing and scratching and burning. *Come on. Come on.* He felt a
tremor in her belly, just beneath him, as though something
had broken there, and it rolled tremendously upward, seeming to divide her breasts, as though he had split her all her
length. And she moaned. It was a curiously warning sound,
as though she were holding up one hand against the ocean.
The sound of her helplessness caused all of his affection, tenderness, desire, to return. They were almost there. *Come on
come on come on come on. Come on!* He began to gallop her,
whinnying a little with delight, and, for the first time, became
a little cold with fright, that so much of himself, so long
damned up, must now come pouring out. Her moans gave
way to sobs and cries. *Vivaldo. Vivaldo. Vivaldo.* She was over
the edge. He hung, hung, clinging to her as she clung to him,
calling her name, wet, itching, bursting, blind. It began to

pour out of him like the small weak trickle that precedes disaster in the mines. He felt his whole face pucker, felt the wind in his throat, and called her name again, while all the love in him rushed down, rushed down, and poured itself into her.

After a long time, he felt her fingers in his hair and he looked into her face. She was smiling—a thoughtful, baffled smile. "Get your big, white self off me. I can't move."

He kissed her, weary as he could be, and peaceful.

"Tell me something first."

She looked sly and amused and mocking; very much like a woman and very much like a shy, little girl. "What do you want to know?"

He shook her, laughing. "Come on. Tell me."

She kissed him on the tip of his nose. "It never happened to me before—not like this, never."

"Never?"

"Never. Almost—but no, never." Then, "Was I good for you?"

"Yes. Yes. Don't ever leave me."

"Let me get up."

He rolled over on his back and she got out of bed and walked into the bathroom. He watched the tall, dusty body, which now belonged to him, disappear. He heard water running in the bathroom, then he heard the shower. He fell asleep.

He woke up in the early afternoon. Ida was standing before the stove, singing.

> *If you can't give me a dollar,*
> *Give me a lousy dime—*

She had washed the dishes, cleaned up the kitchen, and hung up his clothes. Now she was making coffee.

> *Just want to feed*
> *This hungry man of mine.*

BOOK TWO:

ANY DAY NOW

Why don't you take me in your
arms and carry me out of this lonely place?
        —CONRAD, *Victory*

I

ERIC SAT NAKED in his rented garden. Flies buzzed and boomed in the brilliant heat, and a yellow bee circled his head. Eric remained very still, then reached for the cigarettes beside him and lit one, hoping that the smoke would drive the bee away. Yves' tiny black-and-white kitten stalked the garden as though it were Africa, crouching beneath the mimosas like a panther and leaping into the air.

The house and the garden overlooked the sea. Far down the slope, beyond the sand of the beach, in the thunderous blue of the Mediterranean, Yves' head went under, reappeared, went under again. He vanished entirely. Eric stood up, looking out over the sea, almost poised to run. Yves liked to hold his breath under water for as long as possible, a test of endurance which Eric found pointless and, in Yves' case, frightening. Then Yves' head appeared again, and his arm flashed. And, even from this distance, Eric could see that Yves was laughing—he had known that Eric would be watching from the garden. Yves began swimming toward the beach. Eric sat down. The kitten rushed over and rubbed itself against his legs.

It was the end of May. They had been in this house for more than two months. Tomorrow they were leaving. Not for a long time, perhaps never again, would Eric sit in a garden watching Yves in the water. They would take the train for Paris in the morning and, after two days there, Yves would put Eric on the boat for New York. Eric was to get settled there and then Yves was to join him.

Now that it had all been decided and there could be no turning back, Eric felt a sour and savage apprehension. He watched as Yves stepped out of the water. His brown hair was bleaching from the sun and glowed about his head; his long, wiry body was as brown as bread. He bent down to lift off the scarlet bikini. Then he pulled on an old pair of blue jeans which he had expropriated from Eric. They were somewhat too short for him, but no matter—Yves was not very fond of Americans, but he liked their clothes. He stalked up the slope, toward the house, the red cloth of the bikini dangling from one hand.

Yves had never mentioned going to America and had never given Eric any reason to suppose that he nourished such a desire. The desire arrived, or was, in any case, stated, only when the possibility arose: for Eric had slowly graduated from near-starvation to dubbing French films to bit roles in some of the American films produced abroad. One of these bits had led to television work in England; and then a New York director had offered him one of the principal supporting parts in a Broadway play.

This offer had presented Eric with the enormous question he had spent three years avoiding. To accept it was to bring his European sojourn to an end; not to accept it was to transform his sojourn into exile. He and Yves had been together for more than two years and, from the time of their meeting, his home had been with Yves. More precisely and literally, it was Yves who had come to live with him, but each was, for the other, the dwelling place that each had despaired of finding.

Eric did not want to be separated from Yves. But when he told Yves that, for this reason, he had decided to reject the offer, Yves looked at him shrewdly, and sighed. "Then you should have rejected it right away, or you should never have told me about it at all. You are being sentimental—you are maybe being, even, a little cowardly, no? You will never make a *carrière* here in France, you know that as well as I. You will just grow old and discontented and you will make me a terrible life and then *I* will leave *you*. But you can become a great star, I think, if you play this part. Wouldn't you like that?"

He paused, smiling, and Eric shrugged, then blushed. Yves laughed.

"How silly you are!" Then, "I, too, have dreams that I have never spoken of to you," he said. He was still smiling, but there was an expression in his eyes which Eric had come to know. It was the look of a seasoned and able adventurer, trying to decide between pouncing on his prey and luring his prey into a trap. Such decisions are necessarily swift and so it was also the look of someone who was already irresistibly in motion toward whatever it was he wanted; who would certainly have it. This expression always frightened Eric a little. It seemed not to belong in Yves' twenty-one-year-old face, to have no relation to his open, childlike grin, his puppylike playfulness, the adolescent ardor with which he embraced, then rejected, people, doctrines, theories. This expression made his face extremely bitter, profoundly cruel, ageless; the nature, the ferocity, of his intelligence was then all in his eyes; the extraordinary austerity of his high forehead prefigured his maturity and decay.

He touched Eric lightly on the elbow, as a very young child might do.

"I have no wish to stay here," he said, "in this wretched mausoleum of a country. Let us go to New York. I will make my future there. There is no future here, for a boy like me."

The word *future* caused in Eric a small trembling, a small recoil.

"You'll hate America," he said, with vehemence. Yves looked at him in surprise. "What kind of future are you dreaming of?"

"I am sure that there is something I can do there," Yves said, stubbornly. "I can find my way. Do you really think that I want to be protected by you forever?" And he considered Eric for a moment as though they were enemies or strangers.

"I didn't know you minded being—*protected*—by me."

"*Ne te fâche pas.* I do not *mind* it; if I minded it, I would be gone." He smiled and said, gently, reasonably, "But it cannot go on forever, I also am a *man*."

"*What* cannot go on forever?" But he knew what Yves meant and he knew that what Yves said was true.

"Why," said Yves, "my youth. It cannot last forever." Then he grinned. "I have always been sure that you would be returning to your country one day. It might as well be now, while you are still fond of me, and I can seduce you into taking me along."

"You're a great little old seducer," said Eric, "and that's the truth."

"Ah," said Yves, wickedly, "with you it was easy." Then he looked at Eric gravely. "So it is decided." It was not a question. "I suppose that I must go and visit my whore of a mother and tell her that she will never see me any more."

And his face darkened and his large mouth grew bitter. His mother had been a bistro waitress when the Germans came to Paris. Yves had then been five years old and his father had vanished so long before that Yves could scarcely remember him. But he remembered watching his mother with the Germans.

"She was really a *putain*. I remember many times sitting in the café, watching her. She did not know I was watching— anyway, old people think that children never see anything. The bar was very long, and it curved. I would always be sitting behind it, at the far end, around the curve. There was a mirror above me and I could see them in the mirror. And I could see them in the zinc of the bar. I remember their uniforms and the shine on their leather boots. They were always extremely *correct*—not like the Americans who came later. She would always be laughing, and she moved very fast. Someone's hand was always on her—in her bosom, up her leg. There was always another one at our house, the whole German army, coming all the time. How horrible a people."

And then, as though to give his mother a possible, reluctant justice:

"Later, she says that she do it for me, that we would not have eaten otherwise. But I do not believe that. I think she liked that. I think she was always a whore. She always managed everything that way. When the Americans came, she found a very pretty officer. He was very nice to me, I must say—he had a son of his own in the States that he had only seen one time, and he pretended that *I* was his son, though I was much older than his son would have been. He made me wish that *I* had a father, *one* father, especially"—he grinned—"an American father, who liked to buy you things and take you on his shoulder everywhere. I was sorry when he went away. I am sure that it was he who kept her from getting her head shaved, as she deserved. She told all kinds of lies about her work in the Resistance. *Quelle horreur!* that whole time, it was not very pretty. Many women had their heads shaved, sometimes for nothing, you know? just because they were pretty or someone was jealous or they had refused to sleep with someone. But not my mother. *Nous, nous étions tranquille avec nôtre petit officier* and our beefsteak and our chocolate candy."

Then, with a laugh:

"Now, she owns that bistro where she used to work. You see what kind of woman she is? I never go there."

This was not entirely true. He had run away from his mother at fifteen. Or, more accurately, they had established a peculiar truce, to the effect that he would make no trouble for her—that is, he would stay out of the hands of the law; and she would make no trouble for him—that is, she would not use his minority status as a means of having him controlled by the law. So Yves had lived by his wits in the streets of Paris, as a semi-*tapette*, and as a *rat d'hôtel*, until he and Eric had met. And during all this time, at great intervals, he visited his mother—when he was drunk or unbearably hungry or unbearably sad; or, rather, perhaps, he visited the bistro, which was different now. The long, curving counter had been replaced by a long, straight one. Neon swirled on the ceiling and above the mirrors. There were small, plastic-topped tables, in bright colors, and bright, plastic chairs instead of the wooden tables and chairs Yves remembered. There was a juke box now where the soldiers had clumsily manipulated the metal football players of the *baby-foot*; there were Coca-Cola signs, and Coca-Cola. The wooden floor had been covered with black plastic. Only the WC remained the same, a hole in the floor with foot-rests next to it, and torn newspaper hanging from a string. Yves went to the bistro blindly, looking for something he had lost, but it was not there any longer.

He sat in the old, vanished corner and watched his mother. The hair which had been brown was now of a chemical and improbably orange vitality. The figure which had been light was beginning to thicken and spread and sag. But her laugh remained, and she still seemed, in a kind of violent and joyless helplessness, to be seeking and fleeing the hands of men.

Eventually, she would come to his end of the bar.

"*Je t'offre quelque chose, M'sieu?*" With a bright, forced, wistful smile.

"*Un cognac, Madame.*" With a wry grin, and the sketch of a sardonic bow. When she was halfway down the bar, he yelled. "*Un double!*"

"*Ah! Bien sûr, M'sieu.*"

She brought him his drink and a small drink for herself, and watched him. They touched glasses.

"*A la vôtre, Madame.*"

"*A la vôtre, M'sieu.*"

But sometimes he said:

"*A nos amours.*"

And she repeated dryly:

"*A nos amours!*"

They drank in silence for a few seconds. Then she smiled.

"You look very well. You have become very handsome. I'm proud of you."

"Why should you be proud of me? I am just a good-for-nothing, it is just as well that I am good-looking, that's how I live." And he watched her. "*Tu comprends, hein?*"

"If you talk that way, I want to know nothing, nothing, of your life!"

"Why not? It is just like yours, when you were young. Or maybe even now, how can I tell?"

She sipped her cognac and raised her chin. "Why don't you come back? You can see for yourself how well the bar does, it would be a good situation for you. *Et puis*——"

"*Et puis quoi?*"

"I am no longer very, very young, it would be *un soulagement* if my son and I could be friends."

And Yves laughed. "You need friends? Go dig up some of those that you buried in order to get this bar. Friends! *Je veut vivre, moi!*"

"Ah, you are ungrateful." Sometimes, when she said this, she dabbed at her eyes with a handkerchief.

"Don't bother me any more, you know what I think of you, go back to your clients." And the last word was thrown at his mother, like a curse; sometimes, if he were drunk enough, there were tears in his eyes.

He would let his mother get halfway down the bar before he shouted.

"*Merci, pour le cognac, Madame!*"

And she turned, with a slight bow, saying,

"*De rien, M'sieu.*"

Eric had been there with him once, and had rather liked Yves' mother, but they had never gone back. And they had scarcely ever spoken of it. There was something hidden in it which Yves did not want to see.

Now, Yves leapt over the low stone wall and entered the garden, grinning.

"You should have come in the water with me, it was wonderful. It would do wonders for your figure; do you know how fat you are getting?"

He flicked at Eric's belly with his bikini and fell on the ground beside him. The kitten approached cautiously, sniffing Yves' foot as though it were investigating some prehistoric monstrosity, and Yves grabbed it, holding it against his shoulder, and stroking it. The kitten closed its eyes and began to purr.

"You see how she loves me? It is a pity to leave her here, let us take her with us to New York."

"Getting *you* into America is going to be hassle enough, baby, let's not rock the boat. Besides, New York is full of alley cats. And alleys." He said this with his eyes closed, drinking in the sun and the odors of the garden and the dark, salty odors of Yves. The children from the nearby house were still on the beach; he could hear their voices.

"You have no sympathy for animals. She will suffer terribly when we go away."

"She'll recover. Cats are much stronger than people."

He kept his eyes closed. He felt Yves turn to look down at him.

"Why are you so troubled about going to New York?"

"New York's a very troubling place."

"I am not afraid of trouble." He touched Eric lightly on the chest and Eric opened his eyes. He stared up into Yves' grave, brown, affectionate face. "But *you* are. You are afraid of trouble in New York. Why?"

"I'm not *afraid*, Yves. But I *have* had a lot of trouble there."

"We have had much trouble here, too," said Yves, with his abrupt and always rather shocking gravity, "and we have always come out of it and now we are better than ever, I think, no?"

"Yes," said Eric, slowly, and watched Yves' face.

"Well, then, what use is there to worry?" He pushed Eric's

hair back from his forehead. "Your head is hot. You have been in the sun too long."

Eric grabbed his hand. The kitten leapt away. "Jesus. I'm going to miss you."

"It is for so short a time. You will be busy, I will be in New York before you know we have been apart." He grinned and put his chin on Eric's chest. "Tell me about New York. You have many friends there? Many *famous* friends?"

Eric laughed. "Not many famous friends, no. I don't know if I have *any* friends there now, I've been away so long."

"Who were your friends when you left?" He grinned again and rubbed his cheek against Eric's. "Boys like me?"

"There *are* no boys like you. Thank God."

"You mean not so pretty as I? Or not so warm?"

He put his hands on Yves' salty, sandy shoulders. He heard the children's voices from the sea and the buzzing and booming in the garden. "No. Not so impossible."

"Naturally, now that you are about to leave, you find me impossible. And from what point of view?"

He drew Yves closer. "From every point of view."

"C'est dommage. Moi, je t'aime bien."

These words were whispered against his ear, and they lay still for a few moments. Eric wanted to ask, Is that true? but he knew that it was true. Perhaps he did not know what it meant, but, there, Yves could not help him. Only time might help, time which surrendered all secrets but only on the inexorable condition, as far as he could tell, that the secret could no longer be used.

He put his lips to Yves' shoulder and tasted the Mediterranean salt. He thought of his friends—what friends? He was not sure that he had ever really been friends with Vivaldo or Richard or Cass; and Rufus was dead. He was not certain who, long, long after the event, had sent him the news—he had the feeling that it had to be Cass. It could scarcely have been Vivaldo, who was made too uneasy by what he knew of Eric's relation to Rufus—knew without being willing to admit that he knew; and it would certainly not have been Richard. No one, in any case, had written very often; he had not really wanted to know what was happening among the people he had fled; and he felt that they had always protected themselves against any knowledge of what was happening in him. No, Rufus had been his only friend among them. Rufus had made him suffer, but Rufus had dared to know him. And when Eric's pain had faded, and Rufus was far away, Eric remembered only the joy that they had sometimes shared, and the timbre of Rufus' voice, his half-beat, loping, cocky walk, his smile, the way he held a cigarette, the way he threw back his head when he laughed. And there was something in Yves which reminded him of Rufus—something in his trusting smile and his brave, tough vulnerability.

It was a Thursday when the news came. It was pouring down rain, all of Paris was wavering and gray. He had no money at all that day, was waiting for a check which was mysteriously entangled in one of the bureaucratic webs of the French cinema industry. He and Yves had just divided the last of their cigarettes and Yves had gone off to try and borrow money from an Egyptian banker who had once been fond of him. Eric had then lived on the Rue de la Montagne Ste. Geneviève, and he labored up this hill, in the flood, bareheaded, with water dripping down his nose and eyelashes and behind his ears and down his back and soaking through his trench-coat pocket, where he had unwisely placed the cigarettes. He could practically feel them disintegrating in the moist, unclean darkness of his pocket, not at all protected by his slippery hand. He was in a kind of numb despair and intended simply to get home and take off his clothes and stay in bed until help came; help would probably be Yves, with the money for sandwiches; it would be just enough help to enable them to get through yet another ghastly day.

He traversed the great courtyard and started up the steps of his building; and behind him, near the *porte-cochère*, the bell of the concierge's *loge* sounded, and she called his name.

He went back, hoping that she was not going to ask him about his rent. She stood in her door, with a letter in her hand.

"This just came," she said. "I thought it might be important."

"Thank you," he said.

She, too, hoped that it might be the money he was waiting

for, but she closed her door behind her. It was nearly suppertime and she was cooking; in fact, the entire street seemed
to be cooking, and his legs threatened to give way beneath
him.

He did not look carefully at the outside of the envelope
because his mind was entirely occupied by the recalcitrant
check, and he was not expecting a check from America, which
was where the letter came from; and he crumpled it up, un-
read, in his trench-coat pocket and crossed the courtyard and
went upstairs to his room. There, he put the letter on the
table, dried himself, and undressed and got under the covers.
Then he lay the cigarettes out to dry, lit the driest one, and
looked at the letter again. It seemed a very ordinary letter,
until the paragraph beginning *We were all very fond of him,
and I know that you were, too*—yes, it must have been Cass
who wrote. Rufus was dead, and by his own hand. Rufus was
dead.

Boys like me? Yves had teased. How could he tell the boy
who lay beside him now anything about Rufus? It had taken
him a long while to realize that one of the reasons Yves had
so stirred his heart, stirred it in a way he had almost forgotten
it could be stirred, was because he reminded him, somehow,
somewhere, of Rufus. And it had taken him almost until this
very moment, on the eve of his departure, to begin to recognize that part of Rufus' great power over him had to do
with the past which Eric had buried in some deep, dark place;
was connected with himself, in Alabama, *when I wasn't nothing but a child*; with the cold white people and the warm,
black people, warm at least for him, and as necessary as the
sun which bathed the bodies of himself and his lover now.
Lying in this garden now, so warm, covered, and apprehensive, he saw them on the angular, blazing streets of his childhood, and in the shuttered houses, and in the fields. They
laughed differently from other people, so it had seemed to
him, and moved with more beauty and violence, and they
smelled like good things in the oven.

But had he ever loved Rufus? Or had it simply been rage
and nostalgia and guilt? and shame? Was it the body of Rufus
to which he had clung, or the bodies of dark men, seen briefly,
somewhere, in a garden or a clearing, long ago, sweat running

down their chocolate chests and shoulders, their voices ringing out, the white of their jock-straps beautiful against their skin, one with his head tilted back before a dipper—and the water splashing, sparkling, singing down!—one with his arm raised, laying an axe to the base of a tree? Certainly he had never succeeded in making Rufus believe he loved him. Perhaps Rufus had looked into his eyes and seen those dark men Eric saw, and hated him for it.

He lay very still, feeling Yves' unmoving, trusting weight, feeling the sun.

"Yves——?"

"Oui, mon chou?"

"Let's go inside. I think, maybe, I'd like to take a shower and have a drink. I'm beginning to feel sticky."

"*Ah, les américains avec leur* drinks! I will surely become an alcoholic in New York." But he raised his head and kissed Eric swiftly on the tip of his nose and stood up.

He stood between Eric and the sun; his hair very bright, his face in shadow. He looked down at Eric and grinned.

"Alors tu es toujours prêt, toi, d'après ce que je vois."

Eric laughed. *"Et toi, salaud?"*

"Mais moi, je suis français, mon cher, je suis pas puritain, fort heureusement. T'aura du te rendre compte d'ailleurs." He pulled Eric to his feet and slapped him on the buttocks with the red bikini. "*Viens.* Take your shower. I think we have almost nothing left to drink, I will bicycle down to the village. What shall I get?"

"Some whiskey?"

"Naturally, since that is the most expensive. Are we eating in or out?"

They started into the house, with their arms around each other.

"Try to get Madame Belet to come and cook something for us."

"What do you want to eat?"

"I don't care. Whatever you want."

The house was long and low, built of stone, and very cool and dark after the heat and brightness of the kitchen. The kitten had followed them in and now murmured insistently at their feet.

"Perhaps I will feed her before I go. It will only take a minute."

"She can't be hungry yet, she eats all the time," said Eric. But Yves had already begun preparing the kitten's food.

They had entered through the kitchen and Eric walked through it and through the dining salon, into their bedroom, and threw himself down on the bed. The bedroom also had an entrance on the garden. The mimosas pressed against the window, and beyond these were two or three orange trees, holding hard, small oranges, like Christmas balls. There were olive trees in the garden, too, but they had been long untended; it was not worth anyone's while to pick the olives.

The script of the new play was on the plain wooden table which, along with the fireplace in the dining room, had persuaded them to rent the house; on the table, too, were a few books, Yves' copies of Blaise Cendrars and Jean Genet and Marcel Proust, Eric's copies of *An Actor Prepares* and *The Wings of the Dove* and *Native Son*. Yves' sketch pad was on the floor. So were his tennis shoes and his socks and his underwear, all of these embracing Eric's sport shirts and sandals and bathing trunks—less explicit and more somber than Yves' bikini, these last, as Eric himself was less explicit and more sombre.

Yves clattered into the bedroom.

"Are you going to take that shower or not?"

"Yes. Right away."

"Well, start. I am leaving now, I will be back in a moment."

"I know your moments. Try not to get too drunk with the natives." He grinned and stood up.

Yves picked up a pair of socks from the floor, put them on, and put on his tennis shoes, and a faded blue pullover. "Ah. *Celui-là, je te jure.*" He took a comb from his pocket and pulled it through his hair, with the result that it stood up more wildly than ever.

"I'll put you on your bicycle."

They walked past the mimosas. "Hurry back," said Eric; smiling, staring at Yves.

Yves picked up his bicycle. "I will be back before you are dry." He rolled the bicycle through the gate and onto the road. Eric stood in the garden, watching him. The light was still very bright but, in the mysterious way of southern light, was gathering itself together and would soon be gone. Already, the sea looked darker.

Once past the gate, Yves did not look back. Eric turned into the house.

He stepped into the shower, which was off the bedroom. He fumbled with the knobs, and the water came crashing over him, first too cold, but he forced himself to take it, then too hot; he fumbled with the knobs until the water became more bearable. He soaped himself, wondering if he were really getting fat. His belly seemed firm enough, but he had always had a tendency to be chunky and square; it was just as well that he would soon, in New York, be going again to the gym. And the thought of the gym, while the water fell down over him, he was alone with his body and the water, caused many painful and buried things to stir in him. Now that his flight was so rigorously approaching its end, a light appeared, a backward light, throwing his terrors into relief.

And what were these terrors? They were buried beneath the impossible language of the time, lived underground where nearly all of the time's true feeling spitefully and incessantly fermented. Precisely, therefore, to the extent that they were inexpressible, were these terrors mighty; precisely because they lived in the dark were their shapes obscene. And because the taste for obscenity is universal and the appetite for reality rare and hard to cultivate, he had nearly perished in the basement of his private life. Or, more precisely, his fantasies.

These fantasies began as fantasies of love and soured imperceptibly into fantasies of violence and humiliation. When he was little he had been very much alone, for his mother was a civic leader, always busy with clubs and banquets and speeches and proposals and manifestoes, aloft forever on a sea of flowered hats; and his father, rather submerged by this glittering and resounding tide, made his home in the bank and on the golf course, in hunting lodges, and at poker tables. There seemed to be very little between his father and his mother, very little, that is, beyond habit and courtesy and coercion; and perhaps each had loved him, but this was never real to him, since they so clearly did not love each other. He had loved the cook, a black woman named Grace, who fed

him and spanked him and scolded and coddled him, and dried
the tears which scarcely anyone else in the household ever saw.
But, even more than he had loved Grace, he had loved her
husband, Henry.

Henry was younger, or seemed younger, than his wife. He
was a trial to Grace, and probably to them all, because he
drank too much. He was the handyman and one of his duties
was the care of the furnace. Eric still remembered the look
and the smell of the glaring furnace room, the red shadows
from the furnace playing along the walls, and the sticky-sweet
smell of Henry's breath. They had spent many hours together
there, Eric on a box at Henry's knee, Henry with his hand on
Eric's neck or shoulder. His voice fell over Eric like waves of
safety. He was full of stories. He told the story of how he had
met Grace, and how he had seduced her, and how (as he
supposed) he had persuaded her to marry him; told stories of
preachers and gamblers in his part of town—they seemed, in
his part of town, to have much in common, and, often, to be
the same people—how he had outwitted this one and that
one, and how, once, he had managed to escape being put on
the chain gang. (And he had explained to Eric what a chain
gang was.) Once, Eric had walked into the furnace room
where Henry sat alone; when he spoke, Henry did not answer;
and when he approached him, putting his hand on Henry's
knee, the man's tears scalded the back of his hand. Eric no
longer remembered the cause of Henry's tears, but he would
never forget the wonder with which he then touched Henry's
face, or what the shaking of Henry's body had caused him to
feel. He had thrown himself into Henry's arms, almost sobbing himself, and yet somehow wise enough to hold his own
tears back. He was filled with an unutterably painful rage
against whatever it was that had hurt Henry. It was the first
time he had felt a man's arms around him, the first time he
had felt the chest and belly of a man; he had been ten or
eleven years old. He had been terribly frightened, obscurely
and profoundly frightened, but he had not, as the years were
to prove, been frightened enough. He knew that what he felt
was somehow wrong, and must be kept a secret; but he
thought that it was wrong because Henry was a grown man,
and colored, and he was a little boy, and white.

Henry and Grace were eventually banished, due to some lapse or offense on Henry's part. Since Eric's parents had never approved of those sessions in the furnace room, Eric always suspected this as the reason for Henry's banishment, which made his opposition to his parents more bitter than ever. In any case, he lived his life far from them, at school by day and before his mirror by night, dressed up in his mother's old clothes or in whatever colorful scraps he had been able to collect, posturing and, in a whisper, declaiming. He knew that this was wrong, too, though he could not have said why. But by this time he knew that everything he did was wrong in the eyes of his parents, and in the eyes of the world, and that, therefore, everything must be lived in secret.

The trouble with a secret life is that it is very frequently a secret from the person who lives it and not at all a secret for the people he encounters. He encounters, because he *must* encounter, those people who see his secrecy before they see anything else, and who drag these secrets out of him; sometimes with the intention of using them against him, sometimes with more benevolent intent; but, whatever the intent, the moment is awful and the accumulating revelation is an unspeakable anguish. The aim of the dreamer, after all, is merely to go on dreaming and not to be molested by the world. His dreams are his protection against the world. But the aims of life are antithetical to those of the dreamer, and the teeth of the world are sharp. How could Eric have known that his fantasies, however unreadable they were for him, were inscribed in every one of his gestures, were betrayed in every inflection of his voice, and lived in his eyes with all the brilliance and beauty and terror of desire? He had always been a heavy, healthy boy, had played like other children, and fought as they did, made friends and enemies and secret pacts and grandiose plans. And yet none of his playmates, after all, had ever sat with Henry in the furnace room, or ever kissed Henry on his salty face. They did not, weighed down with discarded hats, gowns, bags, sashes, earrings, capes, and necklaces, turn themselves into make-believe characters after everyone in their house was asleep. Nor could they possibly, at their most extended, have conceived of the people he, in the privacy of night, became: his mother's friends, or his mother—his mother as he conceived her to have been when she was young, his mother's friends as his mother was now; the heroines and heroes of the novels he read, and the movies he saw; or people he simply put together out of his fantasies and the available rags. No doubt, at school, the boy with whom he was wrestling failed to feel the curious stabs of terror and pleasure that Eric felt, as they grappled with each other, as one boy pinned the other to the ground; and if Eric saw the girls at all, he saw mainly their clothes and their hair; they were not, for him, as were the boys, creatures in a hierarchy, to be adored or feared or despised. None of them looked on each other as he looked on all of them. His dreams were different—subtly and cruelly and criminally different: this was not known yet, but it was felt. He was menaced in a way that they were not, and it was perhaps this sense, and the instinct which compels people to move away from the doomed, which accounted for the invincible distance, increasing with the years, which stretched between himself and his contemporaries.

And, of course, in Eric's case, in Alabama, his increasing isolation and strangeness was held, even by himself, to be due to the extreme unpopularity of his racial attitudes—or, rather, as far as the world in which he moved was concerned, the lack of any responsible attitudes at all. The town in which Eric lived was celebrated and well-to-do, but it was not very big; as far as Eric was concerned, the South was not very big, certainly, as it turned out, not big enough for him; and he was the only son of very prominent people. So it was not long before his appearance anywhere caused heads to shake, lips to purse, tongues to stiffen or else, violently, venomously, to curl around his name. Which was also, however, his father's name, and Eric, therefore, encountered, very often and very soon, the hideous obsequiousness of people who depised him but who did not dare to say so. They had long ago given up saying anything which they really felt, had given it up so long ago that they were now incapable of feeling anything which was not felt by a mob.

Now, Eric stepped out of the shower, rubbing his body with the enormous, rough, white towel Yves had placed in the bathroom for him. Yves did not like showers, he preferred long, scalding baths, with newspapers, cigarettes, and whiskey on a chair next to the bathtub, and with Eric nearby to talk to, to shampoo his hair, and to scrub his back. The thought of the Oriental opulence which overtook Yves each time he bathed caused Eric to smile. He smiled, but he was troubled, too. And as he put on his bathrobe, his body tingled less from the effect of the towel and the toilet water than from his image, abruptly overwhelming, of Yves leaning back in the bathtub, whistling, the washrag in his hand, a peaceful, abstracted look on his face and his sex gleaming and bobbing in the soapy water like a limp, cylindrical fish; and from his memory, to which his image was somehow the gateway, of that moment, nearly fifteen years ago, when the blow had inexorably fallen and his shame and his battle and his exile had begun. He walked into the dining room and poured himself a drink. Then the bottle was empty and he dropped it in the waste basket. He lit a cigarette and sat down in a chair near the window, overlooking the sea. The sun was sinking and the sea was on fire.

The sun had been sinking on that far-off day, a Sunday, a hot day. The church bells had ceased and the silence of the South hung heavy over that town. The trees along the walks gave no shade. The white houses, with their blank front doors, their blackly shadowed porches, seemed to be in battle with the sun, laboring and shuddering beneath the merciless light. Occasionally, passing a porch, one might discern in its depths a still, shadowed, faceless figure. The interminable pickaninnies were playing in the invincible dirt—where Eric was walking that day, on a back road, near the edge of town, with a colored boy. His name was LeRoy, he was seventeen, a year older than Eric, and he worked as a porter in the courthouse. He was tall and very black, and taciturn; Eric always wondered what he was thinking. They had been friends for a long time, from the time of Henry's banishment. But now their friendship, their effort to continue an impossible connection, was beginning to be a burden for them both. It would have been simpler—perhaps—if LeRoy had worked for Eric's family. Then all would have been permitted, would have been covered by the assumption of Eric's responsibility for his colored boy. But, as things were, it was suspect, it was indecent, that a white boy, especially of Eric's class and difficult reputation, should "run," as Eric incontestably did, after one of his inferiors. Eric had no choice but to run, to insist—LeRoy could certainly not come visiting him.

And yet there was something absolutely humiliating in his position; he felt it very sharply and sadly, and he knew that LeRoy felt it, too. Eric did not know, or perhaps he did not want to know, that he made LeRoy's life more difficult and increased the danger in which LeRoy walked—for LeRoy was considered "bad," as lacking, that is, in respect for white people. Eric did not know, though of course LeRoy did, what was already being suggested about him all over town. Eric had not guessed, though LeRoy knew only too well, that the Negroes did not like him, either. They suspected the motives of his friendliness. They looked for the base one and naturally they found it.

So, shortly before, when Eric had appeared in the road, his hands in his pockets, a hoarse, tuneless whistle issuing from his lips, LeRoy had jumped off his porch and come to meet him, striding toward Eric as though he were an enemy. There was a snicker from LeRoy's porch, quickly muffled; a screen door slammed; every eye on the street was on them.

Eric stammered, "I just dropped by to see what you were doing."

LeRoy spat in the dusty road. "Ain't doing nothing. Ain't you got nothing to do?"

"You want to take a walk?" Eric asked.

For a moment it really seemed that LeRoy was going to refuse, for his scowl deepened. Then a faint smile touched his lips. "Okay. But I can't walk far. I got to get back."

They began to walk. "I want to get out of this town," Eric said, suddenly.

"You and me both," said LeRoy.

"Maybe we can go North together," Eric said, after a moment, "where do you think's best? New York? or Chicago? or maybe San Francisco?" He had wanted to say Hollywood, because he had a dim notion of trying to become a movie star. But he could not really imagine LeRoy as a movie star, and he did not want to seem to want anything LeRoy could not have.

"I can't be thinking about leaving. I got my Ma and all them kids to worry about." He looked at Eric and laughed, but it was not an entirely pleasant laugh. "Ain't everybody's old man runs a bank, you know." He picked up a pebble and threw it at a tree.

"Hell, my old man don't give me no money. He certainly won't give me any money to go North. He wants me to stay right here."

"He going to die one day, Eric, he going to have to leave it to somebody, now who you think it's going to be? Me?" And he laughed again.

"Well, I'm not going to hang around here the rest of my life, waiting for my papa to die. That's certainly not much to look forward to."

And he tried to laugh, to match his tone to LeRoy's. But he did not really understand LeRoy's tone. What was wrong between them today? For it was no longer merely the world—there was something unspoken between them, something unspeakable, undone, and hideously desired. And yet, on that far-off, burning day, though this knowledge clamored in him and fell all around him, like the sun, and everything in him was aching and yearning for the act, he could not, to save his soul, have named it. It had yet to reach the threshold of his imagination; and it had no name, no name for him anyway, though for other people, so he had heard, it had dreadful names. It had only a shape and the shape was LeRoy and LeRoy contained the mystery which had him by the throat.

And he put his arm around LeRoy's shoulder and rubbed the top of his head against LeRoy's chin.

"Well, you got it to look forward to, whether you like it or not," LeRoy said. He put one hand on Eric's neck. "But I guess you know what *I* got to look forward to." And Eric felt that he wished to say more, but did not know how. They walked on a few seconds in silence and LeRoy's opportunity came. A cream-colored roadster, bearing six young people, three white boys and three white girls, came up the road in a violent swirl and wake of dust. Eric and LeRoy did not have time to move apart, and a great laugh came from the car, and the driver beat out a mocking version of the wedding march on his horn—then kept his entire palm on it as the car shot down the road, away. All the people in the car were people with whom Eric had grown up.

He felt his face flame and he and LeRoy moved away from each other; and LeRoy looked at him with a curiously non-committal pity.

"Now *that's* what you supposed to be doing," he said—he said it very gently, looking at Eric, licking his lower lip—"and *that's* where you supposed to be. You *ain't* supposed to be walking around this damn country road with no nigger."

"I don't give a damn about those people," Eric said—but he knew that he was lying and he knew that LeRoy knew it, too—"those people don't mean a thing to me."

LeRoy looked more pitying than ever, and also looked exasperated. The road now was empty, not a creature moved on it; it was yellow-red and brown and trees leaned over it, with fire falling through the leaves; and the road now began to drop beneath them, toward the railroad tracks and the warehouse. This was the town's dividing line and they always turned off the road at this point, into a clump of trees and a rise which overlooked a stream. LeRoy now turned Eric into this haven. His touch was different today; insistent, gentle, ferocious, and resigned.

"Besides," said Eric, helplessly, "you're not a nigger, not for me, you're LeRoy, you're my friend, and I love you." The words took his breath away and tears came to his eyes and they paused in the fiery shadow of a tree. LeRoy leaned against the tree, staring at Eric, with a terrible expression on his black face. The expression on LeRoy's face frightened him, but he labored upward against his fear, and brought out, "I don't know why people can't do what they want to do; what *harm* are we doing to anybody?"

LeRoy laughed. He reached out and pulled Eric against him, under the shadow of the leaves. "Poor little rich boy," he said, "tell me what you want to *do*." Eric stared at him. Nothing could have moved him out of LeRoy's arms, away from his smell, and the terrible, new touch of his body; and yet, in the same way that he knew that everything he had ever wanted or done was wrong, he knew that this was wrong, and he felt himself falling. Falling where? He clung to LeRoy,

whose arms tightened around him. "Poor boy," LeRoy murmured again, "poor boy." Eric buried his face in LeRoy's
neck and LeRoy's body shook a little—*the chest and belly of a
man!*—and then he pushed Eric away and guided him toward
the stream and they sat down beside it.

"I guess you know, now," LeRoy said, after a long silence,
while Eric trailed his hand in the water, "what they saying
about us in this town. I don't care but it can get us in a lot
of trouble and you got to stop coming to see me, Eric."

He had *not* known what they were saying, or he had been
unable to allow himself to know; but he knew now. He said,
staring into the water, and with a totally mysterious abandon,
"Well, if we've got the name, we might as well have the game
is how I see it. I don't give a shit about those people, let them
all go to hell; what have they got to do with you and me?"

LeRoy looked briefly over at Eric and smiled. "You a nice
boy, Eric, but you don't know the score. Your Daddy *owns*
half the folks in this town, ain't but so much they can do to
you. But what they can do to *me*——!" And he spread his
hands wide.

"I won't let anything happen to you."

LeRoy laughed. "You *better* get out of this town. Declare,
they going to lynch you before they get around to me." He
laughed again and rubbed his hand in Eric's bright red hair.

Eric grabbed his hand. They looked at each other, and a
total, a dreadful silence fell. "Boy," LeRoy said, weakly. And
then, after a moment, "You really out for trouble, ain't you?"
And then nothing was said. They lay together beside the
stream.

That day. That day. Had he known where that day would
lead him would he have writhed as he did, in such an anguished joy, beneath the great weight of his first lover? But if
he had known, or been capable of caring, where such a day
might lead him, it could never have been his necessity to bring
about such a day. He was frightened and in pain and the boy
who held him so relentlessly was suddenly a stranger; and yet
this stranger worked in Eric an eternal, a healing transformation. Many years were to pass before he could begin to accept
what he, that day, in those arms, with the stream whispering
in his ear, discovered; and yet that day was the beginning of

his life as a man. What had always been hidden was to him, that day, revealed and it did not matter that, fifteen years later, he sat in an armchair, overlooking a foreign sea, still struggling to find the grace which would allow him to bear that revelation. For the meaning of revelation is that what is revealed is true, and must be borne.

But how to bear it? He rose from his seat and paced restlessly into the garden. The kitten lay curled on the stone doorstep, in the last of the sun, asleep. Then he heard Yves' bicycle bell and, shortly, Yves' head appeared above the low stone wall. He passed, looking straight ahead, and then Eric heard him in the kitchen, bumping into things and opening and closing the icebox door.

Then Yves stood beside him.

"Madame Belet will be here in a few moments. She is cooking for us a chicken. And I have bought some whiskey and some cigarettes." Then he looked at Eric and frowned. "You are mad to be standing here in your bathrobe. The sun is down and it is getting cold. Come in and get dressed, I will make us both a drink."

"What would I do without you?"

"I wonder." Eric followed him into the house. "I also bought some champagne," Yves said, suddenly, and he turned to face Eric with a small, shy smile, "to celebrate our last night here." Then he walked into the kitchen. "Get dressed," he called, "Madame Belet will be here soon."

Eric stepped into the bedroom and began putting on his clothes. "Are we going out after dinner?"

"Perhaps. That depends. If we are not too drunk on champagne."

"I'd just as soon stay in, I think."

"Oh, perhaps we must have just one last look at our little seaside town."

"We have to get packed, you know, and clean up this house a little, and try to get some sleep."

"Madame Belet will clean it for us. Anyway, we would never be able to get it done. We can sleep on the train. And we do not have so very much to pack."

Eric heard him washing the glasses. Then he began to whistle a tune which sounded like a free improvisation on Bach.

Eric combed his hair, which was too long. He decided that he would get it cut very short before he went back to the States.

Eventually, they sat, as they had sat so many evenings, before the window which overlooked the sea. Yves sat on the hassock, the back of his head resting on Eric's knee.

"I will be very sad to leave here," Yves said, suddenly. "I have never been happier than I have been in this house."

Eric stroked Yves' hair and said nothing. He watched the lights that played on the still, black sea, from the sky and the shore.

"I have been very happy, too," he said at last. And then: "I wonder if we will ever be so happy again."

"Yes, why not? But that is not so important—anyway, no matter how happy I may become, and I am sure that I shall have great moments yet, this house will always stay with me. I found out something here."

"And what was that?"

Yves turned his head and looked up at Eric. "I was afraid that I would just remain a street boy forever, that I was no better than my mother." He turned away, toward the window again. "But, somehow, down here in this house with you, I finally realized that that is not so. I have not to be a whore just because I come from whores. I am better than that." He stopped. "I learned that from you. That is really strange, for, you know? in the beginning I thought you thought of me like that. I thought that you were just another sordid American, looking for a pretty, degenerate boy."

"But you are not pretty," Eric said, and sipped his whiskey. "*Au fait, tu es plutôt moche.*"

"Oh. *Ça va.*"

"Your nose turns up." He stroked the tip of Yves' nose. "And your mouth's too big"—Yves laughed—"and your forehead's too high and soon you won't have any hair." He stroked Yves' forehead, stroked his hair. "And those ears, baby! you look like an elephant or a flying machine."

"You are the first person who ever say that I am ugly. Perhaps that is why I am intrigued." He laughed.

"Well. Your eyes are not too bad."

"*Tu parle. J'ai du chien, moi.*"

"Well, yes, baby, now that you mention it, I'm afraid you've got a point."

They were silent for a moment.

"I have been with so many horrible people," Yves said, gravely, "so soon, and for so long. Really, it is a wonder that I am not completely *sauvage*." He sipped his whiskey. Eric could not see his face, but he could imagine the expression it held: hard and baffled and terribly young, with the cruelty that comes from pain and fear. "First, my mother and all those soldiers, *ils étaient mes oncles, tous*," and he laughed, "and then all those awful, slimy men, I no longer know how many." He was silent again. "I lay in the bed, sometimes we never got to bed, and let them grunt and slobber. Some of them were really fantastic, no whore has ever told the truth about who comes to her, I am sure of that, they would chop off her head before they would dare to hear it. But it is happening, it is happening all the time." He leaned up, hugging his knees, staring at the sea. "Then I would take their money; if they made difficulties I could scare them because I was *mineur*. Anyway, it was very easy to scare them. Most of those people are cowards." Then he said, in a low voice, "I never thought that I would be happy to have a man touch me and hold me. I never thought that I would be able, truly, to make love with a man. Or with anyone."

"Why," Eric asked at last, "didn't you use women instead of men, as you despised the men so much?"

Yves was silent. Then, "I don't know. *D'abord*, I took what there was—or allowed what there was to take *me*," and he looked at Eric and grinned. He sipped his whiskey and stood up. "It is simpler with men, it is usually shorter, the money is easier. Women are much more cunning than men, especially those women who would go after a boy like me, and even more unattractive, really." He laughed. "It is much harder work, and it is not so sure." His face dropped again into its incongruous, austere melancholy. "You do not meet many women in the places I have been; you do not meet many human persons at all. They are all dead. Dead." He stopped, his lips pursed, his eyes glittering in the light that fell through the window. "There were many whores in my mother's place, but—well, yes, there have been a few women, but I couldn't stand them, either." He moved to the window and stood there with his back to Eric. "I do not like *l'elégance des femmes*. Every time I see a woman wearing her fur coats and her jewels and her gowns, I want to tear all that off her and drag her someplace, to a *pissoir*, and make her smell the smell of many men, the *piss* of many men, and make her know that *that* is what she is for, she is no better than that, she does not fool me with all those shining rags, which, anyway, she only got by blackmailing some stupid man."

Eric laughed, but he was frightened. *"Comme tu es feroce!"* He watched Yves turn from the window and slowly pace the room—long and lean, like a stalking cat, and in the heavy shadows. And he saw that Yves' body was changing, was losing the adolescent, poverty-stricken harshness. He was becoming a man.

And he watched that sullen, wiry body. He watched his face. The dome of his forehead seemed more remarkable than ever, and more pure, and his mouth seemed, at once, more cruel and more defenseless. This nakedness was the proof of Yves' love and trust, and it was also the proof of Yves' force. Yves, one day, would no longer need Eric as he needed Eric now.

Now, Yves tilted back his head and finished his drink and turned to Eric with a smile.

"You are drinking very slowly tonight. What is the matter?"

"I'm getting old." But he laughed and finished his drink and handed his glass to Yves.

And, as Yves walked away from him, as he heard him in the kitchen, as he looked out over the yellow, winking lights along the shore, something opened in him, an unspeakable despair swept over him. Madame Belet had arrived and he heard Yves and the old peasant woman in the kitchen. Their voices were muted.

On the day that Yves no longer needed him, Eric would drop back into chaos. He remembered that army of lonely men who had used him, who had wrestled with him, caressed him, and submitted to him, in a darkness deeper than the darkest night. It was not merely his body they had used, but something else; his infirmity had made him the receptacle of an anguish which he could scarcely believe was in the world.

This anguish rendered him helpless, though it also lent him his weird, doomed grace and power, and it baffled him and set the dimensions of his trap. Perhaps he had sometimes dreamed of walking out of the drama in which he was entangled and playing some other role. But all the exits were barred—were barred by avid men; the role he played was necessary, and not only to himself.

And he thought of these men, that ignorant army. They were husbands, they were fathers, gangsters, football players, rovers; and they were everywhere. Or they were, in any case, in all of the places he had been assured they could not be found and the need they brought to him was one they scarcely knew they had, which they spent their lives denying, which overtook and drugged them, making their limbs as heavy as those of sleepers or drowning bathers, and which could only be satisfied in the shameful, the punishing dark, and quickly, with flight and aversion as the issue of the act. They fled, with the infection lanced but with the root of the infection still in them. Days or weeks or months might pass—or even years—before, once again, furtively, in an empty locker room, on an empty stairway or a roof, in the shadow of a wall in the park, in a parked car, or in the furnished room of an absent friend, they surrendered to the hands, to the stroking and fondling and kissing of the despised and anonymous sex. And yet the need did not seem to be predominantly physical. It could not be said that they were attracted to men. They did not make love, they were passive, they were acted on. The need seemed, indeed, to be precisely this passivity, this gift of illicit pleasure, this adoration. They came, this army, not out of joy but out of poverty, and in the most tremendous ignorance. Something had been frozen in them, the root of their affections had been frozen, so that they could no longer accept affection, though it was from this lack that they were perishing. The dark submission was the shadow of love—if only someone, somewhere, loved them enough to caress them this way, in the light, with joy! But then they could no longer be passive.

Chaos. For the great difference between these men and himself was also the terms of their connection. He saw their vulnerability and they saw his. But they did not love him for this. They used him. He did not love them, either, though he dreamed of it. And the encounter took place, at last, between two dreamers, neither of whom could wake the other, except for the bitterest and briefest of seconds. Then sleep descended again, the search continued, chaos came again.

And there was more to it than that. When the liaison so casually begun survived the first encounters, when a kind of shy affection began to force itself up through the frozen ground, and shame abated, chaos more than ever ruled. For shame had not so much abated as found a partner. Affection had appeared, but through a fissure, a crevice, in the person, through which, behind affection, came all the winds of fear. For the act of love is a confession. One lies about the body but the body does not lie about itself; it cannot lie about the force which drives it. And Eric had discovered, inevitably, the truth about many men, who then wished to drive Eric and the truth together out of the world.

And where was honor in all this chaos? He watched the winking lights and listened to Yves and Madame Belet in the kitchen. Honor. He knew that he had no honor which the world could recognize. His life, passions, trials, loves, were, at worst, filth, and, at best, disease in the eyes of the world, and crimes in the eyes of his countrymen. There were no standards for him except those he could make for himself. There were no standards for him because he could not accept the definitions, the hideously mechanical jargon of the age. He saw no one around him worth his envy, did not believe in the vast, gray sleep which was called security, did not believe in the cures, panaceas, and slogans which afflicted the world he knew; and this meant that he had to create his standards and make up his definitions as he went along. It was up to him to find out who he was, and it was his necessity to do this, so far as the witchdoctors of the time were concerned, alone.

"*Mais, bien sûr,*" he heard Yves saying to Madame Belet, "*je suis tout à fait à votre avis.*" Madame Belet was very fond of Yves and gave him the benefit, entirely unsolicited, of her seventy-two years' experience each time she was able to corner him. He could see Yves now, in the kitchen, holding the two drinks in his hand, edging toward the door, a pale, polite, and lonely smile on his face—for he had great respect for old people—waiting for the pause in Madame Belet's flow which would allow him to escape.

Madame Belet was fond of Eric, too, but he had the feeling that this was mainly because she recognized him as Yves' somewhat unlikely benefactor. If Eric had been French, she would have despised him. But France did not, *Dieu merci!* produce such conundrums as Eric, and he was not to be judged by the civilized standards which obtained in her own country.

"And what time are you leaving?" she asked.

"Oh, surely not before noon, Madame."

She laughed and Yves laughed. There was something bawdy in their laughter and he could not avoid the feeling, though he suppressed it at once, that they were laughing in league, against him. "I hope you will like America," said Madame Belet.

"I will become very rich there," said Yves, "and when I come back, I will take you on a pilgrimage to Rome."

For Madame Belet was devout and had never been to Rome, and it was her great hope to see the Holy City before she died.

"Ah. You will never come back."

"I will come back," Yves said. But his voice was full of doubt. And Eric realized, for the first time, that Yves was afraid.

"People who go to America," said Madame Belet, "never come back."

"Au contraire," said Yves, "they are coming back all the time."

Coming back to what? Eric asked himself. Madame Belet laughed again. Then their voices dropped. Yves came back into the room. He handed Eric his drink and sat again on the hassock, with his head on Eric's knee.

"I thought I would never get away," he murmured.

"I was thinking of going in to rescue you." He leaned down and kissed Yves on the neck.

Yves put one hand on Eric's cheek and closed his eyes. They were still. A pulse beat in Yves' neck. He turned and he and Eric kissed each other on the mouth. They pulled slightly away. Yves' eyes were very black and bright in the unlit, leaping room. They stared into each other's eyes for a long time, and kissed again. Then Eric sighed and leaned back and Yves rested once more against him.

Eric wondered what Yves was thinking. Yves' eyes had carried him back to that moment, nearly two years before, when, in a darkened hotel room, in the town of Chartres, he and Yves had first become lovers. Yves had visited the cathedral once, years before, and he had wanted Eric to see it. And this gesture, this desire to share with Eric something he had loved, marked the end of a testing period, signaled Yves' turning out of that dark distrust with which he was accustomed to regard the world and with which he had held Eric at bay. They had known each other for more than three months and had seen each other every day, but they had never touched.

And Eric had waited, attentive and utterly chaste. The change in him was like the change in a spendthrift when his attention is captured by something worth more than all his gold, worth more than all the baubles he has ever purchased; then, instead of scattering, he begins to assess and hoard and gather up; all that he has becomes valuable because all that he has may prove to be an unacceptable sacrifice. So Eric waited, praying that this violated urchin would learn to love and trust him. And he knew that the only way he could hope to bring this about was to cease violating himself: if *he* did not love himself, then Yves would never be able to love him, either.

So he did what he alone could do, purified, as well as he could, his house, and opened his doors; established a precarious order in the heart of his chaos; and waited for his guest.

Yves shifted and sat up and lit a cigarette, then lit one for Eric. "I am beginning to be quite hungry."

"So am I. But we'll be eating soon." The kitten wandered in and leapt into Eric's lap. He stroked it with one hand. "Do you remember how we met?"

"I will never forget it. I owe a great deal to Beethoven."

Eric smiled. "*And* to the wonders of modern science."

He had been walking along the Rue des St. Pères on a spring evening, and his thoughts had not been pretty. Paris seemed, and had seemed for a long time, the loneliest city under heaven. And whoever prolongs his sojourn in that city—who tries, that is, to make a home there—is doomed to discover that there is no one to be blamed for whatever happens to him. Contrary to its legend, Paris does not offer many distractions; or, those distractions that it offers are like French pastry, vivid and insubstantial, sweet on the tongue and sour in the belly. Then the discontented wanderer is thrown back on himself—if his life is to become bearable, only he can make it so. And, on that spring evening, walking up the long, dark, murmuring street toward the Boulevard, Eric was in despair. He knew that he had a life to make, but he did not seem to have the tools.

Then, as he neared the Boulevard, he heard music. At first, he thought it came from the houses, but then he realized that it was coming from the shadows across the street, where there were no houses. He stood still and listened; to Beethoven's "Emperor" Concerto, which was moving away from him. Then, out of the shadows, ahead of him, and on the other side of the street, he saw the long, lean figure of a boy. He stood on the corner, waiting for the lights to change, and Eric saw that he was carrying a small portable radio, holding it with both hands. Eric walked to the corner, the lights changed, the boy crossed the street, and Eric followed. Down the long, dark street, the boy on one side and he on the other, and with the violence of the music, which was like the violence in his heart, filling the soft, spring air.

They reached the corner of the Rue de Rennes. The concerto was approaching its end. To the right, far from them, squatted the bulk of the Gare Montparnasse; to the left, and somewhat nearer, were the cafés and the Boulevard, and the clean, gray spire of St. Germain-des-Près.

The boy hesitated on the corner; looked over, briefly, and his eyes met Eric's. He turned in the direction of St. Germain-des-Près. Eric crossed the street. *Tum-ta-tum, tum-ta-tum, tum-ta-tum, tum-ta-tum!* went the music.

"Hello," Eric said. "I'm afraid I've got to hear the end of that concerto."

Yves turned and Eric was immediately struck by his eyes. In the candor with which they regarded him, they were like the eyes of a child; and yet there was also something in that scrutiny which was not childish at all. Eric felt his heart pound once, hard, against his chest. Then Yves smiled.

"It is almost ended," he said.

"I know." They walked in silence, listening to the end of the concerto. When it ended, Yves clicked the radio off.

"Will you have a drink with me?" Eric asked. He said, quickly, "I'm all by myself, I've got no one to talk to—and—and you don't run into people playing Beethoven every day."

"That is true," said Yves, with a smile. "You have a funny accent, where are you from?"

"America."

"I thought it *must* be America. But which section you are from?"

"The South. Alabama."

"Oh," said Yves, and looked at him with interest, "then you are *raciste*."

"Why, no," said Eric, feeling rather stunned, "we are not all like that."

"Oh," said Yves, majestically, "I read your newspapers. And I have many African friends and I have noticed that Americans do not like that."

"Well," said Eric, "that's not *my* problem. I left Alabama as fast as I could and if I ever go back there, they'll probably kill me."

"Have you been here long?"

"About a year."

"And you still know *no one*?"

"It's hard to make friends with the French."

"Well. It is only that we are more *réservé* than you."

"I'll say you are." They stopped before the Royal St. Germain. "Shall we have a drink here?"

"It does not matter." Yves looked over the tables, which were full; looked through the glass walls into the bar, which was crowded, mostly with young males. "But it is terribly crowded."

"Let's go someplace else."

They walked to the corner and crossed the street. All of the cafés were full. They crossed the street again, and passed the Brasserie Lipp. Eric had been watching Yves with more inten-

sity than he realized; as they passed the brasserie, it suddenly
flashed through him that Yves was hungry. He did not know
how he knew it, for Yves said nothing, did not pause or sigh;
and yet Eric could not have been more certain that the boy
was faint with hunger had he abruptly collapsed on the sidewalk.

"Look," Eric said, "I've got an idea. I'm starving, I haven't
eaten any supper. Come on over to Les Halles with me and
let's get something to eat. And by the time we get back, it
won't be so crowded over here." Yves looked at him, his head
tilted in a kind of wary, waiting surprise.

"It is so far," he murmured. And he stared at Eric with a
bright, suspicious bafflement; as though he were thinking, I
am willing to play all games, my friend, but what are the rules
of this one? and what are the penalties?

"I'll bring you back." He grinned and grabbed Yves' arm
and started for the taxi stand. "Come on, be my guest, you'll
be doing me a favor. What's your name?"

"Je m'appel Yves."

"My name is Eric."

He had often thought since that, had it not been for that
sudden apprehension before the brasserie, he and Yves would
never have met again. Their first meal together had given
them time, so to speak, to circle around one another. Eric did
most of the talking; the burden of proof was on him. And
Yves became less wary and less tight. Eric chattered on, delighted by Yves' changing face, waiting for his smile, waiting
for his laugh. He wanted Yves to know that he was not trying
to strike with him the common, brutal bargain; was not buying him a dinner in order to throw him into bed. And by and
by this unspoken declaration caused Yves to nod gravely, as
though he were turning it over in his mind. There also appeared in his face a certain fear. It was this fear which Eric
sometimes despaired of conquering, in Yves, or in himself. It
was the fear of making a total commitment, a vow: it was the
fear of being loved.

That day in Chartres they had passed through town and
watched women kneeling at the edge of the water, pounding
clothes against a flat, wooden board. Yves had watched them
for a long time. They had wandered up and down the old

crooked streets, in the hot sun; Eric remembered a lizard darting across a wall; and everywhere the cathedral pursued them.
It is impossible to be in that town and not be in the shadow
of those great towers; impossible to find oneself on those
plains and not be troubled by that cruel and elegant, dogmatic
and pagan presence. The town was full of tourists, with their
cameras, their three-quarter coats, bright flowered dresses and
shirts, their children, college insignia, Panama hats, sharp,
nasal cries, and automobiles crawling like monstrous gleaming
bugs over the laming, cobblestoned streets. Tourist buses,
from Holland, from Denmark, from Germany, stood in the
square before the cathedral. Tow-haired boys and girls, earnest, carrying knapsacks, wearing khaki-colored shorts, with
heavy buttocks and thighs, wandered dully through the town.
American soldiers, some in uniform, some in civilian clothes,
leaned over bridges, entered bistros in strident, uneasy, smiling packs, circled displays of colored post cards, and picked
up meretricious mementos, of a sacred character. All of the
beauty of the town, all the energy of the plains, and all the
power and dignity of the people seemed to have been sucked
out of them by the cathedral. It was as though the cathedral
demanded, and received, a perpetual, living sacrifice. It tow-
ered over the town, more like an affliction than a blessing,
and made everything seem, by comparison with itself,
wretched and makeshift indeed. The houses in which the people lived did not suggest shelter, or safety. The great shadow
which lay over them revealed them as mere doomed bits of
wood and mineral, set down in the path of a hurricane which,
presently, would blow them into eternity. And this shadow
lay heavy on the people, too. They seemed stunted and mis-
shapen; the only color in their faces suggested too much bad
wine and too little sun; even the children seemed to have been
hatched in a cellar. It was a town like some towns in the
American South, frozen in its history as Lot's wife was trapped
in salt, and doomed, therefore, as its history, that overwhelming, omnipresent gift of God, could not be questioned, to be
the property of the gray, unquestioning mediocre.

   Sometime in the course of the afternoon, though they had
only come down from Paris for the day, they decided to spend
the night. It was Yves' suggestion, made when they returned

to the cathedral and stood on the steps, looking at the saints and martyrs trapped in stone. Yves had been unusually silent all day. And Eric knew him well enough by now not to push him, not to prod, even not to worry. He knew that Yves' silences meant that he was fighting some curious war of his own, was coming to some decision of his own; presently, later today, tomorrow, next week, Yves would abruptly retrace, in speech, the steps he was taking in silence now. And, oddly enough, for it seems not to be the way we live now, for Eric, merely hearing Yves' footfalls at his side, feeling Yves beside him, and watching that changing face, was joy enough—or almost joy enough.

They found a hotel which overlooked a stream and took a double room. Their windows overlooked the water; the towers of the cathedral loomed to the right of them, far away. When they took the room, the sun was setting and great streaks of fire and dull gold were splashed across the still, blue sky.

There were trees just outside the window, bending into the water; and there were a few tables and chairs, but they were empty; there did not seem to be many people in the hotel.

Yves seated himself in the large window and lit a cigarette, looking down at the tables and chairs. Eric stood next to him, his hand on Yves' shoulder.

"Shall we have a drink down there, old buddy?"

"My God, no; we shall be eaten up by bugs. Let's go and find a bistro."

"Okay."

He moved away. Yves stood up. They stared at each other.

"I imagine that we must come back early," Yves said, "there is surely nothing to do in this town." Then he grinned, mischievously. *"Ça va?"*

"It was your idea to come here," Eric said.

"Yes." He turned to the window again. "It is peaceful, yes? And we can be gentle with each other, we can have a moment together." He threw his cigarette out of the window. When he turned to Eric again, his eyes were clouded, and his mouth was very vulnerable. After a moment he said, softly, "Let us go."

But it was very nearly a question. And, now, both of them

were frightened. For some reason, the towers seemed closer
than they had been; and, suddenly, the two large beds, placed
close together, seemed the only objects in the room. Eric felt
his heart shake and his blood begin to race and then to
thicken. He felt that Yves was waiting for him to move, that
everything was in his hands; and he could do nothing.

Then it lifted, the red, dangerous shadow, the moment
passed, they smiled at each other. Yves walked to the door
and opened it. They descended again into the sleepy, the
beautiful town.

For it was not quite the same town it had been a few hours
before. In that second in the room, something had melted
between them, a gap between them had closed; and now the
irresistible current was tugging at them, dragging them slowly,
and absolutely surely, to the fulfillment of that promise.

And for this reason they hesitated, they dawdled, they deliciously put it off. They chose to eat in an unadorned bistro
because it was empty—empty when they walked in, anyway,
though it was taken over after they had been there for a while,
by half a dozen drunk and musical French soldiers. The noise
they made might have been unbearable at any other time, but,
now, it operated as a kind of protective wall between themselves and the world. It gave them something to laugh at—
and they needed to laugh; the distraction the soldiers afforded
the other people who had entered the bistro allowed them,
briefly, to clasp hands; and this small preamble to terror
steadied their hearts and minds.

And then they walked through the town, in which not even
a cat seemed to be moving; and everywhere they walked, the
cathedral was watching them. They crossed a bridge and
watched the moon in the water. Their footfalls rang on the
cobblestones. The walls of the houses were all black, they
walked through great patches of blackness between one far-
off street light to another. But the cathedral was lighted.

The trees and the tables and chairs and the water were lit
by the moon. Yves locked their door behind them and Eric
walked to the window and looked at the sky, at the mighty
towers. He heard the murmur of the water and then Yves
called his name. He turned. Yves stood on the other side of
the room, between the two beds, naked.

"Which bed do you think is better?" he asked.

And he sounded genuinely perplexed, as though it were a difficult decision.

"Whichever you prefer," Eric said, gravely.

Yves pulled back the covers of the bed nearest the window and placed himself between the sheets. He pulled the covers up to his chin and lay on his back, watching Eric. His eyes were dark and enormous in the dark room. A faint smile touched his lips.

And this look, this moment, entered into Eric, to remain with him forever. There was a terrifying innocence in Yves' face, a beautiful yielding: in some marvelous way, for Yves, this moment in this bed obliterated, cast into the sea of forgetfulness, all the sordid beds and squalid grappling which had led him here. He was turning to the lover who would not betray him, to his first lover. Eric crossed the room and sat down on the bed and began to undress. Again, he heard the murmur of the stream.

"Will you give me a cigarette?" Yves asked. He had a new voice, newly troubled, and when Eric looked at him he saw for the first time how the face of a lover becomes a stranger's face.

"Bien sûr." He lit two cigarettes and gave one to Yves. They watched each other in the fantastic, tiny glow—and smiled, almost like conspirators.

Then Eric asked, "Yves, do you love me?"

"Yes," said Yves.

"That's good," said Eric, "because I'm crazy about you. I love you."

Then, in the violent moonlight, naked, he slowly pulled the covers away from Yves. They watched each other and he stared at Yves' body for a long time before Yves lifted up his arms, with that same sad, cryptic smile, and kissed him. Eric felt beneath his fingers Yves' slowly stirring, stiffening sex. This sex dominated the long landscape of his life as the cathedral towers dominated the plains.

Now, Yves, as though he were also remembering that day and night, turned his head and looked at Eric with a wondering, speculative, and triumphant smile. And at that moment, Madame Belet entered, with a sound of knives and forks and plates, and switched on the lights. Yves' face changed, the sea vanished. Yves rose from the hassock, blinking a little. Madame Belet put the utensils on the table, carefully, and marched out again, returning immediately with a bottle of wine, and a corkscrew. She placed these on the table. Yves went to the table and began opening the wine.

"She thinks you are going to abandon me," said Yves. He poured a tiny bit of wine into his own glass, then poured for Eric. He looked at Eric, quickly, and added more wine to the first glass, and set the bottle down.

"Abandon you?" Eric laughed. Yves looked relieved and a little ashamed. "You mean—she thinks I'm running away from you?"

"She thinks that perhaps you do not really intend to bring me to New York. She says that Americans are very different—when—in their own country."

"Well, how the hell does *she* know?" He was suddenly angry. "And it's none of her fucking business, anyway." Madame Belet entered, and he glared at her. Imperturbably, she placed on the table a platter containing *les crudités*, and a basket full of bread. She re-entered the kitchen, Eric staring malevolently at her straight, chauvinistic back. "If there's one thing I can't stand, it's malicious old ladies."

They sat down. "She does not really mean any harm," Yves said. "She thought that she was speaking for my good."

"She thinks it's good for you to distrust me—just when I'm about to get on a boat? Doesn't she think we have enough to worry about?"

"Oh, well. People do not take the relations between boys seriously, you know that. We will never know many people who believe we love each other. They do not believe there can be tears between men. They think we are only playing a game and that we do it to shock them."

Eric was silent, chewing on the raw vegetables which seemed to have no taste. He took a swallow of wine, but it did not help. His belly tightened and his forehead began to be damp. "I know. And it's going to be worse in New York."

"Oh, well," said Yves, with an odd and moving note of finality in his voice, "as long as you do not abandon me, I will not be afraid."

Eric smiled—at the tone, at the statement; but he felt his forehead flush hotter, and a strange fear closed his throat. "Is that a promise?" he asked. He asked it lightly, but his voice sounded stifled; and Yves, who had lowered his head to his plate, looked up. They watched each other. Eric stared into Yves' dark eyes, terribly aware of Yves' forehead, which gleamed like a skull; and, at the same time, with the most immense desire, he watched Yves' curving, parted lips. His teeth gleamed. Eric had felt those teeth on his tongue and on his cheek, and those lips had made him moan and tremble many times. And the short length of the table seemed to tremble between them.

"Why don't we pay Madame Belet now?" Eric asked, "and let her go home?"

Yves rose and walked into the kitchen. Eric munched again on the raw, garlic-flavored vegetables, thinking, *This is our last night here. Our last night.* Again, he heard their voices in the kitchen, Madame Belet seeming to protest, then agreeing to come in the morning. He finished the last of his wine. Then the kitchen door closed and Yves returned.

"I think, perhaps, she is a little angry," Yves said, smiling, "but she is gone. She will come again in the morning, especially to say good-bye to you. I think that is because she wants to make certain that you know how much she dislikes you." He did not sit down again, but stood at his end of the table, his hands on his hips. "She says the chicken is ready, we should not let it get cold." He laughed, and Eric laughed. "I told her it does not matter with chicken, if it is cold or hot, I like it either way." They both laughed again. Then, abruptly, silence fell between them.

Eric rose and crossed to Yves, and they stood for a moment like two wrestlers, watching each other with a kind of physical calculation, smiling and pale. Yves always seemed, a moment before the act, tentative and tremulous; not like a girl—like a boy: and this strangely innocent waiting, this virile helplessness, always engendered in Eric a positive storm of tenderness. Everything in him, from his heights and depths, his mysterious, hidden source, came rushing together, like a great flood barely channeled in a narrow mountain stream. And it chilled him like that—like icy water; and roared in him like that, and with the menace of things scarcely understood, barely to be controlled; and he shook with the violence with which he flowed toward Yves. It was this violence which made him gentle, for it frightened him. And now he touched Yves lightly and wonderingly on the cheek. Yves' smile faded, he watched Eric, they moved into each other's arms.

There were the wine bottle and the glasses on the table, their plates, the platter, the bread; Yves had left a cigarette burning in an ashtray on the table, it was nearly nothing but ash now, long and gray; and the kitchen light was on. "You say you don't care about the chicken?" Eric whispered, laughing. Yves laughed, giving off a whiff of garlic, of peppery sweat. Their arms locked around each other, then they drew apart, and, holding hands, stumbled into the bedroom, into the great haven of their bed. Perhaps it had never before seemed so much like a haven, so much their own, now that the terrible floodwaters of time were about to overtake it. And perhaps they had never before so belonged to each other, had never before given or taken so much from each other, as they did now, burning and sobbing on the crying bed.

They labored together slowly, violently, a long time: both feared the end. Both feared the morning, when the moon and stars would be gone, when this room would be harsh and sorrowful with sunlight, and this bed would be dismantled, waiting for other flesh. *Love is expensive*, Yves had once said, with his curiously dry wonder. *One must put furniture around it, or it goes.* Now, for a while, there would be no furniture—how long would this night have to last them? What would the morning bring? the imminent morning, behind which were hidden so many mornings, so many nights.

And they moaned. *Soon*, Yves whispered, sounding insistent, like a child, and with a terrible regret. *Soon.* Eric's hands and mouth opened and closed on his lover's body, their bodies strained yet closer together, and Yves' body shook and he called Eric's name as no one had ever called this name before. *Eric. Eric. Eric.* The sound of his breath filled Eric, heavier than the far-off pounding of the sea.

Then they were silent, breathing hard. The sound of the sea returned. They were aware of the light in the living room, the light left burning in the kitchen. But they did not move.

They remained still in one another's arms, in their slowly chilling bed. Soon, one of them, it would be Yves, would move, would light two cigarettes. They would lie in bed, smoking, talking and giggling. Then they would shower: *what a mess we are!* Yves would cry, laughing a laugh of triumph. Then they would dress, they would probably eat, they would probably go out. And soon the night would end. But, for the moment, they were simply exhausted and at peace with one another and loath to leave the only haven either of them had ever found.

And, in fact, they did not move again that night, smoked no cigarettes, ate no chicken, did no talking, drank no champagne. They fell asleep as they were, cradled, spoon-fashion, against each other, lulled by the pounding of the sea. Eric woke once, when the kitten crawled into bed, trying to place itself around Yves' neck. But he forced it to the foot of the bed. He turned around, leaning on one elbow, watching Yves' sleeping face. He thought of getting up and turning off all the lights; he felt a little hungry. But nothing seemed important enough to take him out of bed, to take him away from Yves, even for a moment. He lay down again, closing his eyes, and listening to Yves' breathing. He fell asleep, thinking, *Life is very different in New York,* and he woke up with this thought, just as the sun was beginning to rise. Yves was awake and was watching him. Eric thought, *Maybe he'll hate New York. And then, maybe he'll hate me, too.* Yves looked frightened and determined. They were silent. Yves suddenly pulled Eric into his arms as though he were angry, or as though he were lost. By and by they were at peace again, and then they lay there in silence, blue cigarette smoke circling around them in the sunny air, the kitten purring in the sunlight at their feet. Then the sound of Madame Belet in the kitchen told Eric it was time to make tracks.

2

EIGHT DAYS LATER, Eric was in New York, with Yves' last words still ringing in his ears, and his touch and his smell all over his body. And Yves' eyes, like the searchlight of the Eiffel Tower or the sweep of a lighthouse light, lit up, at intervals, the grave darkness around him and afforded him, in the black distance, his only frame of reference and his only means of navigation.

On the last day in Paris, at the last moment, they both suffered from terrible hangovers, having both been up all night, drinking, at a friend's house; their faces were gray and damp; they stank with weariness. There was great shouting and confusion all around them, and the train breathed over them like some unimaginably malevolent beetle. They were almost too tired for sorrow, but not too tired for fear. It steamed out of them both, like the miasma rising from the Gare St. Lazare. In the deep black shadow of this shed, while their friends stood at a discreet distance from them; and the station attendant moved up and down the platform, shouting, *"En voiture, s'il vous plaît! En voiture! En voiture!"*; and the great hand of the great clock approached the zero hour; they stared into each other's faces like comrades who have been through a war.

"T'ne fait pas," Eric murmured.

"En voiture!"

Eric moved up to stand in the crowded doorway of the train. There was nothing to say; there was too much to say.

"I hate waiting," he said. "I hate good-byes." He suddenly felt that he was going to cry, and panic threatened to overtake him because of all these people watching. "We will see each other," he said, "very soon. I promise you, Yves. I promise you. *Tu me fait toujours confiance, j'espère?"* And he tried to smile.

Yves said nothing, but nodded, his eyes very bright, his mouth very vulnerable, his forehead very high, and full of trouble. People were screaming out of windows, were passing last minute items to each other through windows. Eric was the last person standing in the door. He had an awful feeling that he had forgotten something very important. He had paid for Yves' hotel room, they had visited the American embassy and the French authorities, he had left Yves some money— what else? what else? The train began to move. Yves looked stunned for a moment, Eric raised his eyes from Yves' face to say good-bye to all the others. Yves trotted along the platform, then suddenly leapt up on the step, holding on with one hand, and kissed Eric hard on the mouth.

"Ne m'oublie pas," he whispered. "You are all I have in this world."

Then he jumped down, just as the train began to pick up speed. He ran along the platform a little longer, then stopped, his hands in his pockets, staring, and with the wind raising his hair. Eric watched him, waving. The platform narrowed, sloped, ended, the train swerved, and Yves vanished from his sight. It did not seem possible and he stared stupidly at the flying poles and wires, at the sign saying PARIS–ST. LAZARE, at the blank, back walls of buildings. Then tears rolled down his face. He lit a cigarette and stood in the vestibule, while the hideous outskirts of Paris rolled by. Why am I going home? he asked himself. But he knew why. It was time. In order not to lose all that he had gained, he had to move forward and risk it all.

New York seemed very strange indeed. It might, almost, for strange barbarity of manner and custom, for the sense of danger and horror barely sleeping beneath the rough, gregarious surface, have been some impenetrably exotic city of the East. So superbly was it in the present that it seemed to have nothing to do with the passage of time: time might have dismissed it as thoroughly as it had dismissed Carthage and Pompeii. It seemed to have no sense whatever of the exigencies of human life; it was so familiar and so public that it became, at last, the most despairingly private of cities. One was continually being jostled, yet longed, at the same time, for the sense of others, for a human touch; and if one was never—it was the general complaint—left alone in New York, one had, still, to fight very hard in order not to perish of loneliness. This fight, carried on in so many different ways, created the strange climate of the city. The girls along Fifth Avenue wore their bright clothes like semaphores, trying helplessly to bring to the male attention the news of their mysterious trouble. The men could not read this message. They strode purposefully along, wearing little anonymous hats, or bareheaded, with youthfully parted hair, or crew cuts, accoutered with attaché cases, rushing, on the evidence, to the smoking cars of trains. In this haven, they opened up their newspapers and caught up on the day's bad news. Or they were to be found, as five o'clock fell, in discreetly dim, anonymously appointed bars, uneasy, in brittle, uneasy, female company, pouring down joyless martinis.

This note of despair, of buried despair, was insistently, constantly struck. It stalked all the New York avenues, roamed all the New York streets; was as present in Sutton Place, where the director of Eric's play lived and the great often gathered, as it was in Greenwich Village, where he had rented an apartment and been appalled to see what time had done to people he had once known well. He could not escape the feeling that a kind of plague was raging, though it was officially and publicly and privately denied. Even the young seemed blighted— seemed most blighted of all. The boys in their blue jeans ran together, scarcely daring to trust one another, but united, like their elders, in a boyish distrust of the girls. Their very walk, a kind of anti-erotic, knee-action lope, was a parody of locomotion and of manhood. They seemed to be shrinking away from any contact with their flamboyantly and paradoxically outlined private parts. They seemed—but could it be true? and how had it happened?—to be at home with, accustomed to, brutality and indifference, and to be terrified of human affection. In some strange way they did not seem to feel that they were worthy of it.

Now, late on a Sunday afternoon, having been in New York four days, and not yet having written his parents in the South, Eric moved through the tropical streets on his way to visit Cass and Richard. He was having a drink with them to celebrate his return.

"I'm glad you think it's something to celebrate," he had told Cass over the phone.

She laughed. "That's not very nice. You sound as though you haven't missed us at all."

"Oh, I certainly want to see all of *you*. But I don't know if I ever really missed the city very much. Did you ever notice how ugly it is?"

"It's getting uglier all the time," Cass said. "A perfect example of free enterprise gone mad."

"I wanted to thank you," he said, after a moment, "for writing me about Rufus." And he thought, with a rather surprising and painful venom, Nobody else thought to do it.

"Well, I knew," she said, "that you'd want to know." Then there was a silence. "You never knew his sister, did you?"

"Well, I knew he *had* one. I never met her; she was just a kid in those days."

"She's not a kid now," Cass said. "She's going to be singing Sunday, down in the Village, with some friends of Rufus's. For the first time. We promised to bring you along. Vivaldo will be there."

He thought of Rufus. He did not know what to say. "She's something like her brother, huh?"

"I wouldn't say that. Yes and no." Briefly: "You'll see." This brought them to another silence, and, after a few seconds, they hung up.

He entered their building, stepped into the elevator, and told the elevator man where he was going. He had forgotten the style of American elevator men, but now it came back to him. The elevator man, without a surly word, slammed the elevator gates shut and drove the car upward. The nature of his silence conveyed his disapproval of the Silenskis and all their friends and his vivid sense of being as good as they.

He rang the bell. Cass opened the door at once, looking as bright as the bright day.

"Eric!" She looked him over with the affectionate mockery he now remembered. "How nice you look with your hair so short!"

"How nice," he returned, smiling, "you look with yours so long. Or was it always long. It's that kind of thing a long absence makes you forget."

"Let me look at you." She pulled him into the apartment and closed the door. "You really look wonderful. Welcome home." She leaned forward suddenly and kissed him on the cheek. "Is that the way they do it in Paris?"

"You have to kiss me on both cheeks," he said, gravely.

"Oh." She seemed slightly embarrassed but kissed him again. "Is that better?"

"Much," he said. Then, "Where *is* everybody?" For the large living room was empty, and filled with the sound of the blues. It was the voice of a colored woman, the voice of Bessie Smith, and it hurled him, with violence, into the hot center of his past: *It's raining and it's storming on the sea. I feel like somebody has shipwrecked poor me.*

For a moment Cass looked as though she were sardonically echoing his question. She crossed the room and lowered the volume of the music slightly. "The children are over in the park with some friends of theirs. Richard's in his study, working. But they should all be appearing almost any moment now."

"Oh," he said, "then I'm early. I'm sorry."

"You aren't early, you're on time. And *I'm* glad. I was hoping to have a chance to talk to you alone before we go down to this jam session."

"You've got a pretty agreeable jam session going on right now," he said. Cass went over to the bar, and he threw himself down on the sofa. "It's mighty nice and cool in here. It's awful outside. I'd forgotten how hot New York could be."

The large windows were open and the water stretched beyond the windows, very bright and peaceful, but murkier than the Mediterranean. The breeze that filled the room came directly from the water; seemed, almost, to bring with it the spice and stink of Europe and the murmur of Yves' voice. Eric leaned back, held in a kind of peaceful melancholy, comforted by the beat of Bessie's song, and looked over at Cass.

The sun surrounded her golden hair which was piled on top of her head and fell over her brow in girlish, somewhat too artless and incongruous curls. This was meant to soften a face, the principal quality of which had always been a spare, fragile boniness. There was a fine crisscross of wrinkles now around the large eyes; the sun revealed that she was wearing a little too much make-up. This, and something indefinably sorrowful in the line of her mouth and jaw, as she stood silently at the bar, looking down, made Eric feel that Cass was beginning to fade, to become brittle. Something icy had touched her.

"Do you want gin or vodka or bourbon or Scotch or beer? or tequila?" She looked up, smiling. Though the smile was genuine, it was weary. It did not contain the mischievous delight that he remembered. And there were tiny lines now around her neck, which he had never noticed before.

We're getting old, he thought, and it damn sure didn't take long.

"I think I'd better stick to whiskey. I get too drunk too fast on gin—and I don't know what this evening holds."

"Ah," she said, "farsighted Eric! And what *kind* of whiskey?"

"In Paris, when we order whiskey—which, for a very long time, I didn't dare to do—we always mean Scotch."

"You loved Paris, didn't you? You must have, you were gone so long. Tell me about it."

She made two drinks and came and sat beside him. From far away, he heard the muffled *cling!* of a typewriter bell.

It's a long old road, Bessie sang, *but I'm going to find an end.*

"It doesn't seem so long," he said, "now that I'm back." He felt very shy now, for when Cass said *You loved Paris* he at once thought, Yves is there. "It's a great city, Paris, a beautiful city—and—it was very good for me."

"I see that. You seem much happier. There's a kind of light around you."

She said this very directly, with a rueful, conspiratorial smile: as though she knew the cause of his happiness, and rejoiced for him.

He dropped his eyes, but raised them again. "It's just the sun," he said, and they both laughed. Then, irrepressibly, "I *was* very happy there, though."

"Well, you didn't leave because you weren't happy there any more?"

"No." *And when I get there, I'm going to shake hands with a friend.* "A guy I know who thinks he has great psychic powers"—he sipped his whiskey, smiling—"Frenchman, persuaded me that I'd become a great star if I came home and did this play. And I just haven't got the guts to go against the stars, to say nothing of arguing with a Frenchman. So."

She laughed. "I didn't know the French went in for things like that. I thought they were very logical."

"French logic is very simple. Whatever the French do is logical because the French are doing it. That's the really unbeatable advantage French logic has over all others."

"I see," she said, and laughed again. "I hope you read the play before your friend consulted the stars. Is it a good part?"

"It's the best part," he said, after a moment, "that I've ever had."

Again, briefly, he heard the typewriter bell. Cass lit a cigarette, offered one to Eric, and lit it for him. "Are you going to settle here now, or are you planning to go back, or what?"

"I don't," he said, quickly, "have any plans for going back, a lot—maybe everything—depends on what happens with this play."

She sensed his retreat, and took her tone from him. "Oh. I'd love to come and watch rehearsals. I'd run out and get coffee for you, and things like that. It would make me feel that I'd contributed to your triumph."

"Because you're sure it's going to be a triumph," he said, smiling. "Wonderful Cass. I guess it's a habit great men's wives get into."

Weeping and crying, tears falling on the ground.

The atmosphere between them stiffened a little, nevertheless, with their knowledge of why he had allowed his career in New York to lapse for so long. Then he allowed himself to think of opening night, and he thought, Yves will be here. This thought exalted him and made him feel safe. He did not feel safe now, sitting here alone with Cass; he had not felt safe since stepping off the boat. His ears ached for the sound of Yves' footfalls beside him: until he heard this rhythm, all other sounds were meaningless. *Weeping and crying, tears falling on the ground.* All other faces were obliterated for him by the blinding glare of Yves' absence. He looked over at Cass, longing to tell her about Yves, but not daring, not knowing how to begin.

"Great men's wives, indeed!" said Cass. "How I'd love to explode *that* literary myth." She looked at him, gravely sipping her whiskey, without seeming to taste it. *When I got to the end, I was so worried down.* "You seem very sure of yourself," she said.

"I do?" He was profoundly astonished and pleased. "I don't *feel* very sure of myself."

"I remember you before you went away. You were miserable then. We all wondered—*I* wondered—what would become of you. But you aren't miserable now."

"No," he said, and, under her scrutiny, blushed. "I'm not miserable any more. But I still don't know what's going to become of me."

"Growth," she said, "is what will become of you. It's what *has* become of you." And she gave him again her oddly intimate, rueful smile. "It's very nice to see, it's very—enviable. I don't envy many people. I haven't found myself envying *anyone* for a long, long time."

"It's mighty funny," he said, "that you should envy *me*." He rose from the sofa, and walked to the window. Behind him, beneath the mighty lament of the music, a heavy silence gathered: Cass, also, had something to talk about, but he did not want to know what it was. *You can't trust nobody, you might as well be alone.* Staring out over the water, he asked, "What was Rufus like—near the end?"

After a moment, he turned and looked at her. "I hadn't meant to ask you that—but I guess I really want to know."

Her face, despite the softening bangs, grew spare and contemplative. Her lips twisted. "I told you a little of it," she said, "in my letter. But I didn't know how you felt by that time and I didn't see any point in burdening you." She put out her cigarette and lit another one. "He was very unhappy, as—as you know." She paused. "Actually, we never got very close to him. Vivaldo knew him better than—than *we* did, anyway." He felt a curious throb of jealousy: *Vivaldo!* "We didn't see much of him. He became very involved with a Southern girl, a girl from Georgia——"

Found my long lost friend, and I might as well stayed at home!

"You didn't tell me *that*," he said.

"No. He wasn't very nice to her. He beat her up a lot——"

He stared at her, feeling himself grow pale, remembering

more than he wanted to remember, feeling his hope and his hope of safety threatened by invincible, unnamed forces within himself. He remembered Rufus' face, his hands, his body, and his voice, and the constant humiliation. "Beat her up? What for?"

"Well—who knows? Because she was Southern, because she was white. I don't know. Because he was Rufus. It was very ugly. She was a nice girl, maybe a little pathetic—"

"Did she like to be beaten up? I mean—did something in her like it, did she like to be—debased?"

"No, I don't think so. I really don't think so. Well, maybe there's something in everybody that likes to be debased, but I don't think life's that simple. I don't trust all these formulas." She paused. "To tell the truth, I think she probably loved Rufus, really loved him, and wanted Rufus to love her."

"How abnormal," he said, "can you get!" He finished his drink.

A very faint, wry amusement crossed her face. "Anyway, their affair dragged on from bad to worse and she was finally committed to an institution—"

"You mean, a madhouse?"

"Yes."

"Where?"

"In the South. Her family came and got her."

"My God," he said. "Go on."

"Well, then, Rufus disappeared—for quite a long time, that's when I met his sister, she came to see us, looking for him—and came back once, and—*died*." Helplessly, she opened one bony hand, then closed it into a fist.

Eric turned back to the window. "A Southern girl," he said. He felt a very dull, very distant pain. It all seemed very long ago, that gasping and trembling, freezing and burning time. The pain was distant now because it had scarcely been bearable then. It could not really be recollected because it had become a part of him. Yet, the power of this pain, though diminished, was not dead: Rufus' face again appeared before him, that dark face, with those dark eyes and curving, heavy lips. It was the face of Rufus when he had looked with love on Eric. Then, out of hiding, leapt his other faces, the crafty, cajoling face of desire, the remote face of desire achieved.

Then, for a second, he saw Rufus' face as he stared on death, and saw his body hurtling downward through the air: into that water, the water which stretched before him now. The old pain receded into the home it had made in him. But another pain, homeless as yet, began knocking at his heart—not for the first time: it would force an entry one day, and remain with him forever. *Catch them. Don't let them blues in here. They shakes me in my bed, can't sit down in my chair.*

"Let me fix you a fresh drink," Cass said.

"Okay." She took his glass. As she walked to the bar, he said, "You knew about us, I guess? I guess everybody knew—though we thought we were being so smart, and all. And, of course, he always had a lot of girls around."

"Well, so did you," she said. "In fact, I vaguely remember that you were thinking of getting married at one point."

He took his drink from the bar, and paced the room. "Yes. I haven't thought of her in a long time, either." He paused and grimaced sourly. "That's right, I certainly did have a few girls hanging around. I hardly even remember their names." As he said this, the names of two or three old girl friends flashed into his mind. "I haven't thought about them for years." He came back to the sofa, and sat down. Cass watched him from the bar. "I might," he said, painfully, "have had them around just on account of Rufus—trying to prove something, maybe, to him and to myself."

The room was growing darker. Bessie sang, *The blues has got me on the go. They runs around my house, in and out of my front door.* Then the needle scratched aimlessly for a second, and the record player clicked itself off. Eric's attention had painfully snagged itself on the memory of those unloved, but not wholly undesired, girls. Their texture and their odor floated back to him: and it was abruptly astonishing that he had not thought of that side of himself for so long. It had been because of Yves. This thought filled him with a hideous, unwilling resentment: he remembered Yves' hostile adventures with the girls of the Latin Quarter and St. Germain-des-Près. These adventures had not touched Eric because they so clearly had not touched Yves. But now, superbly, like a diver coming to the surface, his terror bobbed, naked, to the surface of his mind: he would lose Yves, here. It would happen here.

And he, he would have no woman, and he would have no Yves. His flesh began to itch, he felt himself beginning to sweat.

He turned and smiled at Cass, who had moved to the sofa, and sat very still beside him in the gloom. She was not watching him. She sat with her hands folded in her lap, busy with thoughts of her own.

"This is one hell of a party," he said.

She rose, smiling, and shook herself a little. "It is, isn't it? I was beginning to wonder where the children are—they should be home by now. And maybe I'd better turn on some lights." She switched on a lamp near the bar. Now, the water and the lights along the water glowed more softly, suggesting the imminent night. Everything was pearl gray, shot with gold. "I'd better go and rouse Richard."

"I didn't know," he said, "that it would be so easy to feel at home again."

She looked at him quickly, and grinned. "Is that good?"

"I don't know yet." He was about to say something more, something about Yves, but he heard Richard's study door open and close. He turned to face Richard as he came into the room; he looked very handsome and boyish and big.

"So we finally got you back here! I'm told it took every penny Shubert Alley could scrape together. How are you, you old bastard?"

"I'm fine, Richard, it's good to see you." They clung together, briefly, in the oddly truncated, shrinking, American embrace, and stepped back to look at one another. "I hear that you're selling more books than Frank Yerby."

"Better," said Richard, "but not more." He looked over at Cass. "How are you, chicken? How's the headache?"

"Eric started telling me about Paris, and I forgot all about it. Why don't *we* go to Paris? I think it would do wonders for us."

"Do wonders for our bank account, too. Don't you let this lousy ex-expatriate come here and turn your head." He walked over to the bar and poured himself a drink. "Did you leave many broken hearts over there?"

"They were very restrained about it. Those centuries of breeding mean something, you know."

"That's what they kept telling me when I was over there.

It didn't seem to mean much, though, beyond poverty and corruption and disease. How did you find it?"

"I had a ball. I loved it. Of course, I wasn't in the Army—"

"Did you like the French? I couldn't stand them; I thought they were as ugly and as phony as they come."

"I didn't feel that. They can be pretty damn exasperating— but, hell, I liked them."

"Well. Of course, you're a far more patient sort than I've ever been." He grinned. "How's your French?"

"*Du trottoir*—of the sidewalk. But fluent."

"You learn it in bed?"

He blushed. Richard watched him and laughed.

"Yes. As a matter of fact."

Richard carried his drink to the sofa and sat down. "I can see that traveling hasn't improved your morals any. You going to be around awhile?"

Eric sat down in the armchair across the room from Richard. "Well, I've got to be here at least until the play opens. But after that—who knows?"

"Well," said Richard, and raised his glass, "here's hoping. May it run longer than *Tobacco Road*."

Eric shuddered. "Not with me in it, bud." He drank, he lit a cigarette; a certain familiar fear and anger began to stir in him. "Tell me about yourself, bring me up to date."

But, as he said this, he realized that he did not care what Richard had been doing. He was merely being polite because Richard was married to Cass. He wondered if he had always felt this way. Perhaps he had never been able to admit it to himself. Perhaps Richard had changed—but *did* people change? He wondered what he would think of Richard if he were meeting him for the first time. Then he wondered what Yves would think of these people and what these people would think of Yves.

"There isn't much to tell. You know about the book—I'll get a copy for you, a coming-home present—"

"*That* should make you glad you've returned," said Cass.

Richard looked at her, smiling. "No sabotage, please." He said to Eric, "Cass still likes to make fun of me." Then, "There's a new book coming, Hollywood may buy the first one, I've got a TV thing coming up."

"Anything for me in the TV bit?"

"It's cast. Sorry. We probably couldn't have afforded you, anyway." The doorbell rang. Cass went to answer it.

There was suddenly a tremendous commotion at the door, sobbing and screaming, but Eric did not react until he saw the change in Richard's face, and heard Cass' cry. Then Richard and Eric stood up and the children came pounding into the room. Michael was sobbing and blood dripped from his nose and mouth onto his red-and-white-striped T-shirt. Paul was behind him, pale and silent, with blood on his knuckles and smeared across his face; and his white shirt was torn.

"It's all right, Cass," Richard said, quickly, "it's all right. They're not dead." Michael ran to his father and buried his bloody face in his father's belly. Richard looked at Paul. "What the hell's been going on?"

Cass pulled Michael away and looked into his face. "Come on, baby, let me wash this blood away and see what's happened to you." Michael turned to her, still sobbing, in a state of terror. Cass held him. "Come on, darling, everything's all right, hush now, darling, come on." Michael was led away, his hand in Cass' trembling hand, and Richard looked briefly at Eric, over Paul's head.

"Come on," he said to Paul, "what happened? You get into a fight or did you beat him up, or what?"

Paul sat down, pressing his hands together. "I don't really know what happened." He was on the edge of tears himself; his father waited. "We had been playing ball and then we were getting ready to come home, we weren't doing anything, just fooling around and walking. I wasn't paying much attention to Mike, he was behind me with some friends of his. Then"— he looked at his father—"some colored—colored boys, they came over this hill and they yelled something, I couldn't hear what they yelled. One of them tripped me up as he passed me and they started beating up the little kids and we came running down to stop them." He looked at his father again. "We never saw any of them before, I don't know where they came from. One of them had Mike down on the ground, and was punching him, but I got him off." He looked at his bloody fist. "I think I knocked a couple teeth down his throat."

"Good for you. You didn't get hurt yourself? How do you feel?"

"I feel all right." But he shuddered.

"Stand up, come over here, let me look at you."

Paul stood up and walked over to his father, who knelt down and stared into his face, prodding him gently in the belly and the chest, stroking his neck and his face. "You got a pretty bad crack in the jaw, didn't you?"

"Mike's hurt worse than I am." But he suddenly began to cry. Richard's lips puckered; he gathered his son into his arms. "Don't cry, Paul, it's all over now."

But Paul could not stop, now that he had begun. "Why would they want to do a thing like that, Daddy? We never even *saw* them before!"

"Sometimes—sometimes the world is like that, Paul. You just have to watch out for people like that."

"Is it because they're colored and we're white? Is that why?"

Again, Richard and Eric looked at each other. Richard swallowed. "The world is full of all kinds of people, and sometimes they do terrible things to each other, but—that's not why."

"Some colored people are very nice," said Eric, "and some are not so nice—like white people. Some are nice and some are terrible." But he did not sound very convincing and he wished he had held his peace.

"This kind of thing's been happening more and more here lately," Richard said, "and, frankly, I'm willing to cry Uncle and surrender the island back to the goddam Indians. I don't think that they ever intended that we should be happy here." He gave a small, dry laugh, and turned his attention to Paul again. "Would you recognize any of these boys if you saw them again?"

"I think so," Paul said. He caught his breath and dried his eyes. "I know I'd recognize one of them, the one I hit. When the blood came out of his nose and his mouth, it looked so— *ugly*—against his skin."

Richard watched him a moment. "Let's go inside and clean up and see what's happening to old Michael."

"Michael can't fight," Paul said, "you know? And kids are always going to be picking on him."

"Well, we're going to have to do something about that. He'll have to *learn* how to fight." He walked to the door, with his arm on Paul's shoulder. He turned to Eric. "Make yourself at home, will you? We'll be back in a few minutes." And he and Paul left the room.

Eric listened to the voices of the children and their parents, racing, indistinct, bewildered. "All kids get into fights," said Richard, "let's not make a big thing out of it." "They didn't really get into a fight," Cass said. "They were *attacked*. That's not the same thing at all, it seems to me." "Cass, let's not make it any worse than it is." "I still think we ought to call the doctor; *we* don't know anything about the human body, how do *we* know there isn't something broken or bleeding inside? It happens all the time, people dropping dead two days after an accident." "Okay, okay, stop being so hysterical. You want to scare them to death?" "I am not hysterical and *you* stop being the Rock of Gibraltar. I'm not part of your public, I *know* you!" "Now, what does that mean?" "Nothing. Nothing. Will you please call the *doctor*?" Michael's voice broke in, high and breaking, with a child's terror. "Why, that's the silliest thing I ever heard," Cass said, in another tone and with great authority; "of course no one's going to come in here while you're asleep. Mama and Daddy are here and so is Paul." Michael's voice interrupted her again. "It's all right, we aren't *going* out," Cass said. "We aren't going out *to-night*," Richard said, "and Paul and I are going to teach you some tricks so kids won't be bothering *you* any more. By the time *we* get through, those guys will be afraid of *you*. If they just see you coming, boy, they'll take off in a cloud of dust." He heard Michael's unsteady laugh. Then he heard the sound of the phone being dialed, and Richard's voice, and the small ring of the phone as Richard hung up.

"I guess we won't be going downtown with you, after all," Richard said, coming back into the room. "I'm sorry. I'm sure they're all right but Cass wants the doctor to look at them and we have to wait for him to get here. Anyway, I don't think we should leave them alone tonight." He took Eric's glass from his hand. "Let me spike this for you." He walked over to the bar; he was not as calm as he pretended to be. "Little black bastards," he muttered, "they could have killed the kid. Why the hell can't they take it out on each other, for Christ's sake!"

"They beat Michael pretty badly?"

"Well—they loosened one of his teeth and bloodied his nose—but, mainly, they *scared* the shit out of him. Thank God Paul was with him." Then he was silent. "I don't know. This whole neighborhood, this whole city's gone to hell. I keep telling Cass we ought to move—but she doesn't want to. Maybe this will help her change her mind."

"Change my mind about what?" Cass asked. She strode to the low table before the sofa, picked up her cigarettes, and lit one.

"Moving out of town," Richard said. He watched her as he spoke and spoke too quietly, as though he were holding himself in.

"I've no objection to moving. We just haven't been able to agree on where to move."

"We haven't agreed on where to move because all you've done is offer objections to every place I suggest. And, since you haven't made any counter-suggestions, I conclude that you don't really want to move."

"Oh, Richard. I simply am not terribly attracted to any of those literary colonies you want us to become a part of——"

Richard's eyes turned as dark as deep water. "Cass doesn't like writers," he said, lightly, to Eric, "not if they make a living at it, anyway. She thinks writers should never cease starving and whoring around, like our good friend, Vivaldo. That's fine, boy, that's really being responsible and artistic. But all the rest of us, trying to love a woman and raise a family and make some loot—we're whores."

She was very pale. "I have never said anything at all like that."

"No? There are lots of ways of saying"—he mimicked her— "things like that. You've said it a thousand times. You must think I'm dumb, chicken." He turned again to Eric, who stood near the window, wishing he could fly out of it. "If she was *stuck* with a guy like Vivaldo—"

"Leave Vivaldo out of this! What has *he* got to do with it?"

Richard gave a surprisingly merry laugh, and repeated, "If she was stuck with a guy like that, maybe you wouldn't hear some pissing and moaning! Oh, what a martyrdom! And how she'd love it!" He took a swallow of his drink and crossed the room toward her. "And you know why? You want to know why?" There was a silence. She lifted her enormous eyes to meet his. "Because you're just like all the other American cunts. You want a guy you can feel sorry for, you love him as long as he's helpless. Then you can *pitch in*, as you love to say, you can be his *helper. Helper!*" He threw back his head and laughed. "Then, one fine day, the guy feels chilly between his legs and feels around for his cock and balls and finds she's helped herself to them and locked them in the linen closet." He finished his drink and, roughly, caught his breath. His voice changed, becoming almost tender with sorrow. "That's the way it is, isn't it, sugar? You don't like me now as well as you did once."

She looked terribly weary; her skin seemed to have loosened. She put one hand lightly on his arm. "No," she said, "that's not the way it is." Then a kind of fury shook her and tears came to her eyes. "You haven't any right to say such things to me; you're blaming me for something I haven't anything to do with at all!" He reached out to touch her shoulder; she moved away. "You'd better go, Eric, this can't be much fun for you. Make our excuses, please, to Vivaldo and Ida."

"You can say that the Silenskis, that model couple, were having their Sunday fight," said Richard; his face very white, breathing hard, staring at Cass.

Eric set his drink down, carefully; he wanted to run. "I'll just say you had to stay in on account of the kids."

"Tell Vivaldo to take it as a warning. This is what happens if you have kids, this is what happens if you get what you want." And, for a moment, he looked utterly baffled and juvenile. Then, "Hell, I'm sorry, Eric. We never meant to submit you to such a melodramatic afternoon. Please come and see us again; we don't do this all the time, we really don't. I'll walk you to the door."

"It's all right," Eric said. "I'm a big boy, I understand."

He walked over to Cass and they shook hands. "It was nice seeing you."

"It was good seeing you. Don't let all that light fade."

He laughed, but these words chilled him, too. "I'll try to keep burning," he said. He and Richard walked to the hall door. Cass stood still in the center of the living room.

Richard opened the door. "So long, kid. Can we call you—has Cass got your number?"

"Yes. And I have yours."

"Okay. See you soon."

"Sure thing. So long."

"So long."

The door closed behind him. He was again in the anonymous, breathing corridor, surrounded by locked doors. He found his handkerchief and wiped his forehead, thinking of the millions of disputes being waged behind locked doors. He rang for the elevator. It arrived, driven by another, older man who was eating a sandwich; he was dumped into the streets again. The long block on which Cass and Richard lived was quiet and empty now, waiting for the night. He hailed a cab on the Avenue and was whirled downtown.

His destination was a bar on the eastern end of the Village, which had, until recently, been merely another neighborhood bar. But now it specialized in jazz, and functioned sometimes as a showcase for younger but not entirely untried or unknown talents or personalities. The current attraction was advertised in the small window by a hand-printed, cardboard poster; he recognized the name of a drummer he and Rufus had known years ago, who would not remember him; in the window, too, were excerpts from newspaper columns and magazines, extolling the unorthodox virtues of the place.

The unorthodox, therefore, filled the room, which was very small, low-ceilinged, with a bar on one side and tables and chairs on the other. At the far end of the bar, the room widened, making space for more tables and chairs, and a very narrow corridor led to the rest rooms and the kitchen; and in this widened space, catty-corner to the room, stood a small, cruelly steep bandstand.

Eric had arrived during a break. The musicians were leaping down from the stand, and mopping their brows with large handkerchiefs, and heading for the street door which would remain open for about ten minutes. The heat in the room was terrifying, and the electric fan in the center of the ceiling could have done nothing to alleviate it. And the room stank: of years of dust, of stale, of regurgitated alcohol, of cooking, of urine, of sweat, of lust. People stood three and four deep at the bar, sticky and shining, far happier than the musicians, who had fled to the sidewalk. Most of the people at the tables had not moved, and they seemed quite young; the boys in sport shirts and seersucker trousers, the girls in limp blouses and wide skirts.

On the sidewalk, the musicians stood idly together, still fanning themselves with their handkerchiefs, their faces blandly watchful, ignoring the occasional panhandlers, and the policeman who walked up and down with his lips pursed and his eyes blind with unnameable suspicions and fears.

He wished he had not come. He was afraid of seeing Vivaldo, he was afraid of meeting Ida; and he began to feel, standing helplessly in the center of this sweltering mob, unbearably odd and visible, unbearably a stranger. It was not a new sensation, but he had not felt it for a long time: he felt marked, as though, presently, someone would notice him and then the entire mob would turn on him, laughing and calling him names. He thought of leaving, but, instead, inched into the bar and ordered a drink. He had no idea how he would go about finding Ida or Vivaldo. He imagined that he would have to wait until she began to sing. But, presumably, they would also be watching for him, for his red hair.

And he sipped his drink, standing uncomfortably close to a burly college boy, unpleasantly jostled by the waiter, who was loading his tray next to him. And he was, indeed, beginning to attract a certain, covert attention; he did not look American, exactly: they were wondering how to place him.

He saw them before they saw him. Something made him turn around and look out through the door, to the sidewalk; and Ida and Vivaldo, loosely swinging hands, walked up and began talking to the musicians. Ida was wearing a tight, white, low-cut dress, and her shoulders were covered with a bright shawl. On the little finger of one hand, she wore a ruby-eyed snake ring; on the opposite wrist, a heavy, barbaric-looking bracelet, of silver. Her hair was swept back from her forehead, piled high, and gleaming, like a crown. She was far more beautiful than Rufus and, except for a beautifully sorrowful, quicksilver tension around the mouth, she might not have reminded him of Rufus. But this detail, which he knew so well, caught him at once, and so did another detail, harder, for a moment, to place. She laughed at something said by one of the musicians, throwing her head back: her heavy silver earrings caught the light. Eric felt a pounding in his chest and between his shoulderblades, as he stared at the gleaming metal and the laughing girl. He felt, suddenly, trapped in a dream from which he could not awaken. The earrings were heavy and archaic, suggesting the shape of a feathered arrow: *Rufus never really liked them.* In that time, eons ago, when they had been cufflinks, given him by Eric as a confession of his love, Rufus had hardly ever worn them. But he had kept them. And here they were, transformed, on the body of his sister. The burly college boy, looking straight ahead, seemed to nudge Eric with his knee. Eric moved a little out from the bar and moved nearer the door, so that they would see him when they looked his way.

He stood sipping his drink in the bar; they stood on the twilit sidewalk. Eric watched Vivaldo and used these moments to remember him. Vivaldo seemed more radiant than he had ever been, and less boyish. He was still very slim, very lean, but he seemed, somehow, to have more weight. In Eric's memory, Vivaldo always put one foot down lightly, like a distrustful colt, ready, at any moment, to break and run; but now he stood where he stood, the ground bore him, and his startled, sniffing, maverick quality was gone. Or perhaps not entirely gone: his black eyes darted from face to face as he spoke, as he listened, investigating, weighing, watching, his eyes hiding more than they revealed. The conversation took a more somber turn. One of the musicians had brought up the subject of money—of unions, and, with a gesture toward the spot where Eric stood, of working conditions. Vivaldo's eyes darkened, his face became still, and he looked briefly down at Ida. She watched the musician who was speaking with a proud, bitter look on her face. "So maybe you better give it another thought, gal," the musician concluded. "I've thought about it," she said, looking down, touching one of the earrings. Vivaldo took this hand in his, and she looked up at him; he kissed her lightly on the tip of the nose. "Well," said another musician, wearily, "we better be making it on in." He turned and entered the bar, saying, "Excuse me, man" to Eric as he passed. Ida whispered something in Vivaldo's ear; he listened, frowning. His hair fell over his forehead, and he threw his head back, sharply, with a look of annoyance, and saw Eric.

For a moment they simply stared at each other. Another musician, entering the bar, passed between them. Then, Vivaldo said, "So there you are. I didn't really believe you'd make it; I didn't really believe you'd be back."

"But I'm here," said Eric, grinning, "now, what do you think of that?"

Vivaldo suddenly raised his arms and laughed—and the policeman moved directly behind him, glowering, seeming to wait for an occult go-ahead signal—and covered the space between himself and Eric and threw both arms around him. Eric nearly dropped the glass he was holding, for Vivaldo had thrown him off balance; he grinned up into Vivaldo's grinning face; and was aware, behind Vivaldo, of Ida, inscrutably watching, and the policeman, waiting.

"You fucking red-headed Rebel," Vivaldo shouted, "you haven't changed a bit! Christ, I'm glad to see you, I'd no *idea* I'd be so glad to see you." He released Eric, and stepped back, oblivious, apparently, to the storm he was creating. He dragged Eric out of the bar, into the street, over to Ida. "Here's the sonofabitch we've been talking about so long, Ida; here's Eric. He's the last human being to get out of Alabama."

The policeman seemed to take a dim, even a murderous view of this, and, ceasing to wait on occult inspiration, peered commandingly into the bar. The signal he then received caused him, slowly, to move a little away. But Vivaldo beamed on Eric as though Eric were his pride and joy; and said again, to Ida, staring at Eric, "Ida, this is Eric. Eric, meet Ida." And he took their hands and placed them together.

Ida grasped his hand, laughing, and looked into his eyes. "Eric," she said, "I think I've heard more about you than I've ever heard about any living human being. I'm so glad to meet you, I can't tell you. I'd decided you weren't nothing but a myth."

The touch of her hand shocked him, as did her eyes and her warmth and her beauty. "I'm delighted to meet you, too," he said. "You can't have heard more about me—you can't have heard *better* about me—than I've heard about you."

They held each other's eyes for a second, she still smiling, wearing all her beauty as a great queen wears her robes—and establishing that distance between them, too—and then one of the musicians came to the doorway, and said, "Ida, honey, the man says come on with it if you coming." And he disappeared.

Ida said, "Come on, follow me. They've got a table for us way in back somewhere." She took Eric's arm. "They're doing me a favor, letting me sit in. I've never sung in public before. So I can't afford to bug them."

"You see," said Vivaldo, behind them, "you got off the boat just in time for a great occasion."

"You should have let *him* say that," said Ida.

"I was just about to," said Eric, "believe me." They squeezed through the crowd to the slightly wider area in the back. Here, Ida paused, looking about her.

She looked up at Eric. "What happened to Richard and Cass?"

"They asked me to apologize for them. They couldn't come. One of the kids was sick."

He felt, as he said this, a faint tremor of disloyalty—to Ida: as though she were mixed up in his mind with the colored children who had attacked Paul and Michael in the park.

"*Today* of all days," she sighed—but seemed, really, scarcely to be concerned about their absence. Her eyes continued to search the crowd; she sighed again, a sigh of private resignation. The musicians were ready, attempts were being made to silence the mob. A waiter appeared and seated them at a tiny table in a corner next to the ladies' room, and took their order. The malevolent heat, now that they were trapped in this spot, began rising from the floor and descending from the ceiling.

Eric did not really listen to the music, he could not; it remained entirely outside him, like some minor agitation of the air. He watched Ida and Vivaldo, who sat opposite him, their profiles turned toward the music. Ida watched with a bright, sardonic knowingness, as though the men on the stand were beating out a message she had commanded them to convey; but Vivaldo's head was slightly lowered and he looked up at the bandstand with a wry, uncertain bravado; as though there were an incipient war going on between himself and the musicians, having to do with rank and color and authority. He and Ida sat very still, very straight, not touching—it was as though, before this altar, touch was forbidden them.

The musicians sweated on the stand, like horses, played loudly and badly, with a kind of reckless contempt, and failed, during their first number, to agree on anything. This did not, of course, affect the applause, which was loud, enthusiastic, and prolonged. Only Vivaldo made no sound. The drummer, who, from time to time, had let his eyes travel from Ida to Vivaldo—then bowed his head to the drums again—registered Vivaldo's silence with a broad, mocking grin, and gestured to Ida.

"It's your turn now," he said. "Come on up here and see what *you* can do to civilize these devils." And, with the merest of glances at Eric and Vivaldo, "I think you might have had enough practice by now."

Ida looked into his eyes with an unreadable smile, which yet held some hint of the vindictive. She crushed out her cigarette, adjusted her shawl, and rose, demurely. "I'm glad you think I'm ready," she said. "Keep your fingers crossed for me, sugar," she said to Vivaldo, and stepped up on the stand.

She was not announced; there was merely a brief huddle with the piano-player; and then she stepped up to the mike. The piano-player began the first few bars, but the crowd did not take the hint.

"Let's try it again," said Ida, in a loud, clear voice.

At this, heads turned to look at her; she looked calmly down on them. The only sign of her agitation was in her hands, which were tightly, restlessly clasped before her—she was wringing her hands, but she was not crying.

Somebody said, in a loud whisper, "Dig, man, that's the Kid's kid sister."

There were beads of sweat on her forehead and on her nose, and one leg moved out, trembling, moved back. The piano-player began again, she grabbed the mike like a drowning woman, and abruptly closed her eyes:

> *You*
> *Made me leave my happy home.*
> *You took my love and now you've gone,*
> *Since I fell for you.*

She was not a singer yet. And if she were to be judged solely on the basis of her voice, low, rough-textured, of no very great range, she never would be. Yet, she had something which made Eric look up and caused the room to fall silent; and Vivaldo stared at Ida as though he had never seen her before. What she lacked in vocal power and, at the moment, in skill, she compensated for by a quality so mysteriously and implacably egocentric that no one has ever been able to name it. This quality involves a sense of the self so profound and so powerful that it does not so much leap barriers as reduce them to atoms—while still leaving them standing, mightily, where they were; and this awful sense is private, unknowable, not to be articulated, having, literally, to do with something else; it transforms and lays waste and gives life, and kills.

She finished her first number and the applause was stunned and sporadic. She looked over at Vivaldo with a small, childish shrug. And this gesture somehow revealed to Eric how desperately one could love her, how desperately Vivaldo was in love with her. The drummer went into a down-on-the-levee-type song, which turned out to be a song Eric had never heard before:

> *Betty told Dupree*
> *She wanted a diamond ring.*
> *And Dupree said, Betty,*
> *I'll get you most any old thing.*

"My God," muttered Vivaldo, "she's been working."

His tone unconsciously implied that he had not been, and held an unconscious resentment. And this threw Eric in on himself. Neither had he been working—for a long time; he

had merely been keeping his hand in. It had been because of
Yves; so he had told himself; but was this true? He looked at
Vivaldo's white, passionate face and wondered if Vivaldo were
now thinking that he had not been working because of Ida:
who had not, however, allowed *him* to distract *her*. There she
was, up on the stand, and unless all the signs were false, and
no matter how hard or long the road might be, she was on
her way. She had started.

> *Give Mama my clothes,*
> *Give Betty my diamond ring.*
> *Tomorrow's Friday,*
> *The day I got to swing.*

   She and the musicians were beginning to enjoy each other
and to egg each other on as they bounced through this ballad
of cupidity, treachery, and death; and Ida had created in the
room a new atmosphere and a new excitement. Even the heat
seemed less intolerable. The musicians played for her as
though she were an old friend come home and their pride in
her restored their pride in themselves.
   The number ended and Ida stepped off the stand, wet and
triumphant, the applause crashing about her ears like foam.
She came to the table, looking at Vivaldo with a smile and a
small, questioning frown, and, standing, took a sip of her
drink. They called her back. The drummer reached down and
lifted her, bodily, onto the stand, and the applause continued.
Eric became aware of a shift in Vivaldo's attention. He looked
at Vivaldo's face, which was stormier than ever, and followed
his eyes. Vivaldo was looking at a short square man with curly
hair and a boyish face who was standing at the end of the bar,
looking up at Ida. He grinned and waved and Ida nodded and
Vivaldo looked up at the stand again: with narrowed eyes and
pursed lips, with an air of grim speculation.
   "Your girl friend's got something," Eric said.
   Vivaldo glanced over at him. "It runs in the family," he
said. His tone was not friendly; it was as though he suspected
Eric of taunting him; and so referred, obliquely, to Rufus,
with the intention of humbling Eric. Yet, in a moment he
relented. "She's going to be terrific," he said, "and, Lord,

I'm going to have to buy me a baseball bat to keep all the hungry cats away." He grinned and looked again at the short man at the bar.

Ida stepped up to the microphone. "This song is for my brother," she said. She hesitated and looked over at Vivaldo. "He died just a little before Thanksgiving, last year." There was a murmur in the room. Somebody said, "What did I tell you?"—triumphantly; there was a brief spatter of applause, presumably for the dead Rufus; and the drummer bowed his head and did an oddly irreverent riff on the rim of his drum: *klook-a-klook, klook-klook, klook-klook!*

Ida sang:

> *Precious Lord, take my hand,*
> *Lead me on, let me stand.*

Her eyes were closed and the dark head on the long dark neck was thrown back. Something appeared in her face which had not been there before, a kind of passionate, triumphant rage and agony. Now, her fine, sensual, free-moving body was utterly still, as though being held in readiness for a communion more total than flesh could bear; and a strange chill came into the room, along with a strange resentment. Ida did not know how great a performer she would have to become before she could dare expose her audience, as she now did, to her private fears and pain. After all, her brother had meant nothing to them, or had never meant to them what he had meant to her. They did not wish to witness her mourning, especially as they dimly suspected that this mourning contained an accusation of themselves—an accusation which their uneasiness justified. They endured her song, therefore, but they held themselves outside it; and yet, at the same time, the very arrogance and innocence of Ida's offering compelled their admiration.

> *Hear my cry, hear my call,*
> *Take my hand, lest I fall,*
> *Precious Lord!*

The applause was odd—not quite unwilling, not quite free; wary, rather, in recognition of a force not quite to be trusted but certainly to be watched. The musicians were now both jubilant and watchful, as though Ida had abruptly become their property. The drummer adjusted her shawl around her shoulders, saying, "You been perspiring, don't you let yourself catch cold"; and, as she started off the stand, the piano-player rose and, ceremoniously, kissed her on the brow. The bass-player said, "Hell, let's tell the folks her *name*." He grabbed the microphone and said, "Ladies and gentlemen, you've been listening to Miss Ida Scott. This is her first—*exposure*," and he mopped his brow, ironically. The crowd laughed. He said, "But it won't be her last." The applause came again, more easily this time, since the role of judge and bestower had been returned to the audience. "We have been present," said the bass-player, "at an historic event." This time the audience, in a paroxysm of self-congratulation, applauded, stomped, and cheered.

"Well," said Vivaldo, taking both her hands in his, "it looks like you're on your way."

"Were you proud of me?" She made her eyes very big: the curve of her lips was somewhat sardonic.

"Yes," he said, after an instant, gravely, "but, then, I'm always proud of you."

Then she laughed and kissed him quickly on the cheek. "My darling Vivaldo. You ain't seen nothing yet."

"I'd like," said Eric, "to add my voice to the general chorus of joy and gratitude. You were great, you really were."

She looked at him. Her eyes were still very big and something in her regard made him feel that she disliked him. He brushed the thought away as he would have brushed away a fly. "I'm not great yet," she said, "but I will be," and she raised both hands and touched her earrings.

"They're very beautiful," he said, "your earrings."

"Do you like them? My brother had them made for me—just before he died."

He paused. "I knew your brother a little. I was very sorry to hear about his—his death."

"Many, many people were," said Ida. "He was a very beautiful man, a very great artist. But he made"—she regarded him with a curious, cool insolence—"some very bad connections. He was the kind who believed what people said. If you told Rufus you loved him, well, he believed you and he'd stick with you till death. I used to try to tell him the world wasn't like that." She smiled. "He was much nicer than I am. It doesn't pay to be too nice in this world."

"That may be true. But you seem nice—you seem very nice—to me."

"That's because you don't know me. But ask Vivaldo!" And she turned to Vivaldo, putting her arm on his.

"I have to beat her up from time to time," said Vivaldo, "but, otherwise, she's great." He stuck out his hand to the short man, who now stood behind Ida. "Hello there, Mr. Ellis. What brings you all the way down here?"

Ellis raised his eyebrows exaggeratedly and threw out his palms. "What do you think brings me down here? I had an uncontrollable desire to see Sammy's Bowery Follies."

Ida turned, smiling, still leaning on Vivaldo. "My God. I saw you down there at the bar, but I scarcely dared believe it was you."

"None other," he said, "and you know"—he looked at her with tremendous admiration—"you are an extraordinary young woman. I've always thought so, I must say, but now I've seen it. I doubt if even you know how great a career is within your grasp."

"I've got an awfully long way to go Mr. Ellis, I've got such an awful lot to learn."

"If you ever stop feeling that way, I will personally take a hairbrush to you." He looked up at Vivaldo. "You have not called me and I take that very unkindly."

Vivaldo suppressed whatever rude retort was on his tongue. He said, mildly, "I just don't think I've got much of a future in TV."

"*Oh*, what an abysmal lack of imagination!" He shook Ida playfully by the shoulder. "Can't you do anything with this man of yours? *Why* does he insist on hiding his light under a bushel?"

"The truth is," said Ida, "that the last time anybody made up Vivaldo's mind for him was the last time they changed his diapers. And that was *quite* a long time ago. Anyway," and she rubbed her cheek against Vivaldo's shoulder, "I wouldn't dream of trying to change him. I like him the way he is."

There was something very ugly in the air. She clung to

Vivaldo, but Eric felt that there was something in it which was meant for Ellis. And Vivaldo seemed to feel this, too. He moved slightly away from Ida and picked up her handbag from the table—to give his hands something to do?—and said, "You haven't met our friend, he just came in from Paris. This is Eric Jones; this is Steve Ellis."

They shook hands. "I know your name," said Ellis. "Why?"

"He's an actor," said Ida, "and he's opening on Broadway in the fall."

Vivaldo, meanwhile, was paying the check. Eric took out his wallet, but Vivaldo waved it away.

"I *have* heard of you. I've heard quite a *lot* about you," and he looked Eric appraisingly up and down. "Bronson's signed you for *Happy Hunting Ground*. Is that right?"

"That's right," said Eric. He could not tell whether he liked Ellis or not.

"It's kind of an interesting play," Ellis said, cautiously, "and, from what I've heard of you, it ought to do very good things for you." He turned back to Ida and Vivaldo. "Could I persuade you to have *one* drink with me in some secluded, *air-conditioned* bar? I really don't think," he said to Ida, "that you ought to make a habit of working in such infernos. You'll end up dying of tuberculosis, like Spanish bullfighters, who are always either too hot or too cold."

"Oh, I guess we have time for *one* drink," said Ida, looking doubtfully at Vivaldo, "what do you think, sweetie?"

"It's your night," said Vivaldo. They started toward the door.

"I'd like to mix maybe just a *little* bit of business in with this drink," said Ellis.

"I figured that," said Vivaldo. "What an eager beaver you are."

"The secret," said Ellis, "of my not inconsiderable success." He turned to Ida. "I thought you told me yesterday that Dick Silenski and his wife would be here—?"

Something happened, then, in her face and in his—in his, wry panic and regret, quickly covered; in hers, an outraged warning, quickly dissembled. They entered the wide, hot street. "Eric saw them," she said, calmly, "something happened, they couldn't come."

"The kids got into a fight in the park," said Eric. "Some colored kids beat them up." He heard Ida's breathing change; he told himself he was a bastard. "I left them waiting for the doctor."

"You didn't tell me that," cried Vivaldo, "Jesus! I'd better call them up!"

"That isn't what you told me, either," said Ida.

"They weren't very badly hurt," said Eric, "just bloody noses. But they thought they'd better have a doctor look at them and of course they didn't want to leave them alone."

"I'll call them," said Vivaldo, "as soon as we get to a bar."

"Yes, sweetie," said Ida, "you'd better do that. What a terrible thing to have happen."

Vivaldo said nothing; kicked at a beer can on the sidewalk. They were walking west through a dark wilderness of tenements, of dirty children, of staring adolescents, and sweating grownups. "When you say colored boys," Ida pursued, after a moment, "do you mean that was the *reason* for the fight?"

"There didn't," said Eric, "seem to be any *other* reason. They'd never seen the boys before."

"I imagine," said Ida, "that it was in some kind of retaliation—for something some other boys had done to them."

"I guess that must be it," said Eric.

They reached the crowded park at the bottom of Fifth Avenue. Eric had not seen the park for many years and the melancholy and distaste which weighed him down increased as they began to walk through it. Lord, here were the trees and the benches and the people and the dark shapes on the grass; the children's playground, deserted now, with the swings and the slides and the sandpile; and the darkness surrounding this place, in which the childless wretched gathered to act out their joyless rituals. His life, his entire life, rose to his throat like bile tonight. The sea of memory washed over him, again and again, and each time it receded another humiliated Eric was left writhing on the sands. How hard it was to be despised! how impossible not to despise oneself! Here were the peaceful men in the lamplight, playing chess. A sound of singing and guitar-playing came from the center of the park; idly, they walked toward it; they each seemed to be waiting and fearing the resolution of their evening. There was a great crowd gathered in the small fountain; this crowd broke down, upon examination, into several small crowds, each surrounding one, two, or three singers. The singers, male and female, wore blue jeans and long hair and had more zest than talent. Yet, there was something very winning, very moving, about their unscrubbed, unlined faces, and their blankly shining, infantile eyes, and their untried, unhypocritical voices. They sang as though, by singing, they could bring about the codification and the immortality of innocence. Their listeners were of another circle, aimless, empty, and corrupt, and stood packed together in the stone fountain merely in order to be comforted or inflamed by the touch and the odor of human flesh. And the policemen, in the lamplight, circled around them all.

Ida and Vivaldo walked together, Eric and Ellis walked together: but all of them were far from one another. Eric felt, dimly, that he ought to make some attempt to talk to the man beside him, but he had no desire to talk to him; he wanted to leave, and he was afraid to leave. Ida and Vivaldo had also been silent. Now, as they walked from group to singing group, intermittently, through romanticized Western ballads and toothless Negro spirituals, he heard their voices. And he knew that Ellis was listening, too. This knowledge forced him, finally, to speak to Ellis.

He heard Ida. "——sweetie, don't *be* like that."

"Will you stop calling me *sweetie*? That's what you call every miserable cock sucker who comes sniffing around your ass."

"*Must* you talk that way?"

"Look, don't you pull any of that *lady* bullshit on me."

"——you talk. I'll never understand white people, never, never, never! How *can* you talk that way? How can you expect anyone else to respect you if you don't respect yourselves?"

"*Oh.* Why the fuck did I ever get tied up with a *house* nigger? And I am not *white people!*"

"——I warn you, I warn you!"

"——*you're* the one who starts it! You *always* start it!"

"——I knew you would be *jealous. That's* why!"

"You picked a fine way to keep me from being—jealous, baby."

"Can't we talk about it *later*? Why do you always have to spoil everything?"

"Oh, sure, sure, I'm the one who spoils everything, all right!"

Eric said, to Ellis, "Do you think any of these singers have a future on TV?"

"On daytime TV maybe," Ellis said, and laughed.

"You're a hard man," said Eric.

"I'm just realistic," Ellis said. "I figure everybody's out for himself, to make a buck, whether he says so or not. And there's nothing wrong with that. I just wish more people would admit it, that's all. Most of the people who think they disapprove of me don't disapprove of me at all. They just wish that they were me."

"I guess that's true," said Eric—mortally bored.

They began walking away from the music. "Did you live abroad a long time?" Ellis asked, politely.

"About three years."

"Where?"

"Paris, mostly."

"What made you go? There's nothing for an actor to do over there, is there? I mean, an American actor."

"Oh, I did a couple of things for American TV." Coming toward them, on the path, were two glittering, loud-talking fairies. He pulled in his belly, looking straight ahead. "And I saw a lot of theater—I don't know—it was very good for me." The birds of paradise passed; their raucous cries faded.

Ida said, "I always feel so *sorry* for people like that."

Ellis grinned. "Why should you feel sorry for them? They've got each other."

The four of them now came abreast, Ida putting her arm through Eric's.

"A couple of the waiters on my job are like that. The way some people treat them—! They tell me about it, they tell me everything. I like them, I really do. They're very sweet. And, of course, they make wonderful escorts. You haven't got to worry about them."

"They don't cost much, either," said Vivaldo. "I'll pick one up for you next week and we can keep him around the house as a pet."

"I simply am not able, today, am I, to say anything that will please you?"

"Stop trying so hard. Ellis, where are you taking us for this business-mixed-with-pleasure drink?"

"Curb your enthusiasm. We're practically there." They turned away from the park, toward Eighth Street, and walked into a downstairs bar. Ellis was known here, naturally; they found a booth and ordered.

"Now, the extent of the *business*," Ellis said, looking from Ida to Vivaldo, "is very simple. I've helped other people and I think I can help Miss Scott." He looked at Ida. "You aren't ready yet. You've got a hell of a lot of work to do and a hell of a lot to learn. And I'd like you to drop by my office one afternoon this week so we can go into all this in detail. You've got to study and work and you've got to keep alive while you're doing all that and maybe I can help you work that out." Then he looked at Vivaldo. "And you can come, too, if you think I'm trying to exploit Miss Scott unfairly. Is it your intention to act as her agent?"

"No."

"You don't have any reason to distrust me; you just don't like me, is that it?"

"Yes," said Vivaldo after a moment, "I guess that's right."

"Oh, Vivaldo," Ida moaned.

"That's all right. It's always good to know where you stand. But you certainly aren't going to allow this—*prejudice*—to stand in Miss Scott's way?"

"I wouldn't dream of it. Anyway, Ida does what she wants."

Ellis considered him. He looked briefly at Ida. "Well. That's reassuring." He signaled for the waiter and turned to Ida. "What day shall we make it? Tuesday, Wednesday?"

"Wednesday might be better," she said, hesitantly.

"Around three o'clock?"

"Yes. That's fine."

"It's settled, then." He made a note in his engagement book, then took out his billfold, picked up the check and gave a ten-dollar bill to the waiter. "Give these people anything they want," he said, "it's on me."

"Oh, are you going now?" asked Ida.

"Yes. My wife will kill me if I don't get home in time to see the kids before I go to the studio. See you Wednesday." He held out his hand to Eric. "Glad to have met you, Red;

all the best. Maybe you'll do a show for me, one day." He looked down at Vivaldo. "So long, genius. I'm sorry you don't like me. Maybe one of these days you ought to ask yourself why. It's no good blaming *me*, you know, if you don't know how to get or how to hold on to what you want." Then he turned and left. Vivaldo watched the short legs going up the stairs into the street.

He wiped his forehead with his wet handkerchief and the three of them sat in silence for a moment. Then, "I'm going to call Cass," Vivaldo said, and rose and walked toward the phone booth in the back.

"I understand," said Ida, carefully, "that you were a very good friend of my brother's."

"Yes," he said, "I was. Or at least I tried to be."

"Did you find it so very hard—to be his friend?"

"No. No, I hadn't meant to suggest that." He tried to smile. "He was very wrapped up in his music, he was very much—himself. I was younger then, I may not always have—understood." He felt sweat in his armpits, on his forehead, between his legs.

"Oh." She looked at him from very far away. "You may have wanted more from him than he could give. Many people did, men *and* women." She allowed this to hang between them for an instant. Then, "He was terribly attractive, wasn't he? I always think that that was the reason he died, that he was too attractive and didn't know how—how to keep people away." She sipped her drink. "People don't have any mercy. They tear you limb from limb, in the name of love. Then, when you're dead, when they've killed you by what they made you go through, they say you didn't have any character. They weep big, bitter tears—not for *you*. For themselves, because they've lost their toy."

"That's a terribly grim view," he said, "of love."

"I know what I'm talking about. That's what most people mean, when they say love." She picked up a cigarette and waited for him to light it. "Thank you. You weren't here, you never saw Rufus's last girl friend—a terrible little whore of a nymphomaniac, from Georgia. She *wouldn't* let him go, he tried all kinds of ways of getting away from her. He even thought of running away to Mexico. She got him so he couldn't work—I swear, there's nothing like a Southern white person, especially a Southern *woman*, when she gets her hooks into a Negro man." She blew a great cloud of smoke above his head. "And now she's still living, the filthy white slut, and Rufus is dead."

He said, hoping that she would really hear him but knowing she would not, perhaps *could* not, "I hope you don't think *I* loved your brother in that terrible way that you describe. I think we really *were* very good friends, and—and it was an awful shock for me to hear that he was dead. I was in Paris when I heard."

"Oh! I'm not accusing *you*. You and I are going to be friends. Don't you think so?"

"I certainly hope so."

"Well, that settles it, as far as I'm concerned." Then, smiling, with her eyes very big, "What did you do in Paris all that time?"

"Oh"—he smiled—"I tried to grow up."

"Couldn't you have done that here? Or didn't you want to?"

"I don't know. It was more fun in Paris."

"I'll bet." She crushed out her cigarette. "*Have* you grown up?"

"I don't know," he said, "any longer, if people *do*."

She grinned. "You've got a point there, Buster."

Vivaldo came back to the table. She looked up at him. "Well? How are the kids?"

"They're all right. Cass sounded a little distraught, but she sends her love to both of you and hopes to see you soon. Are we going to hang around here, or what are we going to do?"

"Well, let's have supper," Ida said.

Vivaldo and Eric looked at each other for the briefest of seconds. "You'll have to count me out," said Eric, quickly. "I'm bushed, I've had it, I'm going to go home and hit the sack."

"It's so *early*," Ida said.

"Well, I just got off a boat and I'm still vibrating." He stood up. "I'll take a rain check on it."

"Well," she looked at Vivaldo, humorously, "I'm sorry the lord and master isn't in a better mood." She moved herself out of the booth. "I've got to go to the little girl's room. Wait for me upstairs."

"I'm sorry," said Vivaldo, as they climbed the stairs into the street, "I'd really looked forward to sitting around and bullshitting with you tonight and all, but I guess you really better leave us alone. You understand, don't you?"

"Of course I understand," said Eric. "I'll give you a call next week sometime." They stood on the sidewalk, watching the aimless mob.

"It must feel very strange for you," said Vivaldo, "to be back here. But I hope you won't think we're not friends any more, because we are. I care a lot about you, Eric. I just want you to know that, so you won't think I'm putting you down gently, sort of, tonight. It's just one of those things." He stared outward, looking very weary. "Sometimes that girl gets me so I don't know if I'm coming or going."

"I know a little bit about it," Eric said. "No sweat." He held out his hand; Vivaldo held it for a moment. "I'll give you a call in a couple of days, all right? Say good-bye to Ida for me."

"All right, Eric. Be well."

Eric smiled. "Stay well."

He turned and started walking toward Sixth Avenue, but he did not really know where he was going. He felt Vivaldo's eyes on his back; then Vivaldo was swallowed up in the press of people behind him.

On the corner of Sixth Avenue, he watched and waited, the lights banged on and off. A truck came by; he looked up into the face of the truck driver, and felt an awful desire to join that man and ride in that truck wherever the truck was going.

But he crossed the street and started walking toward his apartment. It was the safest place to be, it was the only place to be. Strange people—they seemed strange to him now, but, one day, again, he might be one of them—passed him with that ineffable, sidelong, desperate look; but he kept his eyes on the pavement. *Not yet, not you. Not yet. Not yet.*

3

On the Wednesday afternoon that Ida went off to see Ellis, Cass called Vivaldo at the midtown bookshop where he worked and asked if she could buy him a drink when his day was over. The sound of her voice, swift, subdued, and unhappy, had the effect of jolting him out of his own bewilderment. He asked her to pick him up at the shop at six.

She arrived at the exact time, wearing a green summer dress which made her look very young, carrying an absurdly large straw handbag. Her hair was pulled back and fell over her shoulders; and, for a moment, watching her push through the doors, both blurred and defined by the heavy sunlight, she looked like the Cass of his adolescence, of years ago. She had then been the most beautiful, the most golden girl on earth. And Richard had been the greatest, most beautiful man.

She seemed terribly wound up—seemed to blaze, nearly, with some private, barely contained passion. She smiled at him, looking both young and weary; and for a moment he was faintly aware of her personal heat, her odor.

"How are you, Vivaldo? It's been rather a while since we've seen each other."

"I guess it has. And it's been my fault. How are things with you?"

She shrugged humorously, raising her hands like a child. "Oh. Up and down." Then, after a moment, "Rather down right now." She looked around the store. People were peering into bookshelves rather the way children peered in at the glass-enclosed fish in the aquarium. "Are you free? Can we leave now?"

"Yes. I was just waiting for you." He said good night to his employer and they walked into the scalding streets. They were in the Fifties, on the East Side. "Where shall we have this drink?"

"I don't care. Someplace with air conditioning. And without a TV set. I couldn't care less about baseball."

They started walking uptown, and east, as though each wished to get as far away as possible from the world they knew and their responsibilities in it. The presence of others, walking past them, walking toward them, erupting rudely out of doorways and taxicabs, and springing up from the curbs, intruded painfully on their stillness and seemed to menace their connection. And each man or woman that passed seemed also to be carrying some intolerable burden; their private lives screamed from their hot and discontented faces.

"On days like this," Cass said, suddenly, "I remember what it was like—I *think* I remember—to be young, *very* young." She looked up at him. "When everything, touching and tasting—everything—was so new, and even suffering was wonderful because it was so complete."

"That's hindsight, Cass. I wouldn't want to be that young again for anything on earth."

But he knew what she meant. Her words had taken his mind away—for a moment—from his cruel visions of Ida and Ellis. ("You told me you hadn't seen him since that party." "Well. I *did* go to see him once, just to tell him about the jam session." "Why did you have to see him, why didn't you just call?" "I wasn't sure he'd *remember* me from just over the phone. And then I didn't tell you because I knew how you'd behave." "I don't care what you say, baby, I know what he's after, he just wants to get inside your drawers." "Oh, Vivaldo. You think I don't know how to handle little snots like that?" And she gave him a look, which he did not know how to answer, which almost stated *Look how I handled you.*)

But now he thought of himself at fifteen or sixteen—swimming in the Coney Island surf, or in the pool in his neighborhood; playing handball in the playground, sometimes with his father; lying in the gutter after a street fight, vomiting, praying that no enemy would take this occasion to kick his brains in. He remembered the fear of those days, fear of everything, covered with a mocking, staccato style, defended with the bullets of dirty words. Everything was for the first time; at fifteen or sixteen; and what was her name? Zelda. Could that possibly be right? On the roof, in the summertime, under the dirty city stars.

All for the first time, in the days when acts had no consequences and nothing was irrecoverable, and love was simple and even pain had the dignity of enduring forever: it was un-imaginable that time could do anything to diminish it. Where was Zelda now? She might easily have been transformed into the matron with fleshy, spreading buttocks and metallically unlikely blonde hair who teetered on high heels just before them now. She, too, somewhere, some day, had looked on and touched everything for the first time and felt the summer air on her breasts like a blessing and been entered and had the blood run out, for the first time.

And what was Cass thinking?

"Oh, no," she said, slowly, "I certainly don't mean that I want to *be* that miserable girl again. I was just remembering how different it was then—how different from now."

He put one arm around her thin shoulders. "You sound sad, Cass. Tell me what's the matter."

He guided her into a dark, cool cocktail lounge. The waiter led them to a small table for two, took their orders, and disappeared. Cass looked down at the tabletop and played with the salted peanuts in the red plastic dish.

"Well, that's why I called you—to talk to you. But it's not so easy. I'm not sure I *know* what's the matter." The waiter returned and set their drinks down before them. "That's not true. I guess I *do* know what's the matter."

Then she was silent. She sipped her drink nervously and lit a cigarette.

"I guess it's about Richard and me," she said at last. "I don't know what's going to become of us. There doesn't seem to be anything between us any more." She spoke in an odd, breathless way, almost like a schoolgirl, and as though she did not believe what she was saying. "Or I guess that's not right. There's a hell of a lot between us, there *must* be. But none of it seem to work. Sometimes—sometimes I think he hates me—for being married, for the children, for the work he does. And other times I know that isn't true, that can't be true." She bit her lower lip and stubbed out her cigarette and tried to laugh. "Poor Vivaldo. I know you've got troubles of your own and don't know *what* to do about the maunderings of a middle-aged, self-centered matron."

"Now that you mention it," he said, "I guess you *are* practically decrepit." He tried to smile; he did not know what to say. Ida and Ellis, thrust hastily to the back of his mind, were, nevertheless, dimly accomplishing their unspeakable violations of his manhood. "It really just sounds like a kind of summer storm—don't *all* married people have them?"

"I really don't know anything *about* all married people. I'm not sure I know anything about marriage." She sipped her drink again, saying, irrelevantly, "I wish I could get drunk." Then she giggled, her proud face suddenly breaking. "I wish I could get drunk and go out and pick up a truck driver or a taxi driver or anybody who'd touch me and make me feel like a woman again." She hid her face with one bony hand and her tears dripped through her fingers. Keeping her head down, she searched fiercely through the absurd straw handbag and finally came up with a small bit of Kleenex. With this, miraculously, she managed to blow her nose and dry her eyes. "I'm sorry," she said, "I've just been sitting around brooding too long."

"What have you been brooding about, Cass? I thought you and Richard had it made." These words sounded, in his own ears, stiff and uncaring. But he had known Cass and Richard too long and been too young when he met them; he had never really thought of Cass and Richard as lovers. Sometimes, of course, he had watched Cass move, realizing that, small as she was, she was all woman and all there, had good legs and nice breasts and knew how to twist her small behind; and, sometimes, watching Richard's great paw on her wrist, wondered how she bore his weight. But he had the tendency of all wildly disorganized people to suppose that the lives of others were tamer and less sensual and more cerebral than his own. And for the very first time he had the sense of Cass as a passionate woman who had merely been carrying on a legal love affair; who writhed as beautifully and shamelessly in Richard's arms as the women Vivaldo had dreamed about for all these years. "I guess," he added, "I must sound pretty dumb. Forgive me."

She smiled—smiled as though she had read his thoughts. "No, you don't. Perhaps I also thought we had it made. But nobody ever has it made." She lit another cigarette, straightening her shoulders, slowly circling, as she had for many weeks now, around some awful decision. "I keep telling myself it's because of the way our lives have changed, now that Richard's becoming so well known. But it isn't that. It's something that's been there all along." Now she was very grave and dry. She looked at Vivaldo through the smoke of her cigarette, narrowing her eyes. "You know, I used to look at you and all your horrible adventures and compare you to Richard and me and think how lucky we were. He was the first"—she faltered and looked down—"the very first man I ever had, and I was the first for him, too—*really* the first, the first girl, anyway, he ever *loved*."

And she looked down again, as though the burden of confession were too great. Yet they were united in the knowledge that what she had begun she must now finish.

"And you think he doesn't love you any more?"

She did not answer. She covered her forehead with her ringed left hand and stared into the dish of salted peanuts as though the answer to all riddles were hidden there. The tiny arrows on her wrist watch said it was twenty-five minutes to seven. Ida would have left Ellis hours ago and would have visited her singing teacher. She would now be in the restaurant, her station set up, and her uniform on, preparing for the dinner rush. He could see her closed, haughty face as she approached a table, manipulating her pad and pencil as though it were a sword and shield. She would not have stayed long with Ellis—he was a busy man. But how long did it take for those guys to bang off a quick one, in the middle of the afternoon, in their inviolable offices? He tried to concentrate on Cass and her trouble. Perhaps he had taken her out for a drink; perhaps he had persuaded her not to go to work, and had invited her for dinner; perhaps they were together now. (Where?) Perhaps Ellis had persuaded her to meet him at midnight in a theatrical bar, the kind of place where it would do her good to be seen with him. But no, not that; it would certainly not do Ellis any good to be seen with *her*. Ellis was far too smart for that—just as he was far too smart to make any verbal comparisons between his power and Vivaldo's. But he would lose no opportunity to force Ida to make these comparisons for herself.

He was making himself sick with his fears and his fantasies. If Ida loved him, then Ellis and the whole great glittering

world did not matter. If she did not love him, there was nothing he could do about it and the sooner everything came to
an end between them, the better. But he knew that it was not
as simple as that, that he was not being honest. She might
very well love him and yet—he shuddered and threw down
his drink—be groaning on some leather couch under the
weight of Ellis. Her love for him would in no way blunt the
force of her determination to become a singer—to pursue the
career which now seemed so easily within her grasp. He could
even see the truth of her loving and vehement assertion that
it was he, his love, which had given her the courage to begin.
This did not cheer him, the assertion containing to his ears
the suggestion that his role now was finished and he was foul-
ing up everything by failing to deliver his exit lines. He shook
his head. In half an hour—no, an hour—he would call the
restaurant.

"Oh, Cass," he heard himself saying, "I wish I could do
something to help."

She smiled and touched his hand. The tiny arrows on her
wrist had not moved. "Thank you," she said—very gravely.
Then, "I don't know if Richard loves me any more or not.
He doesn't see me any more—he doesn't see me. He hasn't
touched me"—she raised her eyes to Vivaldo's and two tears
spilled over and rolled down her face; she made no move to
check them—"he hasn't touched me in, oh, I don't know
how long. I've never been very aggressive; I've never had to
be." She struck at her tears with the back of her hand. "I sit
in that house like—like a housekeeper. I take care of the kids
and make meals and scrub toilet bowls and answer the phone
and he just—doesn't see me. He's always *working*. He's always
busy with deals with—with Ellis, I guess, and his agent and
all those horrible people. Maybe he's mad at me because I
don't like them very much and I can't help it." She caught
her breath, found another wad of Kleenex, and again accomplished miracles with it. "In the beginning, I sort of teased
him about them. I don't any more, but I guess it's too late.
I know they're busy and important but I can't help it, I don't
think it's serious *work*. Maybe Richard's right, he says I'm a
New England snob and a man-killer but God knows I don't
mean to be and—I don't think Richard's work is any good

any more and he can't forgive me for *that*. What am I to do?"
And she put both hands to her forehead, looking down, and
began to cry again. He looked cautiously around the dark
lounge. No one was noticing them. It was, suddenly a quarter
to seven.

Ineptly, he asked, "Have you and Richard talked about this
at all?"

She shook her head. "No. We've just had fights. We don't
seem to be able to talk to each other any more. I know that
people say that there comes a time in marriage when everything goes out of it except companionship, but this *can't* be
what they were talking about, not this, not so soon. I won't
have it!" And now the extraordinary violence in her voice did
cause a few heads to turn in their direction.

He took both her hands, smiling. "Easy, girl, easy. Let me
buy you another drink."

"That would be nice." The drink before her was mainly
water, but she finished it. Vivaldo signaled the waiter for another round.

"Does Richard know where you are now?"

"No—yes. I told him I was going to have a drink with
you."

"What time does he expect you back?"

She hesitated. "I don't know. I left supper in the oven. I
told him if I wasn't back in time for supper to feed the children and eat himself. He just grunted and walked into his
study." She lit a cigarette, looking both desperate and distant;
and he knew that there was more in her mind than she was
telling. "I guess I'll go on back, though. Or maybe I'll go to
a movie."

"Would you like to have supper with me?"

"No. I don't feel like eating. Besides"—the waiter came
with their drinks; she waited until he left—"Richard's a little
jealous of you."

"Of *me*? Why is he jealous of *me*?"

"Because you may become a real writer. And now he never
will be. And he knows it. And *that's* the whole trouble." She
made this pronouncement with the utmost coolness and
Vivaldo began to see, for the first time, how deadly it must
be for Richard, now, to deal with a woman like Cass. "God-

damnit. I wouldn't care if he couldn't *read*." And she grinned and took a swallow of her drink.

"Yes, you would," he said. "You can't help it."

"Well. If he couldn't read, and knew it, he could learn. I could teach him. But *I* don't care if he's a writer or not. He's the one who dreamed all that up." She paused, bony and thoughtful. "He's a carpenter's son," she said, "the fifth son of a carpenter who came from Poland. Maybe that's why it's so important. A hundred years ago he'd have been like his father and opened a carpenter's shop. But now he's got to be a writer and help Steve Ellis sell convictions and soap." Ferociously, she ground out her cigarette. "And neither he, nor anyone else in that gang, can tell the difference between them." She lit another cigarette at once. "Don't misunderstand me; I've got nothing against Ellis, or any of those people. They're just ordinary Americans, trying to get ahead. So is Richard, I guess."

"And so is Ida," he said.

"Ida?"

"I think she's been seeing him. I know she had a date to see Ellis this afternoon. He's promised to help her—with her career." And he smiled, bleakly.

Suddenly, she laughed. "My God. Aren't we a wonderful pair of slobs. Sitting here in this dark place, full of self-pity and alcohol, while our lovers are out there in the real world, seeing real people, doing real things, bringing real bacon into real homes—are they real? are they? Sometimes I wake up at night with that question in my mind and I walk around the house and go and look at the children. I don't want them to be like *that*. I don't want them to be like me, either." She turned her face sideways, looking helplessly at the wall. With her golden hair down, and all the trouble in her face, she looked unbelievably young. "What am I to do?"

"I always thought," he ventured, "that it was easier for women."

She turned and looked at him; she did not look as young any more. "That *what* was easier?"

"Knowing what to do."

She threw back her head and laughed. "Oh, Vivaldo. Why?"

"I don't know. Men have to think about so many things. Women only have to think about men."

She laughed again. "What's so easy about that?"

"It isn't? I guess it isn't."

"Vivaldo. If men don't know what's happening, what they're doing, where they're going—what are women to do? If Richard doesn't know what kind of world he wants, how am I to help him make it? What am I to tell our sons?" The question hung in the air between them; sluggishly (it was ten past seven) it struck echoes in him of Ida's tone and Ida's eyes when they quarreled. *Oh. All you white boys make me sick. You want to find out what's happening, baby, all you got to do is pay your dues!*

Was there, in all that rage, a plea?

"I'll buy you one more drink," he said.

"Yes. Let me go home or do whatever I'm going to do with just a tiny hint of drunkenness. Excuse me a moment." Jauntily, she signaled the waiter; then gathered up her great handbag and walked to the ladies' room.

All you got to do is pay your dues. He sat, islanded by the vague hum, the meaningless music, of the cocktail lounge, and re-called lapses and errors from his life with Ida which, at the time, he had blamed on her. Their first quarrel had occurred about a month after she had moved in, in April. His mother had called, one Sunday afternoon, to remind him of a birthday party, the following week, for his younger brother, Stevie. His mother as-sumed that he would not want to come, that he would try to get out of it, and this made her voice, before he could say anything, querulous and complaining. This he could not bear, which made *his* tone sharp and hostile. And there they were, then, the aging, frightened woman and her grown son, acting out their kindergarten drama. Ida, in the kitchen, watched and listened. Vivaldo, watching her, suddenly laughed and before he realized what he was saying, he asked, "Do you mind if I bring a girl friend?" And, as he said this, he felt Ida stiffen and become absolutely concentrated with rage.

"If she's a nice girl," his mother was saying. "You know we love to meet your friends."

He felt immediate contrition, seeing, in his mind's eye, her bewildered face, knowing how she wondered why her eldest son should cause, and appear to wish to cause her, so much pain. At the same time he was aware of Ida's ominous humming in the kitchen.

"She's a very nice girl," he said, promptly, sincerely. Then he faltered, involuntarily stealing a glance at Ida. He did not know how to say, *Mama, she's a colored girl,* knowing that his mother, and who on earth could blame her? would immediately decide that this was but one more attempt on his part to shock and humiliate his family. "I want you two to meet one day, I really do." And this sounded totally insincere. He was thinking, *I guess I really am going to have to tell them, I'm going to have to make them accept it.* And then, at once, *Oh, fuck it, why?* He glanced again at Ida. She was smoking a cigarette and leafing through a magazine.

"Well," said his mother, doubtfully, more than willing, albeit in her fashion, to come flying down the road to meet him, "try to bring her to the party. Everybody will be here and they all ask about you, we haven't seen you in so long. I know your father misses you though he'll never say a thing and Stevie misses you, too, and we all do, Danny." They called him Danny at home.

Everybody: his sister and his brother-in-law, his brother and father and mother, the uncles and aunts and cousins, and the resulting miasma of piety and malice and suspicion and fear. The invincible chatter of people, concerning people, who had no reality for him, the talk about money, of children's illnesses, of doctor's bills, of pregnancies, of unlikely and unlovely infidelities occurring between ciphers and neuters in a vacuum, the ditchwater-dull, infantile dirty stories, and the insane talk about politics. They should, really, all of them, still be living in stables, with horses and cows, and should not be expected to tax themselves with matters beyond their comprehension. He hated himself for the sincerity of this reflection and was baffled, as always, by the particular and dangerous nature of its injustice.

"Okay," he said, trying to stop his mother's flow. She was telling him that his father's stomach trouble had returned. *Stomach trouble, my ass. He just hasn't got any liver left any more, that's all. One of these days he's just going to spatter all over those walls, and what a stench.*

"Are you going to bring your girl friend?"

"I don't know. I'll see."

He could just see Ida with all of them. He, alone, was bad enough; he, alone, distressed and frightened them enough. Ida would reduce them to a kind of speechless hysteria and God knew what his father would say under the impression that he was putting the dark girl at her ease.

More chatter from his mother: it was as though each of her contacts with Vivaldo was so brief and so menaced that she tried to establish in minutes a communion which had not been accomplished in years.

"I'll *be* there," he said, "good-bye," and hung up.

Yet, he had loved her once, he loved her still, he loved them all.

He looked at the silent telephone, then looked over at Ida.

"Want to come to a birthday party?"

"No, thank you, sweetie. You want to educate your family, you get them some slides, you hear? *Colored* slides," and she raised her eyes, mockingly, from the magazine.

He laughed, but felt so guilty about Ida and about his mother that he was unable to let well enough alone.

"I'd like to take you over with me one of these days. It might do them some good. They're such cornballs."

"What might do them some good?" Her attention was still on her magazine.

"Why—meeting you. They're not bad people. They're just very limited."

"I've told you, I'm not at all interested in the education of your family, Vivaldo."

Obscurely, deeply, he was stung. "Don't you think there's any hope for them?"

"I don't give a damn if there's any hope for them or not. But I know that I am not about to be bugged by any more white jokers who still can't figure out whether I'm human or not. If they don't know, baby, sad on them, and I hope they drop dead slowly, in great pain."

"That's not very Christian," he said, lightly. But he was ready to drop it.

"It's the best I can do. I learned all my Christianity from white folks."

"Oh, shit," he said, "here we go again."

The magazine came flying at him and hit him across the bridge of the nose.

"What do you mean, you white motherfucker!" She mimicked him. "*Here we go again!* I've been living in this house for over a month and you *still* think it would be a big joke to take me home to see your mother! Goddammit, you think she's a better woman than I am, you big, white, liberal asshole?" She caught her breath and started toward him, crouching, her hands on her hips. "Or do you think it would serve your whore of a mother right to bring your nigger whore home for her to see? Answer me, goddamnit!"

"Will you shut up? You're going to have the police down here in a minute."

"Yes, and when they come, I'm going to tell them you dragged me in off the streets and refused to pay me, yes, I am. You think I'm a whore, well, you treat me like a whore, goddamn your white prick, *pay!*"

"Ida, it was a dumb thing to say, and I'm sorry, all *right.* I didn't mean what you thought I meant. I wasn't trying to put you down."

"Yes, you did. You meant exactly what I thought you meant. And you know why? Because you can't help it, that's why. Can't none of you white boys help it. Every damn one of your sad-ass white chicks think they got a cunt for peeing through, and they don't piss nothing but the best ginger ale, and if it wasn't for the spooks wouldn't a damn one of you white cock suckers *ever* get laid. That's *right.* You are a fucked-up group of people. You hear me? A *fucked*-up group of people."

"All right," he said, wearily, "so we're a fucked-up group of people. So shut up. We're in enough trouble here, as it is."

And they were, because the landlord and the neighbors and the cop on the corner disapproved of Ida's presence. But it was not the most tactful thing he could have said at that moment.

She said, with a contrition absolutely false and murderous, "That's true. I forgot." She turned from him into the kitchen again, reached up in the cupboard and hurled all of his dishes, of which, thank heaven, there were not many, to the floor. "I just think I'll give them something to complain about," she said. There were only two glasses and she smashed these against the refrigerator. Vivaldo had placed himself against the record player, and, as Ida stalked the kitchen, water standing in her eyes, he began to laugh. She rushed at him, slapping and clawing, and he held her off with one hand, still laughing. His belly hurt. Other people in the building were pounding on their pipes and on the walls and on the ceiling, but he could not stop laughing. He ended up on the floor, on his back, howling, and finally, Ida, unwillingly, began to laugh, too. "Get up off the floor, you fool. Lord, what a fool you are."

"I'm just a fucked-up group of people," he said. "Lord, have mercy on me." Ida laughed, helplessly, and he pulled her down on top of him. "Have mercy on me, baby," he said. "Have mercy." The pounding continued, and he said, "There sure are a fucked-up group of people in this house, they won't even let you make love in peace."

Now, Cass returned, with her hair recombed and new make-up on and with her eyes bright and dry. She seated herself in the booth again and picked up her drink. "I'm ready whenever you are," she said. Then, "Thank you, Vivaldo. If I couldn't have found a friend to talk to, I think I would have died."

"You wouldn't have," he said, "but I know what you mean. Here's to you, Cass." And he raised his glass. It was twenty minutes to eight, but, now, he was afraid to call the restaurant. He would wait until he and Cass had separated.

"What are you going to do?" he asked.

"I don't know. I think I may break—is it the sixth commandment? Adultery."

"I mean, right now."

"That's what I thought you meant."

They both laughed. Yet, it crossed his mind that she meant it. "Anyone I know?"

"Are you kidding? Just *think* of the people you know."

He smiled. "All right. But please don't do anything silly, Cass."

She looked down. "I don't think I will," she murmured. Then, "Let's get the bill."

They signaled the waiter, and paid him, and walked into the streets again. The sun was going down, but the heat had not lessened. The stone and steel and wood and brick and asphalt which had soaked in the heat all day would be giving it back all night. They walked two blocks, to the corner of Fifth Avenue, in silence; and in this silence something lived which made Vivaldo oddly reluctant to leave Cass alone.

The corner on which they stood was absolutely deserted, and there was very little traffic.

"Which way are you going?" he asked her.

She looked up and down the Avenue—up and down. From the direction of the park there came a green and yellow cab.

"I don't know. But I think I'll go to that movie."

The cab stopped, several blocks from them, waiting for a red light. Cass abruptly put up her hand.

Again, he volunteered. "Would you like me to come with you? I could act as your protection."

She laughed. "No, Vivaldo, thank you. I don't want to be protected any more." And the cab swerved toward them. They both watched it approach, it slowed and stopped. He looked at her with his eyebrows very high.

"Well—" he said.

She opened the door and he held it. "Thank you, Vivaldo," she said. "Thank you for everything. I'll be in touch with you in a few days. Or call me, I'll be home."

"Okay, Cass." He made a fist and touched her on the chin. "Be good."

"You, too. Good-bye." She got into the cab and he slammed the door. She leaned forward to the driver, the cab rolled forward, downtown. She turned back to wave at him and the cab turned west.

It was like waving good-bye to land: and she could not guess what might have befallen her when, and if, she ever saw land again.

At Twelfth Street and Seventh Avenue she made the driver carry her one block more, to the box office of the Loew's Sheridan; then she paid him and walked out and actually climbed the stairs to the balcony of this hideous place of worship, and sat down. She lit a cigarette, glad of the darkness but not protected by it; and she watched the screen, but all she saw were the extraordinarily unconvincing wiggles of a girl whose name, incredibly enough, appeared to be Doris Day. She thought, irrelevantly, *I never should come to movies, I can't stand them,* and then she began to cry. She wept looking straight ahead, this latter rain coming between her and James Cagney's great, red face, which seemed, at least, thank heaven, to be beyond the possibilities of make-up. Then she looked at her watch, noting that it was exactly eight o'clock. Is that good or bad? she wondered idiotically—knowing, which was always part of her trouble, that she was being idiotic. *My God, you're thirty-four years old, go on downstairs and call him.* But she forced herself to wait, wondering all the time if she were waiting too long or would be calling too early. Finally, during the heaviest of the wide screen's technicolored stormy weather, she walked down the stairs and entered the phone booth. She dialed his number and got the answering service. She crawled back upstairs and found her seat again.

But she could not bear the movie, which showed no signs of ever ending. At nine o'clock, she walked downstairs again, intending to walk and have a drink somewhere and go home. Home. And she dialed the number again.

It rang once, twice; then the receiver was picked up; there was a silence. Then, in an aggressive drawl,

"Hello?"

She caught her breath.

"Hello?"

"Hello. Eric?"

"Yes."

"Well, it's me. Cass."

"Oh," and then, quickly, "How are you, Cass, it's good of you to call me. I've been sitting here trying to read this play and going out of my mind and feeling suicidal."

"I imagine," she said, "that you may have been expecting this call." For never let it be said, she thought, now really in the teeth of irreality and anguish, that I don't lay my cards on the table.

"What did you say, Cass?" But she knew, from the rhythm of his question, that he had understood her.

"I said, 'You may have been expecting this call.' "

After a moment, he said, "Yes. In a way." Then, "Where are you, Cass?"

"I'm around the corner from your house. Can I come up?"

"Please do."

"All right. I'll be there in about five minutes."

"Okay. Oh, Cass—"

"Yes?"

"I haven't got anything in the house to drink. If you'll pick up a bottle of Scotch, I'll pay you for it when you get here."

"Any special kind?"

"Oh, I don't care. Any kind *you* like."

A stone, miraculously enough, seemed to rise from her heart for a moment. She laughed. "Black Label?"

"Crazy."

"In a minute, then."

"In a minute. I'll be here."

She hung up, staring for a moment at the shining black instrument of her—deliverance? She marched into the street, found a liquor store and bought a bottle; and the weight of the bottle in her straw handbag somehow made everything real; as the purchase of a railroad ticket proves the imminence of a journey.

What would she say to him? what would he say to her?

He called, "Is that you, Cass?" She called back, "Yes!" and ran clumsily up the steps, like a schoolgirl. She reached his doorway out of breath, and he stood there, in a T-shirt and a pair of old army pants, smiling and pale. His reality shocked her and so did his beauty—or his vigor, which, in a man, is so nearly the same thing. She might have been seeing him for the first time—his short, disordered red hair, a rather square forehead with lines burned into it, heavier eyebrows than she remembered and darker eyes, set farther back. His chin had a tiny cleft—she had never noticed it before. His mouth was wider than she remembered, his lips were fuller, his teeth were slightly crooked. He had not shaved and his red beard bristled and gleamed in the weak yellow light on the landing. His trousers had no belt and his bare feet were in leather sandals. He said, "Come in," and she brushed quickly past his body. He closed the door behind her.

She walked into the center of the room and stared about her, seeing nothing; then they stared at each other, terribly driven, terribly shy, not daring to imagine what came next. He was frightened, but very self-contained. She felt that he was studying her, preparing himself for whatever this new co-nundrum might prove to be. He had made no decisions at all as yet, was trying to attune himself to her; which placed her under the necessity of finding out what was in his heart by revealing what was in hers. And she did not yet know what was in her heart—or did not want to know.

He took her bag from her and set it on the bookcase. The way he did this made her realize that he was unaccustomed to having women in his room. The Shostakovich Fifth Sym-phony was on his record player; the play, *Happy Hunting Ground*, lay open on his bed, under his night light. The only other light in the room came from a small lamp on his desk. His apartment was small and spare, absolutely monastic; it was less a place to live in than it was a place to work; and she felt, suddenly and sharply, how profoundly he might resent the intrusion into his undecorated isolation of the feminine order and softness.

"Let's have a drink," he said, and took the bottle from her bag. "How much do I owe you?"

She told him, and he paid her, shyly, with some crumpled bills which were lying on the mantelpiece, next to his keys. He moved into the kitchen, tearing the wrapper off the bottle. She watched him as he found glasses and ice. His kitchen was a mess and she longed to offer to clean it up for him, but she did not dare, not yet. She moved heavily to the bed and sat down on the edge of it and picked up the play.

"I can't tell if that play's any good or not. I can't tell any more, anyway." Whenever he was unsure, his Southern accent became more noticeable.

"Which character are you playing?"

"Oh, I'm playing one of the bad cats, the one they call Malcolm." She looked at the cast of characters and found that Malcolm was the son of Egan. The script was heavily under-lined and there were long notes in the margin. One of these notes read, *On this, maybe remember what you know of Yves,* and she looked at the underlined sentence, *No, I don't want no damn aspirin. Man got a headache, why don't you let him find out what kind of headache it* is? Eric called, "Do you want water, or just ice?"

"A little water, thanks."

He came back into the room and handed her her highball. "I play the last male member of a big, rich American family. They got rich by all kinds of swindles and by shooting down people, and all that jazz. But I can't do that by the time I'm a man because it's all been done and they've changed the laws. So I get to be a big labor leader instead, and my Dad tries to get me railroaded to jail as a Communist. It gives us a couple of nice scenes. The point is, there's not a pin to choose between us." He grinned. "It'll probably be a big, fat flop."

"Well, just make sure we have tickets to opening night." A brief silence fell, and her *we* resounded more insistently than the drums of Shostakovich.

"Oh, I'm going to try to pack the house with my friends," he said, "never fear." Silence fell again. He sat down on the bed beside her, and looked at her. She looked down.

"You make me feel very strange," he said. "You make me feel things I didn't think I'd ever feel again."

"What do I make you feel?" she asked. And then, "You do the same for me." She sensed that he was taking the initiative for her sake.

He leaned forward and put one hand on her hand; then rose, and walked away from her, leaving her alone on the bed. "What about Richard?"

"I don't know," she said. "I don't know what's going to happen between Richard and me." She forced herself to look into his eyes, and she put her drink down on the night table. "But it isn't *you* that's come between Richard and me—*you* don't have anything to do with that."

"I don't *now*, you mean. Or I don't yet." He put his cigarette down in the ashtray on the mantelpiece behind him. "But I guess I know what you mean, in a way." He still seemed very troubled and his trouble now propelled him toward her again, to the bed. He felt her trembling, but still he did not touch her, only stared at her with his troubled and searching eyes, and with his lips parted. "Dear Cass," he said, and smiled, "I know we have *now*, but I don't think we have much of a future." She thought, Perhaps if we take *now*, we can have a future, too. It depends on what we mean by "future." She felt his breath on her face and her neck, then he leaned closer, head down, and she felt his lips there. She raised her hands to stroke his head and his red hair. She felt his violence and his uncertainty, and this made him seem much younger than she. And this excited her in a way that she had never been excited before; she glimpsed, for the first time, the force that drove older women to younger men; and then she was frightened. She was frightened because she had never before found herself playing so anomalous a role and because nothing in her experience had ever suggested that her body could become a trap for boys, and the tomb of her self-esteem. She had embarked on a voyage which might end years from now in some horrible villa, near a blue sea, with some unspeaking, unspeakably phallic, Turk or Spaniard or Jew or Greek or Arabian. Yet, she did not want it to stop. She did not quite know what was happening now, or where it would lead, and she was afraid; but she did not want it to stop. She saw the smoke from Eric's cigarette curling up from the mantelpiece—she hoped it was still in the ashtray; the play script was beneath her head, the symphony was approaching its end. She was aware, as though she stood over them both with a camera, of how sordid the scene must appear: a married woman, no longer young, already beginning to moan with lust, pinned down on this untidy and utterly transient bed by a stranger who did not love her and whom she could not love. Then she wondered about that: love; and wondered if anyone really knew anything about it. Eric put one hand on her breast, and it was a new touch, not Richard's, no; but she knew that it was Eric's; and was it love or not? and what did Eric feel? *Sex*, she thought, but that was not really the answer, or if it was, it was an answer which clarified nothing. For now, Eric leaned up from her with a sigh and walked back to his cigarette. He leaned there for a moment, watching her; and she understood that the weight between them, of things unspoken, made any act impossible. On what basis were they to act? for their blind seeking was not a foundation which could be expected to bear any weight.

He came back to the bed and sat down; and he said, "Well.

Listen. I know about Richard. I don't altogether believe you when you say that I don't have anything to do with what's happening between you and Richard, because obviously I do, I do *now*, anyway, if only because I'm here." She started to say something, but he raised his hand to silence her. "But that's all right. I don't want to make an issue out of that, I'm not very well placed to defend—conventional morality." And he smiled. "Something is happening between us which I don't really understand, but I'm willing to trust it. I have the feeling, somehow, that I *must* trust it." He took her hand and raised it to his unshaven cheek. "But I have a lover, too, Cass; a boy, a French boy, and he's supposed to be coming to New York in a few weeks. I really don't know what will happen when he gets here, but"—he dropped her hand and rose and paced his room again—"he *is* coming, and we *have* been together for over two years. And that means something. Probably, if it hadn't been for him, I would never have stayed away so long." And he turned on her now all of his intensity. "No matter *what* happens, I loved him very much, Cass, and I still do. I don't think I've ever loved anyone quite like that before, and"—he shuddered—"I'm not sure I'll ever love anyone quite like that again."

She felt not at all frightened by his lover. She remembered the name written in the margin: *Yves*. But it was better for the name of his lover to fall from his lips. She felt very strangely moved, as though she might be able to help him endure the weight of the boy who had such power over him.

"He sounds very remarkable," she said. "Tell me his name, tell me about him."

He came back to the bed and sat down. His drink was finished, and he sipped from hers.

"There isn't much to tell. His name is Yves." He paused. "I can't imagine what he'll think of the States."

"Or of all of us," she said.

He assented, with a smile. "Or of all of us. I'm not sure I know what *I* think." They laughed; she took a sip of her highball; the atmosphere between them began to be easier, as though they were friends. "But—I'm responsible for him when he gets here. He wouldn't be coming if it weren't for me." He looked at her. "He's the son of somebody he can scarcely remember at all, and his mother runs a bistro in Paris. He hates his mother, or thinks he does."

"That's not the usual pattern, is it?" Then she wished that she had held her tongue, or could call the words back. But it was too late, really, to do more than blandly compound her error: "I mean, from what we're told, most men with a sexual bias toward men love their mothers and hate their fathers."

"We haven't been told much," he observed, mildly sardonic. "I used to know street boys in Paris who hadn't had any opportunity to hate their mother *or* their fathers. Of course, they hated *les flics*—the cops—and I suppose some safe slug of an American would work it out that they hated the cops because they were father-figures—we know a hell of a lot about father-figures here because we don't know anything about fathers, we've made them obsolete—but it seems just as likely to me that they hated the cops because the cops liked to beat the shit out of them."

It was strange how she now felt herself holding back—not from him, but from such a vision of the world. She did not want him to see the world this way because such a vision could not make him happy, and whatever made him unhappy menaced her. She had never had to deal with a policeman in her life, and it had never entered her mind to feel menaced by one. Policemen were neither friends nor enemies; they were part of the landscape, present for the purpose of upholding law and order; and if a policeman—for she had never thought of them as being very bright—seemed to forget his place, it was easy enough to make him remember it. Easy enough if one's own place was more secure than his, and if one represented, or could bring to bear, a power greater than his own. For all policemen were bright enough to know who they were working for, and they were not working, anywhere in the world, for the powerless.

She stroked Eric's hair, remembering how she and Richard, when they had first met, had argued over this very question: for he had been very conscious, in those days, of his poverty and her privilege. He had called her the icebound heiress of all the ages, and she had worked very hard to prove him wrong and to dissociate herself, in his mind, from those who wielded the knout of power.

Eric put his head in her lap. He said, "Well, anyway, that's the story, or all the story I know how to tell you now. I just thought you ought to know." He hesitated; she watched his Adam's apple move as he swallowed; and he said, "I can't promise you anything, Cass."

"I haven't asked you to promise me anything." She bent down and kissed him on the mouth. "You're very beautiful," she said, "and very strong. I'm not afraid."

He looked up at her, looking upside down, so that he was for her at that moment both child and man, and her thighs trembled. He kissed her again and took the two clips out of her hair, so that her golden hair fell over him. He turned and held her beneath him on the bed. Like children, with that very same joy and trembling, they undressed and uncovered and gazed on each other; and she felt herself carried back to an unremembered, unimaginable time and state when she had not been Cass, as she was now, but the plain, mild, arrogant, waiting *Clarissa*, when she had not been weary, when love was on the road but not yet at the gates. He looked on her body as though such a body were a new creation, still damp from the vast firmament; and his wonder infected her. She watched his naked body as he crossed the room to turn off the lamp, and thought of the bodies of her children, Paul and Michael, which had come, so miraculously formed, and so heavy and secret with promise, out of her; and, like the water which sprang in the desert when Moses struck the rock with his rod, tears sprang to her eyes. He glowed in the light which came from the lamp above her head. She could not bear to turn it off. She watched him as he bent to take the long-silent record off the machine, and the green eye of the machine clicked off; then he turned to face her, very grave indeed, and with his eyes darker and set farther back than ever. Now, less than ever, did she know what love was—but she smiled, for joy, and he answered her with a small, triumphant laugh. They were oddly equal: perhaps each could teach the other, concerning love, what neither now knew. And they were equal in that both were afraid of what unanswerable and unimaginable riddles might be uncovered in so merciless a light.

She switched off the lamp at the head of the bed, and watched him come to her in the gloom. He took her like a boy, with that singlemindedness, and with a boy's passion to please: and she had awakened something in him, an animal long caged, which came pounding out of its captivity now with a fury which astounded and transfigured them both. Eventually, he slept on her breast, like a child. She watched him, watched his parted lips and the crooked teeth dully gleaming, and the thin, silver trickle of saliva, flowing on to her; and watched the tiny pulsations in the vein of one arm, the red hairs gleaming on it, thrown heavily across her hip; one leg was thrust out behind him, one knee pointed toward her; the little finger of the hand farthest from her, on the edge of the bed, palm upward, twitched; his sex and his belly were hidden.

She looked at her watch. It was ten past one. She would have to go home and she was relieved to discover that she was apprehensive, but not guilty. She really felt that a weight had rolled away, and that she was herself again, in her own skin, for the first time in a long time.

She moved slowly out from beneath his weight, kissed his brow and covered him. Then she went into the bathroom and stepped into the shower. She sang to herself in an undertone as the water crashed over her body, and used the towel which smelled of him with joy. She dressed, still humming, and combed her hair. But the pins were on the night table. She came out, to find him sitting up, smoking a cigarette. They smiled at each other.

"How are you, baby?" he asked.

"I feel wonderful. How are you?"

"I feel wonderful, too," and he laughed, sheepishly. Then, "You have to go?"

"Yes. Yes, I do." She came to the night table and put the pins in her hair. He reached up and pulled her down on the bed and kissed her. It was a strange kiss, in its sad insistence. His eyes seemed to be seeking in her something he had despaired of finding, and did not yet trust.

"Will Richard be awake?"

"I don't think so. It doesn't matter. We're very seldom together in the evenings; he works, I read, or go out to the movies, or watch TV." She touched his cheek. "Don't worry."

"When will I see you?"

"Soon. I'll call you."

"Does it matter if I call you? Or would you rather I didn't?"

She hesitated. "It doesn't matter." They both thought, *It doesn't matter yet.* He kissed her again.

"I wish you could spend the night," he said. He laughed again. "We were just beginning to get started, I hope you know that."

"Oh, yes," she said, "I can tell." He placed his rough cheek next to hers. "But I've got to go now."

"Shall I walk you to a taxi?"

"Oh, Eric, don't be silly. There's just no point to that at all."

"I'd like to. I'll only be a minute." He jumped out of bed and entered the bathroom. She listened to the water splashing and flushing and looked around his apartment, which already seemed terribly familiar. She would try to get down and clean it up sometime in the next few days. It would be difficult to get away in the daytime, except, perhaps, on Saturdays. Then it occurred to her that she needed a smoke screen for this affair and that she would have to use Vivaldo and Ida.

Eric came out of the bathroom and pulled on his shorts and his trousers and his T-shirt. He stuck his feet into his sandals. He looked scrubbed and sleepy and pale. His lips were swollen and very red, like those of heroes and gods of antiquity.

"All ready?" he asked.

"All ready." He picked up her bag and gave it to her. They kissed briefly again, and walked down the stairs into the streets. He put his arm around her waist. They walked in silence, and the street they walked was empty. But there were people in the bars, gesticulating and seeming to howl in the yellow light, behind the smoky glass; and people in the side streets, loitering and skulking; dogs on leashes, sniffing with their masters. They passed the movie theater, and were on the Avenue, facing the hospital. And in the shadow of the great, darkened marquee, they smiled into each other's faces.

"I'm glad you called me," he said. "I'm so glad."

She said, "I'm glad you were home."

They saw a cab coming crosstown and Eric put up his hand.

"I'll call you in a few days," she said, "around Friday or Saturday."

"All right, Cass." The cab stopped and he opened the door and put her in, leaned in and kissed her. "Be good, little gal."

"You, too." He closed the door on her, and waved. The cab began to move, and she watched him move, alone, into the long, dark street.

There were no phone booths on deserted Fifth Avenue and Vivaldo walked the high, silent block to Sixth Avenue and entered the first bar he came to, heading straight for the phone booth. He rang the number of the restaurant and waited quite a while before an irritated male voice answered. He asked for Miss Ida Scott.

"She didn't come in tonight. She called in sick. Maybe you can get her at home."

"Thank you," he said. But the man had already hung up. He felt nothing at all, certainly not astonishment; yet, he leaned against the phone for an instant, freezing and faint. Then he dialed his own number. There was no answer.

He walked out of the phone booth into the bar, which was a workingman's bar, and there was a wrestling match on the TV screen. He ordered a double shot and leaned on the bar. He was surrounded by precisely those men he had known from his childhood, from his earliest youth. It was as though, hideously, after a long and fruitless voyage, he had come home, to find that he had become a stranger. They did not look at him—or did not seem to look at him; but, then, that was the style of these men; and if they usually saw less than was present, they also, often, saw more than one guessed. Two Negroes near him, in working clothes, seemed to have a bet on the outcome of the wrestling match, which they did not, however, appear to be watching very closely. They kept talking to each other in a rumbling, humorous monotone—a smile kept playing on both their faces—and every once in a while they ordered a new round of drinks, or exploded with laughter, or turned their attention again to the screen. All up and down the bar, men stood silently, usually singly, watching the TV screen, or watching nothing. There were booths beside the bar, near the back. An elderly Negro couple and a young

Negro couple shared one booth, another booth held three aimless youths, drinking beer, in the very last booth an odd-looking man, who might have been a Persian, was feeling up a pasty-faced, string-haired girl. The Negro couples were in earnest conversation—the elderly Negro woman leaned forward with great vehemence; and the three youths were giggling and covertly watching the dark man and the pasty girl; and if this evening ended as all the others had, they would presently drive off to some haven and watch each other masturbate. The bartender was iron-haired and pablum-faced, with spectacles, and leaned on a barrel at one end of the bar, watching the screen. Vivaldo watched the screen, seeing two ancient, flabby men throwing each other around on a piece of canvas; from time to time a sensually grinning blonde advertised soap—but her grin was far less sensual than the wrestling match—and a strong-jawed neuter in a crew cut puffed rapaciously, with unnerving pleasure, on a cigarette. Then, back to the groaning wrestlers, who really should have been home in bed, possibly with each other.

Where was she? *Where* was she? With Ellis, certainly. Where? She had called the restaurant; but she had not called him. And she would say, "But we didn't have any plans for tonight, sweetie, I *knew* you were seeing Cass, and I was sure you'd have supper with *her*!" Where was she? the hell with her. She would say, "Oh, honey, don't be like that, suppose I made a fuss every time you went out and had a drink with someone else? I trust you, now, you've got to trust me. Suppose I really make it as a singer and have to see lots of people, what're you going to do *then*?" She trusted him because she didn't give a damn about him, the hell with her. The hell with her. The hell with her.

Oh, Ida. She would say, "Mama called me after you left and she was real upset; Daddy got into a fight this week end and he was cut kind of bad and I just left the hospital this very minute. Mama wanted me to stay with her but I knew you'd be worried, so I came on home. You know, they don't like the idea of my living down here with you one bit, maybe they'll get used to it, but I'm sure that's what makes my Daddy so evil, he just can't get over Rufus, you know, sugar, please make me a little drink, I'm just about dead."

The hell with her. The hell with her.

She would say, "Oh, Vivaldo, why do you want to be so mean when you know how much I love you?" She would sound exasperated and very close to tears. And then, even though he knew that she was using him against himself, hope rose up hard in him, his throat became tight with pain, he willed away all his doubts. Perhaps she loved him, perhaps she did: but if she did, how was it, then, that they remained so locked away from one another? Perhaps it was he who did not know how to give, did not know how to love. Love was a country he knew nothing about. And he thought, very unwillingly, that perhaps he did not love her. Perhaps it was only because she was not white that he dared to bring her the offering of himself. Perhaps he had felt, somewhere, at the very bottom of himself, that she would not dare despise him.

And if this was what she suspected, well, then, her rage was bottomless and she would never be conquered by him.

He walked out of the bar into the streets again, not knowing what to do but knowing he could not go home. He wished he had a friend, a male friend, with whom he could talk; and this made him realize that, with the dubious exception of Rufus, he had never had a friend in his life. He thought of calling Eric, but Eric had been away too long. He no longer knew anything about Eric's life and tonight he did not want to know.

So he walked. He passed the great livid scar of Forty-second Street, knowing that he could not endure sitting through a movie tonight; and on, down lonely Sixth Avenue, until he came to the Village. Again, he thought of calling Eric and again dismissed it. He walked eastward to the park; there were no singers there tonight, only shadows in the shadows of the trees; and a policeman coming into the park as he walked out of it. He walked along MacDougal Street. Here were the black-and-white couples, defiantly white, flamboyantly black; and the Italians watched them, hating them, hating, in fact, all the Villagers, who gave their streets a bad name. The Italians, after all, merely wished to be accepted as decent Americans and probably could not be blamed for feeling that they might have had an easier time of it if they had not been afflicted with so many Jews and junkies and drunkards and queers and spades. Vivaldo peered into the bars and coffee houses, half-hoping to see a familiar and bearable face. But there were only the rat-faced boys, with beards, and the infantile, shapeless girls, with the long hair.

"How're you and your spade chick making it?"

He turned, and it was Jane. She was drunk and with an uptown, seersucker type, who probably worked in advertising.

He stared at her and she said, quickly, with a laugh, "Oh, now, don't get mad, I was only teasing you. Don't old girl friends have *some* rights?" And to the man beside her, she said, "This is an old friend of mine, Vivaldo Moore. And *this* is Dick Lincoln."

Vivaldo and Dick Lincoln acknowledged each other with brief, constrained nods.

"How are you, Jane?" Vivaldo asked, politely; beginning to move, at the same time, in what he hoped was not their direction.

But they, naturally, began to move with him.

"Oh, I'm fine," she said. "I seem to have made an incredible recovery—"

"Have you been ill?"

She looked at him. "Yes, as a matter of fact. Nerves. Due to a love affair that didn't work out."

"Someone I know?"

She laughed, breathily. "You bastard."

"It's just that I'm terribly accustomed to your dramatics. But I'm glad that everything's working out for you now."

"Oh, everything's fine now," she said, and made a grotesquely girlish little skip, holding heavily onto Lincoln's hand. "Dick doesn't care much about soul-searching, but he's good at what he cares about." The man she thus described moved stiffly beside her, his face a ruddy mask of uncertainty, clearly determined to do the right thing, whatever the right thing might prove to be.

"Come and have a drink with us," Jane said. They were standing on the corner, in the lights spilling outward from a bar. The light illumined and horribly distorted her face, so that her eyes looked like coals of fire and her mouth stretched joylessly back upon the gums. "For old times' sake."

"No, thank you," he said. "I'm going on home. I've had a long, hard day."

"Rushing home to your chick?"

"Good thing to rush home to, if you've got one," Dick Lincoln said, putting his pink, nerveless hand on Jane's shoulder.

Somehow, she bore it; but not without another girlish twitch. She said, "Vivaldo's got a great chick." She turned to Dick Lincoln. "I bet you think you're a liberal," she said, "but this boy, baby, he's miles ahead of you. He's miles ahead of *me*; why, if I was as liberal as my friend, Vivaldo, here"— she laughed; a very tall Negro boy passed them, looking at them briefly—"why, I wouldn't be with *you*, you poor white slob. I'd be with the biggest, blackest buck I could find!" Vivaldo felt his skin prickling, Dick Lincoln blushed. Jane laughed, and Vivaldo realized that others, both black and white, were watching them. "Maybe I should have gone with her brother," Jane said, "would you have liked me better if I had? Or were you going with *him*, too? Can't ever tell about a liberal," and she turned her face, laughing, into Dick Lincoln's shoulder.

Lincoln stared helplessly into Vivaldo's eyes. "She's all yours, mister," Vivaldo said, and at this Jane looked up at him, not laughing at all, her face livid, and old with rage. And all his anger left him at once.

"So long," he said, and turned away. He wanted to leave before Jane precipitated a race riot. And he also realized that he had become the focus of two very different kinds of attention. The blacks now suspected him of being an ally—though not a friend, never a friend!—and the whites, particularly the neighborhood Italians, now knew that he could not be trusted. "Hurry home," Jane called behind him, "hurry home! Is it true that they've got hotter blood than ours? Is her blood hotter than mine?" And laughter rang down the street behind this call, the suppressed, bawdy laughter of the Italians—for, after all, Vivaldo was one of them, and a male, and apparently, a gifted one—and the delighted, vindictive laughter of the Negroes. For a moment, behind him, they were almost united—but then, each, hearing the other's laughter, choked their laughter off. The Italians heard the laughter of black men; the black men remembered that it was a black girl Vivaldo was screwing.

He crossed the Avenue. He wanted to go home and he wanted to eat and he wanted to get drunk and, also, perhaps out of simple fury, he wanted to get laid—but he did not feel that anything good would happen to him tonight. And he felt that if he were a real writer, he would simply go home and work and throw everything else out of his mind, as Balzac had done and Proust and Joyce and James and Faulkner. But perhaps they had never held in their minds the nameless things he held in his. He felt a very peculiar, a deadly resignation: he knew that he would not go home until it was too late for him to go anywhere else, or until Ida answered the phone. Ida: and he felt an eerie premonition, as though he were old, walking years from now through familiar streets where no one knew or noticed him, thinking of his lost love, and wondering, *Where is she now? Where is she now?* He passed the movie theater and the tough boys and tough men who always stood outside it. It was ten o'clock. He turned west on Waverly Place and walked to a crowded bar where he could get a hamburger. He forced himself to have a hamburger and a beer before he called his apartment again. There was no answer. He went back to the bar and ordered a whiskey and realized that he was running out of money. If he were going to keep on drinking he would have to go to Benno's, where he had a tab.

He drank his whiskey very slowly, watching and listening to the crowd around him. They had been college boys, mostly, in his day, but both he and they had grown older and he gathered, from the conversations around him, that the college boys had graduated into the professions. He had his eye, vaguely, on a frail, blonde girl, who also seemed, somewhat less vaguely, to have her eye on him: incredibly enough, she seemed to be a lawyer. And he was abruptly very excited, as he had been years ago, at the prospect of making it with a chick above his station, a chick he was not even supposed to be able to look at. He was from the slums of Brooklyn and that stink was on him, and it turned out to be the stink that they were looking for. They were tired of boys who washed too much, who had no odor in their armpits and no sweat on their balls. He looked at the blonde again, wondering what she was like with no clothes on. She was sitting at a table near the door, facing him, toying with a daiquiri glass, and talking to a heavy, gray-haired man, who had a high giggle, who was a little drunk, and whom Vivaldo recognized as a fairly well-known poet. The blonde reminded him of Cass. And this made him realize—for the first time, it is astonishing how well the obvious can be hidden—that when he had met Cass, so many years ago, he had been terribly flattered that so high-born a lady noticed such a stinking boy. He had been over-whelmed. And he had adored Richard without reserve, not, as it now turned out, because of Richard's talent, which, in any case, he had then been quite unable to judge, but merely because Richard possessed Cass. He had envied Richard's prowess, and had imagined that this envy was love.

But, surely, there had been love in it, or they could never have been friends for so long. (Had they been friends? what had they ever, really, said to one another?) Perhaps the proof of Vivaldo's love resided in the fact that he had never thought of Cass carnally, as a woman, but only as a lady, and Richard's wife. But, more probably, it was only that they were older and he had needed older people who cared about him, who took him seriously, whom he could trust. For this, he would have paid any price whatever. They were not much older now, he was nearly twenty-nine, Richard was thirty-seven or thirty-eight, Cass was thirty-three or thirty-four: but they had seemed, especially in the blazing haven of their love, much older then.

And now—now it seemed that they were all equal in misery, confusion, and despair. He looked at his face in the mirror behind the bar. He still had all his hair, there was no gray in it yet; his face had not yet begun to fall at the bottom and shrivel at the top; and he wasn't yet all ass and belly. But, still—and soon; and he stole a look at the blonde again. He wondered about her odor, juices, sounds; for a night, only for a night; then abruptly, with no warning, he found himself wondering how Rufus would have looked at this girl, and an odd thing happened: all desire left him, he turned absolutely cold, and then desire came roaring back, with legions. *Aha,* he heard Rufus snicker, *you don't be careful, motherfucker, you going to get a* black *hard on.* He heard again the laughter which had followed him down the block. And something in him was breaking; he was, briefly and horribly, in a region where there were no definitions of any kind, neither of color, nor of male and female. There was only the leap and the rending and the terror and the surrender. And the terror: which all seemed to begin and end and begin again—forever—in a cavern behind the eye. And whatever stalked there *saw*, and spread the news of what it saw throughout the entire kingdom of whomever, though the eye itself might perish. What order could prevail against so grim a privacy? And yet, without order, of what value was the mystery? Order. Order. *Set thine house in order.* He sipped his whiskey, light-years removed now from the blonde and the bar and yet, more than ever and most unpleasantly present. When people no longer knew that a mystery could only be approached through form, people became—what the people of this time and place had become, what he had become. They perished within their despised clay tenements, in isolation, passively, or actively together, in mobs, thirsting and seeking for, and eventually reeking of blood. Of rending and tearing there can never be any end, and God save the people for whom passion becomes impersonal!

He went into the phone booth again, and, hopelessly, rang his number. It rang and rang. He hung up and stood in the booth for a moment. Now he wondered if something had happened to Ida, if there really had been some family crisis: but it was too late, now, to call the woman who lived next door to Ida's family. Again, he thought of calling Eric and again decided against it. He walked through the bar, slowly, for he was down to carfare and hot-dog money, and would have to leave.

He said, to the poet, but looking at the girl, as he came up to the table, "I just want to say that I know who you are and I've admired your work for a long time and—thank you."

The poet looked up, astonished, and the girl laughed, and said, "That's very sweet of you. Are you a poet, too?"

"No," he said. He found himself thinking that it had been

a long time since he had been with a white girl. He could not help wondering what it might now be like. "I'm a novelist. Unpublished."

"Well, when you *do* get published, you may make some money," the poet said. "Clever bastard you were, to choose a field which *may* allow you to pay at least a modest rent."

"I don't know if I'm clever," Vivaldo said, "it just turned out like that." He was curious about the girl, curious indeed; but other necessities crowded the center of his mind; perhaps they would meet again. "Well, I just wanted to say thank you, that's all. So long."

"Thank *you*," said the poet.

"Good luck!" cried the girl.

He waved his hand in a kind of parody of a hipster and walked out. He walked over to Benno's. It looked as desolate as a graveyard. There were a couple of people there whom he knew, though he usually avoided them; but he was on a tab tonight, as everyone, instinctively, seemed to know; and, anyway, no one in a bar on a Wednesday night was in a position to be choosy.

Certainly not the three people whose table he joined, who were also running out of money and who were *not* on a tab. One of these was the Canadian-born poet, Lorenzo, moon-faced, with much curly hair; and his girl, a refugee from the Texas backwater, scissor-faced, with much straight hair, and a thumb-chewing giggle; and their sidekick, older, lantern-jawed, with tortured lips, who scowled when he was pleased—which was rare—and smiled a pallid smile when he was frightened—which was almost always—so that he enjoyed the reputation of being extremely good-natured.

"Hi, Vi," cried the poet. "Come on over and join us!"

There was, indeed, nothing else to do, unless he left the bar; so he ordered himself a drink and sat down. They were all drinking beer, and most of their beer was gone. He was introduced, for perhaps the thirtieth time, to Belle and to Harold.

"How *are* you, man?" Lorenzo asked. "Nobody ever sees you any more." He had an open, boyish grin, and it summed him up precisely, even though he was beginning to be rather old for a boy. Still, and especially by contrast with his boy and his girl, he seemed the most vivid person at the table and Vivaldo rather liked him.

"I'm up and I'm down," Vivaldo said—and Belle giggled, chewing on her thumb—"and I'm turning into a serious person; that's why you never see me any more."

"You writing?" asked Lorenzo, still smiling. For he was one of those poets who escaped the terrors of writing by writing all the time. He carried a small notebook with him wherever he went and scribbled in it, and when he got drunk enough, read the results aloud. It lay before him, closed, on the table now.

"I'm trying," said Vivaldo. He looked above their heads at the window, out into the streets. "It's a dead night."

"It sure is," said Harold. He looked over at Vivaldo with his little smile. "Where's your chick, man? Don't tell me she's got away."

"No. She's uptown, at some kind of family deal." He leaned forward. "We have a deal, dig, she won't bug me with her family and I won't bug her with mine."

Belle giggled again. Lorenzo laughed. "You ought to bring them together. It'd be the biggest battle since the Civil War."

"Or since Romeo and Juliet," Belle suggested.

"I've been trying to do that in a long poem," Lorenzo said, "you know, Romeo and Juliet today, only she's black and he's white—"

"And Mercutio's passing," grinned Vivaldo.

"Yes. And everybody else is *all* fucked up—"

"Call it," suggested Harold, "*Pickaninnies Everywhere.*"

"Or *Everybody's Pickaninnies.*"

"Or, *Checkers, Anyone?*"

They all howled. Belle, still clinging to her thumbnail, laughed until tears rolled down her face.

"You people are *high*!" said Vivaldo.

This sent them off again. "Baby," cried Lorenzo, "one day, you've got to tell me how you figured *that* out!"

"You want to turn on?" Harold asked.

It had been a long time. He had become bored by the people with whom one turned on, and really rather bored with marijuana. Either it did not derange his senses enough, or he was already more than sufficiently deranged. And he found the hangover crushing and it interfered with his work and he had never been able to make love on it.

Still, it had been a long time. It was only ten past eleven, he did not know what he was going to do with himself. He wanted to enter into, or to forget, the chaos at his center.

"Maybe," he said. "Let me buy a round first. What're you drinking?"

"We could make it on back to my pad," said Harold, scowling his little scowl.

"I'm having beer," said Lorenzo. His expression indicated that he would rather have had something else, but did not wish to seem to be taking advantage of Vivaldo.

Vivaldo turned to Belle. "And you?"

She dropped her hand and leaned forward. "Do you think I could have a brandy Alexander?"

"God," he said, "if you can drink it, I guess they can make it." She leaned back again, unsmiling, oddly ladylike, and he looked at Harold.

"Beer, dad," Harold said. "Then we'll split."

So he walked over to the bar, and ordered the round, making a special trip to carry the brimming, viscous Alexander. He knew that Lorenzo liked rye and so he bought him a straight one and a bottle of beer, and a beer for Harold, and a double bourbon for himself. Let's go for broke, he thought, the hell with it. Let's see what happens. And he really could not tell, because he did not want to know, whether he was acting out of panic or recklessness or pain. There was certainly something he did not want to think about: he did not want to think about where Ida was, or what she was doing now. Not now, later for you, baby. He did not want to go home and lie awake, waiting, or walk up and down, staring at his typewriter and staring at the walls. Later for all that, later. And beneath all this was the void where anguish lived and questions crouched, which referred only to Vivaldo and to no one else on earth. Down there, down there, lived the raw, unformed substance for the creation of Vivaldo, and only he, Vivaldo, alone, could master it.

"Here's how," he said, and, unsteadily, they raised their glasses, and drank.

"Thanks, Vivaldo," said Lorenzo, and downed his whiskey in a single swallow. Vivaldo looked at the young face, which was damp and a little gray and would soon be damper and grayer. The veins in the nose were thickening and darkening; and, sometimes, as now, when Lorenzo looked straight before him, the eyes were more baffled and infinitely lonelier than those of a child.

And at such moments Belle watched him, too, sympathy struggling to overcome the relentless vacuity in her face. And Harold seemed hooded then, like a great bird watching from a tree.

"I'd love to go back to Spain," said Lorenzo.

"Do you know Spain?" asked Vivaldo.

"He used to live there," Belle said. "He always talks about Spain when we get high. We were supposed to go this summer." She bent her head over her cocktail glass, disappearing for a moment, like some unprecedented turtle, behind the citadel of her hair. "Are we going to go, baby?"

Lorenzo spread his hands, helplessly. "If we can get enough bread, we'll go."

"It shouldn't cost much to get to Spain," Harold said. "And you can live there for almost nothing."

"It's a wonderful place," said Lorenzo. "I lived in Barcelona, on a fellowship, for over a year. And I traveled all over Spain. You know, I think they're the grooviest people in the world, the sweetest cats I ever met, I met in Spain. That's right. They'll do anything for you, baby, lend you their shirts, tell you the time, show you the ropes—"

"Lend you their sisters," Harold laughed.

"No, man, they love their sisters—"

"But hate their mothers?"

"No, man, they love them, too. Like they never heard of Freud." Harold laughed. "They'll take you home and feed you, they'll share anything they've got with you and they'll be hurt if you don't take it."

"Mothers, sisters, or brothers," Harold said. "Take them away. Open up that window and let that foul air out."

Lorenzo ignored this, looking around the table and nodding gravely. "That's the truth, men, they're great people."

"What about Franco?" Belle asked. She seemed rather proud to know that Franco existed.

"Oh, Franco's an asshole, he doesn't count."

"Bull*shit* he doesn't count," cried Harold, "you think all those uniforms that *we* help Franco pay for are walking around Spain just for kicks? You think they don't have real bullets in those guns? Let me tell you, dad, those cats are for real, they *shoot* people!"

"Well. That doesn't have anything to do with the people," said Lorenzo.

"Yeah. But I bet you wouldn't like to be a Spaniard," Harold said.

"I'm sick of all this jazz about the happy Spanish peasant," Vivaldo said. He thought of Ida. He leaned over to Lorenzo. "I bet you you wouldn't want to be a nigger here, would you?"

"Oh!" laughed Lorenzo, "your chick sure has you brainwashed!"

"Brainwashed, hell. You wouldn't want to be colored here and you wouldn't want to be Spanish there." There was a curious tension in his chest and he took a large swallow of his whiskey. "The question is—what *do* we want to be?"

"I want to be me," said Belle, with an unexpected ferocity, and chewed at her thumbnail.

"Well," asked Vivaldo, and looked at her, "what's stopping you?"

She giggled and chewed; she looked down. "I don't know. It's hard to get straight." She looked over at him as though afraid he might reach over and strike him. "You know what I mean?"

"Yes," he said, after a long moment and a long sigh, "I sure do know what you mean."

They all dropped abruptly into silence. Vivaldo thought of his spade chick, his dark girl, his beloved Ida, his mysterious torment and delight and hope, and thought of his own white skin. What did she see when she looked at him? He dilated his nostrils, trying to smell himself: what was that odor like for her? When she tangled her fingers in his hair, his "fine Italian hair," was she playing with water, as she claimed, or was she toying with the notion of uprooting a forest? When he entered that marvelous wound in her, *rending and tearing! rending and tearing!* was she surrendering, in joy, to the Bridegroom, Lord, and Savior? or was he entering a fallen and humiliated city, entering an ambush, watched from secret places by hostile eyes? Oh, Ida, he thought, I'd give up my color for you, I would, only take me, take me, love me as I am! Take me, take me, as I take you. How did he take her, what did he bring to her? Was it his pride and his glory that he brought, or his shame? If he despised his flesh, then he must despise hers—and *did* he despise his flesh? And if she despised her flesh, then she must despise his. Who can blame her, he thought, wearily, if she does? and then he thought, and the thought surprised him, who can blame *me*? They were always threatening to cut the damn thing off, and what were all those fucking confessions about? *I have sinned in thought and deed.* I have sinned, I have sinned, I have sinned—and it was always better, to undercut Hell's competition, to sin, if you had to sin, alone. What a pain in the ass old Jesus Christ had turned out to be, and it probably wasn't even the poor, doomed, loving, hopheaded old Jew's fault.

Harold was watching him. He asked, "You want to turn on now or you want another drink first?" His voice was extremely rough, and he was scowling and smiling at the same time.

"Oh, I don't care," Vivaldo said, "I'm with the crowd." He thought of making another phone call, but realized that he was afraid to. The hell with it. It was one-fifteen. And he was, at last, thank heaven, at least a little drunk.

"Oh, let's split," said Lorenzo. "We've got beer at home."

They rose and left Benno's and walked west to Harold's pad. He lived in a narrow dark street near the river, on the top floor. The climb was discouraging, but the apartment was clean and not too disordered—it was not at all the kind of apartment one would have expected Harold to have—with carpets on the floor and burlap covering the windows. There was a hi-fi set, and records; and science-fiction magazines lay scattered about. Vivaldo flopped down on the narrow couch against the wall, in a kind of alcove formed by two bookcases. Belle sat on the floor near the window. Lorenzo went to the john, then to the kitchen, and returned with a quart bottle of beer.

"You forgot to bring glasses," Belle told him.

"So who needs glasses? We're all friends." But he obediently returned to the kitchen.

Harold, meanwhile, like a meticulous and scientific host, was busily preparing the weed. He seated himself at the coffee table, near Vivaldo, and placed on a sheet of newspaper tweezers, cigarettes, cigarette papers, and a Bull Durham sack full of pot.

"It's great stuff," he told Vivaldo, "chick brought it in from Mexico only yesterday. And, baby, this shit travels *well*!"

Vivaldo laughed. Lorenzo returned with the glasses and looked worriedly over at Vivaldo.

"You feeling all right?"

"I feel fine. Just quiet. You know."

"Groovy." He set a glass of beer carefully on the floor near Vivaldo, and poured a glass for Harold.

"He's going to feel just swinging," said Harold, as happy and busy as bees, "just as soon as he connects with old Mother Harold's special recessed filter-tips. Baby! Are you going to wail!"

Lorenzo poured a glass of beer for Belle, and set the bottle on the floor beside her. "How about some sides?"

"Go, baby."

Vivaldo closed his eyes, feeling an anticipatory languor and lewdness. Lorenzo put on something at once bell-like and doleful, by the Modern Jazz Quartet.

"Here."

He looked up. Harold stood above him with a glowing stick.

He sat up, smiling vaguely, and carefully picked up his beer from the floor before taking the stick from Harold. Harold watched him, smiling intensely, as he took a long, shaky drag. He took a swallow of his beer and gave the stick back. Harold inhaled deeply and expertly, and rubbed his chest.

"Come on over to the window," Belle called.

Her voice sounded high and pleased, like a child's. And, exactly as though he were responding to a child, Vivaldo, though he preferred to remain alone on the sofa, walked over to the window. Harold followed him. Belle and Lorenzo sat on the floor, sharing a stick between them, and staring out at the New York rooftops.

"It's strange," Belle said. "It's so ugly by day and so beautiful at night."

"Let's go up on the roof," said Lorenzo.

"Oh! What a groovy idea!"

They gathered up the makings, and the beer, and Belle picked up a blanket; and, like children, they tiptoed out of the apartment, up the stairs to the roof. And there they seemed bathed in silence, all alone. Belle spread the blanket, which was not big enough for them all. She and Lorenzo shared it. Vivaldo took another large drag and squatted on the edge of the roof, his arms hugging his knees.

"Don't *do* that, man," Lorenzo whispered, "you're too near the edge, I can't bear to watch it."

Vivaldo smiled and moved back, stretching out on his belly beside them.

"I'm sorry. I'm like that, too. I can hang over the edge myself, but I can't watch anybody else do it."

Belle grabbed his hand. He looked up at her pale, thin face, framed by the black hair. She smiled, and she was prettier than she had seemed in the bar. "I like you," she said. "You're a real groovy cat. Lorenzo always said you were, but I never believed him." Her accent, too, was more noticeable now; she sounded like the simplest and most innocent of country girls—if country girls were innocent, and he supposed, at some point in their lives, they had to be.

"Why, thank you," he said. Lorenzo, palely caught in the lights of heaven and earth, grinned over at him. Vivaldo pulled his hand from Belle's hand and reached over and struck Lorenzo lightly on the cheek. "I like you, too, both of you."

"How you feeling, dad?" It was Harold, who seemed to be quite far away.

"I feel wonderful." And he did, in a strange, untrustworthy way. He was terribly aware of his body, the length of his limbs, and the soft wind ruffling his hair, and of Lorenzo and Belle, poised like two cherubim together, and of Harold, the prince of darkness, industrious, indefatigable keeper of the weed. Harold was sitting in the shadow of the chimney, rolling another stick. Vivaldo laughed. "Baby, you really love your work."

"I just love to see people happy," said Harold, and suddenly grinned; he, too, seemed very different from what he had been in the bar, younger and softer; and somewhere beneath it all, much sadder, so that Vivaldo regretted all his harsh, sardonic judgments. What happened to people? why did they suffer so hideously? And at the same time he knew that he and Harold could never be friends and that none of them, really, would ever get any closer to each other than they were right now.

Harold lit his stick and passed it to Vivaldo. "Go, baby," he said—very tenderly, watching Vivaldo with a smile.

Vivaldo took his turn, while the others watched him. It was a kind of community endeavor, as though he were a baby just learning to use the potty or just learning how to walk. They all but applauded when he passed it on to Lorenzo, who took his turn and passed it on to Belle. "Ooh," said Lorenzo, "I'm flying," and leaned back with his head in Belle's lap.

Vivaldo turned over on his back, head resting on his arms, knees pointing to the sky. He felt like singing. "My chick's a singer," he announced.

The sky looked, now, like a vast and friendly ocean, in which drowning was forbidden, and the stars seemed stationed there, like beacons. To what country did this ocean lead? for oceans always led to some great good place: hence, sailors, missionaries, saints, and Americans.

"Where's she singing?" asked Lorenzo. His voice seemed to drop gently from the air: Vivaldo was watching heaven.

"She's not, right now. But she will be soon. And she's going to be great."

"I've seen her," Belle said, "she's beautiful."

He turned his head in the direction of the voice. "You've seen her? Where?"

"In the restaurant where she works. I went there with somebody—not with Lorenzo," and he heard her giggle, "and the cat I was with told me she was your girl." There was a silence. Then, "She's very tough."

"Why do you say that?"

"Oh, I don't know. She just seemed—very tough, that's

all. I don't mean she wasn't nice. But she was very sure of herself, you could tell she wasn't going to take any shit."

He laughed. "Sounds like my girl, all right."

"I wish I looked like her," Belle said. "My!"

"I like you just the way you are," said Lorenzo. Out of the corner of his eye, and from far away, Vivaldo watched his arms go up and saw Belle's dark hair fall.

Just above my head.

That was a song that Ida sometimes sang, puttering inefficiently about the kitchen, which always seemed sandy with coffee grinds and vaguely immoral with dead cigarettes on the burnt, blistered paint of the shelves.

Perhaps the answer was in the songs.

> *Just above my head,*
> *I hear music in the air.*
> *And I really do believe*
> *There's a God somewhere.*

But was it *music* in the air, or *trouble* in the air? He began whistling another song:

> *Trouble in mind, I'm blue,*
> *But I won't be blue always,*
> *'Cause the sun's going to shine*
> *In my back door someday.*

Why *back* door? And the sky now seemed to descend, no longer phosphorescent with possibilities, but rigid with the mineral of choices, heavy as the weight of the finite earth, onto his chest. He was being pressed: *I'm pressing on,* Ida sometimes sang, *the upward way!*

What in the world did these songs mean to her? For he knew that she often sang them in order to flaunt before him privacies which he could never hope to penetrate and to convey accusations which he could never hope to decipher, much less deny. And yet, if he could enter this secret place, he would, by that act, be released forever from the power of her accusations. His presence in this strangest and grimmest of sanctuaries would prove his right to be there; in the same way that the prince, having outwitted all the dangers and slaughtered the lion, is ushered into the presence of his bride, the princess.

> *I loves you, Porgy, don't let him take me.*
> *Don't let him handle me with his hot hands.*

To whom, to whom, did she sing this song?

The blues fell down this morning. The blues my baby gave to me. Water trickled past his ear, onto his wrist. He did not move and the slow tears rolled from the corners of his eyes.

"You're groovy, too," he heard Belle say.

"For real?"

"For real."

"Let's try to make it to Spain. Let's really try."

"I'll get dressed up Monday, uptown style"—she giggled—"and I'll get a job as receptionist somewhere. I hate it, it's such a drag, but, that way, we can get away from here."

"Do that, baby. And I'll get a job, too, I promise."

"You don't have to promise."

"But I do."

He heard their kiss, it seemed light and loving and dry, and he envied them their deadly and unshakable innocence.

"Let's ball."

"Not here. Let's go downstairs."

He heard Lorenzo's laugh. "What's the matter, you shy?"

"No." He heard a giggle and a whisper. "Let's go down."

"They're stoned out of their heads, they don't care."

She giggled again. "Look at them."

He closed his eyes. He felt another weight on his chest, a hand, and he looked into Harold's face. Terribly weary and lined and pale, and his hair was damp and curled on his forehead. And yet, beneath this spectacular fatigue, it was the face of a very young boy which stared at him.

"How're you doing?"

"Great. It was great charge."

"I knew you'd dig it. I like you, man."

He was surprised and yet not surprised by the intensity in Harold's eyes. But he could not bear it; he turned his face away; then he put the weight of Harold's head on his chest.

"Please, man," he told him after a moment, "don't bother. It's not worth it, nothing will happen. It's been too long."

"What's been too long?"

And Vivaldo smiled to himself suddenly, a smile as sad as his tears, thinking of shooting matches and other contests on rooftops and basements and in locker-rooms and cars half his lifetime ago. And he had dreamed of it since, though it was only now that he remembered the dreams that he had dreamed. Feeling very cold now, inwardly cold, with Harold's hand on his cock and Harold's head on his chest, and knowing that: yes, something *could* happen, he recalled his fantasies—of the male mouth, male hands, the male organ, the male ass. Sometimes, a boy—who always rather reminded him of his younger brother, Stevie, and perhaps this was the prohibition, as, in others, it might be the key—passed him, and he watched the boy's face and watched his ass, and he felt something, wanting to touch the boy, to make the boy laugh, to slap him across his young behind. So he knew that it was there, and he probably wasn't frightened of it any more; but it was, possibly, too expensive for him, it did not matter enough. So he said to Harold, gently, "Understand me, man, I'm not putting you down. But my time with boys was a long time ago. I've been busy with girls. I'm sorry."

"And nothing can happen now?"

"I'd rather not. I'm sorry."

Harold smiled. "I'm sorry, too." Then, "Can I lie here with you, like this, just the same?"

Vivaldo held him and closed his eyes. When he opened them, the sky was a great brass bowl above him. Harold lay near him, one hand on Vivaldo's leg, asleep. Belle and Lorenzo lay wrapped in the blanket, like two dirty children. He stood up, moving too close to the edge, getting a dreadful glimpse of the waiting, baking streets. His mouth felt like Mississippi in the days when cotton was king. He hurried down the stairs into the streets, hurrying home to Ida. She would say, "My God, Vivaldo, where've you been? I've been calling this house all night long to let you know I had to go and sit in with some fellows in Jersey City. I keep telling you we better get an answering service, but you never hear anything *I* say!"

4

And the summer came, the New York summer, which is like no summer anywhere. The heat and the noise began their destruction of nerves and sanity and private lives and love affairs. The air was full of baseball scores and bad news and treacly songs; and the streets and the bars were full of hostile people, made more hostile by the heat. It was not possible in this city, as it had been for Eric in Paris, to take a long and peaceful walk at any hour of the day or night, dropping in for a drink at a bistro or flopping oneself down at a sidewalk café—the half-dozen grim parodies of sidewalk cafés to be found in New York were not made for flopping. It was a city without oases, run entirely, insofar, at least, as human perception could tell, for money; and its citizens seemed to have lost entirely any sense of their right to renew themselves. Whoever, in New York, attempted to cling to this right, lived in New York in exile—in exile from the life around him; and this, paradoxically, had the effect of placing him in perpetual danger of being forever banished from any real sense of himself.

In the evenings, and on week ends, Vivaldo sat in his undershorts at the typewriter, his buttocks sticking to the chair, sweat rolling down his armpits and behind his ears and dripping into his eyes and the sheets of paper sticking to each other and to his fingers. The typewriter keys moved sluggishly, striking with a dull, wet sound—moved, in fact, rather the way his novel moved, lifelessly, pushed forward, inch by inch by recalcitrant inch, almost entirely by the will. He scarcely knew what his novel was about any longer, or why he had ever wished to write it, but he could not let it go. He could not let it go, nor could he close with it, for the price of that embrace was the loss of Ida's, or so he feared. And this fear kept him suspended in a pestilential, dripping limbo.

Their physical situation, in any case, was appalling. Their apartment was too small. Even had they both kept regular hours, had worked all day and come home only in the evenings, they would have been cramped; but some weeks Vivaldo worked nights in the bookstore and some weeks he

worked days; and Ida, too, was on a kind of universal, unpredictable shift at the restaurant, sometimes working lunch and
supper, sometimes either, sometimes both. They each hated
their jobs—which did not help their relationship with one another—but Ida was the most popular waitress her boss had,
which gave her a certain leeway, and Vivaldo could no longer
accept those more demanding and more lucrative jobs which
offered him a future he did not want. They were both, as it
were, racing before a storm, struggling to "make it" before
they were sucked into that quicksand, which they saw all
around them, of an aimless, defeated, and defensive bohemia.
And this meant that they could not hope to improve their
physical situation, being scarcely able to maintain the apartment that they had.

Vivaldo had often suggested that they move out of the Village, into the lower East Side, where cheap lofts were available, lofts which could be made extremely attractive. But Ida
had vetoed this. Her most important reason was never stated,
but Vivaldo eventually realized that she had a horror of that
neighborhood because Rufus' last attempt at domestic life, or
at life itself, had been made down there.

She told Vivaldo, "I wouldn't feel safe, honey, coming
home at night or coming home in the daytime. You don't
know those people the way I do, because they've never treated
you the way they've treated me. Some of those cats, baby, if
they catch you alone on a subway platform, or coming up the
steps to *your* apartment, they don't think nothing of opening
up their pants and asking you to give them a blow job. That's
right. And, look, baby, I was down there, it was on Mott
Street, with Rufus, a couple of years ago, to see some
people for Sunday brunch. They were white. And we went
out on the fire escape to look at a wedding procession down
the street. So some of the people on the block saw us. Well,
do you know that three white men came up to that apartment, one with a blackjack and one with a gun and one with
a knife, and they threw us out of there. They said"—and
she laughed—"that we were giving their street a bad
name."

She watched his face for a moment. "It's true," she said,

gently. Then, "Let's just stay here, Vivaldo, until we can do better. It's rough, but it's not as rough as it might be."

So they tried to keep their door open, but there were risks attached to this, particularly if Ida were home, lounging on the sofa in her brief blue playsuit or practicing arrangements with the help of the record player. The sound of Vivaldo's typewriter, the sound of Ida's voice, the sound of the record player, attracted the attention of people coming up and down the stairs and the glimpse the open door afforded of Ida inflamed the transient imagination. People used the open door as an incitement—to stop, to listen, to stare, to knock, pretending that a friend of theirs had once lived in this very apartment, and did they know whatever had become of good old Tom or Nancy or Joanna? Or inviting them to a party upstairs or down the street, or inviting themselves to a party at Vivaldo's. Once, absolutely beside himself, Vivaldo had beaten from the landing to the streets a boy who stood in the hot shadow of the landing, his hands in his pockets and his eyes on Ida—or, rather, on the spot from which, with a furious cry and a curse, she had hastily removed herself. The boy had not taken his hands from his pockets, only kept up a small, ugly animal moaning; and fallen, when Vivaldo had pushed him through the street door, heavily, on one shoulder. The police came shortly afterward, their own combustible imaginations stiffening their ready civic pride. After that, they kept the doors not only closed but locked. Yet, the entire shapeless, unspeakable city seemed to be in the room with them, some summer nights.

He worked, she worked, he paced the room, she paced. She wanted him to become a "great" writer, but, unless *she* was working, she was incapable of being left alone. If she was working, the sound of her voice, the sound of her music, menaced, and, most often, drowned out that other orchestra in his head. If she was not working, she poured him another beer, ruffling his hair; she observed that his cigarette had burned itself out in the ashtray and lit him a new one; or she read over his shoulder, which he could not bear—but it was easier to bear this than to hear himself accused of having no respect for her intelligence. On the evenings they were together in the house, he really could not work, for he could not move far enough away from her, he could not enter himself. But he tried not to resent this, for the evenings she was away were worse.

Once or twice a week, sometimes, or once every two or three weeks, she went to Harlem, never inviting him to come along. Or she was sitting in with some musicians in Peekskill or Poughkeepsie or Washington or Philadelphia or Baltimore or Queens. He drove down with her once, with the other musicians, to a joint in Washington. But the atmosphere was deadly; the musicians had not wanted him along. The people in the joint had liked him well enough but had also seemed to wonder what he was doing there—or perhaps it was only *he* who wondered it; and Ida had sung only two songs, which did not seem much after such a long trip, and she had not sung them well. He felt that this had something to do with the attitude of the musicians, who seemed to want to punish her, and with the uneasy defiance with which she forced herself to face their judgment. It was only too clear that if he had been a powerful white man, their attitudes would have been modified by the assumption that she was using *him*; but it was obvious that, as things were, he could do her no good whatever and, therefore, he must be using *her*. Neither did Ida have the professional standing which would force them to accept him as the whim, the house pet, or husband of a star. He had *no* function, they did: they pulled rank on him, they closed ranks against him.

There was speedily accumulating, then, between Ida and Vivaldo, great areas of the unspoken, vast minefields which neither dared to cross. They never spoke of Washington, nor did he ever again accompany her on such out-of-town jaunts. They never spoke of her family, or of his. After his long, tormenting Wednesday night, Vivaldo found that he lacked the courage to mention the name of Steve Ellis. He knew that Ellis was sending her to a more exclusive and celebrated singing teacher, as well as to a coach, and intended to arrange a recording date for her. Ida and Vivaldo buried their disputes in silence, in the mined field. It seemed better than finding themselves hoarse, embittered, gasping, and more than ever alone. He did not wish to hear himself accused, again, of trying to stand between her and her career—did not wish to hear it because there was more than a little truth to this accusation. Of course, he also felt that she, although unconsciously, was attempting to stand between himself and his fulfillment. But he did not want to say this. It would have made too clear their mutual panic, their terror of being left alone.

So, there they were, as the ghastly summer groaned and bubbled on, he working in order not to be left behind by her, and she working—in order to be free of him? or in order to create a basis on which they could be, more than ever, together? "I've *got* to make it," she sometimes said, "I'm *going* to make it. And you better make it, too, sweetie. I've just about had it, down here among the garbage cans."

As for Ellis:

"Vivaldo, if you want to believe I'm two-timing you with that man, that's your problem. If you want to believe it, you're *going* to believe it. I will not be put in the position of having to *prove* a damn thing. It's up to you. You don't trust me, well, so long, baby, I'll pack my bags and *go*."

Some nights, when Ida came in, from the restaurant, her singing teacher, her parents, wherever she had been, bringing him beer and cigarettes and sandwiches, her face weary and peaceful and her eyes soft with love, it seemed unthinkable that they could ever part. They ate and drank and talked and laughed together, and lay naked on their narrow bed in the darkness, near the open windows through which an occasional limp breeze came, and tasted each other's lips and caressed each other in spite of the heat, and made great plans for their indisputable tomorrow. And often fell asleep like that, at perfect ease with one another. But at other times they could not find each other at all. Sometimes, unable to reach her and unable to reach the people in his novel, he stalked out and walked the summer streets alone. Sometimes she declared she couldn't stand him another minute, his grumpy ways, and was going out to a movie. And sometimes they went out together, down to Benno's, or over to visit Eric—though these days, it was usually Eric and Cass.

Ida professed herself very struck by the change in Eric—she meant by this that she disapproved of surprises and that Eric had surprised her—and the implacable, unaccountable Puritan in her disapproved of his new and astonishing affair. She said that Cass was foolish and that Eric was dishonest.

Vivaldo's feelings were much milder—it was not Eric who had surprised him, but Cass. She had certainly jeopardized everything; and he remembered her declaration: *No, thank you, Vivaldo, I don't want to be protected any more.* And, insofar as his own confusion allowed him to consider hers at all, he was proud of her—not so much because she had placed herself in danger as because she knew she had.

A French movie in which Eric played a bit part came to New York that summer and the four of them made an appointment to go and see it. Ida and Vivaldo were to meet Eric and Cass at the box office.

"What does she think she's doing?" Ida asked. She and Vivaldo were walking toward the theater through the July streets.

"She's trying to live," said Vivaldo, mildly.

"Oh, shit, baby, Cass is a grown woman with two kids. What about those kids? Eric's not the fatherly type, at least not with boys *that* age."

"What a filthy little moralist you are. What Cass does with Cass's life is her business. Not yours. Maybe she knows more about those kids than you do; maybe she's trying to live the way she thinks she ought to live so that they won't be afraid to do it when their time comes." He felt himself beginning to be angry. "And you don't know enough about Eric to talk about him that way."

"Those kids are going to hate her before it's over, believe me. And don't tell me I don't know about Eric; I knew all about him the minute I laid eyes on him."

"You knew what you'd *heard*. And you'd never heard that he was going to have an affair with Cass. So you're bugged."

"Eric may have *you* fooled, and he may have Cass fooled—of course, I think she's just fooling herself—but *I'm* not fooled. You'll see."

"You're not a singer at all, you're a fortune-teller. We should get you some big brass earrings and a vivid turban and set you up in business."

"Laugh, clown," she said.

"Well, what do you care? If he wants to make it with her and she wants to make it with him, what do *we* care?"

"Don't *you* care? Richard's *your* friend."

"Cass is more my friend than Richard," he said.

"She *can't* realize what she's doing. She's got a good man and he's really starting to get someplace, and she can't find anything *better* to do than start screwing some poor-white faggot from Alabama. I swear, I don't understand white folks worth a damn."

"Eric's not poor-white; his family's very well off," he said, beginning to sweat with more than the heat, wishing her voice would cease.

"Well, I hope they haven't disowned him. Do you think Eric's ever going to make it as an actor?"

"I don't see what that has to do with anything. But, yes, I do, he's a very good actor."

"He's getting kind of old to be so unknown. What was he doing in Paris all that time?"

"I don't know, baby, but I hope he was having a ball. You know? Like whatever he digs most, that's what I hope he was doing."

"Well," she said, "that isn't what he's doing now."

He sighed, telling himself to drop the subject or change it. But he said, "I just don't see why it should matter to you, that's all. So he likes a roll in the hay with a man. So what?"

"He wanted a roll in the hay with my brother, too," she said. "He wanted to make him as sick as he is."

"If anything happened between Eric and your brother, it didn't happen because Eric threw him down and raped him. Let me cool you, honey, you don't know as much about men as you think you know."

She turned on him a small, grim smile. "*If* anything happened. You're a damn liar, and a coward, too."

He looked at her; for that moment he hated her. "Why do you say that?"

"Because you know damn well what happened. It's only that you don't want to know—"

"Ida, it was none of my damn business, I never talked about it with Rufus *or* with Eric. Why *should* I have?"

"Vivaldo, you haven't got to *talk* about what's happening to *know* what's happening. Rufus never talked to me about what was happening to him—but I knew just the same."

He was silent for a moment. Then, "You're never going to forgive me, are you? for your brother's death."

Then she, too, was silent. He said, "I loved your brother, too, Ida. You don't believe that, I know, but I did. But he was just a man, baby. He wasn't a saint."

"I never said he was a saint. But I'm black, too, and I know how white people treat black boys and girls. They think you're something for them to wipe their pricks on."

He saw the lights of the movie theater three blocks down the Avenue. The summer streets were full. His throat closed and his eyes began to burn.

"After all this time we've been together," he said, at last, "you still think that?"

"Our being together doesn't change the world, Vivaldo."

"It does," he said, "for me."

"That," she said, "is because you're white."

He felt, suddenly, that he was going to scream, right there in the crowded streets, or close his heavy fingers around her neck. The lights of the movie theater wavered before him, and the sidewalk seemed to tilt. "You stop that," he said, in a voice which he did not recognize. "You stop that. You stop trying to kill me. It's not my fault I'm white. It's not my fault you're black. It's not my fault he's dead." He threw back his head, sharply, to scatter away his tears, to bring the lights into focus, to make the sidewalk even. And in another voice, he said, "He's dead, sweetheart, but we're alive. We're alive, and I love you, I love you. Please don't try to kill me." And then, "Don't you love me? Do you love me, Ida? Do you?" And he turned his head and looked at her.

She did not look at him; and she said nothing; said nothing for a block or more. The theater came closer and closer. Cass and Eric were standing under the marquee, and they waved. "What I don't understand," she said, slowly, "is how you can talk about love when you don't want to know what's happening. And *that's* not *my* fault. How can you say you loved Rufus when there was so much about him you didn't want to know?

How can I believe you love me?" And, with a curious help-lessness, she took his arm. "How can you love somebody you don't know anything about? You don't know where I've been. You don't know what life is like for me."

"But I'm willing," he said, "to spend the rest of my life finding out."

She threw back her head and laughed. "Oh, Vivaldo. You *may* spend the rest of your life finding out—but it won't be because you're willing." And then, with ferocity, "And it won't be *me* you'll be finding out about. Oh, Lord." She dropped his arm. She gave him a strange side glance; he could not read it, it seemed both pitying and cold. "I'm sorry to have hurt your feelings, I'm not trying to kill you. I know you're not responsible for—for the world. And, listen: I don't blame you for not being willing. I'm not willing, nobody's willing. Nobody's willing to pay their dues."

Then she moved forward, smiling, to greet Eric and Cass.

"Hello, kids," she said—and Vivaldo watched her, that ur-chin grin, those flashing eyes—"how you been making it?" She tapped Eric lightly on the cheek. "They tell me you're beginning to enjoy New York almost as much as you enjoyed Paris. How about that? We're not so bad over here, now, are we?"

Eric blushed, and humorously pursed his lips. "I'd enjoy it a whole lot more if you'd put your rivers and bridges in the middle of the city instead of having them all pushed off on the edges this way. You can't *breathe* in this city in the sum-mertime; it's frightening." He looked at Vivaldo. "I don't know how you barbarians stand it."

"If it wasn't for us barbarians," said Vivaldo, "you man-darins would be in one hell of a fix." He kissed Cass on the forehead, and struck Eric lightly on the back of the neck. "It's good to see you, anyway."

"We've got good news," said Cass, "though I guess I really ought to let Eric tell it."

"Well, we're not absolutely certain that it's good news," said Eric. He looked at Ida and Vivaldo. "Anyway, I think we ought to keep them in suspense for awhile. If they don't think I'm the greatest thing they ever saw in this movie, why, then, I think we just ought to let them find out what's happening when the general public finds out." And he threw his chin in the air and swaggered toward the box office.

"Oh, Eric," cried Cass, "*can't* I tell them?" She said, to Ida and Vivaldo, "It's got something to do with this movie we're going to see."

"Well, you've got to tell us," Ida said, "or we simply won't go in." She raised her voice in the direction of Eric's back: "We *do* know other actors."

"Come on, Cass," said Vivaldo, "you've got to tell us now."

But Cass looked again in Eric's direction, with a small, frowning smile. "*Let* me tell them, sweetheart."

He turned, smiling, with the tickets in his hand. "I don't know how to stop you," he said. He moved over to Cass, and put one arm around her shoulder.

"Well," said Cass, smaller than ever, and more radiant— and, as she spoke, Eric watched her with an amused and loving smile—"Eric doesn't have much of a part in this movie, he only appears in one or two scenes and he's only got a couple of lines—"

"*Three* scenes," said Eric, "*one* line. If one of you sneezes, you die."

"—but on the strength of *this*—" cried Cass.

"Well, not *only* on the strength of this," said Eric.

"Will you let the girl talk?" asked Vivaldo. "Go on, Cass."

"—on the strength of this particular performance"—

"—exposure," said Eric.

"Oh, shit," cried Vivaldo.

"He's a perfectionist," Cass said.

"He's going to be a dead one, too," said Ida, "if he doesn't stop hogging this scene. Lord, would I hate to work with you. Please go on, Cass."

"Well, telegrams and phone calls have been coming out of Hollywood asking Eric if he will play——" and she looked up at Eric.

"Well, don't stop now," cried Ida.

Eric, now, was very pale. "They've got some wild idea out there of making a movie version of *The Possessed*—"

"The Dostoievski novel," said Cass.

"Thanks," said Vivaldo, "and——?"

"They want me to play Stavrogin," said Eric.

A total silence fell, and they all stared at Eric, who looked uneasily back at them. There gleamed a small crown of sweat on his forehead, just below the hairline. Vivaldo felt a mighty tug of jealousy and fear. "Wow!" he said. Eric looked at him, seeming to see into his heart; and his brow puckered slightly, as though he were stiffening himself for a quarrel.

"It's probably going to be an awful movie," he said, "can you imagine them doing *The Possessed*? I didn't really take it seriously until my agent called me. And then Bronson called me, too, because, you see, there's going to be a kind of conflict with *Happy Hunting Ground*. We're set to go into rehearsal next month, and, who knows? maybe it'll be a hit. So we've got to iron that out."

"But they're willing to do almost anything to get Eric," Cass said.

"That's not entirely true," said Eric, "don't listen to her. They're just very interested, that's all. I don't believe anything until it happens." He took a blue handkerchief out of his back pocket and wiped his face. "Let's go in," he said.

"Baby," said Vivaldo, "you're going to be a star." He kissed Eric on the forehead. "You son of a bitch."

"Nothing is set," said Eric, and he looked at Cass. He grinned. "I'm really part of an economy drive. They can get me cheap, you know, and they've got almost everybody you ever heard of lined up for the other roles—so my agent explained to me that my name goes *below* the title—"

"*But* in equal size," said Cass.

"One of those *and introducing* deals," said Eric, and laughed. He looked pleased about his good news for the first time.

"Well, baby, it looks like you've made it now," said Ida. "Congratulations."

"Your clairvoyant Frenchman," Cass said, "was right."

"Only what are they going to do about that ante-bellum accent?" asked Vivaldo.

"Look," said Eric, "let's go see this movie. I speak French in it." He threw an arm around Vivaldo's shoulder. "Impeccably."

"Hell," Vivaldo said, "I don't really feel like seeing a

movie. I'd much rather take you out and get you stinking drunk."

"You're going to," said Eric, "as soon as the movie's over."

And they came, laughing, through the doors just as the French film began. The titles were superimposed over a montage of shots of Paris in the morning: laborers on their bicycles, on their way to work, coming down from the hills of Montmartre, crossing the Place de la Concorde, rolling through the great square before Notre Dame. In great close-ups, the traffic lights flashed on and off, the white batons of the traffic policemen rose and fell; it soon became apparent that one had already picked up the central character and would follow him to his destination; which, if one could judge from the music would be a place of execution. The film was one of those politics, sex, and vengeance dramas the French love to turn out, and it starred one of the great French actors, who had died when this film was completed. So the film, which was not remarkable in itself, held this undeniable necrophilic fascination. Working with this actor, being on the set while this man worked, had been one of the great adventures of Eric's life. And though Cass, Vivaldo, and Ida were interested in the film principally because Eric appeared in it, the attention which they brought to it was dictated by the silent intensity of Eric's adoration. They had all heard of the great actor, and they all admired him. But they could not see, of course, as Eric could, with what economy of means he managed great effects and turned an indifferent role into a striking creation.

On the other hand, just as the politics of the film were made helplessly frivolous by the French passion for argument and distrust of community, so was the male star's overwhelming performance rendered suspect by the question of just why so much energy and talent had been expended on so little.

Ida grabbed Vivaldo's hand in the darkness, and clung to it as though she were a child, mutely begging for reassurance and forgiveness. He pressed his shoulder very close to hers, and they leaned against one another. The film unrolled. Cass whispered to Eric, Eric whispered to Cass. Cass turned toward them, whispering, "Here he comes!" and the camera trucked into a crowded café, resting finally on a group of students. "That's our boy!" cried Ida, disturbing the people around them—who sounded, for a second, like the weirdest cloud of insects. Cass leaned over and kissed Eric on the nose; and, "You look very good," Vivaldo whispered. Eric was compelled to be still during this entire brief scene, while the students around him wrangled; his head was thrown back and up, against the wall, his eyes were closed; and he seemed scarcely to move at all. Yet, the director had so placed him that his drunken somnolence held the scene together, and emphasized the futility of the passionate talkers. Someone jostled the table and Eric's position shifted slightly. He seemed to be made of rubber, and seemed, indeed, to be fleeing from the controversy which raged around him—in which, nevertheless, he was fatally involved. Vivaldo had been with Eric when he was drunk and knew that this was not at all the way Eric behaved—on the contrary, it was the Southern rebel and a certain steel-rod quality which came out in Eric then; and Vivaldo, at the same time that he realized that Eric was doing a great deal by doing very little, also, for the first time, caught a glimpse of who Eric really was. It was very strange—to see more of Eric when he was acting than when he was being, as the saying goes, himself. The camera moved very little during this scene and Eric was always kept in range. The light in which he was trapped did not alter, and his face, therefore, was exposed as it never was in life. And the director had surely placed Eric where he had because this face operated, in effect, as a footnote to the twentieth-century torment. Under the merciless light, the lined, tense, coarse-grained forehead also suggested the patient skull; an effect which was underlined by the promontory of the eyebrows and the secret place of the eyes. The nose was flaring and slightly pug, more bone, nevertheless, than flesh. And the full, slightly parted lips were lonely and defenseless, barely protected by the stubborn chin. It was the face of a man, of a tormented man. Yet, in precisely the way that great music depends, ultimately, on great silence, this masculinity was defined, and made powerful, by something which was not masculine. But it was not feminine, either, and something in Vivaldo resisted the word *androgynous*. It was a quality to which great numbers of people would respond without knowing to what it was they were responding. There was great force in the face, and great gentleness. But, as most women are not gentle, nor most men strong, it was a face which suggested, resonantly, in the depths, the truth about our natures.

Eric, without moving his head, suddenly opened his eyes and looked blankly around the table. Then he looked sick, rose, and hurriedly vanished. All the students laughed. They were caustic about their vanished comrade, feeling that the character represented by Eric lacked courage. The film ground on, and Eric appeared twice more, once, silent, deep in the background, during a youthful council of war, and, finally, at the very end of the film, on a rooftop, with a machine gun in his hand. As he delivered his one line—*"Nom de Dieu, que j'ai soif!"*—the camera shifted to show him framed in the sights of an enemy gun; blood suddenly bubbled from Eric's lips and he went sliding off the rooftop, out of sight. With Eric's death, the movie also died for them, and, luckily, very shortly, it was over. They walked out of the cool darkness into the oven of July.

"Who's going to buy me that drink?" Eric asked. He smiled a pale smile. It was something of a shock to see him, standing on the sidewalk, shorter than he had appeared in the film, in flesh and blood. "Anyway, let's get away from here before people start asking me for my autograph." And he laughed.

"It might happen, my dear," said Cass, "you've got great presence on the screen."

"The movie's not so much," said Vivaldo, "but you were terrific."

"I didn't really have anything to do," said Eric.

"No," said Ida, "you didn't. But you sure did the hell out of it."

They walked in silence for a few moments.

"I'm afraid I can only have one drink with you," Cass said, "and then I'll have to go home."

"That's right," Ida said, "let's don't be hanging out with these cats until all hours of the morning. I got too many people to face tomorrow. Besides"—she glanced at Vivaldo with a small smile—"I don't believe they've seen each other alone one *time* since Eric got off the boat."

"And you think we better give them an evening off," Cass said.

"If we don't give it to them, they going to take it. But, this way, we can make ourselves look good—and that always comes in handy." She laughed. "That's right, Cass, you got to be *clever* if you want to keep your man."

"I should have started taking lessons from you years ago," Cass said.

"Now, be careful," said Eric, mildly, "because I don't think that's very flattering."

"I was joking," Cass said.

"Well, I'm insecure," said Eric.

They walked into Benno's, which was half-empty tonight, and sat, in a rather abrupt and mysterious silence, at one of the tables in the back. This silence was produced by the fact that each of them had more on their minds than they could easily say. Their sexes, so to speak, obstructed them. Perhaps the women wished to talk to each other concerning their men, but they could not do this with the men present; and neither could Eric and Vivaldo begin to unburden themselves to each other in the presence of Ida and Cass. They made small-talk, therefore, about the movie they had seen and the movie Eric was to make. Even this chatter was constricted and cautious, there being an unavowed reluctance on Eric's part to go to Hollywood. The nature of this reluctance Vivaldo could not guess; but a certain thoughtfulness, a certain fear, played in Eric's face like a lighthouse light; and Vivaldo thought that perhaps Eric was afraid of being trapped on a height as he had previously been trapped in the depths. Perhaps he was afraid, as Vivaldo knew himself to be afraid, of any real change in his condition. And he thought, The women have more courage than we do. Then he thought, Maybe they don't have any choice.

After one drink, they put Ida and Cass in a cab, together. Ida said, "Now don't you wake me up when you come falling in," and Cass said, "I'll call you sometime tomorrow." They waved to their women and watched the red lights of the cab disappear. They looked at each other.

"Well!" Vivaldo grinned. "Let's make the most of it, baby. Let's go and get drunk."

"I don't want to go back into Benno's," Eric said. "Let's go on over to my place, I've got some liquor."

"Okay," said Vivaldo, "I'd just as soon see you pass out at your place as have to *drag* you to your place." He grinned at Eric. "I'm very glad to see you," he said.

They started toward Eric's house. "Yes, I've wanted to see you," said Eric, "but"—they looked at each other briefly, and both smiled—"we've been kept pretty busy."

Vivaldo laughed. "Good men, and true," he said. "I certainly hope that Cass isn't as—unpredictable—as Ida can be."

"Hell," said Eric, "I hope that you're not as unpredictable as *I* am."

Vivaldo smiled, but said nothing. The streets were very dark and still. On a side street, there stood a lone city tree on which the moonlight gleamed. "We're all unpredictable," he finally said, "one way or another. I wouldn't like you to think that you're special."

"It's very hard to live with that," said Eric. "I mean, with the sense that one is never what one seems—never—and yet, what one seems to be is probably, in some sense, almost exactly what one *is*." He turned his half-smiling face to Vivaldo. "Do you know what I mean?"

"I wish I didn't," said Vivaldo, slowly, "but I'm afraid I do."

Eric's building was on a street with trees, westbound, not far from the river. It was very quiet except for the noise coming from two taverns, one on either far corner. Eric had visited each of them once. "One of them's gay," he said, "and what a cemetery *that* is. The other one's for longshoremen, and that's pretty deadly, too. The longshoremen never go to the gay bar and the gay boys never go to the longshoremen's bar—but they know where to find each other when the bars close, all up and down this street. It all seems very sad to me, but maybe I've been away too long. *I* don't go for back-alley cock-sucking. *I* think sin should be fun."

Vivaldo laughed, but thought, with wonder and a little fear, My God, he *has* changed. He never talked like this before. And he looked at the quiet street, at the shadows thrown by houses and trees, with a new sense of its menace, and its terrifying loneliness. And he looked at Eric again, in very much the same way he had looked at him in the film, wondering again who Eric was, and how he bore it.

They entered Eric's small, lighted vestibule and climbed the stairs to his apartment. One light, the night light over the bed, was burning, "To keep away robbers," Eric said; and the apartment was in its familiar state of disorder, with the bed unmade and Eric's clothes draped over chairs and hanging from knobs.

"Poor Cass," Eric laughed, "she keeps trying to establish some order here, but it's uphill work. Anyway, the way things are between us, I don't give her much time to do much in the way of straightening up." He walked about, picking up odds and ends of clothing, which he then piled all together on top of the kitchen table. He turned on the kitchen light and opened his icebox. Vivaldo flopped down on the unmade bed. Eric poured two drinks and sat down opposite him on a straight-backed easy chair. Then there was silence for a moment.

"Turn out that kitchen light," Vivaldo said, "it's in my eyes."

Eric rose and switched off the kitchen light and came back with the bottle of whiskey and put it on the floor. Vivaldo flipped off his shoes and drew his legs up, playing with the toes of one foot.

"Are you in love with Cass?" he asked, abruptly.

Eric's red hair flashed in the dim light, as he looked down into his drink, then looked up at Vivaldo. "No. I don't think I'm in love with her. I think I wish I were. I care a lot about her—but, no, I'm not in love."

And he sipped his drink.

"But she's in love with you," said Vivaldo. "Isn't she?"

Eric raised his eyebrows. "I guess she is. She thinks she is. I don't know. What does it mean, to be in love? Are you in love with Ida?"

"Yes," said Vivaldo.

Eric rose and walked to the window. "You didn't even have to think about it. I guess that tells me where *I* am." He laughed. With his back to Vivaldo, he said, "I used to envy you, you know that?"

"You must have been out of your mind," said Vivaldo. "Why?"

"Because you were normal," Eric said. He turned and faced Vivaldo.

Vivaldo threw back his head and laughed. "Flattery will get you nowhere, son. Or is that a subtle put-down?"

"It's not a put-down at all," said Eric. "But I'm glad I don't envy you any more."

"Hell," said Vivaldo, "I might just as easily envy *you*. You can make it with both men and women and sometimes I've wished I could do that, I really have." Eric was silent. Vivaldo grinned. "We've all got our troubles, Buster."

Eric looked very grave. He grunted, noncommittally, and sat down again. "You've wished you could—you *say*. And I wish I couldn't."

"*You* say."

They looked at each other and smiled. Then, "I hope you get along with Ida better than I did with Rufus," Eric said.

Vivaldo felt chilled. He looked away from Eric, toward the window; the dark, lonely streets seemed to come flooding in on them. "*How*," he asked, "did you get along with Rufus?"

"It was terrible, it drove me crazy."

"I figured that." He watched Eric. "Is that all over now? I mean—is Cass kind of the wave of your future?"

"I don't know. I thought I could make myself fall in love with Cass, but—but, no. I love her very much, we get on beautifully together. But she's not all tangled up in my guts the way—the way I guess Ida is all tangled up in yours."

"Maybe you're just not in love with *her*. You haven't got to be in love every time you go to bed. You haven't *got* to be in love to have a good affair."

Eric was silent. Then, "No. But once you *have* been—!"

And he stared into his drink. "Yes," Vivaldo said at last, "yes, I know."

"I think," said Eric, "that I've really got to accept—or decide—some very strange things. Right away."

He walked into the dark kitchen, returned with ice, and spiked his drink, and Vivaldo's. He sat down again in his straight chair. "I've spent years now, it seems to me, thinking that one fine day I'd wake up and all my torment would be over, and all my indecision would end—and that no man, no boy, no *male*—would ever have power over me again.''

Vivaldo blushed and lit a cigarette. ''*I* can't be sure,'' he said, ''that one fine day, I won't get all hung up on some boy—like that cat in *Death In Venice*. So *you* can't be sure that there isn't a woman waiting for you, just for you, somewhere up the road.''

''Indeed,'' said Eric, ''I can't be sure. And yet I must decide.''

''*What* must you decide?''

Eric lit a cigarette, drew one foot up, and hugged one knee. ''I mean, I think you've got to be truthful about the life you *have*. Otherwise, there's no possibility of achieving the life you *want*.'' He paused. ''Or *think* you want.''

''Or,'' said Vivaldo, after a moment, ''the life you think you *should* want.''

''The life you think you *should* want,'' said Eric, ''is always the life that looks safest.'' He looked toward the window. The one light in the room, coming from behind Vivaldo, played on his face like firelight. ''When I'm with Cass, it's fun, you know, and sometimes it's, well, really quite fantastic. And it makes me feel kind of restful and protected—and strong— there *are* some things which only a woman can give you.'' He walked to the window, peering down through the slats in the Venetian blinds as though he were awaiting the moment when the men in their opposing camps would leave their tents and meet in the shadow of the trees. ''And yet, in a way, it's all a kind of superior calisthenics. It's a great challenge, a great test, a great game. But I don't really feel that—*terror*—and that anguish and that joy I've sometimes felt with—a few men. Not enough of myself is invested; it's almost as though I'm doing something—for Cass.'' He turned and looked at Vivaldo. ''Does that make sense to you?''

''I think it does,'' said Vivaldo. ''I think it does.''

But he was thinking of some nights in bed with Jane, when she had become drunk enough to be insatiable; he was thinking of her breath and her slippery body, and the eerie impersonality of her cries. Once, he had had a terrible stomachache, but Jane had given him no rest, and finally, in order to avoid shoving his fist down her throat, he had thrown himself on her, hoping, desperately, to exhaust her so that he could get some sleep. And he knew that this was not what Eric was talking about.

"Perhaps," said Vivaldo, haltingly, thinking of the night on the roof with Harold, and Harold's hands, "it's something like the way I might feel if I went to bed with a man only because I—*liked* him—and he wanted me to."

Eric smiled, grimly. "I'm not sure that there *is* a comparison, Vivaldo. Sex is too private. But if you went to bed with a guy just because he wanted you to, *you* wouldn't have to take any responsibility for it; *you* wouldn't be doing any of the work. *He'd* do all the work. And the idea of being passive is very attractive to many men, maybe to most men."

"It is?" He put his feet on the floor and took a long swallow of his drink. He looked over at Eric and sighed and smiled. "You make the whole deal sound pretty rough, old buddy."

"Well, that's the way it looks from where I'm sitting." Eric grimaced, threw back his head, and sipped his whiskey. "Maybe I'm crying because I wanted to believe that, somewhere, for some people, life and love are easier—than they are for me, than they are. Maybe it was easier to call myself a faggot and blame my sorrow on that."

Then silence filled the room, like a chill. Eric and Vivaldo stared at each other with an oddly belligerent intensity. There was a great question in Eric's eyes and Vivaldo turned away as though he were turning from a mirror and walked to the kitchen door. "You really think it makes no difference?"

"I don't know. Does the difference *make* any difference?"

"Well," said Vivaldo, tapping with his thumbnail against the hinges of the door, "I certainly think that the real ball game is between men and women. And it's physically easier." He looked quickly at Eric. "Isn't it? And then," he added, "there are children." And he looked quickly at Eric again.

Eric laughed. "I never heard of two cats who wanted to make it failing because they were the wrong size. Love always finds a way, dad. I don't know anything about baseball, so I don't know if life's a baseball game or not. Maybe it is for you. It isn't for me. And if it's children you're after, well, you can do that in five minutes and you haven't got to love anybody to do it. If all the children who get here every year were brought here by love, wow! baby, what a bright world this would *be*!"

And now Vivaldo felt, at the very bottom of his heart, a certain reluctant hatred rising, against which he struggled as he would have struggled against vomiting. "I can't decide," he said, "whether you want to make everybody as miserable as you are, or whether everybody *is* as miserable as you are."

"Well, don't put it that way, baby. How happy are *you*? That's got nothing to do with me, nothing to do with how I live, or what I think, or how miserable I am—how are *you* making it?"

The question hung in the room, like the smoke which wavered between Eric and Vivaldo. The question was as thick as the silence in which Vivaldo looked down, away from Eric, searching his heart for an answer. He was frightened; he looked up at Eric; Eric was frightened, too. They watched each other. "I'm in love with Ida," Vivaldo said. Then, "And sometimes we make it, beautifully, beautifully. And sometimes we don't. And it's hideous."

And he remained where he was, in the doorway, still.

"I, too, am in love," said Eric, "his name is Yves; he's coming to New York very soon. I got a letter from him today."

He stood up and walked to his desk, picked up the play and opened it and took out an airmail envelope. Vivaldo watched his face, which had become, in an instant, weary and transfigured. Eric opened the letter and read it again. He looked at Vivaldo. "Sometimes we make it, too, and it's beautiful. And when we don't, it's hideous." He sat down again. "When I was talking before about accepting or deciding, I was thinking about him." He paused, and threw his letter on the bed. There was a very long silence, which Vivaldo did not dare to break.

"I," said Eric, "must understand that if I dreamed of escape, and I *did*—when this thing with Cass began, I thought that perhaps here was my opportunity to change, and I was *glad*—well, Yves, who is much younger than I, will also dream of escape. I must be prepared to let him go. He *will* go. And I think"—he looked up at Vivaldo—"that he *must* go, probably, in order to become a man."

"You mean," said Vivaldo, "in order to become himself."

"Yes," said Eric. And silence came again.

"All I can do," said Eric, at last, "is love him. But this means—doesn't it?—that I can't delude myself about loving someone else. I can't make any promise greater than this promise I've made already—not now, not now, and maybe I'll never make any greater promise. I can't be safe and sorry, too. I can't act as though I'm free when I know I'm not. I've got to live with that, I've got to learn to live with that. Does that make sense? or am I mad?" There were tears in his eyes. He walked to the kitchen door and stared at Vivaldo. Then he turned away. "You're right. You're right. There's nothing here to decide. There's everything to accept."

Vivaldo moved from the door, and threw himself face down on the bed, his long arms dangling to the floor. "Does Cass know about Yves?"

"Yes. I told her before anything happened." He smiled. "But you know how that is—we were trying to be honorable. Nothing could really have stopped us by that time; we needed each other too much."

"What are you going to do now? When does"—he gestured toward the letter, which was somewhere beneath his belly button—"Yves get here?"

"In about two weeks. According to that letter. It may be a little longer. It may be sooner."

"Have you told Cass that?"

"No. I'll tell her tomorrow."

"How do you think she'll take it?"

"Well, she's always known he was on his way. I don't know how she'll take—his actual *arrival*."

In the streets, they heard footsteps, walking fast, and someone whistling.

Eric stared at the wall again, frowning heavily. Other voices were heard in the street. "I guess the bars are beginning to close," said Eric.

"Yes." Vivaldo leaned up, looking toward the blinds which held back the jungle. "Eric. How's one going to get through it all? How can you live if you can't love? And how can you live if you *do*?"

And he stared at Eric, who said nothing, whose face gleamed in the yellow light, as mysteriously impersonal and as fearfully moving as might have been a death mask of Eric as a boy. He realized that they were both beginning to be drunk.

"I don't see how I can live with Ida, and I don't see how I can live without her. I get through every day on a prayer. Every morning, when I wake up, I'm surprised to find that she's still beside me." Eric was watching him, perfectly rigid and still, seeming scarcely to breathe, only his unmoving eyes were alive. "And yet"—he caught his breath—"sometimes I wish she weren't there, sometimes I wish I'd never met her, sometimes I think I'd go anywhere to get this burden off me. She never lets me forget I'm white, she never lets me forget she's colored. And I don't care, I don't care—did Rufus do that to you? Did he try to make you pay?"

Eric dropped his eyes, and his lips tightened. "Ah. He didn't *try*. I paid." He raised his eyes to Vivaldo's. "But I'm not sad about it any more. If it hadn't been for Rufus, I would never have had to go away, I would never have been able to deal with Yves." And then, rising and walking to the window, from which more and more voices rose, "Maybe that's what love is for."

"Are you sleeping with anyone besides Cass?"

Eric turned. "No."

"I'm sorry. I just thought you might be. I'm not sleeping with anyone except Ida."

"We can't be everywhere at once," said Eric.

They listened to the footfalls and voices in the street: someone was singing, someone called, someone was cursing. Someone ran. Then silence, again.

"You know," said Eric, "it's true that you can make kids without love. But if you *do* love the person you make the kids with, it must be something fantastic."

"Ida and I could have great kids," said Vivaldo.

"Do you think you will?"

"I don't know. I'd love to—but"—he fell back on the bed, staring at the ceiling. "I don't know."

He allowed himself, for a moment, the luxury of dreaming of Ida's children, though he knew that these children would never be born and that this moment was all he would ever have of them. Nevertheless, he dreamed of a baby boy who had Ida's mouth and eyes and forehead, his hair, only curlier, his build, *their* color. What would that color be? From the streets, again, came a cry and a crash and a roar. Eric switched off the night light and opened the blinds and Vivaldo joined him at the window. But now there was nothing to see, the street was empty, dark, and still, though an echo of voices, diminishing, floated back.

"One of the last times I saw Rufus," Vivaldo said, abruptly—and stopped. He had not thought about it since that moment; in a way, he had never thought about it at all.

"Yes?" He could barely make out Eric's face in the darkness. He turned away from Eric and sat down on the bed again, and lit a cigarette. And in the tiny flare, Eric's face leapt at him, then dropped back into darkness. He watched the red-black silhouette of Eric's head against the dim glow of the Venetian blinds.

He remembered that terrible apartment again, and Leona's tears, and Rufus with the knife, and the bed with the twisted gray sheet and the thin blanket: and it all seemed to have happened many, many years ago.

But, in fact, it had only been a matter of months.

"I never told this to anybody before," he said, "and I really don't know why I'm telling you. It's just that the last time I saw Rufus, before he disappeared, when he was still with Leona"—he caught his breath, he dragged on his cigarette and the glow brought the room back into the world, then dropped it again into chaos—"we had a fight, he said he was going to kill me. And, at the very end, when he was finally in bed, after he'd cried, and after he'd told me—so many terrible things—I looked at him, he was lying on his side, his eyes were half open, he was looking at me. I was taking off my pants, Leona was staying at my place and I was going to stay there, I was afraid to leave him alone. Well, when he looked at me, just before he closed his eyes and turned on his side away from me, all curled up, I had the weirdest feeling that he wanted me to take him in my arms. And not for sex, though maybe sex would have happened. I had the feeling that he wanted someone to hold him, to hold him, and that, that night, it had to be a man. I got in the bed and I thought about it and I watched his back, it was as dark in that room, then, as it is in this room, now, and I lay on my back and I didn't touch him and I didn't sleep. I remember that night as a kind of vigil. I don't know whether he slept or not, I kept trying to tell from his breathing—but I couldn't tell, it was too choppy, maybe he was having nightmares. I loved Rufus, I loved him, I didn't want him to die. But when he was dead, I thought about it, thought about it—isn't it funny? I didn't know I'd thought about it as much as I have—and I wondered, I guess I still wonder, what would have happened if I'd taken him in my arms, if I'd held him, if I hadn't been— afraid. I was afraid that he wouldn't understand that it was— only love. Only love. But, oh, Lord, when he died, I thought that maybe I could have saved him if I'd just reached out that quarter of an inch between us on that bed, and held him." He felt the cold tears on his face, and he tried to wipe them away. "Do you know what I mean? I haven't told Ida this, I haven't told anyone, I haven't thought about it, since he died. But I guess I've been living with it. And I'll never know. I'll never know."

"No," said Eric, "you'll never know. If I had been there, I'd have held him—but it wouldn't have helped. His little girl tried to hold him, and that didn't help."

He sat down on the bed beside Vivaldo. "Would you like a cup of coffee?"

"Hell, no." Vivaldo dried his eyes with the back of his hand. "Let's have another drink. Let's watch the dawn come up."

"Okay." Eric started to move away. Vivaldo grabbed his hand.

"Eric—" He watched Eric's dark, questioning eyes and the slightly parted, slightly smiling lips. "I'm glad I told you about that. I guess I couldn't have told anybody else."

Eric seemed to smile. He took Vivaldo's face between his hands and kissed him, a light, swift kiss, on the forehead. Then his shadow vanished, and Vivaldo heard him in the kitchen.

"I'm out of ice."

"The hell with the ice."

"Water?"

"No. Well, maybe a little."

Eric returned with two glasses and put one in Vivaldo's hand. They touched glasses.

"To the dawn," said Eric.

"To the dawn," Vivaldo said.

Then they sat together, side by side, watching the light come up behind the window and insinuate itself into the room. Vivaldo sighed, and Eric turned to look at his lean, gray face, the long cheeks hollowed now, and the stubble coming up, the marvelous mouth resigned, and the black eyes staring straight out—staring out because they were beginning to look inward. And Eric felt, for perhaps the first time in his life, the key to the comradeship of men. Here was Vivaldo, long, lean, and weary, dressed, as he almost always was, in black and white; his white shirt was open, almost to the navel, and the shirt was dirty now, and the hair on his chest curled out; the hair on his head, which was always too long, was tousled, and fell over his forehead; and he smelled Vivaldo's sweat, his armpits and his groin, and was terribly aware of his long legs. Here Vivaldo sat, on Eric's bed. Not a quarter of an inch divided them. His elbow nearly touched Vivaldo's elbow, as he listened to the rise and fall of Vivaldo's breath. They were like two soldiers, resting from battle, about to go into battle again.

Vivaldo fell back on the bed, one hand covering his forehead, one hand between his legs. Presently, he was snoring, then he shuddered, and turned into Eric's pillow, toward Eric's wall. Eric sat on the bed, alone, and watched him. He took off Vivaldo's shoes, he loosened Vivaldo's belt, turning Vivaldo to face him. The morning light bathed the sleeper. Eric made himself another drink, with ice this time, for the ice was ready. He thought of reading Yves' letter again, but he knew it by heart; and he was terrified of Yves' arrival. He sat on the bed again, looking at the morning. . . . *Mon plus cher. Je te previendra la jour de mon arrivée. Je prendrai l'avion. J'ai dit au revoir à ma mère. Elle a beaucoup pleurée. J'avoue que ça me faisait quelque chose. Bon. Paris est mortelle sans toi. Je t'adore mon petit et je t'aime. Comme j'ai envie de te serre très fort entre mes bras. Je t'embrasse. Toujours à toi. Ton* YVES.

Oh, yes. Somewhere, someone turned on a radio. The day was here. He finished his drink, took off his shoes, loosened his belt, and stretched out beside Vivaldo. He put his head on Vivaldo's chest, and, in the shadow of that rock, he slept.

Ida told the taxi driver, "Uptown, please, to *Small's Paradise*," then turned, with a rueful smile, to Cass.

"*Their* night," she said, indicating the vanished Eric and Vivaldo, "is just beginning. So is mine, only mine won't be as much fun."

"I thought you were going home," Cass said.

"Well. I'm not. I've got some people to meet." She looked thoughtfully at her fingernails, then looked over to Cass. "I couldn't tell Vivaldo, so don't you tell him, please. He just gets upset when he's around—some of those musicians. I can't blame him. I really can't blame them, either; I know how they feel. But I don't like for them to take it out on Vivaldo, he's having a rough enough time as it is."

And, after a moment, she added, under her breath, "So am I."

Cass said nothing, for she was too astonished. So far from imagining herself and Ida to be friends, she had long ago decided that Ida disliked and distrusted her. But she did not sound that way now. She sounded lonely and troubled.

"I wish you'd come up and have one drink with me up there," Ida said. She kept twisting the ring on her little finger.

Cass thought, at once, I'll feel terribly out of place up there, and if you're meeting someone, what's the good of my coming along? But she sensed, somehow, that she could not say this, that Ida needed a woman to talk to, if only for a few minutes, even if the woman were white.

"Okay," she said, "but just one drink. I've got to hurry home to Richard." As she said this, both she and Ida laughed. It was almost the first time they had ever laughed together; and this laughter revealed to Cass that Ida's attitude toward her had been modified by Ida's knowledge of her adultery. Perhaps Ida felt that Cass was more to be trusted and more of a woman, now that her virtue, and her safety, were gone. And there was also, in that sudden and spontaneous laughter, the very faintest hint of blackmail. Ida could be freer with Cass now, since the world's judgment, should it ever be necessary to face it, would condemn Cass yet more cruelly than Ida. For Ida was not white, nor married, nor a mother. The world assumed Ida's sins to be natural, whereas those of Cass were perverse.

Ida said, "Men are a bitch, aren't they, baby?" She sounded sad and weary. "I don't understand them, I swear I don't."

"I always thought you did," said Cass, "much better than I ever have."

Ida smiled. "Well, that's all a kind of act. Besides it's not hard to deal with a man if you don't *give* a damn about him. Most of the jokers I've had to deal with weren't worth shit. And I've always expected all of them to be like that." Then she was silent. She looked over at Cass, who sat very still, looking down. The cab was approaching Times Square. "Do you know what I mean?"

"I don't know if I do, or not," Cass said. "I guess I don't. I've only dealt with—two men—in my whole life."

Ida looked at her, speculatively, a small, sardonic smile touching her lips. "That's very hard to believe. It's hard to imagine."

"Well! I was never very pretty. I guess I led a kind of sheltered life. And—I got married very young." She lit a cigarette, she crossed her legs.

Ida looked out at the lights, and the crowds. "I'm wondering if I'm ever going to marry. I guess I'm not. I'll never marry Vivaldo, and"—she tapped her ring again—"it's hard to see what's coming, up the road. But I don't seem to see a bridegroom."

Cass was silent. Then, "*Why* will you never marry Vivaldo? Don't you love him?"

Ida said, "Love doesn't have as much to do with it as everybody seems to think. I mean, you know, it doesn't change everything, like people say. It can be a goddam pain in the ass." She shifted, restlessly, in their narrow, dark space, and looked out of the window again. "Sure, I love Vivaldo; he's the sweetest man I've ever known. And I know I've given him a rough time sometimes. I can't help it. But I can't marry him, it would be the end of him, and the end of me."

"Well, why?" She paused; then, carefully, "You don't mean just because he's white—?"

"Well, yes," said Ida, forcefully, "in a way, I *do* mean that. That probably sounds terrible to you. I don't care about the color of his skin. I don't mean that." She stopped, clearly trying to discover what she *did* mean. "I've only known one man better than Vivaldo, and that man was my brother. Well, you know, Vivaldo was his best friend—and Rufus was *dying*, but Vivaldo didn't know it. And I was miles away, and I *did*!"

"How do you know that Vivaldo didn't know it? You're being very unjust. And *your* knowing it didn't stop anything, didn't change anything—"

"Maybe nothing can be stopped, or changed," Ida said, "but you've got to *know*, you've got to know what's happening."

"But, Ida, nobody really does know what's happening—not really. Like, perhaps you know things that I don't know. But isn't it possible that I also know things that you don't know? I know what it's like to have a child, for example. You don't."

"Oh, hell, Cass, I can *have* a damn baby, and then I'll know. Babies aren't my kick, but, you know, I can find out if I want to. The way Vivaldo carries on, I'm likely to find out, whether I want to or not," and, incongruously, she giggled. "But"—she sighed—"it doesn't work the other way around. *You* don't know, and there's no way in the world for you to find out, what it's like to be a black girl in this world, and the way white men, and black men, too, baby, treat you. You've never decided that the whole world was just one big whorehouse and so the only way for you to make it was to decide to be the biggest, coolest, hardest whore around, and make the world pay you back that way." They were in the park. Ida leaned forward and lit a cigarette with trembling hands, then gestured out the window. "I bet you think we're in a goddam park. You don't know we're in one of the world's great jungles. You don't know that behind all them damn dainty trees and shit, people are screwing and sucking and fixing and dying. Dying, baby, right now while we move through this darkness in this man's taxicab. And you don't know it, even when you're told; you don't know it, even when you see it."

She felt very far from Ida, and very small and cold. "How *can* we know it, Ida? How can you blame us if we don't know? We never had a chance to find out. I hardly knew that Central Park existed until I was a married woman." And she, too, looked out at the park, trying to see what Ida saw; but, of course, she saw only the trees and the lights and the grass and the twisting road and the shape of the buildings beyond the park. "There were hardly any colored people in the town I grew up in—how am I to know?" And she hated herself for her next question, but she could not hold it back: "Don't you think I deserve some credit, for trying to be human, for not being a part of all that, for—walking out?"

"What the hell," asked Ida, "have you walked out on, Cass?"

"That world," said Cass, "that empty life, that meaningless life!"

Ida laughed. It was a cruel sound and yet Cass sensed, very powerfully, that Ida was not trying to be cruel. She seemed to be laboring, within herself, up some steep, unprecedented slope. "Couldn't we put it another way, honey—just for kicks? Couldn't we, sort of, blame it on nature? and say that you saw Richard and he got you hot, and so you didn't really walk out—you just got married?"

Cass began to be angry; and she asked herself, Why? She said, "No. Long before I met Richard, I knew that that wasn't the life for me." And this was true, and yet her voice lacked conviction. And Ida, relentlessly, put Cass' unspoken question into words.

"And what would have happened if Richard hadn't come?"

"I don't know. But this is silly. He *did* come. I *did* leave."

Now the air thickened between them, as though they were on opposite sides of a chasm in the mountains, trying to discern each other through the cloud and the fog, but terribly frightened of the precipice at their feet. For she had left Richard, or had, anyway, betrayed him—and what did that failure mean? And what was she doing, now, with Eric, and where was the meaning there? She began, dimly and unwillingly, to sense the vast dimensions of Ida's accusation at the same time that her ancient, incipient guilt concerning her life with Richard nosed its way, once more, into the front hall of her mind. She had always seen much farther than Richard, and known much more; she was more skillful, more patient, more cunning, and more single-minded; and he would have had to be a very different, stronger, and more ruthless man, *not* to have married her. But this was the way it always had been, always would be, between men and women, everywhere. Was it? She threw her cigarette out of the window. *He* did *come. I* did *walk out.* Had she, indeed? The cab was approaching Harlem. She realized, with a small shock, that she had not been here since the morning of Rufus' funeral.

"But, imagine," Ida was saying, "that he came, *that* man who's *your* man—because you always know, and he damn sure don't come every day—and there wasn't any place for you to walk out of or into, because he came too late. And no matter when he arrived would have been too late—because too much had happened by the time you were born, let alone by the time you met each other."

I don't believe that, Cass thought. That's too easy. I don't believe it. She said, "If you're talking of yourself and Vivaldo—there are other countries—have you ever thought of that?"

Ida threw back her head and laughed. "Oh, yes! And in another five or ten years, when we get the loot together, we can pack up and go to one of those countries." Then, savagely, "And what do you think will have happened to us in those five years? How much will be left?" She leaned toward Cass. "How much do you think will be left between you and Eric in five years—because I *know* you know you're not going to marry him, you're not *that* crazy."

"We'll be friends, we'll be friends," said Cass. "I hope we'll be friends forever." She felt cold; she thought of Eric's hands and lips; and she looked at Ida again.

Ida had turned again to the window.

"What you people don't know," she said, "is that life is a *bitch*, baby. It's the biggest hype going. You don't have any experience in paying your dues and it's going to be rough on you, baby, when the deal goes down. There're lots of back dues to be collected, and I know damn well you haven't got a penny saved."

Cass looked at the dark, proud head, which was half-turned away from her. "Do you hate white people, Ida?"

Ida sucked her teeth in anger. "What the hell has that got to do with anything? Hell, yes, sometimes I hate them, I could see them all dead. And sometimes I don't. I *do* have a couple of other things to occupy my mind." Her face changed. She looked down at her fingers, she twisted her ring. "If any *one* white person gets through to you, it kind of destroys your—single-mindedness. They say that love and hate are very close together. Well, that's a fact." She turned to the window again. "But, Cass, ask yourself, look out and ask yourself—wouldn't you hate all white people if they kept you in prison here?" They were rolling up startling Seventh Avenue. The entire population seemed to be in the streets, draped, almost, from lampposts, stoops, and hydrants, and walking through the traffic as though it were not there. "Kept you here, and stunted you and starved you, and made you watch your mother and father and sister and lover and brother and son and daughter die or go mad or go under, before your very eyes? And not in a hurry, like from one day to the next, but, every day, every day, for years, for generations? Shit. They keep you here because you're black, the filthy, white cock suckers, while they go around jerking themselves off with all that jazz about the land of the free and the home of the brave. And they want you to jerk yourself off with that same music, too, only, keep your distance. Some days, honey, I wish I could turn myself into one big fist and grind this miserable country to powder. Some days, I don't believe it has a right to exist. Now, you've never felt like that, and Vivaldo's never felt like that. Vivaldo didn't want to know my brother was dying because he doesn't want to know that my brother would still be alive if he hadn't been born black."

"I don't know if that's true or not," Cass said, slowly, "but I guess I don't have any right to say it *isn't* true."

"No, baby, you sure don't," Ida said, "not unless you're really willing to ask yourself how *you'd* have made it, if they'd dumped on you what they dumped on Rufus. And you can't ask yourself that question because there's no way in the world for you to know what Rufus went through, not in this world, not as long as you're white." She smiled. It was the saddest smile Cass had ever seen. "That's right, baby. That's where it's at."

The cab stopped in front of Small's.

"Here we go," said Ida, jauntily, seeming, in an instant, to drag all of herself up from the depths, as though she were about to walk that mile from the wings to the stage. She glanced quickly at the meter, then opened her handbag.

"Let me," said Cass. "It's just about the only thing that a poor white woman can still do."

Ida looked at her, and smiled. "Now, don't you be like that," she said, "because you *can* suffer, and you've got some suffering to do, believe me." Cass handed the driver a bill. "You stand to lose everything—your home, your husband, even your children."

Cass sat very still, waiting for her change. She looked like a defiant little girl.

"I'll never give up my children," she said.

"They *could* be taken from you."

"Yes. It *could* happen. But it won't."

She tipped the driver, and they got out of the cab.

"It happened," said Ida, mildly, "to my ancestors every day."

"Maybe," said Cass, with a sudden flash of anger, and very close to tears, "it happened to all of us! Why was my husband ashamed to speak Polish all the years that he was growing up?—and look at him now, he doesn't *know* who he is. Maybe we're worse off than you."

"Oh," said Ida, "you are. There's no maybe about that."

"Then have a little mercy."

"You're asking a lot."

The men on the sidewalk looked at them with a kind of merciless calculation, deciding that they were certainly unattainable, that their studs or their johns were waiting inside; and, anyway, three white policemen, walking abreast, came up the Avenue. Cass felt, suddenly, exposed, and in danger, and wished she had not come. She thought of herself, later, alone, looking for a taxi; but she did not dare say anything to Ida. Ida opened the doors, and they walked in.

"We're really not dressed for this place," Cass whispered.

"It doesn't matter," Ida said. She stared imperiously over the heads of the people at the bar, into the farther room, where the bandstand seemed to be, and the raised dance floor. And her arrogance produced, out of the smoke and confusion, a heavy, dark man who approached them with raised eyebrows.

"We're with Mr. Ellis's party," said Ida. "Will you lead us to him, please?"

He seemed checked; seemed, indeed almost to bow. "Oh, yes," he said. "Please follow me." Ida moved back slightly, to allow Cass to go before her, giving her the briefest of winks as she did so. Cass felt overcome with admiration and with rage, and at the same time she wanted to laugh. They walked, or, rather, marched through the bar, two lone and superbly improbable women, whose respectability had been, if not precisely defined, placed beyond the gates of common speculation. The place was crowded, but at a large table which gave the impression, somehow, of taking up more than its share of space, sat Steve Ellis, with two couples, one black and one white.

He rose, and the waiter vanished.

"I'm delighted to see you again, Mrs. Silenski," he said, smiling, holding out that regal hand. "Each time I see Richard, I beg to be remembered to you—but has he ever given you any of my messages? Of course not."

"Of course not," Cass said, laughing. She felt, suddenly, unaccountably, extremely lighthearted. "Richard simply has no memory at all. But I kept imagining that you would come back to see us, and you never have."

"Oh, but I will. You'll be seeing much more of me, dear lady, than you have the courage to imagine." He turned to the table. "Let me introduce you all." He gestured toward the dark couple. "Here are Mr. and Mrs. Barry—Mrs. Silenski." He bowed ironically in Ida's direction. "Miss Scott." Ida responded to this bow with an ironical half-curtsey.

Mr. Barry rose and shook their hands. He wore a small mustache over narrow lips; and he smiled a tentative smile which did not quite mask his patient wonder as to who *they* were. His wife looked like a retired showgirl. She glittered and gleamed, and she was one of those women who always seem to be dying to get home and take off their cruel and intricate and invisible lacings. Her red lower lip swooped or buckled down over her chin when she smiled, which was always. The other couple were named Nash. The male was red-faced, gray-haired, heavy, with a large cigar and a self-satisfied laugh; he was much older than his wife, who was pale, blonde and thin, and wore bangs. Ida and Cass were distributed around the table, Ida next to Ellis, Cass next to Mrs. Barry. They ordered drinks.

"Miss Scott," said Ellis, "spends a vast amount of her time pretending to be a waitress. Don't ever go anywhere near the joint she works in—I won't even tell you where it is—she's the *worst*. As a waitress. But she's a great singer. You're going to be hearing a lot from Miss Ida Scott." And he grabbed her hand and patted it hard for a moment, held it for a moment. "We might be able to persuade those boys on the stand to let her sing a couple of numbers for us."

"Oh, please. I didn't come dressed for anything. Cass picked me up at work, and we just came on as we were."

Ellis looked around the table. "Does anyone object to the way Miss Scott is dressed?"

"My God, no," said Mrs. Barry, swooping and buckling and perspiring and breathing hard, "she's perfectly charming."

"If a man's word means anything," said Mr. Nash, "I couldn't care less *what* Miss Scott took it into her beautiful head to wear. There are women who look well in—well, I guess I better not say that in front of my wife," and his heavy, merry laugh rang out, almost drowning the music for a few seconds.

His wife did not, however, seem to be easily amused.

"Anyway," said Ida, "they've got a vocalist, and she won't like it. If *I* was the vocalist, *I* wouldn't like it."

"Well. We'll see." And he took her hand again.

"I'd much rather not."

"We'll *see*. Okay?"

"All right," said Ida, and took her hand away, "we'll see."

The waiter came and set their drinks before them. Cass looked about her. The band was out, the stage was empty; but on the dance floor a few couples were dancing to the juke box. She watched one large, ginger-colored boy dancing with a tall, much darker girl. They danced with a concentration at once effortless and tremendous, sometimes very close to one another, sometimes swinging far apart, but always joined, each body making way for, responding to, and commenting on the other. Their faces were impassive. Only the eyes, from time to time, flashed a signal or acknowledged an unexpected nuance. It all seemed so effortless, so simple; they followed the music, which also seemed to follow them; and yet Cass knew that she would never be able to dance that way; never. Never? She watched the girl; then she watched the boy. Part of their ease came from the fact that it was the boy who led—indisputably—and the girl who followed; but it also came, more profoundly, from the fact that the girl was, in no sense, appalled by the boy and did not for an instant hesitate to answer his rudest erotic quiver with her own. It all seemed so effortless, so simple, and yet, when one considered whence it came, it began to be clear that it was not at all simple: on the contrary, it was difficult and delicate, dangerous and deep. And she, Cass, who watched them with such envy (for first she watched the girl, then she watched the boy) began to feel uneasy; but they, oddly, on the gleaming floor, under the light, were at ease. In what sense, and for what reason, and why would it be forever impossible for her to dance as they did?

Mr. Barry was saying, "We have been hearing the most wonderful things about your husband, Mrs. Silenski. I've read his book, and I must say"—he smiled his cordial smile, everything about him was held within decent bounds—"it's a very remarkable achievement."

For an instant, Cass said nothing. She sipped her drink and watched his face, which was as smooth as a black jellybean. At first, she was tempted to dismiss the face as empty. But it was not empty; it was only that it was desperately trying to empty itself, decently, inward; an impossibility leading to God alone could guess what backing up of bile. Deep, deep behind the carefully hooded and noncommittal eyes, the jungle howled and lunged and bright dead birds lay scattered. He was like his wife, only he would never be able to step out of his iron corsets.

She felt very sorry for him, then she trembled; he hated her; and somehow his hatred was connected with her barely conscious wish to have the ginger-colored boy on the floor make love to her. He hated her—therefore?—far more than Ida could, and was far more at the mercy of his hatred; which, from ceaseless trampling down, yearned to go upward, blowing up the world.

But he could not afford to know this.

She said, smiling, with stiff lips, "Thank you very much."

Mrs. Barry said, "You must be very proud of your husband."

Cass and Ida glanced briefly at each other, and Cass smiled and said, "Well, I've always been proud of him, really; none of this comes as any surprise to me."

Ida laughed. "That's the truth. Cass thinks Richard can do *no* wrong."

"Not even when she catches him at it," Ellis grinned. Then, "We've been together quite a lot lately, and he often speaks of what a happy man he is."

For some reason, this frightened her. She wondered when, and how often, Richard and Ellis met and what Richard really had to say. She swallowed her fear. "Blind faith," she said, inanely, "I've got it," and thought, *God*. She looked toward the dance floor. But that particular couple had vanished.

"Your husband's a lucky man," said Mr. Barry. He looked at his wife, and reached for her hand. "So am I."

"Mr. Barry's just become a part of our publicity department," Ellis said. "We're awfully proud to have him on board. And I'm sorry if I sound like I'm bragging—hell, I'm not sorry, I *am* bragging—but I think it represents a tremendous breakthrough in our pussyfooting, hidebound industry." He grinned, and Mr. Barry smiled. "And hidebound so soon!"

"It was hidebound the instant it was born," said Mr. Nash, "just as your cinema industry was hidebound, and for the same reason. It immediately became the property of the banks—part of what you people quaintly call free enterprise, though God knows there's nothing free about it, and nothing even remotely enterprising about the lot of you."

Cass and Ida stared at him. "Where are you from?" Cass demanded.

He smiled at her from a great, tolerant distance. "Belfast," he said.

"Oh," cried Ida, "I have a friend whose father was born in Dublin! Do you know Dublin? Is it very far from Belfast?"

"Geographically? Yes, some distance. Otherwise, the distance is negligible—though the population of either city would hang me if they heard me say so." And he laughed his cheerful, lubricated laugh.

"What have you got against us?" Cass asked.

"I? Why, nothing," said Mr. Nash, laughing, "I make a great deal of money out of you."

"Mr. Nash," said Ellis, "is an impresario who no longer lives in Belfast."

"Free enterprise, you see," said Mr. Nash, and winked at Mr. Barry.

Mr. Barry laughed. He leaned toward Mr. Nash. "Well, I'm on the side of Mrs. Silenski. What *have* you got against our system? I think we've all made great strides under it." He raised one bony hand, one manicured finger. "What would you replace it with?"

"What," asked Cass, unexpectedly, "*does* one replace a dream with? I wish I knew."

Mr. Nash laughed, then stopped, as if embarrassed. Ida was watching her—watching her without seeming to watch. Then Cass sensed, for the first time in her life, the knowledge that black people had of white people—though what, really, did Ida know about her, except that she was lying, was unfaithful, and was acting? and was in trouble—and, for a second, she hated Ida with all her heart. Then she felt very cold again, the second passed.

"I suppose," said Ida, in an extraordinary voice, "that one replaces a dream with reality."

Everybody laughed, nervously. The music began again. She looked again toward the dance floor, but those dancers were gone. She grabbed her drink as though it were a spar, and held it in her mouth as though it were ice.

"Only," said Ida, "that's not so easy to do." She held her drink between her two thin hands and looked across at Cass. Cass swallowed the warm fluid she had been holding in her mouth, and it hurt her throat. Ida put down her drink and grabbed Ellis by the hand. "Come on, honey," she said, "let's dance."

Ellis rose. "You will excuse us," he said, "but I am summoned."

"Indeed you are," said Ida, and smiled at them all, and swept onto the dance floor. Ellis followed, rather like something entangled in her train.

"She reminds me of the young Billie Holiday," said Mr. Barry, wistfully.

"Yes, I'd love to hear her sing," said Mrs. Nash—rather venomously, and most unexpectedly. They all turned expectantly toward her, as though this were a seance and she were the medium. But she sipped her drink and said nothing more.

Cass turned again toward the dance floor, watching Ida and Ellis. The light was still as bright, the floor somewhat more crowded; the juke box blared. There was a vast amount of cunning, conscious or not, in Ida's choice of a costume for the place. She wore a very simple pale orange dress, and flat shoes, and very little make-up; and her hair, which was usually piled high, was pulled back tonight and held tightly in a severe, old-maidish bun. Therefore, she looked even younger than she was, almost like a very young girl; and the effect of this was to make Ellis, who was so much shorter than she, look older than he was, and more corrupt. They became an odd and unprecedented beauty and the beast up there; and, for the first time consciously, Cass wondered about their real relationship to one another. Ida had said that she did not want Vivaldo "bugged" by any of the musicians; but she had not come to meet any musicians. She had come to meet Ellis. And she had brought Cass along as a kind of smoke screen—and she and Ellis could not have met often in public before. In private then? And she wondered about this as she watched them. Their dance, which was slow and should have been fluid, was awkward and dry and full of hesitations. She was holding him at bay, he could not lead her; yet, she was holding him fast.

"I wonder if his wife knows where he is." Mrs. Nash again, *sotto voce*, to her husband, with a small, smug smile.

Cass thought of Vivaldo, then thought of Richard, and

immediately hated Mrs. Nash. *You evil-minded whore*, she thought, and broke the table's uneasy silence by saying,

"Mrs. Ellis and Miss Scott have known each other for quite a long time, long before Mrs. Ellis's marriage."

Why did I say that? she wondered. *She can easily find out if I'm lying.* She looked steadily at Mrs. Nash, making no attempt to hide her dislike. *She won't, though. She hasn't got the wit or the guts.*

Mrs. Nash looked at Cass with that absolutely infuriating superciliousness achieved only by chambermaids who have lately become great ladies. "How strange that is," she murmured.

"Not at all," Cass said, recklessly, "they both worked in the same factory."

Mrs. Nash watched her, the faintest tremor occurring somewhere around her upper lip. Cass smiled and looked briefly at Mr. Nash. "Did you and your wife meet in Belfast?"

"No," said Mr. Nash, smiling—and Cass felt, with a surge of amusement and horror, how much his wife despised him at that moment—"we met in Dublin, while I was there on a business trip." He took his wife's limp hand. Her pale eyes did not move, her pale face did not change. "The most important trip I ever made."

Ah, yes, thought Cass, *I don't doubt it, for both of you*. But suddenly she felt weary and inexplicably sad. What in the world was she doing here, and why was she needling this absurd little woman? The music changed, becoming louder and swifter and more raucous; and all their attention returned, with relief, to the dance floor. Ida and Ellis had begun a new dance; or, rather, Ida had begun a new cruelty. Ida was suddenly dancing as she had probably not danced since her adolescence, and Ellis was attempting to match her—he could certainly not be said to be leading her now, either. He tried, of course, his square figure swooping and breaking, and his little boy's face trying hard to seem abandoned. And the harder he tried—*the fool!* Cass thought—the more she eluded him, the more savagely she shamed him. He was not on those terms with his body, or with hers, or anyone's body. He moved his buttocks by will, with no faintest memory of love, no hint of grace; his thighs were merely those of a climber, his feet might have been treading grapes. He did not know what to do with his arms, which stuck out at angles to his body as though they were sectioned and controlled by strings, and also as though they had no communion with his hands— hands which had grasped and taken but never caressed. Was Ida being revenged? or was she giving him warning? Ellis' forehead turned slick with sweat, his short, curly hair seemed to darken, Cass almost heard his breathing. Ida circled around him, in her orange dress, her legs flashing like knives, and her hips cruelly grinding. From time to time she extended to him, his fingers touched her lean, brown, fiery hand. Others on the floor made way for them—for her: it must have seemed to Ellis that the music would never end.

But the juke box fell silent, at last, and the colored lights stopped whirling, for the band was coming on again. Ida and Ellis returned to the table.

The lights began to dim. Cass stood up.

"Ida," she said, "I promised to have one drink, and I have, and now I must go. I really must. Richard will kill me if I stay out any longer."

Her voice unaccountably shook, and she felt herself blushing as she said this. At the same time, she realized that Ida was in an even more dangerous mood now than she had been before her dance.

"Oh, call him up," Ida said. "Even the most faithful of wives deserves a night out."

Cass, very nearly, in her fear and despair, sank slowly into her seat again; but Ellis, mopping his brow, and gleaming, was more cheerful than ever. "I don't think that's necessarily so," he said—and wrung from the table the obligatory laugh—"and, anyway, Mrs. Silenski is responsible for a very heavy investment. Her husband is very valuable, we must take good care of his morale." Ida and Cass watched each other. Ida smiled.

"*Will* Richard's morale suffer if you do not get home?"

"Unquestionably," said Cass. "I must go."

Ida's face changed, and she looked down. She seemed, abruptly, weary and sad. "I guess you're right," she said, "and there's no point in putting it off." She looked at Ellis. "Walk her to a cab, sweetie."

"My pleasure," said Ellis.

"Good night, all," said Cass. "I'm sorry I have to run, but I must." She said, to Ida, "I'll see you soon——?"

"Shall I expect to see you at the usual place?"

"If it's still standing," Cass said, after a moment, "yes." She turned and made her way through the darkening room, with Ellis padding behind her. They gained the street, she feeling limp and frightened. Ellis put her into a cab. The cab was driven by a young Puerto Rican.

"Good night, Mrs. Silenski," Ellis said, and gave her his wet, hard hand. "Please give Richard my best, and tell him I'll be calling him in a couple of days."

"Yes, I'll tell him. Thank you. Good night."

He was gone, and she was alone in the cab, behind the unspeaking shoulders of the Puerto Rican. Idly, she sought out his face in the glass, then looked down, lighting a cigarette. The cab began to move. She did not look out. She sat huddled in the darkness, burning with a curious kind of shame. She was not ashamed—was she?—of anything she had done; but she was ashamed, as it were in anticipation, of what she might, now, helplessly, find herself doing. She had been using Ida and Vivaldo as smoke screens to cover her affair with Eric: why should not Ida use *her*, then, to cover from Vivaldo her assignation with Ellis? She had silenced *them*, in relation to Richard—now she was silenced, in relation to Vivaldo. She smiled, but the smoke she inhaled was bitter. When she had been safe and respectable, so had the world been safe and respectable; now the entire world was bitter with deceit and danger and loss; and which was the greater illusion? She was uncomfortably aware of the driver, his shoulders, his untried face, his color, and his soft, dark eyes. He glanced at her from time to time in the mirror—after all, she had glanced at him first; and her mood, perhaps, had set up a tension between them, a sexual tension. She thought, again, unwillingly, of the ginger-colored boy on the dance floor. And she knew (as though her mind, for a moment, were a clear pool, and she saw straight down into its depths) that, yes, yes, had he touched her, had he insisted, he could have had his way, she would have been glad. She would have been glad to know his body, even though the body might be all that she could know.

Eric's entrance into her, her fall from—grace?—had left her prey to ambiguities whose power she had never glimpsed before. Richard had been her protection, not only against the evil in the world, but also against the wilderness of herself. And now she would never be protected again. She tried to feel jubilant about this. But she did not feel jubilant. She felt frightened and bewildered.

The driver coughed. The cab stopped for a red light, just before entering the park, and the driver lit a cigarette. She, too, lit a fresh cigarette: and the two tiny flames almost seemed to be signaling one another. Just so, she now remembered, as the cab lurched forward, had she wandered, aimlessly and bitterly, through the city, when Richard first began to go away from her. She had wanted to be noticed, she had wanted a man to notice her. And they had: they had noticed that she was a sexual beggar, no longer young. Terrifying, that the loss of intimacy with one person results in the freezing over of the world, and the loss of oneself! And terrifying that the terms of love are so rigorous, its checks and liberties so tightly bound together.

There were many things she could not demand of Eric. Their relationship depended on her restraint. She could not go to him now, for example, at two in the morning: this liberty was not in their contract. The premise of their affair, or the basis of their comedy, was that they were two independent people, who needed each other for a time, who would always be friends, but who, probably, would not always be lovers. Such a premise forbids the intrusion of the future, or too vivid an exhibition of need. Eric, in effect, was marking time, waiting—waiting for something to be resolved. And when it was resolved—by the arrival of Yves, the signing of a contract, or the acceptance, in Eric, of a sorrow neither of them could name—she would be locked out of his bed. He would use everything life had given him, or taken from him, in his work—*that* would be his life. He was too proud to use her, or anyone, as a haven, too proud to accept any resolution of his sorrow not forged by his own hands. And she could not be bitter about this, or even sorrowful, for this was precisely why she loved him. Or, if not why, the *why* of such matters being securely locked away from human perception, it was this quality in him which she most admired, and which she knew he could not live without. Most men could—did: this was why she was so menaced.

Therefore, she too, was marking time, waiting—for the blow to fall, for the bill to come in. Only after she had paid this bill would she really know what her resources were. And she dreaded this moment, dreaded it—her terror of this moment sometimes made her catch her breath. The terror was not merely that she did not know how she would rebuild her life, or that she feared, as she grew older, coming to despise herself: the terror was that her children would despise her. The rebuilding of her own life might have reduced itself, simply, to moving out of Richard's house—*Richard's* house! how long had she thought of it as Richard's house?—and getting a job. But holding the love of her children, and helping them to grow from boys into men—this was a different matter.

The cab driver was singing to himself, in Spanish.

"You have a nice voice," she heard herself say.

He turned his head, briefly, smiling, and she watched his young profile, the faint gleam of his teeth, and his sparkling eyes. "Thank you," he said. "We are all singers where I come from." His accent was heavy, and he lisped slightly.

"In Puerto Rico? there can't be very much to sing about."

He laughed. "Oh, but we sing, anyway." He turned to her again. "There is nothing to sing about here, either, you know—nobody sings here."

She smiled. "That's true. I think singing—for pleasure, anyway—may have become one of the great American crimes."

He did not follow this, except in spirit. "You are all too serious here. Cold and ugly."

"How long have you been here?"

"Two years." He smiled at her again. "I was lucky, I work hard, I get along." He paused. "Only, sometimes, it's lonely. So I sing." They both laughed. "It makes the time go," he said.

"Don't you have any friends?" she asked.

He shrugged. "Friends cost money. And I have no money and no time. I must send money home to my family."

"Oh, are you married?"

He shrugged again, turning his profile to her again, not

smiling. "No, I am not married." Then he grinned. "That also costs money."

There was a silence. They turned into her block.

"Yes," she said, idly, "you're right about that." She pointed to the house. "Here we are." The cab stopped. She fumbled in her handbag. He watched her.

"*You* are married?" he asked at last.

"Yes." She smiled. "With two children."

"Boy or girl?"

"Two boys."

"That is very good," he said.

She paid him. "Good-bye. I wish you well."

He smiled. It was a really friendly smile. "I also wish you well. You are very nice. Good night."

"Good night."

She opened the door and the light shone full on their faces for a moment. His face was very young and direct and hopeful, and caused her to blush a little. She slammed the cab door behind her, and walked into her house without looking back. She heard the cab drive away.

The light was on in the living room, and Richard, fully dressed except for his shoes, lay on the sofa, asleep. He was usually in bed, or at work, when she came home. She stared at him for a moment. There was a half-glass of vodka on the table next to him, and a dead cigarette in the ashtray. He slept very silently and his face looked tormented and very young.

She started to wake him, but left him there, and tiptoed into the room where Paul and Michael slept. Paul lay on his belly, the sheet tangled at his feet, and his arms thrown up. With a shock, she saw how heavy he was, and how tall: he was already at the outer edge of his boyhood. It had happened so fast, it seemed almost to have happened in a dream. She looked at the sleeping head and wondered what thoughts it contained, what judgments, watched one twitching leg and wondered what his dreams were now. Gently, she pulled the sheet up to his shoulders. She looked at the secretive Michael, curled on his side like a worm or an embryo, hands hidden between his legs, and the hair damp on his forehead. But she did not dare to touch his brow: he woke too easily. As quietly as possible, she retrieved his sheet from the floor and lay it over him. She left their room and walked into the bathroom. Then she heard, in the living room, Richard's feet hit the floor.

She washed her face, combed her hair, staring at her weary face in the mirror. Then she walked into the living room. Richard sat on the sofa, the glass of vodka in his hands, staring at the floor.

"Hello," she said. "What made you fall asleep in here?" She had left her handbag in the bathroom. She walked to the bar and picked up a package of cigarettes and lit one. She asked, mockingly, "You weren't, were you, waiting up for me?"

He looked at her, drained his glass, and held it out. "Pour me a drink. Pour yourself a drink, too."

She took his glass. Now, his face which in sleep had looked so young, looked old. A certain pain and terror passed through her. She thought, insanely, as she turned her back on him, of Cleopatra's lament for Antony: *His face was as the heavens.* Was that right? She could not remember the rest of it. She poured two drinks, vodka for him, whiskey for her. The ice bucket was empty. "Do you want ice?"

"No."

She handed him his drink. She poured a little water into her whiskey. She looked, covertly, at him again—her guilt began. *His face was as the heavens, Wherein were set the stars and moon.*

"Sit down, Cass."

She left the bar and sat down in the easy chair facing him. She had left the cigarettes on the bar. *Which kept their course and lighted, This little O, the earth.*

He asked, in a friendly tone, "Where are you just coming from, Cass?" He looked at his watch. "It's past two o'clock."

"I often get in past two o'clock," she said. "Is this the first time you've noticed it?" She was astounded at the hostility in her voice. She sipped her drink. Her mind began to play strange tricks on her: her mind was filled, abruptly, with the memory of a field, long ago, in New England, a field with blue flowers in patches here and there. The field was absolutely silent and empty, it sloped gently toward a forest; they were hidden by tall grass. The sun was hot. Richard's face was above her, his arms and his hands held and inflamed her, his weight pressed her down into the flowers. A little way from them lay his army cap and jacket; his shirt was open to the navel, and the rough, glinting hairs of his chest tortured her breasts. But she was resisting, she was frightened, and his face was full of pain and anger. Helplessly, she reached up and stroked his hair. *Oh. I can't.*

We're getting married, remember? And I'm going overseas next week.

Anybody can find us here!

Nobody ever comes this way. Everybody's gone away.

Not here.

Where?

"No," he said, with a dangerous quietness, "it's not the first time I've noticed it."

"Well. It doesn't matter. I've just left Ida."

"With Vivaldo?"

She hesitated, and he smiled. "We were all together earlier. Then she and I went up to Harlem and had a drink."

"Alone?"

She shrugged. "With lots of other people. Why?" But before he could answer, she added, "Ellis was there. He said he's going to call you in a couple of days."

"Ah," he said, "Ellis was there." He sipped his drink. "And you left Ida with Ellis?"

"I left Ida with Ellis's party." She stared at him. "What's going on in your mind?"

"And what did you do when you left Ida?"

"I came home."

"You came straight home?"

"I got into a taxi and I came straight home." She began to be angry. "What are you cross-examining me for? I will not *be* cross-examined, you know, not by you, not by anyone."

He was silent—finished his vodka, and walked to the bar. "I think you're drunk enough already," she said, coldly. "If you have a question you want to ask me, ask it. Otherwise, I'm going to bed."

He turned and looked at her. This look frightened her, but she willed herself to be calm. "You are *not* going to bed for a while yet. And I have a great many questions I want to ask you."

"You may ask," she said. "I may not answer. You've waited a very long time, it seems to me, to ask me questions. Maybe you've waited too long." They stared at each other. And she saw, with a sense of triumph that made her ill, that, yes, she was stronger than he. She could break him: for, to match her will, he would be compelled to descend to stratagems far beneath him.

And her mind was filled again with that bright, blue field. She shook with the memory of his weight, her desire, her terror, and her cunning. *Not here. Where? Oh, Richard.* The cruel sun, and the indifferent air, and the two of them burning on a burning field. She knew that, yes, she must now surrender, now that she had him; she knew that she could not let him go; and, oh, his hands, his hands. But she was frightened, she realized that she knew nothing: *Can't we wait? Wait. No. No.* And his lips burned her neck and her breasts. *Then let's go to the woods. Let's go to the woods.* And he grinned. The memory of that grin rushed up from its hiding place and splintered her heart now. *You'd have to carry me, or I'd have to crawl, can't you feel it?* Then, *Let me in Cass, take me, take me, I swear I won't betray you, you know I won't!*

"I love you, Cass," he said, his lips twitching and his eyes stunned with grief. "Tell me where you've been, tell me why you've gone so far away from me."

"Why *I*," she said, helplessly, "have gone away from *you?*" The smell of crushed flowers rose to her nostrils. She began to cry.

She did not look down. She looked straight up at the sun; then she closed her eyes, and the sun roared inside her head. One hand had left her—where his hand had been, she was cold.

I won't hurt you.

Please.

Maybe just a little. Just at first.

Oh. Richard. Please.

Tell me you love me. Say it. Say it now.

Oh, yes. I love you. I love you.

Tell me you'll love me forever.
Yes. Forever. Forever.

He was looking at her, leaning on the bar, looking at her from far away. She dried her eyes with the handkerchief he had thrown in her lap. "Give me a cigarette, please."

He threw her the pack, threw her some matches. She lit a cigarette.

"When was the last time you saw Ida and Vivaldo? Tell me the truth."

"Tonight."

"And you've been spending all this time—every time you come in here in the early morning—with Ida and Vivaldo?"

She was frightened again, and she knew that her tone betrayed her. "Yes."

"You're lying. Ida hasn't been with Vivaldo. She's been with Ellis. And it's been going on a long time." He paused. "The question is—where have *you* been? Who's been with Vivaldo while Ida's been away—till two o'clock in the morning?"

She looked at him, too stunned for an instant, to calculate. "You mean, Ida's been having an affair with Steve Ellis? For how long? And how do *you* know that?"

"How do *you*—*not* know it?"

"Why—every time I saw them, they seemed perfectly natural and happy together——"

"But many of the times you say you've been with them, you couldn't have been with them because Ida's been with *Steve*!"

She still could not quite get it through her head, even though she knew that it was true and although she knew that precious seconds were passing, and that she must soon begin to fight for herself. "How do you *know*?"

"Because Steve told me! He's got a real thing about her, he's going out of his mind."

Now, she did begin to calculate—desperately, cursing Ida for not having given her warning. But how could she have? She said, coldly, "Ellis at the mercy of a great passion—? don't make me laugh."

"Oh, I know you think we're made of the coarsest of coarse

clay, and are insensitive to all the higher vibrations. I don't care. You *can't* have been seeing much of Ida—that I know. Have you been seeing much of Vivaldo? Answer me, Cass."

She said, wonderingly—for it was *this* she could not get through her head: "And Vivaldo doesn't *know*——"

"And you don't, either? You're the only two in town who don't. What mighty distractions have you two found?"

She winced and looked up at him. She saw that he was controlling himself with a great and terrible effort; that he both wanted to know the truth, and feared to know it. She could not bear the anguish in his eyes, and she looked away.

How could she ever have doubted that he loved her!

"Have you been seeing a lot of Vivaldo? Tell me."

She rose and walked to the window. She felt sick—her stomach seemed to have shrunk to the size of a small, hard, rubber ball. "Leave me alone. You've always been jealous of Vivaldo, and we both know why, though you won't admit it. Sometimes I saw Vivaldo, sometimes I saw Vivaldo with Ida, sometimes I just walked around, sometimes I went to the movies."

"Till two o'clock in the morning?"

"Sometimes I've come in at midnight, sometimes I've come in at four! Leave me alone! Why is it so important to you now? I've lived in this house like a ghost for months, half the time you haven't *known* I was here—what does it matter now?"

His face was wet and white and ugly. "*I* have lived here like a ghost, not you. I've known you were here, how could I not know it?" He took one step toward her. He dropped his voice. "Do you know how you made your presence known? By the way you look at me, by the contempt in your eyes when you look at me. What have I done to deserve your contempt? What have I done, Cass? You loved me once, you loved me, and everything I've done I've done for you."

She heard her voice saying coldly, "Are you sure? For me?"

"Who else? who *else*? You *are* my life. Why have you gone away from me?"

She sat down. "Let's talk about this in the morning."

"No. We'll talk about it now."

He walked about the room—in order, she sensed, not to

come too close to her, not to touch her; he did not know
what would happen if he did. She covered her face with one
hand. She thought of the ginger-colored boy and the Puerto
Rican, Eric blazed up in her mind for a moment, like salvation. She thought of the field of flowers. Then she thought
of the children, and her stomach contracted again. And the
pain in her stomach somehow defeated lucidity. She said, and
knew, obscurely, as she said it, that she was making a mistake,
was delivering herself up, "Stop torturing yourself about
Vivaldo—we have not been sleeping together."

He came close to the chair she sat in. She did not look up.

"I know that you've always admired Vivaldo. More than
you admire me."

There was a terrible mixture of humility and anger in his
tone, and her heart shook; she saw what he was trying to
accept. She almost looked up to reach out to him, to help
him and comfort him, but something made her keep still.

She said, "Admiration and love are very different."

"Are they? I'm not so sure. How can you touch a woman
if you know she despises you? And if a woman admires a man,
what is it, really, that she admires? A woman who admires you
will open her legs for you at once, she'll give you anything
she's got." She felt his heat and his presence above her like a
cloud; she bit one knuckle. "You did—you did, for me, don't
you remember? Won't you come back?"

Then she did look up at him, tears falling down her face.
"Oh, Richard. I don't know if I can."

"Why? Do you despise me so much?" She looked down,
twisting the handkerchief. He squatted beside the chair. "I'm
sorry we've got so far apart—I really don't even know how it
happened, but I guess I got mad at you because—because you
seemed to have so little respect for"—he tried to laugh—"my
success. Maybe you're right, I don't know. I know you're
smarter than I am, but how are we going to eat, baby, what
else can I do? Maybe I shouldn't have let myself get so jealous
of Vivaldo, but it seemed so logical, once I thought about it.
Once I thought about it, I thought about it all the time. I
know he must be alone a lot, and—and you've been alone."
She looked at him, looked away. He put one hand on her
arm; she bit her lip to control her trembling. "Come back to

me, please. Don't you love me any more? You can't have
stopped loving me. I can't live without you. You've always
been the only woman in the world for me."

She could keep silence and go into his arms, and the last
few months would be wiped away—he would never know
where she had been. The world would return to its former
shape. Would it? The silence between them stretched. She
could not look at him. He had existed for too long in her
mind—now, she was being humbled by the baffling reality of
his presence. Her imagination had not taken enough into account—she had not foreseen, for example, the measure or the
quality or the power of his pain. He was a lonely and limited
man, who loved her. Did she love him?

"I don't despise you," she said. "I'm sorry if I've made you
think that." Then she said nothing more. Why tell him? What
good would it do? He would never understand it, she would
merely have given him an anguish which he would never be
able to handle. And he would never trust her again.

Did she love him? And if she did, what should she do? Very
slowly and gently, she took her arm from beneath his hand;
and she walked to the window. The blinds were drawn against
the night, but she opened them a little and looked out: on
the lights and the deep black water. Silence rang its mighty
gongs in the room behind her. She dropped the blinds, and
turned and looked at him. He sat, now, on the floor, beside
the chair that she had left, his glass between his feet, his great
hands loosely clasped below his knees, his head tilted up toward her. It was a look she knew, a listening, trusting look.
She forced herself to look at him; she might never see that
look again; and it had been her sustenance so long! His face
was the face of a man entering middle age, and it was also—
and always would be, for her—the face of a boy. His sandy
hair was longer than usual, it was beginning to turn gray, his
forehead was wet, and his hair was wet. Cass discovered that
she loved him during the fearful, immeasurable second that
she stood there watching him. Had she loved him less, she
might have wearily consented to continue acting as the bul-
wark which protected his simplicity. But she could not do that
to Richard, nor to his children. He had the right to know his
wife: she prayed that he would take it.

She said, "I have to tell you something, Richard. I don't know how you'll take it, or where we can go from here." She paused, and his face changed. *Be quick!* she told herself. "I have to tell you because we can never come back together, we can never have any future if I don't." Her stomach contracted again, dryly. She wanted to run to the bathroom, but she knew that that would do no good. The spasm passed. "Vivaldo and I have never touched each other. I've"—*be quick!*—"been having an affair with Eric."

His voice, when he spoke, seemed to have no consciousness behind it, to belong to no one; it was a mere meaningless tinkle on the air: "Eric?"

She walked to the bar and leaned on it. "Yes."

How the silence rang and gathered! "Eric?" He laughed. *"Eric?"*

It's his turn now, she thought. She did not look at him; he was rising to his feet; he stumbled, suddenly drunken, to the bar. She felt him staring at her—for some reason, she thought of an airplane trying to land. Then his hand was on her shoulder. He turned her to face him. She forced herself to look into his eyes.

"Is that the truth?"

She felt absolutely cold and dry and wanted to go to sleep. "Yes, Richard. That's the truth."

She moved away and sat down in the chair again. She had, indeed, delivered herself up: she thought of the children and fear broke over her like a wave, chilling her. She stared straight before her, sitting perfectly still, listening: for no matter what else was lost, she would not give up her children, she would not let them go.

"It's *not* true. I don't believe you. Why Eric? Why did you go to him?"

"He has something—something I needed very badly."

"What is that, Cass?"

"A sense of himself."

"A sense of himself," he repeated, slowly. "A sense of himself." She felt his eyes on her, and also felt, with dread, how slowly the storm in him gathered, how long it would take to break. "Forgive your coarse-grained husband, but I've always felt that he had no sense of himself at all. He's not even sure he knows what's between his legs, or what to do with it—but I guess I have to take that back now."

Here we go, she thought.

She said, wearily, helplessly, "I know it sounds strange, Richard." Tears came to her eyes. "But he's a very wonderful person. I know. I know him better than you do."

He said, making a sound somewhere between a grunt and a sob, "I guess you *do*—though *he* may have preferred it the other way around. Did you ever think of that? You must be one of the very few women in the world—"

"Don't, Richard. Don't. It won't change anything, it won't help."

He came and stood over her. "Let's get this straight. We've been married almost thirteen years, and I've been in love with you all that time, and I've trusted you, and, except for a couple of times in the army, I haven't had anything to do with any other woman. Even though I've thought about it. But it never seemed worth it. And I've worked, I've worked very hard, Cass, for you and our children, so we could be happy and so our marriage would work. Maybe you think that's old-fashioned, maybe you think I'm dumb, I don't know, you're so much more—*sensitive* than I am. And now—and then—" He walked over to the bar and set his glass down. "Suddenly, for no reason, just when it begins to seem that things are really going to work out for us, all of a sudden—you begin to make me feel that I'm something that stinks, that I ought to be out of doors. I didn't know what had happened, I didn't know where you'd gone—all of a sudden. I've listened to you come into this house and go and look at the boys, and then crawl into bed—I swear, I could hear every move you made—and I'd stay on in the office like a little boy, because I didn't know how, *how*, to come close to you again. I kept thinking, She'll get over it, it's just some strange kind of feminine shift that I can't understand. I even thought, my God, that maybe you were going to have another baby and didn't want to tell me yet." He bowed his head on the bar. "And, Jesus, Jesus— Eric! You walk in and tell me you've been sleeping with Eric." He turned and looked at her. "How long?"

"A few weeks."

"Why?" She did not answer. He came toward her again.

"Answer me, baby. Why?" He leaned over her, imprisoning her in the chair. "Is it that you wanted to hurt me?"

"No. I have never wanted to hurt you."

"Why, then?" He leaned closer. "Did you get bored with me? Does he make love to you better than I; does he know tricks I don't know? Is that it?" He wrapped the fingers of one hand in her hair. "Is that it? Answer me!"

"Richard, you're going to wake the children—"

"*Now* she worries about the children!" He pulled her head forward, then slammed it back against the chair, and slapped her across the face, twice, as hard as he could. The room dropped into darkness for a second, then came reeling back, in light; tears came to her eyes, and her nose began to bleed. "Is that it? Did he fuck you in the ass, did he make you suck his cock? Answer me, you bitch, you slut, you *cunt*!"

She tried to throw back her head, choking and gasping, she felt her thick blood on her lips, and it fell onto her breasts. "No, Richard, no, no. Please, Richard."

"Oh, God. Oh, God." He fell away from her, and, as though in a dream, she saw his great body stagger to the sofa; and he fell beside the sofa, on his knees, weeping. She listened, listened to hear a sound from the children, and looked toward the door, where they would be standing if they were up; but they were not there, there was no sound. She looked at Richard, and covered her face for a moment. She could not bear the sound of his weeping, or the sight of those breaking shoulders. Her face felt twice its size; when she took her hands away, they were covered with blood. She rose, and staggered into the bathroom.

She ran the water, the bleeding slowly began to stop. Then she sat down on the bathroom floor. Her mind swung madly back and forth, like the needle of some broken instrument. She wondered if her face would be swollen in the morning, and how she would explain this to Paul and Michael. She thought of Ida and Vivaldo and Ellis, and wondered what Vivaldo would do when he discovered the truth; and felt very sorry for him, sad enough for her tears to begin again, dripping down on her clenched hands. She thought of Eric, and wondered if she had also betrayed *him* by telling Richard the truth. And what would she say to Eric now, or he to her? She did not want, ever, to leave the white, lighted haven of the bathroom. The center of her mind was filled with the sight and sound of Richard's anguish. She wondered if there was any hope for them, if there was anything left between them which they could use. This last question made her rise at last, her dry belly still contracting, and take off her bloody dress. She wanted to burn it, but she put it in the dirty-clothes hamper. She walked into the kitchen and put coffee on the stove. Then she walked back into the bathroom, put on a bathrobe, and took the cigarettes out of her handbag. She lit a cigarette and sat down at the kitchen table. It was three o'clock in the morning. She sat and waited for Richard to rise and come to her.

BOOK THREE:

TOWARD BETHLEHEM

How with this rage shall beauty hold a plea,
Whose action is no stronger than a flower?
　　　　—SHAKESPEARE, *Sonnet LXV*

I

VIVALDO DREAMED that he was running, running, running, through a country he had always known, but could not now remember, a rocky country. He was blinded by the rain beating down, the tough, wet vines dragged at his legs and feet, and thorns and nettles tormented his hands and arms and face. He was both fleeing and seeking, and, in his dream, the time was running out. There was a high wall ahead of him, a high, stone wall. Broken glass glittered on top of the wall, sharp points standing straight up, like spears. He was reminded of music, though he heard none: the music was created by the sight of the rain which fell in long, cruel, gleaming shafts, and by the bright glass which reared itself bitterly against it. And he felt an answering rearing in his own body, a pull fugitive and powerful and dimly troubling, such as he might have felt for a moment had there been the movement and power of a horse beneath him. And, at the same time, in his dream, as he ran or as he was propelled, he was weighed down and made sick by the certainty that he had forgotten—forgotten—what? some secret, some duty, that would save him. His breath was a terrible captive weight in his chest. He reached the wall. He grasped the stone with his bleeding hands, but the stone was slippery, he could not hold it, could not lift himself up. He tried with his feet; his feet slipped; the rain poured down.

And now he knew that his enemy was upon him. Salt burned his eyes. He dared not turn; in terror he pressed himself against the rough, wet wall, as though a wall could melt or could be entered. He had forgotten—what? how to escape or how to defeat his enemy. Then he heard the wail of trombones and clarinets and a steady, enraged beating on the drums. They were playing a blues he had never heard before, they were filling the earth with a sound so dreadful that he knew he could not bear it. Where was Ida? she could help him. But he felt rough hands on him and he looked down into Rufus' distorted and vindictive face. *Go on up*, said Rufus. *I'm helping you up. Go up!* Rufus' hands pushed and pushed and soon Vivaldo stood, higher than Rufus had ever stood, on the wintry bridge, looking down on death. He knew that this death was what Rufus most desired. He tried to look down, to beg Rufus for mercy, but he could not move without falling off the wall, or falling on the glass. From far away, far beyond this flood, he saw Ida, on a sloping green meadow, walking alone. The sun was beautiful on her blue-black hair and on her Aztec brow, and gathered in a dark, glinting pool at the hollow of her throat. She did not look toward him, walked in a measured way, looking down at the ground; yet, he felt that she saw him, was aware of him standing on the cruel wall, and waited, in collusion with her brother, for his death. Then Rufus came hurtling from the air, impaling himself on the far, spiked fence which bounded the meadow. Ida did not look: she waited. Vivaldo watched Rufus' blood run down, bright red over the black spikes, into the green meadow. He tried to shout, but no words came; tried to reach out to Ida and fell heavily on his hands and knees on the rearing, uplifted glass. He could not bear the pain; yet, he felt again the random, voluptuous tug. He felt entirely helpless and more terrified than ever. But there was pleasure in it. He writhed against the glass. *Don't kill me, Rufus. Please. Please. I love you.* Then, to his delight and confusion, Rufus lay down beside him and opened his arms. And the moment he surrendered to this sweet and overwhelming embrace, his dream, like glass, shattered, he heard the rain at the windows, returned, violently, into his body, became aware of his odor and the odor of Eric, and found that it was Eric to whom he clung, who clung to him. Eric's lips were against Vivaldo's neck and chest.

Vivaldo hoped that he was dreaming still. A terrible sorrow entered him, because he was dreaming and because he was awake. Immediately, he felt that he had created his dream in order to create this opportunity; he had brought about something that he had long desired. He was frightened and then he was angry—at Eric or at himself? he did not know—and started to pull away. But he could not pull away, he did not want to, it was too late. He thought to keep his eyes closed in order to take no responsibility for what was happening. This thought made him ashamed. He tried to reconstruct the way in which this monstrous endeavor must have begun. They must have gone to sleep, spoon-fashion. Eric curled against him—oh, what did this cause him, nearly, to remember? He had curled his legs, himself, around Eric, since Eric's body was there; and desire had entered this monastic, this boyish bed. Now it was too late, thank God it was too late; it was necessary for them to disentangle themselves from the drag and torment of their undershorts, their trousers, and the sheets. He opened his eyes. Eric was watching him with a small half-smile, a troubled smile, and this smile caused Vivaldo to realize that Eric loved him. Eric really loved him and would be proud to give Vivaldo anything Vivaldo needed. With a groan and a sigh, with an indescribable relief, Vivaldo came full awake and pulled Eric closer. It had been a dream and not a dream, how long could such dreams last? this one could not last long. Instantaneously, then, they each seemed to become intent on carrying this moment, which belonged to them, as far as it could go. They kicked their trousers to the floor, saying nothing—what was there to say?—and not daring to let go of one another. Then, as in a waking dream, helpless and trustful, he felt Eric remove his shirt and caress him with his parted lips. Eric bowed and kissed Vivaldo on the belly button, half-hidden in the violent, gypsy hair. This was in honor of Vivaldo, of Vivaldo's body and Vivaldo's need, and Vivaldo trembled as he had never trembled before. And this caress was not entirely pleasant. Vivaldo felt terribly ill at ease, not knowing what was expected of him, or what he could expect from Eric. He pulled Eric up and kissed him on the mouth, kneading Eric's buttocks and stroking his sex. How strange it felt, this violent muscle, stretching and throbbing, so like his own, but belonging to another! And this chest, this belly, these legs, were like his, and the tremor of Eric's breath echoed his own earthquake. Oh, what was it that he could not remember? It was his first sexual encounter with a male in many years, and his very first sexual encounter with a friend. He associated the act with the humiliation and the debasement of one male by another, the inferior male of less importance than the crumpled, cast-off handkerchief; but he did not feel this way toward Eric; and therefore he did not know what he felt. This tormented self-consciousness caused

Vivaldo to fear that their moment might, after all, come to nothing. He did not want this to happen, he knew his need to be too great, and they had come too far, and Eric had risked too much. He was afraid of what might happen if they failed. Yet, his lust remained, and rose, chafing within and battering against the labyrinth of his bewilderment; his lust was unaccustomedly arrogant and cruel and irresponsible, and yet there was mingled in it a deep and incomprehensible tenderness: he did not want to cause Eric pain. The physical pain he had sometimes brought to vanished, phantom girls had been necessary for them, he had been unlocking, for them, the door to life; but he was now involved in another mystery, at once blacker and more pure. He tried to will himself back into his adolescence, grasping Eric's strange body and stroking that strange sex. At the same time, he tried to think of a woman. (But he did not want to think of Ida.) And they lay together in this antique attitude, the hand of each on the sex of the other, and with their limbs entangled, and Eric's breath trembling against Vivaldo's chest. This childish and trustful tremor returned to Vivaldo a sense of his own power. He held Eric very tightly and covered Eric's body with his own, as though he were shielding him from the falling heavens. But it was also as though he were, at the same instant, being shielded—by Eric's love. It was strangely and insistently double-edged, it was like making love in the midst of mirrors, or it was like death by drowning. But it was also like music, the highest, sweetest, loneliest reeds, and it was like the rain. He kissed Eric again and again, wondering how they would finally come together. The male body was not mysterious, he had never thought about it at all, but it was the most impenetrable of mysteries now; and this wonder made him think of his own body, of its possibilities and its imminent and absolute decay, in a way that he had never thought of it before. Eric moved against him and beneath him, as thirsty as the sand. He wondered what moved in Eric's body which drove him, like a bird or a leaf in a storm, against the wall of Vivaldo's flesh; and he wondered what moved in his own body: what virtue were they seeking, now, to share? what was he doing here? This was as far removed as anything could be from the necessary war one underwent with women. He would have entered her by now, this woman who was not here, her sighs would be different and her surrender would never be total. Her sex, which afforded him his entry, would nevertheless remain strange to him, an incitement and an anguish, and an everlasting mystery. And even now, in this bright, laboring and doubting moment, with only the rain as their witness, he knew that he was condemned to women. What was it like to be a man, condemned to men? He could not imagine it and he felt a quick revulsion, quickly banished, for it threatened his ease. But at the very same moment his excitement increased: he felt that he could do with Eric whatever he liked. Now, Vivaldo, who was accustomed himself to labor, to be the giver of the gift, and enter into his satisfaction by means of the satisfaction of a woman, surrendered to the luxury, the flaming torpor of passivity, and whispered in Eric's ear a muffled, urgent plea.

The dream teetered on the edge of nightmare: how old was this rite, this act of love, how deep? in impersonal time, in the actors? He felt that he had stepped off a precipice into an air which held him inexorably up, as the salt sea holds the swimmer: and seemed to see, vastly and horribly down, into the bottom of his heart, that heart which contained all the possibilities that he could name and yet others that he could not name. Their moment was coming to its end. He moaned and his thighs, like the thighs of a woman, loosened, he thrust upward as Eric thrust down. How strange, how strange! Was Eric, now, silently sobbing and praying, as he, over Ida, silently sobbed and prayed? But Rufus had certainly thrashed and throbbed, feeling himself mount higher, as Vivaldo thrashed and throbbed and mounted now. *Rufus. Rufus.* Had it been like this for him? And he wanted to ask Eric, What was it like for Rufus? What was it like for him? Then he felt himself falling, as though the weary sea had failed, had wrapped him about, and he were plunging down—plunging down as he desperately thrust and struggled upward. He heard his own harsh breath, coming from far away; he heard the drumming rain; he was being overtaken. He remembered how Ida, at the unbearable moment, threw back her head and thrashed and bared her teeth. And she called his name. And Rufus? Had he murmured at last, in a strange voice, as he now heard himself murmur, *Oh, Eric. Eric.* What was that fury like? *Eric.* He pulled Eric to him through the ruined sheets and held him tight. And, *Thank you,* Vivaldo whispered, *thank you, Eric, thank you.* Eric curled against him like a child and salt from his forehead dripped onto Vivaldo's chest.

Then they lay together, close, hidden and protected by the sound of the rain. The rain came down outside like a blessing, like a wall between them and the world. Vivaldo seemed to have fallen through a great hole in time, back to his innocence, he felt clear, washed, and empty, waiting to be filled. He stroked the rough hair at the base of Eric's skull, delighted and amazed by the love he felt. Eric's breath trembled against the hairs of his chest; from time to time he touched Vivaldo with his lips. This luxury and this warmth made Vivaldo heavy and drowsy. He slowly began drifting off to sleep again, beams of light playing in his skull, behind his eyes, like the sun. But beneath this peace and this gratitude, he wondered what Eric was thinking. He wanted to open his eyes, to look into Eric's eyes, but this was too great an effort and risked, furthermore, shattering his peace. He stroked Eric's neck and back slowly, hoping that his joy was conveyed by his fingertips. At the same time he wondered, and it almost made him laugh, *after all that shit I was talking last night,* what he was doing, in this bed, in the arms of this man? who was the dearest man on earth, for him. He felt fantastically protected, liberated, by the knowledge that, no matter where, once the clawing day descended, he felt compelled to go, no matter what happened to him from now until he died, and even, or perhaps especially, if they should never lie in each other's arms again, there was a man in the world who loved him. All of his hope, which had grown so pale, flushed into life again. He loved Eric: it was a great revelation. But it was yet more strange and made for an unprecedented steadiness and freedom, that Eric loved him. "Eric—?"

They opened their eyes and looked at each other. Eric's dark blue eyes were very clear and candid, but there was a terrible fear in their depth, too, waiting. Vivaldo said, "It was wonderful for me, Eric." He watched Eric's face. "Was it for you?"

"Yes," Eric said, and he blushed. They spoke in whispers. "I suppose that I needed it, more than I knew."

"It may never happen again."

"I know." There was a silence. Then, "Would you *like* it to happen again?"

Then Vivaldo was silent, feeling frightened for the first time. "I don't know how to answer that," he said. "Yes—yes and no. But, just the same, I love you, Eric, I always will, I hope you know that." He was astonished to hear how his voice shook. "Do you love me? Tell me that you do."

"You know I do," said Eric. He stared into Vivaldo's worn, white face and raised one hand to stroke the stubble which began just below the cheekbone. "I love you very much, I'd do anything for you. You must have known it, no? somewhere, for a very long time. Because I must have loved you for a very long time."

"Is that true? I didn't *know* I knew it."

"I didn't know it, either," Eric said. He smiled. "What a funny day this is. It begins with revelations."

"They're opening up," said Vivaldo, "all those books in heaven." He closed his eyes. The telephone rang. "Oh, shit."

"More revelations," Eric grinned. He reached over Vivaldo for a cigarette, and lit it.

"It's too *early*, baby. Can't we go back to sleep?"

The phone rang and rang.

"It's one o'clock," said Eric. He looked doubtfully from Vivaldo to the ringing telephone. "It's probably Cass. She'll call back."

"Or it may be Ida. She probably *won't* call back."

Eric picked up the receiver. "Hello?"

Vivaldo heard, dimly, from far away, Cass' voice rushing through the wires. "Good morning, baby, how are you?" cried Eric. Then he fell into silence. Something in the quality of that silence caused Vivaldo to come full awake and sit straight up. He watched Eric's face. Then he lit himself a cigarette, and waited.

"Oh," said Eric, after a moment. Then, "Jesus. Oh, my poor Cass." The voice went on and on, Eric's face becoming more troubled and more weary. "Yes. But now it *has* happened. It's here. It's upon us." He looked briefly at Vivaldo, then looked over at his watch. "Yes, certainly, where?" He looked toward the window. "Cass, it doesn't *look* as though it's likely to let up." Then, "Please, Cass. Please don't." His face changed again, registering shock; he glanced at Vivaldo, and said quickly, "Vivaldo's here. *We* didn't go anywhere, we just stayed here." A dry, bitter smile touched his lips. "That's what they say and it sure as hell is pouring to beat the band now." He laughed: "No, nobody lives without clichés—what?" He listened. He said, gently, "But I'm going to be in rehearsal very soon, Cass, and I *may* be going to the Coast, and besides—" He looked over at Vivaldo with a heavy, helpless frown. "Yes, I understand that, Cass. Yes. At four. Okay. You hold on, baby, you just hold on."

He hung up. He sat for a moment, turned, staring toward the rain, then lowered his gaze to Vivaldo with a small smile, both sad and proud. He looked at his watch again, put out his cigarette, and lay back, staring at the ceiling, his head resting on his arms. "Well. Guess what. The shit has hit the fan. Cass got in late last night and she and Richard had a fight—about us. Richard knows about us."

Vivaldo whistled, his eyes very big. "I knew you shouldn't have answered that phone. What a mess. Is Richard on his way down here with a shotgun? and *how* did he find out?"

Eric looked strangely guilty, then he said, "Oh, Cass wasn't at her most coherent, I don't really know. Anyway, *how* he found out hardly matters now, since he *has*." He sat up. "Apparently, he *has* been suspicious—but he was suspicious of *you*——"

"Of *me*? He must be crazy!"

"Well, Cass kept coming to see you all the time, that's what she told him, anyway—"

"And what did he think Ida was doing while Cass and I were screwing? Reading us bedtime stories?"

Again, Eric looked uncomfortable, but he laughed. "I don't know what he thought. Anyway, Cass says that he's very bitter against you because"—he faltered for a moment and looked down—"because you knew about the affair and you're supposed to be his friend and you didn't tell him." He watched Vivaldo. "Do you think you should have told him?"

Vivaldo put out his cigarette. "What a wild idea. I'm nobody's goddam Boy Scout. Besides, you and Cass are my friends, not Richard."

"Well, he didn't know that; you've known him much longer than you've known me, and—Richard doesn't really like me very much—so he'd naturally expect you to be loyal to him."

Vivaldo sighed. "There's a hell of a lot that Richard doesn't know and that's too bad but it's not my fault. And he's being dishonest. He *knows* that we haven't really been friends for a long time. And I *won't* be made to feel guilty." Then he grinned. "I've got enough to feel guilty about."

"*Do* you feel guilty?"

They stared at each other for a moment. Vivaldo laughed. "That wasn't what I had in mind. But, no, I don't feel guilty and I hope to God that I never feel guilty again. It's a monstrous waste of time."

Eric looked down. "Yes, Cass says that Richard may try to see *you* today."

"Sounds just like him. Well, I'm not at home." Suddenly, he laughed. "Wouldn't it be funny if Richard came *here*?"

"And found you here, you mean?" They laughed, rolling in the bed like children. "I wonder what he'd think."

"Poor man. He wouldn't know *what* to think."

They looked at each other and began to laugh again. "We certainly aren't giving him an awful lot of sympathy," Eric said.

"That's true." Vivaldo sat up and lit two cigarettes, giving one to Eric. "The poor bastard must really be suffering; after all, he doesn't know what hit him." They were silent. "And I'm sure Cass isn't laughing."

"No. Not at Richard, not at anything. She sounded half out of her mind."

"Where was she calling from?"

"Home. Richard had just gone out."

"I wonder if he really did go to my house. Maybe I should call and see if Ida's there." But he did not move toward the phone.

"It's all just about as messy as it can possibly be," Eric said, after a moment, "Richard's talking about suing for divorce and getting custody of the children."

"Yes, and he's probably gone out shopping for a brand with the letter *A* on it and if he could, he'd arrange for Cass to peddle her ass in the streets and drop dead of syphilis. Slowly. Because the cat's been wounded, man, in his self-esteem."

"Well," said Eric, slowly, "he *has* been wounded. You haven't got to be—admirable—in order to feel pain."

"No. But I think that perhaps you can begin to *become* admirable if, when you're hurt, you don't try to pay back." He looked at Eric and put one hand on the back of Eric's neck. "Do you know what I mean? Perhaps if you can accept the pain that almost kills you, you can use it, you can become better."

Eric watched him, smiling a strange half-smile, with his face full of love and pain. "That's very hard to do."

"One's got to *try*."

"I know." He said, very carefully, watching Vivaldo, "Otherwise, you just get stopped with whatever it was that ruined you and you make it happen over and over again and your life has—ceased, really—because you can't move or change or love any more."

Vivaldo let his hand fall. He leaned back. "You're trying to tell me something. What is it that you're trying to tell me?"

"I was talking about myself."

"Maybe. But I don't believe you."

"I just hope," said Eric, suddenly, "that Cass will never hate me."

"Why should she hate you?"

"I can't do her much good. I *haven't* done her much good."

"You don't know that. Cass knew what she was doing. I think she had a much clearer idea than you—because you, you know," and he grinned, "you aren't very clear-headed."

"I think I was hoping—perhaps *we* were hoping—that Richard would never find out and that Yves would get here—before——"

"Yes. Well, life isn't ever that tidy."

"*You're* very clear-headed," Eric said.

"Naturally." He grinned and reached out and pulled Eric to him. "And you must do the same for me, baby, when I'm in trouble. Be *clear*-headed."

"I'll do my best," said Eric, gravely.

Vivaldo laughed. "No one could ever hate you. You're

much too funny." He pulled away. "What time are you meeting Cass?"

"At four. At the Museum of Modern Art."

"God. How's she going to get away? Or is Richard coming
along?"

Eric hesitated. "She isn't sure that Richard's coming back
today."

"I see. I think, maybe, we'd better have a cup of coffee—?
I'm going to the john." And he leapt out of bed and slammed
the bathroom door behind him.

Eric walked into the kitchen, which was only slightly less
disordered than he now felt himself to be, and put coffee on
the stove. He stood there a moment, watching the blue flame
in the gloom of the small room. He took down two coffee
cups and found the milk and sugar. He returned to the big
room and cleared the night table of books and of urgently
scrawled notes—nearly all of which, beneath his eyes, as he
wrote them on small scraps of paper, had hardened into ir-
relevance—and emptied the ashtray. He picked up his clothes,
and Vivaldo's, from the floor, piling them on a chair, and
straightened the sheets on the bed. He put the cups and the
milk and sugar on the night table, discovered that there were
only five cigarettes left, and searched in his pockets for more,
but there were none. He was hungry, but the refrigerator was
empty. He thought that, perhaps, he could find the energy to
dress and run down to the corner delicatessen for something—Vivaldo was probably hungry, too. He walked to the
window and peeked out through the blinds. The rain poured
down like a wall. It struck the pavements with a vicious sound,
and spattered in the swollen gutters with the force of bullets.
The asphalt was wide and white and blank with rain. The gray
pavements danced and gleamed and sloped. Nothing
moved—not a car, not a person, not a cat; and the rain was
the only sound. He forgot about going to the store, and
merely watched the rain, comforted by the anonymity and the
violence—this violence was also peace. And just as the speeding rain distorted, blurred, blunted, all the familiar outlines of
walls, windows, doors, parked cars, lamp posts, hydrants,
trees, so Eric, now, in his silent watching, sought to blur and
blunt and flee from all the conundrums which crowded in on

him. *How will I ever get to the museum in all this rain?* he wondered: but did not dare to wonder what he would say to Cass, what she would say to him. He thought of Yves, thought of him with a sorrow that was close to panic, feeling doubly faithless, feeling that the principal support of his life had shifted—had shifted and would shift again, might fail beneath the dreadful, the accumulating and secret weight. Faintly, from the closed door behind him, he heard Vivaldo whistling. How could he not have known what he was capable of feeling for Vivaldo? And the answer drummed at him as relentlessly as the falling rain fell: he had not known because he had not dared to know. There were so many things one did not dare to know. And were they all patiently waiting, like demons in the dark, to spring from hiding, to reveal themselves, on some rainy Sunday morning?

He dropped the blind and turned back into the room. The telephone rang. He stared at it sourly, thinking *More revelations*, and picked up the receiver.

His agent, Harman, shouted in his ear. "Hello there—Eric? I'm sorry to bother you on a Sunday morning, but you're a pretty hard man to reach. I was thinking of sending you a telegram."

"*Am* I hard to find? I've just been staying home, it seems to me, curled up with that lovely script."

"Don't shit *me*, sweetheart. I know you've got a hard on for that play, but it's not *that* big. You just haven't been answering your phone. Listen——"

"Yes?"

"About your screen test—you got a pencil?"

"Wait a minute."

He found a pencil on his desk, and a scrap of paper, and returned to the phone.

"Go ahead, Harman."

"You're not going to the Coast. It's fixed up for you to do it here. You know where the Allied Studios are?"

"Yes, naturally."

"Well, it's set for Wednesday morning. Allied, at ten. Listen. Can you have lunch with me tomorrow?"

"Yes. I'd love to."

"Good. I'll fill you in on all the details. Downey's okay?"

"Right. What time?"

"One o'clock. Now—you still with me?"

"All ears, baby."

"Well, we finally got that *meshugena* of a broken-down movie star in town and the rehearsal date is definitely set for a week from tomorrow."

"Next week?"

"Right."

"Wonderful. God, I'll be so glad to be working again."

Vivaldo came out of the bathroom, seeming unutterably huge in his blank, white nakedness, and walked into the kitchen. He looked critically at the coffee pot, came back into the room, and threw himself into the bed.

"You're going to be working from now on, Eric. You're on your way, sweetheart; you're going to go right over the top, and, baby, I couldn't be more delighted."

"Thanks, Harman. I certainly hope you're right."

"I've been in the business longer than you've been in the world, Eric. I know a winner when I see one and I've never made a mistake, not about that. You be good now, I'll see you tomorrow. Good-bye."

"Good-bye."

He put down the receiver, filled with a fugitive excitement.

"Good news?"

"That was my agent. We're going into rehearsal next week and we're doing my screen test Wednesday." Then his triumph blazed up in him and he turned to Vivaldo. "Isn't that fantastic?"

Vivaldo watched him, smiling. "I think we ought to drink to *that*, baby." He watched as Eric picked up the empty bottle from the floor. "Ah. Too sad."

"But I've got a little bourbon," Eric said.

"Crazy."

Eric poured two bourbons and lowered the flame under the coffee. "Bourbon's really much more fitting," he said, happily, "since that's what they drink in the South, where I come from."

He sat on the bed again, and they touched glasses.

"To your first Oscar," said Vivaldo.

Eric laughed. "That's touching. To your Nobel prize."

"That's *very* touching." Eric pulled the sheet up to his navel. Vivaldo watched him. "You're going to be very lonely,"
he said, suddenly.

Eric looked over at Vivaldo, and shrugged. "So are you, if
it comes to that. If it comes to *that*," he added, after a moment, "I'm lonely now."

Vivaldo was silent for a moment. When he spoke, he
sounded very sad and gentle. "Are you? *Will* you be—when
your boy gets here?"

Then Eric was silent. "No," he said, finally. He hesitated.
"Well—yes and no." Then he looked at Vivaldo. "Are you
lonely with Ida?"

Vivaldo looked down. "I've been thinking about that—or
I've been trying not to think about that—all morning." He
raised his eyes to Eric's eyes. "I hope you don't mind my
saying—well, hell, anyway, you know it—that I'm sort of hiding in your bed now, hiding even in your arms maybe—from
Ida, in a way. I'm trying to get something straight in my mind
about my life with Ida." He looked down again. "I keep feeling that it's up to me to resolve it, one way or another. But
I don't seem to have the guts. I don't know how. I'm afraid
to force anything because I'm afraid to lose her." He seemed
to flounder in the depths of Eric's silence. "Do you know
what I mean? Does it make any sense to you?"

"Oh, yes," said Eric, bleakly, "it makes sense, all right."
He looked over at Vivaldo with a smile, and dared to say,
"Maybe, at this very moment, while both of us are huddled
here, hiding from things which frighten us—maybe you love
me and I love you as well as we'll ever love, or be loved, in
this world."

Vivaldo said, "I don't know if I can accept that, not yet.
Not yet. As *well*—maybe. Well, surely." He looked up at Eric.
"But it's not, really, is it? very complete. Look. This day is
almost over. How long will it be before such a day comes for
us again? Because we're not kids, we know what life is like,
and how time just vanishes, runs away—I can't, really, like
from moment to moment, day to day, month to month, make
you less lonely. Or you, me. We aren't driven in the same
directions and I can't help that, any more than you can." He
paused, watching Eric with enormous, tormented eyes. He

smiled. "It would be wonderful if it could be like that; you're very beautiful, Eric. But I don't, really, dig you the way I guess you must dig me. You know? And if we tried to arrange it, prolong it, control it, if we tried to take more than what we've—by some miracle, some miracle, I swear—stumbled on, then I'd just become a parasite and we'd both shrivel. So what can we really do for each other except—just love each other and be each other's witness? And haven't we got the right to hope—for more? So that we can really stretch into whoever we really are? Don't you think so?" And, before Eric could answer, he took a large swallow of his whiskey and said in a different tone, a lower voice, "Because, you know, when I was in the bathroom, I was thinking that, yes, I loved being in your arms, holding you"—he flushed and looked up into Eric's face again—"why not, it's warm, I'm sensual, I like—you—the way you love me, but"—he looked down again—"it's not my battle, not my *thing*, and I know it, and I can't give up my battle. If I do, I'll die and if I die"—and now he looked up at Eric with a rueful, juvenile grin—"you won't love me any more. And I want you to love me all my life."

Eric reached out and touched Vivaldo's face. After a moment, Vivaldo grabbed his hand. "For you, the moon, baby," Eric said. His voice, to his surprise, was a grave, hoarse whisper. He cleared his throat. "Do you want some coffee now?"

Vivaldo shook his head. He emptied his glass and put it on the table.

"Drink up," he said to Eric.

Eric finished his drink. Vivaldo took the glass from him and set it down.

"I don't want any coffee now," he said. He opened his arms. "Let's make the most of our little day."

By ten minutes to four, Eric was, somehow, showered, shaved, and dressed, with his raincoat and his rain cap on. The coffee was too hot, he only managed to drink half a cup. Vivaldo was still undressed.

"You go on," he said. "I'll clean up a little and I'll lock the door."

"All right." But Eric dreaded leaving in the same way that Vivaldo dreaded getting dressed. "I'll leave you the cigarettes, I'll buy some."

"That's big of you. Go on, now. Give my love to Cass."

"Give *my* love," he said, "to Ida."

They both grinned. "I'm going to call her," Vivaldo said, "just as soon as you get your ass out of here."

"*Okay*, I'm gone." Yet, at the door, he stopped, looking at Vivaldo, who stood in the center of the room, holding a cup of coffee. He stared at the floor with a harsh bewilderment in his face. Then he felt Eric's eyes and looked up. He put down his coffee cup and walked to the door. He kissed Eric on the mouth and looked into his eyes.

"See you soon, baby."

"Yes," said Eric, "see you soon." He opened the door and left.

Vivaldo listened to him go down the stairs. Then he walked to the window and opened the blinds and watched him. Eric appeared in the street as though he had been running, or as though he had been propelled. He looked first in one direction and then in the other; then, his hands in his pockets, head lowered and shoulders raised, he walked the long block, hugging the sides of buildings. Vivaldo watched him till he turned the corner.

Then he turned back into the room, pale with assessments, with guilt deliciously beginning to gnaw at the rope with which he had tied it, sharpening its teeth for him. And yet, at the same time, he felt radiantly, wonderfully spent. He poured himself another small drink and sat on the edge of the bed. Slowly, he dialed his number.

The receiver was lifted almost at once, and Ida's voice came at him: with the force of an electric shock. "Hello?"

In the background, he heard Billie Holiday singing *Billie's Blues.*

"Hello, sugar. This is your man, checking on his woman."

"Do you know what time it is? Where the hell are you?"

"I'm at Eric's. We passed out here. I'm just pulling myself together."

There was a peculiar relief in her voice. He was aware of it because she tried to hide it. "You've been there all *night*? ever since I left you?"

"Yes. We came on over here and started talking and finished

up Eric's whiskey. And he had quite a lot of whiskey—so, you see."

"Yes, I know you think it's against the law to stop drinking as long as there's anything left to drink. Listen. Has Cass called?"

"Yes."

"Did you talk to her?"

"No. Eric did."

"Oh? What did Eric tell you?"

"What do you mean, what did Eric tell me?"

"I mean, what did Cass *say?*"

"She said she was in trouble. Richard's found out about them."

"Isn't that awful? What else did she say?"

"Well—I think that that sort of cluttered up her mind. She doesn't seem to have said anything else. Did you know anything about all this?"

"*Yes.* Richard was here. Has he been there?"

"No."

"Oh, Vivaldo, it was awful. I felt so sorry for him. I thought that you *might* be at Eric's, but I said you'd gone off to see your family in Brooklyn and I didn't have the phone number or the address. It's very sad, Vivaldo, he's very bitter, he wants to hurt you. He feels that you betrayed him—"

"Yes, well, I think it may be easier for him to feel that way. How long was he there?"

"Not long. Only about ten minutes. But it seemed longer. He said some terrible things—"

"I'm sure. Does he still want to see me?"

"I don't know." There was a pause. "Are you coming home now?"

"Yes, right away. Are you going to be there?"

"I'll be here. Come on. Oh. Where's Eric?"

"He's gone—uptown—"

"To meet Cass?"

"Yes."

She sighed. "Lord, what a mess. Come on home, sweetie, if Richard's going to shoot you you don't want him to do it while you're wandering around Eric's house. That would really be too much."

He laughed. "You're right. You seem to be in a good mood today."

"I'm really in a terrible mood. But I'm being brave about it, I'm pretending to be Greer Garson."

He laughed again. "Does it help?"

"Well, no, baby, but it makes everything pretty funny."

"All right. I'll be along in a minute."

"Okay, sweetie. 'Bye."

"Good-bye."

He hung up with an exultant relief that no trouble seemed to be awaiting him at home with Ida. He felt that he had got away with something. He stepped into Eric's shower, scrubbed and sang; but when he stepped out he realized that he was terribly hungry and weak. While he was dressing, Eric's doorbell rang.

He was sure that it was Richard, at last, and he hurriedly buckled his belt and pulled on his shoes before pressing the buzzer. He started, idiotically, to make up the bed, but realized that there would not be time, and, anyway, it could not possibly make any difference to Richard whether the bed was made or not. He waited, hearing the downstairs door open and close. He opened Eric's door. But he heard no footsteps. A voice called, "Eric Jones!"

"Here!" cried Vivaldo. He let out his breath. He walked to the landing. A Western Union boy came up the steps.

"You Eric Jones?"

"He's gone out. But I can take it."

The boy handed him a telegram and a book for him to sign. He gave the boy twenty cents and walked back into the apartment. He thought that the telegram came, probably, from Eric's agent or producer; but he looked at it more carefully and realized that it was a cable and that it came from Europe. He propped it against Eric's telephone. He scribbled a note: *I've borrowed your other raincoat. NOTE CABLEGRAM.* He paused. Then he scribbled, *It was a great day.* And added, *love, Vivaldo.* He placed the note in the center of Eric's desk, weighting it down with an ink bottle.

Then he was ready, he looked about the room. The bed was still unmade; he left it that way; the bottle was still on the floor, the glasses on the night table. Everything was absolutely still, silent, except for the rain. He looked again at the cablegram, which leaned lightly, charged, waiting, against the telephone. Telegrams always frightened him a little. He closed the door behind him, tested it to make certain that it was locked, and walked out, at last, into the unfriendly rain.

Eric saw her at once, standing near the steps, just beyond the ticket-taker. She was pacing in a small circle and her back, as he entered, was to him. She wore her loose brown raincoat and her head was covered with a matching hood; and she played with the tip, white bone in the shape of a claw, of her thin umbrella. The museum was crowded, full of the stale, Sunday museum stink, aggravated, now, by the damp. He came through the doors behind a great cloud of windy, rainy, broad-beamed ladies; and they formed, before him, a large, loud, rocking wall, as they shook their umbrellas and themselves and repeated to each other, in their triumphant voices, how awful the weather was. Three young men and two young girls, scrubbed and milky, gleaming with their passion for improvement and the ease with which they moved among abstractions, were surrendering their tickets and passing through the barrier. Others were on the steps, going down, coming up, stationary, peering at each other like half-blinded birds and setting up a hideous whirr, as of flying feathers and boastful wings. Cass, small, pale, and old-fashioned in her hood, restlessly pacing, disenchantedly watched all this; she glanced indifferently toward the resounding ladies, but did not see him; he was still trying to get through, or around, the wall. He looked toward the people on the steps again, wondering why Cass had wished to meet here; it was only too probable that these sacred and sterile halls contained, blocking a corridor or half-hidden by a spinning mass of statuary, someone that they knew. Cass, resignedly lit a cigarette half-turning in her small, imaginary cage. People now came crushing in through the doors behind him, and their greater pressure spat him past the ladies. He touched Cass on the shoulder.

At his touch, she seemed to spring. Her eyes came alive at once, and her pale lips tensed. And her smile was pale. She said, "Oh. I thought you'd never get here."

He had surmounted a desperate temptation not to come at

all, and had half-hoped that he would not find her there. She was so pale and seemed, in this cold, dazzling place, so helpless, that his heart turned over. He was half an hour late. He said, "Dear Cass, please forgive me, it's hard to get anywhere in weather like this. How are you?"

"Dead." She did not move, merely stared at the tip of her cigarette as though she were hypnotized by it. "I've had no sleep." Her voice was very light and calm.

"You picked a strange place for us to meet."

"Did I?" She looked unseeingly around; then looked at him. The blank despair in her face seemed to take notice, in the far distance, of him, and her face softened into sorrow. "I guess I did. I just thought—well, nobody's likely to overhear us, and I—I just couldn't think of any other place."

He had been about to suggest that they leave, but her white face and the fact of the rain checked him. "It's all right," he said. He took her arm, they started aimlessly up the steps. He realized that he was terribly hungry.

"I can't stay with you very long, because I left the kids alone. But I told Richard that I was coming out—that I was going to try to see you today."

They reached the first of a labyrinthine series of rooms, shifting and crackling with groups of people, with bright paintings above and around them, and stretching into the far distance, like tombstones with unreadable inscriptions. The people moved in waves, like tourists in a foreign graveyard. Occasionally, a single mourner, dreaming of some vanished relationship, stood alone in adoration or revery before a massive memorial—but they mainly evinced, moving restlessly here and there, the democratic gaiety. Cass and Eric moved in some panic through this crowd, trying to find a quieter place; through fields of French impressionists and cubists and cacophonous modern masters, into a smaller room dominated by an enormous painting, executed, principally, in red, before which two students, a girl and a boy, stood holding hands.

"Was it very bad, Cass? last night?"

He asked this in a low voice as they stood before a painting in cool yellow, of a girl with a long neck, in a yellow dress, with yellow hair.

"Yes." Her hood obscured her face; it was hot in the museum; she threw the hood back. Her hair was disheveled on the brow and trailing at the neck: she looked weary and old. "At first, it was awful because I hadn't realized how much I'd hurt him. He *can* suffer, after all," and she looked at Eric quickly, and looked away. They moved away from the yellow painting and faced another one, of a street with canals, somewhere in Europe. "And—no matter what has happened since, I *did* love him very much, he was my whole life, and he'll always be very important to me." She paused. "I suppose he made me feel terribly guilty. I didn't know that would happen. I didn't think it could—but—it did." She paused again, her shoulders sagging with a weary and proud defeat. Then she touched his hand. "I hate to tell you that—but I must try to tell you all of it. He frightened me, too, he frightened me because I was suddenly terribly afraid of losing the children and I cannot live without them." She moved one hand over her brow, uselessly pushing up her hair. "I didn't *have* to tell him; he didn't really know, he didn't suspect you at all, of course; he thought it was Vivaldo. I told him because I thought he had a right to know, that if we were going to—continue—together, we could begin again on a new basis, with everything clear between us. But I was wrong. Some things cannot *be* clear."

The boy and girl were coming to their side of the room. Cass and Eric crossed over, to stand beneath the red painting. "Or perhaps some things *are* clear, only one won't face those things. I don't know. . . . Anyway—I didn't think he'd threaten me, I didn't think he'd try to frighten me. If *he* were leaving *me*, if he were being unfaithful to *me*—unfaithful, what a word!—I don't think I'd try to hold him that way. I don't think I'd try to punish him. After all—he doesn't belong to me, nobody *belongs* to anybody."

They began walking again, down a long corridor, toward the ladies. "He said these terrible things to me, he said that he would sue me for divorce and take Paul and Michael away from me. And I listened to him, it didn't seem real. I didn't see how he could say those things, if he'd ever loved me. And I watched him. I could see that he was just saying these things to hurt me, to hurt me because he'd been hurt—like a child. And I saw that I'd loved him like that, like a child, and now the bill for all that dreaming had come in. How can one have dreamed so long? And I thought it was real. Now I don't know what's real. And I felt betrayed, I felt that I'd betrayed myself, and you, and everything—of value, everything, anyway, that one aspires to become, one doesn't want to be simply another grey, shapeless monster." They passed the cheerful ladies and Cass looked at them with wonder and with hatred. "Oh, God. It's a miserable world."

He said nothing, for he did not know what to say, and they continued their frightening promenade through the icy and angular jungle. The colors on the walls blared at them—like frozen music; he had the feeling that these rooms would never cease folding in on each other, that this labyrinth was eternal. And a sorrow entered him for Cass stronger than any love he had ever felt for her. She stood as erect as a soldier, moving straight ahead, and no bigger, as they said in the South, than a minute. He wished that he could rescue her, that it was within his power to rescue her and make her life less hard. But it was only love which could accomplish the miracle of making a life bearable—only love, and love itself mostly failed; and he had never loved her. He had used her to find out something about himself. And even this was not true. He had used her in the hope of avoiding a confrontation with himself which he had, nevertheless, and with a vengeance, been forced to endure. He felt as far removed from Cass now, in her terrible hour, as he was physically removed from Yves. Space howled between them like a flood. And whereas, with every moment now, Yves was coming closer, defeating all that water, and, as he approached, becoming more unreal, Cass was being driven farther away, was already in the unconquerable distance where she would be wrapped about by reality, unalterable forever, as a corpse is wrapped in a shroud. Therefore, his sorrow, now that he was helpless, luxuriously stretched and reached. "You'll never be a monster," he said, "never. What's happening is unspeakable, I know, but it can't defeat you. You can't go under, you've come too far."

"I think I know what I *won't* be. But what I'm going to become—that I don't see at all. And I'm afraid."

They passed not far from a weary guard, who looked blinded and dazzled, as though he had never been able to escape the light. Before them was a large and violent canvas in greens and reds and blacks, in blocks and circles, in daggerlike exclamations; it took a flying leap, as it were, from the wall, poised for the spectator's eyeballs; and at the same time it seemed to stretch endlessly and adoringly in on itself, reaching back into an unspeakable chaos. It was aggressively and superbly uncharming and unreadable, and might have been painted by a lonely and bloodthirsty tyrant, who had been cheated of his victims. "How horrible," Cass murmured, but she did not move; for they had this corner, except for the guard, to themselves.

"You said once," he said, "that you wanted to grow. Isn't that always frightening? Doesn't it always hurt?"

It was a question he was asking himself—of course; she turned toward him with a small, grateful smile, then turned to the painting again.

"I'm beginning to think," she said, "that growing just means learning more and more about anguish. That poison becomes your diet—you drink a little of it every day. Once you've seen it, you can't stop seeing it—that's the trouble. And it can, it can"—she passed her hand wearily over her brow again—"drive you mad." She walked away briefly, then returned to their corner. "You begin to see that you yourself, innocent, upright you, have contributed and do contribute to the misery of the world. Which will never end because we're what we are." He watched her face from which the youth was now, before his eyes, departing; her girlhood, at last, was falling away from her. Yet, her face did not seem precisely faded, or, for that matter, old. It looked scoured, there was something invincibly impersonal in it. "I watched Richard this morning and I thought to myself, as I've thought before, how much responsibility I must take for who he is, for what he's become." She put the tip of her finger against her lips for a moment, and closed her eyes. "I score him, after all, for being second-rate, for not having any real passion, any real daring, any real thoughts of his own. But he never did, he hasn't changed. I was delighted to give him *my* opinions; when I was with him, *I* had the daring and the passion. And he took them all, of course, how could he tell they weren't his? And I was happy because I'd succeeded so brilliantly, I thought, in making him what I wanted him to be. And of course he can't understand that it's just that triumph which is intolerable now. I've made myself—less than I might have been—by leading him to water which he doesn't know how to drink. It's not *for* him. But it's too late now." She smiled. "He doesn't have any real work to do, that's his trouble, that's the trouble with this whole unspeakable time and place. And I'm trapped. It doesn't do any good to blame the people or the time—one is oneself all those people. We *are* the time."

"You think that there isn't any hope for us?"

"Hope?" The word seemed to bang from wall to wall. "Hope? No, I don't think there's any hope. We're too empty here"—her eyes took in the Sunday crowd—"too empty—here." She touched her heart. "This isn't a country at all, it's a collection of football players and Eagle Scouts. Cowards. We think we're happy. We're not. We're doomed." She looked at her watch. "I must get back." She looked at him. "I only wanted to see you for a moment."

"What are you going to do?"

"I don't know yet. I'll let you know when I do. Richard's gone off, he may not be back for a couple of days. He wants to think, he says." She sighed. "I don't know." She said, carefully, looking at the painting, "I imagine, for the sake of the children, he'll decide that we should weather this, and stick together. I don't know if I want that or not, I don't know if I can bear it. But he won't sue me for divorce, he hasn't got the courage to name you as corespondent." Each to the other's astonishment, laughed. She looked at him again. "I can't come to you," she said.

There was a silence.

"No," he said, "you can't come to me."

"So it's really—though I'll see you again—good-bye."

"Yes," he said. Then, "It had to come."

"I know. I wish it hadn't come as it *has* come, but"—she smiled—"you did something very valuable for me, Eric, just the same. I hope you'll believe me. I hope you'll never forget it—what I've said. I'll never forget you."

"No," he said, and suddenly touched her arm. He felt that he was falling, falling out of the world. Cass was releasing him into chaos. He held on to her for the last time.

She looked into his face, and she said, "Don't be frightened, Eric. It will help me not to be frightened, if you're not. Do that for me." She touched his face, his lips. "Be a man. It can be borne, everything can be borne."

"Yes." But he stared at her still. "Oh, Cass. If only I could do more."

"You can't," she said, "do more than you've done. You've been my lover and now you're my friend." She took his hand in hers and stared down at it. "That was you you gave me for a little while. It was really you."

They turned away from the ringing canvas, into the crowds again, and walked slowly down the stairs. Cass put up her hood; he had never taken off his cap.

"When will I see you?" he asked. "Will you call me, or what?"

"I'll call you," she said, "tomorrow, or the day after." They walked to the doors and stopped. It was still raining.

They stood watching the rain. No one entered, no one left. Then a cab rolled up to the curb and stopped. Two women, wearing plastic hoods, fumbled with their umbrellas and handbags and change purses, preparing to step out of the cab.

Without a word, Eric and Cass rushed out into the rain, to the curb. The women ran heavily into the museum. Eric opened the cab door.

"Good-bye, Eric." She leaned forward and kissed him. He held her. Her face was wet but he did not know whether it was rainwater or tears. She pulled away and got into the cab.

"I'll be expecting your call," he said.

"Yes. I'll call you. Be good."

"God bless you, Cass. So long."

"So long."

He closed the door on her and the cab moved away, down the long, blank, shining street.

Darkness was beginning to fall. The lights of the city would soon begin to blaze; it would not be long, now, before these lights would carry his name. An errant wind, a cold wind, ruffled the water in the gutter at Eric's feet. Then everything was still, with a bleakness that was almost comforting.

Ida heard Vivaldo's step and rushed to open the door for

him, just as he began fumbling for his key. She threw back her head and laughed.

"You look like you narrowly escaped a lynching, dad. And where did you get that coat?" She looked him up and down, and laughed again. "Come on in, you poor, drowned rat, before the posse gets here."

She closed the door behind him and he took off Eric's coat and hung it in the bathroom and dried his dripping hair. "Do we have anything to eat in this house?"

"Yes. Are you hungry?"

"Starving." He came out of the bathroom. "What did Richard have to say?"

She was in the kitchen with her back to him, digging in the cupboard beneath the sink where the pots and pans were kept. She came up with a frying pan; looked at him briefly; and this look made him feel that Richard had managed, somehow, to frighten her.

"Nothing very pleasant. But it's not important now." She put the pan on the stove and opened the icebox door. "I think you and Cass were his whole world. And now both of you have treated him so badly that he doesn't know where he is." She took tomatoes and lettuce and a package of pork chops out of the icebox and put them on the table. "He tried to make me angry—but I just felt terribly sad. He'd been so hurt." She paused. "Men are so helpless when they're hurt."

He came up behind her and kissed her. "Are they?"

She returned his kiss, and said gravely, "Yes. You don't believe it's happening. You think that there must have been some mistake."

"How wise you are!" he said.

"I'm not wise. I'm just a poor, ignorant, black girl, trying to get along."

He laughed. "If you're just a poor, ignorant, black girl, trying to get along, I'd sure hate like hell to tangle with one who'd made it."

"But you wouldn't know. You think women tell the truth. They don't. They can't." She stepped away from him, busy with another saucepan and water and flame. And she gave him a mocking look. "Men wouldn't *love* them if they did."

"You just don't like *men*."

She said, "I can't say that I've met very many. Not what *I* call men."

"I hope I'm one of them."

"Oh, there's hope for you," she said, humorously, "you might make it yet."

"That's probably," he said, "the nicest thing you've ever said to me."

She laughed, but there was something sad and lonely in the sound. There was something sad and lonely in her whole aspect, which obscurely troubled him. And he began to watch her closely, without quite knowing that he was doing so.

She said, "Poor Vivaldo. I've given you a hard time, haven't I, baby?"

"I'm not complaining," he said, carefully.

"No," she said, half to herself, running her fingers thoughtfully through a bowl of dry rice, "I'll say that much for you. I dish it out, but you sure as hell can take it."

"You think maybe," he said, "that I take too much?"

She frowned. She dumped the rice into the boiling water. "Maybe. Hell, I don't think women know what they want, not a damn one of them. Look at Cass—do you want a drink," she asked, suddenly, "before dinner?"

"Sure." He took down the bottle and the glasses and took out the ice. "What do you mean—women don't know what they want? Don't *you* know what you want?"

She had taken down the great salad bowl and was slicing tomatoes into it; it seemed that she did not dare be still. "Sure. I thought I did. I was sure once. Now I'm not so sure." She paused. "And I only found that out—last night." She looked up at him humorously, gave a little shrug, and sliced savagely into another tomato.

He set her drink beside her. "What's happened to confuse you?"

She laughed—again he heard that striking melancholy. "Living with you! Would you believe it? I fell for that jive."

He dragged his work stool in from the other room and teetered on it, watching her, a little above her.

"*What* jive, sweetheart, are you talking about?"

She sipped her drink. "That love jive, sweetheart. Love, love, love!"

His heart jumped up; they watched each other; she smiled a rueful smile. "Are you trying to tell me—without my having to ask you or anything—that you love me?"

"Am I? I guess I am." Then she dropped the knife and sat perfectly still, looking down, the fingers of one hand drumming on the table. Then she clasped her hands, the fingers of one hand playing with the ruby-eyed snake ring, slipping it half-off, slipping it on.

"But—that's wonderful." He took her hand. It lay cold and damp and lifeless in his. A kind of wind of terror shook him for an instant. "Isn't it? It makes me very happy—*you* make me very happy."

She took his hand and rested her cheek against it. "Do I, Vivaldo?" Then she rose and walked to the sink to wash the lettuce.

He followed her, standing beside her, and looking into her closed, averted face. "What's the matter, Ida?" He put one hand on her waist; she shivered, as if in revulsion, and he let his hand fall. "Tell me, please."

"It's nothing," she said, trying to sound light about it, "I told you, I'm in a bad mood. It's probably the time of the month."

"Now, come on, baby, don't try to cop out that way."

She was tearing the lettuce and washing it, and placing it in a towel. She continued with this in silence until she had torn off the last leaf. She was trying to avoid his eyes; he had never seen her at such a loss before. Again, he was frightened. "What *is* it?"

"Leave me alone, Vivaldo. We'll talk about it later."

"We will *not* talk about it later. We'll talk about it now."

The rice came to a boil and she moved hastily away from him to turn down the flame.

"My Mama always told me, honey, you can't cook and talk."

"Well, stop *cooking*!"

She gave him that look, coquettish, wide-eyed, and amused, which he had known so long. But now there was something desperate in it; had there always been something desperate in this look? "But you *said* you were hungry!"

"Stop that. It's not funny, okay?" He led her to the table.

"I want to know what's happening. Is it something Richard said?"

"I am not trying to be funny. I *would* like to feed you." Then, with a sudden burst of anger, "It's got nothing to do with Richard. What, after all, can Richard *say?*"

He had had some wild idea that Richard had made up a story about himself and Eric, and he had been on the point of denying it. He recovered, hoping that she had not been aware of his panic; but his panic increased.

He said, very gently, "Well, then, what *is* it, Ida?"

She said, wearily, "Oh, it's too many things, it goes too far back, I can never make you understand it, never."

"Try me. You say you love me. Why can't you trust me?"

She laughed. "Oh. You think life is so simple." She looked up at him and laughed again And this laughter was unbearable. He wanted to strike her, not in anger, only to make the laughter stop; but he forced himself to stand still, and did nothing. "Because—I know you're older than I am—I always think of you as being much younger. I always think of you as being a very nice boy who doesn't know what the score is, who'll maybe never find out. And I don't want to be the one to teach you."

She said the last in a venomous undertone, looking down again at her hands.

"Okay. Go on."

"Go *on?*" She looked up at him in a strange, wild way. "You want me to go *on?*"

He said, "Please stop tormenting me, Ida. Please go on."

"*Am* I tormenting you?"

"You want it in writing?"

Her face changed, she rose from the table and walked back to the stove. "I'm sure it must seem like that to you," she said—very humbly. She moved to the sink and leaned against it, watching him. "But I wasn't trying to torment you—whenever I did. I don't think that I thought about that at all. In fact, I know I didn't, I've never had the time." She watched his face. "I've just realized lately that I've bitten off more than I can chew, certainly more than I can swallow." He winced. She broke off suddenly: "Are you sure you're a man, Vivaldo?"

He said, "I've got to be sure."

"Fair enough," she said. She walked to the stove and put a light under the frying pan, walked to the table and opened the meat. She began to dust it with salt and pepper and paprika, and chopped garlic into it, near the bone. He took a swallow of his drink, which had no taste whatever; he splashed more whiskey into his glass. "When Rufus died, something happened to me," she said. She sounded now very quiet and weary, as though she were telling someone else's story; also, as though she herself, with a faint astonishment, were hearing it for the first time. But it was yet more astonishing that he now began to listen to a story he had always known, but never dared believe. "I can't explain it. Rufus had always been the world to me. I loved him."

"So did I," he said—too quickly, irrelevantly; and for the first time it occurred to him that, possibly, he was a liar; had never loved Rufus at all, but had only feared and envied him.

"I don't need your credentials, Vivaldo," she said.

She watched the frying pan critically, waiting for it to become hot enough, then dropped in a little oil. "The point, anyway, at the moment, is that *I* loved him. He was my big brother, but as soon as I knew anything, I knew that I was stronger than he was. He was nice, he was really very nice, no matter what any of you might have thought of him later. None of you, anyway, knew anything about him, you didn't know how."

"You often say that," he said, wearily. "Why?"

"How could you—how *can* you?—dreaming the way you dream? You people think you're free. That means you think you've got something other people want—or need. Shit." She grinned wryly and looked at him. "And you *do*, in a way. But it isn't what you think it is. And you're going to find out, too, just as soon as some of those other people start getting what you've got now." She shook her head. "I feel sorry for them. I feel sorry for you. I even feel kind of sorry for myself, because God knows I've often wished you'd left me where I was——"

"Down there in the jungle?" he taunted.

"Yes. Down there in the jungle, black and funky—and myself."

His small anger died down as quickly as it had flared up. "Well," he said, quietly, "sometimes I'm nostalgic, too, Ida." He watched her dark, lonely face. For the first time, he had an intimation of how she would look when she grew old. "What I've never understood," he said, finally, "is that you always accuse me of making a thing about your color, of penalizing you. But you do the same thing. You always make me feel white. Don't you think that hurts me? You lock me out. And all I want is for you to be a part of me, for me to be a part of you. I wouldn't give a damn if you were striped like a zebra."

She laughed. "Yes, you would, really. But you say the cutest things." Then, "If I lock you out, as you put it, it's mainly to protect you—"

"Protect me from what? and I don't *want* to be protected. Besides——"

"Besides?"

"I don't believe you. I don't believe that's why. You want to protect yourself. You want to hate me because I'm white, because it's easier for you that way."

"I don't hate you."

"Then why do you always bring it up? What *is* it?"

She stirred the rice, which was almost ready, found a collander, and placed it in the sink. Then she turned to face him.

"This all began because I said that you people—"

"Listen to yourself. *You people!*"

"—didn't know anything about Rufus—"

"Because we're white."

"No. Because he was black."

"Oh. I give *up*. And, anyway, why must we always end up talking about Rufus?"

"I had started to tell you something," she said, quietly; and watched him.

He swallowed some more of his whiskey, and lit a cigarette. "True. Please go on."

"*Because* I'm black," she said, after a moment, and sat at the table near him, "I know more about what happened to my brother than you can ever know. I watched it happen— from the beginning. I was there. He shouldn't have ended up the way he did. That's what's been so hard for me to accept.

He was a very beautiful boy. Most people aren't beautiful, I knew that right away. I watched them, and I knew. But he didn't because he was so much nicer than I." She paused, and the silence grumbled with the sound of the frying pan and the steady sound of the rain. "He loved our father, for example. He really loved him. I didn't. He was just a loud-mouthed, broken-down man, who liked to get drunk and hang out in barber shops—well, maybe he didn't like it but that was all he could find to do, except work like a dog, for nothing—and play the guitar on the week ends for his only son." She paused again, smiling. "There was something very nice about those week ends, just the same. I can still see Daddy, his belly hanging out, strumming on that guitar and trying to teach Rufus some down-home song and Rufus grinning at him and making fun of him a little, really, but very nicely, and singing with him. I bet my father was never happier, all the days of his life, than when he was singing for Rufus. He's got no one to sing to now. He was so proud of him. He bought Rufus his first set of drums."

She was not locking him out now; he felt, rather, that he was being locked in. He listened, seeing, or trying to see, what she saw, and feeling something of what she felt. But he wondered, just the same, how much her memory had filtered out. And he wondered what Rufus must have looked like in those days, with all his bright, untried brashness, and all his hopes intact.

She was silent for a moment, leaning forward, looking down, her elbows on her knees and the fingers of one hand restlessly playing with her ring.

"When Rufus died, all the light went out of that house, all of it. That was why I couldn't stay there, I knew I couldn't stay there, I'd grow old like they were, suddenly, and I'd end up like all the other abandoned girls who can't find anyone to protect them. I'd always known I couldn't end up like that, I'd always known it. I'd counted on Rufus to get me out of there—I knew he'd do anything in the world for me, just like I would for him. It hadn't occurred to me that it wouldn't happen. I *knew* it would happen."

She rose and returned to the stove and took the rice off the fire and poured it into the collander and ran water over it; put water in the saucepan and put it back on the fire, placing the collander on top of it and covering the rice with a towel. She turned the chops over. Then she sat down.

"When we saw Rufus's body, I can't tell you. My father stared at it, he stared at it, and stared at it. It didn't look like Rufus, it was—terrible—from the water, and he must have *struck* something going down, or in the water, because he was so broken and lumpy—and ugly. *My* brother. And my father stared at it—at it—and he said, They don't leave a man much, do they? His own father was beaten to death with a hammer by a railroad guard. And they brought his father home like that. My mother got frightened, she wanted my father to pray. And he said, he shouted it at the top of his lungs, Pray? *Who*, pray? I bet you, if I ever get anywhere near that white devil you call God, I'll tear my son and my father out of his white hide! Don't you never say the word Pray to me again, woman, not if you want to *live*. Then he started to cry. I'll never forget it. Maybe I hadn't loved him before, but I loved him then. That was the last time he ever shouted, he hasn't raised his voice since. He just sits there, he doesn't even drink any more. Sometimes he goes out and listens to those fellows who make speeches on 125th Street and Seventh Avenue. He says he just wants to live long enough—long enough——."

Vivaldo said, to break the silence which abruptly roared around them, "To be paid back."

"Yes," she said. "And I felt that way, too."

She walked over to the stove again.

"I felt that I'd been robbed. And I *had* been robbed—of the only hope I had. By a group of people too cowardly even to know what they had done. And it didn't seem to me that they deserved any better than what they'd given me. I didn't care what happened to them, just so they suffered. I didn't really much care what happened to me. But I wasn't going to let what happened to Rufus, and what was happening all around me, happen to me. I was going to get through the world, and get what I needed out of it, no matter how."

He thought, *Oh, it's coming now*, and felt a strange, bitter relief. He finished his drink and lit another cigarette, and watched her.

She looked over at him, as though to make certain that he was still listening.

"Nothing you've said so far," he said, carefully, "seems to have much to do with being black. Except for what you make out of it. But nobody can help you there."

She sighed sharply, in a kind of rage. "That could be true. But it's too easy for you to say that."

"Ida, a lot of what you've had to say, ever since we met, has been—too easy." He watched her. "Hasn't it?" And then, "Sweetheart, suffering doesn't *have* a color. Does it? Can't we step out of this nightmare? I'd give anything, I'd give anything if we could." He crossed to her and took her in his arms. "Please, Ida, whatever has to be done, to set us free— let's do that."

Her eyes were full of tears. She looked down. "Let me finish my story."

"Nothing you say will make any difference."

"You don't know that. Are you afraid?"

He stepped back. "No." Then, "Yes. Yes. I can't take any more of your revenge."

"Well, I can't either. Let me finish."

"Come away from the stove. I can't eat now."

"Everything will be ruined."

"Let it be ruined. Come and sit down."

He wished that he were better prepared for this moment, that he had not been with Eric, that his hunger would vanish, that his fear would drop, and love lend him a transcendent perception and concentration. But he knew himself to be physically weak and tired, not drunk, but far from sober; part of his troubled mind was far away, gorging on the conundrum of himself.

She put out the fire under the frying pan and came and sat at the table. He pushed her drink toward her, but she did not touch it.

"I knew there wasn't any hope uptown. A lot of those men, they got their little deals going and all that, but they don't really have anything, Mr. Charlie's not going to let them get but so far. Those that really do have something would never have any use for me; I'm too dark for them, they see girls like me on Seventh Avenue every day. I knew what they would do to me."

And now he knew that he did not want to hear the rest of her story. He thought of himself on Seventh Avenue; perhaps he had never left. He thought of the day behind him, of Eric and Cass and Richard, and felt himself now being sucked into the rapids of a mysterious defeat.

"There was only one thing for me to do, as Rufus used to say, and that was to hit the A train. So I hit it. Nothing was clear in my mind at first. I used to see the way white men watched me, like dogs. And I thought about what I could do to them. How I hated them, the way they looked, and the things they'd say, all dressed up in their damn white skin, and their clothes just so, and their little weak, white pricks jumping in their drawers. You could do any damn thing with them if you just led them along, because they wanted to do something dirty and they knew that you knew how. All black people knew that. Only, the polite ones didn't say dirty. They said real. I used to wonder what in the world they did in bed, white people I mean, between themselves, to get them so sick. Because they *are* sick, and I'm telling you something that I know. I had a couple of girl friends and we used to go out every once in a while with some of these shitheads. But they were smart, too, they knew that they were white, and they could always go back home, and there wasn't a damn thing you could do about it. I thought to myself, Shit, this scene is not for me. Because I didn't want their little change, I didn't want to be at their mercy. I wanted them to be at mine."

She sipped her drink.

"Well, you were calling me all the time about that time, but I didn't really think about you very much, not seriously anyway. I liked you, but I certainly hadn't planned to get hung up on a white boy who didn't have any money—in fact, I hadn't planned to get hung up on anybody. But I liked you, and the few times I saw you it was a kind of—*relief*—from all those other, horrible people. You were really nice to me. You didn't have that look in your eyes. You just acted like a real sweet boy and maybe, without knowing it, I got to depend on it. Sometimes I'd just see you for a minute or so, we'd just

have a cup of coffee or something like that, and I'd run off—
but I felt better, I was kind of protected from their eyes and
their hands. I was feeling so sick most of the time through
there. I didn't want my father to know what I was doing and
I tried not to think about Rufus. That was when I decided
that I ought to try to sing, I'd do it for Rufus, and then all
the rest wouldn't matter. I would have settled the score. But
I thought I needed somebody to help me, and it was then,
just at the time that I—" She stopped and looked down at
her hands. "I think I wanted to go to bed with you, not to
have an affair with you, but just to go to bed with somebody
that I *liked*. Somebody who wasn't old, because all those men
are old, no matter how young they are. I'd only been to bed
with one boy I liked, a boy on our block, but he got religion,
and so it all stopped and he got married. And there weren't
any other colored men, I was afraid, because look what happened to them, they got cut down like grass! And I didn't see
any way out, except—finally—you. And Ellis."

Then she stopped. They listened to the rain. He had finished his drink and he picked up hers. She looked down, he
had the feeling that she could not look up, and he was afraid
to touch her. And the silence stretched; he longed for it to
end, and dreaded it; there was nothing he could say.

She straightened her shoulders and reached out for a cigarette. He lit it for her.

"Richard knows about me and Ellis," she said in a matter-
of-fact tone, "but that's not why I'm telling you. I'm telling
you because I'm trying to bring this whole awful thing to a
halt. If that's possible."

She paused. She said, "Let me have a sip of your drink,
please."

"It's yours," he said. He gave it to her and poured himself
another one.

She blew a cloud of smoke toward the ceiling. "It's funny
the way things work. If it hadn't been for you, I don't think
Ellis would ever have got so hung up on me. *He* saw, better
than I did, that I really liked you and that meant that I could
really like somebody and so why not him, since he could give
me so much more? And I thought so, too, that it was a kind
of dirty trick for life to play on me, for me to like you better

than I liked him. And, after all, the chances of its lasting were just about equal, only with him, if I played it right, I might have something to show for it when it was all over. And he was smart, he didn't bug me about it, he said, Sure, he wanted me but he was going to help me, regardless, and the one thing had nothing to do with the other. And he did—he was very nice to me, in his way, he was as good as his word, he was nicer to me than anyone had ever been before. He used to take me out to dinner, to places where nobody would know him or where it wouldn't matter if they did. A lot of the time we went up to Harlem, or if he knew I was sitting in somewhere, he'd drop in. He didn't seem to be trying to hype me, not even when he talked about his wife and his kids—you know? He sounded as though he really *was* lonely. And, after all, I owed him a lot—and—it was nice to be treated that way and to know the cat had enough money to take you anywhere, and—ah! well, it started, I guess I'd always known it was going to start, and then, once it started, I didn't think I could stand it but I didn't know how to stop it. Because it's one thing for a man to be doing all these things for you while you're not having an affair with him and it's another thing for him to be doing them after you've *stopped* having an affair with him. And I had to go on, I had to get up there on top, where maybe I could begin to breathe. But I saw why he'd never been upset about you. He really is smart. He was *glad* I was with you, he told me so; he was glad I had another boy friend because it made it easier for him. It meant I wouldn't make any scenes, I wouldn't think I'd fallen in love with him. It gave him another kind of power over me in a way because he knew that I was afraid of your finding out and the more afraid I got, the harder it was to refuse him. Do you understand that?"

"Yes," he said, slowly, "I think I understand that."

They stared at each other. She dropped her eyes.

"But, you know," she said, slowly, "I think you knew all the time."

He said nothing. She persisted, in a low voice, "Didn't you?"

"You told me that you weren't," he said.

"But did you believe me?"

He stammered: "I—I *had* to believe you."

"Why?"

Again, he said nothing.

"Because you were afraid?"

"Yes," he said at last. "I was afraid."

"It was easier to let it happen than to try to stop it?"

"Yes."

"Why?"

Her eyes searched his face. It was his turn to look away.

"I used to hate you for that sometimes," she said, "for pretending to believe me because you didn't want to know what was happening to me."

"I was trying to do what I thought you wanted! I was afraid that you would *leave* me—you *told* me that you would!" He rose and stalked the kitchen, his hands in his pockets, water standing in his eyes. "I worried about it, I thought about it—but I put it out of my mind. You had made it a matter of my trusting you—don't you remember?"

He looked at her with hatred, standing above her; but she seemed to be beyond his anger.

"Yes, I remember. But you didn't start trusting me. You just gave in to me and pretended to trust me."

"What would you have done if I had called you on it?"

"I don't know. But if you had faced it, I would have had to face it—as long as you were pretending, I had to pretend. I'm not blaming you. I'm just telling it to you like it is." She looked up at him. "I saw that it could go on a long time like that," and her lips twisted wearily. "I sort of had you where I wanted you. I'd got my revenge. Only, it wasn't *you* I was after. It wasn't *you* I was trying to beat."

"It was Ellis?"

She sighed and put one hand to her face. "Oh. I don't know, I really don't know what I was thinking. Sometimes I'd leave Ellis and I'd come and find you here—like my dog or my cat, I used to think sometimes, just waiting. And I'd be afraid you'd be here and I'd be afraid you'd gone out, afraid you'd ask me, *really* ask me where I'd been, and afraid you wouldn't. Sometimes you'd try, but I could always stop you, I could see in your eyes when you were frightened. I hated that look and I hated me and I hated you. I could see

how white men got that look they so often had when they
looked at me; somebody had beat the shit out of them, had
scared the shit out of them, long ago. And now I was doing
it to you. And it made it hard for me when you touched me,
especially—" She stopped, picked up her drink, tasted it, set
it down. "I couldn't stand Ellis. You don't know what it's
like, to have a man's body over you if you can't stand that
body. And it was worse now, since I'd been with you, than it
had ever been before. Before, I used to watch them wriggle
and listen to them grunt, and, God, they were so solemn
about it, sweating yellow pigs, and so *vain*, like that sad little
piece of meat was making miracles happen, and I guess it was,
for them—and I wasn't touched at all, I just wished I could
make them come down lower. Oh, yes, I found out all about
white people, *that's* what they were like, alone, where only a
black girl could see them, and the black girl might as well
have been blind as far as they were concerned. Because they
knew they were white, baby, and they ruled the world. But
now it was different, sometimes when Ellis put his hands on
me, it was all I could do not to scream, not to vomit. It had
got to me, it had got *to* me, and I felt that I was being pumped
full of—I don't know what, not poison exactly, but dirt, *waste*,
filth, and I'd never be able to get it out of me, never be able
to get that stink out of me. And sometimes, sometimes, sometimes—" She covered her mouth, her tears spilled down over
her hand, over the red ring. He could not move. "Oh, Lord
Jesus. I've done terrible things. Oh, Lord. Sometimes. And
then I'd come home to you. He always had that funny little
smile when I finally left him, that smile he has, I've seen it
many times now, when he's outsmarted somebody who
doesn't know it yet. He can't help it, that's him, it was as
though he were saying, 'Now that I'm through with you, have
a nice time with Vivaldo. And give him my regards.' And,
funny, funny—I couldn't hate him. I saw what he was doing,
but I couldn't hate him. I wondered what it felt like, to be
like that, not to have any real feelings at all, except to say,
Well, now, let's do this and now let's do that and now let's
eat and now let's fuck and now let's go. And do that all your
life. And then I'd come home and look at you. But I'd bring
him with me. It was as though I was dirty, and you had to

wash me, each time. And I knew you never could, no matter how hard we tried, and I didn't hate him but I hated you. And I hated me."

"Why didn't you stop it, Ida? You could have stopped it, you didn't have to go on with it."

"Stop it and go where? Stop it and do what? No, I thought to myself, Well, you're in it now, girl, close your eyes and grit your teeth and get through it. It'll be worth it when it's over. And that's why I've been working so hard. To get away."

"And what about me? What about us?"

She looked up at him with a bitter smile. "What about us? I hoped I'd get through this and then we'd see. But last night something happened, I couldn't take it any more. We were up at *Small's Paradise*——"

"Last night? You and Ellis?"

"Yes. *And* Cass."

"Cass?"

"I asked her to come and have a drink with me."

"Did you leave together?"

"No."

"So that's why she got in late last night." He looked at her. "It's a good thing I didn't come home then, isn't it?"

"What would you have done," she cried, "if you had? You'd have sat at that typewriter for a while and then you'd have played some music and then you'd have gone out and got drunk. And when I came home, no matter *when* I came home, you'd have believed any lie I told you because you were afraid not to."

"What a bitch you are," he said.

"Yes," she said, with a terrible sobriety, "I know." She lit a cigarette. The hand that held the match trembled. "But I'm trying not to be. I don't know if there's any hope for me or not." She dropped the match on the table. "He made me sing with the band. They didn't really want me to, and I didn't want to, but they didn't want to say No, to him. So I sang. And of course I knew some of the musicians and some of them had known Rufus. Baby, if musicians don't want to work with you, they sure can make you know it. I sang *Sweet Georgia Brown*, and something else. I wanted to get off that stand in the worst way. When it was over, and the people were clapping, the bass player whispered to me, he said, 'You black white man's whore, don't you never let me catch you on Seventh Avenue, you hear? I'll tear your little black pussy *up*.' And the other musicians could hear him, and they were grinning. 'I'm going to do it twice, once for every black man you castrate every time you walk, and once for your poor brother, because I loved that stud. And he going to thank me for it, too, you can bet on that, black girl.' And he slapped me on the ass, hard, everybody could see it and, you know, those people up there aren't fools, and before I could get away, he grabbed my hand and raised it, and he said, 'She's the *champion*, ain't she, folks? Talk about walking, this girl ain't *started* walking!' And he dropped my hand, hard, like it was too hot or too dirty, and I almost fell off the stand. And everybody laughed and cheered, they knew what he meant, and I did, too. And I got back to the table. Ellis was grinning like it was all a big joke. And it was. On me."

She rose, and poured herself a fresh drink.

"Then he took me to that place he has, way over on the East River. I kept wondering what I was going to do. I didn't know what to do. I watched his face in the taxicab. He put his hand on my leg. And he tried to take my hand. But I couldn't move. I kept thinking of what that black man had said to me, and his face when he said it, and I kept thinking of Rufus, and I kept thinking of you. It was like a merry-go-round, all these faces just kept going around in my mind. And a song kept going around in my head, *Oh, Lord, is it I?* And there he sat, next to me, puffing on his cigar. The funny thing was that I knew if I really started crying or pleading, he'd take me home. He can't stand scenes. But I couldn't even do that. And God knows I wanted to get home, I hoped you wouldn't be here, so I could just crawl under the sheets and die. And, that way, when you came home, I could tell you everything before you came to bed, and—maybe—but, no, we were going to his place and I felt that I deserved it. I felt that I couldn't fall much lower, I might as well go all the way and get it over with. And then we'd see, if there was anything left of me after that, we'd see." She threw down about two fingers of whiskey and immediately poured herself another drink. "There's always further to fall, always, always." She moved from the table, holding her glass, and leaned against the ice-box door. "And I did everything he wanted, I let him have his way. It wasn't me. It wasn't me." She gestured aimlessly with her glass, tried to drink from it, dropped it, and suddenly fell on her knees beside the table, her hands against her belly, weeping.

Stupidly, he picked up the glass, afraid that she would cut herself. She was kneeling in the spilt whiskey, which had stained the edges of her skirt. He dropped the broken glass in the brown paper bag they used for garbage. He was afraid to go near her, he was afraid to touch her, it was almost as though she had told him that she had been infected with the plague. His arms trembled with his revulsion, and every act of the body seemed unimaginably vile. And yet, at the same time, as he stood helpless and stupid in the kitchen which had abruptly become immortal, or which, in any case, would surely live as long as he lived, and follow him everywhere, his heart began to beat with a newer, stonier anguish, which destroyed the distance called pity and placed him, very nearly, in her body, beside that table, on the dirty floor. The single yellow light beat terribly down on them both. He went to her, resigned and tender and helpless, her sobs seeming to make his belly sore. And, nevertheless, for a moment, he could not touch her, he did not know how. He thought, unwillingly, of all the whores, black whores, with whom he had coupled, and what he had hoped for from them, and he was gripped in a kind of retrospective nausea. What would they see when they looked into each other's faces again? "Come on, Ida," he whispered, "come on, Ida. Get up," and at last he touched her shoulders, trying to force her to rise. She tried to check her sobs, she put both hands on the table.

"I'm all right," she murmured, "give me a handkerchief."

He knelt beside her and thrust his handkerchief, warm and wadded, but fairly clean, into her hand. She blew her nose. He kept his arm around her shoulder. "Stand up," he said. "Go wash your face. Would you like some coffee?"

She nodded her head, Yes, and slowly rose. He rose with her. She kept her head down and moved swiftly, drunkenly, past him, into the bathroom. She locked the door. He had the spinning sensation of having been through all this before.

He lit a flame under the coffee pot, making a mental note to break down the bathroom door if she were silent too long, if she were gone too long. But he heard the water running, and, beneath it, the sound of the rain. He ate a pork chop, greedily, with a piece of bread, and drank a glass of milk; for he was trembling, it had to be because of hunger. Otherwise, for the moment, he felt nothing. The coffee pot, now beginning to growl, was real, and the blue fire beneath it and the pork chops in the pan, and the milk which seemed to be turning sour in his belly. The coffee cups, as he thoughtfully washed them, were real, and the water which ran into them, over his heavy, long hands. Sugar and milk were real, and he set them on the table, another reality, and cigarettes were real, and he lit one. Smoke poured from his nostrils and a detail that he needed for his novel, which he had been searching for for months, fell, neatly and vividly, like the tumblers of a lock, into place in his mind. It seemed impossible that he should not have thought of it before: it illuminated, justified, clarified everything. He would work on it later tonight; he thought that perhaps he should make a note of it now; he started toward his work table. The telephone rang. He picked up the receiver at once, stealthily, as though someone were ill or sleeping in the house, and whispered into it, "Hello?"

"Hello, Vivaldo. It's Eric."

"Eric!" He was overjoyed. He looked quickly toward the bathroom door. "How did things go?"

"Well. Cass is beautiful, as you know. But life is grim."

"As I know. Has anything been decided?"

"Not really, no. She just called me a few minutes ago—I haven't been home long. Oh, thanks for your note. She thinks that she might go up to New England for a little while, with the kids. Richard hasn't come home yet."

"Where is he?"

"He's probably out getting drunk."

"Who with?"

"Well, Ellis, maybe—"

They both halted at the name. The wires hummed. Vivaldo looked at the bathroom door again.

"You knew about that, Eric, didn't you, this morning."

"Knew about what?"

He dropped his voice lower, and struggled to say it: "Ida. You knew about Ida and Ellis. Cass told you."

There was silence for a moment. "Yes." Then, "Who told *you*?"

"Ida."

"Oh. Poor Vivaldo." After a moment: "But it's better that way, isn't it? I didn't think that *I* was the one to tell you—especially—well, especially not this morning."

Vivaldo was silent.

"Vivaldo—?"

"Yes?"

"Don't you think I was right? Are you sore at me?"

"Don't be silly. Never in this world. It's—much better this way." He cleared his throat, slowly, deliberately, for he suddenly wanted to weep.

"Vivaldo, it's a terrible time to ask you, I know—but do you think it's at all likely that you—and Ida—will feel up to coming over to my joint tomorrow night, or the night after?"

"What's up?"

"Yves will be here in the morning. I know he'd like to meet my friends."

"That was the cablegram, huh?"

"Yes."

"Are you glad, Eric?"

"I guess so. Right now, I'm just scared. I don't know whether to try to sleep—it's so *early*, but it feels like midnight—or go to a movie, or what."

"I'd love to go to a movie with you. But—I guess I can't."

"No. When will you let me know about tomorrow?"

"I'll call you later tonight. Or I'll call you in the morning."

"Okay. If you call in the morning and miss, call back. I've got to go to Idlewild."

"What time is he getting in?"

"Oh, at dawn, practically. Naturally. Seven A.M., something convenient like that."

Vivaldo laughed. "Poor Eric."

"Yes. Life's catching up with us. Good night, Vivaldo."

"Good night, Eric."

He hung up, smiling thoughtfully, switched on his work-table lamp, and scribbled his note. Then he walked into the kitchen, turned off the gas, and poured the coffee. He knocked on the bathroom door.

"Ida? Your coffee's getting cold."

"Thank you. I'll be right out."

He sat down on his work stool, and, presently, here she came, scrubbed and quiet, looking like a child. He forced himself to look into her eyes; he did not know what she would see in them; he did not know what he felt.

"Vivaldo," she said, standing, speaking quickly, "I just want you to know that I wouldn't have been with you so long, and wouldn't have given you such a hard time, if"—she faltered, and held on with both hands to the back of a chair—"I didn't love you. That's why I had to tell you everything I've told you. I mean—I know I'm giving you a tough row to hoe." She sat down, and picked up her coffee. "I had to say that while I could."

She had the advantage of him, for he did not know what to say. He realized this with shame and fear. He wanted to say, *I love you*, but the words would not come. He wondered what her lips would taste like now, what her body would be like for him now: he watched her quiet face. She seemed utterly passive; yet, she was waiting, in a despair which steadily chilled and hardened, for some word, some touch, of his. And he could not find himself, could not summon or concentrate enough of himself to make any sign at all. He stared into his cup, noting that black coffee was not black, but deep brown. Not many things in the world were really black, not even the night, not even the mines. And the light was not white, either, even the palest light held within itself some hint of its origins, in fire. He thought to himself that he had at last got what he wanted, the truth out of Ida, or the true Ida; and he did not know how he was going to live with it.

He said, "Thank you for telling me—everything you've told me. I know it wasn't easy." She said nothing. She made a faint, steamy sound as she sipped her coffee, and this sound was unaccountably, inexpressibly annoying. "And forgive me, now, if I don't seem to know just what to say, I'm maybe a little—stunned." He looked over at her, and a wilderness of anger, pity, love, and contempt and lust all raged together in him. She, too, was a whore; how bitterly he had been betrayed! "I'm not trying to deny anything you've said, but just the same, there are a lot of things I didn't—don't—understand, not really. Bear with me, please give me a little time—"

"Vivaldo," she said, wearily, "just one thing. I don't want you to be *understanding*. I don't want you to be kind, okay?" She looked directly at him, and an unnameable heat and tension flashed violently alive between them, as close to hatred as it was to love. She softened and reached out, and touched his hand. "Promise me that."

"I promise you that," he said. And then, furiously, "You seem to forget that I love you."

They stared at each other. Suddenly, he reached out and pulled her to him, trembling, with tears starting up behind his eyes, burning and blinding, and covered her face with kisses, which seemed to freeze as they fell. She clung to him; with a sigh she buried her face in his chest. There was nothing erotic in it; they were like two weary children. And it was she who was comforting him. Her long fingers stroked his back, and he began, slowly, with a horrible, strangling sound, to weep, for she was stroking his innocence out of him.

By and by, he was still. He rose, and went to the bathroom and washed his face, and then sat down at his work table. She put on a record by Mahalia Jackson, *In the Upper Room*, and sat at the window, her hands in her lap, looking out over the sparkling streets. Much, much later, while he was still working and she slept, she turned in her sleep, and she called his name. He paused, waiting, staring at her, but she did not move again, or speak again. He rose, and walked to the window. The rain had ceased, in the black-blue sky a few stars were scattered, and the wind roughly jostled the clouds along.

2

THE SUN struck, on steel, on bronze, on stone, on glass, on the gray water far beneath them, on the turret tops and the flashing windshields of crawling cars, on the incredible highways, stretching and snarling and turning for mile upon mile upon mile, on the houses, square and high, low and gabled, and on their howling antennae, on the sparse, weak trees, and on those towers, in the distance, of the city of New York. The plane tilted, dropped and rose, and the whole earth slanted, now leaning against the windows of the plane, now dropping out of sight. The sky was a hot, blank blue, and the static light invested everything with its own lack of motion. Only things could be seen from here, the work of people's hands: but the people did not exist. The plane rose up, up, as though loath to descend from this high tranquility; tilted, and Yves looked down, hoping to see the Statue of Liberty, though he had been warned that it could not be seen from here; then the plane began, like a stone, to drop, the water rushed up at them, the motors groaned, the wings trembled, resisting the awful, downward pull. Then, when the water was at their feet, the white strip of the landing flashed into place beneath them. The wheels struck the ground with a brief and heavy thud, and wires and lights and towers went screaming by. The hostess' voice came over the speaker, congratulating them on their journey, and hoping to see them soon again. The hostess was very pretty, he had intermittently flirted with her all night, delighted to discover how easy this was. He was drunk and terribly weary, and filled with an excitement which was close to panic; in fact, he had burned his way to the outer edge of drunkenness and weariness, into a diamond-hard sobriety. With the voice of the hostess, the people of this planet sprang out of the ground, pushing trucks and waving arms and crossing roads and vanishing into, or erupting out of buildings. The voice of the hostess asked the passengers please to remain seated until the aircraft had come to a complete halt. Yves touched the package which contained the brandy and cigarettes he had bought in Shannon, and he folded his copies of *France-Soir* and *Le Monde* and *Paris-Match*, for he knew that Eric would like to see them. On the top of a brightly colored building, people were driven against the sky; he looked for Eric's flaming hair, feeling another excitement, an excitement close to pain, well up in him. But the people were too far away, they were faceless still. He watched them move, but there was no movement which reminded him of Eric. Still, he knew that Eric was there, somewhere in that faceless crowd, waiting for him, and he was filled, all at once, with an extraordinary peace and happiness.

Then the plane came slowly to a halt. As the plane halted, the people in the cabin seemed, collectively, to sigh, and discovered that the power of movement had been returned to them. Off came safety belts, down came packages, papers, and coats. The faces they had worn when hanging, at the mercy of mysteries they could not begin to fathom, in the middle of the air, were now discarded for the faces which they wore on earth. The housewife, traveling alone, who had been, during their passage, a rather flirtatious girl, became a housewife once again: her face responded to her proddings as abjectly as her hat. The businessman who had spoken to Yves about the waters of Lake Michigan, and the days when he had hiked and fished there, relentlessly put all of this behind him, and solemnly and cruelly tightened the knot in his tie. Yves was not wearing a tie, he was wearing a light blue shirt, with short sleeves, and he carried a light sport jacket; and he thought now, with some terror, that this had probably been a mistake; he was not really in America yet, after all, and might not be allowed to enter. But there was nothing he could do about it now. He straightened his collar and put on his jacket and ran his fingers through his hair—which was probably too long. He cursed himself and wished that he could ask one of his fellow passengers for reassurance. But his seatmate, a young man who played the organ in Montana, was now frowning and breathing hard and straightening as much of himself as could decently be reached. He had been very friendly during the journey and had even asked Yves to come and see him, if he ever came to Montana; but now Yves realized that he had not been given any address, and that he knew only the man's first name, which was Peter. And it was only too clear that he could not ask for any information now. Nearly everyone on the plane knew—for he had been very high-spirited and talkative—that he was French, and coming to the States for the first time; and some of them knew that he had a friend in New York, who was an actor. This had all seemed perfectly all right while they were in the middle of the air. But now, on the ground, and in the light, hard and American, of sober second thought, it all seemed rather suspect. He felt helplessly French: and he had never felt French before. And he felt their movement away from him, decently but definitely, with nervous, and, as it were, backward smiles; they were making it clear that he could make no appeal to them, for they did not know who he was. It flashed through him that of course he had a test to pass; he had not yet entered the country; perhaps he would not pass the test. He watched them fill the aisles, and he moved backward from them, into his familiar loneliness and contempt. "Good luck," said his seatmate quickly, and took his place in the line; he would probably have said the same words, as quickly, and in the same tone of voice, to a friend about to be carried off to prison. Yves sighed, and remained in his seat, waiting for the load in the aisle to lighten. He thought, bleakly, *Le plus dur reste à faire.*

Then he joined the line, and moved slowly toward the door. The hostesses stood there, smiling and saying good-bye. The sun was bright on their faces, and on the faces of the disembarking passengers; they seemed, as they turned and disappeared, to be stepping into a new and healing light. He held his newspapers under one arm, shifted his package from hand to hand, straightened his belt, trembling. The hostess with whom he had flirted was nearest the door. *"Au revoir,"* she said, with the bright and generous and mocking smile possessed by so many of his countrywomen. He suddenly realized that he would never see her again. It had not occurred to him, until this moment, that he could possibly have left behind him anything which he might, one day, long for and need, with all his heart. *"Bon courage,"* she said. He smiled and said, *"Merci, madamoiselle. Au revoir!"* And he wanted to say, *Vous êtes très jolie,* but it was too late, he had hit the light, the sun glared at him, and everything wavered in the heat. He started down the extraordinary steps. When he hit the ground, a voice above him said, *"Bonjour, mon gar. Soyez le bienvenue."* He looked up. Eric leaned on the rail of the observation deck, grinning, wearing an open white shirt and khaki trousers. He looked very much at ease, at home, thinner than he had been, with his short hair spinning and flaming about his head. Yves looked up joyously, and waved, unable to say anything. *Eric.* And all his fear left him, he was certain, now, that everything would be all right. He whistled to himself as he followed the line which separated him from the Americans, into the examination hall. But he passed his examination with no trouble, and in a very short time; his passport was eventually stamped and handed back to him, with a grin and a small joke, the meaning but not the good nature of which escaped him. Then he was in a vaster hall, waiting for his luggage, with Eric above him, smiling down on him through glass. Then even his luggage belonged to him again, and he strode through the barriers, more high-hearted than he had ever been as a child, into that city which the people from heaven had made their home.

Istanbul, Dec. 10, 1961

GOING TO MEET THE MAN

For Beauford Delaney

Contents

The Rockpile

ACROSS the street from their house, in an empty lot between two houses, stood the rockpile. It was a strange
place to find a mass of natural rock jutting out of the ground;
and someone, probably Aunt Florence, had once told them
that the rock was there and could not be taken away because
without it the subway cars underground would fly apart, killing all the people. This, touching on some natural mystery
concerning the surface and the center of the earth, was far too
intriguing an explanation to be challenged, and it invested the
rockpile, moreover, with such mysterious importance that Roy
felt it to be his right, not to say his duty, to play there.

Other boys were to be seen there each afternoon after
school and all day Saturday and Sunday. They fought on the
rockpile. Sure footed, dangerous, and reckless, they rushed
each other and grappled on the heights, sometimes disappearing down the other side in a confusion of dust and
screams and upended, flying feet. "It's a wonder they don't
kill themselves," their mother said, watching sometimes from
the fire escape. "You children stay away from there, you hear
me?" Though she said "children," she was looking at Roy,
where he sat beside John on the fire escape. "The good Lord
knows," she continued, "I don't want you to come home
bleeding like a hog every day the Lord sends." Roy shifted
impatiently, and continued to stare at the street, as though in
this gazing he might somehow acquire wings. John said nothing. He had not really been spoken to: he was afraid of the
rockpile and of the boys who played there.

Each Saturday morning John and Roy sat on the fire escape
and watched the forbidden street below. Sometimes their
mother sat in the room behind them, sewing, or dressing their
younger sister, or nursing the baby, Paul. The sun fell across
them and across the fire escape with a high, benevolent indifference; below them, men and women, and boys and girls,
sinners all, loitered; sometimes one of the church-members
passed and saw them and waved. Then, for the moment that
they waved decorously back, they were intimidated. They

watched the saint, man or woman, until he or she had disappeared from sight. The passage of one of the redeemed
made them consider, however vacantly, the wickedness of the
street, their own latent wickedness in sitting where they sat;
and made them think of their father, who came home early
on Saturdays and who would soon be turning this corner and
entering the dark hall below them.

But until he came to end their freedom, they sat, watching
and longing above the street. At the end of the street nearest
their house was the bridge which spanned the Harlem River
and led to a city called the Bronx; which was where Aunt
Florence lived. Nevertheless, when they saw her coming, she
did not come from the bridge, but from the opposite end of
the street. This, weakly, to their minds, she explained by saying that she had taken the subway, not wishing to walk, and
that, besides, she did not live in *that* section of the Bronx.
Knowing that the Bronx was across the river, they did not
believe this story ever, but, adopting toward her their father's
attitude, assumed that she had just left some sinful place which
she dared not name, as, for example, a movie palace.

In the summertime boys swam in the river, diving off the
wooden dock, or wading in from the garbage-heavy bank.
Once a boy, whose name was Richard, drowned in the river.
His mother had not known where he was; she had even come
to their house, to ask if he was there. Then, in the evening,
at six o'clock, they had heard from the street a woman screaming and wailing; and they ran to the windows and looked out.
Down the street came the woman, Richard's mother, screaming, her face raised to the sky and tears running down her
face. A woman walked beside her, trying to make her quiet
and trying to hold her up. Behind them walked a man,
Richard's father, with Richard's body in his arms. There were
two white policemen walking in the gutter, who did not seem
to know what should be done. Richard's father and Richard
were wet, and Richard's body lay across his father's arms like
a cotton baby. The woman's screaming filled all the street;
cars slowed down and the people in the cars stared; people
opened their windows and looked out and came rushing out
of doors to stand in the gutter, watching. Then the small procession disappeared within the house which stood beside the

rockpile. Then, *"Lord, Lord, Lord!"* cried Elizabeth, their mother, and slammed the window down.

One Saturday, an hour before his father would be coming home, Roy was wounded on the rockpile and brought screaming upstairs. He and John had been sitting on the fire escape and their mother had gone into the kitchen to sip tea with Sister McCandless. By and by Roy became bored and sat beside John in restless silence; and John began drawing into his schoolbook a newspaper advertisement which featured a new electric locomotive. Some friends of Roy passed beneath the fire escape and called him. Roy began to fidget, yelling down to them through the bars. Then a silence fell. John looked up. Roy stood looking at him.

"I'm going downstairs," he said.

"You better stay where you is, boy. You know Mama don't want you going downstairs."

"I be right *back*. She won't even know I'm gone, less you run and tell her."

"I ain't *got* to tell her. What's going to stop her from coming in here and looking out the window?"

"She's talking," Roy said. He started into the house.

"But Daddy's going to be home soon!"

"I be back before *that*. What you all the time got to be so *scared* for?" He was already in the house and he now turned, leaning on the windowsill, to swear impatiently, "I be back in *five* minutes."

John watched him sourly as he carefully unlocked the door and disappeared. In a moment he saw him on the sidewalk with his friends. He did not dare to go and tell his mother that Roy had left the fire escape because he had practically promised not to. He started to shout, *Remember, you said five minutes!* but one of Roy's friends was looking up at the fire escape. John looked down at his schoolbook: he became engrossed again in the problem of the locomotive.

When he looked up again he did not know how much time had passed, but now there was a gang fight on the rockpile. Dozens of boys fought each other in the harsh sun: clambering up the rocks and battling hand to hand, scuffed shoes sliding on the slippery rock; filling the bright air with curses and jubilant cries. They filled the air, too, with flying weapons:

stones, sticks, tin cans, garbage, whatever could be picked up and thrown. John watched in a kind of absent amazement—until he remembered that Roy was still downstairs, and that he was one of the boys on the rockpile. Then he was afraid; he could not see his brother among the figures in the sun; and he stood up, leaning over the fire-escape railing. Then Roy appeared from the other side of the rocks; John saw that his shirt was torn; he was laughing. He moved until he stood at the very top of the rockpile. Then, something, an empty tin can, flew out of the air and hit him on the forehead, just above the eye. Immediately, one side of Roy's face ran with blood, he fell and rolled on his face down the rocks. Then for a moment there was no movement at all, no sound, the sun, arrested, lay on the street and the sidewalk and the arrested boys. Then someone screamed or shouted; boys began to run away, down the street, toward the bridge. The figure on the ground, having caught its breath and felt its own blood, began to shout. John cried, "Mama! Mama!" and ran inside.

"Don't fret, don't fret," panted Sister McCandless as they rushed down the dark, narrow, swaying stairs, "don't fret. Ain't a boy been born don't get his knocks every now and again. *Lord!*" They hurried into the sun. A man had picked Roy up and now walked slowly toward them. One or two boys sat silent on their stoops; at either end of the street there was a group of boys watching. "He ain't hurt bad," the man said. "Wouldn't be making this kind of noise if he was hurt real bad."

Elizabeth, trembling, reached out to take Roy, but Sister McCandless, bigger, calmer, took him from the man and threw him over her shoulder as she once might have handled a sack of cotton. "God bless you," she said to the man, "God bless you, son." Roy was still screaming. Elizabeth stood behind Sister McCandless to stare at his bloody face.

"It's just a flesh wound," the man kept saying, "just broke the skin, that's all." They were moving across the sidewalk, toward the house. John, not now afraid of the staring boys, looked toward the corner to see if his father was yet in sight.

Upstairs, they hushed Roy's crying. They bathed the blood away, to find, just above the left eyebrow, the jagged, superficial scar. "Lord, have mercy," murmured Elizabeth, "another inch and it would've been his eye." And she looked with apprehension toward the clock. "Ain't it the truth," said Sister McCandless, busy with bandages and iodine.

"When did he go downstairs?" his mother asked at last.

Sister McCandless now sat fanning herself in the easy chair, at the head of the sofa where Roy lay, bound and silent. She paused for a moment to look sharply at John. John stood near the window, holding the newspaper advertisement and the drawing he had done.

"We was sitting on the fire escape," he said. "Some boys he knew called him."

"When?"

"He said he'd be back in five minutes."

"Why didn't you tell me he was downstairs?"

He looked at his hands, clasping his notebook, and did not answer.

"Boy," said Sister McCandless, "you hear your mother a-talking to you?"

He looked at his mother. He repeated:

"He said he'd be back in five minutes."

"He said he'd be back in five minutes," said Sister Mc-Candless with scorn, "don't look to me like that's no right answer. You's the man of the house, you supposed to look after your baby brothers and sisters—you ain't supposed to let them run off and get half-killed. But I expect," she added, rising from the chair, dropping the cardboard fan, "your Daddy'll make you tell the truth. Your Ma's way too soft with you."

He did not look at her, but at the fan where it lay in the dark red, depressed seat where she had been. The fan advertised a pomade for the hair and showed a brown woman and her baby, both with glistening hair, smiling happily at each other.

"Honey," said Sister McCandless, "I got to be moving along. Maybe I drop in later tonight. I don't reckon you going to be at Tarry Service tonight?"

Tarry Service was the prayer meeting held every Saturday night at church to strengthen believers and prepare the church for the coming of the Holy Ghost on Sunday.

"I don't reckon," said Elizabeth. She stood up; she and

Sister McCandless kissed each other on the cheek. "But you be sure to remember me in your prayers."

"I surely will do that." She paused, with her hand on the door knob, and looked down at Roy and laughed. "Poor little man," she said, "reckon he'll be content to sit on the fire escape *now*."

Elizabeth laughed with her. "It sure ought to be a lesson to him. You don't reckon," she asked nervously, still smiling, "he going to keep that scar, do you?"

"Lord, no," said Sister McCandless, "ain't nothing but a scratch. I declare, Sister Grimes, you worse than a child. Another couple of weeks and you won't be able to *see* no scar. No, you go on about your housework, honey, and thank the Lord it weren't no worse." She opened the door; they heard the sound of feet on the stairs. "I expect that's the Reverend," said Sister McCandless, placidly, "I *bet* he going to raise cain."

"Maybe it's Florence," Elizabeth said. "Sometimes she get here about this time." They stood in the doorway, staring, while the steps reached the landing below and began again climbing to their floor. "No," said Elizabeth then, "that ain't her walk. That's Gabriel."

"Well, I'll just go on," said Sister McCandless, "and kind of prepare his mind." She pressed Elizabeth's hand as she spoke and started into the hall, leaving the door behind her slightly ajar. Elizabeth turned slowly back into the room. Roy did not open his eyes, or move; but she knew that he was not sleeping; he wished to delay until the last possible moment any contact with his father. John put his newspaper and his notebook on the table and stood, leaning on the table, staring at her.

"It wasn't my fault," he said. "I couldn't stop him from going downstairs."

"No," she said, "you ain't got nothing to worry about. You just tell your Daddy the truth."

He looked directly at her, and she turned to the window, staring into the street. What was Sister McCandless saying? Then from her bedroom she heard Delilah's thin wail and she turned, frowning, looking toward the bedroom and toward the still open door. She knew that John was watching her. Delilah continued to wail, she thought, angrily, *Now that girl's getting too big for that,* but she feared that Delilah would awaken Paul and she hurried into the bedroom. She tried to soothe Delilah back to sleep. Then she heard the front door open and close—too loud, Delilah raised her voice, with an exasperated sigh Elizabeth picked the child up. Her child and Gabriel's, her children and Gabriel's: Roy, Delilah, Paul. Only John was nameless and a stranger, living, unalterable testimony to his mother's days in sin.

"What happened?" Gabriel demanded. He stood, enormous, in the center of the room, his black lunchbox dangling from his hand, staring at the sofa where Roy lay. John stood just before him, it seemed to her astonished vision just below him, beneath his fist, his heavy shoe. The child stared at the man in fascination and terror—when a girl down home she had seen rabbits stand so paralyzed before the barking dog. She hurried past Gabriel to the sofa, feeling the weight of Delilah in her arms like the weight of a shield, and stood over Roy, saying:

"Now, ain't a thing to get upset about, Gabriel. This boy sneaked downstairs while I had my back turned and got hisself hurt a little. He's alright now."

Roy, as though in confirmation, now opened his eyes and looked gravely at his father. Gabriel dropped his lunchbox with a clatter and knelt by the sofa.

"How you feel, son? Tell your Daddy what happened?"

Roy opened his mouth to speak and then, relapsing into panic, began to cry. His father held him by the shoulder.

"You don't want to cry. You's Daddy's little man. Tell your Daddy what happened."

"He went downstairs," said Elizabeth, "where he didn't have no business to be, and got to fighting with them bad boys playing on that rockpile. That's what happened and it's a mercy it weren't nothing worse."

He looked up at her. "Can't you let this boy answer me for hisself?"

Ignoring this, she went on, more gently: "He got cut on the forehead, but it ain't nothing to worry about."

"You call a doctor? How you know it ain't nothing to worry about?"

"Is you got money to be throwing away on doctors? No, I

ain't called no doctor. Ain't nothing wrong with my eyes that I can't tell whether he's hurt bad or not. He got a fright more'n anything else, and you ought to pray God it teaches him a lesson."

"You got a lot to say *now*," he said, "but I'll have *me* something to say in a minute. I'll be wanting to know when all this happened, what you was doing with your eyes *then*." He turned back to Roy, who had lain quietly sobbing eyes wide open and body held rigid: and who now, at his father's touch, remembered the height, the sharp, sliding rock beneath his feet, the sun, the explosion of the sun, his plunge into darkness and his salty blood; and recoiled, beginning to scream, as his father touched his forehead. "Hold still, hold still," crooned his father, shaking, "hold still. Don't cry. Daddy ain't going to hurt you, he just wants to see this bandage, see what they've done to his little man." But Roy continued to scream and would not be still and Gabriel dared not lift the bandage for fear of hurting him more. And he looked at Elizabeth in fury: "Can't you put that child down and help me with this boy? John, take your baby sister from your mother—don't look like neither of you got good sense."

John took Delilah and sat down with her in the easy chair. His mother bent over Roy, and held him still, while his father, carefully—but still Roy screamed—lifted the bandage and stared at the wound. Roy's sobs began to lessen. Gabriel re-adjusted the bandage. "You see," said Elizabeth, finally, "he ain't nowhere near dead."

"It sure ain't your fault that he ain't dead." He and Elizabeth considered each other for a moment in silence. "He came mightly close to losing an eye. Course, his eyes ain't as big as your'n, so I reckon you don't think it matters so much." At this her face hardened; he smiled. "Lord, have mercy," he said, "you think you ever going to learn to do right? Where was you when all this happened? Who let him go downstairs?"

"Ain't nobody let him go downstairs, he just went. He got a head just like his father, it got to be broken before it'll bow. I was in the kitchen."

"Where was Johnnie?"

"He was in here."

"Where?"

"He was on the fire escape."

"Didn't he know Roy was downstairs?"

"I reckon."

"What you mean, you reckon? He ain't got your big eyes for nothing, does he?" He looked over at John. "Boy, you see your brother go downstairs?"

"Gabriel, ain't no sense in trying to blame Johnnie. You know right well if you have trouble making Roy behave, he ain't going to listen to his brother. He don't hardly listen to me."

"How come you didn't tell your mother Roy was downstairs?"

John said nothing, staring at the blanket which covered Delilah.

"Boy, you hear me? You want me to take a strap to you?"

"No, you ain't," she said. "You ain't going to take no strap to this boy, not today you ain't. Ain't a soul to blame for Roy's lying up there now but you—you because you done spoiled him so that he thinks he can do just anything and get away with it. I'm here to tell you that ain't no way to raise no child. You don't pray to the Lord to help you do better than you been doing, you going to live to shed bitter tears that the Lord didn't take his soul today." And she was trembling. She moved, unseeing, toward John and took Delilah from his arms. She looked back at Gabriel, who had risen, who stood near the sofa, staring at her. And she found in his face not fury alone, which would not have surprised her; but hatred so deep as to become insupportable in its lack of personality. His eyes were struck alive, unmoving, blind with malevolence—she felt, like the pull of the earth at her feet, his longing to witness her perdition. Again, as though it might be propitiation, she moved the child in her arms. And at this his eyes changed, he looked at Elizabeth, the mother of his children, the helpmeet given by the Lord. Then her eyes clouded; she moved to leave the room; her foot struck the lunchbox lying on the floor.

"John," she said, "pick up your father's lunchbox like a good boy."

She heard, behind her, his scrambling movement as he left

the easy chair, the scrape and jangle of the lunchbox as he picked it up, bending his dark head near the toe of his father's heavy shoe.

The Outing

EACH SUMMER the church gave an outing. It usually took place on the Fourth of July, that being the day when most of the church-members were free from work; it began quite early in the morning and lasted all day. The saints referred to it as the 'whosoever will' outing, by which they meant that, though it was given by the Mount of Olives Pentecostal Assembly for the benefit of its members, all men were free to join them, Gentile, Jew or Greek or sinner. The Jews and the Greeks, to say nothing of the Gentiles—on whom, for their livelihood, most of the saints depended—showed themselves, year after year, indifferent to the invitation; but sinners of the more expected hue were seldom lacking. This year they were to take a boat trip up the Hudson as far as Bear Mountain where they would spend the day and return as the moon rose over the wide river. Since on other outings they had merely taken a subway ride as far as Pelham Bay or Van Cortlandt Park, this year's outing was more than ever a special occasion and even the deacon's two oldest boys, Johnnie and Roy, and their friend, David Jackson, were reluctantly thrilled. These three tended to consider themselves sophisticates, no longer, like the old folks, at the mercy of the love or the wrath of God.

The entire church was going and for weeks in advance talked of nothing else. And for weeks in the future the outing would provide interesting conversation. They did not consider this frivolous. The outing, Father James declared from his pulpit a week before the event, was for the purpose of giving the children of God a day of relaxation; to breathe a purer air and to worship God joyfully beneath the roof of heaven; and there was nothing frivolous about *that*. And, rather to the alarm of the captain, they planned to hold church services aboard the ship. Last year Sister McCandless had held an impromptu service in the unbelieving subway car, she played the tambourine and sang and exhorted sinners and passed through the train distributing tracts. Not everyone had found this admirable, to some it seemed that Sister McCandless was being a little ostentatious. "I praise my Redeemer wherever I go," she retorted defiantly. "Holy Ghost don't leave *me* when I leave the church. I got a every day religion."

Sylvia's birthday was on the third, and David and Johnnie and Roy had been saving money for her birthday present. Between them they had five dollars but they could not decide what to give her. Roy's suggestion that they give her underthings was rudely shouted down: did he want Sylvia's mother to kill the girl? They were all frightened of the great, rawboned, outspoken Sister Daniels and for Sylvia's sake went to great pains to preserve what remained of her good humor. Finally, and at the suggestion of David's older sister, Lorraine, they bought a small, gold-plated pin cut in the shape of a butterfly. Roy thought that it was cheap and grumbled angrily at their combined bad taste ("Wait till it starts turning her clothes green!" he cried) but David did not think it was so bad; Johnnie thought it pretty enough and he was sure that Sylvia would like it anyway ("When's *your* birthday?" he asked David). It was agreed that David should present it to her on the day of the outing in the presence of them all. ("Man, I'm the oldest cat here," David said, "you know that girl's crazy about me.") This was the summer in which they all abruptly began to grow older, their bodies becoming troublesome and awkward and even dangerous and their voices not to be trusted. David perpetually boasted of the increase of down on his chin and professed to have hair on his chest—"and somewhere else, too," he added slyly, whereat they all laughed. "You ain't the only one," Roy said. "No," Johnnie said, "I'm almost as old as you are." "Almost ain't got it," David said. "Now ain't this a hell of a conversation for church boys?" Roy wanted to know.

The morning of the outing they were all up early; their father sang in the kitchen and their mother, herself betraying an excitement nearly youthful, scrubbed and dressed the younger children and laid the plates for breakfast. In the bedroom which they shared Roy looked wistfully out of the window and turned to Johnnie.

"Got a good mind to stay home," he said. "Probably have more fun." He made a furious gesture toward the kitchen. "Why doesn't *he* stay home?"

Johnnie, who was looking forward to the day with David and who had not the remotest desire to stay home for any reason and who knew, moreover, that Gabriel was not going to leave Roy alone in the city, not even if the heavens fell, said lightly, squirming into clean underwear: "Oh, he'll probably be busy with the old folks. We can stay out of his way."

Roy sighed and began to dress. "Be glad when I'm a man," he said.

Lorraine and David and Mrs. Jackson were already on the boat when they arrived. They were among the last; most of the church, Father James, Brother Elisha, Sister McCandless, Sister Daniels and Sylvia were seated near the rail of the boat in a little semi-circle, conversing in strident tones. Father James and Sister McCandless were remarking the increase of laxity among God's people and debating whether or not the church should run a series of revival meetings. Sylvia sat there, saying nothing, smiling painfully now and then at young Brother Elisha, who spoke loudly of the need for a revival and who continually attempted to include Sylvia in the conversation. Elsewhere on the boat similar conversations were going on. The saints of God were together and very conscious this morning of their being together and of their sainthood; and were determined that the less enlightened world should know who they were and remark upon it. To this end there were a great many cries of "Praise the Lord!" in greeting and the formal holy kiss. The children, bored with the familiar spectacle, had already drawn apart and amused themselves by loud cries and games that were no less exhibitionistic than that being played by their parents. Johnnie's nine year old sister, Lois, since she professed salvation, could not very well behave as the other children did; yet no degree of salvation could have equipped her to enter into the conversation of the grown-ups; and she was very violently disliked among the adolescents and could not join them either. She wandered about, therefore, unwillingly forlorn, contenting herself to some extent by a great display of virtue in her encounters with the unsaved children and smiling brightly at the grown-ups. She came to Brother Elisha's side. "Praise the Lord," he cried, stroking her head and continuing his conversation.

Lorraine and Mrs. Jackson met Johnnie's mother for the

first time as she breathlessly came on board, dressed in the airy and unreal blue which Johnnie would forever associate with his furthest memories of her. Johnnie's baby brother, her youngest, happiest child, clung round her neck; she made him stand, staring in wonder at the strange, endless deck, while she was introduced. His mother, on all social occasions, seemed fearfully distracted, as though she awaited, at any moment, some crushing and irrevocable disaster. This disaster might be the sudden awareness of a run in her stocking or private knowledge that the trump of judgment was due, within five minutes, to sound: but, whatever it was, it lent her a certain agitated charm and people, struggling to guess what it might be that so claimed her inward attention, never failed, in the process, to be won over. She talked with Lorraine and Mrs. Jackson for a few moments, the child tugging at her skirts, Johnnie watching her with a smile; and at last, the child becoming always more restive, said that she must go—into what merciless arena one dared not imagine—but hoped, with a despairing smile which clearly indicated the improbability of such happiness, that she would be able to see them later. They watched her as she walked slowly to the other end of the boat, sometimes pausing in conversation, always (as though it were a duty) smiling a little and now and then considering Lois where she stood at Brother Elisha's knee.

"She's very friendly," Mrs. Jackson said. "She looks like you, Johnnie."

David laughed. "Now why you want to say a thing like that, Ma? That woman ain't never done nothing to you."

Johnnie grinned, embarrassed, and pretended to menace David with his fists.

"Don't you listen to that old, ugly boy," Lorraine said. "He just trying to make you feel bad. Your mother's real good-looking. Tell her I said so."

This embarrassed him even more, but he made a mock bow and said, "Thank you, Sister." And to David: "Maybe now you'll learn to keep your mouth shut."

"Who'll learn to keep whose mouth shut? What kind of talk is that?"

He turned and faced his father, who stood smiling on them as from a height.

"Mrs. Jackson, this is my father," said Roy quickly. "And this is Miss Jackson. You know David."

Lorraine and Mrs. Jackson looked up at the deacon with polite and identical smiles.

"How do you do?" Lorraine said. And from Mrs. Jackson: "I'm very pleased to meet you."

"Praise the Lord," their father said. He smiled. "Don't you let Johnnie talk fresh to you."

"Oh, no, we were just kidding around," David said. There was a short, ugly silence. The deacon said: "It looks like a good day for the outing, praise the Lord. You kids have a good time. Is this your first time with us, Mrs. Jackson?"

"Yes," said Mrs. Jackson. "David came home and told me about it and it's been so long since I've been in the country I just decided I'd take me a day off. And Lorraine's not been feeling too strong, I thought the fresh air would do her some good." She smiled a little painfully as she spoke. Lorraine looked amused.

"Yes, it will, nothing like God's fresh air to help the feeble." At this description of herself as feeble Lorraine looked ready to fall into the Hudson and coughed nastily into her handkerchief. David, impelled by his own perverse demon, looked at Johnnie quickly and murmured, "That's the truth, deacon." The deacon looked at him and smiled and turned to Mrs. Jackson. "We been hoping that your son might join our church someday. Roy brings him out to service every Sunday. Do you like the services, son?" This last was addressed in a hearty voice to David; who, recovering from his amazement at hearing Roy mentioned as his especial pal (for he was Johnnie's friend, it was to be with Johnnie that he came to church!) smiled and said, "Yes sir, I like them alright," and looked at Roy, who considered his father with an expression at once contemptuous, ironic and resigned and at Johnnie, whose face was a mask of rage. He looked sharply at the deacon again; but he, with his arm around Roy, was still talking.

"This boy came to the Lord just about a month ago," he said proudly. "The Lord saved him just like that. Believe me, Sister Jackson, ain't no better fortress for nobody, young or old, than the arms of Jesus. My son'll tell you so, ain't it, Roy?"

They considered Roy with a stiff, cordial curiosity. He muttered murderously, "Yes sir."

"Johnnie tells me you're a preacher," Mrs. Jackson said at last. "I'll come out and hear you sometime with David."

"Don't come out to hear me," he said. "You come out and listen to the Word of God. We're all just vessels in His hand. Do you know the Lord, sister?"

"I try to do His will," Mrs. Jackson said.

He smiled kindly. "We must all grow in grace." He looked at Lorraine. "I'll be expecting to see you too, young lady."

"Yes, we'll be out," Lorraine said. They shook hands. "It's very nice to have met you," she said.

"Goodbye." He looked at David. "Now you be good. I want to see you saved soon." He released Roy and started to walk away. "You kids enjoy yourselves. Johnnie, don't you get into no mischief, you hear me?"

He affected not to have heard; he put his hands in his pants' pockets and pulled out some change and pretended to count it. His hand was clammy and it shook. When his father repeated his admonition, part of the change spilled to the deck and he bent to pick it up. He wanted at once to shout to his father the most dreadful curses that he knew and he wanted to weep. He was aware that they were all intrigued by the tableau presented by his father and himself, that they were all vaguely cognizant of an unnamed and deadly tension. From his knees on the deck he called back (putting into his voice as much asperity, as much fury and hatred as he dared):

"Don't worry about me, Daddy. Roy'll see to it that I behave."

There was a silence after he said this; and he rose to his feet and saw that they were all watching him. David looked pitying and shocked, Roy's head was bowed and he looked apologetic. His father called:

"Excuse yourself, Johnnie, and come here."

"Excuse me," he said, and walked over to his father. He looked up into his father's face with an anger which surprised and even frightened him. But he did not drop his eyes, knowing that his father saw there (and he wanted him to see it) how much he hated him.

"What did you say?" his father asked.

"I said you don't have to worry about me. I don't think I'll get into any mischief." And his voice surprised him, it was more deliberately cold and angry than he had intended and there was a sardonic stress on the word 'mischief.' He knew that his father would then and there have knocked him down if they had not been in the presence of saints and strangers.

"You be careful how you speak to me. Don't you get grown too fast. We get home, I'll pull down those long pants and we'll see who's the man, you hear me?"

Yes we will, he thought and said nothing. He looked with a deliberate casualness about the deck. Then they felt the lurch of the boat as it began to move from the pier. There was an excited raising of voices and "I'll see you later," his father said and turned away.

He stood still, trying to compose himself to return to Mrs. Jackson and Lorraine. But as he turned with his hands in his pants' pockets he saw that David and Roy were coming toward him and he stopped and waited for them.

"It's a bitch," Roy said.

David looked at him, shocked. "That's no language for a saved boy." He put his arm around Johnnie's shoulder. "We're off to Bear Mountain," he cried, "*up* the glorious Hudson"—and he made a brutal gesture with his thumb.

"Now suppose Sylvia saw you do that," said Roy, "what would you say, huh?"

"We needn't worry about her," Johnnie said. "She'll be sitting with the old folks all day long."

"Oh, we'll figure out a way to take care of *them*," said David. He turned to Roy. "Now you the saved one, why don't you talk to Sister Daniels and distract her attention while we talk to the girl? You the baby, anyhow, girl don't want to talk to you."

"I ain't got enough salvation to talk to that hag," Roy said. "I got a Daddy-made salvation. I'm saved when I'm with Daddy." They laughed and Roy added, "And I ain't no baby, either, I got everything my Daddy got."

"And a lot your Daddy don't dream of," David said.

Oh, thought Johnnie, with a sudden, vicious, chilling anger, *he doesn't have to dream about it!*

"Now let's act like we Christians," David said. "If we was

real smart now, we'd go over to where she's sitting with all
those people and act like we wanted to hear about God. Get
on the good side of her mother."

"And suppose *he* comes back?" asked Johnnie.

Gabriel was sitting at the other end of the boat, talking with
his wife. "Maybe he'll stay there," David said; there was a
note of apology in his voice.

They approached the saints.

"Praise the Lord," they said sedately.

"Well, praise Him," Father James said. "How are you
young men today?" He grabbed Roy by the shoulder. "Are
you coming along in the Lord?"

"Yes, sir," Roy muttered, "I'm trying." He smiled into
Father James's face.

"It's a wonderful thing," Brother Elisha said, "to give up
to the Lord in your youth." He looked up at Johnnie and
David. "Why don't you boys surrender? Ain't nothing in the
world for you, I'll tell you that. He says, 'Remember thy
Creator in the days of thy youth when the evil days come
not.'"

"Amen," said Sister Daniels. "We're living in the last days,
children. Don't think because you're young you got plenty of
time. God takes the young as well as the old. You got to hold
yourself in readiness all the time lest when He comes He catch
you unprepared. Yes sir. Now's the time."

"You boys going to come to service today, ain't you?"
asked Sister McCandless. "We're going to have service on the
ship, you know." She looked at Father James. "Reckon we'll
start as soon as we get a little further up the river, won't we,
Father?"

"Yes," Father James said, "we're going to praise God right
in the middle of the majestic Hudson." He leaned back and
released Roy as he spoke. "Want to see you children there. I
want to hear you make a *noise* for the Lord."

"I ain't never seen none of these young men Shout," said
Sister Daniels, regarding them with distrust. She looked at
David and Johnnie. "Don't believe I've ever even heard you
testify."

"We're not saved yet, sister," David told her gently.

"That's alright," Sister Daniels said. "You *could* get up and praise the Lord for your life, health and strength. Praise Him for what you got, He'll give you something more."

"That's the truth," said Brother Elisha. He smiled at Sylvia. "I'm a witness, bless the Lord."

"They going to make a noise yet," said Sister McCandless. "Lord's going to touch every one of these young men one day and bring them on their knees to the altar. You mark my words, you'll see." And she smiled at them.

"You just stay around the house of God long enough," Father James said. "One of these days the Spirit'll jump on you. I won't never forget the day It jumped on me."

"That *is* the truth," Sister McCandless cried, "so glad It jumped on me one day, hallelujah!"

"Amen," Sister Daniels cried, "amen."

"Looks like we're having a little service right now," Brother Elisha said smiling. Father James laughed heartily and cried, "Well, praise Him anyhow."

"I believe next week the church is going to start a series of revival meetings," Brother Elisha said. "I want to see you boys at every one of them, you hear?" He laughed as he spoke and added as David seemed about to protest, "No, no, brother, don't want no excuses. You *be* there. Get you boys to the altar, then maybe you'll pay more attention in Sunday School."

At this they all laughed and Sylvia said in her mild voice, looking mockingly at Roy, "Maybe we'll even see Brother Roy Shout." Roy grinned.

"Like to see you do some Shouting too," her mother grumbled. "You got to get closer to the Lord." Sylvia smiled and bit her lip; she cast a glance at David.

"Now everybody ain't got the same kind of spirit," Brother Elisha said, coming to Sylvia's aid. "Can't *all* make as much noise as you make," he said, laughing gently, "we all ain't got your energy."

Sister Daniels smiled and frowned at this reference to her size and passion and said, "Don't care, brother, when the Lord moves inside you, you bound to do something. I've seen that girl Shout all night and come back the next night and Shout some more. I don't believe in no dead religion, no sir. The saints of God need a revival."

"Well, we'll work on Sister Sylvia," said Brother Elisha.

Directly before and behind them stretched nothing but the river, they had long ago lost sight of the point of their departure. They steamed beside the Palisades, which rose rough and gigantic from the dirty, broad and blue-green Hudson. Johnnie and David and Roy wandered downstairs to the bottom deck, standing by the rail and leaning over to watch the white, writhing spray which followed the boat. From the river there floated up to their faces a soft, cool breeze. They were quiet for a long time, standing together, watching the river and the mountains and hearing vaguely the hum of activity behind them on the boat. The sky was high and blue, with here and there a spittle-like, changing cloud; the sun was orange and beat with anger on their uncovered heads.

And David muttered finally, "Be funny if they were right."

"If who was right?" asked Roy.

"Elisha and them—"

"There's only one way to find out," said Johnnie.

"Yes," said Roy, "and I ain't homesick for heaven yet."

"You always got to be so smart," David said.

"Oh," said Roy, "you just sore because Sylvia's still up there with Brother Elisha."

"You think they going to be married?" Johnnie asked.

"Don't talk like a fool," David said.

"Well it's a cinch you ain't never going to get to talk to her till you get saved," Johnnie said. He had meant to say 'we.' He looked at David and smiled.

"Might be worth it," David said.

"*What* might be worth it?" Roy asked, grinning.

"Now be nice," David said. He flushed, the dark blood rising beneath the dark skin. "How you expect me to get saved if you going to talk that way? You supposed to be an example."

"Don't look at me, boy," Roy said.

"I want you to talk to Johnnie," Gabriel said to his wife.

"What about?"

"That boy's pride is running away with him. Ask him to tell you what he said to me this morning soon as he got in front of his friends. He's your son, alright."

"What did he say?"

He looked darkly across the river. "You ask him to tell you about it tonight. I wanted to knock him down."

She had watched the scene and knew this. She looked at her husband briefly, feeling a sudden, outraged anger, barely conscious; sighed and turned to look at her youngest child where he sat involved in a complicated and strenuous and apparently joyless game which utilized a red ball, jacks, blocks and a broken shovel.

"I'll talk to him," she said at last. "He'll be alright." She wondered what on earth she would say to him; and what he would say to her. She looked covertly about the boat, but he was nowhere to be seen.

"That proud demon's just eating him up," he said bitterly. He watched the river hurtle past. "Be the best thing in the world if the Lord would take his soul." He had meant to say 'save' his soul.

Now it was noon and all over the boat there was the activity of lunch. Paper bags and huge baskets were opened. There was then revealed splendor: cold pork chops, cold chicken, bananas, apples, oranges, pears, and soda-pop, candy and cold lemonade. All over the boat the chosen of God relaxed; they sat in groups and talked and laughed; some of the more worldly gossiped and some of the more courageous young people dared to walk off together. Beneath them the strong, indifferent river raged within the channel and the screaming spray pursued them. In the engine room children watched the motion of the ship's gears as they rose and fell and chanted. The tremendous bolts of steel seemed almost human, imbued with a relentless force that was not human. There was something monstrous about this machine which bore such enormous weight and cargo.

Sister Daniels threw a paper bag over the side and wiped her mouth with her large handkerchief. "Sylvia, you be careful how you speak to these unsaved boys," she said.

"Yes, I am, Mama."

"Don't like the way that little Jackson boy looks at you. That child's got a demon. You be careful."

"Yes, Mama."

"You got plenty of time to be thinking about boys. Now's the time for you to be thinking about the Lord."

"Yes'm."

"You *mind* now," her mother said.

"Mama, I want to go home!" Lois cried. She crawled into her mother's arms, weeping.

"Why, what's the matter, honey?" She rocked her daughter gently. "Tell Mama what's the matter? Have you got a pain?"

"I want to go home, I want to go home," Lois sobbed.

"A very fine preacher, a man of God and a friend of mine will run the service for us," said Father James.

"Maybe you've heard about him—a Reverend Peters? A real man of God, amen."

"I thought," Gabriel said, smiling, "that perhaps I could bring the message some Sunday night. The Lord called me a long time ago. I used to have my own church down home."

"You don't want to run too fast, Deacon Grimes," Father James said. "You just take your time. You been coming along right well on Young Ministers' Nights." He paused and looked at Gabriel. "Yes, indeed."

"I just thought," Gabriel said humbly, "that I could be used to more advantage in the house of God."

Father James quoted the text which tells us how preferable it is to be a gate-keeper in the house of God than to dwell in the tent of the wicked; and started to add the dictum from Saint Paul about obedience to those above one in the Lord but decided (watching Gabriel's face) that it was not necessary yet.

"You just keep praying," he said kindly. "You get a little closer to God. He'll work wonders. You'll see." He bent closer to his deacon. "And try to get just a little closer to the *people*."

Roy wandered off with a gawky and dazzled girl named Elizabeth. Johnnie and David wandered restlessly up and down the boat alone. They mounted to the topmost deck and leaned over the railing in the deserted stern. Up here the air was sharp and clean. They faced the water, their arms around each other.

"Your old man was kind of rough this morning," David said carefully, watching the mountains pass.

"Yes," Johnnie said. He looked at David's face against the sky. He shivered suddenly in the sharp, cold air and buried his face in David's shoulder. David looked down at him and tightened his hold.

"Who do you love?" he whispered. "Who's your boy?"

"You," he muttered fiercely, "I love you."

"Roy!" Elizabeth giggled, "*Roy Grimes*. If you *ever* say a thing like that *again*."

Now the service was beginning. From all corners of the boat there was the movement of the saints of God. They gathered together their various possessions and moved their chairs from top and bottom decks to the large main hall. It was early afternoon, not quite two o'clock. The sun was high and fell everywhere with a copper light. In the city the heat would have been insupportable; and here, as the saints filed into the huge, high room, once used as a ballroom, to judge from the faded and antique appointments, the air slowly began to be oppressive. The room was the color of black mahogany and coming in from the bright deck, one groped suddenly in darkness; and took one's sense of direction from the elegant grand piano which stood in the front of the room on a little platform.

They sat in small rows with one wide aisle between them, forming, almost unconsciously, a hierarchy. Father James sat in the front next to Sister McCandless. Opposite them sat Gabriel and Deacon Jones and, immediately behind them, Sister Daniels and her daughter. Brother Elisha walked in swiftly, just as they were beginning to be settled. He strode to the piano and knelt down for a second before rising to take his place. There was a quiet stir, the saints adjusted themselves, waiting while Brother Elisha tentatively ran his fingers over the keys. Gabriel looked about impatiently for Roy and Johnnie, who, engaged no doubt in sinful conversation with David, were not yet in service. He looked back to where Mrs. Jackson sat with Lorraine, uncomfortable smiles on their faces, and glanced at his wife, who met his questioning regard quietly, the expression on her face not changing.

Brother Elisha struck the keys and the congregation joined in the song, *Nothing Shall Move Me from the Love of God*, with tambourine and heavy hands and stomping feet. The walls and the floor of the ancient hall trembled and the candelabra wavered in the high ceiling. Outside the river rushed past under the heavy shadow of the Palisades and the copper sun beat down. A few of the strangers who had come along on the outing appeared at the doors and stood watching with an uneasy amusement. The saints sang on, raising their strong voices in praises to Jehovah and seemed unaware of those unsaved who watched and who, some day, the power of the Lord might cause to tremble.

The song ended as Father James rose and faced the congregation, a broad smile on his face. They watched him expectantly, with love. He stood silent for a moment, smiling down upon them. Then he said, and his voice was loud and filled with triumph:

"Well, let us all say, Amen!"

And they cried out obediently, "Well, Amen!"

"Let us all say, praise Him!"

"Praise Him!"

"Let us all say, hallelujah!"

"Hallelujah!"

"Well, glory!" cried Father James. The Holy Ghost touched him and he cried again, "Well, bless Him! Bless His holy name!"

They laughed and shouted after him, their joy so great that they laughed as children and some of them cried as children do; in the fullness and assurance of salvation, in the knowledge that the Lord was in their midst and that each heart, swollen to anguish, yearned only to be filled with His glory. Then, in that moment, each of them might have mounted with wings like eagles far past the sordid persistence of the flesh, the depthless iniquity of the heart, the doom of hours and days and weeks; to be received by the Bridegroom where He waited on high in glory; where all tears were wiped away and death had no power; where the wicked ceased from troubling and the weary soul found rest.

"Saints, let's praise Him," Father James said. "Today, right in the middle of God's great river, under God's great roof, beloved, let us raise our voices in thanksgiving that God has seen fit to save us, amen!"

"Amen! Hallelujah!"

"—and to keep us saved, amen, to keep us, oh glory to God, from the snares of Satan, from the temptation and the lust and the evil of this world!"

"Talk about it!"

"Preach!"

"Ain't nothing strange, amen, about worshiping God *wherever* you might be, ain't that right? Church, when you get this mighty salvation you just can't keep it in, hallelujah! you got to talk about it—"

"Amen!"

"You got to live it, amen. When the Holy Ghost touches you, you *move*, bless God!"

"Well, it's so!"

"Want to hear some testimonies today, amen! I want to hear some *singing* today, bless God! Want to see some *Shouting*, bless God, hallelujah!"

"Talk about it!"

"And I don't want to see none of the saints hold back. If the Lord saved you, amen, He give you a witness *every*where you go. Yes! My soul is a witness, bless our God!"

"Glory!"

"If you ain't saved, amen, get up and praise Him anyhow. Give God the glory for sparing your sinful life, *praise* Him for the sunshine and the rain, praise Him for all the works of His hands. Saints, I want to hear some praises today, you hear me? I want you to make this old boat *rock*, hallelujah! I want to *feel* your salvation. Are you saved?"

"Amen!"

"Are you sanctified?"

"Glory!"

"Baptized in fire?"

"Yes! So glad!"

"Testify!"

Now the hall was filled with a rushing wind on which forever rides the Lord, death or healing indifferently in His hands. Under this fury the saints bowed low, crying out "holy!" and tears fell. On the open deck sinners stood and watched, beyond them the fiery sun and the deep river, the black-brown-green, unchanging cliffs. That sun, which covered earth and water now, would one day refuse to shine, the river would cease its rushing and its numberless dead would rise; the cliffs would shiver, crack, fall and where they had been would then be nothing but the unleashed wrath of God.

"Who'll be the first to tell it?" Father James cried. "Stand up and talk about it!"

Brother Elisha screamed, "Have mercy, Jesus!" and rose from the piano stool, his powerful frame possessed. And the Holy Ghost touched him and he cried again, bending nearly double, while his feet beat ageless, dreadful signals on the floor, while his arms moved in the air like wings and his face, distorted, no longer his own face not the face of a young man, but timeless, anguished, grim with ecstasy, turned blindly toward heaven. *Yes, Lord,* they cried, *yes!*

"Dearly beloved . . ."

"Talk about it!"

"Tell it!"

"I want to thank and praise the Lord, amen . . ."

"Amen!"

". . . for being here, I want to thank Him for my life, health, and strength. . . ."

"Amen!"

"Well, glory!"

". . . I want to thank Him, hallelujah, for saving my soul one day. . . ."

"Oh!"

"Glory!"

". . . for causing the light, bless God, to shine in *my* heart one day when I was still a child, amen, I want to thank Him for bringing me to salvation in the days of my *youth*, hallelujah, when I have all my faculties, amen, before Satan had a chance to destroy my body in the world!"

"Talk about it!"

"He saved me, dear ones, from the world and the things of the world. Saved me, amen, from cardplaying . . ."

"Glory!"

". . . saved me from drinking, bless God, saved me from the streets, from the movies and all the filth that is in the world!"

"I *know* it's so!"

"He saved me, beloved, and sanctified me and filled me with the blessed Holy Ghost, *hallelujah!* Give me a new song, amen which I didn't know before and set my feet on the King's highway. Pray for me beloved, that I will stand in these last and evil days."

"Bless your name, Jesus!"

During his testimony Johnnie and Roy and David had stood quietly beside the door, not daring to enter while he spoke. The moment he sat down they moved quickly, together, to the front of the high hall and knelt down beside their seats to pray. The aspect of each of them underwent always, in this company, a striking, even an exciting change; as though their youth, barely begun, were already put away; and the animal, so vividly restless and undiscovered, so tense with power, ready to spring had been already stalked and trapped and offered, a perpetual blood-sacrifice, on the altar of the Lord. Yet their bodies continued to change and grow, preparing them, mysteriously and with ferocious speed, for manhood. No matter how careful their movements, these movements suggested, with a distinctness dreadful for the redeemed to see, the pagan lusting beneath the blood-washed robes. In them was perpetually and perfectly poised the power of revelation against the power of nature; and the saints, considering them with a baleful kind of love, struggled to bring their souls to safety in order, as it were, to steal a march on the flesh while the flesh still slept. A kind of storm, infernal, blew over the congregation as they passed; someone cried, "Bless them, Lord!" and immediately, honey-colored Sister Russell, while they knelt in prayer, rose to her feet to testify.

From the moment that they closed their eyes and covered their faces they were isolated from the joy that moved everything beside them. Yet this same isolation served only to make the glory of the saints more real, the pulse of conviction, how-

ever faint, beat in and the glory of God then held an undertone of abject terror. Roy was the first to rise, sitting very
straight in his seat and allowing his face to reveal nothing; just
as Sister Russell ended her testimony and sat down, sobbing,
her head thrown back and both hands raised to heaven. Immediately Sister Daniels raised her strong, harsh voice and hit
her tambourine, singing. Brother Elisha turned on the piano
stool and hit the keys. Johnnie and David rose from their
knees and as they rose the congregation rose, clapping their
hands singing. The three boys did not sing; they stood together, carefully ignoring one another, their feet steady on the
slightly tilting floor but their bodies moving back and forth
as the music grew more savage. And someone cried aloud, a
timeless sound of wailing; fire splashed the open deck and
filled the doors and bathed the sinners standing there; fire
filled the great hall and splashed the faces of the saints and a
wind, unearthly, moved above their heads. Their hands were
arched before them, moving, and their eyes were raised to
heaven. Sweat stained the deacon's collar and soaked the tight
headbands of the women. Was it true then? and had there
indeed been born one day in Bethlehem a Saviour who was
Christ the Lord? who had died for them—for *them!*—the spat-
upon and beaten with rods, who had worn a crown of thorns
and seen His blood run down like rain; and who had lain in
the grave three days and vanquished death and hell and risen
again in glory—*was it for them?*

Lord, I want to go, show me the way!

For unto us a child is born, unto us a son is given—and
His name shall be called Wonderful, the mighty God, the everlasting Father, the Prince of Peace. Yes, and He was coming
back one day, the King of glory; He would crack the face of
heaven and descend to judge the nations and gather up His
people and take them to their rest.

Take me by my hand and lead me on!

Somewhere in the back a woman cried out and began the
Shout. They looked carefully about, still not looking at one
another, and saw, as from a great distance and through intolerable heat, such heat as might have been faced by the Hebrew children when cast bound into the fiery furnace, that
one of the saints was dancing under the arm of the Lord. She

danced out into the aisle, beautiful with a beauty unbearable, graceful with grace that poured from heaven. Her face was lifted up, her eyes were closed and the feet which moved so surely now were not her own. One by one the power of God moved others and—as it had been written—the Holy Ghost descended from heaven with a Shout. Sylvia raised her hands, the tears poured down her face, and in a moment, she too moved out into the aisle, Shouting. Is it true then? the saints rejoiced, Roy beat the tambourine. David, grave and shaken, clapped his hands and his body moved insistently in the rhythm of the dancers. Johnnie stood beside him, hot and faint and repeating yet again his struggle, summoning in panic all his forces, to save him from this frenzy. And yet daily he recognized that he was black with sin, that the secrets of his heart were a stench in God's nostrils. *Though your sins be as scarlet they shall be white as snow. Come, let us reason together, saith the Lord.*

Now there was a violent discord on the piano and Brother Elisha leapt to his feet, dancing. Johnnie watched the spinning body and listened, in terror and anguish, to the bestial sobs. Of the men it was only Elisha who danced and the women moved toward him and he moved toward the women. Johnnie felt blow over him an icy wind, all his muscles tightened, as though they furiously resisted some imminent bloody act, as the body of Isaac must have revolted when he saw his father's knife, and, sick and nearly sobbing, he closed his eyes. It was Satan, surely, who stood so foully at his shoulder; and what, but the blood of Jesus, should ever set him free? He thought of the many times he had stood in the congregation of the righteous—and yet he was not saved. He remained among the vast army of the doomed, whose lives—as he had been told, as he now, with such heart-sickness, began to discover for himself—were swamped with wretchedness and whose end was wrath and weeping. Then, for he felt himself falling, he opened his eyes and watched the rejoicing of the saints. His eyes found his father where he stood clapping his hands, glittering with sweat and overwhelming. Then Lois began to shout. For the first time he looked at Roy; their eyes met in brief, wry wonder and Roy imperceptibly shrugged. He watched his mother standing over Lois, her own face obscurely troubled. The light from the door was on her face, the entire room was filled with this strange light. There was no sound now except the sound of Roy's tambourine and the heavy rhythm of the saints; the sound of heavy feet and hands and the sound of weeping. Perhaps centuries past the children of Israel led by Miriam had made just such a noise as they came out of the wilderness. *For unto us is born this day a Saviour who is Christ the Lord.*

Yet, in the copper sunlight Johnnie felt suddenly, not the presence of the Lord, but the presence of David; which seemed to reach out to him, hand reaching out to hand in the fury of flood-time, to drag him to the bottom of the water or to carry him safe to shore. From the corner of his eye he watched his friend, who held him with such power; and felt, for that moment, such a depth of love, such nameless and terrible joy and pain, that he might have fallen, in the face of that company, weeping at David's feet.

Once at Bear Mountain they faced the very great problem of carrying Sylvia sufficiently far from her mother's sight to present her with her birthday present. This problem, difficult enough, was made even more difficult by the continual presence of Brother Elisha; who, inspired by the afternoon's service and by Sylvia's renewal of her faith, remained by her side to bear witness to the goodness and power of the Lord. Sylvia listened with her habitual rapt and painful smile. Her mother, on the one side and Brother Elisha on the other, seemed almost to be taking turns in advising her on her conduct as a saint of God. They began to despair, as the sun moved visibly westward, of ever giving her the gold-plated butterfly which rested uncomfortably in David's waistcoat pocket.

Of course, as Johnnie once suggested, there was really no reason they could not go up to her, surrounded as she was, and give her the jewel and get it over with—the more particularly as David evinced a desire to explore the wonders of Bear Mountain until this mission should have been fulfilled. Sister Daniels could scarcely object to an innocuous memento from three young men, all of whom attended church devoutly and one of whom professed salvation. But this was far from satisfactory for David, who did not wish to hear Sylvia's "thank-you's" in the constricting presence of the saints. Therefore they waited, wandering about the sloping park, lingering near the lake and the skating rink and watching Sylvia.

"God, why don't they go off somewhere and sleep? or pray?" cried David finally. He glared at the nearby rise where Sylvia and her mother sat talking with Brother Elisha. The sun was in their faces and struck from Sylvia's hair as she restlessly moved her head, small blue-black sparks.

Johnnie swallowed his jealousy at seeing how Sylvia filled his comrade's mind; he said, half-angrily, "I still don't see why we don't just go over and give it to her."

Roy looked at him. "Boy, you sound like you ain't got good sense," he said.

Johnnie, frowning, fell into silence. He glanced sidewise at David's puckered face (his eyes were still on Sylvia) and abruptly turned and started walking off.

"Where you going, boy?" David called.

"I'll be back," he said. And he prayed that David would follow him.

But David was determined to catch Sylvia alone and remained where he was with Roy. "Well, make it snappy," he said; and sprawled, full length, on the grass.

As soon as he was alone his pace slackened; he leaned his forehead against the bark of a tree, shaking and burning as in the teeth of a fever. The bark of the tree was rough and cold and though it offered no other comfort he stood there quietly for a long time, seeing beyond him—but it brought no peace—the high clear sky where the sun in fading glory traveled; and the deep earth covered with vivid banners, grass, flower, thorn and vine, thrusting upward forever the brutal trees. At his back he heard the voices of the children and the saints. He knew that he must return, that he must be on hand should David at last outwit Sister Daniels and present her daughter with the golden butterfly. But he did not want to go back, now he realized that he had no interest in the birthday present, no interest whatever in Sylvia—that he had had no interest all along. He shifted his stance, he turned from the tree as he turned his mind from the abyss which suddenly yawned, that abyss, depthless and terrifying, which he had encountered already in dreams. And he slowly began to walk, away from the saints and the voices of the children, his hands in his pockets, struggling to ignore the question which now screamed and screamed in his mind's bright haunted house.

It happened quite simply. Eventually Sister Daniels felt the need to visit the ladies' room, which was a long ways off. Brother Elisha remained where he was while Roy and David, like two beasts crouching in the underbrush, watched him and waited their opportunity. Then he also rose and wandered off to get cold lemonade for Sylvia. She sat quietly alone on the green rise, her hands clasped around her knees, dreaming.

They walked over to her, in terror that Sister Daniels would suddenly reappear. Sylvia smiled as she saw them coming and waved to them merrily. Roy grinned and threw himself on his belly on the ground beside her. David remained standing, fumbling in his waistcoat pocket.

"We got something for you," Roy said.

David produced the butterfly. "Happy birthday, Sylvia," he said. He stretched out his hand, the butterfly glinted oddly in the sun, and he realized with surprise that his hand was shaking. She grinned widely, in amazement and delight, and took the pin from him.

"It's from Johnnie too," he said. "I—we—hope you like it—"

She held the small gold pin in her palm and stared down at it; her face was hidden. After a moment she murmured, "I'm so surprised." She looked up, her eyes shining, almost wet. "Oh, it's wonderful," she said. "I never expected anything. I don't know what to say. It's marvelous, it's wonderful." She pinned the butterfly carefully to her light blue dress. She coughed slightly. "Thank you," she said.

"Your mother won't mind, will she?" Roy asked. "I mean—" he stammered awkwardly under Sylvia's sudden gaze—"we didn't know, we didn't want to get you in any trouble—"

"No," David said. He had not moved; he stood watching Sylvia. Sylvia looked away from Roy and up at David, his eyes met hers and she smiled. He smiled back, suddenly robbed of speech. She looked away again over the path her mother had taken and frowned slightly. "No," she said, "no, she won't mind."

Then there was silence. David shifted uncomfortably from one foot to the other. Roy lay contentedly face down on the grass. The breeze from the river, which lay below them and out of sight, grew subtly more insistent for they had passed the heat of the day; and the sun, moving always westward, fired and polished the tips of trees. Sylvia sighed and shifted on the ground.

"Why isn't Johnnie here?" she suddenly asked.

"He went off somewhere," Roy said. "He said he'd be right back." He looked at Sylvia and smiled. She was looking at David.

"You must want to grow real tall," she said mockingly. "Why don't you sit down?"

David grinned and sat down cross-legged next to Sylvia. "Well, the ladies like 'em tall." He lay on his back and stared up at the sky. "It's a fine day," he said.

She said, "Yes," and looked down at him; he had closed his eyes and was bathing his face in the slowly waning sun. Abruptly, she asked him:

"Why don't you get saved? You around the church all the time and you not saved yet? Why don't you?"

He opened his eyes in amazement. Never before had Sylvia mentioned salvation to him, except as a kind of joke. One of the things he most liked about her was the fact that she never preached to him. Now he smiled uncertainly and stared at her.

"I'm not joking," she said sharply. "I'm perfectly serious. Roy's saved—at least he *says* so—" and she smiled darkly, in the fashion of the old folks, at Roy—"and anyway, you ought to be thinking about your soul."

"Well, I don't know," David said. "I *think* about it. It's—well, I don't know if I can—well, live it—"

"All you got to do is make up your mind. If you really want to be saved, He'll save you. Yes, and He'll keep you too." She did not sound at all hysterical or transfigured. She spoke very quietly and with great earnestness and frowned as she spoke. David, taken off guard, said nothing. He looked embarrassed and pained and surprised. "Well, I don't know," he finally repeated.

"Do you ever pray?" she asked. "I mean, *really* pray?"

David laughed, beginning to recover himself. "It's not fair," he said, "you oughtn't to catch me all unprepared like that. Now I don't know what to say." But as he looked at her earnest face he sobered. "Well, I try to be decent. I don't bother nobody." He picked up a grass blade and stared at it. "I don't know," he said at last. "I do my best."

"*Do* you?" she asked.

He laughed again, defeated. "Girl," he said, "you *are* a killer."

She laughed too. "You black-eyed demon," she said, "if I don't see you at revival services I'll never speak to you again." He looked up quickly, in some surprise, and she said, still smiling, "Don't look at me like that. I mean it."

"All right, sister," he said. Then: "If I come out can I walk you home?"

"I got my mother to walk me home—"

"Well, let your mother walk home with Brother Elisha," he said, grinning. "Let the old folks stay together."

"Loose him, Satan!" she cried, laughing, "loose the boy!"

"The brother needs prayer," Roy said.

"Amen," said Sylvia. She looked down again at David. "I want to see you at church. Don't you forget it."

"All right," he said. "I'll be there."

The boat whistles blew at six o'clock, punctuating their holiday; blew, fretful and insistent, through the abruptly dispirited park and skaters left the skating rink; boats were rowed in furiously from the lake. Children were called from the swings and the seesaw and the merry-go-round and forced to leave behind the ball which had been lost in the forest and the torn kite which dangled from the top of a tree. ("Hush now," said their parents, "we'll get you another one—come along." *"Tomorrow?"*—"Come along, honey, it's time to go!") The old folks rose from the benches, from the grass, gathered together the empty lunch-basket, the half-read newspaper, the Bible which was carried everywhere; and they started down the hillside, an army in disorder. David walked with Sylvia and Sister Daniels and Brother Elisha, listening to their conversation (good Lord, thought Johnnie, don't they ever mention anything but sin?) and carrying Sylvia's lunch-basket. He seemed interested in what they were saying; every now and then he looked at Sylvia and grinned and she grinned back. Once, as Sylvia stumbled, he put his hand on her elbow to steady her and held her arm perhaps a moment too long. Brother Elisha, on the far side of Sister Daniels, noticed this and a frown passed over his face. He kept talking, staring now and then hard at Sylvia and trying, with a certain almost humorous helplessness, to discover what was in her mind. Sister Daniels talked of nothing but the service on the boat and of the forthcoming revival. She scarcely seemed to notice David's presence, though once she spoke to him, making some remark about the need, on his part, of much prayer. Gabriel carried the sleeping baby in his arms, striding beside his wife and Lois—who stumbled perpetually and held tightly to her mother's hand. Roy was somewhere in the back, joking with Elizabeth. At a turn in the road the boat and the dock appeared below them, a dead gray-white in the sun.

Johnnie walked down the slope alone, watching David and Sylvia ahead of him. When he had come back, both Roy and David had disappeared and Sylvia sat again in the company of her mother and Brother Elisha; and if he had not seen the gold butterfly on her dress he would have been aware of no change. She thanked him for his share in it and told him that Roy and David were at the skating rink.

But when at last he found them they were far in the middle of the lake in a rowboat. He was afraid of water, he could not row. He stood on the bank and watched them. After a long while they saw him and waved and started to bring the boat in so that he could join them. But the day was ruined for him; by the time they brought the boat in, the hour, for which they had hired it, was over; David went in search of his mother for more money but when he came back it was time to leave. Then he walked with Sylvia.

All during the trip home David seemed preoccupied. When he finally sought out Johnnie he found him sitting by himself on the top deck, shivering a little in the night air. He sat down beside him. After a moment Johnnie moved and put his head on David's shoulder. David put his arms around him. But now where there had been peace there was only panic and where there had been safety, danger, like a flower, opened.

The Man Child

A s the sun began preparing for her exit, and he sensed the waiting night, Eric, blond and eight years old and dirty and tired, started homeward across the fields. Eric lived with his father, who was a farmer and the son of a farmer, and his mother, who had been captured by his father on some far-off, unblessed, unbelievable night, who had never since burst her chains. She did not know that she was chained any more than she knew that she lived in terror of the night. One child was in the churchyard, it would have been Eric's little sister and her name would have been Sophie: for a long time, then, his mother had been very sick and pale. It was said that she would never, really, be better, that she would never again be as she had been. Then, not long ago, there had begun to be a pounding in his mother's belly, Eric had sometimes been able to hear it when he lay against her breast. His father had been pleased. *I did that,* said his father, big, laughing, dreadful, and red, and Eric knew how it was done, he had seen the horses and the blind and dreadful bulls. But then, again, his mother had been sick, she had had to be sent away, and when she came back the pounding was not there anymore, nothing was there anymore. His father laughed less, something in his mother's face seemed to have gone to sleep forever.

Eric hurried, for the sun was almost gone and he was afraid the night would catch him in the fields. And his mother would be angry. She did not really like him to go wandering off by himself. She would have forbidden it completely and kept Eric under her eye all day but in this she was overruled: Eric's father liked to think of Eric as being curious about the world and as being daring enough to explore it, with his own eyes, by himself.

His father would not be at home. He would be gone with his friend, Jamie, who was also a farmer and the son of a farmer, down to the tavern. This tavern was called the Rafters. They went each night, as his father said, imitating an Englishman he had known during a war, *to destruct the Rafters, sir.* They had been destructing The Rafters long before Eric had kicked in his mother's belly, for Eric's father and Jamie had grown up together, gone to war together, and survived together—never, apparently, while life ran, were they to be divided. They worked in the fields all day together, the fields which belonged to Eric's father. Jamie had been forced to sell his farm and it was Eric's father who had bought it.

Jamie had a brown and yellow dog. This dog was almost always with him; whenever Eric thought of Jamie he thought also of the dog. They had always been there, they had always been together: in exactly the same way, for Eric, that his mother and father had always been together, in exactly the same way that the earth and the trees and the sky were together. Jamie and his dog walked the country roads together, Jamie walking slowly in the way of country people, seeming to see nothing, head slightly bent, feet striking surely and heavily on the earth, never stumbling. He walked as though he were going to walk to the other end of the world and knew it was a long way but knew that he would be there by the morning. Sometimes he talked to his dog, head bent a little more than usual and turned to one side, a slight smile playing about the edges of his granite lips; and the dog's head snapped up, perhaps he leapt upon his master, who cuffed him down lightly, with one hand. More often he was silent. His head was carried in a cloud of blue smoke from his pipe. Through this cloud, like a ship on a foggy day, loomed his dry and steady face. Set far back, at an unapproachable angle, were those eyes of his, smoky and thoughtful, eyes which seemed always to be considering the horizon. He had the kind of eyes which no one had ever looked into—except Eric, only once. Jamie had been walking these roads and across these fields, whistling for his dog in the evenings as he turned away from Eric's house, for years, in silence. He had been married once, but his wife had run away. Now he lived alone in a wooden house and Eric's mother kept his clothes clean and Jamie always ate at Eric's house.

Eric had looked into Jamie's eyes on Jamie's birthday. They had had a party for him. Eric's mother had baked a cake and filled the house with flowers. The doors and windows of the great kitchen all stood open on the yard and the kitchen table was placed outside. The ground was not muddy as it was in

winter, but hard, dry, and light brown. The flowers his mother
so loved and so labored for flamed in their narrow borders
against the stone wall of the farmhouse; and green vines covered the grey stone wall at the far end of the yard. Beyond
this wall were the fields and barns, and Eric could see, quite
far away, the cows nearly motionless in the bright green pasture. It was a bright, hot, silent day, the sun did not seem to
be moving at all.

This was before his mother had had to be sent away. Her
belly had been beginning to grow big, she had been dressed
in blue, and had seemed—that day, to Eric—younger than
she was ever to seem again.

Though it was still early when they were called to table,
Eric's father and Jamie were already tipsy and came across the
fields, shoulders touching, laughing, and telling each other
stories. To express disapproval and also, perhaps, because she
had heard their stories before and was bored, Eric's mother
was quite abrupt with them, barely saying, "Happy Birthday,
Jamie" before she made them sit down. In the nearby village
church bells rang as they began to eat.

It was perhaps because it was Jamie's birthday that Eric was
held by something in Jamie's face. Jamie, of course, was very
old. He was thirty-four today, even older than Eric's father,
who was only thirty-two. Eric wondered how it felt to have
so many years and was suddenly, secretly glad that he was only
eight. For today, Jamie *looked* old. It was perhaps the one
additional year which had done it, this day, before their very
eyes—a metamorphosis which made Eric rather shrink at the
prospect of becoming nine. The skin of Jamie's face, which
had never before seemed so, seemed wet today, and that rocky
mouth of his was loose; loose was the word for everything
about him, the way his arms and shoulders hung, the way he
sprawled at the table, rocking slightly back and forth. It was
not that he was drunk. Eric had seen him much drunker.
Drunk, he became rigid, as though he imagined himself in the
army again. No. He was old. It had come upon him all at
once, today, on his birthday. He sat there, his hair in his eyes,
eating, drinking, laughing now and again, and in a very
strange way, and teasing the dog at his feet so that it sleepily
growled and snapped all through the birthday dinner.

"Stop that," said Eric's father.

"Stop what?" asked Jamie.

"Let that stinking useless dog alone. Let him be quiet."

"Leave the beast alone," said Eric's mother—very wearily, sounding as she often sounded when talking to Eric.

"Well, now," said Jamie, grinning, and looking first at Eric's father and then at Eric's mother, "it *is* my beast. And a man's got a right to do as he likes with whatever's his."

"That dog's got a right to bite you, too," said Eric's mother, shortly.

"This dog's not going to bite me," said Jamie, "he knows I'll shoot him if he does."

"That dog knows you're not going to shoot him," said Eric's father. "Then you *would* be all alone."

"All alone," said Jamie, and looked around the table. "All alone." He lowered his eyes to his plate. Eric's father watched him. He said, "It's pretty serious to be all alone at *your* age." He smiled. "If I was you, I'd start thinking about it."

"I'm thinking about it," said Jamie. He began to grow red.

"No, you're not," said Eric's father, "you're dreaming about it."

"Well, goddammit," said Jamie, even redder now, "it isn't as though I haven't tried!"

"Ah," said Eric's father, "that was a *real* dream, that was. I used to pick *that* up on the streets of town every Saturday night."

"Yes," said Jamie, "I bet you did."

"I didn't think she was as bad as all that," said Eric's mother, quietly. "*I* liked her. I was surprised when she ran away."

"Jamie didn't know how to keep her," said Eric's father. He looked at Eric and chanted: *"Jamie, Jamie, pumkin-eater, had a wife and couldn't keep her!"* At this, Jamie at last looked up, into the eyes of Eric's father. Eric laughed again, more shrilly, out of fear. Jamie said:

"Ah, yes, you can talk, you can."

"It's not my fault," said Eric's father, "if you're getting old—and haven't got anybody to bring you your slippers when night comes—and no pitter-patter of little feet—"

"Oh, leave Jamie alone," said Eric's mother, "he's *not* old, leave him alone."

Jamie laughed a peculiar, high, clicking laugh which Eric had never heard before, which he did not like, which made him want to look away and, at the same time, want to stare. "Hell, no," said Jamie, "I'm not old. I can still do all the things we used to do." He put his elbows on the table, grinning. "I haven't ever told you, have I, about the things we used to do?"

"No, you haven't," said Eric's mother, "and I certainly don't want to hear about them now."

"He wouldn't tell you anyway," said Eric's father, "he knows what I'd do to him if he did."

"Oh, sure, sure," said Jamie, and laughed again. He picked up a bone from his plate. "Here," he said to Eric, "why don't you feed my poor mistreated dog?"

Eric took the bone and stood up, whistling for the dog; who moved away from his master and took the bone between his teeth. Jamie watched with a smile and opened the bottle of whiskey and poured himself a drink. Eric sat on the ground beside the dog, beginning to be sleepy in the bright, bright sun.

"Little Eric's getting big," he heard his father say.

"Yes," said Jamie, "they grow fast. It won't be long now."

"Won't be long *what?*" he heard his father ask.

"Why, before he starts skirt-chasing like his Daddy used to do," said Jamie. There was mild laughter at the table in which his mother did not join; he heard instead, or thought he heard, the familiar, slight, exasperated intake of her breath. No one seemed to care whether he came back to the table or not. He lay on his back, staring up at the sky, wondering—wondering what he would feel like when he was old—and fell asleep.

When he awoke his head was in his mother's lap, for she was sitting on the ground. Jamie and his father were still sitting at the table; he knew this from their voices, for he did not open his eyes. He did not want to move or speak. He wanted to remain where he was, protected by his mother, while the bright day rolled on. Then he wondered about the uncut birthday cake. But he was sure, from the sound of Jamie's voice, which was thicker now, that they had not cut it yet; or if they had, they had certainly saved a piece for him.

"—ate himself just as full as he could and then fell asleep in the sun like a little animal," Jamie was saying, and the two men laughed. His father—though he scarcely ever got as drunk as Jamie did, and had often carried Jamie home from The Rafters—was a little drunk, too.

Eric felt his mother's hand on his hair. By opening his eyes very slightly he would see, over the curve of his mother's thigh, as through a veil, a green slope far away and beyond it the everlasting, motionless sky.

"—she was a no-good *bitch*," said Jamie.

"She was beautiful," said his mother, just above him.

Again, they were talking about Jamie's wife.

"Beauty!" said Jamie, furious. "Beauty doesn't keep a house clean. Beauty doesn't keep a bed warm, neither."

Eric's father laughed. "You were so—poetical—in those days, Jamie," he said. "Nobody thought you cared much about things like that. I guess she thought you didn't care, neither."

"I cared," said Jamie, briefly.

"In fact," Eric's father continued, "I *know* she thought you didn't care."

"*How* do you know?" asked Jamie.

"She told me," Eric's father said.

"What do you mean," asked Jamie, "what do you mean, she told you?"

"I mean just that. She told me."

Jamie was silent.

"In those days," Eric's father continued after a moment, "all you did was walk around the woods by yourself in the daytime and sit around The Rafters in the evenings with me."

"You two were always together then," said Eric's mother.

"Well," said Jamie, harshly, "at least that hasn't changed."

"Now, you know," said Eric's father, gently, "it's not the same. Now I got a wife and kid—and another one coming—"

Eric's mother stroked his hair more gently, yet with something in her touch more urgent, too, and he knew that she was thinking of the child who lay in the churchyard, who would have been his sister.

"Yes," said Jamie, "you really got it all fixed up, you did. You got it all—the wife, the kid, the house, and all the land."

"I didn't steal your farm from you. It wasn't my fault you lost it. I gave you a better price for it than anybody else would have done."

"I'm not blaming you. I know all the things I have to thank you for."

There was a short pause, broken, hesitantly, by Eric's mother. "What I don't understand," she said, "is why, when you went away to the city, you didn't *stay* away. You didn't really have anything to keep you here."

There was the sound of a drink being poured. Then, "No. I didn't have nothing—*really*—to keep me here. Just all the things I ever knew—all the things—*all* the things—I ever cared about."

"A man's not supposed to sit around and mope," said Eric's father, wrathfully, "for things that are over and dead and finished, things that can't *ever* begin again, that can't ever be the same again. That's what I mean when I say you're a dreamer—and if you hadn't kept on dreaming so long, you might not be alone now."

"Ah, well," said Jamie, mildly, and with a curious rush of affection in his voice, 'I know you're the giant-killer, the hunter, the lover—the real old Adam, that's you. I know you're going to cover the earth. I know the world depends on men like you."

"And you're damn right," said Eric's father, after an uneasy moment.

Around Eric's head there was a buzzing, a bee, perhaps, a blue-fly, or a wasp. He hoped that his mother would see it and brush it away, but she did not move her hand. And he looked out again, through the veil of his eyelashes, at the slope and the sky, and then saw that the sun had moved and that it would not be long now before she would be going.

"—just like you already," Jamie said.

"You think my little one's like me?" Eric knew that his father was smiling—he could almost feel his father's hands.

"Looks like you, walks like you, talks like you," said Jamie.

"*And* stubborn like you," said Eric's mother.

"Ah, yes," said Jamie, and sighed. "You married the stubbornest, most determined—most selfish—man I know."

"I didn't know you felt that way," said Eric's father. He was still smiling.

"I'd have warned you about him," Jamie added, laughing, "if there'd been time."

"Everyone who knows you feels that way," said Eric's mother, and Eric felt a sudden brief tightening of the muscle in her thigh.

"Oh, *you*," said Eric's father, "I know *you* feel that way, women like to feel that way, it makes them feel important. But," and he changed to the teasing tone he took so persistently with Jamie today, "I didn't know my fine friend, Jamie, here—"

It was odd how unwilling he was to open his eyes. Yet, he felt the sun on him and knew that he wanted to rise from where he was before the sun went down. He did not understand what they were talking about this afternoon, these grown-ups he had known all his life; by keeping his eyes closed he kept their conversation far from him. And his mother's hand lay on his head like a blessing, like protection. And the buzzing had ceased, the bee, the blue-fly, or the wasp seemed to have flown away.

"—if it's a boy this time," his father said, "we'll name it after you."

"That's touching," said Jamie, "but that really won't do me—or the kid—a hell of a lot of good."

"Jamie can get married and have kids of his own any time he decides to," said Eric's mother.

"No," said his father, after a long pause, "Jamie's thought about it too long."

And, suddenly, he laughed and Eric sat up as his father slapped Jamie on the knee. At the touch, Jamie leaped up, shouting, spilling his drink and overturning his chair, and the dog beside Eric awoke and began to bark. For a moment, before Eric's unbelieving eyes, there was nothing in the yard but noise and flame.

His father rose slowly and stared at Jamie. "What's the matter with you?"

"What's the matter with me!" mimicked Jamie, "what's the matter with me? what the hell do you care what's the matter with me! What the hell have you been riding me for all day like this? What do you want? what do you *want*?"

"I want you to learn to hold your liquor for one thing," said his father, coldly. The two men stared at each other. Jamie's face was red and ugly and tears stood in his eyes. The dog, at his legs, kept up a furious prancing and barking. Jamie bent down and, with one hand, with all his might, slapped his dog, which rolled over, howling, and ran away to hide itself under the shadows of the far grey wall.

Then Jamie stared again at Eric's father, trembling, and pushed his hair back from his eyes.

"You better pull yourself together," Eric's father said. And, to Eric's mother, "Get him some coffee. He'll be all right."

Jamie set his glass on the table and picked up the over-turned chair. Eric's mother rose and went into the kitchen. Eric remained sitting on the ground, staring at the two men, his father and his father's best friend, who had become so unfamiliar. His father, with something in his face which Eric had never before seen there, a tenderness, a sorrow—or perhaps it was, after all, the look he sometimes wore when approaching a calf he was about to slaughter—looked down at Jamie where he sat, head bent, at the table. "You take things too hard," he said. "You always have. I was only teasing you for your own good."

Jamie did not answer. His father looked over to Eric, and smiled.

"Come on," he said. "You and me are going for a walk."

Eric, passing on the side of the table farthest from Jamie, went to his father and took his hand.

"Pull yourself together," his father said to Jamie. "We're going to cut your birthday cake as soon as me and the little one come back."

Eric and his father passed beyond the grey wall where the dog still whimpered, out into the fields. Eric's father was walking too fast and Eric stumbled on the uneven ground. When they had gone a little distance his father abruptly checked his pace and looked down at Eric, grinning.

"I'm sorry," he said. "I guess I said we were going for a walk, not running to put out a fire."

"What's the matter with Jamie?" Eric asked.

"Oh," said his father, looking westward where the sun was moving, pale orange now, making the sky ring with brass and copper and gold—which, like a magician, she was presenting only to demonstrate how variously they could be transformed—"Oh," he repeated, "there's nothing wrong with Jamie. He's been drinking a lot," and he grinned down at Eric, "and he's been sitting in the sun—you know, his hair's not as thick as yours," and he ruffled Eric's hair, "and I guess birthdays make him nervous. Hell," he said, "they make me nervous, too."

"Jamie's *very* old," said Eric, "isn't he?"

His father laughed. "Well, butch, he's not exactly ready to fall into the grave yet—he's going to be around awhile, is Jamie. Hey," he said, and looked down at Eric again, "you must think I'm an old man, too."

"Oh," said Eric, quickly, "I know you're not as old as Jamie."

His father laughed again. "Well, thank you, son. That shows real confidence. I'll try to live up to it."

They walked in silence for awhile and then his father said, not looking at Eric, speaking to himself, it seemed, or to the air: "No, Jamie's not so old. He's not as old as he should be."

"How old *should* he be?" asked Eric.

"Why," said his father, "he ought to be his age," and, looking down at Eric's face, he burst into laughter again.

"Ah," he said, finally, and put his hand on Eric's head again, very gently, very sadly, "don't you worry now about what you don't understand. The time is coming when you'll have to worry—but that time hasn't come yet."

Then they walked till they came to the steep slope which led to the railroad tracks, down, down, far below them, where a small train seemed to be passing forever through the countryside, smoke, like the very definition of idleness, blowing out of the chimney stack of the toy locomotive. Eric thought, resentfully, that he scarcely ever saw a train pass when he came here alone. Beyond the railroad tracks was the river where they sometimes went swimming in the summer. The river was hidden from them now by the high bank where there were houses and where tall trees grew.

"And this," said his father, "is where your land ends."

"What?" said Eric.

His father squatted on the ground and put one hand on Eric's shoulder. "You know all the way we walked, from the house?" Eric nodded. "Well," said his father, "that's your land."

Eric looked back at the long way they had come, feeling his father watching him.

His father, with a pressure on his shoulder made him turn; he pointed: "And over there. It belongs to you." He turned him again. "And that," he said, "that's yours, too."

Eric stared at his father. "Where does it end?" he asked.

His father rose. "I'll show you that another day," he said. "But it's further than you can walk."

They started walking slowly, in the direction of the sun.

"When did it get to be mine?" asked Eric.

"The day you were born," his father said, and looked down at him and smiled.

"My father," he said, after a moment, "had some of this land—and when he died, it was mine. He held on to it for me. And I did my best with the land I had, and I got some more. I'm holding on to it for you."

He looked down to see if Eric was listening. Eric was listening, staring at his father and looking around him at the great countryside.

"When I get to be a real old man," said his father, "even older than old Jamie there—you're going to have to take care of all this. When I die it's going to be yours." He paused and stopped; Eric looked up at him. "When you get to be a big man, like your Papa, you're going to get married and have children. And all this is going to be theirs."

"And when *they* get married?" Eric prompted.

"All this will belong to *their* children," his father said.

"Forever?" cried Eric.

"Forever," said his father.

They turned and started walking toward the house.

"Jamie," Eric asked at last, "how much land has *he* got?"

"Jamie doesn't have any land," his father said.

"Why not?" asked Eric.

"He didn't take care of it," his father said, "and he lost it."

"Jamie doesn't have a wife anymore, either, does he?" Eric asked.

"No," said his father. "He didn't take care of her, either."

"And he doesn't have any little boy," said Eric—very sadly.

"No," said his father. Then he grinned. "But *I* have."

"*Why* doesn't Jamie have a little boy?" asked Eric.

His father shrugged. "Some people do, Eric, some people don't."

"Will I?" asked Eric.

"Will you what?" asked his father.

"Will I get married and have a little boy?"

His father seemed for a moment both amused and checked. He looked down at Eric with a strange, slow smile. "Of course you will," he said at last. "Of course you will." And he held out his arms. "Come," he said, "climb up. I'll ride you on my shoulders home."

So Eric rode on his father's shoulders through the wide green fields which belonged to him, into the yard which held the house which would hear the first cries of his children. His mother and Jamie sat at the table talking quietly in the silver sun. Jamie had washed his face and combed his hair, he seemed calmer, he was smiling.

"Ah," cried Jamie, "the lord, the master of this house arrives! And bears on his shoulders the prince, the son, and heir!" He described a flourish, bowing low in the yard. "My lords! Behold your humble, most properly chastised servant, desirous of your—compassion, your love, and your forgiveness!"

"Frankly," said Eric's father, putting Eric on the ground, "I'm not sure that this is an improvement." He looked at Jamie and frowned and grinned. "Let's cut that cake."

Eric stood with his mother in the kitchen while she lit the candles—thirty-five, one, as they said, to grow on, though Jamie, surely, was far past the growing age—and followed her as she took the cake outside. Jamie took the great, gleaming knife and held it with a smile.

"Happy Birthday!" they cried—only Eric said nothing—and then Eric's mother said, "You have to blow out the candles, Jamie, before you cut the cake."

"It looks so pretty the way it is," Jamie said.

"Go ahead," said Eric's father, and clapped him on the back, "be a man."

Then the dog, once more beside his master, awoke, growling, and this made everybody laugh. Jamie laughed loudest. Then he blew out the candles, all of them at once, and Eric watched him as he cut the cake. Jamie raised his eyes and looked at Eric and it was at this moment, as the suddenly blood-red sun was striking the topmost tips of trees, that Eric had looked into Jamie's eyes. Jamie smiled that strange smile of an old man and Eric moved closer to his mother.

"The first piece for Eric," said Jamie, then, and extended it to him on the silver blade.

That had been near the end of summer, nearly two months ago. Very shortly after the birthday party, his mother had fallen ill and had had to be taken away. Then his father spent more time than ever at The Rafters; he and Jamie came home in the evenings, stumbling drunk. Sometimes, during the time that his mother was away, Jamie did not go home at all, but spent the night at the farm house; and once or twice Eric had awakened in the middle of the night, or near dawn, and heard Jamie's footsteps walking up and down, walking up and down, in the big room downstairs. It has been a strange and dreadful time, a time of waiting, stillness, and silence. His father rarely went into the fields, scarcely raised himself to give orders to his farm hands—it was unnatural, it was frightening, to find him around the house all day, and Jamie was there always, Jamie and his dog. Then one day Eric's father told him that his mother was coming home but that she would not be bringing him a baby brother or sister, not this time, nor in any time to come. He started to say something more, then looked at Jamie who was standing by, and walked out of the house. Jamie followed him slowly, his hands in his pockets and his head bent. From the time of the birthday party, as though he were repenting of that outburst, or as though it had frightened him, Jamie had become more silent than ever.

When his mother came back she seemed to have grown older—old; she seemed to have shrunk within herself, away from them all, even, in a kind of storm of love and helplessness, away from Eric; but, oddly, and most particularly, away from Jamie. It was in nothing she said, nothing she did—or perhaps it was in everything she said and did. She washed and cooked for Jamie as before, took him into account as much as before as a part of the family, made him take second helpings at the table, smiled good night to him as he left the house—it was only that something had gone out of her familiarity. She seemed to do all that she did out of memory and from a great distance. And if something had gone out of her ease, something had come into it, too, a curiously still attention, as though she had been startled by some new aspect of something she had always known. Once or twice at the supper table, Eric caught her regard bent on Jamie, who, obliviously, ate. He could not read her look, but it reminded him of that moment at the birthday party when he had looked into Jamie's eyes. She seemed to be looking at Jamie as though she were wondering why she had not looked at him before; or as though she were discovering, with some surprise, that she had never really liked him but also felt, in her weariness and weakness, that it did not really matter now.

Now, as he entered the yard, he saw her standing in the kitchen doorway, looking out, shielding her eyes against the brilliant setting sun.

"Eric!" she cried, wrathfully, as soon as she saw him, "I've been looking high and low for you for the last hour. You're getting old enough to have some sense of responsibility and I wish you wouldn't worry me so when you know I've not been well."

She made him feel guilty at the same time that he dimly and resentfully felt that justice was not all on her side. She pulled him to her, turning his face up toward hers, roughly, with one hand.

"You're filthy," she said, then. "Go around to the pump and wash your face. And hurry, so I can give you your supper and put you to bed."

And she turned and went into the kitchen, closing the door

lightly behind her. He walked around to the other side of the house, to the pump.

On a wooden box next to the pump was a piece of soap and a damp rag. Eric picked up the soap, not thinking of his mother, but thinking of the day gone by, already half asleep: and thought of where he would go tomorrow. He moved the pump handle up and down and the water rushed out and wet his socks and shoes—this would make his mother angry, but he was too tired to care. Nevertheless, automatically, he moved back a little. He held the soap between his hands, his hands beneath the water.

He had been many places, he had walked a long way and seen many things that day. He had gone down to the railroad tracks and walked beside the tracks for awhile, hoping that a train would pass. He kept telling himself that he would give the train one more last chance to pass; and when he had given it a considerable number of last chances, he left the railroad bed and climbed a little and walked through the high, sweet meadows. He walked through a meadow where there were cows and they looked at him dully with their great dull eyes and moo'd among each other about him. A man from the far end of the field saw him and shouted, but Eric could not tell whether it was someone who worked for his father or not and so he turned and ran away, ducking through the wire fence. He passed an apple tree, with apples lying all over the ground—he wondered if the apples belonged to him, if he were still walking on his own land or had gone past it—but he ate an apple anyway and put some in his pockets, watching a lone brown horse in a meadow far below him nibbling at the grass and flicking his tail. Eric pretended that he was his father and was walking through the fields as he had seen his father walk, looking it all over calmly, pleased, knowing that everything he saw belonged to him. And he stopped and pee'd as he had seen his father do, standing wide-legged and heavy in the middle of the fields; he pretended at the same time to be smoking and talking, as he had seen his father do. Then, having watered the ground, he walked on, and all the earth, for that moment, in Eric's eyes, seemed to be celebrating Eric.

Tomorrow he would go away again, somewhere. For soon

it would be winter, snow would cover the ground, he would not be able to wander off alone.

He held the soap between his hands, his hands beneath the water; then he heard a low whistle behind him and a rough hand on his head and the soap fell from his hands and slithered between his legs onto the ground.

He turned and faced Jamie, Jamie without his dog.

"Come on, little fellow," Jamie whispered. "We got something in the barn to show you."

"Oh, did the calf come yet?" asked Eric—and was too pleased to wonder why Jamie whispered.

"Your Papa's there," said Jamie. And then: "Yes. Yes, the calf is coming now."

And he took Eric's hand and they crossed the yard, past the closed kitchen door, past the stone wall and across the field, into the barn.

"But *this* isn't where the cows are!" Eric cried. He suddenly looked up at Jamie, who closed the barn door behind them and looked down at Eric with a smile.

"No," said Jamie, "that's right. No cows here." And he leaned against the door as though his strength had left him. Eric saw that his face was wet, he breathed as though he had been running.

"Let's go see the cows," Eric whispered. Then he wondered why he was whispering and was terribly afraid. He stared at Jamie, who stared at him.

"In a minute," Jamie said, and stood up. He had put his hands in his pockets and now he brought them out and Eric stared at his hands and began to move away. He asked, "Where's my Papa?"

"Why," said Jamie, "he's down at The Rafters, I guess. I have to meet him there soon."

"I have to go," said Eric. "I have to eat my supper." He tried to move to the door, but Jamie did not move. "I have to go," he repeated, and, as Jamie moved toward him the tight ball of terror in his bowels, in his throat, swelled and rose, exploded, he opened his mouth to scream but Jamie's fingers closed around his throat. He stared, stared into Jamie's eyes.

"That won't do you any good," said Jamie. And he smiled.

Eric struggled for breath, struggled with pain and fright. Jamie relaxed his grip a little and moved one hand and stroked Eric's tangled hair. Slowly, wondrously, his face changed, tears came into his eyes and rolled down his face.

Eric groaned—perhaps because he saw Jamie's tears or because his throat was so swollen and burning, because he could not catch his breath, because he was so frightened—he began to sob in great, unchildish gasps. "Why do you hate my father?"

"I love your father," Jamie said. But he was not listening to Eric. He was far away—as though he were struggling, toiling inwardly up a tall, tall mountain. And Eric struggled blindly, with all the force of his desire to live, to reach him, to stop him before he reached the summit.

"Jamie," Eric whispered, "you can have the land. You can have all the land."

Jamie spoke, but not to Eric: "I don't want the land."

"I'll be your little boy," said Eric. "I'll be your little boy forever and forever and forever—and you can have the land and you can live forever! Jamie!"

Jamie had stopped weeping. He was watching Eric.

"We'll go for a walk tomorrow," Eric said, "and I'll show it to you, all of it—really and truly—if you kill my father I can be your little boy and we can have it all!"

"This land," said Jamie, "will belong to no one."

"Please!" cried Eric, "oh, please! Please!"

He heard his mother singing in the kitchen. Soon she would come out to look for him. The hands left him for a moment. Eric opened his mouth to scream, but the hands then closed around his throat.

Mama. Mama.

The singing was further and further away. The eyes looked into his, there was a question in the eyes, the hands tightened. Then the mouth began to smile. He had never seen such a smile before. He kicked and kicked.

Mama. Mama. Mama. Mama. Mama.

Far away, he heard his mother call him.

Mama.

He saw nothing, he knew that he was in the barn, he heard a terrible breathing near him, he thought he heard the sniffling of beasts, he remembered the sun, the railroad tracks, the cows, the apples, and the ground. He thought of tomorrow—he wanted to go away again somewhere tomorrow. *I'll take you with me,* he wanted to say. He wanted to argue the question, the question he remembered in the eyes—wanted to say, *I'll tell my Papa you're hurting me.* Then terror and agony and darkness overtook him, and his breath went violently out of him. He dropped on his face in the straw in the barn, his yellow head useless on his broken neck.

Night covered the countryside and here and there, like emblems, the lights of houses glowed. A woman's voice called, "Eric! Eric!"

Jamie reached his wooden house and opened his door; whistled, and his dog came bounding out of darkness, leaping up on him; and he cuffed it down lightly, with one hand. Then he closed his door and started down the road, his dog beside him, his hands in his pockets. He stopped to light his pipe. He heard singing from The Rafters, then he saw the lights; soon, the lights and the sound of singing diminished behind him. When Jamie no longer heard the singing, he began to whistle the song that he had heard.

Previous Condition

I WOKE UP shaking, alone in my room. I was clammy cold with sweat; under me the sheet and the mattress were soaked. The sheet was gray and twisted like a rope. I breathed like I had been running.

I couldn't move for the longest while. I just lay on my back, spread-eagled, looking up at the ceiling, listening to the sounds of people getting up in other parts of the house, alarm clocks ringing and water splashing and doors opening and shutting and feet on the stairs. I could tell when people left for work: the hall doorway downstairs whined and shuffled as it opened and gave a funny kind of double slam as it closed. One thud and then a louder thud and then a little final click. While the door was open I could hear the street sounds too, horses' hoofs and delivery wagons and people in the streets and big trucks and motor cars screaming on the asphalt.

I had been dreaming. At night I dreamt and woke up in the morning trembling, but not remembering the dream, except that in the dream I had been running. I could not remember when the dream—or dreams—had started; it had been long ago. For long periods maybe, I would have no dreams at all. And then they would come back, every night, I would try not to go to bed, I would go to sleep frightened and wake up frightened and have another day to get through with the nightmare at my shoulder. Now I was back from Chicago, busted, living off my friends in a dirty furnished room downtown. The show I had been with had folded in Chicago. It hadn't been much of a part—or much of a show either, to tell the truth. I played a kind of intellectual Uncle Tom, a young college student working for his race. The playwright had wanted to prove he was a liberal, I guess. But, as I say, the show had folded and here I was, back in New York and hating it. I knew that I should be getting another job, making the rounds, pounding the pavement. But I didn't. I couldn't face it. It was summer. I seemed to be fagged out. And every day I hated myself more. Acting's a rough life, even if you're white. I'm not tall and I'm not good looking and I can't sing or dance and I'm not white; so even at the best of times I wasn't in much demand.

The room I lived in was heavy ceilinged, perfectly square, with walls the color of chipped dry blood. Jules Weissman, a Jewboy, had got the room for me. It's a room to sleep in, he said, or maybe to die in but God knows it wasn't meant to live in. Perhaps because the room was so hideous it had a fantastic array of light fixtures: one on the ceiling, one on the left wall, two on the right wall, and a lamp on the table beside my bed. My bed was in front of the window through which nothing ever blew but dust. It was a furnished room and they'd thrown enough stuff in it to furnish three rooms its size. Two easy chairs and a desk, the bed, the table, a straight-backed chair, a bookcase, a cardboard wardrobe; and my books and my suitcase, both unpacked; and my dirty clothes flung in a corner. It was the kind of room that defeated you. It had a fireplace, too, and a heavy marble mantelpiece and a great gray mirror above the mantelpiece. It was hard to see anything in the mirror very clearly—which was perhaps just as well—and it would have been worth your life to have started a fire in the fireplace.

"Well, you won't have to stay here long," Jules told me the night I came. Jules smuggled me in, sort of, after dark, when everyone had gone to bed.

"Christ, I hope not."

"I'll be moving to a big place soon," Jules said. "You can move in with me." He turned all the lights on. "Think it'll be all right for a while?" He sounded apologetic, as though he had designed the room himself.

"Oh, sure. D'you think I'll have any trouble?"

"I don't think so. The rent's paid. She can't put you out."

I didn't say anything to that.

"Sort of stay undercover," Jules said. "You know."

"Roger," I said.

I had been living there for three days, timing it so I left after everyone else had gone, coming back late at night when everyone else was asleep. But I knew it wouldn't work. A couple of the tenants had seen me on the stairs, a woman had surprised me coming out of the john. Every morning I waited for the landlady to come banging on the door. I didn't know what would happen. It might be all right. It might not be. But the waiting was getting me.

The sweat on my body was turning cold. Downstairs a radio was tuned in to the Breakfast Symphony. They were playing Beethoven. I sat up and lit a cigarette. "Peter," I said, "don't let them scare you to death. You're a man, too." I listened to Ludwig and I watched the smoke rise to the dirty ceiling. Under Ludwig's drums and horns I listened to hear footsteps on the stairs.

I'd done a lot of traveling in my time. I'd knocked about through St. Louis, Frisco, Seattle, Detroit, New Orleans, worked at just about everything. I'd run away from my old lady when I was about sixteen. She'd never been able to handle me. You'll never be nothin' *but* a bum, she'd say. We lived in an old shack in a town in New Jersey in the nigger part of town, the kind of houses colored people live in all over the U.S. I hated my mother for living there. I hated all the people in my neighborhood. They went to church and they got drunk. They were nice to the white people. When the landlord came around they paid him and took his crap.

The first time I was ever called nigger I was seven years old. It was a little white girl with long black curls. I used to leave the front of my house and go wandering by myself through town. This little girl was playing ball alone and as I passed her the ball rolled out of her hands into the gutter.

I threw it back to her.

"Let's play catch," I said.

But she held the ball and made a face at me.

"My mother don't let me play with niggers," she told me.

I did not know what the word meant. But my skin grew warm. I stuck my tongue out at her.

"I don't care. Keep your old ball." I started down the street.

She screamed after me: "Nigger, nigger, nigger!"

I screamed back: "Your mother was a nigger!"

I asked my mother what a nigger was.

"Who called you that?"

"I heard somebody say it."

"Who?"

"Just somebody."

"Go wash your face," she said. "You dirty as sin. Your supper's on the table."

I went to the bathroom and splashed water on my face and wiped my face and hands on the towel.

"You call that clean?" my mother cried. "Come here, boy!"

She dragged me back to the bathroom and began to soap my face and neck.

"You run around dirty like you do all the time, everybody'll call you a little nigger, you hear?" She rinsed my face and looked at my hands and dried me. "Now, go on and eat your supper."

I didn't say anything. I went to the kitchen and sat down at the table. I remember I wanted to cry. My mother sat down across from me.

"Mama," I said. She looked at me. I started to cry.

She came around to my side of the table and took me in her arms.

"Baby, don't fret. Next time somebody calls you nigger you tell them you'd rather be your color than be lowdown and nasty like some white folks is."

We formed gangs when I was older, my friends and I. We met white boys and their friends on the opposite sides of fences and we threw rocks and tin cans at each other.

I'd come home bleeding. My mother would slap me and scold me and cry.

"Boy, you wanna get killed? You wanna end up like your father?"

My father was a bum and I had never seen him. I was named for him: Peter.

I was always in trouble: truant officers, welfare workers, everybody else in town.

"You ain't never gonna be nothin' *but* a bum," my mother said.

By and by older kids I knew finished school and got jobs and got married and settled down. They were going to settle down and bring more black babies into the world and pay the same rents for the same old shacks and it would go on and on—

When I was sixteen I ran away. I left a note and told Mama not to worry, I'd come back one day and I'd be all right. But when I was twenty-two she died. I came back and put my mother in the ground. Everything was like it had been. Our house had not been painted and the porch floor sagged and there was somebody's raincoat stuffed in the broken window. Another family was moving in.

Their furniture was stacked along the walls and their children were running through the house and laughing and somebody was frying pork chops in the kitchen. The oldest boy was tacking up a mirror.

Last year Ida took me driving in her big car and we passed through a couple of towns upstate. We passed some crumbling houses on the left. The clothes on the line were flying in the wind.

"Are people living there?" asked Ida.

"Just darkies," I said.

Ida passed the car ahead, banging angrily on the horn. "D'you know you're becoming paranoiac, Peter?"

"All right. All right. I know a lot of white people are starving too."

"You're damn right they are. I know a little about poverty myself."

Ida had come from the kind of family called shanty Irish. She was raised in Boston. She's a very beautiful woman who married young and married for money—so now I can afford to support attractive young men, she'd giggle. Her husband was a ballet dancer who was forever on the road. Ida suspected that he went with boys. Not that I give a damn, she said, as long as he leaves me alone. When we met last year she was thirty and I was twenty-five. We had a pretty stormy relationship but we stuck. Whenever I got to town I called her; whenever I was stranded out of town I'd let her know. We never let it get too serious. She went her way and I went mine.

In all this running around I'd learned a few things. Like a prizefighter learns to take a blow or a dancer learns to fall, I'd learned how to get by. I'd learned never to be belligerent with policemen, for instance. No matter who was right, I was certain to be wrong. What might be accepted as just good old

American independence in someone else would be insufferable
arrogance in me. After the first few times I realized that I had
to play smart, to act out the role I was expected to play. I
only had one head and it was too easy to get it broken. When
I faced a policeman I acted like I didn't know a thing. I let
my jaw drop and I let my eyes get big. I didn't give him any
smart answers, none of the crap about my rights. I figured
out what answers he wanted and I gave them to him. I never
let him think he wasn't king. If it was more than routine, if I
was picked up on suspicion of robbery or murder in the neighborhood, I looked as humble as I could and kept my mouth
shut and prayed. I took a couple of beatings but I stayed out
of prison and I stayed off chain gangs. That was also due to
luck, Ida pointed out once. "Maybe it would've been better
for you if you'd been a little less lucky. Worse things have
happened than chain gangs. Some of them have happened to
you."

There was something in her voice. "What are you talking
about?" I asked.

"Don't lose your temper. I said maybe."

"You mean you think I'm a coward?"

"I didn't say that, Peter."

"But you meant that. Didn't you?"

"No. I didn't mean that. I didn't mean anything. Let's not
fight."

There are times and places when a Negro can use his color
like a shield. He can trade on the subterranean Anglo-Saxon
guilt and get what he wants that way; or some of what he
wants. He can trade on his nuisance value, his value as forbidden fruit; he can use it like a knife, he can twist it and get
his vengeance that way. I knew these things long before I
realized that I knew them and in the beginning I used them,
not knowing what I was doing. Then when I began to see it,
I felt betrayed. I felt beaten as a person. I had no honest place
to stand.

This was the year before I met Ida. I'd been acting in stock
companies and little theaters; sometimes fairly good parts.
People were nice to me. They told me I had talent. They said
it sadly, as though they were thinking, What a pity, he'll never

get anywhere. I had got to the point where I resented praise and I resented pity and I wondered what people were thinking when they shook my hand. In New York I met some pretty fine people; easygoing, hard-drinking, flotsam and jetsam; and they liked me; and I wondered if I trusted them; if I was able any longer to trust anybody. Not on top, where all the world could see, but underneath where everybody lives.

Soon I would have to get up. I listened to Ludwig. He shook the little room like the footsteps of a giant marching miles away. On summer evenings (and maybe we would go this summer) Jules and Ida and I would go up to the Stadium and sit beneath the pillars on the cold stone steps. There it seemed to me the sky was far away; and I was not myself, I was high and lifted up. We never talked, the three of us. We sat and watched the blue smoke curl in the air and watched the orange tips of cigarettes. Every once in a while the boys who sold popcorn and soda pop and ice cream climbed the steep steps chattering; and Ida shifted slightly and touched her blue-black hair; and Jules scowled. I sat with my knee up, watching the lighted half-moon below, the black-coated, straining conductor, the faceless men beneath him moving together in a rhythm like the sea. There were pauses in the music for the rushing, calling, halting piano. Everything would stop except the climbing soloist; he would reach a height and everything would join him, the violins first and then the horns; and then the deep blue bass and the flute and the bitter trampling drums; beating, beating and mounting together and stopping with a crash like daybreak. When I first heard the *Messiah* I was alone; my blood bubbled like fire and wine; I cried; like an infant crying for its mother's milk; or a sinner running to meet Jesus.

Now below the music I heard footsteps on the stairs. I put out my cigarette. My heart was beating so hard I thought it would tear my chest apart. Someone knocked on the door.

I thought: Don't answer. Maybe she'll go away.

But the knocking came again, harder this time.

Just a minute, I said. I sat on the edge of the bed and put on my bathrobe. I was trembling like a fool. For Christ's sake,

Peter, you've been through this before. What's the worst thing that can happen? You won't have a room. The world's full of rooms.

When I opened the door the landlady stood there, red-and-whitefaced and hysterical.

"Who are you? I didn't rent this room to you."

My mouth was dry. I started to say something.

"I can't have no colored people here," she said. "All my tenants are complainin'. Women afraid to come home nights."

"They ain't gotta be afraid of me," I said. I couldn't get my voice up; it rasped and rattled in my throat; and I began to be angry. I wanted to kill her. "My friend rented this room for me," I said.

"Well, I'm sorry, he didn't have no right to do that, I don't have nothin' against you, but you gotta get out."

Her glasses blinked, opaque in the light on the landing. She was frightened to death. She was afraid of me but she was more afraid of losing her tenants. Her face was mottled with rage and fear, her breath came rushed and little bits of spittle gathered at the edges of her mouth; her breath smelled bad, like rotting hamburger on a July day.

"You can't put me out," I said. "This room was rented in my name." I started to close the door, as though the matter was finished: "I live here, see, this is my room, you can't put me out."

"You get outa my house!" she screamed. "I got the right to know who's in my house! This is a white neighborhood, I don't rent to colored people. Why don't you go on uptown, like you belong?"

"I can't stand niggers," I told her. I started to close the door again but she moved and stuck her foot in the way. I wanted to kill her, I watched her stupid, wrinkled, frightened white face and I wanted to take a club, a hatchet, and bring it down with all my weight, splitting her skull down the middle where she parted her iron-grey hair.

"Get out of the door," I said. "I want to get dressed."

But I knew that she had won, that I was already on my way. We stared at each other. Neither of us moved. From her came an emanation of fear and fury and something else. You maggot-eaten bitch, I thought. I said evilly, "You wanna come in and watch me?" Her face didn't change, she didn't take her foot away. My skin prickled, tiny hot needles punctured my flesh. I was aware of my body under the bathrobe; and it was as though I had done something wrong, something monstrous, years ago, which no one had forgotten and for which I would be killed.

"If you don't get out," she said, "I'll get a policeman to put you out."

I grabbed the door to keep from touching her. "All right. All right. You can have the goddamn room. Now get out and let me dress."

She turned away. I slammed the door. I heard her going down the stairs. I threw stuff into my suitcase. I tried to take as long as possible but I cut myself while shaving because I was afraid she would come back upstairs with a policeman.

Jules was making coffee when I walked in.

"Good morning, good morning! What happened to you?"

"No room at the inn," I said. "Pour a cup of coffee for the notorious son of man." I sat down and dropped my suitcase on the floor.

Jules looked at me. "Oh. Well. Coffee coming up."

He got out the coffee cups. I lit a cigarette and sat there. I couldn't think of anything to say. I knew that Jules felt bad and I wanted to tell him that it wasn't his fault.

He pushed coffee in front of me and sugar and cream.

"Cheer up, baby. The world's wide and life—life, she is very long."

"Shut up. I don't want to hear any of your bad philosophy."

"Sorry."

"I mean, let's not talk about the good, the true, and the beautiful."

"All right. But don't sit there holding onto your table manners. Scream if you want to."

"Screaming won't do any good. Besides I'm a big boy now."

I stirred my coffee. "Did you give her a fight?" Jules asked. I shook my head. "No."

"Why the hell not?"

I shrugged; a little ashamed now. I couldn't have won it. What the hell.

"You might have won it. You might have given her a couple of bad moments."

"Goddamit to hell, I'm sick of it. Can't I get a place to sleep without dragging it through the courts? I'm goddamn tired of battling every Tom, Dick, and Harry for what everybody else takes for granted. I'm tired, man, tired! Have you ever been sick to death of something? Well, I'm sick to death. And I'm scared. I've been fighting so goddamn long I'm not a person any more. I'm not Booker T. Washington. I've got no vision of emancipating anybody. I want to emancipate myself. If this goes on much longer, they'll send me to Bellevue, I'll blow my top, I'll break somebody's head. I'm not worried about that miserable little room. I'm worried about what's happening to me, *to me*, inside. I don't walk the streets, I crawl. I've never been like this before. Now when I go to a strange place I wonder what will happen, will I be accepted, if I'm accepted, can I accept?—"

"Take it easy," Jules said.

"Jules, I'm beaten."

"I don't think you are. Drink your coffee."

"Oh," I cried, "I know you think I'm making it dramatic, that I'm paranoiac and just inventing trouble! Maybe I think so sometimes, how can I tell? You get so used to being hit you find you're always waiting for it. Oh, I know, you're Jewish, you get kicked around, too, but you can walk into a bar and nobody *knows* you're Jewish and if you go looking for a job you'll get a better job than mine! How can I say what it feels like? I don't know. I know everybody's in trouble and nothing is easy, but how can I explain to you what it feels like to be black when I don't understand it and don't want to and spend all my time trying to forget it? I don't want to hate anybody—but now maybe, I can't love anybody either—are we friends? Can we be really friends?"

"We're friends," Jules said, "don't worry about it." He scowled. "If I wasn't Jewish I'd ask you why you didn't live in Harlem." I looked at him. He raised his hand and smiled—"But I'm Jewish, so I didn't ask you. Ah Peter," he said, "I can't help you—take a walk, get drunk, we're all in this to-gether."

I stood up. "I'll be around later. I'm sorry."

"Don't be sorry. I'll leave my door open. Bunk here for awhile."

"Thanks," I said.

I felt that I was drowning; that hatred had corrupted me like cancer in the bone.

I saw Ida for dinner. We met in a restaurant in the Village, an Italian place in a gloomy cellar with candles on the tables.

It was not a busy night, for which I was grateful. When I came in there were only two other couples on the other side of the room. No one looked at me. I sat down in a corner booth and ordered a Scotch old-fashioned. Ida was late and I had three of them before she came.

She was very fine in black, a high-necked dress with a pearl choker; and her hair was combed page-boy style, falling just below her ears.

"You look real sweet, baby."

"Thank you. It took fifteen extra minutes but I hoped it would be worth it."

"It was worth it. What're you drinking?"

"Oh—what're you drinking?"

"Old-fashioneds."

She sniffed and looked at me. "How many?"

I laughed. "Three."

"Well," she said, "I suppose you had to do something." The waiter came over. We decided on one Manhattan and one lasagna and one spaghetti with clam sauce and another old-fashioned for me.

"Did you have a constructive day, sweetheart? Find a job?"

"Not today," I said. I lit her cigarette. "Metro offered me a fortune to come to the coast and do the lead in *Native Son* but I turned it down. Type casting, you know. It's so difficult to find a decent part."

"Well, if they don't come up with a decent offer soon tell them you'll go back to Selznick. *He'll* find you a part with guts—the very *idea* of offering you *Native Son*! I wouldn't stand for it."

"You ain't gotta tell me. I told them if they didn't find me a decent script in two weeks I was through, that's all."

"Now that's talking, Peter my lad."

The drinks came and we sat in silence for a minute or two. I finished half of my drink at a swallow and played with the toothpicks on the table. I felt Ida watching me.

"Peter, you're going to be awfully drunk."

"Honeychile, the first thing a southern gentleman learns is how to hold his liquor."

"That myth is older than the rock of ages. And anyway you come from Jersey."

I finished my drink and snarled at her: "That's just as good as the South."

Across the table from me I could see that she was readying herself for trouble: her mouth tightened slightly, setting her chin so that the faint cleft showed: "What happened to you today?"

I resented her concern; I resented my need. "Nothing worth talking about," I muttered, "just a mood."

And I tried to smile at her, to wipe away the bitterness.

"Now I know something's the matter. Please tell me."

It sounded trivial as hell: "You know the room Jules found for me? Well, the landlady kicked me out of it today."

"God save the American republic," Ida said. "D'you want to waste some of my husband's money? We can sue her."

"Forget it. I'll end up with lawsuits in every state in the union."

"Still, as a gesture—"

"The devil with the gesture. I'll get by."

The food came. I didn't want to eat. The first mouthful hit my belly like a gong. Ida began cutting up lasagna.

"Peter," she said, "try not to feel so badly. We're all in this together, the whole world. Don't let it throw you. What can't be helped you have to learn to live with."

"That's easy for you to say," I told her.

She looked at me quickly and looked away. "I'm not pretending that it's easy to do," she said.

I didn't believe that she could really understand it; and there was nothing I could say. I sat like a child being scolded, looking down at my plate, not eating, not saying anything. I wanted her to stop talking, to stop being intelligent about it, to stop being calm and grown-up about it; good Lord, none of us has ever grown up, we never will.

"It's no better anywhere else," she was saying. "In all of Europe there's famine and disease, in France and England they hate the Jews—nothing's going to change, baby, people are too empty-headed, too empty-hearted—it's always been like that, people always try to destroy what they don't understand—and they hate almost everything because they understand so little—"

I began to sweat in my side of the booth. I wanted to stop her voice. I wanted her to eat and be quiet and leave me alone. I looked around for the waiter so I could order another drink. But he was on the far side of the restaurant, waiting on some people who had just come in; a lot of people had come in since we had been sitting there.

"Peter," Ida said, "Peter please don't look like that."

I grinned: the painted grin of the professional clown. "Don't worry, baby, I'm all right. I know what I'm going to do. I'm gonna go back to my people where I belong and find me a nice, black nigger wench and raise me a flock of babies."

Ida had an old maternal trick; the grin tricked her into using it now. She raised her fork and rapped me with it across the knuckles. "Now, stop that. You're too old for that."

I screamed and stood up screaming and knocked the candle over: "Don't *do* that, you bitch, don't *ever* do that!"

She grabbed the candle and set it up and glared at me. Her face had turned perfectly white: "Sit down! Sit *down*!"

I fell back into my seat. My stomach felt like water. Everyone was looking at us. I turned cold, seeing what they were seeing: a black boy and a white woman, alone together. I knew it would take nothing to have them at my throat.

"I'm sorry," I muttered, "I'm sorry, I'm sorry."

The waiter was at my elbow. "Is everything all right, miss?"

"Yes, quite, thank you." She sounded like a princess dismissing a slave. I didn't look up. The shadow of the waiter moved away from me.

"Baby," Ida said, "forgive me, please forgive me."

I stared at the tablecloth. She put her hand on mine, brightness and blackness.

"Let's go," I said, "I'm terribly sorry."

She motioned for the check. When it came she handed the waiter a ten dollar bill without looking. She picked up her bag.

"Shall we go to a nightclub or a movie or something?"

"No, honey, not tonight." I looked at her. "I'm tired, I think I'll go on over to Jules's place. I'm gonna sleep on his floor for a while. Don't worry about me. I'm all right."

She looked at me steadily. She said: "I'll come see you tomorrow?"

"Yes, baby, please."

The waiter brought the change and she tipped him. We stood up; as we passed the tables (not looking at the people) the ground under me seemed falling, the doorway seemed impossibly far away. All my muscles tensed; I seemed ready to spring; I was waiting for the blow.

I put my hands in my pockets and we walked to the end of the block. The lights were green and red, the lights from the theater across the street exploded blue and yellow, off and on.

"Peter?"

"Yes?"

"I'll see you tomorrow?"

"Yeah. Come by Jules's. I'll wait for you."

"Goodnight, darling."

"Goodnight."

I started to walk away. I felt her eyes on my back. I kicked a bottle-top on the sidewalk.

God save the American republic.

I dropped into the subway and got on an uptown train, not knowing where it was going and not caring. Anonymous, is-landed people surrounded me, behind newspapers, behind make-up, fat, fleshy masks and flat eyes. I watched the empty faces. (No one looked at me.) I looked at the ads, unreal women and pink-cheeked men selling cigarettes, candy, shav-ing cream, nightgowns, chewing gum, movies, sex; sex with-out organs, drier than sand and more secret than death. The train stopped. A white boy and a white girl got on. She was nice, short, svelte. Nice legs. She was hanging on his arm. He was the football type, blond, ruddy. They were dressed in summer clothes. The wind from the doors blew her print dress. She squealed, holding the dress at the knees and giggled and looked at him. He said something I didn't catch and she looked at me and the smile died. She stood so that she faced him and had her back to me. I looked back at the ads. Then I hated them. I wanted to do something to make them hurt, something that would crack the pink-cheeked mask. The white boy and I did not look at each other again. They got off at the next stop.

I wanted to keep on drinking. I got off in Harlem and went to a rundown bar on Seventh Avenue. My people, my people. Sharpies stood on the corner, waiting. Women in summer dresses pranced by on wavering heels. Click clack. Click clack. There were white mounted policemen in the streets. On every block there was another policeman on foot. I saw a black cop.

God save the American republic.

The juke box was letting loose with "Hamps' Boogie." The place was jumping, I walked over to the man.

"Rye," I said.

I was standing next to somebody's grandmother. "Hello, papa. What you puttin' down?"

"Baby, you can't pick it up," I told her. My rye came and I drank.

"Nigger," she said, "you must think you's somebody."

I didn't answer. She turned away, back to her beer, keeping time to the juke box, her face sullen and heavy and aggrieved. I watched her out of the side of my eye. She had been good looking once, pretty even, before she hit the bottle and started crawling into too many beds. She was flabby now, flesh heaved all over in her thin dress. I wondered what she'd be like in bed; then I realized that I was a little excited by her; I laughed and set my glass down.

"The same," I said. "And a beer chaser."

The juke box was playing something else now, something brassy and commercial which I didn't like. I kept on drinking, listening to the voices of my people, watching the faces of my people. (God pity us, the terrified republic.) Now I was sorry to have angered the woman who still sat next to me, now deep in conversation with another, younger woman. I longed for some opening, some sign, something to make me part of the life around me. But there was nothing except my color. A white outsider coming in would have seen a young Negro drinking in a Negro bar, perfectly in his element, in his place, as the saying goes. But the people here knew differently, as I did. I didn't seem to have a place.

So I kept on drinking by myself, saying to myself after each drink, Now I'll go. But I was afraid; I didn't want to sleep on Jules's floor; I didn't want to go to sleep. I kept on drinking and listening to the juke box. They were playing Ella Fitzgerald, "Cow-Cow Boogie."

"Let me buy you a drink," I said to the woman.

She looked at me, startled, suspicious, ready to blow her top.

"On the level," I said. I tried to smile. "Both of you."

"I'll take a beer," the young one said.

I was shaking like a baby. I finished my drink.

"Fine," I said. I turned to the bar.

"Baby," said the old one, "what's your story?"

The man put three beers on the counter.

"I got no story, Ma," I said.

Sonny's Blues

I READ about it in the paper, in the subway, on my way to work. I read it, and I couldn't believe it, and I read it again. Then perhaps I just stared at it, at the newsprint spelling out his name, spelling out the story. I stared at it in the swinging lights of the subway car, and in the faces and bodies of the people, and in my own face, trapped in the darkness which roared outside.

It was not to be believed and I kept telling myself that, as I walked from the subway station to the high school. And at the same time I couldn't doubt it. I was scared, scared for Sonny. He became real to me again. A great block of ice got settled in my belly and kept melting there slowly all day long, while I taught my classes algebra. It was a special kind of ice. It kept melting, sending trickles of ice water all up and down my veins, but it never got less. Sometimes it hardened and seemed to expand until I felt my guts were going to come spilling out or that I was going to choke or scream. This would always be at a moment when I was remembering some specific thing Sonny had once said or done.

When he was about as old as the boys in my classes his face had been bright and open, there was a lot of copper in it; and he'd had wonderfully direct brown eyes, and great gentleness and privacy. I wondered what he looked like now. He had been picked up, the evening before, in a raid on an apartment downtown, for peddling and using heroin.

I couldn't believe it: but what I mean by that is that I couldn't find any room for it anywhere inside me. I had kept it outside me for a long time. I hadn't wanted to know. I had had suspicions, but I didn't name them, I kept putting them away. I told myself that Sonny was wild, but he wasn't crazy. And he'd always been a good boy, he hadn't ever turned hard or evil or disrespectful, the way kids can, so quick, so quick, especially in Harlem. I didn't want to believe that I'd ever see my brother going down, coming to nothing, all that light in his face gone out, in the condition I'd already seen so many others. Yet it had happened and here I was, talking about algebra to a lot of boys who might, every one of them for all I knew, be popping off needles every time they went to the head. Maybe it did more for them than algebra could.

I was sure that the first time Sonny had ever had horse, he couldn't have been much older than these boys were now. These boys, now, were living as we'd been living then, they were growing up with a rush and their heads bumped abruptly against the low ceiling of their actual possibilities. They were filled with rage. All they really knew were two darknesses, the darkness of their lives, which was now closing in on them, and the darkness of the movies, which had blinded them to that other darkness, and in which they now, vindictively, dreamed, at once more together than they were at any other time, and more alone.

When the last bell rang, the last class ended, I let out my breath. It seemed I'd been holding it for all that time. My clothes were wet—I may have looked as though I'd been sitting in a steam bath, all dressed up, all afternoon. I sat alone in the classroom a long time. I listened to the boys outside, downstairs, shouting and cursing and laughing. Their laughter struck me for perhaps the first time. It was not the joyous laughter which—God knows why—one associates with children. It was mocking and insular, its intent was to denigrate. It was disenchanted, and in this, also, lay the authority of their curses. Perhaps I was listening to them because I was thinking about my brother and in them I heard my brother. And myself.

One boy was whistling a tune, at once very complicated and very simple, it seemed to be pouring out of him as though he were a bird, and it sounded very cool and moving through all that harsh, bright air, only just holding its own through all those other sounds.

I stood up and walked over to the window and looked down into the courtyard. It was the beginning of the spring and the sap was rising in the boys. A teacher passed through them every now and again, quickly, as though he or she couldn't wait to get out of that courtyard, to get those boys out of their sight and off their minds. I started collecting my stuff. I thought I'd better get home and talk to Isabel.

The courtyard was almost deserted by the time I got downstairs. I saw this boy standing in the shadow of a doorway, looking just like Sonny. I almost called his name. Then I saw that it wasn't Sonny, but somebody we used to know, a boy from around our block. He'd been Sonny's friend. He'd never been mine, having been too young for me, and, anyway, I'd never liked him. And now, even though he was a grown-up man, he still hung around that block, still spent hours on the street corners, was always high and raggy. I used to run into him from time to time and he'd often work around to asking me for a quarter or fifty cents. He always had some real good excuse, too, and I always gave it to him, I don't know why.

But now, abruptly, I hated him. I couldn't stand the way he looked at me, partly like a dog, partly like a cunning child. I wanted to ask him what the hell he was doing in the school courtyard.

He sort of shuffled over to me, and he said, "I see you got the papers. So you already know about it."

"You mean about Sonny? Yes, I already know about it. How come they didn't get you?"

He grinned. It made him repulsive and it also brought to mind what he'd looked like as a kid. "I wasn't there. I stay away from them people."

"Good for you." I offered him a cigarette and I watched him through the smoke. "You come all the way down here just to tell me about Sonny?"

"That's right." He was sort of shaking his head and his eyes looked strange, as though they were about to cross. The bright sun deadened his damp dark brown skin and it made his eyes look yellow and showed up the dirt in his kinked hair. He smelled funky. I moved a little away from him and I said, "Well, thanks. But I already know about it and I got to get home."

"I'll walk you a little ways," he said. We started walking. There were a couple of kids still loitering in the courtyard and one of them said goodnight to me and looked strangely at the boy beside me.

"What're you going to do?" he asked me. "I mean, about Sonny?"

"Look. I haven't seen Sonny for over a year, I'm not sure I'm going to do anything. Anyway, what the hell *can* I do?"

"That's right," he said quickly, "ain't nothing you can do. Can't much help old Sonny no more, I guess."

It was what I was thinking and so it seemed to me he had no right to say it.

"I'm surprised at Sonny, though," he went on—he had a funny way of talking, he looked straight ahead as though he were talking to himself—"I thought Sonny was a smart boy, I thought he was too smart to get hung."

"I guess he thought so too," I said sharply, "and that's how he got hung. And how about you? You're pretty god-damn smart, I bet."

Then he looked directly at me, just for a minute. "I ain't smart," he said. "If I was smart, I'd have reached for a pistol a long time ago."

"Look. Don't tell *me* your sad story, if it was up to me, I'd give you one." Then I felt guilty—guilty, probably, for never having supposed that the poor bastard *had* a story of his own, much less a sad one, and I asked, quickly, "What's going to happen to him now?"

He didn't answer this. He was off by himself some place. "Funny thing," he said, and from his tone we might have been discussing the quickest way to get to Brooklyn, "when I saw the papers this morning, the first thing I asked myself was if I had anything to do with it. I felt sort of responsible."

I began to listen more carefully. The subway station was on the corner, just before us, and I stopped. He stopped, too. We were in front of a bar and he ducked slightly, peering in, but whoever he was looking for didn't seem to be there. The juke box was blasting away with something black and bouncy and I half watched the barmaid as she danced her way from the juke box to her place behind the bar. And I watched her face as she laughingly responded to something someone said to her, still keeping time to the music. When she smiled one saw the little girl, one sensed the doomed, still-struggling woman beneath the battered face of the semi-whore.

"I never *give* Sonny nothing," the boy said finally, "but a long time ago I come to school high and Sonny asked me how it felt." He paused, I couldn't bear to watch him, I watched the barmaid, and I listened to the music which seemed to be causing the pavement to shake. "I told him it felt great." The music stopped, the barmaid paused and watched the juke box until the music began again. "It did."

All this was carrying me some place I didn't want to go. I certainly didn't want to know how it felt. It filled everything, the people, the houses, the music, the dark, quicksilver barmaid, with menace; and this menace was their reality.

"What's going to happen to him now?" I asked again.

"They'll send him away some place and they'll try to cure him." He shook his head. "Maybe he'll even think he's kicked the habit. Then they'll let him loose"—he gestured, throwing his cigarette into the gutter. "That's all."

"What do you mean, that's *all?*"

But I knew what he meant.

"I *mean*, that's *all*." He turned his head and looked at me, pulling down the corners of his mouth. "Don't you know what I mean?" he asked, softly.

"How the hell *would* I know what you mean?" I almost whispered it, I don't know why.

"That's right," he said to the air, "how would *he* know what I mean?" He turned toward me again, patient and calm, and yet I somehow felt him shaking, shaking as though he were going to fall apart. I felt that ice in my guts again, the dread I'd felt all afternoon; and again I watched the barmaid, moving about the bar, washing glasses, and singing. "Listen. They'll let him out and then it'll just start all over again. That's what I mean."

"You mean—they'll let him out. And then he'll just start working his way back in again. You mean he'll never kick the habit. Is that what you mean?"

"That's right," he said, cheerfully. "*You* see what I mean."

"Tell me," I said at last, "why does he want to die? He must want to die, he's killing himself, why does he want to die?"

He looked at me in surprise. He licked his lips. "He don't want to die. He wants to live. Don't nobody want to die, ever."

Then I wanted to ask him—too many things. He could not have answered, or if he had, I could not have borne the answers. I started walking. "Well, I guess it's none of my business."

"It's going to be rough on old Sonny," he said. We reached the subway station. "This is your station?" he asked. I nodded. I took one step down. "Damn!" he said, suddenly. I looked up at him. He grinned again. "Damn it if I didn't leave all my money home. You ain't got a dollar on you, have you? Just for a couple of days, is all."

All at once something inside gave and threatened to come pouring out of me. I didn't hate him any more. I felt that in another moment I'd start crying like a child.

"Sure," I said. "Don't sweat." I looked in my wallet and didn't have a dollar, I only had a five. "Here," I said. "That hold you?"

He didn't look at it—he didn't want to look at it. A terrible, closed look came over his face, as though he were keeping the number on the bill a secret from him and me. "Thanks," he said, and now he was dying to see me go. "Don't worry about Sonny. Maybe I'll write him or something."

"Sure," I said. "You do that. So long."

"Be seeing you," he said. I went on down the steps.

And I didn't write Sonny or send him anything for a long time. When I finally did, it was just after my little girl died, he wrote me back a letter which made me feel like a bastard.

Here's what he said:

> Dear brother,
> You don't know how much I needed to hear from you. I wanted to write you many a time but I dug how much I must have hurt you and so I didn't write. But now I feel like a man who's been trying to climb up out of some deep, real deep and funky hole and just saw the sun up there, outside. I got to get outside.
> I can't tell you much about how I got here. I mean I don't know how to tell you. I guess I was afraid of something or I was trying to escape from something and you know I have never been very strong in the head (smile). I'm glad Mama and Daddy are dead and can't see what's happened to their son and I swear if I'd known what I was doing I would never have hurt you

so, you and a lot of other fine people who were nice to me and who believed in me.

I don't want you to think it had anything to do with me being a musician. It's more than that. Or maybe less than that. I can't get anything straight in my head down here and I try not to think about what's going to happen to me when I get outside again. Sometime I think I'm going to flip and *never* get outside and sometime I think I'll come straight back. I tell you one thing, though, I'd rather blow my brains out than go through this again. But that's what they all say, so they tell me. If I tell you when I'm coming to New York and if you could meet me, I sure would appreciate it. Give my love to Isabel and the kids and I was sure sorry to hear about little Gracie. I wish I could be like Mama and say the Lord's will be done, but I don't know it seems to me that trouble is the one thing that never does get stopped and I don't know what good it does to blame it on the Lord. But maybe it does some good if you believe it.

Your brother,
Sonny

Then I kept in constant touch with him and I sent him whatever I could and I went to meet him when he came back to New York. When I saw him many things I thought I had forgotten came flooding back to me. This was because I had begun, finally, to wonder about Sonny, about the life that Sonny lived inside. This life, whatever it was, had made him older and thinner and it had deepened the distant stillness in which he had always moved. He looked very unlike my baby brother. Yet, when he smiled, when we shook hands, the baby brother I'd never known looked out from the depths of his private life, like an animal waiting to be coaxed into the light.

"How you been keeping?" he asked me.

"All right. And you?"

"Just fine." He was smiling all over his face. "It's good to see you again."

"It's good to see you."

The seven years' difference in our ages lay between us like a chasm: I wondered if these years would ever operate between us as a bridge. I was remembering, and it made it hard to catch my breath, that I had been there when he was born; and I had heard the first words he had ever spoken. When he started to walk, he walked from our mother straight to me. I caught him just before he fell when he took the first steps he ever took in this world.

"How's Isabel?"

"Just fine. She's dying to see you."

"And the boys?"

"They're fine, too. They're anxious to see their uncle."

"Oh, come on. You know they don't remember me."

"Are you kidding? Of course they remember you."

He grinned again. We got into a taxi. We had a lot to say to each other, far too much to know how to begin.

As the taxi began to move, I asked, "You still want to go to India?"

He laughed. "You still remember that. Hell, no. This place is Indian enough for me."

"It used to belong to them," I said.

And he laughed again. "They damn sure knew what they were doing when they got rid of it."

Years ago, when he was around fourteen, he'd been all hipped on the idea of going to India. He read books about people sitting on rocks, naked, in all kinds of weather, but mostly bad, naturally, and walking barefoot through hot coals and arriving at wisdom. I used to say that it sounded to me as though they were getting away from wisdom as fast as they could. I think he sort of looked down on me for that.

"Do you mind," he asked, "if we have the driver drive alongside the park? On the west side—I haven't seen the city in so long."

"Of course not," I said. I was afraid that I might sound as though I were humoring him, but I hoped he wouldn't take it that way.

So we drove along, between the green of the park and the stony, lifeless elegance of hotels and apartment buildings, toward the vivid, killing streets of our childhood. These streets hadn't changed, though housing projects jutted up out of them now like rocks in the middle of a boiling sea. Most of the houses in which we had grown up had vanished, as had the stores from which we had stolen, the basements in which we had first tried sex, the rooftops from which we had hurled tin cans and bricks. But houses exactly like the houses of our past yet dominated the landscape, boys exactly like the boys we once had been found themselves smothering in these houses, came down into the streets for light and air and found themselves encircled by disaster. Some escaped the trap, most didn't. Those who got out always left something of themselves behind, as some animals amputate a leg and leave it in the trap. It might be said, perhaps, that I had escaped, after all, I was a school teacher; or that Sonny had, he hadn't lived in Harlem for years. Yet, as the cab moved uptown through streets which seemed, with a rush, to darken with dark people, and as I covertly studied Sonny's face, it came to me that what we both were seeking through our separate cab windows was that part of ourselves which had been left behind. It's always at the hour of trouble and confrontation that the missing member aches.

We hit 110th Street and started rolling up Lenox Avenue. And I'd known this avenue all my life, but it seemed to me again, as it had seemed on the day I'd first heard about Sonny's trouble, filled with a hidden menace which was its very breath of life.

"We almost there," said Sonny.

"Almost." We were both too nervous to say anything more.

We live in a housing project. It hasn't been up long. A few days after it was up it seemed uninhabitably new, now, of course, it's already rundown. It looks like a parody of the good, clean, faceless life—God knows the people who live in it do their best to make it a parody. The beat-looking grass lying around isn't enough to make their lives green, the hedges will never hold out the streets, and they know it. The big windows fool no one, they aren't big enough to make space out of no space. They don't bother with the windows, they watch the TV screen instead. The playground is most popular with the children who don't play at jacks, or skip rope, or roller skate, or swing, and they can be found in it after dark. We moved in partly because it's not too far from where I teach, and partly for the kids; but it's really just like the houses in which Sonny and I grew up. The same things happen, they'll have the same things to remember. The moment Sonny and I started into the house I had the feeling that I was simply bringing him back into the danger he had almost died trying to escape.

Sonny has never been talkative. So I don't know why I was sure he'd be dying to talk to me when supper was over the first night. Everything went fine, the oldest boy remembered him, and the youngest boy liked him, and Sonny had remembered to bring something for each of them; and Isabel, who is really much nicer than I am, more open and giving, had gone to a lot of trouble about dinner and was genuinely glad to see him. And she's always been able to tease Sonny in a way that I haven't. It was nice to see her face so vivid again and to hear her laugh and watch her make Sonny laugh. She wasn't, or, anyway, she didn't seem to be, at all uneasy or embarrassed. She chatted as though there were no subject which had to be avoided and she got Sonny past his first, faint stiffness. And thank God she was there, for I was filled with that icy dread again. Everything I did seemed awkward to me, and everything I said sounded freighted with hidden meaning. I was trying to remember everything I'd heard about dope addiction and I couldn't help watching Sonny for signs. I wasn't doing it out of malice. I was trying to find out something about my brother. I was dying to hear him tell me he was safe.

"Safe!" my father grunted, whenever Mama suggested trying to move to a neighborhood which might be safer for children. "Safe, hell! Ain't no place safe for kids, nor nobody."

He always went on like this, but he wasn't, ever, really as bad as he sounded, not even on weekends, when he got drunk. As a matter of fact, he was always on the lookout for "something a little better," but he died before he found it. He died suddenly, during a drunken weekend in the middle of the war, when Sonny was fifteen. He and Sonny hadn't ever got on too well. And this was partly because Sonny was the apple of his father's eye. It was because he loved Sonny so much and was frightened for him, that he was always fighting with him. It doesn't do any good to fight with Sonny. Sonny just moves back, inside himself, where he can't be reached. But the principal reason that they never hit it off is that they were so much alike. Daddy was big and rough and loud-talking, just the opposite of Sonny, but they both had—that same privacy.

Mama tried to tell me something about this, just after Daddy died. I was home on leave from the army.

This was the last time I ever saw my mother alive. Just the same, this picture gets all mixed up in my mind with pictures I had of her when she was younger. The way I always see her is the way she used to be on a Sunday afternoon, say, when the old folks were talking after the big Sunday dinner. I always see her wearing pale blue. She'd be sitting on the sofa. And my father would be sitting in the easy chair, not far from her. And the living room would be full of church folks and relatives. There they sit, in chairs all around the living room, and the night is creeping up outside, but nobody knows it yet. You can see the darkness growing against the windowpanes and you hear the street noises every now and again, or maybe the jangling beat of a tambourine from one of the churches close by, but it's real quiet in the room. For a moment nobody's talking, but every face looks darkening, like the sky outside. And my mother rocks a little from the waist, and my father's eyes are closed. Everyone is looking at something a child can't see. For a minute they've forgotten the children. Maybe a kid is lying on the rug, half asleep. Maybe somebody's got a kid in his lap and is absent-mindedly stroking the kid's head. Maybe there's a kid, quiet and big-eyed, curled up in a big chair in the corner. The silence, the darkness coming, and the darkness in the faces frightens the child obscurely. He hopes that the hand which strokes his forehead will never stop—will never die. He hopes that there will never come a time when the old folks won't be sitting around the living room, talking about where they've come from, and what they've seen, and what's happened to them and their kinfolk.

But something deep and watchful in the child knows that this is bound to end, is already ending. In a moment someone will get up and turn on the light. Then the old folks will remember the children and they won't talk any more that day. And when light fills the room, the child is filled with darkness. He knows that every time this happens he's moved just a little closer to that darkness outside. The darkness outside is what the old folks have been talking about. It's what they've come from. It's what they endure. The child knows that they won't talk any more because if he knows too much about what's happened to *them*, he'll know too much too soon, about what's going to happen to *him*.

The last time I talked to my mother, I remember I was restless. I wanted to get out and see Isabel. We weren't married then and we had a lot to straighten out between us.

There Mama sat, in black, by the window. She was humming an old church song, *Lord, you brought me from a long ways off.* Sonny was out somewhere. Mama kept watching the streets.

"I don't know," she said, "if I'll ever see you again, after you go off from here. But I hope you'll remember the things I tried to teach you."

"Don't talk like that," I said, and smiled. "You'll be here a long time yet."

She smiled, too, but she said nothing. She was quiet for a long time. And I said, "Mama, don't you worry about nothing. I'll be writing all the time, and you be getting the checks. . . ."

"I want to talk to you about your brother," she said, suddenly. "If anything happens to me he ain't going to have nobody to look out for him."

"Mama," I said, "ain't nothing going to happen to you *or* Sonny. Sonny's all right. He's a good boy and he's got good sense."

"It ain't a question of his being a good boy," Mama said, "nor of his having good sense. It ain't only the bad ones, nor yet the dumb ones that gets sucked under." She stopped, looking at me. "Your Daddy once had a brother," she said, and she smiled in a way that made me feel she was in pain. "You didn't never know that, did you?"

"No," I said, "I never knew that," and I watched her face.

"Oh, yes," she said, "your Daddy had a brother." She looked out of the window again. "I know you never saw your Daddy cry. But *I* did—many a time, through all these years."

I asked her, "What happened to his brother? How come nobody's ever talked about him?"

This was the first time I ever saw my mother look old.

"His brother got killed," she said, "when he was just a little younger than you are now. I knew him. He was a fine boy. He was maybe a little full of the devil, but he didn't mean nobody no harm."

Then she stopped and the room was silent, exactly as it had sometimes been on those Sunday afternoons. Mama kept looking out into the streets.

"He used to have a job in the mill," she said, "and, like all young folks, he just liked to perform on Saturday nights. Saturday nights, him and your father would drift around to different place, go to dances and things like that, or just sit around with people they knew, and your father's brother would sing, he had a fine voice, and play along with himself on his guitar. Well, this particular Saturday night, him and your father was coming home from some place, and they were both a little drunk and there was a moon that night, it was bright like day. Your father's brother was feeling kind of good, and he was whistling to himself, and he had his guitar slung over his shoulder. They was coming down a hill and beneath them was a road that turned off from the highway. Well, your father's brother, being always kind of frisky, decided to run down this hill, and he did, with that guitar banging and clanging behind him, and he ran across the road, and he was making water behind a tree. And your father was sort of amused at him and he was still coming down the hill, kind of slow. Then he heard a car motor and that same minute his brother stepped from behind the tree, into the road, in the moonlight. And he started to cross the road. And your father started to run down the hill, he says he don't know why. This car was full of white men. They was all drunk, and when they seen your father's brother they let out a great whoop and holler and they aimed the car straight at him. They was having fun, they just wanted to scare him, the way they do sometimes, you know. But they was drunk. And I guess the boy, being drunk, too, and scared, kind of lost his head. By the time he jumped it was too late. Your father says he heard his brother scream when the car rolled over him, and he heard the wood of that guitar when it give, and he heard them strings go flying, and he heard them white men shouting, and the car kept on a-going and it ain't stopped till this day. And, time your father got down the hill, his brother weren't nothing but blood and pulp."

Tears were gleaming on my mother's face. There wasn't anything I could say.

"He never mentioned it," she said, "because I never let him mention it before you children. Your Daddy was like a crazy man that night and for many a night thereafter. He says he never in his life seen anything as dark as that road after the lights of that car had gone away. Weren't nothing, weren't nobody on that road, just your Daddy and his brother and that busted guitar. Oh, yes. Your Daddy never did really get right again. Till the day he died he weren't sure but that every white man he saw was the man that killed his brother."

She stopped and took out her handkerchief and dried her eyes and looked at me.

"I ain't telling you all this," she said, "to make you scared or bitter or to make you hate nobody. I'm telling you this because you got a brother. And the world ain't changed."

I guess I didn't want to believe this. I guess she saw this in my face. She turned away from me, toward the window again, searching those streets.

"But I praise my Redeemer," she said at last, "that He called your Daddy home before me. I ain't saying it to throw no flowers at myself, but, I declare, it keeps me from feeling too cast down to know I helped your father get safely through this world. Your father always acted like he was the roughest, strongest man on earth. And everybody took him to be like that. But if he hadn't had *me* there—to see his tears!"

She was crying again. Still, I couldn't move. I said, "Lord, Lord, Mama, I didn't know it was like that."

"Oh, honey," she said, "there's a lot that you don't know. But you are going to find it out." She stood up from the window and came over to me. "You got to hold on to your brother," she said, "and don't let him fall, no matter what it looks like is happening to him and no matter how evil you gets with him. You going to be evil with him many a time. But don't you forget what I told you, you hear?"

"I won't forget," I said. "Don't you worry, I won't forget. I won't let nothing happen to Sonny."

My mother smiled as though she were amused at something

she saw in my face. Then, "You may not be able to stop nothing from happening. But you got to let him know you's *there*."

Two days later I was married, and then I was gone. And I had a lot of things on my mind and I pretty well forgot my promise to Mama until I got shipped home on a special furlough for her funeral.

And, after the funeral, with just Sonny and me alone in the empty kitchen, I tried to find out something about him.

"What do you want to do?" I asked him.

"I'm going to be a musician," he said.

For he had graduated, in the time I had been away, from dancing to the juke box to finding out who was playing what, and what they were doing with it, and he had bought himself a set of drums.

"You mean, you want to be a drummer?" I somehow had the feeling that being a drummer might be all right for other people but not for my brother Sonny.

"I don't think," he said, looking at me very gravely, "that I'll ever be a good drummer. But I think I can play a piano."

I frowned. I'd never played the role of the older brother quite so seriously before, had scarcely ever, in fact, *asked* Sonny a damn thing. I sensed myself in the presence of something I didn't really know how to handle, didn't understand. So I made my frown a little deeper as I asked: "What kind of musician do you want to be?"

He grinned. "How many kinds do you think there are?"

"Be *serious*," I said.

He laughed, throwing his head back, and then looked at me. "I *am* serious."

"Well, then, for Christ's sake, stop kidding around and answer a serious question. I mean, do you want to be a concert pianist, you want to play classical music and all that, or—or what?" Long before I finished he was laughing again. "For Christ's *sake*, Sonny!"

He sobered, but with difficulty. "I'm sorry. But you sound so—*scared!*" and he was off again.

"Well, you may think it's funny now, baby, but it's not going to be so funny when you have to make your living at it, let me tell you *that*." I was furious because I knew he was laughing at me and I didn't know why.

"No," he said, very sober now, and afraid, perhaps, that he'd hurt me, "I don't want to be a classical pianist. That isn't what interests me. I mean"—he paused, looking hard at me, as though his eyes would help me to understand, and then gestured helplessly, as though perhaps his hand would help—"I mean, I'll have a lot of studying to do, and I'll have to study *everything*, but, I mean, I want to play *with*—jazz musicians." He stopped. "I want to play jazz," he said.

Well, the word had never before sounded as heavy, as real, as it sounded that afternoon in Sonny's mouth. I just looked at him and I was probably frowning a real frown by this time. I simply couldn't see why on earth he'd want to spend his time hanging around nightclubs, clowning around on bandstands, while people pushed each other around a dance floor. It seemed—beneath him, somehow. I had never thought about it before, had never been forced to, but I suppose I had always put jazz musicians in a class with what Daddy called "good-time people."

"Are you *serious*?"

"Hell, *yes*, I'm serious."

He looked more helpless than ever, and annoyed, and deeply hurt.

I suggested, helpfully: "You mean—like Louis Armstrong?"

His face closed as though I'd struck him. "No. I'm not talking about none of that old-time, down home crap."

"Well, look, Sonny, I'm sorry, don't get mad. I just don't altogether get it, that's all. Name somebody—you know, a jazz musician you admire."

"Bird."

"Who?"

"Bird! Charlie Parker! Don't they teach you nothing in the goddamn army?"

I lit a cigarette. I was surprised and then a little amused to discover that I was trembling. "I've been out of touch," I said. "You'll have to be patient with me. Now. Who's this Parker character?"

"He's just one of the greatest jazz musicians alive," said Sonny, sullenly, his hands in his pockets, his back to me.

"Maybe *the* greatest," he added, bitterly, "that's probably why *you* never heard of him."

"All right," I said, "I'm ignorant. I'm sorry. I'll go out and buy all the cat's records right away, all right?"

"It don't," said Sonny, with dignity, "make any difference to me. I don't care what you listen to. Don't do me no favors."

I was beginning to realize that I'd never seen him so upset before. With another part of my mind I was thinking that this would probably turn out to be one of those things kids go through and that I shouldn't make it seem important by pushing it too hard. Still, I didn't think it would do any harm to ask: "Doesn't all this take a lot of time? Can you make a living at it?"

He turned back to me and half leaned, half sat, on the kitchen table. "Everything takes time," he said, "and—well, yes, sure, I can make a living at it. But what I don't seem to be able to make you understand is that it's the only thing I want to do."

"Well, Sonny," I said, gently, "you know people can't always do exactly what they *want* to do—"

"*No*, I don't know that," said Sonny, surprising me. "I think people *ought* to do what they want to do, what else are they alive for?"

"You getting to be a big boy," I said desperately, "it's time you started thinking about your future."

"I'm thinking about my future," said Sonny, grimly. "I think about it all the time."

I gave up. I decided, if he didn't change his mind, that we could always talk about it later. "In the meantime," I said, "you got to finish school." We had already decided that he'd have to move in with Isabel and her folks. I knew this wasn't the ideal arrangement because Isabel's folks are inclined to be dicty and they hadn't especially wanted Isabel to marry me. But I didn't know what else to do. "And we have to get you fixed up at Isabel's."

There was a long silence. He moved from the kitchen table to the window. "That's a terrible idea. You know it yourself."

"Do you have a *better* idea?"

He just walked up and down the kitchen for a minute. He

was as tall as I was. He had started to shave. I suddenly had the feeling that I didn't know him at all.

He stopped at the kitchen table and picked up my cigarettes. Looking at me with a kind of mocking, amused defiance, he put one between his lips. "You mind?"

"You smoking already?"

He lit the cigarette and nodded, watching me through the smoke. "I just wanted to see if I'd have the courage to smoke in front of you." He grinned and blew a great cloud of smoke to the ceiling. "It was easy." He looked at my face. "Come on, now. I bet you was smoking at my age, tell the truth."

I didn't say anything but the truth was on my face, and he laughed. But now there was something very strained in his laugh. "Sure. And I bet that ain't all you was doing."

He was frightening me a little. "Cut the crap," I said. "We already decided that you was going to go and live at Isabel's. Now what's got into you all of a sudden?"

"*You* decided it," he pointed out. "*I* didn't decide nothing." He stopped in front of me, leaning against the stove, arms loosely folded. "Look, brother. I don't want to stay in Harlem no more, I really don't." He was very earnest. He looked at me, then over toward the kitchen window. There was something in his eyes I'd never seen before, some thoughtfulness, some worry all his own. He rubbed the muscle of one arm. "It's time I was getting out of here."

"Where do you want to *go*, Sonny?"

"I want to join the army. Or the navy, I don't care. If I say I'm old enough, they'll believe me."

Then I got mad. It was because I was so scared. "You must be crazy. You goddamn fool, what the hell do you want to go and join the *army* for?"

"I just told you. To get out of Harlem."

"Sonny, you haven't even finished *school*. And if you really want to be a musician, how do you expect to study if you're in the *army*?"

He looked at me, trapped, and in anguish. "There's ways. I might be able to work out some kind of deal. Anyway, I'll have the G.I. Bill when I come out."

"*If* you come out." We stared at each other. "Sonny, please.

Be reasonable. I know the setup is far from perfect. But we got to do the best we can."

"I ain't learning nothing in school," he said. "Even when I go." He turned away from me and opened the window and threw his cigarette out into the narrow alley. I watched his back. "At least, I ain't learning nothing you'd want me to learn." He slammed the window so hard I thought the glass would fly out, and turned back to me. "And I'm sick of the stink of these garbage cans!"

"Sonny," I said, "I know how you feel. But if you don't finish school now, you're going to be sorry later that you didn't." I grabbed him by the shoulders. "And you only got another year. It ain't so bad. And I'll come back and I swear I'll help you do *whatever* you want to do. Just try to put up with it till I come back. Will you please do that? For me?"

He didn't answer and he wouldn't look at me.

"Sonny. You hear me?"

He pulled away. "I hear you. But you never hear anything *I* say."

I didn't know what to say to that. He looked out of the window and then back at me. "OK," he said, and sighed. "I'll try."

Then I said, trying to cheer him up a little, "They got a piano at Isabel's. You can practice on it."

And as a matter of fact, it did cheer him up for a minute. "That's right," he said to himself. "I forgot that." His face relaxed a little. But the worry, the thoughtfulness, played on it still, the way shadows play on a face which is staring into the fire.

But I thought I'd never hear the end of that piano. At first, Isabel would write me, saying how nice it was that Sonny was so serious about his music and how, as soon as he came in from school, or wherever he had been when he was supposed to be at school, he went straight to that piano and stayed there until suppertime. And, after supper, he went back to that piano and stayed there until everybody went to bed. He was at the piano all day Saturday and all day Sunday. Then he bought a record player and started playing records. He'd play one record over and over again, all day long sometimes, and he'd improvise along with it on the piano. Or he'd play one section of the record, one chord, one change, one progression, then he'd do it on the piano. Then back to the record. Then back to the piano.

Well, I really don't know how they stood it. Isabel finally confessed that it wasn't like living with a person at all, it was like living with sound. And the sound didn't make any sense to her, didn't make any sense to any of them—naturally. They began, in a way, to be afflicted by this presence that was living in their home. It was as though Sonny were some sort of god, or monster. He moved in an atmosphere which wasn't like theirs at all. They fed him and he ate, he washed himself, he walked in and out of their door; he certainly wasn't nasty or unpleasant or rude, Sonny isn't any of those things; but it was as though he were all wrapped up in some cloud, some fire, some vision all his own; and there wasn't any way to reach him.

At the same time, he wasn't really a man yet, he was still a child, and they had to watch out for him in all kinds of ways. They certainly couldn't throw him out. Neither did they dare to make a great scene about that piano because even they dimly sensed, as I sensed, from so many thousands of miles away, that Sonny was at that piano playing for his life.

But he hadn't been going to school. One day a letter came from the school board and Isabel's mother got it—there had, apparently, been other letters but Sonny had torn them up. This day, when Sonny came in, Isabel's mother showed him the letter and asked where he'd been spending his time. And she finally got it out of him that he'd been down in Greenwich Village, with musicians and other characters, in a white girl's apartment. And this scared her and she started to scream at him and what came up, once she began—though she denies it to this day—was what sacrifices they were making to give Sonny a decent home and how little he appreciated it.

Sonny didn't play the piano that day. By evening, Isabel's mother had calmed down but then there was the old man to deal with, and Isabel herself. Isabel says she did her best to be calm but she broke down and started crying. She says she just watched Sonny's face. She could tell, by watching him, what was happening with him. And what was happening was that they penetrated his cloud, they had reached him. Even if their fingers had been a thousand times more gentle than human fingers ever are, he could hardly help feeling that they had stripped him naked and were spitting on that nakedness. For he also had to see that his presence, that music, which was life or death to him, had been torture for them and that they had endured it, not at all for his sake, but only for mine. And Sonny couldn't take that. He can take it a little better today than he could then but he's still not very good at it and, frankly, I don't know anybody who is.

The silence of the next few days must have been louder than the sound of all the music ever played since time began. One morning, before she went to work, Isabel was in his room for something and she suddenly realized that all of his records were gone. And she knew for certain that he was gone. And he was. He went as far as the navy would carry him. He finally sent me a postcard from some place in Greece and that was the first I knew that Sonny was still alive. I didn't see him any more until we were both back in New York and the war had long been over.

He was a man by then, of course, but I wasn't willing to see it. He came by the house from time to time, but we fought almost every time we met. I didn't like the way he carried himself, loose and dreamlike all the time, and I didn't like his friends, and his music seemed to be merely an excuse for the life he led. It sounded just that weird and disordered.

Then we had a fight, a pretty awful fight, and I didn't see him for months. By and by I looked him up, where he was living, in a furnished room in the Village, and I tried to make it up. But there were lots of other people in the room and Sonny just lay on his bed, and he wouldn't come downstairs with me, and he treated these other people as though they were his family and I weren't. So I got mad and then he got mad, and then I told him that he might just as well be dead as live the way he was living. Then he stood up and he told me not to worry about him any more in life, that he *was* dead as far as I was concerned. Then he pushed me to the door and the other people looked on as though nothing were happening, and he slammed the door behind me. I stood in the hallway, staring at the door. I heard somebody laugh in the room and then the tears came to my eyes. I started down the steps, whistling to keep from crying, I kept whistling to myself, *You going to need me, baby, one of these cold, rainy days.*

I read about Sonny's trouble in the spring. Little Grace died in the fall. She was a beautiful little girl. But she only lived a little over two years. She died of polio and she suffered. She had a slight fever for a couple of days, but it didn't seem like anything and we just kept her in bed. And we would certainly have called the doctor, but the fever dropped, she seemed to be all right. So we thought it had just been a cold. Then, one day, she was up, playing, Isabel was in the kitchen fixing lunch for the two boys when they'd come in from school, and she heard Grace fall down in the living room. When you have a lot of children you don't always start running when one of them falls, unless they start screaming or something. And, this time, Grace was quiet. Yet, Isabel says that when she heard that *thump* and then that silence, something happened in her to make her afraid. And she ran to the living room and there was little Grace on the floor, all twisted up, and the reason she hadn't screamed was that she couldn't get her breath. And when she did scream, it was the worst sound, Isabel says, that she'd ever heard in all her life, and she still hears it sometimes in her dreams. Isabel will sometimes wake me up with a low, moaning, strangled sound and I have to be quick to awaken her and hold her to me and where Isabel is weeping against me seems a mortal wound.

I think I may have written Sonny the very day that little Grace was buried. I was sitting in the living room in the dark, by myself, and I suddenly thought of Sonny. My trouble made his real.

One Saturday afternoon, when Sonny had been living with us, or, anyway, been in our house, for nearly two weeks, I found myself wandering aimlessly about the living room, drinking from a can of beer, and trying to work up the courage to search Sonny's room. He was out, he was usually out whenever I was home, and Isabel had taken the children to see their grandparents. Suddenly I was standing still in front of the living room window, watching Seventh Avenue. The idea of searching Sonny's room made me still. I scarcely dared to admit to myself what I'd be searching for. I didn't know what I'd do if I found it. Or if I didn't.

On the sidewalk across from me, near the entrance to a barbecue joint, some people were holding an old-fashioned revival meeting. The barbecue cook, wearing a dirty white apron, his conked hair reddish and metallic in the pale sun, and a cigarette between his lips, stood in the doorway, watching them. Kids and older people paused in their errands and stood there, along with some older men and a couple of very tough-looking women who watched everything that happened on the avenue, as though they owned it, or were maybe owned by it. Well, they were watching this, too. The revival was being carried on by three sisters in black, and a brother. All they had were their voices and their Bibles and a tambourine. The brother was testifying and while he testified two of the sisters stood together, seeming to say, amen, and the third sister walked around with the tambourine outstretched and a couple of people dropped coins into it. Then the brother's testimony ended and the sister who had been taking up the collection dumped the coins into her palm and transferred them to the pocket of her long black robe. Then she raised both hands, striking the tambourine against the air, and then against one hand, and she started to sing. And the two other sisters and the brother joined in.

It was strange, suddenly, to watch, though I had been seeing these street meetings all my life. So, of course, had everybody else down there. Yet, they paused and watched and listened and I stood still at the window. *"Tis the old ship of Zion,"* they sang, and the sister with the tambourine kept a steady, jangling beat, *"it has rescued many a thousand!"* Not a soul under the sound of their voices was hearing this song for the first time, not one of them had been rescued. Nor had they seen much in the way of rescue work being done around them. Neither did they especially believe in the holiness of the three sisters and the brother, they knew too much about them, knew where they lived, and how. The woman with the tambourine, whose voice dominated the air, whose face was bright with joy, was divided by very little from the woman who stood watching her, a cigarette between her heavy, chapped lips, her hair a cuckoo's nest, her face scarred and swollen from many beatings, and her black eyes glittering like coal. Perhaps they both knew this, which was why, when, as rarely, they addressed each other, they addressed each other as Sister. As the singing filled the air the watching, listening faces underwent a change, the eyes focusing on something within; the music seemed to soothe a poison out of them; and time seemed, nearly, to fall away from the sullen, belligerent, battered faces, as though they were fleeing back to their first condition, while dreaming of their last. The barbecue cook half shook his head and smiled, and dropped his cigarette and disappeared into his joint. A man fumbled in his pockets for change and stood holding it in his hand impatiently, as though he had just remembered a pressing appointment further up the avenue. He looked furious. Then I saw Sonny, standing on the edge of the crowd. He was carrying a wide, flat notebook with a green cover, and it made him look, from where I was standing, almost like a schoolboy. The coppery sun brought out the copper in his skin, he was very faintly smiling, standing very still. Then the singing stopped, the tambourine turned into a collection plate again. The furious man dropped in his coins and vanished, so did a couple of the women, and Sonny dropped some change in the plate, looking directly at the woman with a little smile. He started across the avenue, toward the house. He has a slow, loping walk, something like the way Harlem hipsters walk, only he's imposed on this his own half-beat. I had never really noticed it before.

I stayed at the window, both relieved and apprehensive. As Sonny disappeared from my sight, they began singing again. And they were still singing when his key turned in the lock.

"Hey," he said.

"Hey, yourself. You want some beer?"

"No. Well, maybe." But he came up to the window and stood beside me, looking out. "What a warm voice," he said.

They were singing *If I could only hear my mother pray again!*

"Yes," I said, "and she can sure beat that tambourine."

"But what a terrible song," he said, and laughed. He

dropped his notebook on the sofa and disappeared into the kitchen. "Where's Isabel and the kids?"

"I think they went to see their grandparents. You hungry?"

"No." He came back into the living room with his can of beer. "You want to come some place with me tonight?"

I sensed, I don't know how, that I couldn't possibly say no. "Sure. Where?"

He sat down on the sofa and picked up his notebook and started leafing through it. "I'm going to sit in with some fellows in a joint in the Village."

"You mean, you're going to play, tonight?"

"That's right." He took a swallow of his beer and moved back to the window. He gave me a sidelong look. "If you can stand it."

"I'll try," I said.

He smiled to himself and we both watched as the meeting across the way broke up. The three sisters and the brother, heads bowed, were singing *God be with you till we meet again.* The faces around them were very quiet. Then the song ended. The small crowd dispersed. We watched the three women and the lone man walk slowly up the avenue.

"When she was singing before," said Sonny, abruptly, "her voice reminded me for a minute of what heroin feels like sometimes—when it's in your veins. It makes you feel sort of warm and cool at the same time. And distant. And—and sure." He sipped his beer, very deliberately not looking at me. I watched his face. "It makes you feel—in control. Sometimes you've got to have that feeling."

"Do you?" I sat down slowly in the easy chair.

"Sometimes." He went to the sofa and picked up his notebook again. "Some people do."

"In order," I asked, "to play?" And my voice was very ugly, full of contempt and anger.

"Well"—he looked at me with great, troubled eyes, as though, in fact, he hoped his eyes would tell me things he could never otherwise say—"they *think* so. And *if* they think so—!"

"And what do *you* think?" I asked.

He sat on the sofa and put his can of beer on the floor. "I

don't know," he said, and I couldn't be sure if he were answering my question or pursuing his thoughts. His face didn't tell me. "It's not so much to *play*. It's to *stand* it, to be able to make it at all. On any level." He frowned and smiled: "In order to keep from shaking to pieces."

"But these friends of yours," I said, "they seem to shake themselves to pieces pretty goddamn fast."

"Maybe." He played with the notebook. And something told me that I should curb my tongue, that Sonny was doing his best to talk, that I should listen. "But of course you only know the ones that've gone to pieces. Some don't—or at least they haven't *yet* and that's just about all *any* of us can say." He paused. "And then there are some who just live, really, in hell, and they know it and they see what's happening and they go right on. I don't know." He sighed, dropped the notebook, folded his arms. "Some guys, you can tell from the way they play, they on something *all* the time. And you can see that, well, it makes something real for them. But of course," he picked up his beer from the floor and sipped it and put the can down again, "they *want* to, too, you've got to see that. Even some of them that say they don't—*some*, not all."

"And what about you?" I asked—I couldn't help it. "What about you? Do *you* want to?"

He stood up and walked to the window and remained silent for a long time. Then he sighed. "Me," he said. Then: "While I was downstairs before, on my way here, listening to that woman sing, it struck me all of a sudden how much suffering she must have had to go through—to sing like that. It's *repulsive* to think you have to suffer that much."

I said: "But there's no way not to suffer—is there, Sonny?"

"I believe not," he said and smiled, "but that's never stopped anyone from trying." He looked at me. "Has it?" I realized, with this mocking look, that there stood between us, forever, beyond the power of time or forgiveness, the fact that I had held silence—so long!—when he had needed human speech to help him. He turned back to the window. "No, there's no way not to suffer. But you try all kinds of ways to keep from drowning in it, to keep on top of it, and to make it seem—well, like *you*. Like you did something, all right, and now you're suffering for it. You know?" I said nothing. "Well you know," he said, impatiently, "why *do* people suffer? Maybe it's better to do something to give it a reason, *any* reason."

"But we just agreed," I said, "that there's no way not to suffer. Isn't it better, then, just to—take it?"

"But nobody just takes it," Sonny cried, "that's what I'm telling you! *Everybody* tries not to. You're just hung up on the *way* some people try—it's not *your* way!"

The hair on my face began to itch, my face felt wet. "That's not true," I said, "that's not true. I don't give a damn what other people do, I don't even care how they suffer. I just care how *you* suffer." And he looked at me. "Please believe me," I said, "I don't want to see you—die—trying not to suffer."

"I won't," he said, flatly, "die trying not to suffer. At least, not any faster than anybody else."

"But there's no need," I said, trying to laugh, "is there? in killing yourself."

I wanted to say more, but I couldn't. I wanted to talk about will power and how life could be—well, beautiful. I wanted to say that it was all within; but was it? or, rather, wasn't that exactly the trouble? And I wanted to promise that I would never fail him again. But it would all have sounded—empty words and lies.

So I made the promise to myself and prayed that I would keep it.

"It's terrible sometimes, inside," he said, "that's what's the trouble. You walk these streets, black and funky and cold, and there's not really a living ass to talk to, and there's nothing shaking, and there's no way of getting it out—that storm inside. You can't talk it and you can't make love with it, and when you finally try to get with it and play it, you realize *nobody's* listening. So *you've* got to listen. You got to find a way to listen."

And then he walked away from the window and sat on the sofa again, as though all the wind had suddenly been knocked out of him. "Sometimes you'll do *anything* to play, even cut your mother's throat." He laughed and looked at me. "Or your brother's." Then he sobered. "Or your own." Then: "Don't worry. I'm all right now and I think I'll *be* all right. But I can't forget—where I've been. I don't mean just the physical place I've been, I mean where I've *been*. And *what* I've been."

"What have you been, Sonny?" I asked.

He smiled—but sat sideways on the sofa, his elbow resting on the back, his fingers playing with his mouth and chin, not looking at me. "I've been something I didn't recognize, didn't know I could be. Didn't know anybody could be." He stopped, looking inward, looking helplessly young, looking old. "I'm not talking about it now because I feel *guilty* or anything like that—maybe it would be better if I did, I don't know. Anyway, I can't really talk about it. Not to you, not to anybody," and now he turned and faced me. "Sometimes, you know, and it was actually when I was most *out* of the world, I felt that I was in it, that I was *with* it, really, and I could play or I didn't really have to *play*, it just came out of me, it was there. And I don't know how I played, thinking about it now, but I know I did awful things, those times, sometimes, to people. Or it wasn't that I *did* anything to them—it was that they weren't real." He picked up the beer can; it was empty; he rolled it between his palms: "And other times—well, I needed a fix, I needed to find a place to lean, I needed to clear a space to *listen*—and I couldn't find it, and I—went crazy, I did terrible things to *me*, I was terrible *for* me." He began pressing the beer can between his hands, I watched the metal begin to give. It glittered, as he played with it, like a knife, and I was afraid he would cut himself, but I said nothing. "Oh well. I can never tell you. I was all by myself at the bottom of something, stinking and sweating and crying and shaking, and I smelled it, you know? *my* stink, and I thought I'd die if I couldn't get away from it and yet, all the same, I knew that everything I was doing was just locking me in with it. And I didn't know," he paused, still flattening the beer can, "I didn't know, I still *don't* know, something kept telling me that maybe it was good to smell your own stink, but I didn't think that *that* was what I'd been trying to do—and—who can stand it?" and he abruptly dropped the ruined beer can, looking at me with a small, still smile, and then rose, walking to the window as though it were the lodestone rock. I watched his face, he watched the avenue. "I couldn't tell you when Mama died—but the reason I wanted to leave

Harlem so bad was to get away from drugs. And then, when I ran away, that's what I was running from—really. When I came back, nothing had changed, *I* hadn't changed, I was just—older." And he stopped, drumming with his fingers on the windowpane. The sun had vanished, soon darkness would fall. I watched his face. "It can come again," he said, almost as though speaking to himself. Then he turned to me. "It can come again," he repeated. "I just want you to know that."

"All right," I said, at last. "So it can come again. All right."

He smiled, but the smile was sorrowful. "I had to try to tell you," he said.

"Yes," I said. "I understand that."

"You're my brother," he said, looking straight at me, and not smiling at all.

"Yes," I repeated, "yes. I understand that."

He turned back to the window, looking out. "All that hatred down there," he said, "all that hatred and misery and love. It's a wonder it doesn't blow the avenue apart."

We went to the only nightclub on a short, dark street, downtown. We squeezed through the narrow, chattering, jam-packed bar to the entrance of the big room, where the bandstand was. And we stood there for a moment, for the lights were very dim in this room and we couldn't see. Then, "Hello, boy," said a voice and an enormous black man, much older than Sonny or myself, erupted out of all that atmospheric lighting and put an arm around Sonny's shoulder. "I been sitting right here," he said, "waiting for you."

He had a big voice, too, and heads in the darkness turned toward us.

Sonny grinned and pulled a little away, and said, "Creole, this is my brother. I told you about him."

Creole shook my hand. "I'm glad to meet you, son," he said, and it was clear that he was glad to meet me *there*, for Sonny's sake. And he smiled, "You got a real musician in *your* family," and he took his arm from Sonny's shoulder and slapped him, lightly, affectionately, with the back of his hand.

"Well. Now I've heard it all," said a voice behind us. This was another musician, and a friend of Sonny's, a coal-black, cheerful-looking man, built close to the ground. He imme-

diately began confiding to me, at the top of his lungs, the
most terrible things about Sonny, his teeth gleaming like a
lighthouse and his laugh coming up out of him like the beginning of an earthquake. And it turned out that everyone at
the bar knew Sonny, or almost everyone; some were musicians, working there, or nearby, or not working, some were
simply hangers-on, and some were there to hear Sonny play.
I was introduced to all of them and they were all very polite
to me. Yet, it was clear that, for them, I was only Sonny's
brother. Here, I was in Sonny's world. Or, rather: his kingdom. Here, it was not even a question that his veins bore royal
blood.

They were going to play soon and Creole installed me, by
myself, at a table in a dark corner. Then I watched them,
Creole, and the little black man, and Sonny, and the others,
while they horsed around, standing just below the bandstand.
The light from the bandstand spilled just a little short of them
and, watching them laughing and gesturing and moving
about, I had the feeling that they, nevertheless, were being
most careful not to step into that circle of light too suddenly:
that if they moved into the light too suddenly, without thinking, they would perish in flame. Then, while I watched, one
of them, the small, black man, moved into the light and
crossed the bandstand and started fooling around with his
drums. Then—being funny and being, also, extremely cere-
monious—Creole took Sonny by the arm and led him to the
piano. A woman's voice called Sonny's name and a few hands
started clapping. And Sonny, also being funny and being cer-
emonious, and so touched, I think, that he could have cried,
but neither hiding it nor showing it, riding it like a man,
grinned, and put both hands to his heart and bowed from the
waist.

Creole then went to the bass fiddle and a lean, very bright-
skinned brown man jumped up on the bandstand and picked
up his horn. So there they were, and the atmosphere on the
bandstand and in the room began to change and tighten.
Someone stepped up to the microphone and announced
them. Then there were all kinds of murmurs. Some people at
the bar shushed others. The waitress ran around, frantically
getting in the last orders, guys and chicks got closer to each

other, and the lights on the bandstand, on the quartet, turned to a kind of indigo. Then they all looked different there. Creole looked about him for the last time, as though he were making certain that all his chickens were in the coop, and then he—jumped and struck the fiddle. And there they were.

All I know about music is that not many people ever really hear it. And even then, on the rare occasions when something opens within, and the music enters, what we mainly hear, or hear corroborated, are personal, private, vanishing evocations. But the man who creates the music is hearing something else, is dealing with the roar rising from the void and imposing order on it as it hits the air. What is evoked in him, then, is of another order, more terrible because it has no words, and triumphant, too, for that same reason. And his triumph, when he triumphs, is ours. I just watched Sonny's face. His face was troubled, he was working hard, but he wasn't with it. And I had the feeling that, in a way, everyone on the bandstand was waiting for him, both waiting for him and pushing him along. But as I began to watch Creole, I realized that it was Creole who held them all back. He had them on a short rein. Up there, keeping the beat with his whole body, wailing on the fiddle, with his eyes half closed, he was listening to everything, but he was listening to Sonny. He was having a dialogue with Sonny. He wanted Sonny to leave the shoreline and strike out for the deep water. He was Sonny's witness that deep water and drowning were not the same thing—he had been there, and he knew. And he wanted Sonny to know. He was waiting for Sonny to do the things on the keys which would let Creole know that Sonny was in the water.

And, while Creole listened, Sonny moved, deep within, exactly like someone in torment. I had never before thought of how awful the relationship must be between the musician and his instrument. He has to fill it, this instrument, with the breath of life, his own. He has to make it do what he wants it to do. And a piano is just a piano. It's made out of so much wood and wires and little hammers and big ones, and ivory. While there's only so much you can do with it, the only way to find this out is to try; to try and make it do everything.

And Sonny hadn't been near a piano for over a year. And he wasn't on much better terms with his life, not the life that stretched before him now. He and the piano stammered, started one way, got scared, stopped; started another way, panicked, marked time, started again; then seemed to have found a direction, panicked again, got stuck. And the face I saw on Sonny I'd never seen before. Everything had been burned out of it, and, at the same time, things usually hidden were being burned in, by the fire and fury of the battle which was occurring in him up there.

Yet, watching Creole's face as they neared the end of the first set, I had the feeling that something had happened, something I hadn't heard. Then they finished, there was scattered applause, and then, without an instant's warning, Creole started into something else, it was almost sardonic, it was *Am I Blue*. And, as though he commanded, Sonny began to play. Something began to happen. And Creole let out the reins. The dry, low, black man said something awful on the drums, Creole answered, and the drums talked back. Then the horn insisted, sweet and high, slightly detached perhaps, and Creole listened, commenting now and then, dry, and driving, beautiful and calm and old. Then they all came together again, and Sonny was part of the family again. I could tell this from his face. He seemed to have found, right there beneath his fingers, a damn brand-new piano. It seemed that he couldn't get over it. Then, for awhile, just being happy with Sonny, they seemed to be agreeing with him that brand-new pianos certainly were a gas.

Then Creole stepped forward to remind them that what they were playing was the blues. He hit something in all of them, he hit something in me, myself, and the music tightened and deepened, apprehension began to beat the air. Creole began to tell us what the blues were all about. They were not about anything very new. He and his boys up there were keeping it new, at the risk of ruin, destruction, madness, and death, in order to find new ways to make us listen. For, while the tale of how we suffer, and how we are delighted, and how we may triumph is never new, it always must be heard. There isn't any other tale to tell, it's the only light we've got in all this darkness.

And this tale, according to that face, that body, those strong hands on those strings, has another aspect in every country, and a new depth in every generation. Listen, Creole seemed to be saying, listen. Now these are Sonny's blues. He made the little black man on the drums know it, and the bright, brown man on the horn. Creole wasn't trying any longer to get Sonny in the water. He was wishing him Godspeed. Then he stepped back, very slowly, filling the air with the immense suggestion that Sonny speak for himself.

Then they all gathered around Sonny and Sonny played. Every now and again one of them seemed to say, amen. Sonny's fingers filled the air with life, his life. But that life contained so many others. And Sonny went all the way back, he really began with the spare, flat statement of the opening phrase of the song. Then he began to make it his. It was very beautiful because it wasn't hurried and it was no longer a lament. I seemed to hear with what burning he had made it his, with what burning we had yet to make it ours, how we could cease lamenting. Freedom lurked around us and I understood, at last, that he could help us to be free if we would listen, that he would never be free until we did. Yet, there was no battle in his face now. I heard what he had gone through, and would continue to go through until he came to rest in earth. He had made it his: that long line, of which we knew only Mama and Daddy. And he was giving it back, as everything must be given back, so that, passing through death, it can live forever. I saw my mother's face again, and felt, for the first time, how the stones of the road she had walked on must have bruised her feet. I saw the moonlit road where my father's brother died. And it brought something else back to me, and carried me past it, I saw my little girl again and felt Isabel's tears again, and I felt my own tears begin to rise. And I was yet aware that this was only a moment, that the world waited outside, as hungry as a tiger, and that trouble stretched above us, longer than the sky.

Then it was over. Creole and Sonny let out their breath, both soaking wet, and grinning. There was a lot of applause and some of it was real. In the dark, the girl came by and I asked her to take drinks to the bandstand. There was a long pause, while they talked up there in the indigo light and after awhile I saw the girl put a Scotch and milk on top of the piano for Sonny. He didn't seem to notice it, but just before they started playing again, he sipped from it and looked toward me, and nodded. Then he put it back on top of the piano. For me, then, as they began to play again, it glowed and shook above my brother's head like the very cup of trembling.

This Morning, This Evening, So Soon

"Y ou are full of nightmares," Harriet tells me. She is in her dressing gown and has cream all over her face. She and my older sister, Louisa, are going out to be girls together. I suppose they have many things to talk about—they have *me* to talk about, certainly—and they do not want my presence. I have been given a bachelor's evening. The director of the film which has brought us such incredible and troubling riches will be along later to take me out to dinner.

I watch her face. I know that it is quite impossible for her to be as untroubled as she seems. Her self-control is mainly for my benefit—my benefit, and Paul's. Harriet comes from orderly and progressive Sweden and has reacted against all the advanced doctrines to which she has been exposed by becoming steadily and beautifully old-fashioned. We never fought in front of Paul, not even when he was a baby. Harriet does not so much believe in protecting children as she does in helping them to build a foundation on which they can build and build again, each time life's high-flying steel ball knocks down everything they have built.

Whenever I become upset, Harriet becomes very cheerful and composed. I think she began to learn how to do this over eight years ago, when I returned from my only visit to America. Now, perhaps, it has become something she could not control if she wished to. This morning, at breakfast, when I yelled at Paul, she averted Paul's tears and my own guilt by looking up and saying, "My God, your father is cranky this morning, isn't he?"

Paul's attention was immediately distracted from his wounds, and the unjust inflicter of those wounds, to his mother's laughter. He watched her.

"It is because he is afraid they will not like his songs in New York. Your father is an *artiste, mon chou,* and they are very mysterious people, *les artistes.* Millions of people are waiting for him in New York, they are begging him to come, and they will give him a *lot* of money, but he is afraid they will not like him. Tell him he is wrong."

865

She succeeded in rekindling Paul's excitement about places he has never seen. I was also, at once, reinvested with all my glamour. I think it is sometimes extremely difficult for Paul to realize that the face he sees on record sleeves and in the newspapers and on the screen is nothing more or less than the face of his father—who sometimes yells at him. Of course, since he is only seven—going on eight, he will be eight years old this winter—he cannot know that I am baffled, too.

"Of course, you are wrong, you are silly," he said with passion—and caused me to smile. His English is strongly accented and is not, in fact, as good as his French, for he speaks French all day at school. French is really his first language, the first he ever heard. "You are the greatest singer in France"—sounding exactly as he must sound when he makes this pronouncement to his schoolmates—"the greatest *American* singer"—this concession was so gracefully made that it was not a concession at all, it added inches to my stature, America being only a glamorous word for Paul. It is the place from which his father came, and to which he now is going, a place which very few people have ever seen. But his aunt is one of them and he looked over at her. "Mme. Dumont says so, and she says he is a *great actor, too.*" Louisa nodded, smiling. "And she has seen *Les Fauves Nous Attendent*—five times!" This clinched it, of course. Mme. Dumont is our concierge and she has known Paul all his life. I suppose he will not begin to doubt anything she says until he begins to doubt everything.

He looked over at me again. "So you are wrong to be afraid."

"I was wrong to yell at you, too. I won't yell at you any more today."

"All right." He was very grave.

Louisa poured more coffee. "He's going to knock them dead in New York. You'll see."

"Mais bien sûr," said Paul, doubtfully. He does not quite know what "knock them dead" means, though he was sure, from her tone, that she must have been agreeing with him. He does not quite understand this aunt, whom he met for the first time two months ago, when she arrived to spend the summer with us. Her accent is entirely different from anything

he has ever heard. He does not really understand why, since she is my sister and his aunt, she should be unable to speak French.

Harriet, Louisa, and I looked at each other and smiled. "Knock them dead," said Harriet, "means *d'avoir un succès fou*. But you will soon pick up all the American expressions." She looked at me and laughed. "So will I."

"That's what he's afraid of." Louisa grinned. "We have *got* some expressions, believe me. Don't let anybody ever tell you America hasn't got a culture. Our culture is as thick as clabber milk."

"Ah," Harriet answered, "I know. I know."

"I'm going to be practicing later," I told Paul.

His face lit up. *"Bon."* This meant that, later, he would come into my study and lie on the floor with his papers and crayons while I worked out with the piano and the tape recorder. He knew that I was offering this as an olive branch. All things considered, we get on pretty well, my son and I.

He looked over at Louisa again. She held a coffee cup in one hand and a cigarette in the other; and something about her baffled him. It was early, so she had not yet put on her face. Her short, thick, graying hair was rougher than usual, almost as rough as my own—later, she would be going to the hairdresser's; she is fairer than I, and better-looking; Louisa, in fact, caught all the looks in the family. Paul knows that she is my older sister and that she helped to raise me, though he does not, of course, know what this means. He knows that she is a schoolteacher in the *American* South, which is not, for some reason, the same place as South America. I could see him trying to fit all these exotic details together into a pattern which would explain her strangeness—strangeness of accent, strangeness of manner. In comparison with the people he has always known, Louisa must seem, for all her generosity and laughter and affection, peculiarly uncertain of herself, peculiarly hostile and embattled.

I wondered what he would think of his Uncle Norman, older and much blacker than I, who lives near the Alabama town in which we were born. Norman will meet us at the boat.

*

Now Harriet repeats, "Nightmares, nightmares. Nothing ever turns out as badly as you think it will—in fact," she adds laughing, "I am happy to say that that would scarcely be possible."

Her eyes seek mine in the mirror—dark-blue eyes, pale skin, black hair. I had always thought of Sweden as being populated entirely by blondes, and I thought that Harriet was abnormally dark for a Swedish girl. But when we visited Sweden, I found out differently. "It is all a great racial salad, Europe, that is why I am sure that I will never understand your country," Harriet said. That was in the days when we never imagined that we would be going to it.

I wonder what she is really thinking. Still, she is right, in two days we will be on a boat, and there is simply no point in carrying around my load of apprehension. I sit down on the bed, watching her fix her face. I realize that I am going to miss this old-fashioned bedroom. For years, we've talked about throwing out the old junk which came with the apartment and replacing it with less massive, modern furniture. But we never have.

"Oh, everything will probably work out," I say. "I've been in a bad mood all day long. I just can't sing any more." We both laugh. She reaches for a wad of tissues and begins wiping off the cream. "I wonder how Paul will like it, if he'll make friends—that's all."

"Paul will like any place where you are, where we are. Don't worry about Paul."

Paul has never been called any names, so far. Only, once he asked us what the word *métis* meant and Harriet explained to him that it meant mixed blood, adding that the blood of just about everybody in the world was mixed by now. Mme. Dumont contributed bawdy and detailed corroboration from her own family tree, the roots of which were somewhere in Corsica; the moral of the story, as she told it, was that women were weak, men incorrigible, and *le bon Dieu* appallingly clever. Mme. Dumont's version is the version I prefer, but it may not be, for Paul, the most utilitarian.

Harriet rises from the dressing table and comes over to sit in my lap. I fall back with her on the bed, and she smiles down into my face.

"Now, don't worry," she tells me, "please try not to worry. Whatever is coming, we will manage it all very well, you will see. We have each other and we have our son and we know what we want. So, we are luckier than most people."

I kiss her on the chin. "I'm luckier than most men."

"I'm a very lucky woman, too."

And for a moment we are silent, alone in our room, which we have shared so long. The slight rise and fall of Harriet's breathing creates an intermittent pressure against my chest, and I think how, if I had never left America, I would never have met her and would never have established a life of my own, would never have entered my own life. For everyone's life begins on a level where races, armies, and churches stop. And yet everyone's life is always shaped by races, churches, and armies; races, churches, armies menace, and have taken, many lives. If Harriet had been born in America, it would have taken her a long time, perhaps forever, to look on me as a man like other men; if I had met her in America, I would never have been able to look on her as a woman like all other women. The habits of public rage and power would also have been our private compulsions, and would have blinded our eyes. We would never have been able to love each other. And Paul would never have been born.

Perhaps, if I had stayed in America, I would have found another woman and had another son. But that other woman, that other son are in the limbo of vanished possibilities. I might also have become something else, instead of an actor-singer, perhaps a lawyer, like my brother, or a teacher, like my sister. But no, I am what I have become and this woman beside me is my wife, and I love her. All the sons I might have had mean nothing, since I *have* a son, I named him, Paul, for my father, and I love him.

I think of all the things I have seen destroyed in America, all the things that I have lost there, all the threats it holds for me and mine.

I grin up at Harriet. "Do you love me?"

"Of course not. I simply have been madly plotting to get to America all these years."

"What a patient wench you are."

"The Swedes are very patient."

She kisses me again and stands up. Louisa comes in, also in a dressing gown.

"I hope you two aren't sitting in here yakking about the *subject*." She looks at me. "My, you are the sorriest-looking celebrity I've ever seen. I've always wondered why people like you hired press agents. Now I know." She goes to Harriet's dressing table. "Honey, do you mind if I borrow some of that *mad* nail polish?"

Harriet goes over to the dressing table. "I'm not sure I know *which* mad nail polish you mean."

Harriet and Louisa, somewhat to my surprise, get on very well. Each seems to find the other full of the weirdest and most delightful surprises. Harriet has been teaching Louisa French and Swedish expressions, and Louisa has been teaching Harriet some of the saltier expressions of the black South. Whenever one of them is not playing straight man to the other's accent, they become involved in long speculations as to how a language reveals the history and the attitudes of a people. They discovered that all the European languages contain a phrase equivalent to "to work like a nigger." ("Of course," says Louisa, "they've had black men working for them for a long time.") "Language is experience and language is power," says Louisa, after regretting that she does not know any of the African dialects. "That's what I keep trying to tell those dicty bastards down South. They get their own experience into the language, we'll have a great language. But, no, they all want to talk like white folks." Then she leans forward, grasping Harriet by the knee. "I tell them, honey, white folks ain't saying *nothing*. Not a thing are they saying—and *some* of them know it, they *need* what you got, the whole world needs it." Then she leans back, in disgust. "You think they listen to me? Indeed they do not. They just go right on, trying to talk like white folks." She leans forward again, in tremendous indignation. "You know some of them folks are *ashamed* of Mahalia Jackson? *Ashamed* of her, one of the greatest singers alive! They think she's common." Then she looks about the room as though she held a bottle in her hand and were looking for a skull to crack.

I think it is because Louisa has never been able to talk like this to any white person before. All the white people she has ever met needed, in one way or another, to be reassured, consoled, to have their consciences pricked but not blasted; could not, could not afford to hear a truth which would shatter, irrevocably, their image of themselves. It is astonishing the lengths to which a person, or a people, will go in order to avoid a truthful mirror. But Harriet's necessity is precisely the opposite: it is of the utmost importance that she learn everything that Louisa can tell her, and then learn more, much more. Harriet is really trying to learn from Louisa how best to protect her husband and her son. This is why they are going out alone tonight. They will have, tonight, as it were, a final council of war. I may be moody, but they, thank God, are practical.

Now Louisa turns to me while Harriet rummages about on the dressing table. "What time is Vidal coming for you?"

"Oh, around seven-thirty, eight o'clock. He says he's reserved tables for us in some very chic place, but he won't say where." Louisa wriggles her shoulders, raises her eyebrows, and does a tiny bump and grind. I laugh. "That's right. And then I guess we'll go out and get drunk."

"I hope to God you do. You've been about as cheerful as a cemetery these last few days. And, that way, your hangover will keep you from bugging us tomorrow."

"What about *your* hangovers? I know the way you girls drink."

"Well, we'll be paying for our own drinks," says Harriet, "so I don't think we'll have that problem. But *you're* going to be feted, like an international movie star."

"You sure you don't want to change your mind and come out with Vidal and me?"

"We're sure," Louisa says. She looks down at me and gives a small, amused grunt. "An international movie star. And I used to change your diapers. I'll be damned." She is grave for a moment. "Mama'd be proud of you, you know that?" We look at each other and the air between us is charged with secrets which not even Harriet will ever know. "Now, get the hell out of here, so we can get dressed."

"I'll take Paul on down to Mme. Dumont's."

Paul is to have supper with her children and spend the night there.

"For the last time," says Mme. Dumont and she rubs her hand over Paul's violently curly black hair. *"Tu vas nous manquer, tu sais?"* Then she looks up at me and laughs. "He doesn't care. He is only interested in seeing the big ship and all the wonders of New York. Children are never sad to make journeys."

"I would be very sad to go," says Paul, politely, "but my father must go to New York to work and he wants me to come with him."

Over his head, Mme. Dumont and I smile at each other. *"Il est malin, ton gosse!"* She looks down at him again. "And do you think, my little diplomat, that you will like New York?"

"We aren't only going to New York," Paul answers, "we are going to California, too."

"Well, do you think you will like California?"

Paul looks at me. "I don't know. If we don't like it, we'll come back."

"So simple. Just like that," says Mme. Dumont. She looks at me. "It is the best way to look at life. Do come back. You know, we feel that you belong to us, too, here in France."

"I hope you do," I say. "I hope you do. I have always felt—always felt at home here." I bend down and Paul and I kiss each other on the cheek. We have always done so—but will we be able to do so in America? American fathers never kiss American sons. I straighten, my hand on Paul's shoulder. "You be good. I'll pick you up for breakfast, or, if you get up first you come and pick me up and we can hang out together tomorrow, while your *Maman* and your Aunt Louisa finish packing. They won't want two men hanging around the house."

"D'accord. Where shall we hang out?" On the last two words he stumbles a little and imitates me.

"Maybe we can go to the zoo, I don't know. And I'll take you to lunch at the Eiffel Tower, would you like that?"

"Oh, yes," he says, "I'd love that." When he is pleased, he seems to glow. All the energy of his small, tough, concentrated being charges an unseen battery and adds an incredible luster to his eyes, which are large and dark brown—like mine—and to his skin, which always reminds me of the colors of honey and the fires of the sun.

"OK, then." I shake hands with Mme. Dumont. *"Bonsoir, Madame."* I ring for the elevator, staring at Paul. *"Ciao, Pauli."*

"Bonsoir, Papa."

And Mme. Dumont takes him inside.

Upstairs, Harriet and Louisa are finally powdered, perfumed, and jeweled, and ready to go: dry martinis at the Ritz, supper, "in some *very* expensive little place," says Harriet, and perhaps the Folies Bergère afterwards. "A real cornball, tourist evening," says Louisa. "I'm working on the theory that if I can get Harriet to act like an American now, she won't have so much trouble later."

"I very much doubt," Harriet says, "that I will be able to endure the Folies Bergère for three solid hours."

"Oh, then we'll duck across town to Harry's New York bar and drink mint juleps," says Louisa.

I realize that, quite apart from everything else, Louisa is having as much fun as she has ever had in her life. Perhaps she, too, will be sad to leave Paris, even though she has only known it for such a short time.

"Do people drink those in New York?" Harriet asks. I think she is making a list of the things people do or do not do in New York.

"*Some* people do." Louisa winks at me. "Do you realize that this Swedish chick's picked up an Alabama drawl?"

We laugh together. The elevator chugs to a landing.

"We'll stop and say goodnight to Paul," Harriet says. She kisses me. "Give our best to Vidal."

"Right. Have a good time. Don't let any Frenchmen run off with Louisa."

"I did not come to Paris to be protected, and if I had, this wild chick *you* married couldn't do it. I just *might* upset everybody and come home with a French count." She presses the elevator button and the cage goes down.

I walk back into our dismantled apartment. It stinks of departure. There are bags and crates in the hall which will be taken away tomorrow, there are no books in the bookcases, the kitchen looks as though we never cooked a meal there, never dawdled there, in the early morning or late at night, over coffee. Presently, I must shower and shave but now I pour myself a drink and light a cigarette and step out on our balcony. It is dusk, the brilliant light of Paris is beginning to fade, and the green of the trees is darkening.

I have lived in this city for twelve years. This apartment is on the top floor of a corner building. We look out over the trees and the roof tops to the Champ de Mars, where the Eiffel Tower stands. Beyond this field is the river, which I have crossed so often, in so many states of mind. I have crossed every bridge in Paris, I have walked along every *quai*. I know the river as one finally knows a friend, know it when it is black, guarding all the lights of Paris in its depths, and seeming, in its vast silence, to be communing with the dead who lie beneath it; when it is yellow, evil, and roaring, giving a rough time to tugboats and barges, and causing people to remember that it has been known to rise, it has been known to kill; when it is peaceful, a slick, dark, dirty green, playing host to rowboats and *les bateaux mouches* and throwing up from time to time an extremely unhealthy fish. The men who stand along the *quais* all summer with their fishing lines gratefully accept the slimy object and throw it in a rusty can. I have always wondered who eats those fish.

And I walk up and down, up and down, glad to be alone.

It is August, the month when all Parisians desert Paris and one has to walk miles to find a barbershop or a laundry open in some tree-shadowed, silent side street. There is a single person on the avenue, a paratrooper walking toward École Militaire. He is also walking, almost certainly, and rather sooner than later, toward Algeria. I have a friend, a good-natured boy who was always hanging around the clubs in which I worked in the old days, who has just returned from Algeria, with a recurring, debilitating fever, and minus one eye. The government has set his pension at the sum, arbitrary if not occult, of fifty-three thousand francs every three months. Of course, it is quite impossible to live on this amount of money without working—but who will hire a half-

blind invalid? This boy has been spoiled forever, long before
his thirtieth birthday, and there are thousands like him all over
France.

And there are fewer Algerians to be found on the streets of
Paris now. The rug sellers, the peanut vendors, the postcard
peddlers and money-changers have vanished. The boys I used
to know during my first years in Paris are scattered—or cor-
ralled—the Lord knows where.

Most of them had no money. They lived three and four
together in rooms with a single skylight, a single hard cot, or
in buildings that seemed abandoned, with cardboard in the
windows, with erratic plumbing in a wet, cobblestoned yard,
in dark, dead-end alleys, or on the outer, chilling heights of
Paris.

The Arab cafés are closed—those dark, acrid cafés in which
I used to meet with them to drink tea, to get high on hashish,
to listen to the obsessive, stringed music which has no relation
to any beat, any time, that I have ever known. I once thought
of the North Africans as my brothers and that is why I went
to their cafés. They were very friendly to me, perhaps one or
two of them remained really fond of me even after I could no
longer afford to smoke Lucky Strikes and after my collection
of American sport shirts had vanished—mostly into their
wardrobes. They seemed to feel that they had every right to
them, since I could only have wrested these things from the
world by cunning—it meant nothing to say that I had had no
choice in the matter; perhaps I had wrested these things from
the world by treason, by refusing to be identified with the
misery of my people. Perhaps, indeed, I identified myself with
those who were responsible for this misery.

And this was true. Their rage, the only note in all their
music which I could not fail to recognize, to which I responded, yet had the effect of setting us more than ever at a
division. They were perfectly prepared to drive all Frenchmen
into the sea, and to level the city of Paris. But I could not
hate the French, because they left me alone. And I love Paris,
I will always love it, it is the city which saved my life. It saved
my life by allowing me to find out who I am.

It was on a bridge, one tremendous, April morning, that I

knew I had fallen in love. Harriet and I were walking hand in hand. The bridge was the Pont Royal, just before us was the great *horloge*, high and lifted up, saying ten to ten; beyond this, the golden statue of Joan of Arc, with her sword uplifted. Harriet and I were silent, for we had been quarreling about something. Now, when I look back, I think we had reached that state when an affair must either end or become something more than an affair.

I looked sideways at Harriet's face, which was still. Her dark-blue eyes were narrowed against the sun, and her full, pink lips were still slightly sulky, like a child's. In those days, she hardly ever wore make-up. I was in my shirt sleeves. Her face made me want to laugh and run my hand over her short dark hair. I wanted to pull her to me and say, *Baby, don't be mad at me*, and at that moment something tugged at my heart and made me catch my breath. There were millions of people all around us, but I was alone with Harriet. She was alone with me. Never, in all my life, until that moment, had I been alone with anyone. The world had always been with us, between us, defeating the quarrel we could not achieve, and making love impossible. During all the years of my life, until that moment, I had carried the menacing, the hostile, killing world with me everywhere. No matter what I was doing or saying or feeling, one eye had always been on the world—that world which I had learned to distrust almost as soon as I learned my name, that world on which I knew one could never turn one's back, the white man's world. And for the first time in my life I was free of it; it had not existed for me; I had been quarreling with my girl. It was our quarrel, it was entirely between us, it had nothing to do with anyone else in the world. For the first time in my life I had not been afraid of the patriotism of the mindless, in uniform or out, who would beat me up and treat the woman who was with me as though she were the lowest of untouchables. For the first time in my life I felt that no force jeopardized my right, my power, to possess and to protect a woman; for the first time, the first time, felt that the woman was not, in her own eyes or in the eyes of the world, degraded by my presence.

The sun fell over everything, like a blessing, people were moving all about us, I will never forget the feeling of Harriet's small hand in mine, dry and trusting, and I turned to her, slowing our pace. She looked up at me with her enormous, blue eyes, and she seemed to wait. I said, *"Harriet. Harriet. Tu sais, il y a quelque chose de très grave qui m'est arrivé. Je t'aime. Je t'aime. Tu me comprends,* or shall I say it in English?"

This was eight years ago, shortly before my first and only visit home.

That was when my mother died. I stayed in America for three months. When I came back, Harriet thought that the change in me was due to my grief—I was very silent, very thin. But it had not been my mother's death which accounted for the change. I had known that my mother was going to die. I had not known what America would be like for me after nearly four years away.

I remember standing at the rail and watching the distance between myself and Le Havre increase. Hands fell, ceasing to wave, handkerchiefs ceased to flutter, people turned away, they mounted their bicycles or got into their cars and rode off. Soon, Le Havre was nothing but a blur. I thought of Harriet, already miles from me in Paris, and I pressed my lips tightly together in order not to cry.

Then, as Europe dropped below the water, as the days passed and passed, as we left behind us the skies of Europe and the eyes of everyone on the ship began, so to speak, to refocus, waiting for the first glimpse of America, my apprehension began to give way to a secret joy, a checked anticipation. I thought of such details as showers, which are rare in Paris, and I thought of such things as rich, cold, American milk and heavy, chocolate cake. I wondered about my friends, wondered if I had any left, and wondered if they would be glad to see me.

The Americans on the boat did not seem to be so bad, but I was fascinated, after such a long absence from it, by the nature of their friendliness. It was a friendliness which did not suggest, and was not intended to suggest, any possibility of friendship. Unlike Europeans, they dropped titles and used first names almost at once, leaving themselves, unlike the Europeans, with nowhere thereafter to go. Once one had become "Pete" or "Jane" or "Bill" all that could decently be known was known and any suggestion that there might be further depths, a person, so to speak, behind the name, was taken as a violation of that privacy which did not, paradoxically, since they trusted it so little, seem to exist among Americans. They apparently equated privacy with the unspeakable things they did in the bathroom or the bedroom, which they related only to the analyst, and then read about in the pages of best sellers. There was an eerie and unnerving irreality about everything they said and did, as though they were all members of the same team and were acting on orders from some invincibly cheerful and tirelessly inventive coach. I was fascinated by it. I found it oddly moving, but I cannot say that I was displeased. It had not occurred to me before that Americans, who had never treated me with any respect, had no respect for each other.

On the last night but one, there was a gala in the big ballroom and I sang. It had been a long time since I had sung before so many Americans. My audience had mainly been penniless French students, in the weird, Left Bank bistros I worked in those days. Still, I was a great hit with them and by this time I had become enough of a drawing card, in the Latin Quarter and in St. Germain des Prés, to have attracted a couple of critics, to have had my picture in *France-soir*, and to have acquired a legal work permit which allowed me to make a little more money. Just the same, no matter how industrious and brilliant some of the musicians had been, or how devoted my audience, they did not know, they could not know, what my songs came out of. They did not know what was funny about it. It was impossible to translate: It damn well better be funny, or Laughing to keep from crying, or What did *I* do to be so black and blue?

The moment I stepped out on the floor, they began to smile, something opened in them, they were ready to be pleased. I found in their faces, as they watched me, smiling, waiting, an artless relief, a profound reassurance. Nothing was more familiar to them than the sight of a dark boy, singing, and there were few things on earth more necessary. It was under cover of darkness, my own darkness, that I could sing for them of the joys, passions, and terrors they smuggled about with them like steadily depreciating contraband. Under cover of the midnight fiction that I was unlike them because I was black, they could stealthily gaze at those treasures which they had been mysteriously forbidden to possess and were never permitted to declare.

I sang *I'm Coming, Virginia*, and *Take This Hammer*, and *Precious Lord*. They wouldn't let me go and I came back and sang a couple of the oldest blues I knew. Then someone asked me to sing *Swanee River*, and I did, astonished that I could, astonished that this song, which I had put down long ago, should have the power to move me. Then, if only, perhaps, to make the record complete, I wanted to sing *Strange Fruit*, but, on this number, no one can surpass the great, tormented Billie Holiday. So I finished with *Great Getting-Up Morning* and I guess I can say that if I didn't stop the show I certainly ended it. I got a big hand and I drank at a few tables and I danced with a few girls.

After one more day and one more night, the boat landed in New York. I woke up, I was bright awake at once, and I thought, *We're here*. I turned on all the lights in my small cabin and I stared into the mirror as though I were committing my face to memory. I took a shower and I took a long time shaving and I dressed myself very carefully. I walked the long ship corridors to the dining room, looking at the luggage piled high before the elevators and beside the steps. The dining room was nearly half empty and full of a quick and joyous excitement which depressed me even more. People ate quickly, chattering to each other, anxious to get upstairs and go on deck. Was it my imagination or was it true that they seemed to avoid my eyes? A few people waved and smiled, but let me pass; perhaps it would have made them uncomfortable, this morning, to try to share their excitement with me; perhaps they did not want to know whether or not it was possible for me to share it. I walked to my table and sat down. I munched toast as dry as paper and drank a pot of coffee. Then I tipped my waiter, who bowed and smiled and called me "sir" and said that he hoped to see me on the boat again. "I hope so, too," I said.

And was it true, or was it my imagination, that a flash of wondering comprehension, a flicker of wry sympathy, then appeared in the waiter's eyes? I walked upstairs to the deck.

There was a breeze from the water but the sun was hot and made me remember how ugly New York summers could be. All of the deck chairs had been taken away and people milled about in the space where the deck chairs had been, moved from one side of the ship to the other, clambered up and down the steps, crowded the rails, and they were busy taking photographs—of the harbor, of each other, of the sea, of the gulls. I walked slowly along the deck, and an impulse stronger than myself drove me to the rail. There it was, the great, unfinished city, with all its towers blazing in the sun. It came toward us slowly and patiently, like some enormous, cunning, and murderous beast, ready to devour, impossible to escape. I watched it come closer and I listened to the people around me, to their excitement and their pleasure. There was no doubt that it was real. I watched their shining faces and wondered if I were mad. For a moment I longed, with all my heart, to be able to feel whatever they were feeling, if only to know what such a feeling was like. As the boat moved slowly into the harbor, they were being moved into safety. It was only I who was being floated into danger. I turned my head, looking for Europe, but all that stretched behind me was the sky, thick with gulls. I moved away from the rail. A big, sandy-haired man held his daughter on his shoulders, showing her the Statue of Liberty. I would never know what this statue meant to others, she had always been an ugly joke for me. And the American flag was flying from the top of the ship, above my head. I had seen the French flag drive the French into the most unspeakable frenzies, I had seen the flag which was nominally mine used to dignify the vilest purposes: now I would never, as long as I lived, know what others saw when they saw a flag. "There's no place like home," said a voice close by, and I thought, *There damn sure isn't*. I decided to go back to my cabin and have a drink.

There was a cablegram from Harriet in my cabin. It said: Be good. Be quick. I'm waiting. I folded it carefully and put it in my breast pocket. Then I wondered if I would ever get back to her. How long would it take me to earn the money to get out of this land? Sweat broke out on my forehead and I poured myself some whiskey from my nearly empty bottle. I paced the tiny cabin. It was silent. There was no one down in the cabins now.

I was not sober when I faced the uniforms in the first-class lounge. There were two of them; they were not unfriendly. They looked at my passport, they looked at me. "You've been away a long time," said one of them.

"Yes," I said, "it's been a while."

"What did you do over there all that time?"—with a grin meant to hide more than it revealed, which hideously revealed more than it could hide.

I said, "I'm a singer," and the room seemed to rock around me. I held on to what I hoped was a calm, open smile. I had not had to deal with these faces in so long that I had forgotten how to do it. I had once known how to pitch my voice precisely between curtness and servility, and known what razor's edge of a pickaninny's smile would turn away wrath. But I had forgotten all the tricks on which my life had once depended. Once I had been an expert at baffling these people, at setting their teeth on edge, and dancing just outside the trap laid for me. But I was not an expert now. These faces were no longer merely the faces of two white men, who were my enemies. They were the faces of two white people whom I did not understand, and I could no longer plan my moves in accordance with what I knew of their cowardice and their needs and their strategy. That moment on the bridge had undone me forever.

"That's right," said one of them, "that's what it says, right here on the passport. Never heard of you, though." They looked up at me. "Did you do a lot of singing over there?"

"Some."

"What kind—concerts?"

"No." I wondered what I looked like, sounded like. I could tell nothing from their eyes. "I worked a few nightclubs."

"Nightclubs, eh? I guess they liked you over there."

"Yes," I said, "they seemed to like me all right."

"Well"—and my passport was stamped and handed back to me—"let's hope they like you over here."

"Thanks." They laughed—was it at me, or was it my imagination? and I picked up the one bag I was carrying and threw my trench coat over one shoulder and walked out of the first-class lounge. I stood in the slow-moving, murmuring line which led to the gangplank. I looked straight ahead and watched heads, smiling faces, step up to the shadow of the gangplank awning and then swiftly descend out of sight. I put my passport back in my breast pocket—*Be quick. I'm waiting*—and I held my landing card in my hand. Then, suddenly, there I was, standing on the edge of the boat, staring down the long ramp to the ground. At the end of the plank, on the ground, stood a heavy man in a uniform. His cap was pushed back from his gray hair and his face was red and wet. He looked up at me. This was the face I remembered, the face of my nightmares; perhaps hatred had caused me to know this face better than I would ever know the face of any lover. "Come on, boy," he cried, "come on, come on!"

And I almost smiled. I was home. I touched my breast pocket. I thought of a song I sometimes sang, *When will I ever get to be a man?* I came down the gangplank, stumbling a little, and gave the man my landing card.

Much later in the day, a customs inspector checked my baggage and waved me away. I picked up my bags and started walking down the long stretch which led to the gate, to the city.

And I heard someone call my name.

I looked up and saw Louisa running toward me. I dropped my bags and grabbed her in my arms and tears came to my eyes and rolled down my face. I did not know whether the tears were for joy at seeing her, or from rage, or both.

"How are you? How are you? You look wonderful, but, oh, haven't you lost weight? It's wonderful to see you again."

I wiped my eyes. "It's wonderful to see you, too, I bet you thought I was never coming back."

Louisa laughed. "I wouldn't have blamed you if you hadn't. These people are just as corny as ever, I swear I don't believe there's any hope for them. How's your French? Lord, when I think that it was I who studied French and now I can't speak a word. And you never went near it and you probably speak it like a native."

I grinned. *"Pas mal. Te me défends pas mal."* We started down the wide steps into the street. "My God," I said. "New York." I was not aware of its towers now. We were in the shadow of the elevated highway but the thing which most struck me was neither light nor shade, but noise. It came from a million things at once, from trucks and tires and clutches and brakes and doors; from machines shuttling and stamping and rolling and cutting and pressing; from the building of tunnels, the checking of gas mains, the laying of wires, the digging of foundations; from the chattering of rivets, the scream of the pile driver, the clanging of great shovels; from the battering down and the raising up of walls; from millions of radios and television sets and juke boxes. The human voices distinguished themselves from the roar only by their note of strain and hostility. Another fleshy man, uniformed and red faced, hailed a cab for us and touched his cap politely but could only manage a peremptory growl: "Right this way, miss. Step up, sir." He slammed the cab door behind us. Louisa directed the driver to the New Yorker Hotel.

"Do they take us there?"

She looked at me. "They got laws in New York, honey, it'd be the easiest thing in the world to spend all your time in court. But over at the New Yorker, I believe they've already got the message." She took my arm. "You see? In spite of all this chopping and booming, this place hasn't really changed very much. You still can't hear yourself talk."

And I thought to myself, Maybe that's the point.

Early the next morning we checked out of the hotel and took the plane for Alabama.

I am just stepping out of the shower when I hear the bell ring. I dry myself hurriedly and put on a bathrobe. It is Vidal, of course, and very elegant he is, too, with his bushy gray hair quite lustrous, his swarthy, cynical, gypsylike face shaved and lotioned. Usually he looks just any old way. But tonight his brief bulk is contained in a dark-blue suit and he has an ironical pearl stickpin in his blue tie.

"Come in, make yourself a drink. I'll be with you in a second."

"I am, *hélas!*, on time. I trust you will forgive me for my thoughtlessness."

But I am already back in the bathroom. Vidal puts on a record: Mahalia Jackson, singing *I'm Going to Live the Life I Sing About in My Song.*

When I am dressed, I find him sitting in a chair before the open window. The daylight is gone, but it is not exactly dark. The trees are black now against the darkening sky. The lights in windows and the lights of motorcars are yellow and ringed. The street lights have not yet been turned on. It is as though, out of deference to the departed day, Paris waited a decent interval before assigning her role to a more theatrical but inferior performer.

Vidal is drinking a whiskey and soda. I pour myself a drink. He watches me.

"Well. How are you, my friend? You are nearly gone. Are you happy to be leaving us?"

"No." I say this with more force than I had intended. Vidal raises his eyebrows, looking amused and distant. "I never really intended to go back there. I certainly never intended to raise my kid there—"

"Mais, mon cher," Vidal says, calmly, "you are an intelligent man, you must have known that you would probably be returning one day." He pauses. "And, as for Pauli—did it never occur to you that he might wish one day to see the country in which his father and his father's fathers were born?"

"To do that, really, he'd have to go to Africa."

"America will always mean more to him than Africa, you know that."

"I don't know." I throw my drink down and pour myself another. "Why should he want to cross all that water just to be called a nigger? America never gave him anything."

"It gave him his father."

I look at him. "You mean, his father escaped."

Vidal throws back his head and laughs. If Vidal likes you, he is certain to laugh at you and his laughter can be very unnerving. But the look, the silence which follow this laughter can be very unnerving, too. And, now, in the silence, he asks me, "Do you really think that you have escaped anything? Come. I know you for a better man than that." He walks to the table which holds the liquor. "In that movie of ours which has made you so famous, and, as I now see, so troubled, what are you playing, after all? What is the tragedy of this half-breed troubadour if not, precisely, that he has taken all the possible roads to escape and that all these roads have failed him?" He pauses, with the bottle in one hand, and looks at me. "Do you remember the trouble I had to get a performance out of you? How you hated me, you sometimes looked as though you wanted to shoot me! And do you remember when the role of Chico began to come alive?" He pours his drink. "Think back, remember. I am a very great director, *mais pardon!* I could not have got such a performance out of anyone but you. And what were you thinking of, what was in your mind, what nightmare were you living with when you began, at last, to play the role—truthfully?" He walks back to his seat.

Chico, in the film, is the son of a Martinique woman and a French *colon* who hates both his mother and his father. He flees from the island to the capital, carrying his hatred with him. This hatred has now grown, naturally, to include all dark women and all white men, in a word, everyone. He descends into the underworld of Paris, where he dies. *Les fauves*—the wild beasts—refers to the life he has fled and to the life which engulfs him. When I agreed to do the role, I felt that I could probably achieve it by bearing in mind the North Africans I had watched in Paris for so long. But this did not please Vidal. The blowup came while we were rehearsing a fairly simple, straightforward scene. Chico goes into a sleazy Pigalle dance hall to beg the French owner for a particularly humiliating job. And this Frenchman reminds him of his father.

"You are playing this boy as though you thought of him as the noble savage," Vidal said, icily. "*Ça vient d'où*—all these ghastly mannerisms you are using all the time?"

Everyone fell silent, for Vidal rarely spoke this way. This silence told me that everyone, the actor with whom I was playing the scene and all the people in the "dance hall," shared Vidal's opinion of my performance and were relieved that he was going to do something about it. I was humiliated and too angry to speak; but perhaps I also felt, at the very bottom of my heart, a certain relief, an unwilling respect.

"You are doing it all wrong," he said, more gently. Then, "Come, let us have a drink together."

We walked into his office. He took a bottle and two glasses out of his desk. "Forgive me, but you put me in mind of some of those English *lady* actresses who love to play *putain* as long as it is always absolutely clear to the audience that they are really ladies. So perhaps they read a book, not usually, *hélas!*, *Fanny Hill*, and they have their chauffeurs drive them through Soho once or twice—and they come to the stage with a performance so absolutely loaded with detail, every bit of it meaningless, that there can be no doubt that they are acting. It is what the British call a triumph." He poured two cognacs. "That is what you are doing. Why? Who do you think this boy is, what do you think he is feeling, when he asks for this job?" He watched me carefully and I bitterly resented his look. "You come from America. The situation is not so pretty there for boys like you. I know you may not have been as poor as—as some—but is it really impossible for you to understand what a boy like Chico feels? Have you never, yourself, been in a similar position?"

I hated him for asking the question because I knew he knew the answer to it. "I would have had to be a very lucky black man not to have been in such a position."

"You would have had to be a very lucky *man*."

"Oh, God," I said, "please don't give me any of this equality-in-anguish business."

"It is perfectly possible," he said, sharply, "that there is not another kind."

Then he was silent. He sat down behind his desk. He cut a cigar and lit it, puffing up clouds of smoke, as though to prevent us from seeing each other too clearly. "Consider this," he said. "I am a French director who has never seen your country. I have never done you any harm, except, perhaps, historically—I mean, because I am white—but I cannot be blamed for that—"

"But *I* can be," I said, "and I am! I've never understood why, if *I* have to pay for the history written in the color of my skin, *you* should get off scot-free!" But I was surprised at my vehemence, I had not known I was going to say these things, and by the fact that I was trembling and from the way he looked at me I knew that, from a professional point of view anyway, I was playing into his hands.

"What makes you think I *do*?" His face looked weary and stern. "I am a Frenchman. Look at France. You think that I—we—are not paying for our history?" He walked to the window, staring out at the rather grim little town in which the studio was located. "If it is revenge that you want, well, then, let me tell you, you will have it. You will probably have it, whether you want it or not, our stupidity will make it inevitable." He turned back into the room. "But I beg you not to confuse me with the happy people of your country, who scarcely know that there is such a thing as history and so, naturally, imagine that they can escape, as you put it, scot-free. That is what you are doing, that is what I was about to say. I was about to say that I am a French director and I have never been in your country and I have never done you any harm—but you are not talking to that man, in this room, now. You are not talking to Jean Luc Vidal, but to some other white man, whom you remember, who has nothing to do with me." He paused and went back to his desk. "Oh, most of the time you are not like this, I know. But it is there all the time, it must be, because when you are upset, this is what comes out. So you are not playing Chico truthfully, you are lying about him, and I will not let you do it. When you go back, now, and play this scene again, I want you to remember what has just happened in this room. You brought your past into this room. That is what Chico does when he walks into the dance hall. The Frenchman whom he begs for a job is not merely a Frenchman—he is the father who disowned and betrayed him and all the Frenchmen whom he hates." He smiled and poured me another cognac. "Ah! If it were not for *my* history, I would not have so much trouble to get the truth out of you." He looked into my face, half smiling. "And you, you are angry—are you not?—that I *ask* you for the truth. You think I have no right to ask." Then he said something which he knew would enrage me. "Who are you then, and what good has it done you to come to France, and how will you raise your son? Will you teach him never to tell the truth to anyone?" And he moved behind his desk and looked at me, as though from behind a barricade.

"You have no right to talk to me this way."

"Oh, yes, I do," he said. "I have a film to make and a reputation to maintain and I am going to get a performance out of you." He looked at his watch. "Let us go back to work."

I watch him now, sitting quietly in my living room, tough, cynical, crafty old Frenchman, and I wonder if he knows that the nightmare at the bottom of my mind, as I played the role of Chico, was all the possible fates of Paul. This is but another way of saying that I relived the disasters which had nearly undone me; but, because I was thinking of Paul, I discovered that I did not want my son ever to feel toward me as I had felt toward my own father. He had died when I was eleven, but I had watched the humiliations he had to bear, and I had pitied him. But was there not, in that pity, however painfully and unwillingly, also some contempt? For how could I *know* what he had borne? I knew only that I was his son. However he had loved me, whatever he had borne, I, his son, was despised. Even had he lived, he could have done nothing to prevent it, nothing to protect me. The best that he could hope to do was to prepare me for it; and even at that he had failed. How can one be prepared for the spittle in the face, all the tireless ingenuity which goes into the spite and fear of small, unutterably miserable people, whose greatest terror is the singular identity, whose joy, whose safety, is entirely dependent on the humiliation and anguish of others?

But for Paul, I swore it, such a day would never come. I would throw my life and my work between Paul and the nightmare of the world. I would make it impossible for the world to treat Paul as it had treated my father and me.

Mahalia's record ends. Vidal rises to turn it over. "Well?" He looks at me very affectionately. "Your nightmares, please!"

"Oh, I was thinking of that summer I spent in Alabama, when my mother died." I stop. "You know, but when we finally filmed that bar scene, I was thinking of New York. I was scared in Alabama, but I almost went crazy in New York. I was sure I'd never make it back here—back here to Harriet. And I knew if I didn't, it was going to be the end of me." Now Mahalia is singing *When the Saints Go Marching In.* "I got a job in the town as an elevator boy, in the town's big department store. It was a special favor, one of my father's white friends got it for me. For a long time, in the South, we all—depended—on the—*kindness*—of white friends." I take out a handkerchief and wipe my face. "But this man didn't like me. I guess I didn't seem grateful enough, wasn't enough like my father, what he thought my father was. And I couldn't get used to the town again, I'd been away too long, I hated it. It's a terrible town, anyway, the whole thing looks as though it's been built around a jailhouse. There's a room in the courthouse, a room where they beat you up. Maybe you're walking along the street one night, it's usually at night, but it happens in the daytime, too. And the police car comes up behind you and the cop says, 'Hey, boy. Come on over here.' So you go on over. He says, 'Boy, I believe you're drunk.' And, you see, if you say, 'No, no sir,' he'll beat you because you're calling him a liar. And if you say anything else, unless it's something to make him laugh, he'll take you in and beat you, just for fun. The trick is to think of some way for them to have their fun without beating you up."

The street lights of Paris click on and turn all the green leaves silver. "Or to go along with the ways *they* dream up. And they'll do anything, anything at all, to prove that you're no better than a dog and to make you feel like one. And they hated me because I'd been North and I'd been to Europe. People kept saying, I hope you didn't bring no foreign notions back here with you, boy. And I'd say, 'No sir,' or 'No ma'am,' but I never said it right. And there was a time, all of them remembered it, when I *had* said it right. But now they could tell that I despised them—I guess, no matter what, I wanted them to know that I despised them. But I didn't despise them any more than everyone else did, only the others never let it show. They knew how to keep the white folks happy, and it was easy—you just had to keep them feeling like they were God's favor to the universe. They'd walk around with great, big, foolish grins on their faces and the colored folks loved to see this, because they hated them so much. "Just look at So-and-So," somebody'd say. "His white is *on* him today." And when we didn't hate them, we pitied them. In America, that's usually what it means to have a white friend. You pity the poor bastard because he was born believing the world's a great place to be, and you know it's not, and you can see that he's going to have a terrible time getting used to this idea, if he *ever* gets used to it."

Then I think of Paul again, those eyes which still imagine that I can do anything, that skin, the color of honey and fire, his jet-black, curly hair. I look out at Paris again, and I listen to Mahalia. "Maybe it's better to have the terrible times first. I don't know. Maybe, then, you can have, *if* you live, a better life, a real life, because you had to fight so hard to get it away—you know?—from the mad dog who held it in his teeth. But then your life has all those tooth marks, too, all those tatters, and all that blood." I walk to the bottle and raise it. "One for the road?"

"Thank you," says Vidal.

I pour us a drink, and he watches me. I have never talked so much before, not about those things anyway. I know that Vidal has nightmares, because he knows so much about them, but he has never told me what his are. I think that he probably does not talk about his nightmares any more. I know that the war cost him his wife and his son, and that he was in prison in Germany. He very rarely refers to it. He has a married daughter who lives in England, and he rarely speaks of her. He is like a man who has learned to live on what is left of an enormous fortune.

We are silent for a moment.

"Please go on," he says, with a smile. "I am curious about the reality behind the reality of your performance."

"My sister, Louisa, never married," I say, abruptly, "because, once, years ago, she and the boy she was going with and two friends of theirs were out driving in a car and the police stopped them. The girl who was with them was very fair and the police pretended not to believe her when she said she was colored. They made her get out and stand in front of the headlights of the car and pull down her pants and raise her dress—they said that was the only way they could be sure. And you can imagine what they said, and what they did—and they were lucky, at that, that it didn't go any further. But none of the men could do anything about it. Louisa couldn't face that boy again, and I guess he couldn't face her." Now it is really growing dark in the room and I cross to the light switch. "You know, I know what that boy felt, I've felt it. They want you to feel that you're not a man, maybe that's the only way they can feel like men, I don't know. I walked around New York with Harriet's cablegram in my pocket as though it were some atomic secret, in *code*, and they'd kill me if they ever found out what it meant. You know, there's something wrong with people like that. And thank God Harriet was here, she *proved* that the world was bigger than the world they wanted me to live in, I *had* to get back here, get to a place where people were too busy with their own lives, *their private lives*, to make fantasies about mine, to set up walls around mine." I look at him. The light in the room has made the night outside blue-black and golden and the great search-light of the Eiffel Tower is turning in the sky. "That's what it's like in America, for me, anyway. I always feel that I don't exist there, except in someone else's—usually dirty—mind. I don't know if you know what that means, but I do, and I don't want to put Harriet through that and I don't want to raise Paul there."

"Well," he says at last, "you are not required to remain in America forever, are you? You will sing in that elegant club which apparently feels that it cannot, much longer, so much as open its doors without you, and you will probably accept the movie offer, you would be very foolish not to. You will make a lot of money. Then, one day, you will remember that airlines and steamship companies are still in business and that France still exists. *That* will certainly be cause for astonishment."

Vidal was a Gaullist before de Gaulle came to power. But he regrets the manner of de Gaulle's rise and he is worried about de Gaulle's regime. "It is not the fault of *mon général*," he sometimes says, sadly. "Perhaps it is history's fault. I *suppose* it must be history which always arranges to bill a civilization at the very instant it is least prepared to pay."

Now he rises and walks out on the balcony, as though to reassure himself of the reality of Paris. Mahalia is singing *Didn't It Rain?* I walk out and stand beside him.

"You are a good boy—Chico," he says. I laugh. "You believe in love. You do not know all the things love cannot do, but"—he smiles—"love will teach you that."

We go, after dinner, to a Left Bank discothèque which can charge outrageous prices because Marlon Brando wandered in there one night. By accident, according to Vidal. "Do you know how many people in Paris are becoming rich—to say nothing of those, *hélas!*, who are going broke—on the off chance that Marlon Brando will lose his way again?"

He has not, presumably, lost his way tonight, but the discothèque is crowded with those strangely faceless people who are part of the night life of all great cities, and who always arrive, moments, hours, or decades late, on the spot made notorious by an event or a movement or a handful of personalities. So here are American boys, anything but beardless, scratching around for Hemingway; American girls, titillating themselves with Frenchmen and existentialism, while waiting for the American boys to shave off their beards; French painters, busily pursuing the revolution which ended thirty years ago; and the young, bored, perverted, American *arrivistes* who are buying their way into the art world via flattery and liquor, and the production of canvases as arid as their greedy little faces. Here are boys, of all nations, one step above the pimp, who are occasionally walked across a stage or trotted before a camera. And the girls, their enemies, whose faces are sometimes seen in ads, one of whom will surely have a tantrum before the evening is out.

In a corner, as usual, surrounded, as usual, by smiling young men, sits the drunken blonde woman who was once the mistress of a famous, dead painter. She is a figure of some importance in the art world, and so rarely has to pay for either her drinks or her lovers. An older Frenchman, who was once a famous director, is playing *quatre cent vingt-et-un* with the woman behind the cash register. He nods pleasantly to Vidal and me as we enter, but makes no move to join us, and I respect him for this. Vidal and I are obviously cast tonight in the role vacated by Brando: our entrance justifies the prices and sends a kind of shiver through the room. It is marvelous to watch the face of the waiter as he approaches, all smiles and deference and grace, not so much honored by our presence as achieving his reality from it; excellence, he seems to be saying, gravitates naturally toward excellence. We order two whiskey and sodas. I know why Vidal sometimes comes here. He is lonely. I do not think that he expects ever to love one woman again, and so he distracts himself with many.

Since this is a discothèque, jazz is blaring from the walls and record sleeves are scattered about with a devastating carelessness. Two of them are mine and no doubt, presently, someone will play the recording of the songs I sang in the film.

"I thought," says Vidal, with a malicious little smile, "that your farewell to Paris would not be complete without a brief exposure to the perils of fame. Perhaps it will help prepare you for America, where, I am told, the populace is yet more carnivorous than it is here."

I can see that one of the vacant models is preparing herself to come to our table and ask for an autograph, hoping, since she is pretty—she has, that is, the usual female equipment, dramatized in the usual, modern way—to be invited for a drink. Should the maneuver succeed, one of her boy friends or girl friends will contrive to come by the table, asking for a light or a pencil or a lipstick, and it will be extremely difficult not to invite this person to join us, too. Before the evening ends, we will be surrounded. I don't, now, know what I expected of fame, but I suppose it never occurred to me that the light could be just as dangerous, just as killing, as the dark.

"Well, let's make it brief," I tell him. "Sometimes I wish that you weren't quite so fond of me."

He laughs. "There are some very interesting people here tonight. Look."

Across the room from us, and now staring at our table, are a group of American Negro students, who are probably visiting Paris for the first time. There are four of them, two boys and two girls, and I suppose that they must be in their late teens or early twenties. One of the boys, a gleaming, curly-haired, golden-brown type—the color of his mother's fried chicken—is carrying a guitar. When they realize we have noticed them, they smile and wave—wave as though I were one of their possessions, as, indeed, I am. Golden-brown is a mime. He raises his guitar, drops his shoulders, and his face falls into the lugubrious lines of Chico's face as he approaches death. He strums a little of the film's theme music, and I laugh and the table laughs. It is as though we were all back home and had met for a moment, on a Sunday morning, say, before a church or a poolroom or a barbershop.

And they have created a sensation in the discothèque, naturally, having managed, with no effort whatever, to outwit all the gleaming boys and girls. Their table, which had been of no interest only a moment before, has now become the focus of a rather pathetic attention; their smiles have made it possible for the others to smile, and to nod in our direction.

"Oh," says Vidal, "he does that far better than you ever did, perhaps I will make him a star."

"Feel free, *m'sieu, le bon Dieu*, I got mine." But I can see that his attention has really been caught by one of the girls, slim, tense, and dark, who seems, though it is hard to know how one senses such things, to be treated by the others with a special respect. And, in fact, the table now seems to be having a council of war, to be demanding her opinion or her cooperation. She listens, frowning, laughing; the quality, the force of her intelligence causes her face to keep changing all the time, as though a light played on it. And, presently, with a gesture she might once have used to scatter feed to chickens, she scoops up from the floor one of those dangling rag bags women love to carry. She holds it loosely by the drawstrings, so that it is banging somewhere around her ankle, and walks over to our table. She has an honest, forthright walk, entirely unlike the calculated, pelvic workout by means of which most women get about. She is small, but sturdily, economically, put together.

As she reaches our table, Vidal and I rise, and this throws her for a second. (It has been a long time since I have seen such an attractive girl.)

Also, everyone, of course, is watching us. It is really a quite curious moment. They have put on the record of Chico singing a sad, angry Martinique ballad; my own voice is coming at us from the walls as the girl looks from Vidal to me, and smiles.

"I guess you know," she says, "we weren't *about* to let you get out of here without bugging you just a little bit. We've only been in Paris just a couple of days and we thought for sure that we wouldn't have a chance of running into you anywhere, because it's in all the papers that you're coming home."

"Yes," I say, "yes. I'm leaving the day after tomorrow."

"Oh!" She grins. "Then we really *are* lucky." I find that I have almost forgotten the urchin-like grin of a colored girl. "I guess, before I keep babbling on, I'd better introduce myself. My name is Ada Holmes."

We shake hands. "This is Monsieur Vidal, the director of the film."

"I'm very honored to meet you, sir."

"Will you join us for a moment? Won't you sit down?" And Vidal pulls a chair out for her.

But she frowns contritely. "I really ought to get back to my friends." She looks at me. "I really just came over to say, for myself and all the kids, that we've got your records and we've seen your movie, and it means so much to us"—and she laughs, breathlessly, nervously, it is somehow more moving than tears—"more than I can say. Much more. And we wanted to know if you and your friend"—she looks at Vidal—"your *director*, Monsieur Vidal, would allow us to buy you a drink? We'd be very honored if you would."

"It is we who are honored," says Vidal, promptly, "*and* grateful. We were getting terribly bored with one another, thank God you came along."

The three of us laugh, and we cross the room.

The three at the table rise, and Ada makes the introductions. The other girl, taller and paler than Ada, is named Ruth. One of the boys is named Talley—"short for Talliafero"—and Golden-brown's name is Pete. "Man," he tells me, "I dig you the most. Your tore me up, baby, tore me *up*."

"You tore up a lot of people," Talley says, cryptically, and he and Ruth laugh. Vidal does not know, but I do, that Talley is probably referring to white people.

They are from New Orleans and Tallahassee and North Carolina; are college students, and met on the boat. They have been in Europe all summer, in Italy and Spain, but are only just getting to Paris.

"We meant to come sooner," says Ada, "but we could never make up our minds to leave a place. I thought we'd never pry Ruth loose from Venice."

"I resigned myself," says Pete, "and just sat in the Piazza San Marco, drinking gin fizz and being photographed with the pigeons, while Ruth had herself driven *all* up and down the Grand Canal." He looks at Ruth. "Finally, thank heaven, it rained."

"She was working off her hostilities," says Ada, with a grin. "We thought we might as well let her do it in Venice, the opportunities in North Carolina are really terribly limited."

"There are some very upset people walking around down there," Ruth says, "and a couple of tours around the Grand Canal might do them a world of good."

Pete laughs. "Can't you just see Ruth escorting them to the edge of the water?"

"I haven't lifted my hand in anger yet," Ruth says, "but, oh Lord," and she laughs, clenching and unclenching her fists.

"You haven't been back for a long time, have you?" Talley asks me.

"Eight years. I haven't really lived there for twelve years."

Pete whistles. "I fear you are in for some surprises, my friend. There have been some changes made." Then, "Are you afraid?"

"A little."

"We all are," says Ada, "that's why I was so glad to get away for a little while."

"Then you haven't been back since Black Monday," Talley says. He laughs. "That's how it's gone down in Confederate history." He turns to Vidal. "What do people think about it here?"

Vidal smiles, delighted. "It seems extraordinarily infantile behavior, even for Americans, from whom, I must say, I have never expected very much in the way of maturity." Everyone at the table laughs. Vidal goes on. "But I cannot really talk

about it, I do not understand it. I have never really understood Americans; I am an old man now, and I suppose I never
will. There is something very nice about them, something very
winning, but they seem so ignorant—so ignorant of life. Perhaps it is strange, but the only people from your country with
whom I have ever made contact are black people—like my
good friend, my discovery, here," and he slaps me on the
shoulder. "Perhaps it is because we, in Europe, whatever else
we do not know, or have forgotten, know about suffering. We
have suffered here. You have suffered, too. But most Americans do not yet know what anguish is. It is too bad, because
the life of the West is in their hands." He turns to Ada. "I
cannot help saying that I think it is a scandal—and we may
all pay very dearly for it—that a civilized nation should elect
to represent it a man who is so simple that he thinks the world
is simple." And silence falls at the table and the four young
faces stare at him.

"Well," says Pete, at last, turning to me, "you won't be
bored, man, when you get back there."

"It's much too nice a night," I say, "to stay cooped up in
this place, where all I can hear is my own records." We laugh.
"Why don't we get out of here and find a sidewalk café?" I
tap Pete's guitar. "Maybe we can find out if you've got any
talent."

"Oh, talent I've got," says Pete, "but character, man, I'm
lacking."

So, after some confusion about the bill, for which Vidal has
already made himself responsible, we walk out into the Paris
night. It is very strange to feel that, very soon now, these
boulevards will not exist for me. People will be walking up
and down, as they are tonight, and lovers will be murmuring
in the black shadows of the plane trees, and there will be these
same still figures on the benches or in the parks—but they will
not exist for me, I will not be here. For a long while Paris will
no longer exist for me, except in my mind; and only in the
minds of some people will I exist any longer for Paris. After
departure, only invisible things are left, perhaps the life of the
world is held together by invisible chains of memory and loss
and love. So many things, so many people, depart! And we
can only repossess them in our minds. Perhaps this is what

the old folks meant, what my mother and my father meant, when they counseled us to keep the faith.

We have taken a table at the Deux Magots and Pete strums on his guitar and begins to play this song:

> *Preach the word, preach the word, preach the word!*
> *If I never, never see you any more.*
> *Preach the word, preach the word.*
> *And I'll meet you on Canaan's shore.*

He has a strong, clear, boyish voice, like a young preacher's, and he is smiling as he sings his song. Ada and I look at each other and grin, and Vidal is smiling. The waiter looks a little worried, for we are already beginning to attract a crowd, but it is a summer night, the gendarmes on the corner do not seem to mind, and there will be time, anyway, to stop us.

Pete was not there, none of us were, the first time this song was needed; and no one now alive can imagine what that time was like. But the song has come down the bloodstained ages. I suppose this to mean that the song is still needed, still has its work to do.

The others are all, visibly, very proud of Pete; and we all join him, and people stop to listen:

> *Testify! Testify!*
> *If I never, never see you any more!*
> *Testify! Testify!*
> *I'll meet you on Canaan's shore!*

In the crowd that has gathered to listen to us, I see a face I know, the face of a North African prize fighter, who is no longer in the ring. I used to know him well in the old days, but have not seen him for a long time. He looks quite well, his face is shining, he is quite decently dressed. And something about the way he holds himself, not quite looking at our table, tells me that he has seen me, but does not want to risk a rebuff. So I call him. "Boona!"

And he turns, smiling, and comes loping over to our table, his hands in his pockets. Pete is still singing and Ada and Vidal have taken off on a conversation of their own. Ruth and Talley look curiously, expectantly, at Boona. Now that I have called him over, I feel somewhat uneasy. I realize that I do not know what he is doing now, or how he will get along with any of these people, and I can see in his eyes that he is delighted to be in the presence of two young girls. There are virtually no North African women in Paris, and not even the dirty, rat-faced girls who live, apparently, in cafés are willing to go with an Arab. So Boona is always looking for a girl, and because he is so deprived and because he is not Western, his techniques can be very unsettling. I know he is relieved that the girls are not French and not white. He looks briefly at Vidal and Ada. Vidal, also, though for different reasons, is always looking for a girl.

But Boona has always been very nice to me. Perhaps I am sorry that I called him over, but I did not want to snub him.

He claps one hand to the side of my head, as is his habit. "*Comment vas-tu, mon frère?* I have not see you, oh, for long time." And he asks me, as in the old days, "You all right? Nobody bother you?" And he laughs. "Ah! *Tu as fait le chemin, toi!* Now you are *vedette*, big star—wonderful!" He looks around the table, made a little uncomfortable by the silence that has fallen, now that Pete has stopped singing. "I have seen you in the movies—you know?—and I tell every-body, I know *him*!" He points to me, and laughs, and Ruth and Talley laugh with him. "That's right, man, you make me real proud, you make me cry!"

"Boona, I want you to meet some friends of mine." And I go round the table: "Ruth, Talley, Ada, Pete"—and he bows and shakes hands, his dark eyes gleaming with pleasure—"*et Monsieur Vidal, le metteur en scène du film qui t'a arraché des larmes.*"

"*Enchanté.*" But his attitude toward Vidal is colder, more distrustful. "Of course I have heard of Monsieur Vidal. He is the director of many films, many of them made me cry." This last statement is utterly, even insolently, insincere.

But Vidal, I think, is relieved that I will now be forced to speak to Boona and will leave him alone with Ada.

"Sit down," I say, "have a drink with us, let me have your news. What's been happening with you, what are you doing with yourself these days?"

"Ah," he sits down, "nothing very brilliant, my brother." He looks at me quickly, with a little smile. "You know, we have been having hard times here."

"Where are you from?" Ada asks him.

His brilliant eyes take her in entirely, but she does not flinch. "I am from Tunis." He says it proudly, with a little smile.

"From Tunis. I have never been to Africa, I would love to go one day."

He laughs. "Africa is a big place. Very big. There are many countries in Africa, many"—he looks briefly at Vidal—"different kinds of people, many colonies."

"But Tunis," she continues, in her innocence, "is free? Freedom is happening all over Africa. That's why I would like to go there."

"I have not been back for a long time," says Boona, "but all the news I get from Tunis, from my people, is not good."

"Wouldn't you like to go back?" Ruth asks.

Again he looks at Vidal. "That is not so easy."

Vidal smiles. "You know what I would like to do? There's a wonderful Spanish place not far from here, where we can listen to live music and dance a little." He turns to Ada. "Would you like that?"

He is leaving it up to me to get rid of Boona, and it is, of course, precisely for this reason that I cannot do it. Besides, it is no longer so simple.

"Oh, I'd love that," says Ada, and she turns to Boona. "Won't you come, too?"

"Thank you, mam'selle," he says, softly, and his tongue flicks briefly over his lower lip, and he smiles. He is very moved, people are not often nice to him.

In the Spanish place there are indeed a couple of Spanish guitars, drums, castanets, and a piano, but the uses to which these are being put carry one back, as Pete puts it, to the levee. "These are the wailingest Spanish cats I ever heard," says Ruth. "They didn't learn how to do this in Spain, no, they didn't, they been rambling. You ever hear anything like this going on in Spain?" Talley takes her out on the dance floor, which is already crowded. A very handsome French-woman is dancing with an enormous, handsome black man, who seems to be her lover, who seems to have taught her how to dance. Apparently, they are known to the musicians, who egg them on with small cries of *"Olé!"* It is a very good-natured crowd, mostly foreigners, Spaniards, Swedes, Greeks. Boona takes Ada out on the dance floor while Vidal is answering some questions put to him by Pete on the entertainment situation in France. Vidal looks a little put out, and I am amused.

We are there for perhaps an hour, dancing, talking, and I am, at last, a little drunk. In spite of Boona, who is a very good and tireless dancer, Vidal continues his pursuit of Ada, and I begin to wonder if he will make it and I begin to wonder if I want him to.

I am still puzzling out my reaction when Pete, who has disappeared, comes in through the front door, catches my eye, and signals to me. I leave the table and follow him into the streets.

He looks very upset. "I don't want to bug you, man," he says, "but I fear your boy has goofed."

I know he is not joking. I think he is probably angry at Vidal because of Ada, and I wonder what I can do about it and why he should be telling me.

I stare at him, gravely, and he says, "It looks like he stole some money."

"Stole *money*? Who, Vidal?"

And then, of course, I get it, in the split second before he says, impatiently, "No, are you kidding? Your friend, the Tunisian."

I do not know what to say or what to do, and so I temporize with questions. All the time I am wondering if this can be true and what I can do about it if it is. The trouble is, I know that Boona steals, he would probably not be alive if he didn't, but I cannot say so to these children, who probably still imagine that everyone who steals is a thief. But he has never, to my knowledge, stolen from a friend. It seems unlike him. I have always thought of him as being better than that, and smarter than that. And so I cannot believe it, but neither can I doubt it. I do not know anything about Boona's life, these days. This causes me to realize that I do not really know much about Boona.

"Who did he steal it from?"

"From Ada. Out of her bag."

"How much?"

"Ten dollars. It's not an awful lot of money, but"—he grimaces—"none of us *have* an awful lot of money."

"I know." The dark side street on which we stand is nearly empty. The only sound on the street is the muffled music of the Spanish club. "How do you know it was Boona?"

He anticipates my own unspoken rejoinder. "Who else could it be? Besides—somebody *saw* him do it."

"Somebody saw him?"

"Yes."

I do not ask him who this person is, for fear that he will say it is Vidal.

"Well," I say, "I'll try to get it back." I think that I will take Boona aside and then replace the money myself. "Was it in dollars or in francs?"

"In francs."

I have no dollars and this makes it easier. I do not know how I can possibly face Boona and accuse him of stealing money from my friends. I would rather give him the benefit of even the faintest doubt. But, "Who saw him?" I ask.

"Talley. But we didn't want to make a thing about it—"

"Does Ada know it's gone?"

"Yes." He looks at me helplessly. "I know this makes you feel pretty bad, but we thought we'd better tell you, rather than"—lamely—"anybody else."

Now, Ada comes out of the club, carrying her ridiculous handbag, and with her face all knotted and sad. "Oh," she says, "I hate to cause all this trouble, it's not worth it, not for ten lousy dollars." I am astonished to see that she has been weeping, and tears come to her eyes now.

I put my arm around her shoulder. "Come on, now. You're not causing anybody any trouble and, anyway, it's nothing to cry about."

"It isn't your fault, Ada," Pete says, miserably.

"Oh, I ought to get a sensible handbag," she says, "like you're always telling me to do," and she laughs a little, then looks at me. "Please don't try to do anything about it. Let's just forget it."

"What's happening inside?" I ask her.

"Nothing. They're just talking. I think Mr. Vidal is dancing with Ruth. He's a great dancer, that little Frenchman."

"He's a great talker, too," Pete says.

"Oh, he doesn't mean anything," says Ada, "he's just having fun. He probably doesn't get a chance to talk to many American girls."

"He certainly made up for lost time tonight."

"Look," I say, "if Talley and Boona are alone, maybe you better go back in. We'll be in in a minute. Let's try to keep this as quiet as we can."

"Yeah," he says, "okay. We're going soon anyway, okay?"

"Yes," she tells him, "right away."

But as he turns away, Boona and Talley step out into the street, and it is clear that Talley feels that he has Boona under arrest. I almost laugh, the whole thing is beginning to resemble one of those mad French farces with people flying in and out of doors; but Boona comes straight to me.

"They say I stole money, my friend. You know me, you are the only one here who knows me, you know I would not do such a thing."

I look at him and I do not know what to say. Ada looks at him with her eyes full of tears and looks away. I take Boona's arm.

"We'll be back in a minute," I say. We walk a few paces up the dark, silent street.

"She say I take her money," he says. He, too, looks as though he is about to weep—but I do not know for which reason. "You know me, you know me almost twelve years, you think I do such a thing?"

Talley saw you, I want to say, but I cannot say it. Perhaps Talley only thought he saw him. Perhaps it is easy to see a boy who looks like Boona with his hand in an American girl's purse.

"If you not believe me," he says, "search me. Search me!" And he opens his arms wide, theatrically, and now there are tears standing in his eyes.

I do not know what his tears mean, but I certainly cannot

search him. I want to say, I know you steal, I know you have to steal. Perhaps you took the money out of this girl's purse in order to eat tomorrow, in order not to be thrown into the streets tonight, in order to stay out of jail. This girl means nothing to you, after all, she is only an American, an American like me. Perhaps, I suddenly think, no girl means anything to you, or ever will again, they have beaten you too hard and kept out in the gutter too long. And I also think, if you would steal from her, then of course you would lie to me, neither of us means anything to you; perhaps, in your eyes, we are simply luckier gangsters in a world which is run by gangsters. But I cannot say any of these things to Boona. I cannot say, Tell me the truth, nobody cares about the money any more.

So I say, "Of course I will not search you." And I realize that he knew I would not.

"I think it is that Frenchman who say I am a thief. They think we all are thieves." His eyes are bright and bitter. He looks over my shoulder. "They have all come out of the club now."

I look around and they are all there, in a little dark knot on the sidewalk.

"Don't worry," I say. "It doesn't matter."

"You believe me? My brother?" And his eyes look into mine with a terrible intensity.

"Yes," I force myself to say, "yes, of course, I believe you. Someone made a mistake, that's all."

"You know, the way American girls run around, they have their sack open all the time, she could lost the money anywhere. Why she blame me? Because I come from Africa?" Tears are glittering on his face. "Here she come now."

And Ada comes up the street with her straight, determined walk. She walks straight to Boona and takes his hand. "I am sorry," she says, "for everything that happened. Please believe me. It isn't worth all this fuss. I'm sure you're a very nice person, and"—she falters—"I must have lost the money, I'm sure I lost it." She looks at him. "It isn't worth hurting your feelings, and I'm terribly sorry about it."

"I no take your money," he says. "Really, truly, I no take it. Ask him"—pointing to me, grabbing me by the arm, shaking me—"he know me for years, he will tell you that I never, never steal!"

"I'm sure," she says. "I'm sure."

I take Boona by the arm again. "Let's forget it. Let's forget it all. We're all going home now, and one of these days we'll have a drink again and we'll forget all about it, all right?"

"Yes," says Ada, "let us forget it." And she holds out her hand.

Boona takes it, wonderingly. His eyes take her in again. "You are a very nice girl. Really. A very nice girl."

"I'm sure you're a nice person, too." She pauses. "Goodnight."

"Goodnight," he says, after a long silence.

Then he kisses me on both cheeks. *"Au revoir, mon frère."*

"Au revoir, Boona."

After a moment we turn and walk away, leaving him standing there.

"Did he take it?" asks Vidal.

"I tell you, I *saw* him," says Talley.

"Well," I say, "it doesn't matter now." I look back and see Boona's stocky figure disappearing down the street.

"No," says Ada, "it doesn't matter." She looks up. "It's almost morning."

"I would gladly," says Vidal, stammering, "gladly—"

But she is herself again. "I wouldn't think of it. We had a wonderful time tonight, a wonderful time, and I wouldn't think of it." She turns to me with that urchin-like grin. "It was wonderful meeting you. I hope you won't have too much trouble getting used to the States again."

"Oh, I don't think I will," I say. And then, "I hope you won't."

"No," she says, "I don't think anything they can do will surprise me any more."

"Which way are we all going?" asks Vidal. "I hope someone will share my taxi with me."

But he lives in the sixteenth arrondissement, which is not in anyone's direction. We walk him to the line of cabs standing under the clock at Odéon.

And we look each other in the face, in the growing morning

light. His face looks weary and lined and lonely. He puts both
hands on my shoulders and then puts one hand on the nape
of my neck. "Do not forget me, Chico," he says. "You must
come back and see us, one of these days. Many of us depend
on you for many things."

"I'll be back," I say. "I'll never forget you."

He raises his eyebrows and smiles. *"Alors, Adieu."*

"Adieu, Vidal."

"I was happy to meet all of you," he says. He looks at Ada.
"Perhaps we will meet again before you leave."

"Perhaps," she says. "Goodby, Monsieur Vidal."

"Goodby."

Vidal's cab drives away. "I also leave you now," I say. "I
must go home and wake up my son and prepare for our journey."

I leave them standing on the corner, under the clock, which
points to six. They look very strange and lost and determined,
the four of them. Just before my cab turns off the boulevard,
I wave to them and they wave back.

Mme. Dumont is in the hall, mopping the floor.

"Did all my family get home?" I ask. I feel very cheerful,
I do not know why.

"Yes," she says, "they are all here. Paul is still sleeping."

"May I go in and get him?"

She looks at me in surprise. "Of course."

So I walk into her apartment and walk into the room where
Paul lies sleeping. I stand over his bed for a long time.

Perhaps my thoughts traveled—travel through to him. He
opens his eyes and smiles up at me. He puts a fist to his eyes
and raises his arms. *"Bonjour, Papa."*

I lift him up. *"Bonjour.* How do you feel today?"

"Oh, I don't know yet," he says.

I laugh. I put him on my shoulder and walk out into the
hall. Mme. Dumont looks up at him with her radiant, aging
face.

"Ah," she says, "you are going on a journey! How does it
feel?"

"He doesn't know yet," I tell her. I walk to the elevator
door and open it, dropping Paul down to the crook of my
arm.

She laughs again. "He will know later. What a journey! *Jusqu'au nouveau monde!*"

I open the cage and we step inside. "Yes," I say, "all the way to the new world." I press the button and the cage, holding my son and me, goes up.

Come Out the Wilderness

P AUL did not yet feel her eyes on him. She watched him. He went to the window, peering out between the slats in the Venetian blinds. She could tell from his profile that it did not look like a pleasant day. In profile, all of the contradictions that so confounded her seemed to be revealed. He had a boy's long, rather thin neck but it supported a head that seemed even more massive than it actually was because of its plantation of thickly curling black hair, hair that was always a little too long or else, cruelly, much too short. His forehead was broad and high but this austerity was contradicted by a short, blunt, almost ludicrously upturned nose. And he had a large mouth and very heavy, sensual lips, which suggested a certain wry cruelty when turned down but looked like the mask of comedy when he laughed. His body was really excessively black with hair, which proved, she said, since Negroes were generally less hairy than whites, which race, in fact, had moved farthest from the ape. Other people did not see his beauty, which always mildly astonished her—it was like thinking that the sun was ordinary. He was sloppy about the way he stood and sat, that was true, and so his shoulders were already beginning to be round. And he was a poor man's son, a city boy, and so his body could not really remind anyone of a Michelangelo statue as she—"fantastically," he said—claimed; it did not have that luxury or that power. It was economically tense and hard and testified only to the agility of the poor, who are always dancing one step ahead of the devil.

He stepped away from the window, looking worried. Ruth closed her eyes. When she opened them he was disappearing away from her down the short, black hall that led to the bathroom. She wondered what time he had come in last night; she wondered if he had a hangover; she heard the water running. She thought that he had probably not been home long. She was very sensitive to his comings and goings and had often found herself abruptly upright and wide awake a moment after he, restless at two-thirty in the morning, had closed the door behind him. Then there was no more sleep for her.

She lay there on a bed that inexorably became a bed of ashes and hot coals, while her imagination dwelt on every conceivable disaster, from his having forsaken her for another woman to his having, somehow, ended up in the morgue. And as the night faded from black to gray to daylight, the telephone began to seem another presence in the house, sitting not far from her like a great, malevolent black cat that might, at any moment, with one shrill cry, scatter her life like dismembered limbs all over this tiny room. There were places she could have called, but she would have died first. After all—he had only needed to point it out once, he would never have occasion to point it out again—they were not married. Often she had pulled herself out of bed, her loins cold and all her body trembling, and gotten dressed and had coffee and gone to work without seeing him. But he would call her in the office later in the day. She would have had several stiff drinks at lunch and so could be very offhand over the phone, pretending that she had only supposed him to have gotten up a little earlier than herself that morning. But the moment she put the receiver down she hated him. She made herself sick with fantasies of how she would be revenged. Then she hated herself; thinking into what an iron maiden of love and hatred he had placed her, she hated him even more. She could not help feeling that he treated her this way because of her color, because she was a colored girl. Then her past and her present threatened to engulf her. She knew she was being unfair; she could not help it; she thought of psychiatry; she saw herself transformed, at peace with the world, herself, her color, with the male of indeterminate color she would have found. Always, this journey round her skull ended with tears, resolutions, prayers, with Paul's face, which then had the power to reconcile her even to the lowest circle of hell.

After work, on the way home, she stopped for another drink, or two or three; bought Sen-Sen to muffle the odor; wore the most casually glowing of smiles as he casually kissed her when she came through the door.

She knew that he was going to leave her. It was in his walk, his talk, his eyes. He wanted to go. He had already moved back, crouching to leap. And she had no rival. He was not going to another woman. He simply wanted to go. It would happen today, tomorrow, three weeks from today; it was over, she could do nothing about it; neither could she save herself by jumping first. She had no place to go, she only wanted him. She had tried hard to want other men, and she was still young, only twenty-six, and there was no real lack of opportunity. But all she knew about other men was that they were not Paul.

Through the gloom of the hallway he came back into the room and, moving to the edge of the bed, lit a cigarette. She smiled at him.

"Good morning," she said. "Would you light one for me too?"

He looked down at her with a sleepy and slightly shame-faced grin. Without a word he offered her his freshly lit cigarette, lit another, and then got into bed, shivering slightly.

"Good morning," he said then. "Did you sleep well?"

"Very well," she said, lightly. "Did you? I didn't hear you come in."

"Ah, I was very quiet," he said teasingly, curling his great body toward her and putting his head on her breast. "I didn't want to wake you up. I was afraid you'd hit me with something."

She laughed. "What time *did* you come in?"

"Oh"—he raised his head, dragging on his cigarette, and half-frowned, half-smiled—"about an hour or so ago."

"What did you do? Find a new after-hours joint?"

"No. I ran into Cosmo. We went over to his place to look at a couple new paintings he's done. He had a bottle, we sat around."

She knew Cosmo and distrusted him. He was about forty and he had had two wives; he did not think women were worth much. She was sure that Cosmo had been giving Paul advice as to how to be rid of her; she could imagine, or believed she could, how he had spoken about her, and she felt her skin tighten. At the same moment she became aware of the warmth of Paul's body.

"What did you talk about?" she asked.

"Oh. Painting. His paintings, my paintings, all God's chillun's paintings."

During the day, while she was at work, Paul painted in the back room of this cramped and criminally expensive Village apartment, where the light was bad and where there was not really room enough for him to step back and look at his canvas. Most of his paintings were stored with a friend. Still, there were enough, standing against the wall, piled on top of the closet and on the table, for a sizable one-man show. "If they were any good," said Paul, who worked very hard. She knew this, despite the fact that he said so rather too often. She knew by his face, his distance, his quality, frequently, of seeming to be like a spring, unutterably dangerous to touch. And by the exhaustion, different in kind from any other, with which he sometimes stretched out in bed.

She thought—of course—that his paintings were very good, but he did not take her judgment seriously. "You're sweet, funnyface," he sometimes said, "but, you know, you aren't really very bright." She was scarcely at all mollified by his adding, "Thank heaven. I hate bright women."

She remembered, now, how stupid she had felt about music all the time she had lived with Arthur, a man of her own color who had played a clarinet. She was still finding out today, so many years after their breakup, how much she had learned from him—not only about music, unluckily. If I stay on this merry-go-round, she thought, I'm going to become very accomplished, just the sort of girl no man will every marry.

She moved closer to Paul, the fingers of one hand playing with his hair. He lay still. It was very silent.

"Ruth," he said finally, "I've been thinking . . ."

At once she was all attention. She drew on her cigarette, her fingers still drifting through his hair, as though she were playing with water.

"Yes?" she prompted.

She had always wondered, when the moment came, if she would make things easy for him, or difficult. She still did not know. He leaned up on one elbow, looking down at her. She met his eyes, hoping that her own eyes reflected nothing but calm curiosity. He continued to stare at her and put one hand on her short, dark hair. Then, "You're a nice girl," he said, irrelevantly, and leaned down and kissed her.

With a kiss! she thought.

"My father wouldn't think so," she said, "if he could see me now. What is it you've been thinking?"

He still said nothing but only looked down at her, an expression in his eyes that she could not read.

"I've been thinking," he said, "that it's about time I got started on that portrait of you. I ought to get started right away."

She felt, very sharply, that his nerve had failed him. But she felt, too, that his decision, now, to do a portrait of her was a means of moving far away enough from her to be able to tell her the truth. Also, he had always said that he could do something wonderful with her on canvas—it would be foolish to let the opportunity pass. Cosmo had probably told him this. She had always been flattered by his desire to paint her but now she hoped that he would suddenly go blind.

"Anytime," she said, and could not resist, "Am I to be part of a gallery?"

"Yeah. I'll probably be able to sell you for a thousand bucks," he said, and kissed her again.

"That's not a very nice thing to say," she murmured.

"You're a funny girl. What's not nice about a thousand dollars?" He leaned over her to put out his cigarette in the ash tray near the bed; then took hers and put it out too. He fell back against her and put his hand on her breast.

She said, tentatively: "Well, I suppose if you do it often enough, I could stop working."

His arms tightened but she did not feel that this was due entirely to desire; it might be said that he was striving, now, to distract her. "If I do *what* enough?" he grinned.

"Now, now," she smiled, "you just said that I was a nice girl."

"You're one of the nicest girls I ever met," said Paul soberly. "Really you are. I often wonder . . ."

"You often wonder what?"

"What's going to become of you."

She felt like a river trying to run two ways at once: she felt herself shrinking from him, yet she flowed toward him too; she knew he felt it. "But as long as you're with me," she said, and she could not help herself, she felt she was about to cry; she held his face between her hands, pressing yet closer against him. "As long as you're with me." His face was white, his eyes glowed: there was a war in him too. Everything that divided them charged, for an instant, the tiny space between them. Then the veils of habit and desire covered both their eyes.

"Life is very long," said Paul at last. He kissed her. They both sighed. And slowly she surrendered, opening up before him like the dark continent, made mad and delirious and blind by the entry of a mortal as bright as the morning, as white as milk.

When she left the house he was sleeping. Because she was late for work and because it was raining, she dropped into a cab and was whirled out of the streets of the Village—which still suggested, at least, some faint memory of the individual life—into the grim publicities of midtown Manhattan. Blocks and squares and exclamation marks, stone and steel and glass as far as the eye could see; everything towering, lifting itself against though by no means into, heaven. The people, so surrounded by heights that they had lost any sense of what heights were, rather resembled, nevertheless, these gray rigidities and also resembled, in their frantic motion, people fleeing a burning town. Ruth, who was not so many years removed from trees and earth, had felt in the beginning that she would never be able to live on an island so eccentric; she had, for example, before she arrived, dreamed of herself as walking by the river. But apart from the difficulties of realizing this ambition, which were not inconsiderable, it turned out that a lone girl walking by the river was simply asking to be victimized by both the disturbers and the defenders of the public peace. She retreated into the interior and this dream was abandoned—along with others. For her as for most of Manhattan, trees and water ceased to be realities; the nervous, trusting landscape of the city began to be the landscape of her mind. And soon her mind, like life on the island, seemed to be incapable of flexibility, of moving outward, could only shriek upward into meaningless abstractions or drop downward into cruelty and confusion.

She worked for a life insurance company that had only recently become sufficiently progressive to hire Negroes. This meant that she worked in an atmosphere so positively electric with interracial good will that no one ever dreamed of telling the truth about anything. It would have seemed, and it quite possibly would have been, a spiteful act. The only other Negro there was male, a Mr. Davis, who was very highly placed. He was an expert, it appeared, in some way about Negroes and life insurance, from which Ruth had ungenerously concluded that he was the company's expert on how to cheat more Negroes out of more money and not only remain within the law but also be honored with a plaque for good race relations. She often—but not always—took dictation from him. The other girls, manifesting a rough, girl-scoutish camaraderie that made the question of their sincerity archaic, found him "marvelous" and wondered if he had a wife. Ruth found herself unable to pursue these strangely overheated and yet eerily impersonal speculations with anything like the indicated vehemence. Since it was extremely unlikely that any of these girls would ever even go dancing with Mr. Davis, it was impossible to believe that they had any ambition to share his couch, matrimonial or otherwise, and yet, lacking this ambition, it was impossible to account for their avidity. But they were all incredibly innocent and made her ashamed of her body. At the same time it demanded, during their maddening coffee breaks, a great deal of will power not to take Paul's photograph out of her wallet and wave it before them saying, *"You'll never lay a finger on Mr. Davis. But look what I took from you!"* Her face at such moments allowed them to conclude that she was planning to ensnare Mr. Davis herself. It was perhaps this assumption, despite her phone calls from Paul, that allowed them to discuss Mr. Davis so freely before her, and they also felt, in an incoherent way, that these discussions were proof of their democracy. She did not find Mr. Davis "marvelous," though she thought him good-looking enough in a square, stocky, gleaming, black-boyish sort of way.

Near her office, visible from her window and having the air of contraband in Caesar's market place, was a small gray chapel. An ugly neon cross jutted out above the heads of passers-by, proclaiming "Jesus Saves." Today, as the lunch hour approached and she began, as always, to fidget, debating whether she should telephone Paul or wait for Paul to telephone her, she found herself staring in some irritation at this cross, thinking about her childhood. The telephone rang and rang, but never for her; she began to feel the need of a drink. She thought of Paul sleeping while she typed and became outraged, then thought of his painting and became maternal; thought of his arms and paused to light a cigarette, throwing the most pitying of glances toward the girl who shared her office, who still had a crush on Frank Sinatra. Nevertheless, the sublimatory tube still burning, the smoke tickling her nostrils and the typewriter bell clanging at brief intervals like signals flashing by on a railroad track, she relapsed into bitterness, confusion, fury: for she was trapped, Paul was a trap. She wanted a man of her own and she wanted children and all she could see for herself today was a lifetime of typing while Paul slept or a lifetime of typing with no Paul. And she began rather to envy the stocky girl with the crush on Frank Sinatra, since she would settle one day, obviously, for a great deal less, and probably turn out children as Detroit turned out cars and never sigh for an instant for what she had missed, having indeed never, and especially with a lifetime of movie-going behind her, missed anything.

"Jesus Saves." She began to think of the days of her innocence. These days had been spent in the South, where her mother and father and older brother remained. She had an older sister, married and with several children, in Oakland, and a baby sister who had become a small-time nightclub singer in New Orleans. There were relatives of her father's living in Harlem and she was sure that they wrote to him often complaining that she never visited them. They, like her father, were earnest churchgoers, though, unlike her father, their religion was strongly mixed with an opportunistic respectability and with ambitions to better society and their own place in it, which her father would have scorned. Their ambitions vitiated in them what her father called the "true" religion, and what remained of this religion, which was principally vindictiveness, prevented them from understanding anything whatever about those concrete Northern realities that made them at once so obsequious and so venomous.

Her innocence. It was many years ago. She remembered

their house, so poor and plain, standing by itself, apart from other houses, as nude and fragile on the stony ground as an upturned cardboard box. And it was nearly as dark inside as it might have been beneath a box, it leaked when the rain fell, froze when the wind blew, could scarcely be entered in July. They tried to coax sustenance out of a soil that had long ago gone out of the business. As time went on they grew to depend less and less on the soil and more on the oyster boats, and on the wages and leftovers brought home by their mother, and then herself, from the white kitchens in town. And her mother still struggled in these white kitchens, humming sweet hymns, tiny, mild eyed and bent, her father still labored on the oyster boats; after a lifetime of labor, should they drop dead tomorrow, there would not be a penny for their burial clothes. Her brother, still unmarried, nearing thirty now, loitered through the town with his dangerous reputation, drinking and living off the women he murdered with his love-making. He made her parents fearful but they reiterated in each letter that they had placed him, and all of their children, in the hands of God. Ruth opened each letter in guilt and fear, expecting each time to be confronted with the catastrophe that had at last overtaken her kin; anticipating too, with a selfish annoyance that added to her guilt, the enforced and necessary journey back to her home in mourning; the survivors gathered together to do brief honor to the dead, whose death was certainly, in part, attributable to the indifference of the living. She often wrote her brother asking him to come North, and asked her sister in Oakland to second her in this plea. But she knew that he would not come North—because of her. She had shamed him and embittered him, she was one of the reasons he drank.

Her mother's song, which she, doubtless, still hummed each evening as she walked the old streets homeward, began with the question, *How did you feel when you come out the wilderness?*

And she remembered her mother, half-humming, half-singing, with a steady, tense beat that would make any blues singer sit up and listen (though she thought it best not to say this to her mother):

Come out the wilderness,
Come out the wilderness.
How did you feel when you come out the wilderness,
Leaning on the Lord?

And the answers were many: *Oh, my soul felt happy!* or, *I shouted hallelujah!* or, *I do thank God!*

Ruth finished her cigarette, looking out over the stone-cold, hideous New York streets, and thought with a strange new pain of her mother. Her mother had once been no older than she, Ruth, was today. She had probably been pretty, she had also wept and trembled and cried beneath the rude thrusting that was her master and her life, and children had knocked in her womb and split her as they came crying out. Out, and into the wilderness: she had placed them in the hands of God. She had known nothing but labor and sorrow, she had had to confront, every day of her life, the everlasting, nagging, infinitesimal details; it had clearly all come to nothing, how could she be singing still?

"Jesus Saves." She put out her cigarette and a sense of loss and disaster wavered through her like a mist. She wished, in that moment, from the bottom of her heart, that she had never left home. She wished that she had never met Paul. She wished that she had never been touched by his whiteness. She should have found a great, slow, black man, full of laughter and sighs and grace, a man at whose center there burned a steady, smokeless fire. She should have surrendered to him and been a woman, and had his children, and found, through being irreplaceable, despite whatever shadows life might cast, peace that would enable her to endure.

She had left home practically by accident; it had been partly due to her brother. He had grown too accustomed to thinking of her as his prized, adored little sister to recognize the changes that were occurring within her. This had had something to do with the fact that his own sexual coming of age had disturbed his peace with her—he would, in good faith, have denied this, which did not make it less true. When she was seventeen her brother had surprised her alone in a barn with a boy. Nothing had taken place between herself and this boy, though there was no saying what might not have happened if her brother had not come in. She, guilty though she was in everything but the act, could scarcely believe and had not, until today, ever quite forgiven his immediate leap to the obvious conclusion. She began screaming before he hit her, her father had had to come running to pull her brother off the boy. And she had shouted their innocence in a steadily blackening despair, for the boy was too badly beaten to be able to speak and it was clear that no one believed her. She bawled at last: "Goddamit, I wish I had, I wish I had, I might as well of done it!" Her father slapped her. Her brother gave her a look and said: "You dirty . . . you dirty . . . you black and dirty—" Then her mother had had to step between her father and her brother. She turned and ran and sat down for a long time in the darkness, on a hillside, by herself, shivering. And she felt dirty, she felt that nothing would ever make her clean.

After this she and her brother scarcely spoke. He had wounded her so deeply she could not face his eyes. Her father dragged her to church to make her cry repentance but she was as stubborn as her father, she told him she had nothing to repent. And she avoided them all, which was exactly the most dangerous thing that could have happened, for when she met the musician, Arthur, who was more than twenty years older than she, she ran away to New York with him. She lived with him for more than four years. She did not love him all that time, she simply did not know how to escape his domination. He had never made the big-time himself and he therefore wanted her to become a singer; and perhaps she had ceased to love him when it became clear that she had no talent whatever. He was very disappointed, but he was also very proud, and he made her go to school to study shorthand and typing, and made her self-conscious about her accent and her grammar, and took great delight in dressing her. Through him, she got over feeling that she was black and unattractive and as soon as this happened she was able to leave him. In fleeing Harlem and her relatives there, she drifted downtown to the Village, where, eventually, she found employment as a waitress in one of those restaurants with candles on the tables.

Here, after a year or so, and several increasingly disastrous and desperate liaisons, she met Paul.

The telephone rang several desks away from her and, at the same instant, she was informed that Mr. Davis wanted her in his office. She was sure that it was Paul telephoning but she picked up her pad and walked into Mr. Davis's cubbyhole. Someone picked up the receiver, cutting off the bell, and she closed the door of Mr. Davis's office behind her.

"Good morning," she said.

"Good morning," he answered. He looked out of his window. "Though, between you and me, I've seen better mornings. This morning ain't half trying."

They both laughed, self-consciously amused and relieved by his "ain't."

She sat down, her pencil poised, looking at him questioningly.

"How do you like your job?" he asked her.

She had not expected his question, which she immediately distrusted and resented, suspecting him, on no evidence whatever, of acting now as a company spy.

"It's quite pleasant," she said in a guarded, ladylike tone, and stared hypnotically at him as though she believed that he was about to do her mischief by magical means and she had to resist his spell.

"Are you intending to be a career girl?"

He was giving her more attention this morning than he ever had before, with the result that she found herself reciprocating. A tentative friendliness wavered in the air between them. She smiled. "I guess I ought to say that it depends on my luck."

He laughed—perhaps rather too uproariously, though, more probably, she had merely grown unaccustomed to his kind of laughter. Her brother bobbed briefly to the surface of her mind.

"Well," he said, "does your luck seem likely to take you out of this office anytime in the near future?"

"No," she said, "it certainly doesn't look that way," and they laughed again. But she wondered if he would be laughing if he knew about Paul.

"If you don't mind my saying so, then," he said, "*I'm* lucky." He quickly riffled some papers on his desk, putting on a business air as rakishly as she had seen him put on his hat. "There's going to be some changes made around here—I reckon you have heard that." He grinned. Then, briskly: "I'm going to be needing a secretary. Would you like it? You get a raise"—he coughed—"in salary, of course."

"Why, I'd love it," she heard herself saying before she had had time for the bitter reflection that this professional advance probably represented the absolute extent of her luck. And she was ashamed of the thought, which she could not repress, that Paul would probably hang on a little longer if he knew she was making more money.

She resolved not to tell him and wondered how many hours this resolution would last.

Mr. Davis looked at her with an intentness almost personal. There was a strained, brief silence. "Good," he said at last. "There are a few details to be worked out, like getting me more office space"—they both smiled—"but you'll be hearing directly in a few days. I only wanted to sound you out first." He rose and held out his hand. "I hope you're going to like working with me," he said. "I think I'm going to like working with you."

She rose and shook his hand, bewildered to find that something in his simplicity had touched her very deeply. "I'm sure I will," she said, gravely. "And thank you very much." She reached backward for the doorknob.

"Miss Bowman," he said sharply—and paused. "Well, if I were you I wouldn't mention it yet to"—he waved his hand uncomfortably—"the girls out there." Now he really did look rather boyish. "It looks better if it comes from the front office."

"I understand," she said quickly.

"Also, I didn't ask for you out of any—racial—considerations," he said. "You just seemed, the most *sensible* girl available."

"I understand," she repeated; they were both trying not to smile. "And thank you again." She closed the door of his office behind her.

"A man called you," said the stocky girl. "He said he'd call back."

"Thank you," Ruth said. She could see that the girl wanted to talk so she busily studied some papers on her desk and retired behind the noise of her typewriter.

The stocky girl had gone out to lunch and Ruth was reluctantly deciding that she might as well go too when Paul called again.

"Hello. How's it going up there?"

"Dull. How are things down there? Are you out of bed already?"

"What do you mean, already?" He sounded slightly nettled and was trying not to sound that way, the almost certain signal that a storm was coming. "It's nearly one o'clock. I got work to do too, you know."

"Yes. I know." But neither could she quite keep the sardonic edge out of her voice.

There was a silence.

"You coming straight home from work?"

"Yes. Will you be there?"

"Yeah. I got to go uptown with Cosmo this afternoon, talk to some gallery guy, Cosmo thinks he might like my stuff."

"Oh"—thinking *Damn Cosmo!*—"that's wonderful, Paul. I hope something comes of it."

Nothing whatever would come of it. The gallery owner would be evasive—*if* he existed, if they ever got to his gallery—and then Paul and Cosmo would get drunk. She would hear, while she ached to be free, to be anywhere else, *with* anyone else, from Paul, all about how stupid art dealers were, how incestuous the art world had become, how impossible it was to *do* anything—his eyes, meanwhile, focusing with a drunken intensity, his eyes at once arrogant and defensive.

Well. Most of what he said was true, and she knew it, it was not his fault.

Not his fault. "Yeah. I sure hope so. I thought I'd take up some of my water colors, some small sketches—you know, all the most *obvious* things I've got."

This policy did not, empirically, seem to be as foolproof as

everyone believed but she did not know how to put her uncertain objections into words. "That sounds good. What time
have you got to be there?"

"Around three. I'm meeting Cosmo now for lunch."

"Oh"—lightly—"why don't you two, just this once, order
your lunch before you order your cocktails?"

He laughed too and was clearly no more amused than she.
"Well, Cosmo'll be buying, he'll have to, so I guess I'll leave
it up to him to order."

Touché. Her hand, holding the receiver, shook. "Well, I
hope you two make it to the gallery without falling flat on
your faces."

"Don't worry." Then, in a rush, she recognized the tone
before she understood the words, it was his you-can't-say-I-
haven't-been-honest-with-you tone: "Cosmo says the gallery
owner's got a daughter."

I hope to God she marries you, she thought. I hope she
marries you and takes you off to Istanbul forever, where I will
never have to hear you again, so I can get a breath of air, so
I can get out from under.

They both laughed, a laugh conspiratorial and sophisti-
cated, like the whispered, whiskey laughter of a couple in a
nightclub. "Oh?" she said. "Is she pretty?"

"She's probably a pig. She's had two husbands already,
both artists."

She laughed again. "Where has she buried the bodies?"

"Well"—really amused this time, but also rather grim—
"one of them ended up in the booby hatch and the other
turned into a fairy and was last seen dancing with some soldiers in Majorca."

Now they laughed together and the wires between them
hummed, almost, with the stormless friendship they both
hoped to feel for each other someday. "A powerful pig. Maybe
you *better* have a few drinks."

"You see what I mean? But Cosmo says she's not such a
fool about painting."

"She doesn't seem to have much luck with painters. Maybe
you'll break the jinx."

"Maybe. Wish me luck. It sure would be nice to unload
some of my stuff on somebody."

You're doing just fine, she thought. "Will you call me later?"

"Yeah. Around three-thirty, four o'clock, as soon as I get away from there."

"Right. Be good."

"You too. Goodby."

"Goodby."

She put down the receiver, still amused and still trembling. After all, he had called her. But he would probably not have called her if he were not actually nourishing the hope that the gallery owner's daughter might find him interesting; in that case he would have to tell Ruth about her and it was better to have the way prepared. Paul was always preparing the way for one unlikely exploit or flight or another, it was the reason he told Ruth "everything." To tell everything is a very effective means of keeping secrets. Secrets hidden at the heart of midnight are simply waiting to be dragged to the light, as, on some unlucky high noon, they always are. But secrets shrouded in the glare of candor are bound to defeat even the most determined and agile inspector for the light is always changing and proves that the eye cannot be trusted. So Ruth knew about Paul nearly all there was to know, knew him better than anyone else on earth ever had or probably ever would, only—she did not know him well enough to stop him from being Paul.

While she was waiting for the elevator she realized, with mild astonishment, that she was actually hoping that the gallery owner's daughter would take Paul away. This hope resembled the desperation of someone suffering from a toothache who, in order to bring the toothache to an end, was almost willing to jump out of a window. But she found herself wondering if love really ought to be like a toothache. Love ought—she stepped out of the elevator, really wondering for a moment which way to turn—to be a means of being released from guilt and terror. But Paul's touch would never release her. He had power over her not because she was free but because she was guilty. To enforce his power over her he had only to keep her guilt awake. This did not demand malice on his part, it scarcely demanded perception—it only demanded that he have, as, in fact, he overwhelmingly did have, an instinct for his own convenience. His touch, which should have raised her, lifted her roughly only to throw her down hard; whenever he touched her, she became blacker and dirtier than ever; the loneliest place under heaven was in Paul's arms.

And yet—she went into his arms with such eagerness and such hope. She had once thought herself happy. Was this because she had been proud that he was white? But—it was she who was insisting on these colors. Her blackness was not Paul's fault. Neither was her guilt. She was punishing herself for something, a crime she could not remember. *You dirty . . . you black and dirty . . .*

She bumped into someone as she passed the cigar stand in the lobby and, looking up to murmur, "Excuse me," recognized Mr. Davis. He was stuffing cigars into his breast pocket—though the gesture was rather like that of a small boy stuffing his pockets with cookies, she was immediately certain that they were among the most expensive cigars that could be bought. She wondered what he spent on his clothes—it looked like a great deal. From the crown of rakishly tilted, deafeningly conservative hat to the tips of his astutely dulled shoes, he glowed with a very nearly vindictive sharpness. There were no flies on Mr. Davis. He would always be the best-dressed man in *any*body's lobby.

He was just about the last person she wanted to see. But perhaps his lunch hour was over and he was coming in.

"Miss Bowman!" He gave her a delighted grin. "Are you just going to lunch?"

He made her want to laugh. There was something so incongruous about finding that grin behind all that manner and under all those clothes.

"Yes," she said. "I guess you've had your lunch?"

"*No.* I ain't had no lunch," he said. "I'm hungry, just like you." He paused. "I be delighted to have your company, Miss Bowman."

Very courtly, she thought, amused, and the smile is extremely wicked. Then she realized that she was pleased that a man was *being* courtly with her, even if only for an instant in a crowded lobby, and, at the same instant, made the discovery that what was so widely referred to as a "wicked" smile was really only the smile, scarcely ever to be encountered any more, of a man who was not afraid of women.

She thought it safe to demur. "Please don't think you have to be polite."

"I'm never polite about food," he told her. "Almost drove my mamma crazy." He took her arm. "I know a right nice place nearby." His stride and his accent made her think of home. She also realized that he, like many Negroes of his uneasily rising generation, kept in touch, so to speak, with himself by deliberately affecting, whenever possible, the illiterate speech of his youth. "We going to get on real well, you'll see. Time you get through being *my* secretary, you likely to end up with Alcoholics Anonymous."

The place "nearby" turned out to be a short taxi ride away, but it was, as he had said, "right nice." She doubted that Mr. Davis could possibly eat there every day, though it was clear that he was a man who liked to spend money.

She ordered a dry martini and he a bourbon on the rocks. He professed himself astonished that she knew what a dry martini was. "I thought you was a country girl."

"I *am* a country girl," she said.

"No, no," he said, "no more. You a country girl who came to the city and that's the dangerous kind. Don't know if it's safe, having you for my secretary."

Underneath all his chatter she felt him watching her, sizing her up.

"Are you afraid your wife will object?" she asked.

"You ought to be able to look at me," he said, "and tell that I ain't got a wife."

She laughed. "So you're *not* married. I wonder if I should tell the girls in the office?"

"I don't care what you tell them," he said. Then: "How do you get along with them?"

"We get along fine," she said. "We don't have much to talk about except whether or not you're married but that'll probably last until you *do* get married and then we can talk about your wife."

But thinking, For God's sake let's get off *this* subject, she added, before he could say anything: "You called me a country girl. Aren't you a country boy?"

"I am," he said, "but I didn't *change* my drinking habits when I came North. If bourbon was good enough for me down yonder, it's good enough for me up here."

"I didn't have any drinking habits to change, Mr. Davis," she told him. "I was too young to be drinking when I left home."

His eyes were slightly questioning but he held his peace, while she wished that she had held hers. She concentrated on sipping her martini, suddenly remembering that she was sitting opposite a man who knew more about why girls left home than could be learned from locker-room stories. She wondered if he had a sister and tried to be amused at finding herself still so incorrigibly old fashioned. But he did not, really, seem to be much like her brother. She met his eyes again.

"Where I come from," he said, with a smile, "*nobody* was too young to be drinking. Toughened them up for later life," and he laughed.

By the time lunch was over she had learned that he was from a small town in Alabama, was the youngest of three sons (but had no sisters), had gone to college in Tennessee, was a reserve officer in the Air Force. He was thirty-two. His mother was living, his father was dead. He had lived in New York for two years but was beginning, now, to like it less than he had in the beginning.

"At first," he said, "I thought it would be fun to live in a city where didn't nobody know you and you didn't know nobody and where, look like, you could just do anything you was big and black enough to do. But you get tired not knowing nobody and there ain't really that many things you want to do alone."

"Oh, but you must have friends," she said, "uptown."

"I don't live uptown. I live in Brooklyn. Ain't *nobody* in Brooklyn got friends."

She laughed with him, but distrusted the turn the conversation was taking. They were walking back to the office. He walked slowly, as though in deliberate opposition to the people around them, although they were already a little late—at least *she* was late, but, since she was with one of her superiors, it possibly didn't matter.

"Where do you live?" he asked her. "Do you live uptown?"

"No," she said, "I live downtown on Bank Street." And after a moment: "That's in the Village. Greenwich Village."

He grinned. "Don't tell me you studying to be a writer or a dancer or something?"

"No. I just found myself there. It used to be cheap."

He scowled. "Ain't nothing cheap in this town no more, not even the necessities."

His tone made clear to which necessities he referred and she would have loved to tease him a little, just to watch him laugh. But she was beginning, with every step they took, to be a little afraid of him. She was responding to him with parts of herself that had been buried so long she had forgotten they existed. In his office that morning, when he shook her hand, she had suddenly felt a warmth of affection, of nostalgia, of gratitude even—and again in the lobby—he had somehow made her feel safe. It was his friendliness that was so unsettling. She had grown used to unfriendly people.

Still, she did not *want* to be friends with him: still less did she desire that their friendship should ever become anything more. Sooner or later he would learn about Paul. He would look at her differently then. It would not be—so much—because of Paul as a man, perhaps not even Paul as a white man. But it would make him bitter, it would make her ashamed, for him to see how she was letting herself be wasted—for Paul, who did not love her.

This was the reason she was ashamed and wished to avoid the scrutiny of Mr. Davis. She was doing something to herself—out of shame?—that he would be right in finding indefensible. She was punishing herself. For what? She looked sideways at his black Sambo profile under the handsome lightweight Dobbs hat and wished that she could tell him about it, that he would turn his head, holding it slightly to one side, and watch her with those eyes that had seen and that had learned to hide so much. Eyes that had seen so many girls like her taken beyond the hope of rescue, while all the owner of the eyes could do—perhaps she wore Paul the way Mr. Davis wore his hat. And she looked away from him, half-smiling and yet near tears, over the furious streets on which, here and there, like a design, colored people also hurried, thinking, *And we were slaves here once.*

"Do you like music?" he asked her abruptly. "I don't necessarily mean Carnegie Hall."

Now was the time to stop him. She had only to say, "Mr. Davis, I'm living with someone." It would not be necessary to say anything more than that.

She met his eyes. "Of course I like music," she said faintly.

"Well, I know a place I'd like to take you one of these evenings, after work. Not going to be easy, being *my* secretary."

His smile forced her to smile with him. But, "Mr. Davis," she said, and stopped. They were before the entrance to their office building.

"What's the matter?" he asked. "You forget something?"

"No." She looked down, feeling big, black and foolish. "Mr. Davis," she said, "you don't know anything about me."

"You don't know anything about me, either," he said.

"That's not what I mean," she said.

He sounded slightly angry. "I ain't asked you nothing yet," he said. "Why can't you wait till you're asked?"

"Well," she stammered, "it may be too late by then."

They stared hard at each other for a moment. "Well," he said, "if it turns out to be too late, won't be nobody to blame but me, will it?"

She stared at him again, almost hating him. She blindly felt that he had no right to do this to her, to cause her to feel such a leap of hope, if he was only, in the end, going to give her back all her shame.

"You know what they say down home," she said, slowly. "If you don't know what you doing, you better ask somebody." There were tears in her eyes.

He took her arm. "Come on in this house, girl," he said. "We got insurance to sell."

They said nothing to each other in the elevator on the way upstairs. She wanted to laugh and she wanted to cry. He, ostentatiously, did not watch her; he stood next to her, humming *Rocks in My Bed*.

She waited all afternoon for Paul to telephone, but although, perversely enough, the phone seemed never to cease ringing, it never rang for her. At five-fifteen, just before she left the office, she called the apartment. Paul was not there. She went downstairs to a nearby bar and ordered a drink and called again at a quarter to six. He was not there. She resolved to have one more drink and leave this bar, which she did, wandering a few blocks north to a bar frequented by theater people. She sat in a booth and ordered a drink and at a quarter to seven called again. He was not there.

She was in a reckless, desperate state, like flight. She knew that she could not possibly go home and cook supper and wait in the empty apartment until his key turned in the lock. He would come in, breathless and contrite—or else, truculently, *not* contrite—probably a little drunk, probably quite hungry. He would tell her where he had been and what he had been doing. Whatever he told her would probably be true—there are so many ways of telling the truth! And whether it was true or not did not matter and she would not be able to reproach him for the one thing that *did* matter: that he had left her sitting in the house alone. She could not make this reproach because, after all, leaving women sitting around in empty houses had been the specialty of all men for ages. And, for ages, when the men arrived, women bestirred themselves to cook supper—luckily, it was not yet common knowledge that many a woman had narrowly avoided committing murder by calmly breaking a few eggs.

She wondered where it had all gone to—the ease, the pleasure they had had together once. At one time their evenings together, sitting around the house, drinking beer or reading or simply laughing and talking, had been the best part of all their days. Paul, reading, or walking about with a can of beer in his hand, talking, gesturing, scratching his chest; Paul, stretched out on the sofa, staring at the ceiling; Paul, cheerful, with that lowdown, cavernous chuckle and that foolish grin; Paul, grim, with his mouth turned down and his eyes burning; Paul doing anything whatever, Paul with his eyelids sealed in sleep, drooling and snoring, Paul lighting her cigarette, touching her elbow, talking, talking, talking, in his million ways, to her, had been the light that lighted up her world. Now it was all gone, it would never come again, and that face which was like the heavens was darkening against her.

These present days, after supper, when the chatter each used as a cover began to show dangerous signs of growing thinner, there would be no choice but sleep. She might, indeed, have preferred a late movie, or a round of the bars, lights, noise, other people, but this would scarcely be Paul's desire, already tired from his day. Besides—after all, she had to face the office in the morning. Eventually, therefore, bed; perhaps he or she or both of them might read awhile; perhaps there would take place between them what had sometimes been described as the act of love. Then sleep, black and dreadful, like a drugged state, from which she would be rescued by the scream of the alarm clock or the realization that Paul was no longer in bed.

Ah. Her throat ached with tears of fury and despair. In the days before she had met Paul men had taken her out, she had laughed a lot, she had been young. She had not wished to spend her life protecting herself, with laughter, against men she cared nothing about; but she could not go on like this, either, drinking in random bars because she was afraid to go home; neither could she guess what life might bring her when Paul was gone.

She wished that she had never met him. She wished that he, or she, or both of them were dead. And for a moment she really wished it, with a violence that frightened her. Perhaps there was always murder at the very heart of love: the strong desire to murder the beloved, so that one could at last be assured of privacy and peace and be as safe and unchanging as the grave. Perhaps this was why disasters, thicker and more malevolent than bees, circled Paul's head whenever he was out of her sight. Perhaps in those moments when she had believed herself willing to lay down her life for him she had only been presenting herself with a metaphor for her peace, his death; death, which would be an inadequate revenge for the color of his skin, for his failure, by not loving her, to release her from the prison of her own.

The waitress passed her table and Ruth ordered another drink. After this drink she would go. The bar was beginning to fill up, mostly, as she judged, with theater people, some of them, possibly, on their way to work, most of them drawn here by habit and hope. For the past few moments, without realizing it, she had been watching a lean, pale boy at the bar, whose curly hair leaned electrically over his forehead like a living, awry crown. Something about him, his stance, his profile or his grin, prodded painfully at her attention. But it was not that he reminded her of Paul. He reminded her of a boy she had known, briefly, a few years ago, a very lonely boy who was now a merchant seaman, probably, wherever he might be on the globe at this moment, whoring his unbearably unrealized, mysteriously painful life away. She had been fond of him but loneliness in him had been like a cancer, it had really unfitted him for human intercourse, and she had not been sorry to see him go. She had not thought of him for years; yet, now, this stranger at the bar, whom she was beginning to recognize as an actor of brief but growing reputation, abruptly brought him back to her; brought him back encrusted, as it were, with the anguish of the intervening years. She remembered things she thought she had forgotten and wished that she had been wiser then—then she smiled at herself, wishing she were wiser now.

Once, when he had done something to hurt her, she had told him, trying to be calm but choked and trembling with rage: "Look. This is the twentieth century. We're not down on a plantation, you're not the master's son, and I'm not the black girl you can just sleep with when you want to and kick about as you please!"

His face, then, had held something, held many things—bitterness, amusement, fury; but the startling element was pain, his pain, with which she now invested the face of the actor at the bar. It made her wish that she had held her tongue.

"Well," he said at last. "I guess I'll get on back to the big house and leave you down here with the pickaninnies."

They had seen each other a few times thereafter but that was really the evening on which everything had ended between them.

She wondered if that boy had ever found a home.

The actor at the bar looked toward her briefly, but she knew he was not seeing her. He looked at his watch, frowned, she saw that he was not as young as he looked; he ordered another drink and looked downward, leaning both elbows on the bar. The dim lights played on his crown of hair. He moved his head slightly, with impatience, upward, his mouth slightly open, and in that instant, somehow, his profile was burned into her mind. He reminded her then of Paul, of the vanished boy, of others, of others she had seen and never touched, of an army of boys—boys forever!—an army she feared and hated and loved. In that gesture, that look upward, with the light so briefly on his face, she saw the bones that held his face together and the sorrow beginning to corrode his brow, the blood beating like butterfly wings against the cage of his heavy neck. But there was no name for something blind, cruel, lustful, lost, intolerably vulnerable in his eyes and mouth. She knew that in spite of everything, his color, his power or his coming fame, he was lost. He did not know what had happened to his life. And never would. This was the pain she had seen on the face of that boy so long ago, and it was this that had driven Paul into her arms, and now away. The sons of the masters were roaming the world, looking for arms to hold them. And the arms that might have held them—could not forgive.

A sound escaped her; she was astonished to realize it was a sob. The waitress looked at her sharply. Ruth put some money on the table and hurried out. It was dark now and the rain that had been falling intermittently all day spangled the air and glittered all over the streets. It fell against her face and mingled with her tears and she walked briskly through the crowds to hide from them and from herself the fact that she did not know where she was going.

Going to Meet the Man

W HAT's the matter?" she asked.
"I don't know," he said, trying to laugh, "I guess
I'm tired."

"You've been working too hard," she said. "I keep telling
you."

"Well, goddammit, woman," he said, "it's not my fault!"
He tried again; he wretchedly failed again. Then he just lay
there, silent, angry, and helpless. Excitement filled him like a
toothache, but it refused to enter his flesh. He stroked her
breast. This was his wife. He could not ask her to do just a
little thing for him, just to help him out, just for a little while,
the way he could ask a nigger girl to do it. He lay there, and
he sighed. The image of a black girl caused a distant excitement in him, like a far-away light; but, again, the excitement
was more like pain; instead of forcing him to act, it made
action impossible.

"Go to sleep," she said, gently, "you got a hard day tomorrow."

"Yeah," he said, and rolled over on his side, facing her, one
hand still on one breast. "Goddamn the niggers. The black
stinking coons. You'd think they'd learn. Wouldn't you think
they'd learn? I mean, *wouldn't* you?"

"They going to be out there tomorrow," she said, and took
his hand away, "get some sleep."

He lay there, one hand between his legs, staring at the frail
sanctuary of his wife. A faint light came from the shutters; the
moon was full. Two dogs, far away, were barking at each
other, back and forth, insistently, as though they were agreeing to make an appointment. He heard a car coming north
on the road and he half sat up, his hand reaching for his holster, which was on a chair near the bed, on top of his pants.
The lights hit the shutters and seemed to travel across the
room and then went out. The sound of the car slipped away,
he heard it hit gravel, then heard it no more. Some liver-lipped
students, probably, heading back to that college—but coming
from where? His watch said it was two in the morning. They

could be coming from anywhere, from out of state most likely, and they would be at the court-house tomorrow. The niggers were getting ready. Well, they would be ready, too.

He moaned. He wanted to let whatever was in him out; but it wouldn't come out. Goddamn! he said aloud, and turned again, on his side, away from Grace, staring at the shutters. He was a big, healthy man and he had never had any trouble sleeping. And he wasn't old enough yet to have any trouble getting it up—he was only forty-two. And he was a good man, a God-fearing man, he had tried to do his duty all his life, and he had been a deputy sheriff for several years. Nothing had ever bothered him before, certainly not getting it up. Sometimes, sure, like any other man, he knew that he wanted a little more spice than Grace could give him and he would drive over yonder and pick up a black piece or arrest her, it came to the same thing, but he couldn't do that now, no more. There was no telling what might happen once your ass was in the air. And they were low enough to kill a man then, too, every one of them, or the girl herself might do it, right while she was making believe you made her feel so good. The niggers. What had the good Lord Almighty had in mind when he made the niggers? Well. They were pretty good at that, all right. Damn. Damn. Goddamn.

This wasn't helping him to sleep. He turned again, toward Grace again, and moved close to her warm body. He felt something he had never felt before. He felt that he would like to hold her, hold her, hold her, and be buried in her like a child and never have to get up in the morning again and go downtown to face those faces, good Christ, they were ugly! and never have to enter that jail house again and smell that smell and hear that singing; never again feel that filthy, kinky, greasy hair under his hand, never again watch those black breasts leap against the leaping cattle prod, never hear those moans again or watch that blood run down or the fat lips split or the sealed eyes struggle open. They were animals, they were no better than animals, what could be done with people like that? Here they had been in a civilized country for years and they still lived like animals. Their houses were dark, with oil cloth or cardboard in the windows, the smell was enough to make you puke your guts out, and there they sat, a whole tribe, pumping out kids, it looked like, every damn five minutes, and laughing and talking and playing music like they didn't have a care in the world, and he reckoned they didn't, neither, and coming to the door, into the sunlight, just standing there, just looking foolish, not thinking of anything but just getting back to what they were doing, saying, Yes suh, Mr. Jesse. I surely will, Mr. Jesse. Fine weather, Mr. Jesse. Why, I thank you, Mr. Jesse. He had worked for a mail-order house for a while and it had been his job to collect the payments for the stuff they bought. They were too dumb to know that they were being cheated blind, but that was no skin off his ass—he was just supposed to do his job. They would be late—they didn't have the sense to put money aside; but it was easy to scare them, and he never really had any trouble. Hell, they all liked him, the kids used to smile when he came to the door. He gave them candy, sometimes, or chewing gum, and rubbed their rough bullet heads—maybe the candy should have been poisoned. Those kids were grown now. He had had trouble with one of them today.

"There was this nigger today," he said; and stopped; his voice sounded peculiar. He touched Grace. "You awake?" he asked. She mumbled something, impatiently, she was probably telling him to go to sleep. It was all right. He knew that he was not alone.

"What a funny time," he said, "to be thinking about a thing like that—you listening?" She mumbled something again. He rolled over on his back. "This nigger's one of the ringleaders. We had trouble with him before. We must have had him out there at the work farm three or four times. Well, Big Jim C. and some of the boys really had to whip that nigger's ass today." He looked over at Grace; he could not tell whether she was listening or not; and he was afraid to ask again. "They had this line you know, to register"—he laughed, but she did not—"and they wouldn't stay where Big Jim C. wanted them, no, they had to start blocking traffic all around the court house so couldn't nothing or nobody get through, and Big Jim C. told them to disperse and they wouldn't move, they just kept up that singing, and Big Jim C. figured that the others would move if this nigger would move, him being the ring-leader, but he wouldn't move and he wouldn't let the others move, so they had to beat him and a couple of the others and they threw them in the wagon— but *I* didn't see this nigger till I got to the jail. They were still singing and I was supposed to make them stop. Well, I couldn't make them stop for me but I knew he could make them stop. He was lying on the ground jerking and moaning, they had threw him in a cell by himself, and blood was coming out his ears from where Big Jim C. and his boys had whipped him. Wouldn't you think they'd learn? I put the prod to him and he jerked some more and he kind of screamed—but he didn't have much voice left. "You make them stop that singing," I said to him, "you hear me? You make them stop that singing." He acted like he didn't hear me and I put it to him again, under his arms, and he just rolled around on the floor and blood started coming from his mouth. He'd pissed his pants already." He paused. His mouth felt dry and his throat was as rough as sandpaper; as he talked, he began to hurt all over with that peculiar excitement which refused to be released. "You all are going to stop your singing, I said to him, and you are going to stop coming down to the court house and disrupting traffic and molesting the people and keeping us from our duties and keeping doctors from getting to sick white women and getting all them Northerners in this town to give our town a bad name—!" As he said this, he kept prodding the boy, sweat pouring from beneath the helmet he had not yet taken off. The boy rolled around in his own dirt and water and blood and tried to scream again as the prod hit his testicles, but the scream did not come out, only a kind of rattle and a moan. He stopped. He was not supposed to kill the nigger. The cell was filled with a terrible odor. The boy was still. "You hear me?" he called. "You had enough?" The singing went on. "You had enough?" His foot leapt out, he had not known it was going to, and caught the boy flush on the jaw. *Jesus*, he thought, *this ain't no nigger, this is a goddamn bull*, and he screamed again, "You had enough? You going to make them stop that singing now?"

But the boy was out. And now he was shaking worse than the boy had been shaking. He was glad no one could see him. At the same time, he felt very close to a very peculiar, particular joy; something deep in him and deep in his memory was stirred, but whatever was in his memory eluded him. He took off his helmet. He walked to the cell door.

"White man," said the boy, from the floor, behind him.

He stopped. For some reason, he grabbed his privates.

"You remember Old Julia?"

The boy said, from the floor, with his mouth full of blood, and one eye, barely open, glaring like the eye of a cat in the dark, "My grandmother's name was Mrs. Julia Blossom. *Mrs.* Julia Blossom. You going to call our women by their right names yet.—And those kids ain't going to stop singing. We going to keep on singing until every one of you miserable white mothers go stark raving out of your minds." Then he closed the one eye; he spat blood; his head fell back against the floor.

He looked down at the boy, whom he had been seeing, off and on, for more than a year, and suddenly remembered him: Old Julia had been one of his mail-order customers, a nice old woman. He had not seen her for years, he supposed that she must be dead.

He had walked into the yard, the boy had been sitting in a swing. He had smiled at the boy, and asked, "Old Julia home?"

The boy looked at him for a long time before he answered. "Don't no Old Julia live here."

"This is her house. I know her. She's lived here for years."

The boy shook his head. "You might know a Old Julia someplace else, white man. But don't nobody by that name live here."

He watched the boy; the boy watched him. The boy certainly wasn't more than ten. *White man*. He didn't have time to be fooling around with some crazy kid. He yelled, "Hey! Old Julia!"

But only silence answered him. The expression on the boy's face did not change. The sun beat down on them both, still and silent; he had the feeling that he had been caught up in a nightmare, a nightmare dreamed by a child; perhaps one of the nightmares he himself had dreamed as a child. It had that feeling—everything familiar, without undergoing any other change, had been subtly and hideously displaced: the trees, the sun, the patches of grass in the yard, the leaning porch and the weary porch steps and the card-board in the windows and the black hole of the door which looked like the entrance to a cave, and the eyes of the pickaninny, all, all, were charged with malevolence. *White man.* He looked at the boy. "She's gone out?"

The boy said nothing.

"Well," he said, "tell her I passed by and I'll pass by next week." He started to go; he stopped. "You want some chewing gum?"

The boy got down from the swing and started for the house. He said, "I don't want nothing you got, white man." He walked into the house and closed the door behind him.

Now the boy looked as though he were dead. Jesse wanted to go over to him and pick him up and pistol whip him until the boy's head burst open like a melon. He began to tremble with what he believed was rage, sweat, both cold and hot, raced down his body, the singing filled him as though it were a weird, uncontrollable, monstrous howling rumbling up from the depths of his own belly, he felt an icy fear rise in him and raise him up, and he shouted, he howled, "You lucky we *pump* some white blood into you every once in a while—your women! Here's what I got for all the black bitches in the world—!" Then he was, abruptly, almost too weak to stand; to his bewilderment, his horror, beneath his own fingers, he felt himself violently stiffen—with no warning at all; he dropped his hands and he stared at the boy and he left the cell.

"All that singing they do," he said. "All that singing." He could not remember the first time he had heard it; he had been hearing it all his life. It was the sound with which he was most familiar—though it was also the sound of which he had been least conscious—and it had always contained an obscure comfort. They were singing to God. They were singing for mercy and they hoped to go to heaven, and he had even sometimes felt, when looking into the eyes of some of the old women, a few of the very old men, that they were singing for mercy for his soul, too. Of course he had never thought of their heaven or of what God was, or could be, for them; God was the same for everyone, he supposed, and heaven was where good people went—he supposed. He had never thought much about what it meant to be a good person. He tried to be a good person and treat everybody right: it wasn't his fault if the niggers had taken it into their heads to fight against God and go against the rules laid down in the Bible for everyone to read! Any preacher would tell you that. He was only doing his duty: protecting white people from the niggers and the niggers from themselves. And there were still lots of good niggers around—he had to remember that; they weren't all like that boy this afternoon; and the good niggers must be mighty sad to see what was happening to their people. They would thank him when this was over. In that way they had, the best of them, not quite looking him in the eye, in a low voice, with a little smile: We surely thanks you, Mr. Jesse. From the bottom of our hearts, we thanks you. He smiled. They hadn't all gone crazy. This trouble would pass.—He knew that the young people had changed some of the words to the songs. He had scarcely listened to the words before and he did not listen to them now; but he knew that the words were different; he could hear that much. He did not know if the faces were different, he had never, before this trouble began, watched them as they sang, but he certainly did not like what he saw now. They hated him, and this hatred was blacker than their hearts, blacker than their skins, redder than their blood, and harder, by far, than his club. Each day, each night, he felt worn out, aching, with their smell in his nostrils and filling his lungs, as though he were drowning—drowning in niggers; and it was all to be done again when he awoke. It would never end. It would never end. Perhaps this was what the singing had meant all along. They had not been singing black folks into heaven, they had been singing white folks into hell.

Everyone felt this black suspicion in many ways, but no one knew how to express it. Men much older than he, who had been responsible for law and order much longer than he, were now much quieter than they had been, and the tone of their jokes, in a way that he could not quite put his finger on, had changed. These men were his models, they had been friends to his father, and they had taught him what it meant to be a man. He looked to them for courage now. It wasn't that he didn't know that what he was doing was right—he knew that,

nobody had to tell him that; it was only that he missed the
ease of former years. But they didn't have much time to hang
out with each other these days. They tended to stay close to
their families every free minute because nobody knew what
might happen next. Explosions rocked the night of their tran-
quil town. Each time each man wondered silently if perhaps
this time the dynamite had not fallen into the wrong hands.
They thought that they knew where all the guns were; but
they could not possibly know every move that was made in
that secret place where the darkies lived. From time to time
it was suggested that they form a posse and search the home
of every nigger, but they hadn't done it yet. For one thing,
this might have brought the bastards from the North down
on their backs; for another, although the niggers were scattered throughout the town—down in the hollow near the railroad tracks, way west near the mills, up on the hill, the well-off
ones, and some out near the college—nothing seemed to happen in one part of town without the niggers immediately
knowing it in the other. This meant that they could not take
them by surprise. They rarely mentioned it, but they *knew* that
some of the niggers had guns. It stood to reason, as they said,
since, after all, some of them had been in the Army. There
were niggers in the Army right now and God knows they
wouldn't have had any trouble stealing this half-assed government blind—the whole world was doing it, look at the European countries and all those countries in Africa. They made
jokes about it—bitter jokes; and they cursed the government
in Washington, which had betrayed them; but they had not
yet formed a posse. Now, if their town had been laid out like
some towns in the North, where all the niggers lived together
in one locality, they could have gone down and set fire to the
houses and brought about peace that way. If the niggers had
all lived in one place, they could have kept the fire in one
place. But the way this town was laid out, the fire could hardly
be controlled. It would spread all over town—and the niggers
would probably be helping it to spread. Still, from time to
time, they spoke of doing it, anyway; so that now there was
a real fear among them that somebody might go crazy and
light the match.

    They rarely mentioned anything not directly related to the

war that they were fighting, but this had failed to establish between them the unspoken communication of soldiers during a war. Each man, in the thrilling silence which sped outward from their exchanges, their laughter, and their anecdotes, seemed wrestling, in various degrees of darkness, with a secret which he could not articulate to himself, and which, however directly it related to the war, related yet more surely to his privacy and his past. They could no longer be sure, after all, that they had all done the same things. They had never dreamed that their privacy could contain any element of terror, could threaten, that is, to reveal itself, to the scrutiny of a judgment day, while remaining unreadable and inaccessible to themselves; nor had they dreamed that the past, while certainly refusing to be forgotten, could yet so stubbornly refuse to be remembered. They felt themselves mysteriously set at naught, as no longer entering into the real concerns of other people—while here they were, out-numbered, fighting to save the civilized world. They had thought that people would care—people didn't care; not enough, anyway, to help them. It would have been a help, really, or at least a relief, even to have been forced to surrender. Thus they had lost, probably forever, their old and easy connection with each other. They were forced to depend on each other more and, at the same time, to trust each other less. Who could tell when one of them might not betray them all, for money, or for the ease of confession? But no one dared imagine what there might be to confess. They were soldiers fighting a war, but their relationship to each other was that of accomplices in a crime. They all had to keep their mouths shut.

I stepped in the river at Jordan.

Out of the darkness of the room, out of nowhere, the line came flying up at him, with the melody and the beat. He turned wordlessly toward his sleeping wife. *I stepped in the river at Jordan.* Where had he heard that song?

"Grace," he whispered. "You awake?"

She did not answer. If she was awake, she wanted him to sleep. Her breathing was slow and easy, her body slowly rose and fell.

I stepped in the river at Jordan.
The water came to my knees.

He began to sweat. He felt an overwhelming fear, which yet contained a curious and dreadful pleasure.

I stepped in the river at Jordan.

The water came to my waist.

It had been night, as it was now, he was in the car between his mother and his father, sleepy, his head in his mother's lap, sleepy, and yet full of excitement. The singing came from far away, across the dark fields. There were no lights anywhere. They had said good-bye to all the others and turned off on this dark dirt road. They were almost home.

I stepped in the river at Jordan,

The water came over my head,

I looked way over to the other side,

He was making up my dying bed!

"I guess they singing for him," his father said, seeming very weary and subdued now. "Even when they're sad, they sound like they just about to go and tear off a piece." He yawned and leaned across the boy and slapped his wife lightly on the shoulder, allowing his hand to rest there for a moment. "Don't they?"

"Don't talk that way," she said.

"Well, that's what we going to do," he said, "you can make up your mind to that." He started whistling. "You see? When I begin to feel it, I gets kind of musical, too."

Oh, Lord! Come on and ease my troubling mind!

He had a black friend, his age, eight, who lived nearby. His name was Otis. They wrestled together in the dirt. Now the thought of Otis made him sick. He began to shiver. His mother put her arm around him.

"He's tired," she said.

"We'll be home soon," said his father. He began to whistle again.

"We didn't see Otis this morning," Jesse said. He did not know why he said this. His voice, in the darkness of the car, sounded small and accusing.

"You haven't seen Otis for a couple of mornings," his mother said.

That was true. But he was only concerned about *this* morning.

"No," said his father, "I reckon Otis's folks was afraid to let him show himself this morning."

"But Otis didn't do nothing!" Now his voice sounded questioning.

"Otis *can't* do nothing," said his father, "he's too little." The car lights picked up their wooden house, which now solemnly approached them, the lights falling around it like yellow dust. Their dog, chained to a tree, began to bark.

"We just want to make sure Otis *don't* do nothing," said his father, and stopped the car. He looked down at Jesse. "And you tell him what your Daddy said, you hear?"

"Yes sir," he said.

His father switched off the lights. The dog moaned and pranced, but they ignored him and went inside. He could not sleep. He lay awake, hearing the night sounds, the dog yawning and moaning outside, the sawing of the crickets, the cry of the owl, dogs barking far away, then no sounds at all, just the heavy, endless buzzing of the night. The darkness pressed on his eyelids like a scratchy blanket. He turned, he turned again. He wanted to call his mother, but he knew his father would not like this. He was terribly afraid. Then he heard his father's voice in the other room, low, with a joke in it; but this did not help him, it frightened him more, he knew what was going to happen. He put his head under the blanket, then pushed his head out again, for fear, staring at the dark window. He heard his mother's moan, his father's sigh; he gritted his teeth. Then their bed began to rock. His father's breathing seemed to fill the world.

That morning, before the sun had gathered all its strength, men and women, some flushed and some pale with excitement, came with news. Jesse's father seemed to know what the news was before the first jalopy stopped in the yard, and he ran out, crying, "They got him, then? They got him?"

The first jalopy held eight people, three men and two women and three children. The children were sitting on the laps of the grown-ups. Jesse knew two of them, the two boys; they shyly and uncomfortably greeted each other. He did not know the girl.

"Yes, they got him," said one of the women, the older one,

who wore a wide hat and a fancy, faded blue dress. "They found him early this morning."

"How far had he got?" Jesse's father asked.

"He hadn't got no further than Harkness," one of the men said. "Look like he got lost up there in all them trees—or maybe he just go so scared he couldn't move." They all laughed.

"Yes, and you know it's near a graveyard, too," said the younger woman, and they laughed again.

"Is that where they got him now?" asked Jesse's father.

By this time there were three cars piled behind the first one, with everyone looking excited and shining, and Jesse noticed that they were carrying food. It was like a Fourth of July picnic.

"Yeah, that's where he is," said one of the men, "declare, Jesse, you going to keep us here all day long, answering your damn fool questions. Come on, we ain't got no time to waste."

"Don't bother putting up no food," cried a woman from one of the other cars, "we got enough. Just come on."

"Why, thank you," said Jesse's father, "we be right along, then."

"I better get a sweater for the boy," said his mother, "in case it turns cold."

Jesse watched his mother's thin legs cross the yard. He knew that she also wanted to comb her hair a little and maybe put on a better dress, the dress she wore to church. His father guessed this, too, for he yelled behind her, "Now don't you go trying to turn yourself into no movie star. You just come on." But he laughed as he said this, and winked at the men; his wife was younger and prettier than most of the other women. He clapped Jesse on the head and started pulling him toward the car. "You all go on," he said, "I'll be right behind you. Jesse, you go tie up that there dog while I get this car started."

The cars sputtered and coughed and shook; the caravan began to move; bright dust filled the air. As soon as he was tied up, the dog began to bark. Jesse's mother came out of the house, carrying a jacket for his father and a sweater for Jesse. She had put a ribbon in her hair and had an old shawl around her shoulders.

"Put these in the car, son," she said, and handed everything to him. She bent down and stroked the dog, looked to see if there was water in his bowl, then went back up the three porch steps and closed the door.

"Come on," said his father, "ain't nothing in there for nobody to steal." He was sitting in the car, which trembled and belched. The last car of the caravan had disappeared but the sound of singing floated behind them.

Jesse got into the car, sitting close to his father, loving the smell of the car, and the trembling, and the bright day, and the sense of going on a great and unexpected journey. His mother got in and closed the door and the car began to move. Not until then did he ask, "Where are we going? Are we going on a picnic?"

He had a feeling that he knew where they were going, but he was not sure.

"That's right," his father said, "we're going on a picnic. You won't ever forget *this* picnic—!"

"Are we," he asked, after a moment, "going to see the bad nigger—the one that knocked down old Miss Standish?"

"Well, I reckon," said his mother, "that we *might* see him."

He started to ask, *Will a lot of niggers be there? Will Otis be there?*—but he did not ask his question, to which, in a strange and uncomfortable way, he already knew the answer. Their friends, in the other cars, stretched up the road as far as he could see; other cars had joined them; there were cars behind them. They were singing. The sun seemed, suddenly very hot, and he was, at once very happy and a little afraid. He did not quite understand what was happening, and he did not know what to ask—he had no one to ask. He had grown accustomed, for the solution of such mysteries, to go to Otis. He felt that Otis knew everything. But he could not ask Otis about this. Anyway, he had not seen Otis for two days; he had not seen a black face anywhere for more than two days; and he now realized, as they began chugging up the long hill which eventually led to Harkness, that there were no black faces on the road this morning, no black people anywhere. From the houses in which they lived, all along the road, no smoke curled, no life stirred—maybe one or two chickens were to be seen, that was all. There was no one at the windows, no one in the yard, no one sitting on the porches, and the doors were closed. He had come this road many a time and seen women washing in the yard (there were no clothes on the clotheslines) men working in the fields, children playing in the dust; black men passed them on the road other mornings, other days, on foot, or in wagons, sometimes in cars, tipping their hats, smiling, joking, their teeth a solid white against their skin, their eyes as warm as the sun, the blackness of their skin like dull fire against the white of the blue or the grey of their torn clothes. They passed the nigger church—dead-white, desolate, locked up; and the graveyard, where no one knelt or walked, and he saw no flowers. He wanted to ask, *Where are they? Where are they all?* But he did not dare. As the hill grew steeper, the sun grew colder. He looked at his mother and his father. They looked straight ahead, seeming to be listening to the singing which echoed and echoed in this graveyard silence. They were strangers to him now. They were looking at something he could not see. His father's lips had a strange, cruel curve, he wet his lips from time to time, and swallowed. He was terribly aware of his father's tongue, it was as though he had never seen it before. And his father's body suddenly seemed immense, bigger than a mountain. His eyes, which were grey-green, looked yellow in the sunlight; or at least there was a light in them which he had never seen before. His mother patted her hair and adjusted the ribbon, leaning forward to look into the car mirror. "You look all right," said his father, and laughed. "When that nigger looks at you, he's going to swear he throwed his life away for nothing. Wouldn't be surprised if he don't come back to haunt you." And he laughed again.

The singing now slowly began to cease; and he realized that they were nearing their destination. They had reached a straight, narrow, pebbly road, with trees on either side. The sunlight filtered down on them from a great height, as though they were under-water; and the branches of the trees scraped against the cars with a tearing sound. To the right of them, and beneath them, invisible now, lay the town; and to the left, miles of trees which led to the high mountain range which his ancestors had crossed in order to settle in this valley. Now, all was silent, except for the bumping of the tires against the rocky road, the sputtering of motors, and the sound of a crying child. And they seemed to move more slowly. They were beginning to climb again. He watched the cars ahead as they toiled patiently upward, disappearing into the sunlight of the clearing. Presently, he felt their vehicle also rise, heard his father's changed breathing, the sunlight hit his face, the trees moved away from them, and they were there. As their car crossed the clearing, he looked around. There seemed to be millions, there were certainly hundreds of people in the clearing, staring toward something he could not see. There was a fire. He could not see the flames, but he smelled the smoke. Then they were on the other side of the clearing, among the trees again. His father drove off the road and parked the car behind a great many other cars. He looked down at Jesse.

"You all right?" he asked.

"Yes sir," he said.

"Well, come on, then," his father said. He reached over and opened the door on his mother's side. His mother stepped out first. They followed her into the clearing. At first he was aware only of confusion, of his mother and father greeting and being greeted, himself being handled, hugged, and patted, and told how much he had grown. The wind blew the smoke from the fire across the clearing into his eyes and nose. He could not see over the backs of the people in front of him. The sounds of laughing and cursing and wrath—and something else—rolled in waves from the front of the mob to the back. Those in front expressed their delight at what they saw, and this delight rolled backward, wave upon wave, across the clearing, more acrid than the smoke. His father reached down suddenly and sat Jesse on his shoulders.

Now he saw the fire—of twigs and boxes, piled high; flames made pale orange and yellow and thin as a veil under the steadier light of the sun; grey-blue smoke rolled upward and poured over their heads. Beyond the shifting curtain of fire and smoke, he made out first only a length of gleaming chain, attached to a great limb of the tree; then he saw that this chain bound two black hands together at the wrist, dirty yellow palm facing dirty yellow palm. The smoke poured up; the hands dropped out of sight; a cry went up from the crowd. Then the hands slowly came into view again, pulled upward by the chain. This time he saw the kinky, sweating, bloody head—he had never before seen a head with so much hair on it, hair so black and so tangled that it seemed like another jungle. The head was hanging. He saw the forehead, flat and high, with a kind of arrow of hair in the center, like he had, like his father had; they called it a widow's peak; and the mangled eye brows, the wide nose, the closed eyes, and the glinting eye lashes and the hanging lips, all streaming with blood and sweat. His hands were straight above his head. All his weight pulled downward from his hands; and he was a big man, a bigger man than his father, and black as an African jungle Cat, and naked. Jesse pulled upward; his father's hands held him firmly by the ankles. He wanted to say something, he did not know what, but nothing he said could have been heard, for now the crowd roared again as a man stepped forward and put more wood on the fire. The flames leapt up. He thought he heard the hanging man scream, but he was not sure. Sweat was pouring from the hair in his armpits, poured down his sides, over his chest, into his navel and his groin. He was lowered again; he was raised again. Now Jesse knew that he heard him scream. The head went back, the mouth wide open, blood bubbling from the mouth; the veins of the neck jumped out; Jesse clung to his father's neck in terror as the cry rolled over the crowd. The cry of all the people rose to answer the dying man's cry. He wanted death to come quickly. They wanted to make death wait: and it was they who held death, now, on a leash which they lengthened little by little. *What did he do?* Jesse wondered. *What did the man do? What did he do?*—but he could not ask his father. He was seated on his father's shoulders, but his father was far away. There were two older men, friends of his father's, raising and lowering the chain; everyone, indiscriminately, seemed to be responsible for the fire. There was no hair left on the nigger's privates, and the eyes, now, were wide open, as white as the eyes of a clown or a doll. The smoke now carried a terrible odor across the clearing, the odor of something burning which was both sweet and rotten.

He turned his head a little and saw the field of faces. He watched his mother's face. Her eyes were very bright, her mouth was open: she was more beautiful than he had ever seen her, and more strange. He began to feel a joy he had never felt before. He watched the hanging, gleaming body, the most beautiful and terrible object he had ever seen till then. One of his father's friends reached up and in his hands he held a knife: and Jesse wished that he had been that man. It was a long, bright knife and the sun seemed to catch it, to play with it, to caress it—it was brighter than the fire. And a wave of laughter swept the crowd. Jesse felt his father's hands on his ankles slip and tighten. The man with the knife walked toward the crowd, smiling slightly; as though this were a signal, silence fell; he heard his mother cough. Then the man with the knife walked up to the hanging body. He turned and smiled again. Now there was a silence all over the field. The hanging head looked up. It seemed fully conscious now, as though the fire had burned out terror and pain. The man with the knife took the nigger's privates in his hand, one hand, still smiling, as though he were weighing them. In the cradle of the one white hand, the nigger's privates seemed as remote as meat being weighed in the scales; but seemed heavier, too, much heavier, and Jesse felt his scrotum tighten; and huge, huge, much bigger than his father's, flaccid, hairless, the largest thing he had ever seen till then, and the blackest. The white hand stretched them, cradled them, caressed them. Then the dying man's eyes looked straight into Jesse's eyes— it could not have been as long as a second, but it seemed longer than a year. Then Jesse screamed, and the crowd screamed as the knife flashed, first up, then down, cutting the dreadful thing away, and the blood came roaring down. Then the crowd rushed forward, tearing at the body with their hands, with knives, with rocks, with stones, howling and cursing. Jesse's head, of its own weight, fell downward toward his father's head. Someone stepped forward and drenched the body with kerosene. Where the man had been, a great sheet of flame appeared. Jesse's father lowered him to the ground.

"Well, I told you," said his father, "you wasn't never going to forget *this* picnic." His father's face was full of sweat, his eyes were very peaceful. At that moment Jesse loved his father more than he had ever loved him. He felt that his father had carried him through a mighty test, had revealed to him a great secret which would be the key to his life forever.

"I reckon," he said. "I reckon."

Jesse's father took him by the hand and, with his mother a little behind them, talking and laughing with the other women, they walked through the crowd, across the clearing. The black body was on the ground, the chain which had held it was being rolled up by one of his father's friends. Whatever the fire had left undone, the hands and the knives and the stones of the people had accomplished. The head was caved in, one eye was torn out, one ear was hanging. But one had to look carefully to realize this, for it was, now, merely, a black charred object on the black, charred ground. He lay spread-eagled with what had been a wound between what had been his legs.

"They going to leave him here, then?" Jesse whispered.

"Yeah," said his father, "they'll come and get him by and by. I reckon we better get over there and get some of that food before it's all gone."

"I reckon," he muttered now to himself, "I reckon." Grace stirred and touched him on the thigh: the moonlight covered her like glory. Something bubbled up in him, his nature again returned to him. He thought of the boy in the cell; he thought of the man in the fire; he thought of the knife and grabbed himself and stroked himself and a terrible sound, something between a high laugh and a howl, came out of him and dragged his sleeping wife up on one elbow. She stared at him in a moonlight which had now grown cold as ice. He thought of the morning and grabbed her, laughing and crying, crying and laughing, and he whispered, as he stroked her, as he took her, "Come on, sugar, I'm going to do you like a nigger, just like a nigger, come on, sugar, and love me just like you'd love a nigger." He thought of the morning as he labored and she moaned, thought of morning as he labored harder than he ever had before, and before his labors had ended, he heard the first cock crow and the dogs begin to bark, and the sound of tires on the gravel road.

CHRONOLOGY

NOTE ON THE TEXTS

NOTES

Chronology

1924   Born James Arthur Jones on August 2 in Harlem Hospital,
            New York City, the son of Emma Berdis Jones and a father
            he will never know. (Mother moved from Deal Island,
            Maryland, around the turn of the century and lived briefly
            in Philadelphia before moving to New York City.)

1925–28   Receives name James Arthur Baldwin after mother marries
            David Baldwin in 1927. (Stepfather, a Baptist preacher in
            Harlem who also works at a bottling factory, moved from
            New Orleans to New York City in the early 1920s with his
            mother, Barbara Ann Baldwin, a former slave, and son
            Samuel Baldwin, who is about 12 years old.) Family lives
            in Harlem apartment. Brother George born.

1929–34   Sister Barbara born. Baldwin begins attending Public
            School 24 in 1929, where he is encouraged in his studies
            by school principal, Gertrude E. Ayer. Brother Wilmer is
            born in 1930, brother David in 1931, and sister Gloria in
            1933; during this time step-grandmother dies and Samuel,
            after a dispute with his father, leaves home for good. Bald-
            win helps mother care for growing family. Family is forced
            by lack of money to move several times, always within
            Harlem, and occasionally to accept relief. Orilla Miller, a
            WPA Theater Project worker in the public schools, en-
            courages Baldwin in his reading and takes him to movies,
            museums, and plays.

1935–38   Sister Ruth born in 1935. Baldwin enters Frederick Doug-
            lass Junior High School (P.S. 139) in September 1935,
            where he is influenced by teacher and literary club adviser
            Countee Cullen, a leading poet of the Harlem Renais-
            sance. Contributes essays, sketches, poems, and stories to
            school magazine *The Douglass Pilot* and becomes one of
            its editors. Visits midtown library often and reads vora-
            ciously; his favorite novels are Stowe's *Uncle Tom's Cabin*
            and Dickens' *A Tale of Two Cities*. Sister Elizabeth born
            in 1937. Researches history of Harlem for essay "Har-
            lem—Then and Now." Attends Pentecostalist churches

with family of school friend Arthur Moore; undergoes a conversion experience, becomes a young minister at Fireside Pentecostal Assembly, and for next three years preaches there regularly. Enters De Witt Clinton High School, a prestigeous public school in the Bronx, in September 1938.

1939–41   Works on school journal *The Magpie* along with friends Emile Capouya, Sol Stein, and Richard Avedon; Baldwin's contributions include stories "Woman at the Well," "Mississippi Legend," "Incident in London," and an interview with Countee Cullen, "Rendezvous with Life." Grows troubled at not knowing his real father. Finds it hard to concentrate on schoolwork and fails some courses but does well in English and history. Through Capouya meets Beauford Delaney, an artist living in Greenwich Village; he introduces Baldwin to the art world there, teaches him about music—including blues and jazz, which are forbidden by stepfather at home—and becomes a lifelong friend. Stepfather's health begins to fail. With Capouya's support, Baldwin leaves the church, preaching his last sermon at the end of senior year.

1942–44   Awarded high school diploma in January 1942. Takes laboring job at army depot under construction in Belle Mead, near Princeton, New Jersey, where Capouya is also employed. Rooms with local family but visits New York on weekends and regularly sends money to family. Fired from Belle Mead job; returns home and finds work at a meatpacking plant. Stepfather dies on July 29, 1943, the same day that sister Paula is born. Baldwin loses the meatpacking job. Moves to Greenwich Village to concentrate on writing, staying at first with Delaney and other friends. Works as waiter at Calypso restaurant and enjoys the company of artists and writers who gather there. Has liaisons with both men and women. Around this time tells Capouya that he thinks of himself as homosexual. Becomes good friend of Eugene Worth and meets young actor Marlon Brando while taking a theater class. Begins a novel that he calls "Crying Holy" and "In My Father's House" (later *Go Tell It on the Mountain*). Meets Richard Wright in late 1944; he reads Baldwin's manuscript and recommends it to an editor at Harper and Brothers.

1945–48   Receives $500 grant from Harper's Eugene F. Saxton Memorial Trust in November 1945. Works on novel; a draft is rejected by both Harper and Doubleday. Eugene Worth commits suicide by jumping from George Washington Bridge in the winter of 1946; Baldwin is deeply upset and later uses the incident in *Another Country*. Baldwin begins regularly writing reviews for *The Nation* and *The New Leader*, and in 1948 *Commentary* publishes his essay "The Harlem Ghetto" and story "Previous Condition." Drafts novel "Ignorant Armies," which he abandons. Reads widely in French, Russian, and American literature including Balzac, Flaubert, Dostoevsky, Henry Miller, Walt Whitman, and Henry James. Wins Rosenwald fellowship to do book on Harlem in collaboration with photographer Theodore Pelatowski, whom he met through Avedon (it is never completed). Moves to Paris in November 1948. Sees Richard Wright, who moved to France in 1947, and meets Themistocles Hoetis and Asa Beneviste, friends of Wright who are planning to publish a little magazine called *Zero*, and journalist Otto Friedrich. Stays first at Hôtel de Rome then finds less expensive room at Hôtel de Verneuil, where he makes a number of friends including English socialist Mary Keen and Norwegian journalist Gidske Anderson. Meets Truman Capote, Saul Bellow, and Herbert Gold around this time. Explores the works of Henry James.

1949–50   "Everybody's Protest Novel" (*Zero*, Spring 1949, and *Partisan Review*, June 1949), attacking Stowe's *Uncle Tom's Cabin* and including criticism of Wright's *Native Son*, strains his relationship with Wright. Finds job in summer as clerk for an American lawyer. Works sporadically on his novel (later called *Go Tell It on the Mountain*), then starts another, "So Long at the Fair," about Greenwich Village, which he abandons. Continues writing essays. When clerking job ends in late September, accepts a loan from American acquaintance Frank Price as advance against the publication of his novel. Takes trip with Hoetis and Anderson in fall but becomes ill in the south of France and is hospitalized twice for treatment of inflamed gland. Reads Shakespeare and the Bible during recuperation. Back in Paris is jailed for eight days in December in connection with a friend's theft of a bedsheet; charges are dismissed (later writes of the incident in "Equal in Paris").

Falls in love with Lucien Happersberger, a young Swiss living in Paris.

1951–52   Meets Mary Painter, an economist at the American embassy, with whom he forms an enduring friendship. Low on funds, continues writing for journals but makes little progress on novel. "Many Thousands Gone" (*Partisan Review*, Nov.–Dec. 1951), an explicit attack on Wright, leads to painful break between the writers. Spends three months in winter of 1951–52 with Happersberger at his family's cottage in Loèche-les-Bains in the Bernese Alps, where he completes *Go Tell It on the Mountain*. When Knopf expresses interest in the novel, borrows money from Marlon Brando and sails to New York in June. Receives $250 advance from Knopf and another $750 when revised novel is accepted in July. Meets Ralph Ellison. Spends time with family and friends and begins a play, *The Amen Corner*. Back in France, becomes godfather to Luc James Happersberger, son of Lucien and Suzy Happersberger, who were married earlier in the year. Writes essay "Stranger in the Village," based on stay in Loèche-les-Bains (*Harper's Magazine*, Oct. 1953).

1953   Completes draft of *The Amen Corner*. *Go Tell It on the Mountain* is published by Knopf in May; receives congratulatory letter from Langston Hughes, with laudatory reviews enclosed. Knopf declines to publish play but requests another novel. Spends time with entertainers including Gordon Heath, Bernard Hassell, Bobby Short, Inez Cavanaugh, and meets Maya Angelou around this time. Sees writers including Chester Himes, Gardner Smith, and Frank Yerby. Beauford Delaney moves to France in late summer and settles in Clamart, outside of Paris, where Baldwin sees him often. Goes to Les Quatre-Chemins, near Grasse, for Christmas and remains until March 1954; works on new novel that becomes *Giovanni's Room*.

1954–55   Wins Guggenheim fellowship and returns to New York in June 1954. Agrees to prepare a collection of his essays and reviews at the request of Sol Stein, now an editor at Beacon Press. Works on play, novel, and essays at MacDowell Colony in Peterboro, New Hampshire, and in 1955 at Yaddo in Saratoga Springs, New York. Lucien Happersberger arrives for a visit. Further revises *The Amen Corner* during rehearsals at Howard University, where it is staged by Owen Dodson's Howard Players in May 1955. Meets E. Franklin Frazier and Sterling Brown. Returns to Europe in summer. *Giovanni's Room*, which was rejected by Knopf and several other publishers earlier in 1955, is accepted by Dial Press in New York and Michael Joseph in London. *Notes of a Native Son* (11 essays) published by Beacon in late 1955.

1956   Accepts National Institute of Arts and Letters Award and *Partisan Review* fellowship. At request of editor Philip Rahv of *Partisan Review*, writes "Faulkner and Desegregation." Meets and begins friendship with Norman and Adele Mailer. Covers First Conference of Negro-African Writers and Artists; held at the Sorbonne in September, it is sponsored by *Présence Africaine*, a journal of the *Négritude* movement, and attended by delegates from Africa, the United States, and the Caribbean. Travels to Corsica where he writes article on the conference ("Princes and Powers," *Encounter*, Jan. 1957) and works on new novel, *Another Country*. *Giovanni's Room*, published by Dial in fall, goes into second printing in six weeks.

1957–58   "Sonny's Blues" appears in *Partisan Review*, summer 1957. Sails to New York in July and in September makes first trip to the Deep South on assignment for *Partisan Review* and *Harper's Magazine*. Interviews children who are integrating public schools in Charlotte, North Carolina, and sees Martin Luther King Jr. in Atlanta, Georgia. Travels through Alabama visiting Birmingham (where he meets the Rev. Fred Shuttlesworth), Little Rock, Tuskeegee, and Montgomery (meets Coretta Scott King), and Nashville, Tennessee. Back in New York for casting of Lee Strasberg's Actors Studio workshop production of *Giovanni's Room*, meets Lorraine Hansberry, Rip Torn, and Engin Cezzar, a young Turkish actor cast as Giovanni. At MacDowell Colony, writes essay on southern trip and works on adaptation of novel (staged in May 1958). Through old friend Sam Floyd, leases New York apartment at 81 Horatio Street. Accepts Elia Kazan's invitation to learn more about theater by apprenticing on his productions of Archibald MacLeish's *JB* and Tennessee Williams' *Sweet Bird of Youth*. Returns to Paris for summer of 1958.

1959   Awarded two-year Ford Foundation grant to complete
            Another Country. Hires William "Tony" Maynard as a pri-
            vate secretary. Travels to Sweden to interview film director
            Ingmar Bergman in October. Back in Paris, meets Jean
            Genet and is impressed by his play *Les Nègres* (*The Blacks*).
            "A Letter from the South: Nobody Knows My Name"
            published in *Partisan Review*.

1960   Travels in May to Tallahassee, Florida, to cover sit-in
            movement; meets members of the Congress of Racial
            Equality (CORE), and interviews students at Florida Ag-
            ricultural and Mechanical University, a historically black
            school ("They Can't Turn Back," *Mademoiselle*, Aug.
            1960). In Paris for summer, works on *Another Country*
            and second essay collection, *Nobody Knows My Name*.
            Spends time with William and Rose Styron and moves in
            late fall into studio at their home in Connecticut (uses it
            as his base through summer of 1961). Also sees James and
            Gloria Jones. Speaks at *Esquire Magazine* symposium on
            the writer in America held in San Francisco in October;
            spends time with John Cheever and Philip Roth. After
            sudden death of Richard Wright on November 28, returns
            to France to do research for essays on him (collected in
            Nobody Knows My Name as "Alas, Poor Richard").

1961   Second essay collection, *Nobody Knows My Name: More
            Notes of a Native Son*, published by Dial in summer to
            excellent reviews. Gives speeches, including address to
            CORE rally in Washington, D.C., in June, and makes ra-
            dio and television appearances. Meets Black Muslim lead-
            ers Malcolm X and Elijah Muhammad. Visits Israel and
            Istanbul, Turkey, where he sees family of Engin Cezzar
            and meets David Leeming (will stay in Istanbul often in
            following years). Completes *Another Country* in Decem-
            ber. Spends Christmas in Paris with Mary Painter, then
            goes to Loèche-les-Bains for filming of "Stranger in the
            Village" by Swiss television.

1962   Attends White House dinner honoring American Nobel
            laureates in April. Begins friendship with Katherine Anne
            Porter. *Another Country*, published by Dial in June to
            mixed reviews, becomes a national bestsellar. Travels to
            Africa in July with sister Gloria, who works as his assistant.

Visits Dakar, Senegal; Conakry, Guinea; and Freetown, Sierra Leone. "Letter from a Region in My Mind," published in *The New Yorker* November 17, receives wide attention (essay is printed as "Down at the Cross" in *The Fire Next Time*).

1963   Undertakes lecture tour for CORE. In Jackson, Mississippi, meets James Meredith, the first African American student at the University of Mississippi, and Medgar Evers, state field secretary for the National Association for the Advancement of Colored People (NAACP); accompanies Evers on investigation of a reported lynching. Travels through the South giving talks, often held in churches. *The Fire Next Time*, collecting two essays, published by Dial in January to wide acclaim. Makes television and radio appearances, gives numerous interviews. Wins George Polk Memorial Award for outstanding magazine journalism in April and is subject of *Time* cover story on May 17. Continues lecture tour in New York and California, where he sees half-brother Samuel Baldwin for first time in 30 years. Photo-story on CORE tour appears in *Life* on May 24. Wires Attorney General Robert F. Kennedy on May 12 to protest police assaults on peaceful civil rights demonstrators in Birmingham, Alabama, and blames the violence in part on inaction by President John F. Kennedy. Meets with Robert Kennedy at his home in McLean, Virginia, on May 23. Brings a group of civil rights leaders and entertainers, including freedom rider Jerome Smith, Dr. Kenneth Clark, attorney Clarence B. Jones, Edwin C. Berry of the Chicago Urban League, Lorraine Hansberry, Harry Belafonte, Lena Horne, Rip Torn, and Henry Morgenthau, to meeting with Robert Kennedy and Burke Marshall, head of the Justice Department's Civil Rights Division, held at Kennedy's New York City apartment on May 24. Works on new play, *Blues for Mr. Charlie*, dedicating it to Medgar Evers, who was assassinated in Jackson on June 12, and plans a collaborative book project with Richard Avedon. Participates in March on Washington, a major demonstration for civil rights, in August. Along with brother David assists James Forman and Student Non-Violent Coordinating Committee (SNCC) in drive to register black voters in Selma, Alabama, in October. As part of a group that also includes Thurgood Marshall,

Harry Belafonte, and Sidney Poitier, goes to Nairobi in December for celebration of Kenya's independence.

1964–65   Elected to National Institute of Arts and Letters in February 1964. *Blues for Mr. Charlie,* directed by Burgess Meredith and starring Pat Hingle, Al Freeman Jr., Diana Sands, and Rip Torn, runs at ANTA Theater in New York City from April 23 to August 29, 1964. The play is published by Dial and *Nothing Personal,* with photographs by Richard Avedon, by Atheneum in 1964. In Cambridge Union Society debate at Cambridge University on February 18, 1965, successfully supports motion that "the American dream is at the expense of the American Negro"; opposition is led by William F. Buckley Jr. Malcolm X is assassinated February 21, 1965, in New York City. Participates in civil rights march from Selma to Montgomery, Alabama, led by Martin Luther King Jr. in late March. Speaking engagements include the New School for Social Research and Harvard University. Prepares story collection *Going To Meet the Man* (published by Dial in December). *The Amen Corner* opens April 16 at the Barrymore Theater in New York (runs for 48 performances) and another production of it tours in Europe and Israel. Spends holiday season in Istanbul with friends.

1966–67   Writes essays "Negroes Are Anti-Semitic Because They're Anti-White" and "Anti-Semitism and Black Power." Meets Eldridge Cleaver and Huey Newton. Agrees to write scenario for screen adaptation of *The Autobiography of Malcolm X* for producer Marvin Worth at Columbia Pictures.

1968–69   Visits Tony Maynard in Hamburg, Germany, where he is awaiting extradition to the United States on charges of murder (works on his behalf over several years; charges against Maynard are dismissed in 1974). Becomes a target of criticism by radical activists and is attacked by Eldridge Cleaver in *Soul on Ice.* Appears before congressional subcommittee with Betty Shabazz to propose establishment of a national commission on black history and culture. Works on *Malcolm X* script in Hollywood. Sees Martin Luther King Jr. and Andrew Young in Los Angeles in March during their fundraising drive for Poor People's

Campaign. Play *The Amen Corner* and novel *Tell Me How Long the Train's Been Gone* published by Dial. Martin Luther King Jr. is assassinated on April 4, 1968, in Memphis; Baldwin attends funeral April 9 in Atlanta. Has disputes with Columbia executives over *Malcolm X* script, and they assign screenwriter Arnold Perl to work with him. Addresses assembly of the World Council of Churches in Uppsala, Sweden, on "White Racism or World Community" in July. Writes article "The Price May Be Too High" (*The New York Times Magazine*, Feb. 2, 1969) on the problems of a black writer in a world controlled by whites. Quits the Columbia project in spring; continues working on his own script. In Istanbul directs Turkish stage production of John Herbert's *Fortune and Men's Eyes*.

1970–71   Ill with hepatitis for several weeks. Sedat Pakay makes short documentary film, *James Baldwin from Another Place*, in Istanbul in May 1970. Visits New York to record a conversation with Margaret Mead in August (transcription is published by Lippincott in 1971 as *A Rap on Race*). Becomes ill again and is hospitalized in Paris in October 1970; on advice of Mary Painter, goes to St. Paul-de-Vence, near Nice, to recuperate. Writes "An Open Letter to My Sister, Miss Angela Davis" (*New York Review of Books*, Jan. 7, 1971) after Davis is indicted for kidnapping and murder in connection with the August 1970 shootings at the San Rafael, California, courthouse (she is acquitted in 1972). Buys a large house on 10 acres of land in St. Paul-de-Vence. Hires Bernard Hassell to oversee the estate. Often sees actors Yves Montand and Simone Signoret and has numerous guests. Appears with poet Nikki Giovanni on Ellis Haizlipp's television program *Soul* (transcription is published by Lippincott as *A Dialogue* in 1973).

1972–74   *No Name in the Street* and *One Day When I Was Lost: A Scenario Based on "The Autobiography of Malcolm X"* published by Dial in 1972. Writes screenplay "The Inheritance" (never produced). Helps care for Beauford Delaney, whose mental faculties are failing; writes catalog tribute for major retrospective exhibition of his work in Paris. Becomes close to artist Yoran Cazac. Interviewed in August 1973, along with Josephine Baker, by Henry Louis Gates Jr., at this time a correspondent for *Time* magazine (editor declines to print Gates' story, calls Baldwin "passé"). Novel *If Beale Street Could Talk*, inspired by life of Tony Maynard, published by Dial in 1974. Awarded centennial medal for the "artist as prophet" from Cathedral of St. John the Divine in New York City in March 1974. Celebrates 50th birthday with family and friends in St. Paul-de-Vence.

1975–77   Works on long essay on movies, *The Devil Finds Work*, and children's book, *Little Man, Little Man: A Story of Childhood*, with illustrations by Yoran Cazac; both are published by Dial in 1976. Contributes to American bicentennial symposium *The Nature of a Humane Society* in October 1976; other participants include Toni Morrison, Archibald Cox, Arthur Schlesinger, and Coretta Scott King. Continues publishing in periodicals and gives many interviews.

1978   Teaches spring course in contemporary literature at Bowling Green College in Ohio, first long stay in the United States since 1969 (will return to teach at the college for fall semesters of 1979 and 1981). Awarded Martin Luther King Memorial Medal for "lifelong dedication to humanitarian ideals" at City College of New York. Vacations on Cape Cod before returning to France.

1979–80   Completes novel *Just Above My Head* (published in fall 1979 by Dial). Goes into seclusion after learning of Beauford Delaney's death in Paris on March 26, 1979. Teaches class at University of California, Berkeley, in spring, and speaks at Los Angeles, Santa Barbara, and San Diego campuses; meets Thomas A. Dorsey and sees Angela Davis. Begins writing and lecturing on "Black English." In France in summer writes "Open Letter to the Born Again" (*The Nation*, Sept. 29, 1979) after Andrew Young resigns as U.S. ambassador to the United Nations following disclosure of his unauthorized meetings with representatives of the Palestine Liberation Organization. Gives talks at Youngstown and Wayne state universities in February 1980. Travels to the University of Florida in Gainesville for meeting of African Literature Association, where he participates in conversation on the "African Aesthetic" with Nigerian writer Chinua Achebe. Travels through South accompanied by Dick Fontaine and Pat Hartley, who make a television documentary of his trip (*I Heard It Through the Grapevine*, released in 1982).

1981–82   Spends several weeks in Atlanta researching series of murders of black children for essay "The Evidence of Things Not Seen" (*Playboy*, Dec. 1981).

1983–84   *Jimmy's Blues: Selected Poems* published by Michael Joseph in 1983 (also published in New York by St. Martin's Press in 1985). Begins teaching in the Afro-American studies department at University of Massachusetts, Amherst, in fall 1983 (later teaches alternate semesters to make time for writing and speaking engagements). Hospitalized in Boston for exhaustion in late summer of 1984. Works on play "The Welcome Table." Writes "Freaks and the American Ideal of Manhood" (*Playboy*, Jan. 1985.)

1985–86   *Go Tell It on the Mountain* dramatized on public television's *American Playhouse* in January 1985. *The Evidence of Things Not Seen* (expanded version of his 1981 essay) published by Holt, Rinehart and Winston and *The Price of the Ticket: Collected Non-Fiction, 1948–1985* by St. Martin's Press in 1985. Completes last year of teaching in June 1986. Travels to France where he is made an officer of the Legion of Honor in ceremony presided over by President François Mitterand on June 19. Travels with brother David in October to the Soviet Union for international conference. Suffers from weakness and persistent sore throat. Goes to London for production of *The Amen Corner* (it runs for seven months).

1987   Returns to St. Paul-de-Vence and undergoes tests that reveal cancer of the esophagus. Treatments including surgery on April 25 make it possible to eat. Feels well until middle of summer and works on "The Welcome Table" and other projects. As condition worsens, is cared for by brother David, aided by visiting relatives and friends. Enjoys seeing guests and speaks regulary by phone with mother. Interviewed by Quincy Troupe in November and later that month insists on hosting a Thanksgiving dinner party, although he is too weak to walk to table. Dies at home on December 1 with David, Happersberger, and Hassell at bedside. After viewings in St. Paul-de-Vence and Harlem and funeral service at Episcopal Cathedral of St. John the Divine, with eulogists including Toni Morrison, Maya Angelou, and Amiri Baraka, buried December 8 in Ferncliff Cemetery, Hartsdale, New York.

Note on the Texts

This volume contains James Baldwin's first three published novels, *Go Tell It on the Mountain* (1953), *Giovanni's Room* (1956), and *Another Country* (1962), along with *Going To Meet the Man* (1965), his only collection of short stories.

In late 1944 Baldwin showed Richard Wright a draft of an unfinished novel, and on the strength of Wright's recommendation he received a Eugene F. Saxton Award of $500 in November 1945 to complete the work. Using "Crying Holy" and "In My Father's House" as titles, Baldwin worked sporadically on the novel after a version was rejected by both Harper and Doubleday in 1946, but he was not able to complete it until a stay in the mountain village of Loèche-les-Bains, Switzerland, in the winter of 1951–52. He further revised the manuscript after it was accepted by Alfred A. Knopf in the summer of 1952. Versions of two passages from the novel appeared in 1952: "Roy's Wound" (pp. 38–47 in the present volume) in *New World Writing*, vol. 2 (New York: New American Library, 1952), and "Exodus" (pp. 65–75 in the present volume) in *American Mercury*, August 1952. *Go Tell It on the Mountain* was published by Knopf on May 11, 1953, and in England by Michael Joseph in 1954. Baldwin was not involved in the English edition, and the text presented here is that of the first American printing.

Baldwin wrote most of *Giovanni's Room* between 1953 and 1955, using the titles "One for My Baby" and "A Fable for Our Children." After a version of the novel was rejected by Knopf and several other publishers in the summer and fall of 1955, it was accepted by Dial Press in the United States and by Michael Joseph in England. Baldwin received editorial suggestions from James Silberman of Dial while revising the novel; on April 8, 1956, he sent off the final version of *Giovanni's Room* to Dial Press. It was published by Dial in the fall of 1956 and by Michael Joseph, using the American plates, in 1957. This volume prints the text of the first 1956 Dial printing.

Another Country was substantially written between 1956 and 1961, while Baldwin was living in various places in Europe, the United States, and the Middle East. An excerpt, titled "Any Day Now" (pp. 413–28 in the present volume), appeared in *Partisan Review* for Spring 1960. Baldwin finished the novel in Istanbul on December 10, 1961; the book was published by Dial Press on June 25, 1962, and in England by Michael Joseph in 1963. Baldwin was not involved in the English edition, and the text presented here is that of the first American printing.

Going To Meet the Man collects eight stories. Five of them had previously been published, between 1948 and 1960: "The Outing" appeared in *New Story* in April 1951; "Previous Condition," the first Baldwin story to be featured in a major publication, in *Commentary* in October 1948; "Sonny's Blues" in *Partisan Review* for Summer 1957; "This Morning, This Evening, So Soon" in *The Atlantic Monthly* in September 1960; and "Come Out the Wilderness" in *Mademoiselle* in March 1958. Baldwin made revisions in some of the stories while preparing the collection in early 1965. "The Rockpile," which had not been previously published, is an early version of a passage in *Go Tell It on the Mountain*, Part One (pp. 38–47 in this volume). "The Man Child" was a previously unpublished story drafted in the 1950s and revised in early 1965 for this collection. "Going To Meet the Man," which was written for the collection, appeared in *Status* in October 1965. *Going To Meet the Man* was published by Dial Press in December 1965; the present volume prints the text of that original edition.

This volume presents the texts of the original printings chosen for inclusion here, but it does not attempt to reproduce features of their typographic design, such as display capitalization of chapter openings. The texts are printed without change, except for the correction of typographical errors. Spelling, punctuation, and capitalization are often expressive features, and they are not altered, even when inconsistent or irregular. Except for clear typographical errors, the spelling and usage of foreign words and phrases are left as they appear in the original texts. The following is a list of typographical errors corrected, cited by page and line number: 15.35, iminent; 16.5, neighbor's; 27.23, was had; 57.29, *may the*; 65.16, in world; 74.14, be here; 75.36, Oh; 81.38, ectasy; 84.12, irrespressibly; 149.12, apalled; 155.3, Good-*bye*?'" "You; 156.37, was was; 163.22, up as; 176.16, its; 177.1, heard,; 178.34, sister.; 178.37, wouldnt; 189.33, Whosover; 242.29, here'; 248.5, hot water; 256.5, once; 259.16, male).; 260.28, *Deiu*; 272.1, Guillaime; 272.15, *sûr.*'; 273.20, sems; 273.23, *bien?*—; 273.34, *M'sieu!*; 276.2, fianceé; 282.37, quais; 295.35, *Mon cher'*,; 298.17, Oh; 298.39, She; 304.22, th; 307.7, *pied-a terre*; 307.25, *parce–qu'il*; 316.21, faltered.' I; 318.11, some; 326.2, smile.; 326.16, fianceé; 327.23, fianceé; 327.28, here'; 329.16, me,; 336.16, fianceé; 338.5–6, what . . . me.; 345.1, hadnd't; 345.4, of; 349.2, its; 355.27, drawers; 367.4–5, afternon; 374.14, cigarette; 383.5, her.; 393.14, himself.; 440.13, thought.; 442.14, thought; 469.24, ladies; 471.33, sing if; 477.13, It; 491.12, Scott,; 498.37, helplessly,; 504.2, barbarian.; 508.6, spectacled,; 540.19, the the; 552.38, fell though; 623.37, where; 624.32, paused,; 629.13, Scott."; 631.37, all; 637.31, poet,; 657.24, pursued; 658.30, If; 667.23, you,; 689.11, touched,; 694.8, said,; 695.25, Ellis??; 697.24, everytime; 697.26, them.; 764.22, they; 764.25, said,; 768.40, here?; 771.34, car; 772.18, anyway;; 772.22, me")·; 774.24, Elishas'; 777.19, bitch.; 779.6, everyone; 782.10, home.; 785.37, Glory?; 786.11, unleased; 787.19, company; 791.18, back"; 794.3, fair,'; 794.19, grinning,; 797.8, anymore; 798.15, heads lightly; 802.31, days"; 805.15, mother.; 808.18, you,; 809.15, Eric",; 813.8–9, 'Why . . . father?'; 822.33, wrinkled; 823.21–22, man. . . . floor."; 826.33, together; 831.2, the the; 834.10, now; 835.31, it last; 859.9, again,; 873.6, *Madame*,; 877.4, *Fe*; 877.5, *Fe*; 877.17, LeHavre; 899.15, nead; 907.2, *Fusqu'au*; 911.18, adding.; 912.2, is you've; 916.39, mother:); 917.33, occuring; 922.15, Cosmos; 925.21, girl.; 934.19, everyone; 937.25, lived her; 946.8, there.

Notes

In the notes below, the reference numbers denote page and line of this volume (the line count includes headings). No note is made for material included in standard desk-reference books such as Webster's *Collegiate, Biographical,* and *Geographical* dictionaries. Biblical quotations are keyed to the King James Version. Quotations from Shakespeare are keyed to *The Riverside Shakespeare,* ed. G. Blakemore Evans (Boston: Houghton Mifflin, 1974). For further background and references to other studies, see *Conversations with James Baldwin* (Jackson: University Press of Mississippi, 1989), ed. by Fred L. Stanley and Louis H. Pratt; Fern Marja Eckmann, *The Furious Passage of James Baldwin* (New York: M. Evans & Co., Inc., 1966); David Leeming, *James Baldwin* (New York: Alfred A. Knopf, 1994); Fred L. Stanley and Nancy V. Stanley, *James Baldwin: A Reference Guide* (Boston: G.K. Hall & Co., 1980); W. J. Weatherby, *James Baldwin: Artist on Fire* (New York: Donald I. Fine, Inc., 1989).

GO TELL IT ON THE MOUNTAIN

3.1–3   *They . . . faint.*]   Isaiah 40:31.

7.3–7   *And . . . freely.*]   Revelation 22:17.

8.1–2   *I . . . wondered*]   From "I Looked Down the Line," a gospel song.

14.15   "walking disorderly"]   Cf. 2 Thessalonians 3:6–7, 11–12.

20.6   *He . . . still.*]   Revelation 22:11.

24.25–30   a man . . . hill]   Sisyphus, in Greek mythology.

25.36–39   *Come . . . you.*]   "The Welcome," lines 1–4, by Irish poet Thomas Osborne Davis (1814–45).

30.12–13   Everything . . . Lord.]   Romans 8:28.

30.14–15   *Set . . . order*]   2 Kings 20:1 and Isaiah 38:1.

36.22   The woman]   Bette Davis as Mildred Rodgers in *Of Human Bondage* (RKO, 1934), John Cromwell's adaptation of Somerset Maugham's 1915 novel.

59.3–7   *And . . . earth?*]   Revelation 6:10.

61.3–4   *Light . . . wings!*]   Charles Wesley, "Hark the Herald Angels Sing" (1734), stanza 3.

66.17–18   herd . . . sea.]   Cf. Matthew 8:30–32, Mark 5:11–13.

77.6   fool . . . God—] Cf. Psalm 14:1

87.3–6   *Now . . . now.*] From "Crying Holy Unto the Lord," a gospel song. ("Crying Holy" was a working title for *Go Tell It on the Mountain*.)

104.12   mincing . . . Zion!] Cf. Isaiah 3:16.

106.17   dog . . . vomit] Cf. Proverbs 26:11.

114.16–17   son . . . Hell] Cf. Isaiah 14:12–15.

168.38–169.3   God . . . door] "Rock-a My Soul (in the Bosom of Abraham)," a spiritual.

185.3–8   *Then . . . hosts.*] Isaiah 6:5.

191.7   accursed . . . Noah] Ham, in Genesis 9:22–27.

201.20–21   text . . . high.] Job 16:19.

GIOVANNI'S ROOM

219.1   *I am . . . there.*] *Leaves of Grass* (1856 edition), "Song of Myself," Sect. 33, line 123.

252.17   *Je m'en fou.*] I don't give a damn.

252.35   *'Va te faire foutre.'*] Go fuck yourself.

259.31   *'tres bon marche'*] Very cheap.

259.40–260.1   *Nom . . . boulot!*] My God, what a job!

260.28   *les fesses*] Buttocks.

260.28–29   *'Fais-moi confiance.'*] Trust me.

261.1–2   *'Il . . . dedans,'*] Young men are inside.

262.1   *pote*] Pal.

264.3   *vache*] A drag.

264.8   *mome*] Buddy.

274.34   *Tant mieux.*] Much better.

279.3   *'Souvenez-vous,'*] Remember.

295.35–36   mais . . . preferé.] But Paris is still my favorite city.

305.35   *'Ne . . . prie.'*] Please don't let me fall.

308.30   *tapette*] Prostitute.

316.34   *'J'espère bien.'*] I hope so.

359.23–25   *When I . . . things.*] 1 Corinthians 13:11.

ANOTHER COUNTRY

365.3–6   *I . . . far.*] In "Yellow Dog Blues" (1914).

378.38–39   Little Eva] Daughter of a slaveholder in Harriet Beecher Stowe's *Uncle Tom's Cabin* (1852).

410.25–27   *When . . . do.*] "Empty Bed Blues."

438.17–18   *I wouldn't . . . long*] Bessie Smith, "Jailhouse Blues."

540.17–18   *The Wings . . . Son.*] Novels by, respectively, Henry James (1902) and Richard Wright (1940).

551.30   *"Au . . . moche."*] Actually, you are rather ugly.

551.40   *"Tu . . . moi."*] Right! I'm very attractive.

555.35   *je . . . avis."*] I agree with you completely.

570.10   *"Ne m'oublie pas,"*] Don't forget me.

573.8–9   *It's . . . me.*] "Shipwrecked Blues."

574.20–21   *It's . . . end.*] This, and the italicized lines at 574.36–37, 575.25, 576.1–2, 576.21–22, and 576.36–37, are from Smith's "Long Old Road."

578.7–8   *Catch . . . chair.*] These, and the lines at 578.26–28, are from Smith's "In the House Blues."

579.24   Shubert Alley] Theatrical "alley" just off Broadway, between 45th and 46th streets in New York City.

579.29   Frank Yerby] Expatriate African American author (1916–91); Yerby's popular novels appeared almost annually after the success of *The Foxes of Harrow* (1946).

580.21   *Tobacco Road*] Jack Kirkland's dramatization of Erskine Caldwell's 1932 novel; it had a continuous Broadway run of 3,182 performances, 1933–41.

594.13–14   *Precious . . . stand.*] Opening of Thomas A. Dorsey's hymn "Precious Lord."

646.27–28   *I'm . . . way!*] Opening of "Higher Ground," words by Johnson Oatman Jr., music by Charles H. Gabriel.

662.14–15   *"Nom . . . soif!"*] My God, how thirsty I am!

667.5   cat . . . *Venice.*] Gustave von Aschenbach, in Thomas Mann's story (1912).

674.35–39   *Je . . . toi.*] I will tell you my arrival date. I'm coming by plane. I said good-bye to my mother. She cried a great deal. I admit that did something to me. Very well. Paris is deadly without you. I adore you my little one and I love you. How I wish to hold you tightly in my arms. I kiss you. Yours always.

694.18–30   *His . . . earth.*]   Shakespeare, *Antony and Cleopatra*, V.ii. 79–81.

755.22   *Le plus . . . faire.*]   The hardest part is yet to come.

GOING TO MEET THE MAN

864.4–5   very cup of trembling]   Cf. Isaiah 51:17, 22.

866.23   *Les Fauves Nous Attendent*]   *The Wild Beasts Await Us.*

872.5–6   *"Tu . . . sais?"*]   We are going to miss you, you know?

872.14   *"Il . . . gosse!"*]   Your kid is a sly one!

874.22   *les bateaux mouches*]   Sightseeing boats.

877.4–5   *Tu . . . comprends*]   You know, something very momentous has happened to me. I love you. I love you. Do you understand me . . .

896.33   Black Monday]   On Monday, May 17, 1954, in the case of *Brown* v. *Board of Education* (of Topeka, Kansas), the Supreme Court by a unanimous vote declared segregation in public schools unconstitutional because "separate but equal" educational facilities are inherently unequal.

899.29–30   *le metteur . . . larmes.*]   The director of the film that made you cry.

Library of Congress Cataloging-in-Publication Data

James, Baldwin, 1924–1987.
    Early novels and stories / James Baldwin.
       p.   cm. — (The Library of America ; 97)
    Contents: Go tell it on the mountain — Giovanni's room
— Another country — Going to meet the man.
    ISBN 1–883011–51–5 (alk. paper)
    I. Title. II Title: Go tell it on the mountain. III Title:
    Giovanni's room. IV Title: Another country. V Title:
    Going to meet the man. VI. Series
PS3552.A45A6   1998   97–23028
813′.54—dc21   CIP

THE LIBRARY OF AMERICA SERIES

This book is set in 10 point Linotron Galliard,
a face designed for photocomposition by Matthew Carter
and based on the sixteenth-century face Granjon. The paper is
acid-free Ecusta Nyalite and meets the requirements for permanence
of the American National Standards Institute. The binding
material is Brillianta, a woven rayon cloth made by
Van Heek-Scholco Textielfabrieken, Holland.
The composition is by The Clarinda
Company. Printing and binding by
R.R.Donnelley & Sons Company.
Designed by Bruce Campbell.